The Kappillan of Malta

The son of a distinguished surgeon, Nicholas Monsarrat was born in Liverpool in 1910 and was educated at Winchester and Trinity College, Cambridge. His first book to attract attention was the largely autobiographical *This Is the Schoolroom*, published in 1939. On the outbreak of war he joined the RNVR, serving mainly with corvettes: his war-time experiences are vividly described in *The Three Corvettes* and *Depends What You Mean by Love*. In 1946 he became director of the UK Information Service in Johannesburg and subsequently in Ottawa. His most famous book, *The Cruel Sea*, published in 1951, is one of the most successful stories of all time and was made into a film starring Jack Hawkins. Other famous novels include: *The Master Mariner*, *The Tribe That Lost Its Head* and its sequel, *Richer Than All His Tribe*, *The Story of Esther Costello*, *The White Rajah* and *The Pillow Fight*. Nicholas Monsarrat died in August 1979.

Nicholas Monsarrat

The Kappillan
of Malta

Pan Books London and Sydney

First published 1973 by Cassell & Company Ltd
This edition published 1975 by Pan Books Ltd,
Cavaye Place, London SW10 9PG
8th printing 1980
© Nicholas Monsarrat 1973
ISBN 0 330 24266 0
Printed and bound in Great Britain by
Hazell Watson & Viney Ltd, Aylesbury, Bucks

To
ANN
without whom

Contents

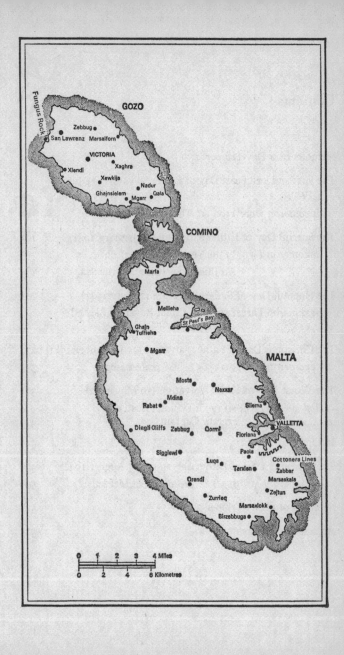

Memoirs of a
Day~Tripper 1

The man in the bar of the Phoenicia Hotel, by the main gate of Valletta, gave me more mis-information, in the space of two hours, than even six gins and tonics could really justify. He was a fattish, pinkish man in bulging blue shorts; a man on a long lazy holiday, but discontented none the less.

He was looking round for a decent place to settle, he told me by way of introduction. He'd already 'done a recce' on the Bahamas, Bermuda, the Channel Islands, the Isle of Man, Jamaica, Geneva, and Capri. Now he was in Malta. Among the Malts.

'Don't get me wrong,' he said, popping salted peanuts into his mouth one by one, like a man on a very strange, measured diet. 'I *like* the Malts! But you know what their trouble is? They're not organized. You can't even get a decent mixed grill here. Well, I mean, that's no bloody use, is it?'

'I suppose not.' I always picked the wrong man at the bar, if I picked anyone, and I had done it again. 'But the fish is pretty good, don't you think?' In the middle of stone history, here I was, talking about fish. It always happened. I tried again. 'Have you been out to Mdina?'

'What's that?'

'The old capital.'

'No.' He inserted two more peanuts. 'That's just architecture, isn't it? Guidebook stuff.'

'And history. Like this place.'

'This hotel? Is it old? I didn't know.'

'No. I mean Valletta. Have you been round Grand Harbour?'

'I've done a recce... My trouble is, I like *people*.' He leant forward, suddenly confidential. 'I met a *very* interesting man last night, right outside here in the carpark. One of those settler fellows. He told me a *very* interesting story.'

I waited.

'It's a way of getting duty-free cars into Malta... He had a brand-new Mercedes, beautiful job, must have cost about six thousand, and he saw me looking at it, and we got to chatting, and he told me how it was done. He said – and he seemed to know what he was talking about – that if you did a year here as a settler, and then said you'd changed your mind, and asked for a tourist visa instead, and extended that for a year, and then after twelve months signed up as a settler again, you could import one new car each year, duty free, and then trade it in for another one. All buckshee, all fixed up in Germany, and no pain at all. What do you think of that?'

'I believe they've changed the rules. Anyway, can you really use a new Mercedes every year, in Malta?'

'That's not quite the point, old boy, is it? All I know is, he was on his third duty-free Merc in three years.' He sat back, deeply content. 'That's what I meant when I said, the Malts aren't properly organized.'

The Maltese, I knew, were organized to the extent of a 40 mph speed limit and roads which disappeared into the sea after an absolute maximum of seventeen miles. A Mercedes owner would be trapped, just as I was trapped. But I still owed him the fourth drink.

'Would you like another drink?'

'Can't fly on one wing.'

The new drinks were brought, the barman rebuked for not providing fresh slices of lemon ('Got to keep them up to the mark, old boy'), and we settled down again. Early convictions of despair warred with late manifestations of a social conscience. I told him that I was crossing to Gozo, the next-door island, tomorrow.

'What? To live?'

'No. Just a day trip.'

'That's about enough... There's nothing on Gozo. Talk about *quiet*! If you draw a cork they think the revolution has started... Of course, it's a quaint sort of place, if you like that kind of thing. Only they don't make anything of it. I would go so far as to say' – all of a sudden he became exceptionally judicial, stabbing the air with a large pink forefinger – 'that Gozo's got *distinct* possibilities, if only it's handled right. It's *exactly* the sort of place that hundreds of people in the upper brackets are looking for, as a holiday spot, or even as a place to live. It's got peace, and sunshine, and a real chance to relax. Of course it needs a complete face-lift... But what's the good if no one knows about it? I mean, who's heard of Gozo? The Malts have got to *sell* the place, if they want to get it organized. And sell it to the right kind of chap. It could be a *top* island for *top* people—'

He droned on. The upper brackets, as time went by, seemed to expand to bursting point, involving thousands of jet-set travellers winging in from all over, top people who must assuredly turn Gozo, which I did not know, into Miami, which I did. Peace, sunshine, and a place to relax... Finally my friend focused his fat eyes, and looked at his watch.

'I make it seven o'clock.'

'Well – eight o'clock.'

'Good grief – I promised my wife—' he levered himself off his stool, his pale-blue shorts nigh to rippling explosion. 'Well, I wish you joy, old boy... Are you catching the early ferry?'

'Yes.'

'At least you've got one good thing going for you. There'll be no one on the boat. Not at 7.30 in the morning.'

By 7.30 in the morning, as I might have guessed, there seemed to be more people on board the boat than there were in Valletta itself. The ferry-boat *Jylland*, which had started life romantically as a British submarine-chaser, switched to Danish registry, and had then been converted to a stubby pedestrian work-horse making approximately 1800 return trips a year between Gozo and Malta (I was interested in ships, just as the man in the bar liked people, and the oldest of the Phoenicia porters had supplied me with her pedigree) – the *Jylland*, by the time the gangways were hauled in, was crammed to the roof with my fellow-passengers.

All the lower-level benches were close-packed with humanity, and it was standing-room only even on the upper deck, where a sea of people had cascaded up the ladders and overflowed.

They were certainly not tourists, on this voyage. Almost without exception, they were Maltese. Almost all were in black, except for children who carried bunches and sheaves of flowers. There were many priests; many men in dark business suits; quite a number of old people in wheelchairs. Some of the oldest women wore that strange black headdress which I had so far only seen in photographs: a kind of arching tent, an arrangement of mourning topsails, which the captions had called *faldettas*. There was some murmuring of prayer, as well as cheerful bustle and clatter. There were some tears.

A priest sitting opposite me on the big slatted bench, a serious and studious young man, had his head buried in a leather-bound breviary. His lips were moving: all else was still. But he was part of this strange throng, in spite of his withdrawal. The whole boatload, as far as I could observe it, had a pilgrim air which I could not quite place.

The *Jylland*, with the minimum of fuss, backed away from the quay of Marfa's tiny harbour, and made a slow 180-degree turn towards Gozo, the north-western target. There was a sudden surge of movement on deck as passengers thrust across to get a better view, and we took a very slight list to port. At this, the young priest looked up for a moment, and crossed himself. So did most of the people round him. ('They do it when they're putting out the dustbins,' my friend in the Phoenicia had said at one point, derisively. 'It's a *journey* – know what I mean? Personally I think they're nuts.') The *Jylland*, now headed in the right direction, started her voyage across a sparkling three-mile channel.

Occasionally she dipped her forefoot, very gently, into the long low northerly swell; but it was nothing – just a reminder that a ship was a ship, married to the restless sea, not a tram nor a long-distance truck. When a bell rang, deep down below, she increased her speed to a throbbing pulse, dividing the blue water with a spreading milk-white wake. Presently the porpoises joined in the fun, darting in at right angles to play last-across-the-road with her advancing prow.

It was a marvellous morning, clear as a mirror, warm as the promise of love, bright as heaven. I had known that it would be.

There was a group of nuns, young and old, either pious like pictures or jolly like housewives bingo-bound, grouped in a close circle near one of the life-boats. Now, at some reverent signal, they started to pray out loud, and people near them joined in. At the end they all crossed themselves in unison. This attracted the attention of the only English-looking family within my range.

I had already christened them: they were Dad, Mum, Charlene, and Grandma. They stood out like stuffed canaries in a flock of crows, or blood-puddings in batter; and though there was no harm in that, there was no merit in it either. Dad – taking him from the top – had a flat green cap, a good red North-country face, a brown suit of honest hard-wearing tweed, and vaguely ecclesiastical sandals. Mum was just Mum, as I imagined she would be, anywhere between the River Tyne and the mysterious upper reaches of the Amazon: a coat-and-skirt mum, a shopping-bag mum, a mum with sensible strap-shoes and corns to match, a placid anchor in a placid sea.

Daughter Charlene had emerged from the chrysalis as a gruesome essay in tourist *baroque*: mauve head-scarf, lime-green stretch pants very near their limit of embrace, and a halter-top which left some six inches of bulging pink midriff for the public to browse on. Her face, in repose a small pudding, was on the way to achieving the large holiday size. Grandma, at the other end of life's magical span, had shot the works on a trouser suit of purest bell-bottomed blue, scarlet ankle socks, and a rakish yachting cap adorned with the crossed anchors of the American Coast Guard.

I might have liked them, anywhere except among this devout and sober pilgrimage. Now, as they stared at the murmuring nuns, and exchanged glances, and began to nudge each other, the tolerant observer could only cringe.

'Did you see that?' Charlene said, theatrically aghast. 'They did it again! They were crossing themselves! Quite openly!'

Mum said: 'It's their religion.' Dad puffed his pipe and said nothing. Grandma was going 'T'ch, t'ch!' through grimly disapproving lips. But she had another complaint, on a social plane.

'All this eating...' She had a low hoarse voice, like an old boxer whose career had not been blessed. 'You'd think people would have more consideration.'

It was a fact that the Maltese passengers, safely embarked on their voyage, were now tucking into breakfast. Bottles of something which looked like cold coffee were going from hand to hand. Wedges of bread, clamped over a filling of raw onion and tomato paste, were disappearing at a steady rate. Old folk ate with a dutiful persistence; children had become bright-eyed, ravening wolves.

For a space the pilgrimage had changed to a picnic, with much moving about, exchange of one food for another, generous sharing, determined munching, wordless smiles, and an honest display of appetite.

Grandma growled again: 'Fancy eating all over the place!' and Charlene added, with a delicate shudder: 'You didn't say you were taking me to the zoo!'

But there were worse things to come than raw onions and tomato paste.

A sudden violent flurry of activity, unmatched on board so far, erupted from below, preceded by a tumult of shouts and cries. For a moment I thought, fancifully, that some gang or other must be rushing the bridge, intent on hijacking the *Jylland*, holding us all as hostages, and sailing her to Libya or Israel. What did the good citizen, ex-Navy, unarmed, past his best years as a combat animal, do in such circumstances? Then the huge good humour of the moment made all this fancy ridiculous.

For the rush was a holiday rush, of laughing cheering people pushing their way up the lower ladder in support of an enormous, labouring old man, who was himself carrying, bodily, a battered wicker wheelchair. Enthroned on this, clinging to its frail sides, rocking like a tiny boat in a storm, seeming to laugh and to weep at the same moment, was a crippled dwarf.

This ludicrous pair was swept upwards on a great wave of strong arms, willing hands, and gusty goodwill. Where a moment ago, on the main deck below us, there had been no room at all, there was suddenly plenty, and the dwarf and his wheelchair and his huge attendant were set down in a prime vantage-point. They began to hold court immediately.

Everyone seemed to know them, and to crowd round: eager to stretch out and pat the dwarf, and thump the old man on his massive back. Food was pressed upon them – crusty horns of bread, gleaming segments of fresh sheep's-milk cheese; people who could not get near waved and shouted, many of the nuns cooed and smiled in the background, a swollen old woman in a black *faldetta* smothered the dwarf in a vast embrace, tears streaming down her cheeks.

Even the young priest looked up from his breviary, surrendered his aloof face to the joyful moment, and called out his blessing.

The old man stood sentinel, like a tide-washed rock, behind the wheelchair, head and shoulders above everyone round him. He was an extraordinary figure, something between a great gaunt oak and an ancient scarecrow; a rusty black frock coat, frayed at the cuffs, bursting at the seams, covered him from his shoulders to his calves: a coat seemingly as old as the man, which placed both of them well into their eighth decade. But it was the tiny dwarf who was the centre of this stage.

He was about fifty: swarthy as an Arab, beak-nosed, deeply lined: above his burnt-olive shrunken face was a shock of black hair, the last evidence of virile, vanished youth. He had a tattered rug over his knees – or rather, his knee; for even this pitiful body was maimed and incomplete.

A chance movement showed that his left leg had at some time been severed at mid-thigh; a chance lifting of his grinning, working face suddenly betrayed the truth – that the harsh lines were those of lasting, grinding pain, that both the man and the face had been a ruin, a stricken wreck, for a very long time.

What on earth was it all about? There were plenty of clues, but absolutely no answers. Dad, a shrewd fellow-observer, broke silence for the first time, to sum it up in his own style. Taking his pipe out of his mouth, he gave his verdict:

'Eh – the things you see when you haven't got a gun!'

'Now, Dad!'

It must have been a hallowed family joke, for they all burst out laughing. Round them, the Maltese smiled and nodded their heads. They could scarcely have understood, even if they had made out the words, but I knew already that they loved to hear laughter.

I had read a guidebook – several guidebooks – during my stay, and it was wonderful to see them unfold, and come true. The *Jylland*, ploughing steadily onwards with her varied cargo, was now half-way across, and passing the small island of Comino, midway between Malta and Gozo. It was a moment of rare beauty; in the clear morning air, the arc of the Maltese sky, flawless and innocent, might indeed have been the canopy of heaven. I felt like nudging the young priest, whose nose was now reburied in his breviary, and telling him: 'Hey! He's up there.'

The ship, like the sky, was deliciously poised. There was the distant view of Malta astern, with its steep rocky cliffs and pink-turreted police station, and then of Gozo ahead, its ridge of honey-coloured houses broken only by the yellow spire of the island's first church.

Close by was Comino : an almost barren rock, laced here and there by tiny strips of tilled fields, already murdered by the summer sun, and by the sort of winds which, though apparently kept secret from the Tourist Board and the men who wrote the advertisements, had been steadily flogging their way across the Maltese Islands for the first week of my stay.

But this morning even bare Comino was beautiful, to match the day. Through a cleft in the rocks, there was a glimpse of an inner lagoon, matchlessly blue, calm, inviolate – except for the miniature fishing boat, a Gozo *luzzu* painted in broad bands of red, blue, and yellow which rose to a slim peak at bow and stern, creeping out from under the cliff shadows to try her luck in deep water. Her helmsman stood tall on the tiny afterdeck, immobile, carved against the sky just as the ship herself was carved, and as much a part of it as the massive rudderhead at his back.

Facing the channel, a square orange-brown tower, eyeless yet watchful, commanded the sea approach. It was the only building to be seen, and it had an ancient purpose. The guidebook told me that Comino had once been a 'pirates' lair', infested with Barbary corsairs who hid among the cliffs and attacked the boats crossing, like the *Jylland*, between Malta and Gozo.

The Knights of Malta had built the tower to cleanse this naughty nest and make the island secure. Grand Master de Wignacourt, a stalwart of 1601, was the man who put up the money, and the tower with it. After 370 years, his work still stood, as solid and serviceable as the rock at its feet.

Presently a bell rang below, the engine lost its steady thumping beat, and the *Jylland* began to slow down, preparing to make the entrance to Mġarr harbour on the southern corner of Gozo. Mġarr lay under an unmarked sky and brilliant warming sunshine; within the small haven, crowded with visiting yachts, the fishing-fleet of *luzzus* swung peacefully at anchor, their garish colours reflected in water of purest, clearest blue.

Ashore, the red-brown nets were drying on roadside trestles; above them the burnt earth rose tier by tier, criss-crossed by yellow tracks, until the summit of the island was reached, and the flat roofs of the village crowning it cut the backcloth of the sky into a turreted silhouette.

Another fort, much larger, guarded the entrance to the harbour, its massive bastions rising sheer from the hill-top, staring across the straits towards the corsairs of Comino and the sisterly embrace of Malta itself. I recognized it – but only from the guidebook – as Fort Chambray, the last stronghold of Napoleon's troops before they were ousted by Nelson in 1798.

So the years turned, and it was the deepest pleasure to keep pace with them. But now it was time to catch up with the morning of today.

From the upper deck, there had for some time been a steady thrust towards the gangways below. The dwarf and the giant had vanished, borne down again by the same willing, loving hands. The ladders leading downwards were now crammed to bursting point with a congealed mass of people. Behind them other people pushed or elbowed or plotted to gain a place or two; behind them again, lazier or more contented passengers such as myself held back from the press, and enjoyed the sunshine and the noble view.

Grandma was another determined stayer. Her jaunty yachting cap bobbed up and down as she declared :

'You don't catch me with that lark! One thing I *must* say about Malta – they don't know how to queue.'

Charlene, who had wandered as the crowds thinned, came back with important news.

'I just heard something from a sailor.[1]

'You watch your step, my girl.'

'No, seriously. All this lot – they're going to a *funeral*! Isn't it *morbid*?'

The hotel at the bottom of Racecourse Street in Victoria, the Gozo capital, promised me 'a real English breakfast', and the waiter who presently appeared at my table confirmed the offer. He was a lively young man of about thirty, with the Australian accent which I had already noted as the most popular in Malta, with its thousands of returned immigrants from Sydney and Melbourne. His recital of the menu was impressive.

'There's a choice of fruit juices,' he began, 'then porridge or cornflakes, fish, eggs any style, bacon, ham, grilled tomatoes, grilled sausages, grilled kidneys.' He paused, but only for breath. 'Toast or rolls. Honey, marmalade, or jam. Tea or coffee.'

Breakfast was not a meal I counted on to sustain me for the whole of the working day. 'What sort of fish?'

'*Dendici*, sir. Caught new this morning.'

'What sort is that?'

'Like a dog-fish. Or a salmon.'

'I'll have that.'

When he brought it – it was actually like a cod, and very good – and saw me settled down, he returned to gossip. The news that I might write a book about Malta filled him with enthusiasm.

'Will it really be printed?'

'I hope so.'

'In the newspapers?'

'No. As a book.' I made book movements with my hands. 'Bound up.'

'A real paperback! Is that why you're here? Have you come for the *kappillan*'s funeral?'

'Not specially. Whose funeral did you say?'

'The *kappillan*. It means a priest. The priest who is dead is Father Salvatore. Dun Salv, we used to call him. We always shorten names. His family would call him Salvu.' But he was surprised. 'Haven't you heard of Dun Salv?'

'No.'

'He was a famous good man.'

The *dendici* was finished; now there was only toast and honey, which didn't matter. 'Tell me about him.'

The waiter shrugged. 'He was very old, so it was a long time ago. He was a priest in Malta during the war. He had a church in the catacombs, near the Cottonera Lines. That's what they called him then – *il-kappillan tal-katakombi* – the priest of the catacombs. He looked after all the people. They lived there because of the bombs. And do you know something' – suddenly his eyes were shining – 'that's where I was born! I was the first baby to be born in the catacombs! Dun Salv baptized me with his own name. Salvatore. That's my name.'

'Can you remember him?'

He shook his head, sadly. 'No. He went away when I was eight months, so my mother said. But *she* knew him. She said he was the best man in the whole world.'

The moving little story invited many questions. I could only think of one. 'Why is the funeral here?'

'He lived here, ever since then. In the monastery. They say he was sent there, or something, but it was never properly told. Anyway he died yesterday. So all the people have come to Gozo for the funeral. You can tell how he is remembered!' The young waiter straightened up. 'There's one thing for sure – I'll be there, if they give me the sack!'

The guidebook came to life again, as I went down the hotel steps and began to walk up Racecourse Street. The sun was now starting to burn rather than shine, and I kept to the shady side of the street as it rose sharply towards the summit of the town.

They actually did hold horse-races here, the printed page told me: once a year, to celebrate a *festa* and, I would have thought, to test a weary animal to the limit of its endurance. The prospect of galloping up this iron slope under a midday sun was enough to make even a jockey yearn for green pastures.

The street itself was like a minor street in Valletta: a haphazard collection of buildings, a proliferation of little wooden balconies which might or might not pass an inspection test, and countless shops which were mere slits in the wall, masked by slatted bamboo curtains. But at the top could be seen, from any angle, the crown of Victoria: the citadel of Gozo, which had served as a secure refuge in the past and was now a monument to determined planning, civic pride, and the limitless capacity of man to place one enormous stone upon another, until a tall rock became an unassailable bastion.

But I had not walked very far before it became clear that Victoria was filling up to capacity; and by the time I had reached the crossroads which split the town into its four quarters, I was only one of an enormous crowd – a single tourist, member of a modest band now outnumbered, and swallowed up, and almost brought to a halt by the nearly impenetrable mass of Maltese and Gozitans who had taken possession of the capital.

For the most part these were the people off the ferry-boat. Many of them were now eating again: munching on the small oval cakes, called *pasti*, with which the day customarily started, sipping the strong Gozo wine which (I had been warned) made the Gozitans so happy and unwary visitors so quarrelsome, or the plastic cups of grey coffee which could also start the day off, for anyone from a dockyard worker to a policeman.

But as they waited and munched and sipped, they seemed to be accumulating a kind of communal purpose. They had a bond, and they knew it; they had one intention, one focus, and it was gradually coming into evidence. As the crowds thickened at the crossroads, and spilled off down the hill towards Item No. 8 in the guidebook – the Capuchin Monastery – they did not have to explain themselves to anyone – to anyone who mattered.

They were on home ground: borrowed home ground, hallowed home ground; they knew why they were there, and could defend their presence, and honour it, against all comers.

I knew why they were there myself; and while growing aware of exclusion, I could not quarrel with it. The fact that strangers, interlopers, men and women without this bond and purpose, were beginning not to matter, had a public and private validity which one could only respect.

To resent it, to try to crack it, would be crass impertinence. I was lucky: I had been allowed to know that this was the crowning day, and the mortal night, of one Father Salvatore... Without offence on either side, I made for the nearest refuge which beckoned naturally to a writer.

In the dusty, cool oasis of the Gozo Museum, which the day's heat had not yet touched, I latched on to a party of tourists which, headed by its guide, was trooping round the display cases.

Our surroundings were handsome, as the guide was quick to point out. This had once been the Bondi Palace: papal inquisitors had lived here, two of them later to become popes. Now, given over to a dry municipal account of the past, the building itself still rang with the live voices of men.

Here Maltese time itself unfolded, ancient beyond comprehension. There were fragments of Phoenician pottery, brought by men flattering themselves to be the first sailors ever to make a Malta landfall – only to find that they were late-comers by fifteen centuries, forestalled by Neolithic man from the north; and Neolithic man was here as well, with his own pottery from the Copper Age, 3,000 years before the birth of Christ.

There were Punic bones and skulls: coins from all the known world of long ago: wine and oil amphoras from the wreck

of a Roman merchant ship, now resting for ever in twenty-
five fathoms of blue water: that ship's own anchor; and a
curious Greek device for extracting stones from olives before
they went to the presses – though this implement, which could
be dismissed as a chunk of granite, needed perhaps a certain
scholarly faith to determine its function.

Probing back through years which must now be reckoned
by the million instead of the thousand, we gazed at a pink
fossil fish, a cousin of the world's first red mullet, its scales
and dorsal fin still as delicately formed as on the last day it
swam. It had been patiently prised from a stone quarry now
standing 600 feet above sea level.

Next stop on my listed tour was the cathedral, but here one
could not linger; it was being put to its proper use by the
devout. Instead of the customary pious and deserted calm, it
was thronged by a constant stream of people – the mourners
of today – who wandered in, prayed briefly, and left in silence
to give place to others. I went on my way, alone. It was still
true: this could never be my party.

The way was uphill again, through tiny winding streets sometimes sliced through the rock, with little gouged-out houses
where people lived and loved, towards the crown which was
the ancient Citadel of Gozo. Soon I passed through a second
maze of huge bastions, where enormous yellow stones were
crumbled and overgrown with weeds and wild olives; and then
into the sunny ruined splendour of an open courtyard, the heart
of the stronghold.

From far off, the citadel had looked impregnable and proud;
close to, the air of neglect was depressing. There were gaps in
the masonry here and there, gaping spaces as if teeth had been
drawn from some mouldering mouth, cascades of fallen stone-
work where someone had dug, and probed, and searched, and
gone away again, on a nightfall perhaps a hundred years ago.
I made one more effort – it had been a hot and breathless
climb – and clambered up on top of the bastions themselves.

From the stage-box of the huge wall, which was thirty feet
across and as solid as the rock on which it was grafted, a
superb view unfolded all round the horizon. The sea, on this
benevolent day, upheld the island with a steady, loving hand.
Malta could be seen, five miles away across the rim of bright
water. Even Sicily could be seen, fifty miles away, crowned by

the troubled smudge which was Mount Etna. All was peaceful, and calm, and reassuring.

Towards the western end of the island there was another view, undeniably beautiful, tranquil as the pale sea beyond it, but simple and pastoral. The only features were the checkerboard of tiny fields cut by dry-stone yellow walls, the complacent domes of four churches, and a squat lighthouse on top of a flat, eroded hill.

Then I heard voices behind me, and turned from the pastoral to the people. My adopted tourists had caught up with me.

The same guide led the way : a middle-aged man with a beaky brown face atop a shrunken body, with an air of genteel starvation about him. He said: 'This way! This way!' on the note of command which a captive audience promotes. Then, when he had them exactly where he wanted them, a few feet from my side, he launched into his speech. Though it was a set-piece, delivered in an eerie monotone like a recorded telephone message, it still spoke loudly – as the museum had done – of ancient turmoils.

'The citadel of Rabat – that is the old name of Victoria – had its origin with the Phoenicians, long before Rome was founded. After the Roman occupation, 216 BC, the Arabs lived here. They were troubled by Barbary pirates, and were expelled in 1224. The citadel was besieged by the Turks in 1551 who came to Gozo with 140 war galleys and many soldiers. The citadel was taken by force after a heroic struggle, and 6,000 people were carried away as slaves to Tripoli. Their descendants are still there today, in a district called Tarhuna. Only forty old people were left on Gozo, though 300 others escaped by means of ropes let down from these bastions. The Turks and other pirates still continued to be troublesome, and up to 1637 there was a law that all Gozitans had to sleep here at night, when the drawbridge was lifted and the citadel sealed.

He paused. But the tourists had their inevitable spokesman, an inquisitive bird-like fellow whose scarlet arms and neck promised agonies of sunburn by nightfall. He did his duty :

'What happened in 1637?'

'The law was changed.'

But at this moment, more interesting than 1637 was today's scene right below the bastions, and it was this which was claiming the most attention. For now, as far as the eye could reach, the crowds were really building up, Victoria itself had become completely clogged; and a great concourse of people, black on yellow, a mourning mass contained only by the burnt fields, was slowly thickening round the Capuchin Monastery on the road northwards.

It was enough to focus the eye irresistibly, and to spark another question from the spokesman.

'Excuse me,' he interrupted the guide, who was talking about the time, as recently as 1798, when the French seemed to have replaced the Turks as Gozo's principal tormentors. 'But what's all the activity down there?'

'It is for a funeral,' the guide answered. He pointed. 'That is the monastery. The funeral begins from there. The funeral of Father Salvatore, a local priest. Everyone is going.'

'You can say that again!'

I was near enough to ask: 'Are you going?'

'Oh, yes!' For a moment the guide came alive, as a man, and as a voice in which private feeling had replaced public performance. His little walnut face positively lit up. 'I knew Dun Salv – Father Salvatore – when I was a little boy. Once he came to our house, here in Gozo, when he was – when he was—' he could not find the phrase he sought, and seemed to decide on something else, 'when he was on holiday here during the war. My blessed mother talked to him many times.' His eyes brightened, as perhaps they had brightened long ago. 'Once I took him some food in a cave!'

'What on earth was he doing in a cave?' the spokesman asked.

The guide repeated: 'He was on holiday from the war,' and that seemed to be that. In any case, he could not have added much more. All round us – from the cathedral close by, from other churches in the town, from villages far and near – the bells began to peal, filling the air with wave after wave of clanging thunder. The concert only lasted for a minute, but it was a division of time which could not be ignored.

As the sounds died, the guide looked at his watch. Never had the hour of eleven been announced with such emphasis.

'Ladies, gentleman,' he called out. 'The tour is completed. I will bid you goodbye, and lead the way downhill.' He bowed. 'The account has been paid... Thank you.' Then he was off.

But he was a small man, and his strides were short. I overtook him at the first breach in the bastions. He looked up as I appeared by his side, but he did not slacken his pace. He was going to the funeral.

'You said the funeral starts from the monastery,' I began after a moment. 'Is there a procession? Where does it go to?'

'To Marsalforn.' He indicated a direction on our left. 'It is a village on the north coast. That is where I am going. There will still be a bus, if it can get through the crowd.' He spread his hands. 'If not, I will walk.'

He was very determined, and so, for some reason never to be explained on land or sea, was I.

'Can anyone go?'

'But of course!' He looked up at me. 'Will you come?'

'I don't want to—' I was not sure how to phrase it. I didn't want to treat it as a free show, a tourist extra – something like that. But before I said another word, he had read me, clear as a bell.

'This is a very holy day,' he said. 'I think you understand... Come with me.'

2

At Marsalforn I lost my friend, who as a boy had brought food to Father Salvatore in a cave. But by the greatest stroke of luck I exchanged him for another, of even higher rank.

Marsalforn – the name meant 'Harbour of the Oven', a reference either to its shape, which was neat and narrow, or to the bakery which used to be there – Marsalforn would not normally have been a place to lose anyone. Though it had a ridge of new flats and 'holiday villas', garish pseudo-smart confections of the kind which was turning parts of Malta into an architectural slaughterhouse, yet its small and simple fabric remained intact.

It was still a fishing-harbour, salty as brine, tucked into a corner of a bay of perfect shape, size, and colour: it still offered all that such a haven should – brilliant sunshine, clear water of limpid blue, a fringe of elegantly shaped *luzzus* hauled out against the recent storm and now waiting to be launched: drying nets threaded with tatters of seaweed, woven fish-traps of delicate filigree bamboo, lithe Maltese hounds like the last companions of some dead Pharaoh, and tables and chairs set out for the innocent enjoyment of this retreat.

That, at least, was the theory. But today, theory had been swamped by intrusive fact. Here, already, were people in the mass. The stiff black suits, the shapeless mourning garb, the close-pressed bodies, the steady rise and fall of prayerful murmuring, the aura of waiting for something of tremendous significance – all were here again, transferred from Victoria, afflicting Marsalforn with the possibility of chaos.

There were street-corner crowds, quayside crowds, sad crowds (for a good man was dead), happy crowds (for such a man must be near to heaven already); crowds which had unaccountably become important and influential, with a status never contemplated on any other day.

They, like myself, were part of the funeral. They *were* the funeral, which was happening now – for as we looked up the dusty hill towards Victoria, and the Capuchin Monastery, and the noble ruined citadel which topped the skyline, a vast sigh, like the breath of heaven itself, suddenly engulfed the whole throng.

We had seen what we were waiting for: movement, the faraway glint of a cross as it caught the sunlight, and the first thin thread of black humanity, spilling out as if from a sluggish wineskin, overflowing like pitch, coming down the valley towards us. Two miles away, the procession had started.

It was at this moment that I looked round for my guide, and could not find him, and found someone else instead. There had been a disturbance in the crowd – someone had fainted, and had been borne away into the shade; a number of us were thrust forward on to the roadway between the harbour and its fringe of houses, and we made our way back as best we could.

My way took me to a new vantage-point, and it was there, with a shock of recognition, that I found myself next to a wicker wheelchair, and to the dwarf, the extraordinary little man from the *Jylland*, and to the grotesque giant who was his escort. Either by accident or by the strange design of their friends, this pair had been left almost alone on the last street corner at the bottom of the valley. The gap round them, the curious considerate isolation, had now been invaded by me.

But within two minutes – such was the welcome of the Maltese for all strangers – the dwarf was answering every question of mine, and sharing every feeling, even his grief. It was only the man with him who would not yield, nor admit me to his company: the frock-coated giant who had manoeuvred the wicker chair into its choice position, and did not want it shared.

It was more than the position, as far as he was concerned. The old guardian – and he really was very old, gaunt and ravaged like a tree still upright on a windswept plain – maintained a manifestly bleak expression: suspicious, fiercely protective, proud. This little man in the wheelchair, it seemed to say, is *my* little man. Leave him alone. Keep your distance. If there has to be any talking, I will do it.

But the dwarf was not in this mood, nor could he see the giant's face. His was a welcome beyond any expectation. Though he had a voice to match his looks – raw, rough, almost gravelly, as if both voice and man, ground down to rubble by the same millstone of the years, had suffered and endured an equal punishment – he spoke excellent English, and gave me all the benefit of it.

'Have you not heard of Father Salvatore?' On his cracked olive face, so much larger and more lively than the wasted little body which sagged sideways in the wheelchair, there was the same surprise as had been voiced by the waiter at breakfast-time. 'I thought that all the world knew his name. Father Salvatore... Our saviour during the war. I do not mean' – the dwarf added quickly – 'Our Saviour—' and he crossed himself, as swiftly and naturally as a man buttoning his coat against the chill. 'I mean that he came to our help when we needed him.'

'Someone told me this morning that he was called' – and I made a wild stab, from memory, at the waiter's words – '*il-kappillan tal-katakombi*.'

He did not even correct my pronunciation. Instead, his face lit up, instantly, delightedly. 'You speak Malti!' he exclaimed, and repeated the information, over his shoulder, for the benefit of the huge old man. But neither of them was going to test it further. Instead, the dwarf went on:

'That's it! That's what he was called in the old days. The priest of the catacombs. What a man he was! ... *Now* people say that he was mad, or that he saw things which were not there. Or that he grew mad after the war. Who can tell?' He spread his hands, which were continuously talkative, in the gesture which meant 'Such matters are beyond me'. Then his right hand, which was a tiny claw, dropped on to the stump of his left leg, and he kneaded and caressed it, in a movement which must, over the years, have become a warning message for all who had any part in caring for him. The old man, concerned, bent down over his shoulder, but was brushed aside. 'All I can say is, the *kappillan* had his senses when we needed him.'

I had to ask : 'But what did he actually *do*?'

After a long pause the dwarf answered : 'He gave us heart.' Then he turned away from my questions – but gently, without discourtesy – and looked up the hill. His face, which had been brooding, grew animated again. 'See there! He comes!'

The river of people was now in full flood, coursing down the valley towards us. Its outline could already be made out. A giant cross – the same which had flashed the first distant signal – was borne at its head. Then there came the glimpse of white, which must be the clergy and the choir. Then came the hearse, an ambling black dot, separate from all else; and then the vast following of the mourners.

Above their moving throng, a pall of yellow dust grew and thickened and followed them on the windless air, down the valley which seemed, even on this bright morning, to have become the Via Dolorosa of all mankind.

Far away up the hill, church bells were tolling faintly, in the five-note descending sequence which by its very repetition seemed the saddest voice with which any bells could speak. They were answered from near at hand, by the thin dialogue of the Marsalforn bell-tower. The place of death was now linked, by grievous music, with the place of burial.

Yet so slow an event, such a gradual unfolding, could not impose silence straight away; the holy ground was still distant, and the watchers still waiting for the actual touch of its solemnity. It was the old man behind the wheelchair who broke the pause. Melting at last, he bent towards me – and it was a long descent, like a tall father to a small child, a great crane to a little load far below – and started a long rambling sentence in Maltese.

Though there seemed no doubt in his mind that it would be understood, not a single word of the non-Latin tongue was recognizable, and my ashamed face must have proclaimed the fact. The dwarf, who had been watching me, broke in. With a gesture he silenced the old man – it was extraordinary to note the command of this shrunken human over the lofty figure behind him – and then he explained.

'He was telling you that this was the day it all started. The Feast of St Barnabas, the' – he fumbled for the right word, and for once failed to find it – 'the tenth day and one more of June, 1940.'

'The eleventh.'

'The eleventh!' The dwarf, just as pleased as I was, gave me a brilliant smile which lit the ugly worn face with sudden childlike beauty. 'Exactly! The eleventh of June, the day his little church was killed.' He saw my look of puzzlement, and tackled it manfully. 'He had a church which was being built. It was to be the church of St Barnabas near Cospicua, where a new village was growing. Dun Salv *loved* St Barnabas, because St Barnabas was a friend of St Paul, and then they had a quarrel, and St Barnabas wandered away and was heard no more.' This sequence seemed so clear in the dwarf's mind that one could not question it. 'His beloved church was nearly finished, and then – BOUM!' the dwarf brought his clenched fist thumping down on his sound right knee, 'a bomb fell, perhaps the first bomb of the first day of the war, and the church disappeared.' He said something in Maltese to the man behind him, and the giant answered, equally swiftly, spreading his hands in a kind of flattening gesture. The dwarf went on : 'This old man was there, on that day. He says that *in one moment* there was nothing left but a heap of stones. So Father Salvatore, who was a brave man, not to be put down, made another church in the catacombs, and there he preached to us.' The dwarf mused for a moment, his gaze seeming to turn inwards. 'I tell you preach, but that is not the correct word. Not a preach like in church. It was more like a film which shows you.'

This was not as clear as I would have wished, but perhaps it did not need to be. Instead of probing further, I put the question to which I must have an answer.

'But who are *you*? You seem to know so much about him.'

'I know so much because I was there.' The answer was as ready as all the other answers. 'Not at the beginning. First it was this old man' – he jerked his head backwards – 'and then it was me. I was his sacristan. They called me' – he smiled suddenly, beautifully – '*is-sagristan tal-katakombi*. The sacristan of the tombs.'

But he had begun to knead and cherish his maimed stump again. Perhaps he had talked too long. Perhaps the pain of the past had become the pain in his blunted thigh. Directing my attention with the same sort of authority as he had shown to his giant guardian, he pointed up the hill towards the funeral procession. 'Look! They will soon be here!'

It was true. Round a bend in the road, marked by a tall fluted pine tree which spread its favours like a huge opened fan, the great and the small were advancing upon us. The black and silver cross, borne by a stalwart friar in the brown habit of the Capuchins, was dominant in the van.

Then came the solid phalanx of white, which was the priestly escort: then the hearse, black draped, drawn by a black plumed horse, but topped by the brightness of summer flowers, to include in the earthly malevolence of death the hope of heaven. After that, the first of the enormous following: black again, shuffling raggedly, seeping down the last slope of the valley as if weight of numbers could bear witness to weight of sorrow.

Now could be heard a swelling tide of prayer from the mourners, and it was answered here and there among the crowd at the quayside: no more than a private muttering of responses, yet loud enough to reach the sky and to rend the heart on the way.

For me, there was a single strand left, if I had time for it. 'Tell me one more thing. Why is he being buried in Gozo? Did he come and live here?'

Perhaps it was not a good moment for such a question, or for any question, but the dwarf, eternally patient with a stranger, was still ready to deal with it.

'Father Salvatore lived here for the last thirty years,' he answered. 'He lived with the brothers in the monastery. I cannot tell you why. Some say he was sent there after the war, as a punishment. *For what?* Some say he went mad, and was put in a cell. I said to you before, who can tell? Some say he chose to live here, instead of Malta, because of something that happened.' His thigh was twitching again, and he calmed it like a fractious child with toothache or a high fever. 'They say he never spoke of it. It was a secret between himself and God. And perhaps the archbishop – who knows? ... But now he rests here for ever.'

There was a cry, a woman's cry, among the crowd a little

way off. It was one of many such cries. Someone else had fainted in the press, under the burning sun, or had given way to inconsolable grief.

The dwarf looked towards the noise. There were beads of sweat on his brow, and he seemed to be holding down his rebellious thigh by main force. But though he spoke with difficulty, he had something more to tell me.

'We loved him always. We can never forget him. Some believe that he will come again to Malta, when we need him. He used to say that himself, of other men, old dead men. That was what he taught us in the catacombs.' The dwarf's glance flickered round him, but whether he saw me, or the crowds, or the fringe of new buildings, or the far horizon of the sea, it was difficult to tell. 'Perhaps we will need him again, before it is our turn to die...' The swaying cross appeared at the corner of the street, upheld by the sandalled friar, whose knotted hempen girdle swung in unison; and a loud voice was heard in prayer. In extreme agitation, the dwarf ended: 'I am sorry. I cannot speak now.'

After the cross and the priests, the ancient hearse came into view. It was black and creaking and shabby, yet with a moving majesty about it – the last majesty of all. Its top, buried under mounds of flowers, rocked crazily as it rumbled onwards. The horse which drew it, caparisoned like the charger of Death, draped and plumed for this dread assignment, strained against the weight.

People fell on their knees as the shadow of the black nodding plumes touched the ground in front of them. When the hearse drew level with the wheelchair, the great old man behind it seemed to crumple earthwards as he knelt, while the dwarf shrank away, and then recovered himself. But it was only to let out a terrible cry, as the shadows slid across his single foot:

'I cannot march, Dun Salv! But I follow you always!'

The First and Last
Feast Day
of Father Salvatore

11 June 1940

I

Father Salvatore hated his boots. They were black, thick-soled, awkward, and ugly; when they grew shabby, as they always did within their first year, the bulging toe-caps reared up like swollen fists; after two years, they became cracked, deformed, bulbous, repellent, like a drunkard's nose. He prayed, often, that this might be the only hate in his heart. But he did hate them.

Once, long ago, as a young seminarian in golden Rome, he had bought himself a pair of elegant Italian shoes, slim and lithe like quick-silver, and earned a fearful rebuke from the Vice-Rector, whose domain was discipline. '*Shoes*, Santo-Nobile?' the voice of authority had thundered, making 'shoes' sound like 'fornication', and his honoured Maltese name like some coarse country joke. 'Dancing-master's shoes? *Pretty* shoes?'

Although he knew that this was not his first outward sign of inward, sinful pride, it seemed condemned as the most gross so far. This was a *seminary*, he was told, not some lounger's café on the Via Veneto – and the eyes of authority, as fierce and as piercing as the voice, forbade Salvatore Santo-Nobile even to *think* of that other coarse joke, that 'seminary' was from the Latin *seminarium*, a seed-bed, and *seminarium* was from the shame-word *semen*, and that, in spite of prayerful continence, there was often ample proof of this among the involuntary young... Take those shoes off instantly! Destroy them! *Burn* them! And as a penance...

Father Salvatore, praying mightily, had forsworn pride on that day, and for ever afterwards; and as a mark of his submission, he still bought, every three years or so, a pair of this same model of black, stuffy, ungainly boot. After more than a quarter of a century, such boots had even become hard to find. 'My humble footwear,' he called them sometimes, and persevered. But there were pitfalls even here.

Once his mother had said : 'I believe you take pride in wearing those terrible boots.' That had been a day of doubt indeed.

Father Salvatore hated his boots, and especially so this morning, as he toiled up the steep street of steps from Lascaris Wharf
to the crown of the city of Valletta, where his mother's house
reigned supreme, alike in its situation and in his heart.

It was nearly six o'clock, and Valletta was already stirring and
bustling as was its habit soon after the dawn of every day.
Across the harbour, in the 'Three Cities' (so christened by Napoleon, of the tidy mind and tyrant will, in his efforts to impose
civic order and logic upon Maltese who were indifferent to both),
the buses were disgorging the endless streams of dockyard
workers, now flocking to their early toil.

The ferries and the *dghajsas*, the slim gondolas of Malta, were
also bustling to and fro, intent on the same job : bringing Three
Cities men from Cospicua and Senglea and Vittoriosa to their
work in Valletta, taking countless return-loads of the citizens
of Valletta across Grand Harbour to the dockyard.

It was a daily exchange, the one sure tide in a tideless sea. If
one had asked such men why they did not live where they
worked, or work where they lived, and so save the time and
money spent on the daily journey, the question would have been
answered with a shrug, and not too friendly a shrug either. Who
could ask such foolish questions? Who had the right to such
impudence?

If a man lived in Senglea, that was where he lived until he
died. If he chose to work across the harbour in Valletta, that
was where he would work until God gave him rest.

Do you want to change our lives? What are you – Napoleon?
A meddler? A dictator? A *Turk*? Away with you! Leave us
alone! We *know* how we want to live!

All round Father Salvatore, as he toiled upward on feet already
cramped and painful, Valletta itself was well into its new
day.

The late fishermen were going one way, down to the harbour;
the early stone-masons were going another, up to the heights
where rich men were always building and poor men always
propping up poor houses. Lawyers were hurrying to catch an
early tide of profitable envy and malice; shop-keepers were
slamming back their barred doors, and rolling down the bamboo
curtains which softly replaced them. Priests, crossing a slit of

sunshine in a narrow street, passed businessmen who predict-
ably kept to the shadows.

Silversmiths marshalled their array of tiny hammers, and
balanced them in stiff hands; lace-makers picked up once more
the intricate threads of life and labour. Goats were being milked
from door to door, as obliging as village taps; dogs nosed and
buffeted against garbage-cans, rocking them adroitly until the
contents spilled out and could be wolfed at leisure. All the
world, in fact, woke to its due endeavour.

Already the first harvest of the day was being offered to the
hungry. On the scored, bloodied market tables, fish caught before
dawn, or perhaps fish less innocent in death, lay in mountainous display, in a Mediterranean rainbow of blue and red and
gold and gleaming silver.

Round them the slippered housewives prowled, sniffing and
peering, appraising, arguing, making up their minds one way
or the other; beneath them the soft-footed cats of Valletta,
tawny orange or sullen black, also prowled, intent on an even
better bargain, if a little cunning, a little feline finesse, could
bring it off.

One-third of his way up, still outside the main bastions of
Valletta, Father Salvatore paused, as he always did, to rest, to
look back, and to enjoy. He could not feel guilty at such indul-
gence. He loved God, and man, and history. God was always
first. But sometimes man lost his place to history (which was the
moment to pray for grace), and this was often so when Father
Salvatore stood silent on a street in Valletta.

For him, this was still, stone upon stone, the city of the
Knights, the shrine of history itself : the 'most humble city', as
Grand Master La Valette himself had called it at its foundation
– 'Humillima Civitas Valettae' – though whether to honour God,
or to dissuade his knights from exulting too much in its magnificence and their own tempestuous pride, was never made
clear, either then or later.

He stood now in the heart of all this splendour, while the
crowds weaved past him, stepping aside, casting curious glances
at his face or his habit, wondering perhaps what a priest (or, if
they knew him, what Dun Salv, never tolerant of idleness in
himself or in others) was doing, standing there like some old
statue on this, the most exciting of all new mornings.

Father Salvatore could never have explained, in simple words, the astonishing awareness of all such moments, which could take hold of him whenever he stood on the good earth of Valletta and felt once more, in piety and pride, the city's ageless embrace.

It was something in the streets, the narrow linkage of their criss-cross pattern; the way the jutting balconies reached out towards each other, the way the wrought-iron grilles insisted on a private world for those within.

It was something in the buildings themselves, simple and solid as the rock they stood on; and in the proud armorial bearings carved as deep as history into the fabric of great porticoes. It was something in the smell of sun-warmed stone which persisted over all other smells; and the sudden startling glimpse, at the end of so many streets, as if at the end of a cave, of blue water with the sunlight sparkling on it.

The Knights, inspired by Grand Master La Valette, a man of enterprise and energy even in his seventy-second year, had built marvellously, and after nearly 400 years the result was still marvellous, even though so swiftly achieved at the end of an exhausting war. Two thousand houses, and certain public buildings of noble elegance, were all built within five years; while most of the Auberges which housed the eight Langues of the Knights, together with the whole of Valletta as it was this very morning, were completed within another quarter of a century.

Not quite completed, his tired feet told him, as he made his pause last as long as possible; those builder–soldiers had had to break off and then leave for ever unfinished the levelling of this mountain on which the city was built, under the threat of new invasion from the Turks, only brought to naught by the Battle of Lepanto.

'Lepanto, Santo-Nobile?'

'Sir, after the death of Suleiman the Magnificent the Turkish fleet, with war galleys manned by Christian galley-slaves chained to their oars, was waylaid in the Gulf of Corinth by Don John of Austria—'

'The date, boy, the date!'

1571, 1571. . . But the threat of Lepanto was still a plague and a nuisance in 1940; it was the reason – still the reason, after three and a half centuries – why he had had to toil so steeply up a street of steps from Lascaris Wharf.

The stone ladder scaling this abandoned ground pierced the

great bastions of Valletta, first of the mighty defences of Grand Harbour, with its girdle of forts and watch-towers; and a reminder of those murderous times could still be given, on any sunny morning such as this, by that glimpse of lapping water at the end of a narrow alleyway which seemed to be tumbling into the sea.

Yet the monument to valour was there, all round him; and it was enshrined for ever in the inscription on the tomb of St John's Co-Cathedral : an inscription he had always known by heart, in Latin and in English, first as a small boy's punishment and then in a man's loving admiration :

> Here lies Valette, worthy of eternal honour. He who was formerly the scourge of Asia and Africa and the shield of Europe, whence by his holy arms he expelled the barbarians, is the first to be buried in this beloved city of which he was the founder.

Indeed, he had been the first to be buried, in a lonely splendour never to be matched again. Until the Knights took formal possession of their new city, the dead Valette was its only inhabitant.

Now it was time to move again, while this blessed old warrior slept on in peace. But as Father Salvatore came to himself, he saw today's people again, instead of yesterday's; and today's people swiftly became important. Man overtook history, as he should, in the hierarchy of love, and claimed his place once more.

Now there seemed to be puzzlement and perplexity on every face he saw, in every pair of eyes which met his. The usual bustle and stir had taken on a new element, the deep infection of doubt; it could even be seen in the way that people were reading their newspapers this morning – whipping urgently through the pages, sharing them with others who leant across their shoulders, passing them from hand to hand among a knot of neighbours.

But always, on the scanning faces, in the bewildered eyes, was the same look of uncertainty, almost of dissatisfaction.

It was because of the rumours of the night, a night which had ended one era of wild speculation and started another. After all the tensions and alarms of the past few days and weeks – was it to be war with Italy, was it to be peace? – they knew that they were at war, because it had been on the radio and was now in the headlines.

Many of them had listened to that actual declaration of war, shouted from a balcony on the Palazzo Venezia in faraway, much-loved Rome, and understood it, or had it translated instantly by the knowing. The word had spread from mouth to mouth among the evening promenaders on every street in Valletta:

'*Mussolini ddikjara l-gwerra!* Mussolini has declared war!'

In a way it had all come as a relief. Now they understood where they were. It was also a laugh. Those Italians! The way they talked! Mussolini's words, in all their bombastic absurdity, had come screaming out of the loudspeakers:

> Fighters of the land, the sea, and the air, Blackshirts of the revolution and of the legions, men and women of Italy, of the Empire and the other kingdom of Albania, listen! The hour marked out by destiny is sounding in the sky of our country! This is the hour of irrevocable decisions! The declaration of war has already been handed to the ambassadors of Britain and France!

It had been followed by an animal roar from the vast crowd below the Roman balcony. It went on and on, like a raging sea, like a mad runaway train coming straight towards them. It seemed to be baying for blood. For Maltese blood? Who could tell? And would blood be shed that night? Again, who could tell? What would happen? *How did such a thing begin?*

Then, within a few minutes of listening to the bellow of the Duce and the howling of his audience, they had heard a very different voice on Malta's loudspeakers. A British voice, measured, low-keyed, almost mournful, yet confident – the voice of the island's Governor, General Sir William Dobbie – assured them that all would be well.

His message was brief, and none the worse for that. It was also clear. Hard times might lie ahead of them, but with divine aid they would maintain the security of their island fortress:

> I therefore call on all humbly to seek God's help, and then in reliance on Him to do their duty unflinchingly.

The contrast in the two styles was almost laughable, but the laugh could only be on Mussolini. There was no doubt which was the man for the Maltese... They already knew Governor Dobbie to be a godly man. Now he sounded like a godly fighter, and that was the best kind of man to be.

After that, because it was so like the first day at school or the first day at work, they had all done as they were told. While men from the Air Raid Precautions toured the island, curtains were drawn, lights turned low, and windows screened with meticulous care. While the fighting men stood to their guns, the people were docile in conformity.

Some thousands flocked to the ready-made shelters of Valletta and Floriana and the Three Cities – the ancient caves beneath the massive bastions, the old railway tunnel so strangely handy to the Porte des Bombes, the scooped-out galleries of the Cottonera Lines. The rest closed their shutters, barred their doors, and waited for what must come. The enemy, as all the world knew, was no more than sixty miles away.

As darkness – God-made, man-made – fell on the troubled city, and the streets were left to the cats, it seemed certain that the bombs must also fall, in that very hour.

Yet nothing had happened: nothing all night, nothing at dawn, nor at sunrise. There was nothing happening now, except a new day, another day – and 'now' was already past six o'clock on the first morning of the war.

What could it mean?

On the faces of all was this same question. Sometimes, as he passed, they looked the question at him. He was a priest; he must know what was happening, and the reason for it. Once it was put into words, by a mountainous market-woman with the arms of a stone-mason, standing on a street corner with a small crowd round her.

She was not known to him, even by sight; perhaps she had come in from the country. She had been talking volubly; her friends had been listening. But when she caught sight of Father Salvatore, she called out to him:

'Eh, Reverend! Can you tell us? When will the war start?'

He did not like the address, which was rough and familiar. But then he saw that, beneath the bold manner, she was worried and anxious, like all the rest.

All he could answer was: 'I know nothing. We must pray. Work and pray.'

The answer was repeated here and there among the crowd. There was agreement in their voices, not on their faces. Though it was an answer to be expected, it was not what they wanted to hear.

He half-raised his hand, palm open, in the traditional, ageless gesture of blessing, and went on his way.

The way he now trod, towards the summit of the city, had left the steps behind, but it was still steep, and tiring to the legs, and especially harsh to the thick boots. Father Salvatore sighed as he toiled upwards. He was forty-five, not a young man with the lithe muscles of a Maltese hound!

The streets were sultry and airless under the encroaching sun, and he began to feel the sweat trickling down his broad face and under the collar-band of his cassock. It was his best cassock, with all the buttons intact and not a stain or mend to be seen, since this was the day for visiting his honoured mother, his beloved sister, both with their immaculate houses where a priest's working clothes seemed twice as shabby as anywhere else.

He wished, as always, that he were taller and leaner, so that he could bound through the streets, and through life itself, like a gazelle in a picture-book; but God had given him a short thick frame, big-boned, strong like a peasant's but slow-moving and awkward.

He could stack clover-ricks or swing a hoe tirelessly in the fields, but he could never walk into a drawing-room, nor even assist at High Mass in the cathedral, with the easy grace which both deserved.

'What have I done, to have such a little farmer for a son?' his mother used to ask, with the loving impatience of all mothers. That was before he became a priest. Now she said nothing – except about his boots – but something of the old look was still there, on certain days, in certain surroundings.

He could sum it up for her in his secret thoughts: I am a small, simple, lumbering priest, with faith, and only faith, to take the place of style. I will always be so. The great family of Santo-Nobile has sired its last cardinal, and it was not myself – it was more than a hundred years ago, in the blessed reign of Gregory XVI.

Ah, those unworthy, shaming old dreams, those hopes scarcely admitted and now vanished – and ah, the steep streets of Valletta! Feeling his cassock clinging to his shoulders, he cursed – no, no, no! – he could find it in his heart to criticize, gently, old Grand Master Lascaris, who had left a handsome wharf behind but had failed to finish the task of levelling the city.

Lascaris had tired him out already, as he had tired his lusty young Knights (but all in the service of God) by making them play mallet-ball (called *pallamaglio* or pall-mall) for hour after hour, in a specially built court, as soon as they had finished their spell of sea-duty in the galleys. His stern intent was to take their minds off the delights of dice, wine, and women. All very well for Grand Master Lascaris! – he was ninety-seven, and could safely admonish : 'Celibacy and chastity are no longer one.'

Celibacy and chastity... Father Salvatore honoured them, and lived them gladly according to his sacred vows, and lived *with* them, among the fathers of the Capuchin Monastery at Il-Wileg, across the harbour beyond the Cottonera Lines. It would be his home until his little church near by was built. He had spent last night there, and had found it in the same state of turmoil and doubt as was now the rule all over Valletta.

The friars had questioned him eagerly, as the market-woman had questioned him this morning. He was from the outside world; his mother was a great lady who knew all those in power; he *must* have heard more than they. But all he knew was what had been shared already, as they listened to the ranting declaration of war from Rome, and then to Governor Dobbie's sober voice afterwards.

At least he could tell them about Sir William Dobbie, whom he had met at his mother's house : how he was a God-fearing old man (well, sixty-one, old for a soldier) and one of the Plymouth Brethren of England, a strict sect of believers : how he had big ears and a grey moustache, a sad face and a steely spirit, how he truly trusted God to protect them, as all those in the monastery trusted Him. But beyond that? – nothing but hopes and fears.

No, he did not know if the bombs would fall that same night. No, he knew nothing of poison gas, which it was said would be the first weapon of war. No, he could not tell if the towns would be sacked and the churches and monasteries left un-harmed. No, he could not say whether there would be a dis-pensation over the eating of meat, if fish could not be caught. No, he had not heard that Catholic Italy must surely spare Catholic Malta, and that there was a secret agreement to this end.

No, he did not wish to keep vigil, and wake and pray all night. He would join them at midnight, and then sleep as best he could, and rise early, and be on his way. God watched over them all, but tomorrow there would be work for the hands of men – perhaps more work than ever.

Though the friars were kind and simple and devout, and housed him lovingly, yet for once it had been a relief to leave their cloistered shelter, where (he could not help feeling) small things became great, and great things small, and submit to the testing world again.

Thus he had kept to his intent, on that first morning of the war. He had attended the earliest Mass of the day ('the fisher-men's Mass', they used to call it as children, with the men on their knees at 4.30 and at their nets by five). He had broken his fast with coffee and dry bread: perhaps the best bread in the world, as the Maltese sometimes said, and the visitors always told the Maltese, but dry bread none the less.

Then he had walked the short distance, from the monastery to the building site below the Cottonera Lines, where the church of St Barnabas – his church, his St Barnabas – was rising to the glory of God.

He went there every morning of every day; sometimes he worked with the men, carrying stones on his broad shoulders, chipping curved blocks for a cornice (though he could never match the masons' fantastic skill), pacing out the length of a wall to enclose, one day, the private chapel which was his mother's gift. But on this bright and ominous morning, the place was deserted; even Rafel, his sacristan, on whom he counted – on whom he counted every day – was not to be seen.

He looked at the walls, strong and thick; he looked at the arches of the roof and the small dome, now nearly completed; he looked at the place where the altar would stand, where he himself would stand. One day, perhaps this time next year, the very feast of the saint... He said his daily prayer to St Barnabas, the lonely outcast saint who 'fell at strife', on whom his special devotion had always been centred.

Like his own people, like all Catholics, he thought of a saint as closer to God than man could ever be. So he did not always bother God directly; he prayed to the saint to intercede on his behalf: such a man, cherished in heaven after a stay on earth, must have an excellent working knowledge of humans and also better access to God. So – honour the saint: petition him: he would know what to do and how best to do it. . .

Blessed St Barnabas, ask God to speed the building of our church. Ask God to take care of today. Ask God that we should win the war, or survive the war, or die in the war, yet in His service, whichever was the most acceptable in His sight. Amen, amen.

Life was so easy, so simple, so wonderful, with the help of God... Now, nearly two hours later, he stood on a street corner, half-way up the cluttered mountain which was Valletta, and renewed those joyous prayers, and then, head down, continued his climb. War or no war, he was on his way to see his mother and sister, as he had done on a certain morning every week for as long as he could remember. This, especially, was not a day to fail either God or man.

Presently he became aware that his way was barred, and that a huge shadow was blocking the sun. A voice, gruff, hesitant, said: '*Bonġu, Dun Salv. Il-festa t-tajjba!*'

It was the man he had been waiting for, down at the church: his mighty sacristan-to-be, Rafel Vella.

Though he had ceased to marvel at Rafel's height, Father Salvatore never failed to be aware of it, whenever they met. He himself, thick-soled boots and all, could not aspire beyond five feet six inches; Rafel Vella must top him by another eighteen inches – nearly seven feet of solid, slow-moving flesh. The Maltese did not grow to such a size!

He was aware also that this was a simple giant; somewhere along the way, somewhere during the last fifty years, the great frame had stopped growing, and it had (as the Maltese said) stopped at the head. Rafel was not stupid – no man should call another stupid – but he was slow in wits and small in imagination. Give him something to do, something precisely stated, and he did it; leave him alone, without direction, and the huge man and the labouring mind often ground to a halt.

He was honest, and good-hearted, and weak. He was also, at this moment of time, feeling a little guilty, as Father Salvatore could easily tell. The tone in which he had said 'il-festa t-tajjba' – 'Happy feast day' – betrayed this. Father Salvatore, before replying, glanced at his watch. It was past 6.30. Rafel had not observed their feast day. Not when he had been expected to.

'Where have you been, Rafel?' he asked, with the necessary emphasis. 'I waited for you.'

The giant bent his mind to this, and the answers came slowly but steadily. 'I had to go to Gozo last night. To see my mother. I got a *luzzu* back this morning. All the way to the salt pans at Salina Bay. And then on a lorry coming in to market. With tomatoes! So early in the year!' Humble and ingratiating, he looked down at the small priest. 'I knew that I would meet you somewhere here, on your way to see the Baroness.'

Rafel never said 'your mother'. It might have been a peasant snobbery, or a decent respect for rank. At no time did it really matter: during thirty years of adult life, Father Salvatore had grown used to every variation on this theme. The variations were often astonishing.

Great men found it impossible to see him as a parish priest, when his family was noble. Small men of no pretensions found it natural, even logical: nothing could be more noble than the calling itself. The only people he could not love were the syco-phants who said: 'With your family connections it should be easy,' and waited for favours.

Now he said: 'But why did you not tell me yesterday?'

Awkwardly, avoiding a direct look, Rafel answered: 'I did not know. It happened so quickly.'

Very well, thought Father Salvatore: he is ashamed, and that is enough for today. If what he says is a lie, his confessor will hear of it. That was one blessed certainty... Seeking for gentle disengagement, he asked:

'How is your mother, Rafel?'

But even as he spoke, he knew the answer. Rafel's mother would not be well.

Rafel's mother was like a character in a play, a character who exerted tremendous pressure on the plot but was never seen on stage, only ominously reported. Father Salvatore knew her solely from hearsay, and from Rafel's halting comments over many years and many family disputes.

It had been established long ago that she did not like Rafel's wife; the idea that her son, a Gozitan, should have married a girl not even from the island itself, but a girl from Malta, was a notable stain on the family honour, a stigma scarcely to be borne, and she had never accepted it.

The rules were simple, and unbreakable. A man married a girl from the same village. If he chose to marry a foreign girl, even a girl from five miles away, there was something wrong with the girl : she must have been rejected by the whole regiment of local suitors, for the very good reason that they knew too much about her.

There was even a proverb which covered this, a proverb which Father Salvatore found crude to the point of indecency. 'A good cow is sold at home,' they would say, when a girl failed to find a serious marriage prospect within the limits of her own village, within a short mile of her own doorstep. If she was a good girl, she should not have to cast her net so wide. She could only be disreputable. And as for a girl from Malta marrying a boy from Gozo...

Worse still, Rafel had chosen to live and work in Malta instead of Gozo : to *emigrate* – one could hardly call it less – with all that this involved in sundered ties and divided loyalties. A son living away from home was expected to visit his mother, and bring his wife with him, two or three times a month at the very least; but Rafel's wife's mother had the same idea, with the added complication that her daughter was 'very close' to her, and would naturally prefer to stay in Malta, at the parental home, *with her husband*, at weekends and on holidays, instead of travelling all that way to Gozo, just to see her mother-in-law.

Poor Rafel, caught in this trap, had come to dread every Saturday and Sunday, every *festa*, every public holiday. And as for Christmas and Easter... Whatever he did was wrong, on one side of the water or the other. At home, it seemed, he was always wrong. He was either a tyrant or a martyr.

Worst of all, in Rafel's long tale of woe, and his mother's enduring opposition, was something which Rafel had only confessed with great shame and embarrassment. From the very beginning, it seemed, his mother had thought that his wife was 'too dark'.

Father Salvatore had heard this scandalous charge before, just as he had heard every other item in the canon of marital strife based on family jealousy, family pride, family greed : on bickering (or worse) between relatives, between mother and daughter-in-law, son and mother-in-law, husband and wife, parent and children, big children and little. But the 'too dark' slur was one of the gravest, none the less.

Such girls were commonly called 'Turkish girls'. It meant that they were likely to prove too ardent, too passionate, too dangerous altogether : that they might sap a man's strength beyond what was seemly, or keep him in bed when he should be in the fields; or, worse still, that they might need more than one man to satisfy their hot blood and outlandish lusts... What mother could bear to see her only son delivered over to such a monster?

Poor Rafel, Father Salvatore thought again. This had been his lot since the dawn of love itself. Now he had been married for thirty years, his mother was still unreconciled, and his wife was still barren.

Rafel said : 'My mother is not well, Dun Salv. She can no longer work as she wishes. Sometimes she can hardly fetch water from the tap. She wants me to come home.'

Father Salvatore found himself making the conventional responses, as he had done a hundred times to Rafel and a thousand times to others in the same case. Rafel's duty was to his wife, first, and then to his mother. His home, and therefore his loyalty, was in Malta. He must explain this – though dutifully and kindly, without hurting anyone's feelings. But one thing was certain : Rafel could not leave his wife and go home to his mother.

He was about to add, with as much impatience as he could find in his heart, that this was a cross which must be borne, and that on the first day of the war, when so many worse things could happen, it must take second place to all the more important problems, when Rafel himself made the point, in a different way.

'She was worried about the war, also,' he told the priest. 'That is why she sent for me. She does not understand.' His stolid face on top of the towering body was showing doubt and confusion. 'I do not understand either, Dun Salv. What is going to happen?'

'We do not know,' Father Salvatore answered. 'War has been declared. Soon it will start. Soon it *must* start. We must be ready, and we must pray for deliverance. That is all I can tell you.'

'How can I be ready, Dun Salv?'

'Go about your work as usual. Wait, and see what happens. Then I will help you.' His heart softened and warmed to the troubled look in the other man's face. 'Rafel! Trust God, and trust me! There will be work to do. When the time comes, I will tell you exactly – *exactly*—' in honest hope, he repeated the last word, 'how to do it.'

'Thank you.' Rafel's simple brow cleared. 'They say it is only the Italians, anyway. They say that a man has only to wave his arms, and they will run away. Do you think that is true, Dun Salv?'

'No.'

But Rafel, secure in new confidence, had not heard him. 'I was told there was fighting in Valletta last night. All the Italians – I mean all the friends of the Italians – had their windows broken. The police had to stop people carrying their furniture away.' He was smiling broadly; this, perhaps, was his idea of war. 'I wish I had been there. I would have broken a window or two! Those Italians!'

Father Salvatore shook his head. 'No, Rafel, you must not say that. Breaking windows and stealing goods in Valletta will not win the war.'

'But it is *something*, Dun Salv.'

'It is wrong.'

With that abrupt dismissal, Father Salvatore became aware, once more, that they were standing on a street corner, under a burning sun, in the middle of a crowded city. The knots of people were still gathering and arguing, the newspapers were still fluttering under the touch of hasty hands; opposite to them, some children had set up a chorus of droning aeroplane noises, with great curving sweeps of their arms, and a simulated rattle of machine-gun fire to counter the invasion. Where did they learn such nonsense? ... He turned back to Rafel. It was time to take up the burden and the business of the day.

'Go back to the church,' he commanded, 'and help the men. There are some baskets of stone chippings to be taken away. I will come later, this afternoon. Go across on the ferry. Have you any money?'

'No, Dun Salv. I spent it.'

Father Salvatore thrust a hand beneath his cassock, extracted a worn leather purse, and picked out some coins.

'Here is two shillings. Remember to put it down in your book.'

'Yes, Dun Salv. Thank you.'

'Go carefully, Rafel. No wine until after the noon Angelus, and then only one glass. And remember – no breaking of windows tonight!'

'I promise you.' The giant saluted with a sweep of a huge hand, and then bent his head submissively. Father Salvatore blessed him. They parted – the big man lumbering and swaying downhill, Father Salvatore starting to climb again.

Before very long, because the slopes were now easier, he stood at the summit of Valletta, on the broad bastion in front of the Auberge de Castile. This was his favourite building, in all the city. No matter if it had been raised less for the glory of God than to house in splendour the fifth Langue of the Knights. God, looking down on its nobility, would surely forgive man for his base intentions, and then bless the result.

It stood four-square against the world, as it had done for nearly 370 years, when it started life as the hostel of the Knights of Spain and Portugal. Girolamo Cassar, the very architect of Valletta (and of the thousands of descendants who bore his name), had built it; Grand Master Pinto had given it a new façade 200 years later. Now it was a marvel of yellow stone, and windows wonderfully ornamented, with a great coat of arms over the door and another on the roof-top.

Today the traffic circled it, and the soldiers moved in and out of that massive front door – for it was still the domain of fighting men, as it had been when soldiers wore curved and vizored helmets, of burnished steel, instead of the ugly snouted gas-masks which themselves seemed to pollute the air. It still remained the fairest of buildings, and the honoured crown of the city.

Father Salvatore, before making the last short detour which would take him to his mother's house, looked at it with pleasure.

It was not a church, nor a cathedral, but it shone with the pious badge of history, none the less.

He was still looking at it, and still finding it fair, when without warning the air-raid sirens began to wail and scream, just above his head.

Father Salvatore was never to forget that moment, nor that sound, nor the sick dismay which siezed hold of him as the first strident note split the air. Though he was to hear hundreds and thousands more such alarms, with a promise – a guarantee – of slaughter not then imaginable, it was always this baptismal one he heard, Malta's first terrible summons to arms. For him, it marked the division between heaven and hell; the heaven of peaceful calm, the hell of wanton death.

As he stood, transfixed, on the plateau in front of the Auberge de Castile, he had a premonition that he would never be the same man again, nor Valletta the same city, nor Malta the same island. 'This is it!' someone in those foolish American films always used to say, when the big fight started or the curtain went up on the tottering musical or the door-bell rang for the bride's first dinner party. For his beloved Malta, this was it.

A soldier, an officer with red tabs on his lapels, had been passing near him when the sirens started. At the sound he paused, and listened, his head on one side. Then he said, crossly: 'Now what?' and walked back into the Auberge de Castile. Father Salvatore wished he could have helped, with a word of comfort for a troubled man; but almost immediately the question was answered by something else – a new and frightful noise, a noise never heard before, a noise such as no one could be ready for, as the air above them was rent by a tremendous barrage of bursting shells.

People started running, while Father Salvatore stood irresolute. They had been told to take shelter at the first warning; he had told many people this himself, from the pulpit and in private homily. But surely someone like himself should stay on watch, the good shepherd who remained faithful as the eyes and ears of his flock? While he waited, breaking the rules in a good cause, he stared upwards, searching the innocent sky for whatever lay in store. Then he saw them.

They were big planes, flying high up, covered by little planes flying even higher. They were coming in from the north-west, from Gozo, making a ruler-straight run over Valletta and Grand Harbour. Father Salvatore found that he had a splendid view of them; he had always known that this was the finest vantage point of the whole city, and now it was proved.

The big planes, which must be bombers, flew overhead in two neat groups, seven first and then three more. There were only ten altogether, but ten was enough. The punctual Italians – after all, it was only the seventh hour of their declared war – whose peaceful sea-planes, under the badge of Alittorio, had up to a few days ago made daily passenger flights across the island, to alight elegantly on the harbour of Marsa Scirocco to the south, were now at hand, not as single spies but in battalions.

Just as no one could have been ready for the first shattering sound of the barrage, so no one could have been steeled for what happened almost immediately afterwards. Fantastically, bombs began to fall: to shake the earth, astonish the city, and kill the people.

The very rock under his feet jumped at the first explosions, and continued so in shuddering waves of shock. Men and women on the exposed plateau cowered back into doorways. Flocks of terrified pigeons soared up and away as the bound humans clung close to the earth. Barking dogs matched the crack and roar of the defiant guns, which rose to a crescendo as the loudest of all, from the monitor well-named HMS *Terror* down in the harbour, launched an ear-splitting broadside into the sky.

Father Salvatore found himself looking down the whole length of St Paul Street, from the Castile Square to the bastions at the lower end. It had become a world of distraught pigmies. There was screaming and panic as people rushed out of their homes, and then darted inside again to crouch and cower under any shelter they could find.

A woman a few yards away from him had fallen on her knees, her head pressed close against the glass front of a shop window, and was screeching '*Gesu! Marija! Gesu!*' in an extremity of fear. A series of rending crashes came from every direction all round him: from nearby Floriana, from Cospicua across the harbour, and then, much louder, from St Elmo at the farther end of Valletta itself.

After a moment, and a prayer which came direct from a

thudding heart, Father Salvatore began to walk downhill, towards the lower town where bombs must have fallen. He lifted and guided the screaming woman through the shop door and under cover. Then, as he walked onwards, he began to meet people coming up the other way : a great sea of people, in fact, a terrorized crowd from whom rose a whimpering and a wailing such as he had hoped never to hear, even in purgatory.

Men, women, and children, stumbling in a helpless tide, flowed past him and away. Some were carrying the first things they had seized on in their panic : sensible things like bedding and cooking pots, foolish things like clocks and pictures and lampshades. Some were pushing laden bicycles, weighed down with mattresses and baskets of food and crates of live chickens.

Many were shouting: 'The tunnel! The tunnel!': making blindly for the deepest womb they could remember, the disused railway tunnel between Valletta and Floriana. They were not to know that there, as cave dwellers under the giant arches, some of them would spend the next four years. Others seemed to be heading for the open country, streaming downhill towards Pieta and Hamrun: anywhere, as long as it was far enough away.

The first bombing had now ceased, and the sky was empty and blameless as a pool of blue water. Stemming the frantic onrush of the fleeing, weaving and fighting his way through it, Father Salvatore kept on walking towards the lower part of the town, until he came to a place where a bomb had fallen. He might have smelled his way there blindfold; a reek of cordite, acrid and horrible, lay over the whole desolate scene.

It was a corner house, now wrenched sideways and sent sprawling into the street. People were wandering round and round it, like crazed dogs, howling, weeping, struck dumb with fear. There were crazed dogs also, snapping and snarling at anything that moved.

Across the doorstep lay an old man, with a leg fearfully gashed by a stone splinter, bleeding to death.

Was it for this that Christ was crucified? ... Father Salvatore dropped on his knees beside the terrible figure. *He must do something.* Just before he flexed his hands to staunch, somehow, the gross flow of blood, which was now seeping across the pavement into the gutter, he glanced naturally up at the sky. As well as the terror of death, surely there must be mercy and help to be found there?

There was. Through the slit of roofs, now rent open like the top of an exploded wine-cask, he saw a glint of metal caught by the sun. Where a moment ago there had been no planes, there was now one, and then another, and then a third; three tiny, strange-looking planes, bulbous and awkward, but streaking across the sky in the direction of Sicily, whence the enemy must have come.

He caught a glimpse, a mere flicker, of red-white-and-blue markings. A man nearby, also staring skywards – perhaps because he could not bear to look at the man on the doorstep – said in utter astonishment:

'They're ours!'

Father Salvatore bent to the shattered human again, and said: 'Let me help you.'

There was a man on that island working on the same side as Father Salvatore, though neither of them knew it. He was an Air Commodore, a New Zealander with a chest-full of medals – as far from Father Salvatore, in fact, as one man could be from another. But he could also say, or think: 'Let me help you,' and flex his hands to staunch a wound and to ward off a worse blow, which could only be death.

He knew, better than most, the official pre-war 'policy line' on Malta: that if the Italians came into any future war, it could never be defended from the air, since Sicily, sixty miles and five minutes' flying time away, was impossibly close: that, though the Navy thought the island crucially important, the Royal Air Force had decided that its air-fields were inadequate, its supply impossible, and the place, a thousand miles from the nearest British bases of Gibraltar or Alexandria, therefore untenable; and that the Army, with all sorts of other things on its mind, had concurred.

Malta, indeed, had been stripped down to the bone and written off before a shot was fired; the definitive brief had been marked *No Action*, like a loan-application from a bankrupt or a diagnosis of terminal cancer. But when the crisis loomed, other men had other thoughts, and the Air Commodore was one of them – not the most august, but certainly the most energetic.

He looked around him. For the island's defence, for the island's life, he needed planes – neither the world's best planes, nor the second-best, but anything which could get up in the air and discourage or outwit enemy raiders. Presently he found them. They did not belong to the Air Force; they were Fleet Air Arm *materiel*, and firmly branded 'Property of the Royal Navy'. But that, he decided, was something which could be left to come out in the wash. If there was such a thing as a wash, when all this uproar in the camp was over.

When he first saw them they were also branded as 'Boxed Spares', which was not at all the same thing as front-line aircraft. They were the various pieces, in numbered thousands neatly crated, of four Gloster Gladiators, left behind at Marsa Scirocco by the aircraft carrier *Glorious* when she sailed away for the Norway campaign, and was sunk.

With the minimum of formality, the Air Commodore appropriated them. They were unpacked, and neatly laid out on the floor, and put together; when this jigsaw was completed they emerged from the chrysalis as four of the last of the bi-plane fighters, with steel fuselages covered with fabric, wooden propellers, armed with four rifle-sized machine-guns (two firing through the props, two housed under the wings), and a maximum speed of 250 mph when going downhill.

They were also found to be 'Sea Gladiators', with arrester-gear and deck-landing hooks, which knocked a bit off that hopeful speed.

No sooner had the muted cheers rung out at Kalafrana, the Marsa Scirocco RAF base, than the Navy asked for them back again, in a way which did not allow for argument. Sadly the planes were pulled to pieces, which were then wrapped in brown paper and re-packed in their crates. Just as that task was finished, the news came that Malta could keep them after all. They were thus unpacked for the second time, by men now experienced as well as profane, and reassembled. The effective date of that was 5 May 1940, a month and a few spare days before the day to remember.

But they could fly – a fact proved a certain distance up the hilt when they were used as target-towing planes for the Army to shoot at. When ready for action on the outbreak of war, with fuel supplied by a submarine, they stood (three at the alert, one kept in reserve for spare parts) on a half-finished airfield defended by Lewis guns and blocked against possible enemy air-borne troop-carriers by old buses, ancient horse-drawn *karrozzini*, junked cars, derelict cranes, lumps of stone, and packing-cases, with one single flight path left clear for their take-off and landing.

Months later, when the trio had been christened Faith, Hope, and Charity, and had actually shot down enemy planes and put the Regia Aeronautica into an operatic turmoil, and had emerged deliriously as Malta's darlings and its only air defenders, Admiral Cunningham, the Commander-in-Chief, was still the target of pained inquiries from the Director of Naval Supplies as to why he had turned over Fleet Air Arm spare-parts to the Royal Air Force.

Chasing the enemy on Raid One of Day One, the three Gladiators – man's answer to the confetti of bureaucracy, man's assertion of hope over foolish myopic fear – were too late on take-off and too slow to intercept. But it was a try, a good try, with more to come on that very morning.

Father Salvatore, having fashioned a tourniquet out of a strip of torn curtain and the handle of a spoon, was relentlessly applying pressure to the leg of a man mercifully unconscious, a man who could only awake to terror and pain. Round about him was a most miserable turmoil: men raising clouds of choking yellow dust as they burrowed under the wreckage of the house, women crying, other women offering advice at the topmost pitch of anguish, children staring avidly at what they should never have seen, dogs licking at spilt blood.

Other people were hurrying past the house with averted eyes, stepping aside like Levites, or like the poor scared human beings they were. An ambulance had got so far up the street, and then been brought to a halt by a pile of rubble.

When the air-raid sirens started to scream again, people screamed with them, and huddled in doorways, or ran away. 'We will have to do better than this,' Father Salvatore thought, as the blood stopped flowing under the pressure of his trembling arms, and a doctor – who suddenly seemed to be the only sane man on the face of the earth – touched him on the shoulder and then took over, with blessed skill, the care of the casualty.

He rose to his feet, his head swimming. His hands were filthy with blood and dust, and his best cassock no longer any better than the one he had lately thrown away as being unfit even for the humblest service of Christ. He had knelt in blood, he observed, though this did not seem at all disreputable. There could be no shame in kneeling, and no longer any astonishment in blood.

The sound of the sirens had died away, and now, with a bitter irony which gave him a moment of superb, unreasoning happiness, it was replaced by the sound of the Angelus. Eight o'clock ... He noticed, still with satisfaction, that many of the people on the street, reverting to a piety no longer universal, had fallen on their knees at the sound of the bells : that men had uncovered their heads, and children been hushed to silence.

He could only be pleased, as he hoped God would be pleased; though whether it was better to pray when in fear, or to pray harder than ever when happy and secure, was something for God to rule on, in His own good time.

A stretcher had at last arrived for the old man, and he was borne away amid wailing lamentations; if to life, or if to death, was something else for divine disposition. A woman with a tear-streaked face – the wife? the daughter? – who now seemed the second most sensible person in the world, brought him a bowl of water, and he washed his hands and tidied up as best he could.

But then a mutter of guns – or were they bombs? – to the north-west told him that all this might happen again, within a few moments. The woman, on the verge of hysteria once more, asked : 'What does it mean? When will it end?'

He comforted her as best he could, speaking of God's will with more authority than he truly felt, even in his most sub-servient heart. The steady procession of people in flight and fear flowed past the house. 'We will have to do better than this,' he thought again. Then he took his leave, and began to make his way towards his mother's house.

He was late, and in great disarray, and sickened by all this terror and pain. But at least, like the planes he knew nothing about, like the Air Commodore he knew nothing about, he had been able to do something for his side, at the first stroke of war.

2

The Most Noble the Baroness Celeste Emilia Santo-Nobile sat in a chair as straight as her own back, in a salon as formal and severe as the style she commanded from her *coiffeuse*, and waited for her son, who was late.

She sat upright, like a long-stemmed flower, because that was the way she had been taught, sixty years ago when she was being schooled for her first drawing-room appearance, and the way in which she had taught her daughter when the turn for this arrived. Her hands were folded in her lap because that was how hands, if they had to be idle, must always be composed.

Her face, exquisitely beautiful when young, markedly handsome in old age, betrayed nothing of her feelings, which on this strange morning were uneasy. Faces, even in private, should behave like people: with good manners, with calm assurance, with absolute control.

Her black silk dress, the dress equally of a widow and a baroness, was composed in the same way, in straight folds which almost reached her footstool. The high silent room, with its louvred windows and tapestried walls, was only a setting for its occupant; when she was there, sole yet paramount, it was, for all its magnificence, scarcely a room in its own right. Rooms, like faces and people, should know their place, and observe it meticulously.

At her feet a tawny Maltese hound, also very well behaved, dozed contentedly, its nose inching towards a tiny bar of sunlight. Its front paws were crossed one over the other, but the effect was heraldic and correct rather than relaxed.

It was only her thoughts which Emilia Santo-Nobile could not quite control. Her son was more than an hour late; morning coffee was at seven-fifteen precisely, and had been so for fifty-two mornings of every year for at least twenty years, with half an hour's grace in mid-winter, and it was very unlike Salvatore – it was impossibly unlike him – to keep her waiting without a message. Especially on a morning such as this, when the city, and even the massive walls of the Palazzo Santo-Nobile, had been so shaken, so beset by intruders, and so insulted.

It was possible that something might have happened to him (she would not phrase it, even to herself, any more concisely than this : the form of words had served for her thoughts about her husband, in the old forgotten war, up till the very moment when bleak death had crudely translated them). She felt herself vulnerable, which was a new idea, and hateful for its novelty as well as its weakness.

With an elder son who passed his time – his life, indeed – in a section of Parisian society so smart, *soigné*, and elegant that it could only be seen as false; with a younger son who was a priest, and no more – God forgive her – than a priest; a dear daughter who was all that she wished, allied with a son-in-law whom she had long found odious—

Far away, a bell rang, and the dog at her feet gave a small, well-bred growl of warning. The Baroness, who knew her great house as intimately and exactly as another woman might know a two-roomed apartment, recognized the sound instantly. It was not the front door, which was below the room in which she sat, but a side door – called the postern door since her grandfather's time – which gave access to the inner courtyard. It was the door used by intimates, and by her family, and thus the bell she had been waiting to hear.

In an unusual movement – because to watch one's guests arriving was an unacceptable vulgarity – she rose, and crossed to a window which gave on to the courtyard. Below her, a huge bougainvillea in full scarlet flower, and a lemon tree with a trunk so massive and gnarled that it was astonishing to see the delicate fruit it now bore, were the frame for what she found herself watching.

A liveried footman – it was Francis, a new well-mannered boy, but he slouched when he thought himself unobserved, and she must remember to tell Gregory to correct him before it became a habit – a footman crossed the courtyard, moving from shadow to bright sunshine and then to shadow again, as an actor with a very small part leaves the wings for the lighted stage and then disappears on the opposite side.

Out of her sight, he opened the postern door a little too energetically, so that the sound was needlessly loud. There had been enough noise that morning... Then there was a pause, and a murmur of voices. Then Salvatore, a black figure extraordinarily distinct against the sleepy, sun-warmed greens and yellows of the courtyard, came into view.

He looked the same as he always did: small, and self-contained, and solid as the Church he served. He was alive after all... This was as much as Baroness Santo-Nobile would allow herself. She drew back from the window, and when Father Salvatore presently came into the salon, his mother was back in her chair, still and authoritative like the tapestry flanking the walls, with the dog at her feet to complete a picture he remembered, and welcomed, and loved.

'Good morning, Mother.' He advanced and kissed her cheek, and was aware, with a pleasure almost sensual, of dry frail flesh, cared-for, old and valuable at the same time. To be young and beautiful was an easy privilege; to be seventy-three years old and beautiful was the greatest of mysteries, an accomplishment and a gift to an undeserving world. 'I am so sorry to be late. I couldn't even send a message.'

'What delayed you, Salvatore?'

He could not be surprised, only pleased. 'Mother, you're magnificent! You must have heard the bombing. I was terribly worried – I was afraid it would be near here.'

'The bombing,' his mother repeated, as she might have said 'the heat' or (if she had been aware of it) 'the price of butter'. 'You mean, it was made difficult to come here? Surely you could have taken a *karrozzin*, or sent a message?' She looked at the great clock standing sentinel against the wall, solemnly ticking away the minutes, as it had done – and a date on its raddled face proudly announced it – since it was first fashioned by Thomas Tompion in 1681. 'Nearly half past eight... Coffee will be ruined!'

She was doing it on purpose, Father Salvatore realized, and he forgave her, and loved her for it. She was seeking to maintain that this was a day like any other day, in spite of cruel surprises; and she must, God bless her, have been anxious about him... He smiled, and met her lively eyes, which were examining him with their customary thoroughness, and said:

'Well, I am here at last. I really am sorry to have kept you waiting.'

'You have a new cassock,' she announced. Her eyes strayed downwards, as they often did. 'I suppose you did not think of a pair of new boots as well.'

'A cassock was all I needed. I bought it on the way here.'

'Ready-made?'

He smiled again. 'I am size one. There are small priests, and medium priests, and large priests, and very large priests. It is really quite simple.'

'*What* your father would have said!'

They were interrupted by the ceremony of coffee. It arrived in a delicately curved silver pot, carried high on a silver salver by a footman. A second footman bore a second tray, on which the blue-and-gold fluted cups gleamed cunningly and cheerfully, like the promise of delight. It was preceded by Gregory, the major-domo, who had himself been a senior footman when Baroness Santo-Nobile awoke to her wedding day: a little gnarled walnut of a man, stooped like a gnome, but majestically dignified in every movement and every stillness.

Now he supervised the setting down of the trays, the pouring, the serving, the offering of sugar and cream, with small directional waves of a gloved hand. Then he nodded to the footmen, who withdrew. Then he bowed, murmured 'Madame', and left the room in his turn. The silver buckled shoes moved soundlessly, even on polished marble; and the doors, twelve feet high, closed behind him with a gentle click, no louder than a footfall at the other end of a church.

One lived by contrast, Father Salvatore thought, as he sipped his coffee, which was not 'ruined' at all but made, as usual, from Colombian beans hand-ground at the moment the doorbell was heard. If he had not lately walked and knelt in fear on the lower streets of Valletta, he would not now so enjoy the deep peace and contentment of this well-ordered house; if he had not the measuring-stick of the Palazzo Santo-Nobile, cherished and loved since he first opened infant eyes to its magnificent ceilings, he might not realize so vividly the violence and cruelty of the world outside, nor be so determined to return to it, and there serve out all the time which God allowed.

But it was those lofty ceilings which now gave him uneasiness.

'You should really be on the ground floor, Mother,' he advised. 'Particularly when the warnings sound. It would be so much safer there.'

'It would be very *peculiar*,' she answered tartly. 'In the kitchens? In the coach house? In the ballroom? In the chapel? Am I a *soldier*, that I should camp out? The idea of this war is ridiculous enough, without people taking it to extremes!'

'Mother, you must treat this seriously!' he admonished her, quite sharply. There were moments when he could presume on the authority of a priest, in place of the duty of a son; such a balance, such a choice, was an enormously subtle one, like a note in music which signals a revolution in tone or colour; it meant that he must be stern, and she submissive – a reversal of roles which tampered with the cycle of life itself.

But at forty-five he no longer hesitated, as he had done when he was a young priest, when the ordainment, the holy authority, the anointing, still had elements of a masquerade. 'There *is* danger,' he insisted. 'You heard the bombs falling. There have been two raids already, and this is only the first day. We are in the war, and it may become terrible. This house can be hit, just as easily as anywhere else.'

She was watching his face, as much as listening to his words. 'Has there been much damage, Salvatore?'

'I'm afraid so.'

'Where?'

'Near St Elmo. Floriana, I think, and Pieta. And across the harbour.'

'There are dead already?'

'Yes.'

She sighed. 'Very well... I will think about it... I hope my son-in-law is satisfied.'

Though the subject had been a matter of family controversy, expressed sometimes in good-natured banter, sometimes in violent collision, for more than a year, it was still a shock to hear his mother make such a remark, on this morning, in such bitter terms. The fact that it *was* a family concern, yet might now invite the attention of a much wider world, made it even more disturbing.

To Father Salvatore, the moment and the remark recalled another mother – the mother of Rafel. Just as she would have said of her daughter-in-law, with the same contempt: 'She is a Turkish girl,' so Baroness Santo-Nobile might one day be prepared to admit of her daughter's husband, for all the world to hear: 'Lewis Debrincat is pro-Italian.'

Father Salvatore had always accepted his brother-in-law's inclination as perfectly understandable, even admirable. It was a matter of aesthetic preference. For Debrincat, Italy, whatever she did, was still the nation of Michelangelo, Bernini, Canaletto, Verdi, Leonardo da Vinci, Dante, and Giotto. There was also the matter of Rome itself, repository of its own genius... But on the morning when the bombs were falling, Italy was none of these men, nor these things.

It could only be seen and felt as the nation of Mussolini, the hated killer and destroyer, the bombastic clown whose obscene jokes could bring the circus of their world down in ruins; and it would ever remain so, for as far as one could see ahead. That was what Lewis Debrincat would now have to face, or else suffer the fate of all suspect traitors.

The Baroness, seeing her son silent, was continuing to speak, in a way which had become familiar, and ominous.

'I know you make allowances for him, Salvatore, but such opinions are really insufferable! To stand up for that ridiculous Mussolini! The man who tells us that the Maltese are a branch of the Italian race, and our language an Italian dialect! That we should now join his Third Empire, before it is too late! Yet I have heard Lewis say, in this very room' – and she mimicked him, a very rare departure from good manners: ' "Italy is closer to us than Britain can ever be".'

'But Mother, you know what he meant – well, the whole range of cultural ties. He did not really mean it politically.'

'He meant that he had made a choice.' The Baroness, sitting straighter than ever, spoke with a steely determination. It was her best style, the core of her proud spirit, and Father Salvatore knew that he could never match it. 'His choice is the people who are bombing Malta this morning... Far too many of his lawyer friends think the same way. Far too many politicians. Far too many priests, also – *I know!*' She spoke with the freedom which only a munificent benefactor of the Church might assert, as of right. 'What can the people of Malta think, when they are set such an example from the top?'

'The people of Malta think Mussolini is a joke. You know they despise the Italians.'

'Then they have more sense than their betters!'

'In any case, I do not think that Lewis will persevere.'

'He will persevere in prison, as far as I am concerned!'

'Oh, Mother!' he began, sick at heart to see her so angry, so eaten up by hatred – or was it fear? – so uncharitable, so less than Christian. If her son-in-law erred so atrociously, then he was to be pitied, not despised. Hate the sin, love the sinner... He was about to admonish her once more – and it would take all his spirit, let alone his skill – when the subject was brought to an abrupt halt, in the most appropriate way imaginable.

The sirens set up their anguished wailing, the guns opened their iron throats, and almost immediately the tormenting bombs began to fall.

This time the raid was short and sharp, yet not less terrifying, less murderous and wicked. Isolated in the huge house, a square castle round an inner courtyard, they could not tell the direction from which the explosions came; they were simply there, all about them – in the trembling air, the shaking floor, the fretful movement of a chandelier, the fall of plaster from the ceiling, and the fearful noise all over the city.

While it endured, they endured: the Baroness in absolute stillness, the priest with hands and finger-tips composed in prayer, prepared to live or die at will – Thy will.

When the noise ceased, as suddenly as it had begun, Father Salvatore crossed himself, and was unreasonably happy to see his mother do the same. Ah, she was a loving and faithful servant still... Then they found that they were smiling at each other, as children smile when a huge growling dog begins to thump its tail, or a thunder-storm dies away in the distance, without striking them dead under their bedroom roof. In some strange way, the terror of the raid brought a cleansing of the spirit, a surcease to pettiness and recrimination.

They spoke no more of Lewis Debrincat, but of smaller matters, matters of before the war – already there was this precious distinction, and perhaps it would prove the one to cling to, in testing times, in tumult and fear. They spoke of his little church of St Barnabas beyond the Cottonera Lines, and the people it would serve, and the Santo-Nobile chapel, dedicated to God and to the memory of her husband. Had ever a British naval officer been so commemorated? Well, there was Nelson, there was Sir Francis Drake...

'You should have been a great historian, Salvatore,' she chided him gently. By this she meant, not a historian instead of a priest, which was an honourable calling, but a historian instead of the priest he had become: a priest without preferment, nor the wish for it.

But he did not mind. Such questions had been settled long ago, by a hundred strands in the weaving of life, by a hundred choices of one answer over another, a turn to the left instead of to the right. It was too late now – and that did not matter either.

He spoke once more of her safety, and the fears he had for it.

'Should you not leave for the country? Valletta *must* be the place they will drop their bombs, because of the harbour. You could move out to Mdina. Or even across to Gozo.'

She shook her head. This was another matter which, for her, had been settled long ago, in sober speculation, in determined choice.

'No,' she answered. 'I will stay here, whatever happens. This house is strong. And I trust General Dobbie.' She was not going to argue about it. 'But what will you do, Salvatore?'

'Whatever I must.'

'Will you go back to the monastery?'

'Yes. And take care of the church, and work in the village. There are people who need me.'

'I know.'

The great door to the salon opened softly, and it was Francis, the young footman, whose back was sometimes not as straight as it should be. But it was straight enough now.

'It is Monsignor Scholti, Baroness. He apologizes for being a little early. Mr Gregory has shown him into the chapel.'

'Ask him to come up.'

Father Salvatore rose. 'Well, I must say goodbye. I have some things to do before lunch.'

'Oh, stay a little longer. Scholti is sure to be full of news. Why do you always avoid him?'

He smiled. It was another old occasion of remonstrance. 'I do not avoid him. I do not avoid anyone. But he is always so busy, and I am – always so busy.'

'Salvatore, he is only a monsignor.'

'*Only?*' But he smiled as he bent to say farewell. She was so much loved, so wilful, so entire a person in the image of God. When she asked the formal '*Benedizzjoni*', he could only bless

her, as he did now. '*Tkun imbierka*... And please think about
going downstairs, when the raids are on.'

'I promise.' Since he had accorded her the whole of God's
protection when she made her dutiful request, she could hardly
answer otherwise. 'Give my love to Giovanna and the children.'

'And Lewis?'

She was entire to the last. 'Give him *your* love!'

Father Salvatore made his way downstairs: unescorted, as
one of the family, and slowly, for the sheer pleasure of savour-
ing, on such a fearful day as this, the tranquil glory of the
house where he was born. The rooms themselves were high
and spacious, with windows small in proportion, according to
the sensible Maltese choice; who, living under a glaring Mediterranean sun, would wish to allow its burning heat to invade the
coolness within?

It was even a pleasure to touch, as he passed, the sleeping
stone of the passageways; sleeping, and holding embalmed for
ever other sleepers of a million years ago – tiny fossilized
molluscs, little seashells which had once been houses themselves, minute fish caught and killed and fixed eternally in the
long-ago sandy bed of the sea.

Great sweeping wrought-iron grilles covered all the outer
windows: a reminder of turbulent times when a house such
as this had to fend for itself, with no one to come to its rescue
if it ever dropped its guard.

Built at the time of the first *auberges* of the Knights, the
Palazzo Santo-Nobile rivalled the best of them in splendour,
even the Auberge de Castile itself. There could be no question
why it should not do so: to the Santo-Nobile barony, a creation
of one of the early kings of Aragon, Alfonso V ('the Mag-
nanimous') in 1434, the Knights of 1530 were newcomers,
interlopers, bringing their rancorous troubles to a peaceful
island and embroiling it in all sorts of excess and violence.

Indeed, most of the Maltese nobility – ten barons, ten counts,
nine marquises, with their great names which had the ring of
history: Saint George, Testaferrata Olivier, Ciantar Paleologo,
Scicluna, Sceberras (it was Mount Sceberras which bore the
whole weight of Valletta on its back) – most of these honoured
families were like the Knights: a little late upon the scene
compared with the Santo-Nobiles, a little new to history. They
must be labelled '*After* the Knights', as Noah, or probably Mrs

Noah in a mood of disparagement, might have murmured: '*After* the Flood.'

This was his mother's pride, not his own, Father Salvatore thought, as he walked down the last flight of a marble staircase, between tall pillars which had been serviceable before the Spanish Armada, to the entrance hall. He had abjured all such worldliness; she had not, and (speaking as a son rather than a priest) he would not expect her to.

She was the guardian of her name, as well as its bearer; the ancient lineage imposed a paramount twin duty, to preserve and to endure, and the family motto – *Stabilitas Contra Mundum, against* the world, not with it or in it – enshrined this for all time. The Santo-Nobiles had always been fiercely and strictly proud. Though their entrance door was necessarily as wide as a travelling coach, their choice of visitors was traditionally narrow.

Grand Masters had certainly never eluded the mesh of this net. Grand Master Nicolas Cotoner, of the Spanish Langue of 1663, *yes*: the splendid fortifications of the Cottonera Lines were alike his monument and his card of entrance. Grand Master Pinto de Fonçeca, *no*: he was Portuguese, and dabbled in alchemy, which by 1745 was no longer reputable. Grand Master Antoine de Paule, accused by an Inquisitor who later became Pope Alexander VII of irreverence, sensuality, duplicity, and an indifference to censure, *yes*: he was excellent company, he entertained *en prince* at the newly-built San Anton Palace, and Inquisitors could often be wrong.

The invader Napoleon, *no* – a more pliant family had obliged him, and been disgraced for ever. Sir Alexander Ball, the first Civil Commissioner of the island, *yes*. Lord Nelson, at the peak of his brilliant career after the Battle of the Nile, *yes*, though it was a pity that Sir William and Lady Hamilton, the one a cuckold in his dotage, the other a public harlot, had to be included in his company.

The young Lord Byron, *yes* – his talent just outweighed a notorious love affair embarked on within the Palazzo Santo-Nobile itself. The ridiculous popinjay Disraeli, who paraded the streets of Valletta with long curls, rings on his fingers, gold chains round his neck, a blue velvet suit, a rainbow-coloured sash, pistols and daggers stuck in his belt, scarlet slippers, and a six-foot-long porcelain Turkish pipe, *no*.

William IV, the Sailor King of England who had fathered ten illegitimate children by a married Irish actress before ascending to the throne, certainly not; and King Edward VII, another monarch much too merry for the Victorian Santo-Nobiles, only once.

Father Salvatore paused at the foot of the stairs, and listened, just as he had listened when a little boy, venturing downstairs into great company and great surroundings. Now there was only silence: silence, and peace, and the feeling of history encased in golden stone. Now it was his mother who ruled here, and preserved, and endured. Now the barony, which in defiance of any nonsense from the Salic Law of exclusion could pass from male to female and back again, had passed to her.

One day it would be his elder brother's, the 'man of the world' whose Parisian follies were as foolish as anything in a foolish universe. It would never be his own; though he loved it, and honoured it, he did not want it. He only bore its name, which by custom persisted even though his father had been a British naval officer.

Father Salvatore was eternally proud of his father. But by English law his name would have to be set down as Salvatore Westgate-Saul. With the best will in the world...

Now, at the courtyard door, a shadow moved to greet him, and then a man. It was old Gregory, the major-domo of the household.

In Father Salvatore's favourite play, which was *Hamlet*, there was a character who always reminded him of old Gregory. But he was not exactly a living man; he was the man who had become a skull by the time the grave-diggers' scene was reached. It was poor Yorick, he that was the King's Jester.

It could never be said that old Gregory was a jester, or anything like it; he was of far too great consequence for that. He never jested, and no one ever jested with him. But for Father Salvatore the remembrance was embedded for ever in a single line, a loving memorial to the past: 'He hath bore me on his back a thousand times.'

This was his prized childhood memory of Gregory, who could always be somehow cajoled or wheedled or tormented or plagued into serving as a mount for a small boy: as a mettle-some steed which could be whipped – well, pretend-whipped

– into a galloping, plunging ride all round the courtyard – this very courtyard where they now met.

Gregory bowed, with a grace which Father Salvatore could never have matched. His small shrunken body – he must be over eighty now – was still as sinewy and controlled as that of a man half his age. Only his face was troubled.

'Dun Salv,' he said, and gestured, to show that he wished, this morning, to conduct Father Salvatore round the court-yard. It was immediately apparent why. 'Dun Salv,' Gregory said again, as he began to walk beside the priest on the shadowed side of the open space. 'What does it all mean? What in the world is happening?'

It was the same question that everyone was asking, the question not he nor anyone else could answer ... 'The war has started, Gregory. That is all I know.'

'I heard the bombs, Dun Salv.' Gregory's face peered up at him, pinched and pale, even trembling. He was, indeed, nearly eighty that morning – and yet he had served their coffee with the same faultless aplomb as ever. Brave old man... There might – there *must* – be many more like him... 'I *felt* the bombs. Is it safe here?'

'It is as safe as anywhere else. But I have asked the Baroness to come downstairs – perhaps to the old armoury – when the warning sounds. She will think about it.'

'The armoury!' Gregory repeated in astonishment. 'But there are no chairs! It is so small!'

'That is why it is safer. Bring down some chairs and a table. Even a bed. Make it a place to live.' He touched the old man on the shoulder. 'There will be many changes like that. You must look after her, Gregory.'

'With my life!' Gregory answered, and the formal phrase took on sudden reality and truth. 'But should we not go to the country?'

'The Baroness does not wish to leave here.'

Silence fell: the answer was enough for Gregory, and for himself. They walked together in the shadows, past the climb-ing bougainvillea with its scarlet and purple veins, past the well which, beneath its crested coping-stone, probed a hundred feet deep into the vitals of Mount Sceberras: past the open-fronted stables where a light travelling-coach and an old two-wheeled *calèche*, slung on leather thongs, panelled with the

Santo-Nobile arms, stood waiting for their next or last journey.

The courtyard still maintained its warm and sleepy peace; it had been the same for himself as a little boy, the same for Gregory as an old man whose course was nearly run. Was it all to be destroyed, to die, as that other old man with the shattered leg must surely now have died? He shook off such thoughts, as they reached the postern door.

'You must look after her, Gregory,' he said again. 'I will come as often as I can. If you need any help or advice, send a message to me. Or to Mr Debrincat: he is nearer.'

Not by a flicker did Gregory's face react to the latter choice. All he said was: 'I will remember you, Dun Salv.'

Then another shadow moved towards him, a bulky shadow emerging from the small chapel as if the chapel had released one of its buttresses for service outside. With a feeling of un-Christian regret which he tried hard to suppress, Father Salvatore saw that it was Bruno Scholti.

Monsignor Scholti, PEP, was all that he could never be. Father Salvatore admitted the fact without vexation, with no feeling of any sort except, occasionally, relief. Just as he had forsworn pride, so he had forsworn envy, another sin prominent in the calendar of mischief. It was already obvious that Scholti was destined to take the high road, he the low. His only regret was that he had to disappoint so many people on the way.

Whereas Father Salvatore was small and bull-like, awkward in his movement, simple in his thoughts, Monsignor Scholti was large and bland and sleek, utterly assured in voice and bearing, never at a loss for an opinion, never without a point of view calculated to set everyone present nodding their agreement. At thirty-five he was still young, though committed already to a certain fleshiness which would advance with age and with advancement itself.

'Fat priest, thin people,' was how some of the more cynical members of the faithful phrased it. Father Salvatore preferred St Jerome's verdict, still stern but more general in tone: 'A fat paunch never breeds fine thoughts', and he coupled this with the same saintly man's crisp directive: 'Avoid, as you would the plague, a priest who is also a man of business.'

Monsignor Scholti was a man of business: not in any crude commercial sense, but in the particular one of being busy at all times – busy with people, busy with Church affairs, busy socially, busy with opening things, and blessing things (new houses, new fishing-boats, new wells and donkeys and tractors), and making speeches on any doctrinal matter which had social significance, and chairing committees on this and that.

He was known to be 'very close' to the bishop – or at least, this was what everyone said of him, which was just as effective, whether it was true or false. His Vatican medal, *Pro Ecclesia et Pontifice*, proclaimed his repute in influential circles. His attachment to the Baroness Santo-Nobile, compounded of a courtier's intimacy, an impeccable social manner, and an attitude to rank which never fell short of the obsequious, was part of the same picture – and not the least revealing aspect of it.

Yet it must be recorded that, with his fine sonorous voice and impressive stance, his celebration of the Mass could be truly beautiful, and moving to the point of tears – which was all to the glory of God, and should never be forgotten in the accounting.

Father Salvatore, divided in thought, wishing to be generous yet beset by a small infection which could only be labelled distrust – Father Salvatore always thought of Monsignor Scholti as 'a churchman'. It was not the same thing as a priest – and one must be meticulously careful of pride there.

But as a future cardinal? It was not impossible. Father Salvatore grudged Scholti nothing, and would not grudge him this : it was – it must be – part of the awesome pattern, proof of the divine love of Christ which they both shared.

What Scholti thought of Father Salvatore was always impenetrably wrapped under layers of *bonhomie*, social calculation, Christian charity (one must not rob him of that, either), and an obvious doubt as to what the other man thought of *him*. Such wariness (so weak was the flesh) was bound to be an important factor, even between priests... This was not the sort of morning when Scholti's opinion would be made any more manifest.

'Salvu!' Monsignor Scholti advanced towards him like a one-man tide of benevolence, cresting to its own flood as it went along. His large brown eyes beamed a princely welcome, as if he were the host, and Father Salvatore, a son of this house, were only a wandering traveller who had made his way to sanctuary. 'How very nice to catch you, on the wing as it

were! Tell me straight away, how is the Baroness? Is she
well? I was so *worried* about her!'

Old Gregory had by now melted away behind the portico,
having first waved Francis out of earshot. The two men were
alone.

'My mother is well,' Father Salvatore answered. He thought:
I speak of *my* mother, not *your* Baroness, and then, to make
up for such a foolish stab of jealousy, such pettiness of spirit,
he added: 'But thank you for asking after her. And for coming
to see her too, on such a terrible day.'

Monsignor Scholti raised eyes and hands heavenwards. 'The
worst day of our lives! Have you heard any news?'

'No. Only the raids.'

'Three raids so far, with more than thirty Italian planes!'
Scholti had naturally heard all the news, and more. 'They say
the bombing in Senglea and Cospicua has been terrible. There
was the whole crew of a gun wiped out at one stroke, at Fort
St Elmo. Other people were killed. Some were buried alive.
Poor souls! They are going to evacuate the whole of Valletta,
if this goes on. As many as a quarter of a million people. They
will have to be *billeted*, all over the island. Perhaps in Gozo as
well. The bishop is to make a statement... Are you going to
the Debrincats for lunch?'

'Yes.'

'I hope Lewis will be all right.'

Something in the other man's tone caught Father Salvatore's
attention. 'How do you mean, all right? Safe? He is as safe in
Sliema as anywhere else.'

Monsignor Scholti assumed a look of diplomatic intensity.
'Oh, I am sure your brother-in-law and sister will be *safe*, so
far as anyone is safe from bombing. That is not quite what I
meant. I meant – well, shall we say, politically.'

Father Salvatore waited.

'I think we both know,' Scholti went on, in his best judicial
manner, 'that Lewis has made himself something of a reputation, these last few months. His sympathies have seemed to
lie with the Italians. Perhaps we have misunderstood him...
You know that there have been arrests already?'

'No.'

Monsignor Scholti flashed his most understanding smile.
'Salvu, you *must* take an interest in these things! Yes, a number

of people were detained, last night and this morning. By the
police. I am told that they will be interned. In some cases
it is certainly unfair. As if a man like Borg-Ganado could be
a spy or a *saboteur*! But in war' – Scholti looked as though he
knew all about war – 'sometimes the innocent have to suffer.
One cannot be too careful. One must guard against the enemy
within.'

So that, Father Salvatore thought, was going to be Bruno
Scholti's line of argument, for public consumption anyway...
One learned a little every day, with God's grace, and this must
be today's lesson... He was about to agree, and thus dispose
of the matter, when he felt suddenly a most acute discomfort
in the region of his neck.

This humbug, this fraud, is sticking in my throat, he thought,
in a moment of real panic. So the phrase actually meant something, the phrase was true; one could swallow so much and
then – even if one were a priest, endowed with all the charity
of heaven, with compassion and understanding formed in the
very image of Christ – something sounded so flagrant and dis-
honest that it lodged in the gullet, and would not go down...
He heard himself saying, with a directness which astounded
him :

'Will *you* be all right?'

Scholti looked back at him, with a most genuine expression
of astonishment. Then the liquid brown eyes grew reproachful
as a cuffed spaniel's. 'My dear Salvu! What *can* you mean?'

Father Salvatore was having none of this. Whether it was the
shock of the bombing, or all the troubled people he had met,
or the danger to his mother, or the peril to Malta, or a private
need to conquer fear, he found himself already set in a most
curious mood of rebellion.

In war, someone had said, the first casualty was truth. Why
should it not be lies as well? ... Why should one countenance
such deceit as this? ... Where had Monsignor Scholti been,
when Father Salvatore knelt in blood? ... He looked up at
the tall figure, and for once he did not mind having to do
so.

'I will tell you. You seemed to be hinting that Lewis Debrincat
might be arrested and interned, for being pro-Italian. You
seemed to be hinting that he *ought* to be, to guard against the
enemy within. But I have heard you agreeing with him many

times, when we were talking about the Italians. You once
said—' he searched his memory for the florid phrases, and
found them easily: '"I would forgive Italy anything for one
line of her poetry! A people of such genius cannot be bad! In
fact they cannot be wrong!"' He saw a sulky look come over
Scholti's face, and a brief flash of something which could even
have been hatred, and he thought: On a morning such as this,
when one needs friends almost as much as one needs the help
of God, I have made an enemy... But, though he would suffer
torments of conscience for his outburst: though a whole night
of prayer, or a whole week of penitence, would not take it
away, he persisted to the end. 'Are the Italians right this
morning? Are they to be forgiven? Do you still admire their
genius?'

'But Salvu—' Monsignor Scholti recovered his self-assurance,
and his utterly reasonable good humour, as easily as a man
picking up a dropped handkerchief, 'you cannot be so unfair!
It is unlike you. You take a few chance words out of context... Of course I was only speaking of poetry. True poets
love all mankind, and we should return that love.'

'Not all the Italian poets love us.'

Monsignor Scholti said: 'You are really being very difficult
today. But I do understand.'

'I was thinking of Gabriele D'Annunzio – "Malta is no
longer an island, but an infection to be cured."'

'Words out of context again...' Mastering his sorrow, Monsignor Scholti looked at his watch, which was worth looking at:
an elegant gold orb of a watch, which sat on his fat wrist
like a favourite canary which would never leave home. Italian-
Swiss, no doubt... 'Well, I am expected, as you know. Goodbye, Salvu. Try not to worry too much. And please give my
greetings to Giovanna and Lewis and the children.'

He turned without waiting for an answer, and began to
walk away. Within a few moments he had been joined by
Gregory, and a stately progress began across the courtyard.

Father Salvatore, watching their diminishing figures – fat
young priest, thin old servant – wondered what Scholti would
tell his mother, exactly how he would phrase it, how he would
manage to convey a certain dissatisfaction – no, that would be
too strong – a certain *regret* that dear Salvatore, who perhaps
was overworked, or too much upset by the thought of war,

had let slip certain observations which, making every Christian allowance, could only be construed as—

And this was the first morning of a bloody war? ... Father Salvatore smiled his goodbye to Francis, who had opened the postern door for him, stepped outside into a narrow crowded street, and, with relief, became once more a citizen of Valletta.

From the great main gate of Valletta to Sliema along the coast was a distance of four miles, and downhill all the way. For Father Salvatore, already ashamed of himself, there was something entirely appropriate in walking downhill; it was what he deserved, a descent into humility after the pride of his confrontation with Monsignor Scholti. This was something he *must* conquer, if he was to have any peace within himself. For it had all happened before, and now he had fallen from grace again.

From any point of view, his collision with his superior was disgraceful. He could not help recalling the last time it had happened, less than a year ago: when Scholti had said something, at a party at the Palazzo Santo-Nobile, which he had thought pompous and affected, and he had said so, in terms too plain: when Scholti had outfaced him, as he had every right to do, with a formal rebuke: and when he had heard from his mother, later, an account of the affair which had driven him nearly desperate with anger and frustration.

'I cannot tell you,' the Baroness had said, 'how *grieved* Monsignor Scholti was when he spoke to me about this. Grieved with himself! Do you know what he said? "My one regret is that I did not give him time to repent." Salvatore, you *must* learn to get on with people!'

The fact that he found Scholti's remark odiously sanctimonious had delayed his repentance almost until it was too late. Now, with this lesson in mind, he was repentant already. Now he walked downhill, into the shadows, into a small annexe of purgatory and shame which was of his own making. *Mea culpa*, he found, not for the first time, was not a pious cry nor a way out. It was a way in, and 'in' was into a world of remorse.

One learned a little every day, he thought again. Today's lesson was the lesson of life, the same for a priest as for everyone else. God's will was made up of small things and great;

the great were often inexplicable, but the small were still too big for private resentment.

One should only fold the hands, and walk downhill. There would come a time – and it would be God's good time, not to be measured by man's little invented ticking clock – when one would walk uphill again.

Presently he found that in walking downhill he was not alone. In fact he had never been less alone, on any walk in Malta. An exodus from the high ground was now in full spate, and he was part of it.

It was a steady flow of the prudent, the fearful, and the desperate which must have been going on all the morning, from the moment – now so long ago – when he had braced himself, after the first fall of the bombs, to walk down St Paul Street towards the dust-clouds and the smell of cordite : when he had first met this jostling tide of people in flight from Valletta.

Now that he was with them, going their way, he could observe them more closely, more individually, and the result was not reassuring. These people had been transformed, within a few hours, into refugees, in fear of their lives; the loss of status, the change from man at home to man on the run, was a bitter degradation.

Under a blazing sun, choked by their own dust, escorted by clouds of flies, men, women, and children shuffled and stumbled downhill in a forlorn torrent, laden with their goods. There was weeping, there was public cursing as he had never heard before; there was entreaty to God, but it was being made, not in loving humility but in rage and resentment and animal terror, as if God were certainly going to be blamed for all this, unless He could give them a convincing answer.

There were even, he thought, some side-glances at himself, glances of suspicion and mistrust; his very cassock made him a uniformed agent of this awful visitation, and he also had better come up with the right answer if he wanted to keep his repute.

Even if this were his own imagination, it was only part of the same evil dream which gripped them all, the private sector of public chaos.

He noticed a slatternly woman walking by his side, with a string of five ragged, noisy children whom she could not control.

Perhaps she had never controlled them, and this was no more wretched a day than any other day. But her repeated shouts of 'Ejja, ejja!' – 'Come on, come on!' – were not only ugly, like the harsh cries of a parrot. They were also totally disregarded, in a way which showed that this, her loving family, had a contempt for the mother which they could only have learned from the adult world, or from another parent.

She was wheeling a pram piled high with worn blankets, and loaves of bread, and tins of olive oil, and tomatoes, and filthy underclothes. Peeping out from under a mattress was a sixth child, a child with enormous frightened eyes and a face the same colour as the bread. Presently one of the other children, lunging out at a brother who was also a tormentor, stumbled under the front wheels of the pram.

It tipped over, and fell on its side. The varied load it bore spewed out over the roadway. The last household object to be thrown clear was the sixth child, which landed softly on a pillow. But it screamed in fear none the less, and the woman began to scream also, on a high note issuing from a mouth which suddenly seemed demented.

Worst of all, the people went on walking past her, unconcerned, indifferent. They stepped to one side if they had to, and that was the extent of their compassion.

Father Salvatore, after calming her, helped her to set the pram to rights. Then, because she seemed so distraught, so defeated by her tribulation, he asked: 'Are you alone? Where is your husband?'

She looked at him with blank eyes. She was unrelievedly ugly, with a sack-like body and great swollen legs. She pointed vaguely ahead, down the hill towards Pieta.

'With the rest of the children.'

'How many children have you?'

'Sixteen,' the woman answered. She looked at his cassock, and then added, with a ferocious snarl: 'Thanks be to God and the Virgin Mary!'

It was no more than the literal translation of the words which accompanied nearly every birth-announcement in Malta – Deo Gratias et Mariae. But because of the tone in which it was said, the way it had suddenly exploded from a dull mind, it was the most shocking thing which Father Salvatore had heard that day, a day of sufficient shocks already.

He could have wept for the woman, and her straggling brood of children, and the wounded faith which her sneering words betrayed. Was this what was happening to Malta, along with all the rest? Was it, so early in the day, already time to weep for Malta itself?

It came almost as a relief, as he neared Msida Creek, the second of the coastal inlets, and the woman, now reduced to silence and despair, had stumbled off down a side street, when the air-raid sirens began to scream, as if to take the place of the woman, and the fourth raid of the first morning began.

Father Salvatore considered what he should do. The road on which they were moving was bounded by cheap shops on one side, and open to the harbour and curiously naked, on the other. It was not the best choice in the world. But within a few moments a helmeted man on a bicycle, blowing a police-whistle, waving his free arm, came pedalling furiously towards them.

'Get off the street!' he shouted. 'Take cover!' He was a fat man with a theatrical air of importance, but very soon he was speaking to the empty air; he had been out-acted and out-shouted by the bark of guns and the snarl of aircraft overhead, and within seconds everyone had fled for sanctuary through the nearest doorway.

The nearest doorway to Father Salvatore was the entrance to a wine-shop, a mere slit in the wall which widened to a broad passageway flanked by wooden trestle-tables. It was half-full already, with men and women who had obviously been there for some time; the place had a sordid, sodden look, and everything about it – the people lolling half-drunk against the walls, the smoke-fouled air, the circling flies, the wine-stains on the scored table-tops, the smell of sweat and cheap wine and vomit – needed a strong stomach to be endured.

Father Salvatore was reminded of a picture he had seen somewhere: a Hogarth print called *Gin Lane*, full of drunken and disgusting people in the ultimate disarray. His surroundings had the same air, and carried the same message of humanity degraded into ape-hood. But this was fair Malta in 1940, not an eighteenth-century London slum!

He felt deeply ashamed – and then he remembered that nearby Pieta had already been bombed that morning. These must be people who were regaining their courage, in the only way they knew, after enduring sights and sounds which he could easily imagine.

Inside the bar, he greeted anyone who would meet his eye, and sat down near the doorway. The contrast between the clear sunny harbour, seen through the open entrance, and the murky bear-pit behind him, was horrible. But the place would serve. The best thing about it was the row of massive stone arches standing guard over all their heads.

He said a prayer, and composed himself. A man in a dirty apron brought him the coffee he ordered, without a word or a smile. He did not want a priest in his shop ... Father Salvatore sat and waited and listened and watched; and what he saw and heard made him sadder still.

There was little talk; most of the people there just drank and stared in front of them, waiting for whatever was to come. But there was one man near the bar repeating the same sort of phrases over and over again, in a loud whining voice.

He said: 'What do we do? – just sit here and be killed, I suppose!' He said: 'Who asked for this war? Only the rich men and the politicians.' He said: 'What has it to do with Malta, I'd like to know!' He said, with a string of foul oaths: 'Fight the — Italians? I'd rather ask them in and let them choke on — spaghetti!' Then he said, surprisingly: 'Let them all come, I say! Perhaps they'll build us a few decent roads.'

A gross man, fat as a pig with dropsy, sitting next to Father Salvatore, called out: 'Why don't you shut up! There's nothing we can do about it anyway.'

No one else seemed to be paying any attention. They just sat and stared and waited for the future, whatever it was. It was going to happen. So let it happen.

Never argue with a drunken man, Father Salvatore thought. They were his father's words, his father's advice, remembered from long ago; naval officers, it seemed, had plenty of experience in this particular realm... It was all so silly, so sad and foolish. But the very fat man's words – 'There's nothing we can do about it anyway' – though they might be equally sad and foolish, were authentic Maltese.

Father Salvatore knew his people well – well enough never to be surprised by what they did. They were highly individual, in a strangely negative sense. Though they could work very well, they preferred to be lazy – or not to be zealous, anyway;

after sweating hard for three days, they would go fishing or loafing or bird-shooting for the next three; and if fishing was their trade, they turned to gardening or picnicking instead. They had earned enough for that week's needs. What man with his wits about him wanted more?

But though they were easygoing, in this sense, they could also be mulishly, brutally obstinate when they felt like it. A family quarrel, on some tiny matter of inheritance – a field wrongly divided, a *senduq* (the massive household chest) mysteriously spirited away – could last for three generations, with an enduring violence, vindictiveness, and spite on both sides, and a self-wounding determination never to give up, never to let go of the prize nor the lust for it.

They could also be brave, but usually they preferred not to be. Bravery was for other people; for fools, for braggarts, and for dead men.

Usually they preferred to be hedgehogs, rolling themselves up in a protective ball at the first sound or smell of danger, and letting the warlike world thunder past above their curled backs. A hundred times in the past, Malta's history had shown this; whenever danger threatened, the Maltese hid their heads, absorbed the shock, learned to live with it, and learned to outlive it altogether.

Only once or twice in the past had they been stung to violence themselves, in self-defence, in pride, in anger or in despair. Then they had been superbly brave, and enduring also.

What was to be their story this time? Would they lie down and wait, or stand up, and be counted, and if necessary killed? There must be some way—

His sombre thoughts were interrupted by an excited man who rushed in through the doorway. He was a street-cleaner, a breed not given to enthusiasm of any kind. But this one was inspired.

'Hey!' he shouted. 'Come and see the fun! There's a dog-fight going on up there!'

A dog-fight... Father Salvatore knew what the expression meant, from the newspapers of the last few weeks, telling about the great air-battles over Holland and Germany and France. Others in the wine-shop must have known too. But scarcely anyone moved, or even raised their heads. Let it happen...
With a handful of men, including the noisy customer at the

bar, Father Salvatore stepped outside on to the pavement. He knew that this was a stupid thing to do, against all regulations. But an actual dog-fight! In Malta!

For a few moments the harsh sunlight, after the gloom of the wine-shop, made it difficult to see anything. The street-cleaner was pointing upwards, and crying 'Look there! Look there!' like a topmast hand who had discovered a distant coast invisible to everyone else. All that Father Salvatore could discover was noise: there were small explosions and large, the drone and snarl and whine of aircraft engines forced to their extreme limit, the rattle and stutter of machine-guns.

It was *very* like what the children had been miming on the streets of Valletta, before the raids ever started.

Then his vision cleared, and he could make out at least part of what was happening. It was beautiful and terrifying at the same time. The sky above him seemed full of planes, weaving and circling like the flies in the wine-shop; but these were pretty dragon-flies, flies gleaming silver and white against the smoke-puffs of exploding shells which punctured the blue sky.

He could not understand much of it, but he understood what happened next. After a sudden high-pitched scream from an engine, the picture seemed to change dramatically. One of the larger planes, with black smoke pouring from its tail, began to spiral down. It fell like a leaf, a silver leaf; it was beautiful, like everything else, and it was dropping down to what Father Salvatore had prayed for, so many times amid a stricken family – a beautiful death.

Had this been done by an anti-aircraft gun, or by one of their own little planes, the kind he had seen earlier that morning? The street-cleaner was quite sure about this; he was positively dancing as he shouted: 'The English plane won! Didn't you see the bullets hitting? It won the fight!' Father Salvatore did not know if this was true. He was not an expert, and he did not want to be. All he knew was that certain brave young men were now falling into eternity.

He prayed for them, while the knot of people round him, with different desires, shouted and laughed and cheered the kill. As the smoking, twisting plane neared the earth – it would fall far out of sight, over the hills towards Naxxar – the drunk man from the bar paused in his shouted obscenities to become a furious finger-biting man, in the Maltese gesture of hatred and contempt: putting the knuckle of his index finger between his teeth and pretending to clench and snap his jaws in the direction of the loathed enemy.

The plane disappeared from their sight over the hill: a funeral pyre of black smoke rose skywards, mingling with the smoke of its downward ruin: the drunk man screamed: 'I spit you out, you bastard!'

Father Salvatore prayed for dying souls unknown, as the dying fell dead.

Then, quite near them in the Msida inlet, there was a shattering explosion as a bomb hit the water. It threw up a gigantic column of muddy grey liquid, which a moment before had been a soft azure blue. Below a plume of spray, the jumble of dirty waves spread outwards, setting the yachts and fishing-boats plunging and rocking, and presently sucking greedily at the foreshore below the road. The blast of shock, reaching the men on the pavement, sent them scurrying back into the wine-shop.

The closeness of the noise, and its violent aftermath, seemed to have cowed them once again. Some – the apathetic – had never changed. A few talked of the plane shot down, but one such victory was not enough for triumph; that bomb in the water had been much too near, it could have killed them all...
The drunk man took up his dreary commentary, with the same theme as before: the futility of such a war, the futility of everything.

He said: 'What is one plane to them? They must be sending hundreds.'

Father Salvatore sat silent, his hands folded. He knew that he should have been praying – and *seen* to be praying, as an example to all – but something quite different was forming in his mind. He did not know what it was: a spark of impatience, a flicker of rebellious thought – no more than that.

When the all-clear sounded he left the wine-shop, gladly and gratefully, and started to walk once more towards his sister's house.

Lewis Debrincat, and Giovanna his wife, together with their two children, one dog, and four maids, lived in some style in one of the elegant old houses bordering the sea-front at Sliema. It was not the style of the Palazzo Santo-Nobile, which was ancient, noble, and hallowed by time. But a tall three-storeyed terraced mansion, with a columned portico to set off its impressive yellow-stone façade – the sort of house scarcely available to Malta's young marrieds in the 1920s, even if they had enough money to run it properly – carried its own stamp of consequence.

The Casa Debrincat looked what it was, inside and out: solid, smart, sophisticated, and expensive. It was exactly the sort of house which Lewis Debrincat, the young lawyer of twenty years ago, still making his way in the world, had always dreamed of; and with the help of a post-war slump, and the massive injection of Santo-Nobile money which came to him as Giovanna's marriage portion, he had achieved it earlier than he had ever hoped.

He had grown into that house, as he had grown into everything else, and the house was still exactly what he wanted.

It always affected Father Salvatore in the same way, whenever he passed through the front door; and it affected him now, as he entered the lofty hall, with its spick-and-span *terrazzo* tiling, its wide marble staircase, its white-painted panels framed in gold, and its wrought-iron sconces so cunningly converted from the gas-lighting of 1840 to the electricity of today.

He found it uncomfortably excellent: too elegant for him, too smart, proclaiming too incisively that when one entered the Casa Debrincat, one stood on superior ground, and had better match it.

It always afflicted him, also, with the most mortal doubt of all, as far as a marriage or a family was concerned. Though the house was handsome, and supremely well-run, a positive power-base of chic entertainment, it was still cold to his senses. Here people lived in luxury. But did they love in the same degree?

The youngest of the maids, Carmelina, who opened the front door to him, was red-eyed from weeping; and she was normally so pretty, so cheerful, and so free from care that he felt able to ask her why. A priest could ask questions which a visitor should not.

'Oh, Dun Salv!' she exclaimed, and began to cry again. 'It is the war,' she said, between sobs. 'Those awful bombs! What is going to happen?'

'You must be brave, Carmelina,' he answered. 'This is a strong house. You are safe here.'

'But my family!' She was only about sixteen, on the very threshold of a life of her own; yet admirably, movingly, it was this she was worrying about. 'They say there has been terrible bombing all over Senglea. My father works in the dockyard!'

'I know.' He touched her shoulder, in a gesture half-way between a human act of comfort and a formal blessing. 'But they have built some deep concrete shelters there, enough for the biggest bombs. I tell you what! I shall be crossing over, later this afternoon. I'll make sure that he is all right, and then I'll send a message.'

'Thank you, Dun Salv. You are so good.' Since she was young, she was also quick to change her mood; a wide smile, which would soon be invitation enough to make any young man's heart miss a beat, now took the place of tears. 'Is it true there was a big battle in Gozo, and the Italian boats were driven away?'

'No.' He shook his head reprovingly. 'Where did you hear such a thing?'

'One of the delivery boys said he heard the guns.'

'They were firing at the aeroplanes, that's all. You mustn't listen to too many stories, Carmelina.' Then he asked the question he always asked. 'What's for lunch today?'

'Chicken in a pie!'

There was a patter, and then a stamping, and then a positive thunder of footsteps coming down the stairs. As Carmelina withdrew, Father Salvatore turned to greet the new arrival. In a final flurry, a cascade of whirling arms and legs which seemed to belong to more than one body, the bright-eyed boy who was the son and heir of this house, Pietru Pawl Hugo Santo-Nobile Debrincat, made his traditional appearance.

He was tall for his age, and fair-haired from his English strain, and coltish in all his movements, and as beautiful as any angel on the most pious of canvases; he was also, at this moment, panting with wild excitement.

'Uncle Salvu! Uncle Salvu! Did you see the aeroplane shot down? Oh, I *wish* I could have been up there, firing all those bullets!'

Father Salvatore, as the only uncle within a thousand miles, felt it his duty to bring the temperature down a little. 'Good morning, Peter Paul. That was a very dangerous way to come downstairs.'

He always called Pietru 'Peter Paul', from some forgotten joke of long ago; he had kept up the habit ever afterwards, perhaps as a hoped-for special link with this boy whom he found such a delight. Since there could be no sons for priests, nephews must fill the void, and bring happiness to it.

The link went back to the very begining; Father Salvatore could remember Pietru's first birthday, when to the Baroness's expressed pleasure and Lewis Debrincat's mortification, they had observed the old country custom of *Il-Quċċija* – the choosing by the child, from a tray-full of various objects, of one item which would give a clue to his future.

Faced with a choice of a bowl of wheat, a quill pen, a dagger, some silver coins, a fish-hook safely stuck in a cork, a mariner's compass, a jewelled mask, a hammer, a pair of scissors, and a paintbrush, the one-year-old Pietru had turned his back on the whole collection and made straight for one of his elder sister's dolls. But now he was thirteen and, it seemed, could not wait to get to grips with the enemy.

Pietru, subdued for at least five seconds, advanced more formally, to be kissed on the forehead and blessed by his uncle. Then he burst out again :

'I saw the whole thing, Uncle Salvu! The bombers came over in *swarms*, and then one of those little British planes went up—'

'But how did you see it, Peter Paul?'

'I was on the roof.'

'That was very silly of you. You know you're meant to take shelter downstairs when the sirens go.'

'But it went on for so long. So I *crept* up—' he began to act the furtive look-out, creeping under murderous fire to the top of the battlements, 'and just *peeped* out, keeping my head well down, and saw the bombs falling, and then all the planes started flying different ways, and the little plane hit the big plane, and smoke poured from it, and it crashed, right in front of my eyes!'

'Where was that?'

'Just up the street, I think.'

'Peter Paul, it was miles away! Somewhere near Naxxar or Mosta.'

'Was it?' Pietru's face, which was always innocent, now took on the cast of a small saint. 'It seemed so much nearer, from the roof. Did you actually see it shot down, Uncle Salvu?'

'Yes, I did.'

'Then you must have been outside yourself.'

'I just happened—' Father Salvatore began, already preparing, in his private mind, for his very next confession, when he was fortunately rescued. His sister Giovanna appeared at the head of the stairs, and called out: 'Salvu! Thank heaven you are here!'

The relief was mutual, as it so often was, in a greater or less degree. This much-loved sister was, next to God and his mother, the staple blessing of Father Salvatore's life. It had started in the nursery, with the arrival, when he was five years old, of a new and exciting stranger – a little sister whom he must love and protect. It had continued without alteration throughout their joint adolescence. It had survived the sad blow of her marriage, at the age of twenty-two, in the face of stern parental opposition, to Lewis Debrincat.

He could remember, to this day, his mother's verdict when this suitor was first mentioned: 'Lewis *Debrincat*? A *lawyer*? I have never heard of such a person!' It had been followed by the fearful tussle of the 'understanding' which became a four-year engagement, and the engagement which became a marriage, solemnized before God and man under the majestic canopy of St John's Co-Cathedral, and the marriage which had become – whatever it was today.

Did Giovanna regret her ferocious determination, which had had to survive and overcome so much in order to bring the two of them to the high altar? Was she happy with such a man? Two children in eighteen years of marriage – what did that mean? A swift aversion? The proud chemistry of the body rejecting the unwelcome invasion? Pure chance? Impure use of methods which were, and would remain for ever, a mortal sin?

Salvatore and Giovanna, brother and sister, might once have discussed such things, in theory at least. Now, constrained by fact, they could not. Now she was forty, loving daughter, loving mother, mistress of an envied household; secure in her

temporal fortune, sure of a visit twice a year to London or
Paris or Rome : sure of all that money and rank could bring
in the way of social pre-eminence.

If love had eluded her, she did not show it; if she had made
a mistake, it was a mistake utterly private, eating into no heart
but her own.

She was still slim, and elegant, and serene of brow; still
beautiful, with those touches of grey in her dark hair which
she had no doubt earned, and disdained to conceal. She was
still all these things, as she came down the last flight of stairs
to greet her brother.

'Good morning, Salvu.' She was smiling as she kissed him.
'When I said, thank heaven you are here, I hope it didn't
sound too dramatic. What I meant was, the sight of you in
the hall turned it into an ordinary day after all, in spite of
the awful things that are happening. Have you come from
Mother?'

'Yes. She is perfectly well, as always. She sent her love to
you.'

'What about the bombing?'

'It was quite a long way from the palazzo.'

'Thank heaven again.' She turned to her son. 'Pietru, I want
to talk to Uncle Salvu for a moment.'

'Can I go upstairs again?'

'No. Have you washed your hands for lunch?'

'Yes, Mother.'

'Then go and pour out our drinks. On the patio. Sherry for
me, and Dubonnet with ice for Uncle Salvu. We'll be out in
a minute or two.'

Pietru, who fancied himself as a barman when he was not
an airman, turned to go.

'And don't eat all the peanuts.'

Pietru turned back again. 'How many can I have?'

'Not more than six.'

'Do you mean, six actual peanuts, or six peanut-shells with
two peanuts in each of them?'

'Pietru . . .'

'Yes, Mother.' He disappeared swiftly.

'That boy will become a Jesuit, unless we are very careful.'
It was the sort of remark which she, like all good Catholics,
could make without the smallest ill-humour or offence, on

either side. 'Salvu, I really am so glad to see you. Come into the drawing-room for a moment.'

When they were there, out of earshot of anyone else, she changed swiftly, as she could always do. In every realm save the intimacy of marriage, they could both do so, and he thanked God for it.

She became a sister, cutting all the corners, falling back on the instinctive understanding of childhood; and the priest became a man and a brother, a confidant quite different from the confidant of the confessional, which imposed its own formal rules; a confidant uncritical, an ally free of the duty to impose discipline.

'I just wanted to tell you about Gigi,' she began immediately. Father Salvatore could never think of Lewis Debrincat as Gigi; the diminutive – Gigi standing for Luigi, and Luigi the Italian gloss for Lewis – was not for him, only for her. 'He is upstairs, of course. He has taken everything very hard. He always said it couldn't possibly happen... He won't talk to anyone. He doesn't want to come down to lunch.'

Salvatore nodded. He could understand, though he could not agree. 'All right. But it's a very bad idea, Giovanna. He mustn't hide. He *needn't* hide, especially from us. Shall I go up and see him?'

'It would be better after lunch.' She sighed. 'That's all I wanted to say, really. I knew you would understand. Now let's have our drinks.'

The screened patio, which gave on to a narrow walled garden, all that Sliema's crowded building plans allowed, was the favourite family meeting ground, and it was Father Salvatore's favourite also, because of its simplicity. No one and nothing was on show here; if one wanted to leave a camera or a work-basket or a stamp-collection or a bicycle bell under repair lying about in the Casa Debrincat, this was the place to leave it.

Lewis Debrincat, in moments of irritation, sometimes called it 'a damned tool-shed'. Yet even he would deploy his expensive fishing-tackle here, and not bother to tidy it away. This morning it had its usual air of jumbled inconsequence. But the welcome drinks were waiting, served by Pietru the barman who, in defiance of his guild's regulations, held a bottle of fizzy lemonade topped by a straw in his free hand.

Prince, the family dog, was also waiting, in panting ecstasy –
the more visitors, and possibly even burglars, there were, the
better he liked it. Prince was a second-class dog, an all-purpose
hound of the kind called *tal-kaċċa* ('of the game'), scarcely to
be mentioned in the same social breath as the Baroness's pure-
bred specialist, which was a Maltese *kelb tal-fenek* ('of the
rabbit').

Waiting also, in dreamy expectation of all the joys of love
and life, which must surely be just round the corner, perhaps
even in the next room, within the next few seconds of time,
was the pride and decoration of the household, Marija Celeste
Debrincat.

At seventeen, she gave promise of great beauty; all the cunning resources of the female line seemed already to be ranged
on her side, only waiting to change her from a very pretty girl
to a lovely one. She was dark, like her mother, and long-legged
(which was a happy accident for a Maltese); with large grey
eyes, and a mouth as happily formed for smiling and kissing
as a ring to a finger.

Her budding figure was something no longer for conceal-
ment under folded arms, but for shy display and shy pride.

What did young girls *really* think about, Father Salvatore
sometimes wondered when he watched Marija. In the confessional they reeled off a lot of acceptable nonsense: 'impure
thoughts', which were only the thoughts of effervescent youth,
or 'impure actions', which might be anything from the forbidden caress to the calculated self-stimulation; or else they
were silent and sullen, which could be ascribed to actual guilt,
or confusion, or stupidity, or blessed innocence.

But their *real* thoughts? What had little Marija (but already
she was taller than he was) been thinking and dreaming about,
when he came out on to the patio and interrupted her? There
was danger in the air today, there was a war. Did she dream
of love still? – of a knight in shining armour who would ride
or fly to her rescue? She was waiting for love, like all young
girls; it would be a dreadful, arid, joyless world if this were not
so. But a lover in the flesh? Today, here and now, tonight?

Did she know what it was that she wanted? Or was she
still as innocently confused as four years ago, when on this
very patio, in the calm and comforting darkness, she had
solemnly confided what she hoped for was a husband who

would never become 'demanding', because he would under-stand, and honour, her special devotion to Saint Agatha, who had died defending her purity.

She had had this special devotion since she was eight. Did not Uncle Salvu think she was right?

Uncle Salvu, who knew where all this came from – a pious picture of Saint Agatha holding a salver containing her severed breasts, together with the pincers used for their removal : Uncle Salvu, cursing all pious pictures, had felt bound to tell her that there was much to be said for both sides, and that time would show the truth. Meanwhile, how was she getting on at school?

The trouble was, the image of chastity outraged persisted just as much in his own mind as it must have done in hers. Celibate priests were far too preoccupied with sex, he thought, not for the first time : let this not be so today... He smiled as he greeted Marija, and blessed her, as he had done a thousand times in the past, and said :

'Your grandmother sent her best love to you. And' – with a side glance at Pietru, 'she said to be sure to take shelter, *down-stairs*, as soon as you hear the sirens.'

'Uncle Salvu,' said Pietru, 'you made that up.'

'I made it up with the best possible motives.' Father Salvatore sipped his iced *apéritif*, sharp and inviting, and hugely welcome after his long walk and all that had gone with it. But how many people would take to drink, irrevocably, before this hor-rible war was over? ... 'It really is dangerous, you know. Not just the bombs.' He could never tell them about the old man with the gashed leg, bleeding his life away on the dusty pave-ment; that was something locked up and barred already. 'But when the guns start firing, anything can happen.'

Giovanna said : 'Do you think we should build a proper shelter here?'

'I don't think so. Not when you have the cellars. They must be very strong.'

Marija, sitting on the swing-divan, her long legs folded under her, a look of concentration on her pretty face, asked :

'Uncle Salvu, how long do you think it will go on for?'

It was a serious question, for young and old alike. 'I don't know, Marija. No one knows. The last war went on for more than four years.'

'That was when grandfather was killed,' said Pietru.

But Marija, just at that moment, did not care about grandfather. 'Four years! I shall be twenty-one!'

'I shall be seventeen,' said Pietru. 'I hope it lasts a year longer. Then I can be conscripted.'

'I shall be forty-nine,' said Father Salvatore.

'I shall be sixty-seven,' said Giovanna.

'Mother, you won't!'

'I saw an American film once,' Father Salvatore told them, looking for a lighter topic. 'A historical film. Edward III was sitting on the throne – that was in 1337,' he added for the benefit of Pietru, whose history reports were sad documents, 'when a courtier rushed in and said: "Your Majesty! The Hundred Years War has just broken out!"'

Giovanna laughed, as did her daughter. But Pietru moved a little more slowly.

'How could he possibly know—' he began, and then looked almost resentfully at his uncle. 'Oh, it's a joke.'

Marija, the loving sister, tapped the side of her head. 'Knock, knock. Don't cut down that tree! It might be alive!'

Lunch was announced. Giovanna stood up immediately, and said: 'Your father won't be coming down today. The bombing has given him a headache. Let's go in.' It was as easy as that.

At the table, they waited with bowed heads for their priest-uncle to say grace. With 'Benedic Domine nos et haec Tua dona' on his lips, he suddenly changed his mind, for reasons he could never afterwards determine, and began instead the first meal-time prayer of the war:

'Is-sliem ghalik, Marija, bil-grazzja mimlija, is-Sinjur Alla mieghek, imbierka int fost in-nisa u mbierek il-frott tal-ġuf tieghek Gesu.'

Pietru, astonished, was not the one to conceal it. He could hardly wait for the end. 'Uncle Salvu, you said it in Maltese!'

'Just for a change.'

There could be no day changed more than today.

Lunch was excellent, as usual: the brightest occasion of his week, compounded of the joy of family life, which he could not command, and the innocent pleasure of good eating, which with such an ally as his sister he could. A gazpacho soup of purest coolest texture gave place to the American-style chicken-pot-pie which was the children's favourite, surviving from the nursery to grace the adult dining table; and then a concoction of garden peaches, ice-cream, and fingers of meringue showed what a talented cook could do with simple ingredients and the cunning of imagination. Would that the good brothers of the Capuchin Monastery could be inspired to glorify God in such a fashion!

Yet it was not an easy meal. Though there were cheerful moments, the anxiety which lay over the city lay over this room also, inducing a nervous tension which infected everything they did and said. There were aeroplane noises, and ambulance noises; the telephone rang several times, and then subsided into silence, which must mean that Giovanna had ordered the same message to be given to any caller – that her husband could not be disturbed.

There was a lengthening pause in the middle of lunch, when they were waiting for vegetables, and she was forced to say: 'I'm so sorry. Everyone is so upset today.' It was the first time that Father Salvatore had ever heard his sister make such an apology.

But it was the missing man – the head of the family whose traditional chair was empty – who most disturbed and worried him. The idea of Lewis Debrincat – or of any human being, whether he was a saint in turmoil or a thief on the run – hiding himself away like a cornered animal, refusing the touch of any hand and the sound of any voice, was not something which could be forgotten because it was not seen.

The missing man was there all the time: in the silences, in the family jokes, in the empty chair. On this day of all days, when every Maltese household should be drawing together under the most dire threat of their lives, the void was a wound, and the wound a witness to raw pain.

As soon as he could after lunch, Father Salvatore went upstairs, in search of the man he had not seen that day.

His knock on the door was unanswered. When he knocked again, he heard a growling sound which might have meant anything. Acting on certain privileges, he opened the door and entered.

The room, heavily louvred and screened from the sun, was almost in darkness; at first he thought it was empty, in spite of the noise he had heard. All he was aware of was a smell, a smell familiar, a smell only puzzling within this secure and privileged house. It was the smell of the confessional *at certain times*; a compound of alcohol and fear which told its story before a pair of lips need be opened.

But then he made out a hunched figure, huddled deep into an armchair as if it would have preferred to be part of the furniture; and a voice said:

'So you have come to see the condemned man.'

It was not the quality of voice he had been expecting; the throaty growl which was Lewis Debrincat's normal speech now had a jeering note, unpleasant and immediately antagonizing. Father Salvatore was reminded of an occasion years ago, when he was doing his best to sort out, in pitiable circumstances, the facts of a case which the law would presently describe as 'the defiling of a female minor', and which must explicitly be called rape.

The young man involved had been truculent and jeering, in the same way. He could not be reached, either with mercy or with stern rebuke. All he said was: 'You can do what you like. *But I had her, didn't I?*'

Lewis Debrincat sounded impenitent, to the point of triumph. He was not a cornered animal at all; he was right, the rest of the world was wrong, and nothing that the world could do would alter that score.

He was also rather drunk, and it did not need the half-empty bottle of whisky at his feet to advertise the fact.

Father Salvatore said gently: 'No one has condemned you, Lewis. Why do you say that? Naturally I am worried. So is Giovanna. But you must not hide like this.'

'*I am not hiding!*' The voice changed from a jeer to a snarl. 'On the first day of their stupid war, I don't choose to see anybody. That is all. Let them sort it out for themselves.'

Father Salvatore advanced until he was standing in front of the armchair. 'But people need you. Your family needs you. There is nothing to be afraid of.'

'*I am not afraid!*'

'May I sit down, Lewis?'

'I suppose so. But spare me the absolution for my sins. I don't feel like it.'

In a moment of anger and dislike, Father Salvatore could not smile. 'I will leave that to God, if you prefer.'

Close to, Lewis Debrincat was a sad sight, to all but his sworn enemies. He had been running to fat during the last few years, and the pudgy body and over-fleshed face were now no more than a caricature of the good-looking young lawyer of twenty years ago. He was sweating freely in the barred room; his shirt was unbuttoned, exposing a chest matted with dank hair, and his trousers, stained by spilt liquor, gaped at the fly. His feet, with their enormous yellow horned toe-nails, were bare. His eyes blinked nervously, and the hand which held the whisky glass was trembling.

The neat black beard, which had been the Italian cult in Malta up to that very morning, seemed the only steadfast thing about him; it stood out like a square-cut badge, imprinted on the sweaty pallor of his face. What, Father Salvatore wondered, were the pro-Italians going to do about their little stylized beards? Shave them off? Grow them until they became Biblical, and safe? Maintain that they were really Royal Navy models, or even Elizabethan?

Lewis Debrincat's nickname had always been *il-volpi* – the fox; he had a certain persistent cunning which was admired among his friends. But today he did not look like a fox. He looked like a raffish, quarrelsome, ill-kept goat. Was this the man with whom Giovanna had to lie, every night of her life? ... Father Salvatore leant forward in his chair, penetrating the reek of whisky.

'You have done nothing wrong, Lewis, have you?'

Lewis Debrincat blinked and glared at the same time. '*No – I – have – not!* In fact, we're the only people who are *right*! But that's not going to help, is it? There have been arrests already. And all because of this stupid war! We're only in it because we're still a damned British colony. What quarrel has Malta got with Italy? We are friends! I tell you' – he wagged a wavering finger, much too near Salvatore's face, 'we're fighting the wrong enemy! You'll see! Don't say I didn't warn you!'

'I'm sure you're absolutely sincere about this—'

'Oh, don't be so damned forgiving! You know you hate me.'

'I hate nobody.'

Lewis Debrincat put his hand to his lips, in an absurd gesture of secrecy. 'Sh! Don't let the government hear you. You've got to hate the Italians! It's an order, because we're still a British colony. We're going to be bombed to hell, because we're still a British colony.' The wild words came tumbling out. 'Direct rule! What happened to Lord Strickland in 1930? He wanted to tie this country hand and foot to Britain. So you people' – he gestured contemptuously towards Father Salvatore's cassock, 'made it a grave sin to vote for him and his Constitutional Party. So they said, to hell with the Pope, and put us all under direct rule. British rule! We weren't even allowed to speak Italian!'

'Lewis, you're so confused. And this is so long ago, anyway. There's a war *today*. We're in the middle of it. We must fight, all of us. You don't want Malta to be ruled by Mussolini, do you?'

'I'd rather have Mussolini than some old idiot like Neville Chamberlain.' Debrincat took another copious swig from the whisky bottle, and smacked his lips in ridiculous triumph. 'I'd rather have the Italians than the British. There, I've said it! Is that a crime?'

'I don't think you really believe it. Not if you think about it properly.'

'I have thought about it *properly*,' Lewis answered savagely, 'for more than twenty years. I'm not going to change my mind now, just because the British have got us into their war.' He set down the bottle on the floor, and passed his hand over his eyes. He said: 'Oh God! Oh God!' and then suddenly he was crying. The working face seemed to collapse into ruin, between one moment and the next. 'You know what will happen?' he said, between sobs. 'They'll put me in prison. They'll break all the windows, like they did last night in Valletta. I won't be allowed to practise. *I'll probably be expelled from the club!*'

Father Salvatore, between pity and aversion, rose suddenly from his chair. He was not sure that he could stand any more of this, or that he could, even with the greatest compassion, help the other man, at this moment. It would be a waste of time even to warn Lewis to guard his tongue. That must come from within, or not at all. Today, he must be allowed his terrors and his fears, and perhaps be purged of hatred and foolishness at the end of them.

He realized now that, in spite of all the surface bravado, Lewis Debrincat was in desperate straits. The test – perhaps

the first real test of his life – had found him out. From being a
secure social man, he had become a sick animal.

The Maltese had words for this, as they had for most
human imperfections. They called such a man, who could be
destroyed by adversity, *kaptan tal-bnazzi* – a fair-weather captain, or, as he had once heard it translated, more melodiously,
a captain of calm waters. When the fierce winds blew, the
cool and arrogant figure on the bridge, though supported by all
the trappings of authority, was to be found cowering behind
any shelter, crying for any help, yielding his office to any
man who would take it.

When the lordly prince became the craven serf, it could be
seen as God's rebuke to pride. But it was not the less disgusting, for all that... Father Salvatore was about to say something – anything – which would serve as a farewell, when
there was a knock on the door, and Giovanna's voice called
out:

'Gigi? Salvu?'

Lewis Debrincat's reaction was immediate. He whipped his
tear-stained face aside, away from the light, and whispered:
'Don't let her in!'

'But—'

'She is not to come in!'

'All right.' Father Salvatore made for the door, ready to inter-
pose himself, if need be, between the head of the household
and his wife. It was the least he could do, in the circumstances.
It was also, he realized sadly, the most that he would do. At
the door he turned. 'Goodbye, Lewis. God bless you. I hope
I'll see you next week. But think about what I've said. People
need you, and you need people.'

There was not a sound from the huddled figure as he closed
the door behind him.

'I'm terribly sorry,' Giovanna said. 'I didn't want to interrupt. But it's Rafel.'

'Rafel? Here?'

'Yes.' She laid her hand on his arm. 'Salvu, I think something
awful has happened. He's crying.'

Everyone was crying today.

Giovanna left the two of them alone, as soon as she reached
the hall. She did not even speak; all she did was to touch the
huge sacristan on the shoulder, by way of saying goodbye:

whereupon he bent and seized her hand, and kissed it, and turned his head aside in wordless anguish.

Rafel had indeed been crying, and he started afresh as soon as he was alone with Father Salvatore; tears coursed freely down his cheeks, which were already stained and streaked with dusty rivulets. It was strange, Father Salvatore thought, as he tried to comfort his friend, how so small a thing as a tear could shake and rack a giant frame, to the edge of distraction and beyond.

'Calm yourself, calm yourself,' he repeated over and over again, as Rafel dropped his face in his hands, and sought to shield it from the world. 'You must tell me what has happened. I did not expect to see you here. But whatever it is you have seen, or heard, you are with friends now.' And, as Rafel burst out into fresh and noisy weeping, Father Salvatore exerted his authority: 'Rafel! You are a man. Stop crying. Tell me what has happened.'

Rafel made a supreme effort to master himself. Finally he uncovered his face, now swollen and ugly beyond belief, and said:

'I ran all the way, Dun Salv.'

'But why? Tell me why?'

Rafel looked at him, wild-eyed. 'The little church is destroyed. It was hit by a bomb. Oh God, that I should have to tell you such a thing!'

It was indeed the most fearful shock of Father Salvatore's life. The great ambitions, the humble hopes, had all been centred on the building of the church of St Barnabas; since it was likely to be all that he would ever achieve, the sum of a devoted life, he had grown to love and care for it, on a scale to match its meaning.

It must stand for all the lost things of life: for the son he would never have, for the cardinal's scarlet thirty-tasselled hat which he did not deserve, for the vision of a great metropolitan ministry which had shrunk down, year by year, to the handful of farmers and fishermen, policemen and stone-masons, women burdened by care, and children, blessed children, who with the greatest of good luck might turn out to be as good as their fathers – his once and future flock.

Could it really be true that there was now no church, and might never be one?

It could be true.

'The little church is gone, Dun Salv,' Rafel said again. 'There is nothing left but stones and dust. I saw it myself, five minutes after the bomb fell.'

'Tell me all that you saw. What happened after you left me this morning?'

What had happened to Rafel Vella, on that first morning of the war, was what had happened to Valletta and Senglea, Floriana and Pieta, Cospicua and St Elmo, and to all their teeming citizens. He had been down at the harbour, just stepping ashore from the ferry which had taken him across from Lascaris Wharf, when the raid started.

There had been buses arriving with dockyard workers, and other men already hammering and welding and planing and measuring, and *dghajsas* going to and fro with shoppers and market-sellers, and the usual crowd of people who had business in the dockyard area; and then suddenly a bomb fell in the water, and another toppled a giant crane, and everyone was running and diving for cover, for any protection they could find from this awful danger – into the new shelters, into the concrete latrines, into the little rock tunnels, or under the steel plates stacked in racks outside the workshops.

'We ran about like mice,' Rafel said fearfully, 'and then we kept very still, hardly daring to breathe. Even the guns were terrible, and the bombs – I thought my ears would crack... When it was over I began to walk through the dockyard, and then out to Cospicua. There were houses smashed, and shops, and cars still burning. I saw dead people, Dun Salv. I saw a dead donkey, split open like a melon, with a little donkey coming out. I saw—'

'Rafel!'

'Yes, Dun Salv?'

'Tell me about the church.'

'But there is nothing to tell, Dun Salv!' Rafel was near to tears again. 'That is why I tell you other things... I noticed the cloud of dust a long way away, and I thought, that must be the church, though I could not really believe it. But when I came there, it was lying on the ground. It had been hit in the very middle. All the stones, all the arches, the beautiful dome. Eight years of work. Now you could not tell which was the roof and which was the floor... I talked to the people, but they had nothing to say. They are very afraid, Dun Salv. They need you. I told them you would come... And I ran all the way.'

Father Salvatore, sick at heart, felt as if he himself had run all the way: all the way to the edge of hell, and back again, with the black tidings of disaster. He felt he could say nothing more to Rafel, nor hear anything more from him: enough was enough, he must think on these things, the soul must have time to breathe again... He found himself in an immense hurry to get rid of the sacristan, and to be alone. It was unworthy, it was weak, it was wrong, but he could not help it, and he did not try to.

'You must go back, Rafel. Do the best you can. Tell the people I will come, as soon as I can.'

'But when, Dun Salv?'

'Soon. Later this afternoon. Go now.'

They walked towards the front door, the small stunned priest leading the tall sacristan. If he was puzzled by the abrupt dismissal, Rafel did not show it; he took orders from so many people, and on such a day he might have been glad that this, at least, had not changed. But then, unluckily, a third person came into the hall. It was the maid Carmelina.

She was only crossing from the kitchen to the patio, to tidy up before the Casa Debrincat settled down to its afternoon siesta. But as soon as he saw her, Rafel stopped as if paralysed. His face, already stricken by grief, grew pale as death. He said, in a terrified voice:

'I must speak to you again, Dun Salv.'

'What is it now?' Father Salvatore asked impatiently.

The girl had passed out of sight, with a smile towards the sacristan. Rafel put a hand to his brow. 'I forgot, I forgot! The police at Senglea told me, just before I got on to the ferry, and I promised to tell you. They knew that the girl worked here, they knew that I was going to see you. So they said, we will leave it to you. May Christ forgive me!'

'But what *is* it?'

'It is Carmelina. Her father. He was killed in a raid. When the sirens went he said "I have work to do," and he did not take shelter. He was blown high into the water, and then he floated like a dead fish. They say he was the first man to be killed, in the whole of Malta.'

3

Father Salvatore never really knew how he got through the rest of the afternoon, and the evening, and the night; if he had known, at any stage of the increasing ordeal, what was to come, perhaps he would not have done so. He wanted, every moment of his time, simply to cross Grand Harbour and go back to his church, or what was left of it, and to his people, or what was left of them.

But inevitably he was delayed, and frustrated, and set on another course; inevitably the minutes and then the hours slipped away, and were forfeited to danger or to fear or to other people who needed him.

A priest could never be his own man. God disposed of him, and to rebel against that Will was wicked. But to wish for better things was surely forgiveable.

In the midst of his own sorrow, he spent a heart-rending hour with the girl Carmelina, who was distraught with grief, and beyond any comfort save the comfort of familiar words. All the time that he was talking to her, an air-raid was in progress, with near and distant explosions, and a constant onslaught of shell-fire overhead.

To tell her: 'Your father is at peace, my child. He is with God. He suffered nothing. Now he has everything, in heaven,' was arid consolation for a daughter's loss of an adored parent. Words were one thing, fact was another. The thud and thunder of the explosions all round them were too strong a reminder of what had happened.

A noise like that, a shock-wave like the one which jolted against the front door and set the heavy iron knocker trembling, was the real truth. It was under such brutal blows that her father had died.

As soon as it was safe to move, he shared a taxi with her as far as her house – a house already shuttered, with a black mourning-band draped over the handle of the front door. He had said all he could to Carmelina; now he had to repeat it to her mother, who had woken as a wife and would soon sleep as a widow: to certain neighbours who were sitting with her: and to brothers and sisters wild-eyed and weeping, who could not believe in God's will, only in the pitiless violence with which He allowed men to execute it.

He went on his way as soon as he could, and then, trudging through the back streets of Floriana, he was caught in another raid. He had lost count of how many there had been, on this appalling day. Each one brought its new terror and agony, as fresh and astonishing as some evil hour which marked another stage of creation.

This time he took refuge alone, for half an hour, under the portico of a shabby old building, solid as a rock, which had perhaps started life as a rich merchant's house and had suffered the decay of centuries. Now it was a sort of warehouse, or garage, or auctioneer's storeroom; tattered posters advertised furniture for sale, and cheap rebuilt tyres, and lottery tickets, and talking films, and election candidates of long ago who urged, without supporting evidence, that a vote for them was a vote for a free Malta.

What a place to live, what a place to die... The flaking stone façade and the ruined paintwork proclaimed that the building would never rise again, in its own esteem or in anyone else's, until it was torn down and replaced. Yet it commanded a superb view of the western arm of Grand Harbour: the yellow stone reflected in the blue water seemed to promise a timeless stability and peace. But the view of the bombers swooping in from the north-west was equally impressive; and as the bombs began to fall, it became clear that one part of this building's future might well be fulfilled, on this very day. It would at least be torn down.

The earth shook; wave after wave of hideous noise assaulted the ear-drums; fierce heat was followed by the thunder of collapsing stone, and then by great wafts of choking dust, which made even nearby buildings invisible. Five bombs burst on Floriana; but they were only a small careless dividend from the main assault, which he could tell was falling on the other edge of the harbour, where he wanted above all places on earth to go: falling on his own people, perhaps on the shattered remains of his own church.

At long last the sirens screamed the all-clear, and eased the terror which gripped him. But after heat and dust came blood and tears; and he did not have to walk far to find either of them.

Just up the street was the same scene as he had witnessed earlier that day: a building collapsed into the roadway, a terrified crowd in attendance, wounded men and women lying about like discarded, bloodied dolls: a crying and a wailing and a sobbing on all sides: a dead child, a dead girl, a dying young man, and another so fearfully mauled about the face and chest that he might well wish to die as soon as he awoke to hideous pain.

Father Salvatore, in a daze of shock and exhaustion, did his best, as he had done before. He bound up wounds, he staunched blood, he wiped away tears. He set a broken leg, though it was done so roughly and clumsily that he feared the man would walk crooked for the rest of his life.

Three times he drew from his pocket the small golden phial of holy oil, and dipped his fingers in it, and gently smoothed across the eyes, the ears, the nostrils, the mouth, the hands, and the feet of a shattered human being who would never find use for any of these gifts of God again, the balm of extreme unction.

As these and other shadows lengthened, and the first evening of the war was upon him, his aching hunger to return across the harbour grew unbearable. It was clear that he would be needed wherever he went; where better, then, than among his own people, who all day must have been suffering dire punishment? And he had not even seen his crucified church... A phrase from a night-vision of St Paul continued to haunt him: a cry from another anguished heart, a lonely man beseeching: 'Come over into Macedonia, and help us.'

His own Macedonia was only a short mile away. *He must reach it.*

The ancient *barklor* who rowed Father Salvatore, and the other chance passengers, across Grand Harbour in his *dghajsa* had already had enough of the war. Though it was only seven o'clock on the calm evening of Day One, he was ready to call a halt to all this nonsense, and go back to peace and plenty.

He was an old man, a very old man with a gnarled face framed by a pair of wispy white side-whiskers: they gave him a raffish operatic air, a touch of the *gondolieri* who were his trade-colleagues across the water in Italy. As he rowed, standing high in the bows of the tall-stemmed *dghajsa*, he grumbled;

and as he grumbled his complaining words floated down upon his boatload of passengers like a dark woolly cloud of doubt, matching the shadows of night which were beginning to shroud the harbour.

'May heaven help us,' the old *barklor* said, though he did not sound as if he believed that this would happen, or would welcome it if it did. 'Another day like this will kill me. It will kill us all! If I could tell you what I have seen ... Four bodies I've fished out of the harbour today. Four bodies in this very boat! They used to pay me five shillings for every one I brought in, and that's little enough, the way some of them stink. But now the police say, they won't pay me *anything* anymore, it's the war and it's my duty as a citizen. A citizen!' He rested on his oars, and looked round at his passengers, with a whole world of contempt in his rheumy eyes. He spat, and the spittle hit the grey water with a solid plop of protest. 'Does a *citizen* have to pull bodies out of the water for nothing? They should pay me *more* because of the war, not less. They should pay me *double* for taking my *dghajsa* across. I might be killed!' His roving glance singled out Father Salvatore, whom he had known for many years, and he put a straight question. 'What do you think, Dun Salv? Is it fair that I should pull out corpses for nothing? Is it fair that I should row you across for the same money, when the bombs are falling?'

Father Salvatore, sitting on a wooden bench amidships, enjoying the hard-won cool of the evening, had been reading his breviary, as swiftly as his conscience would allow. Today he had fallen woefully behindhand in this duty; the reading of the Divine Office, which took him about an hour and must be accomplished every day of his life, under grave peril if he failed ('A mortal sin, Santo-Nobile! A mortal sin!' he could still hear the seminary's Spiritual Director intone) had been forgotten in the rush and turmoil of other events.

He would have preferred to ignore the question – old Angelo was a notorious grumbler, as well as a mean old man who had grown old in meanness; but he found that he could not. On this day of all days, the children of God must surely be more important than the set forms of His worship. But he could still be firm, with such an old reprobate as Angelo the *barklor*.

'We must all help each other,' he answered, lowering the

breviary to his knees. The water lapped against the side of the *dghajsa* as Angelo took up his rowing again, and Father Salvatore raised his voice. 'It is not an ordinary day. It is not an ordinary time. You should do your duty, and not think about money. Money will not bring back the dead.'

'Then why should *I* bring back the dead?' The tart answer showed that Angelo, in churlish mood, was not at all ready for a public rebuke, and he rested on his oars again, to make this fact plain. 'It is all very well for you, Dun Salv. You do not have to earn a living, as I do. Four bodies I've collected—'

There was a murmur among the passengers, and an angry voice called out: 'Less talk, for God's sake! Row us across. I want to get home. Do you think you are the only one who has had a bad day today?'

'Now just a minute—' the *barklor* began, and his white whiskers bristled.

An old woman crouching under an umbrella interrupted him again. 'What is four bodies?' she croaked. 'I have seen *forty* bodies, in Pieta alone. I have seen—'

Suddenly everyone was talking at once, and no one was listening. They all had their own stories of this terrible day of war, and they would not be denied. The phrases flew to and fro as the boat rocked, and Angelo, disgruntled and sulky at the loss of his audience, concentrated on his rowing.

'A bomb hit the hospital where my own sister was having a baby. The doctor was late, and all he said was, is it a boy or a girl?'

'They say we must take people in if they lose their homes, but who wants strangers?'

'The bomb made a great hole in the road, and the bus ran right into it. I heard them screaming.'

'Forty bodies I saw. Laid out like fish in the market. Where will it end?'

'I could not even get a bus from Birkirkara. As soon as the sirens went, they all ran away.'

'She was bleeding all over. It was broken glass, little bits of it, forced through her skin. Why didn't they tell us, that's what I want to know!'

'A chicken with its head blown off. But then it laid an egg!'

'They bombed the cemetery. Why should they do that? The dead are dead already.'

'We have a little shop in Old Bakery Street. When the bomb fell, it broke all the windows, and would you believe it? – A man walking by reached in and stole a box of candles.'

'I saw a policeman with his arm cut off.'

'I saw a horse sliced to ribbons. All covered with flies.'

'I saw the wall falling, and I thought, this is it, but I jumped out of the way, and it hit the vegetable cart instead.'

'But where will it end? What is the point? What do the Italians want? They can have it, as far as I am concerned.'

'They say it is worse in Senglea.'

'We will know soon, if this old devil will only row harder.'

'A new sewing machine. I saved for two years to buy it. Now it's nothing but a lump of metal.'

'My husband says, he's not going to fight. He's just bought a new *luzzu*, with two engines. It's fishing for him!'

'I counted the bombers going over Cospicua. Sixteen of them. What can you do against sixteen bombers?'

'I saw the bomb coming down, like a great balloon, straight at me, and I said, "Gesu Marija! Let it fall somewhere else!" And it did.'

'I was standing right there when it happened. A dead dog came flying through the air. It missed me by an inch, and then it made a mess all over the courtyard.'

'What can we do? I could not even buy oil this morning. The man closed his shop straight away, and now they say he's gone to Naxxar till it's all over.'

'Hit in the face. They say it wasn't a bomb at all, but a bit of shell from one of our own guns. What can you do if your own side goes shooting at you?'

'What can we do?'

Father Salvatore had returned to his breviary, but the voices, with their burden of fear and despair – a burden which, it must be said, often seemed wholly selfish, with a certain pleasurable interest in the blood of others added to it – came between him and the holy words, and he found himself listening instead of reading. What could be done with such a crew as this? They were like the people in the bar – was it ten hours ago, six raids ago? – who had seemed so spiritless, so morbid, and so unworthy of the moment.

Was all Malta so obsessed with its troubles that it could see nothing beyond flying dogs and closed shops and flies swarming over dead horses? What would they find, when they had crossed the harbour? What did they deserve to find? Was old Angelo the *barklor* no better than old Charon the oarsman, rowing them across the river Styx to the infernal regions of hell?

Then his ear, which had heard nothing but tales of private woe, heard one new voice with one new thought. It was a young voice, rough and harsh, coming from behind him in the stern of the *dghajsa*, and it said :

'Who cares about all this? They want to kill us? They want to take our land? We must fight back, that's all! I'd give them dead dogs! I'd give them dead dogs for breakfast!'

Now there, at last, was a man... It might not be strict Christian sentiment, but by all that was holy, it was the spirit of the Lord! He turned round to find out the author of this brave defiance, and discovered that it was not really a man at all. It was a young dwarf, not more than eighteen, sitting on the last single bench just under the stern-post, his stunted legs dangling above the floor-boards.

Father Salvatore had never seen him before, nor noticed him when he came on board the *dghajsa*. He had a little olive-brown face, and a fierce hooked nose, and burning eyes which somehow seemed able to express contempt for everything bigger, or stronger, or better favoured than himself, with a single flicker of a glance.

But he was also a good-humoured, smiling young man, and he was smiling now, all round him – at his startled neighbours in the boat, at Father Salvatore whose eye he had caught, at Angelo bending to his oars as the *dghajsa* glided up Dockyard Creek between Senglea and Vittoriosa : even at the sad discoveries to be made ashore, the missing buildings, toppled cranes, dust clouds still settling, an oil barge still burning, all the wretched aftermath of the first day's raids.

Look about you, the smiling young dwarf seemed to be saying. Look at yourselves. Look at me, if you like. This is war! It is something to be *won*, not cried over, not run away from. I have said my say. You will find I am right.

Father Salvatore found himself drawn irresistibly to the young man. For once, the brash confidence of youth did not seem either laughable or irritating. From this small misshapen frame, from such a tiny grain of mustard seed, all faith and strength could spring... Here was a man at last... But how many more were there like him in Malta this evening, in Malta under attack?

They landed at last – terribly late, nearly half past seven – and Father Salvatore began to walk the last mile of his day, towards Cospicua and the Cottonera Lines and the church of St Barnabas which was no more. He could scarcely visualize what he would find; the idea of a blank space where a beloved building had been, the idea of no shadows where this morning the shadows had fallen so comfortingly, was horrible, unthinkable.

But it must be faced. Ruin and destruction and heart-break were part of life, just as death was part of life. All must be faced, with acceptance, with bravery, with the manhood which a priest, above all others, should be able to summon up intact.

Presently, passing some of the wreckage which was Senglea this evening, he found that he had company. The little dwarf, the young man with the ancient spirit, had fallen into step beside him.

'Fallen into step' was a relative term. Since he had to take two strides to the priest's one, the dwarf's progress was erratic, like a puppy striving to keep up with a full-grown pack. He jumped and ran and skipped on his tiny legs, sometimes lagging a little behind, sometimes achieving a spurt which took him well ahead of Father Salvatore.

All the time he smiled, and chattered, and looked up into the priest's face for approval or agreement or confirmation. His energy and bouncing spirit, at the end of such a day, were the best tonic that Father Salvatore had had, for many hours.

'I liked what you said in the boat,' he told the dwarf, as soon as they were set on their course together.

'Thank you, Dun Salv.'

'You know my name?'

'I heard that old misery Angelo use it. Have you ever heard such rubbish as he talked? You would think we had lost the war already. He was the worst of the bunch because he started it... My name is Nero, Father. Nero Cassar. It's Nazzareno, really, but you know how it is. Who wants to say Nazzareno when they can shorten it? So it's a little name for a little man. But it suits *me*!'

Father Salvatore smiled. The contrast between the holy name of the Nazarene, and Nero, the little monster who became a Roman Emperor, was so absurd that it could only be accepted.

'Where do you live, Nero?'

'Near the Salvatore Gate.' The dwarf, whose sudden burst of energy had taken him several steps ahead, turned round and grinned. 'Your gate, Dun Salv. I'm a carpenter. Not the best in the world, but the best in the village, anyway. I made myself strong, with exercises.'

It was indeed true, Father Salvatore noticed: the small body was sinewy and compact, the shoulders and forearms rippling with muscle.

'One must do something, if one is little,' Nero went on. 'One cannot sit down and cry.' Had there been a time when he had done this? 'Any fool who is six feet high can get a job. But three feet and nine inches – now there's a problem worth having! So I made myself a carpenter. What does a dwarf need to be a good carpenter? Only a longer ladder!' He laughed aloud; it was clear that he had made the joke many times before, and lived with it, as he had learned to live with everything else which might have confined or dispirited him. 'I'd like a girl, too, but that's a bit more difficult. Can you find me a girl, Dun Salv?'

Father Salvatore smiled again. 'You find a girl, Nero. I'm sure you can. And I'll come to the wedding.'

'We'll see, we'll see.' Briefly the little face with its big hooked nose was clouded. 'Even the Italians would touch me for luck, but the girls here... I do not want a – I want an ordinary girl. You understand, Father?'

'Then you'll find an ordinary girl, Nero. Just as you've found a job for yourself, and made a success of it.' Something made him add: 'Malta is small, Nero. Is that what you've been thinking today?'

'Exactly!' The face lit up again, with all its jaunty, irrepressible good humour. 'Why should we sit down and cry?'

They had come to a crossroads in the centre of Cospicua, and to a scene familiar – no better and no worse than what they had already witnessed that day: buildings in ruins, people in ferment or despair, all the aftermath of a savage attack. But there were police everywhere, and two ambulances at work, and an air of official control.

'I go to the left, Dun Salv.'

'Then goodbye, Nero. I'm glad we met. Take care of your-self.'

'I'll take care of others too!' He really meant it; his face and his bearing seemed to express a boundless confidence, and his next words were said with the same perky assurance. 'Bless me, Father!'

'*Tkun imbierek.*'

'Thank you. *Sahha!*'

Nero wheeled round, and began to run and jump and skip up the street, as if he could not wait to confront his next problem. He turned to wave at the first corner. Father Salvatore inclined to the right, and began to walk more soberly, but with something of the same confidence. What a lesson, what a reassurance... Surely there was nothing which, with the help of God and the driving spirit of man, could not be solved.

Almost immediately the sirens sounded.

It was the last raid of the day, though he was not to know this; and it was Malta's eighth, inflicted by twenty-five Italian planes, though he could only work out these sums with the help of later information. For him, it was just another air-raid, at the end of a long crippling day, and this time it fell, with all its crude ferocity, on Cospicua itself. But for Father Salvatore it had at least one difference. For most of the time, he was unconscious.

He scarcely had time to master the sick feeling of fear when it happened. A bomb, screaming down with that eery whistling sound which seemed already to have become part of life in Malta, fell at a street corner about a hundred yards away. The tremendous blast knocked him off his feet, and as he tottered sideways his head caught the sharp edge of a doorway. Stunned, he lowered himself on wavering legs until he was wedged between the step and the upright of the door. Then a scarlet film of blood ran into his eyes, and turned black as his senses left him.

He awoke to a blinding headache, and the touch of careful hands on his face. He could feel also the cool caress of water, and he gradually became aware that someone was sponging his forehead and his eyes. His headache and his vision cleared slowly; when at last he opened his eyes, it was to find an old woman peering into his face as if she had seen a miracle.

'Thanks be to God!' she exclaimed. 'A priest dead on my doorstep – what next?'

Father Salvatore sat upright, and summoned a wan smile. 'This priest is not dead... Thank you, *nanna*.' He was sure she was a grandmother: she had the look and the touch, the worn hands and the compassionate care, of all this honoured tribe. He fingered a tender spot on his head. 'Is it a bad cut?'

She almost smacked his hand away, as she must have done a thousand times before. 'Don't touch it!' Then she recollected herself. 'Excuse me, *sur kappillan*. But the wound is still open. Your hands are dirty. It should be covered up. Wait till I get a clean cloth.'

She disappeared through the open doorway behind him. With an effort, Father Salvatore leant forward and looked down the street. It was the same, and it was not the same. Yellow dust hung in clouds on the twilight air. The cordite reek was strong in his nostrils. There was a sprawl of stones at the further end, where a corner shop had once stood. There were no people at all.

When the old woman, whose black widow's dress was as neat and clean as her touch had been gentle, returned and began to tie a rough bandage round his head, Father Salvatore asked:

'Has the all-clear gone?'

'Eh? What's that?' She was busy with the knot of the bandage.

'Have they sounded the all-clear? Did the sirens go again?'

Before she could answer, the sirens answered for her, in the strident, long-drawn-out, one-note wail which had already lifted his heart several times that day. He waited until she had finished the bandaging, and then said:

'That was the all-clear sound.'

She looked at him, smiling and level-headed in a mad world. 'Was it really? I thought it was another raid... I am too old for all this nonsense, Father.'

'But you have done very well.' He pressed her hand as he rose unsteadily to his feet. 'Thank you for looking after me.'

She clicked her tongue. 'If we can't help each other, what is the world coming to? A priest dying on my doorstep? If my mother was alive, God rest her soul, she'd give those Frenchies a piece of her mind!'

'But it's the Italians who are fighting us now.'

'They're all the same... I can tell you something, Father. When I was a little girl, they still used to say: "You be good, or I'll fetch Napoleon to you!"'

'How old are you, *nanna*?'

'Never you mind!'

Light-headed, he responded to her rough humour.

'Are you sure it wasn't the Turks?'

'*Ejja!*'

He bade her goodbye, promising to return the bandage next day, and took up his walk again. His head was swimming slightly and his weary legs were unsteady. But within a few moments he found that he was walking towards the most terrible sound he had ever heard, a sound which rid his mind of his own troubles on the instant.

It was a noise coming up the street, a kind of lowing, moaning sound which put him in mind of terrified cattle, or of cattle tortured by thirst, in flight from what they feared towards what they hoped would make them safe again.

If he had heard it in a cinema, Father Salvatore would have accepted it. Cattle, he had learned from American western films, did panic, and stampede, and advertise their distress while they were doing so. But this sound, on a street in Cospicua, was not being made by cattle. These cattle were people.

As he marched towards the next crossroads, the noise increased, and with it his own dismay. People came into view: a solid river of people, moving in blind obedience to their fear, and calling all the world to witness it, without shame, without control of any kind. The sound grew horrifying, with such a note of hysteria that it might have signalled the end of the world, with all its terror and remorse. These people were craven fugitives from war.

He heard a man, stumbling blindly up the street, shriek out suddenly: 'I have left my wife and children buried! Buried, I tell you!' and he could only think, between pity and nausea: But why did you not stay, and try to dig them out? Then he was launched into the mob, and forced to join them, and was swept along helplessly. It was the way he wanted to go, towards the Cottonera Lines; but not like this, not like this...

Some of them were his own people. He recognized them, and

they recognized him; they even exclaimed at the sight of his bandaged head. But it changed nothing in their distraught purpose. They were fleeing from the last ordeal of the day, and they would not be stopped, by man or God or wounded priest. It would be useless to try to stem this tide, which carried its own wretched flotsam with it, as he had witnessed that same morning: the snatched-up household goods, the prams and the wheelbarrows laden with clothes and toys, clocks and pictures, half-cooked meals, oil and water in slopping tin cans.

But it was worse than this morning. There was more desperation in this flight; more panic fear, more wild determination to get away at any price, in any direction. And by now it was nearly dark; the gloomy twilight and the tossing shadows added a special element of dread, as it must do for children abandoned, for men trapped underground, for women overtaken in labour, alone at night.

Some had dropped out already, collapsing from exhaustion and fright, lying like tattered bundles in doorways and at street-corners. Four blood-spattered bodies were sprawled on the roadside not far from the Zabbar Gate; seeing them, the people all round him set up a most fearful clamour; they moaned, and howled, and wept, and shouted hysterically. But they never thought to stop.

It would not do. In a world which, for all its cruelty, still lay in the arms of God, it would not do. Whatever their pitch of terror, whatever horrors they had seen and heard during the last obscene hours of this day, this abject surrender was not to be borne... Father Salvatore, on a sudden impulse, wrestled himself free of his companions, dived into an open doorway, and let the crowds swirl past him.

Then he peered out, in the direction whence the people were coming, and saw a most welcome sight. Under a street lamp only a few yards away, Rafel Vella was moving towards him.

Though he towered head and shoulders above all those around him, the giant sacristan was still being carried along like a cork in a stream, the same as any other man trapped in this river of humanity. Father Salvatore called out to him, but his hoarse voice was lost in the general chaos of sound. He jumped up and down in the doorway, waving his arms – and realized, even as he did so, what an absurd figure he must be presenting. But even this extravagance was wasted on the murky twilight, and the confused wailing movement which was all that it contained.

Then he heard a woman's voice call out: 'Rafel! Rafel! Dun Salv wants you! Over there!' and he thanked God, and blessed this unknown Samaritan, for a tiny gleam of common sense in all this madness. Rafel turned, and stared, and a beam of pure joy came over his harassed face. Then he lurched sideways, and somehow fought his way to the doorway. There, the small priest and his huge servant, reunited, embraced like long-lost brothers.

'Oh, Dun Salv, Dun Salv! I thought I would never find you! I thought you must be dead! Where have you been all day?'

'I was delayed, Rafel. Like everyone else.'

'But your head! My God, what has happened?'

'It is nothing,' Father Salvatore reassured him. 'I fell against a doorway, and cut it.'

'But you should go to hospital.'

'The hospital has better things to do than treat a little cut on the forehead.' Father Salvatore looked up at Rafel, whose own brow had cleared magically during the last few moments. 'Where are all these people going?'

'Anywhere. Some to the country, some to the new catacombs. I asked one man, and he said "I am going where they don't ask silly questions," and he spat at me... They are running from the last raid. It was the worst of all.'

'Where were *you* going, Rafel?'

'I was coming to find you, Dun Salv.'

Was that true, Father Salvatore wondered, or had Rafel joined the panic flight and been swept along as part of it? Had he led it, or added to it? Was he just another blind runaway? Perhaps it did not matter. Only God could sort out the strong from the weak, and in His infinite pity He might forbear to judge, on such a day as this. A priest could hardly do less than that.

'Well, here I am,' he said. 'I was on my way to see the church. Then I was caught, the same as you. What happened in the air-raid, Rafel?'

The giant gestured towards the throng moving past the doorway. 'I wonder there are so many people left alive in Cospicua. It was terrible. Whole streets disappeared. The air-raid centre was hit, and everyone in it killed. The police station at the dockyard was the same. I counted twenty bodies in the last half-mile. What can we do, Dun Salv?'

'Work. Work and pray.' But had he not said that already, at the beginning of today? Had it proved a good answer? Rafel, the simple observer, did not think so.

'But all those bodies. All the blood. Where will it end? We can all be killed, *all*!'

'We will all be killed if we do nothing,' Father Salvatore answered firmly. 'Never mind the bodies, Rafel. They are in God's care. They are at rest. We must help the living, then count the dead.' He looked out on to the street, at the marching stumbling moaning crowds. "If we join these for a little while, perhaps we can cut across at San Sebastian Street, and make for the church. I want to see it for a moment. Then we must get back to the people.'

'I told as many of them as I could to go to the catacombs. I promised you would be there.'

The curious word, used for the second time, now caught Father Salvatore's attention. 'Catacombs? What catacombs are these, Rafel?'

Rafel's eyes opened wide. 'They are a new place, Dun Salv. Some time this morning a huge bomb knocked off a piece of the Cottonera bastions, and when all the dust had cleared the people went to look, and it was an old burial-ground. With long passages and caves. I've seen it myself. It goes deep down into the Lines. It's a great shelter, all ready for us. Nothing could hit us there.'

'But why do you say catacombs?'

'It was a word I heard, Dun Salv. Everyone was using it. I walked all round the place. I could have walked for an hour or more. Some people had brought oil lamps already, and made little shelters for themselves. Others had torches. But there were still plenty of ghosts about! I would not like to be there alone, I can tell you!'

'Why not?'

'It was full of little dead brothers.'

'*Brothers?*'

'Have I said something wrong, Dun Salv?'

'No, no. I did not intend to speak sharply. But I don't understand what you mean.'

'I mean they are friars. Like the friars from the monastery

today. Each one is in a little bed in the rock. There must be hundreds of them. Each in his brown habit, with a rope girdle, and his name and the date carved on the rock above his head. I saw one date that said 1725! Of course they are all dried up. Sometimes there is just the skull, and a few bones, and the dust of the habit.' Rafel was looking anxiously at Father Salvatore. 'I know it is holy ground, Dun Salv,' he said. But there is room for people as well. Even if we do not—'

'Push them all to one side,' Father Salvatore said harshly.

'With decency, Dun Salv. You could say a prayer for each, God rest their souls. But even without that, there is one great cave in the middle, where we could all shelter. It is like a church, hollowed out of the rock.' Rafel was looking at him again, with humble persistence. 'Dun Salv, you just said, we should help the living, then count the dead.'

Father Salvatore smiled. Rafel, in all his simplicity, had gone right to the heart of the matter. What harm could there be, under the hand of God, in taking shelter among the dead, if it brought comfort and life and courage to the living? The lonely little brothers of long ago might be glad of the company... He reached up and patted the sacristan on the shoulder.

'You are right, Rafel. We'll go to the church, and then back to your catacombs. We must sleep somewhere tonight. Perhaps I could say a prayer. And then speak to the people. They have suffered so much...' Conscious of his own weary limbs and throbbing head, he braced himself for action, and took Rafel's arm. 'Now then! We have work to do. You move first, and I'll follow.'

Together they launched themselves upon the jostling throng, the throng so desperate, so implacable in its advance. It was like diving into some deep muddy pool, which might hold all sorts of horrors, which might not even support him, which could drown him with a single engulfing wave. But this time, at least, he had a friend.

After all the effort and turmoil of the journey, there was nothing to see, on the site of the church of poor St Barnabas. Almost, there was nothing to feel. Whatever he had hoped or feared, or had been resigned to, it was not to be found here. Here, there was only a sad desolation, the rubble of faith betrayed.

The moonlight fell on tossed hummocks of stone, on jagged corners of wall, on the curved up-ended saucer which was the shattered dome; and on the piles of dust which, stirred by their feet, was bitter in the mouth and nostrils, choking to the spirit. But that was all. It was not even as heart-rending as he had feared. This was no longer a church, nor even part of a church. It was a builders' rubbish tip, formless, derelict, not wanted any more by hopeful man.

It was as if the virtue of this holy place had melted away into the ground, as the stones collapsed one upon another. The gloom of *Tenebrae* – the candles extinguished one by one, the fearful darkness of the crucifixion – seemed to have descended before the little church had even been sanctified. Once again, St Barnabas had disappeared into the wilderness of time, with a second, monstrous thunder-clap of wrath to hurl him into limbo for ever.

All that was left was a heap of stones, and a heart too empty to feel its own sickness.

Perhaps that would come, in the lonely watches of the night, on some awful tomorrow... He became aware that Rafel was looking at him: was indeed peering into his face as if he would not know what to feel until he found out what Father Salvatore himself was feeling. Even when he said: 'It is very sad, Dun Salv,' it was on a tentative note.

Rafel, an earlier witness, had survived his first shock, had shed his first tears. Now the loss of their church would be sad only to the degree that it made Dun Salv sad as well.

Father Salvatore pulled himself together. He must not fall into the sin of Malta, as he had observed it today all over the city: the sin of apathy, the sin of surrender. He nodded, and he saw his moon-shadow nod, coldly black against a yellow corner-stone which was a corner-stone no more.

'Yes, it is very sad, Rafel. We can do nothing more tonight. But tomorrow we must think about clearing things up here.'

'Shall we start building again, Dun Salv?'

'Certainly! As soon as we find men who can be spared. That may take some time.' His mind went off at a tangent. 'Tell me, do you know a boy called Nero Cassar?'

'The little carpenter? Yes, I do. Well, I've met him once, at the *festa* of Vittoriosa.' An unexpected note of derision came into Rafel's voice. 'They say his mother was frightened by a mouse.'

'Rafel! That's a cruel thing to say. Would you like to have someone say, your mother was frightened by an elephant?'

'I'd like to hear them try it!'

'Well, then...' But he could never quarrel with Rafel; only love him, and teach him, and honour his innocence. He continued, on a gentler note: 'I met Nero on the *dghajsa* coming over. I liked what he said about the war. He had plenty of spirit, I can tell you! I was thinking, when we start work again, he would be a good one to have helping us.'

After a pause, Rafel said humbly: 'I have plenty of spirit too, Dun Salv.'

'I know that. Otherwise we would not be friends.'

'And I have great ideas, as well!' In the lonely moonlit silence, the phrase 'great ideas' hung strangely, as if Rafel had said: I have two heads! I have the power of healing! 'And I can prove it too. When I saw all this, I said: "But Dun Salv has no church any more. Therefore he has no altar. How can he pray? How can he bless the people?" So I went home, and fetched the little altar for you. It is here, Dun Salv! So wherever you go, you still have a church.'

'Why, Rafel—' Father Salvatore began, suddenly moved near to tears.

'I hid it in a sack, under a pile of stone,' Rafel said, and walked a few paces away. 'Otherwise someone might steal it,' he called over his shoulder. 'You would not believe the stories I've heard today. Two men in St Ursula Street stole a piano from a bombed house. A whole piano! They hoisted it on their shoulders and walked away, as cheeky as if they were policemen... Ah, here it is.'

Rafel drew near him again, his huge figure like an ambling mountain peak against the moonlight. He had a bundle in his hands, and Father Salvatore recognized its outlines. Always entrusted to Rafel for safe-keeping, it was the small oblong of marble, his 'travelling altar' with the black square on its face which marked where the sacred relic had been plastered in, under the eye and the blessing of authority.

The relic, he had been assured, was a minuscule fragment of bone from the forearm of the blessed Saint and martyr Lawrence. But the altar, and the faith it enshrined, was as big as the whole world, and, at this moment, as precious as the body of Our Lord.

'Why, Rafel,' he said again, 'that was *very* good of you. Very good, and very thoughtful, and very valuable.' He took the altarpiece, and cradled it in his grasp: he knew its weight, and its shape, down to the last ounce, the last centimetre. 'Now we can go anywhere!'

'To the catacombs?'

'Especially to the catacombs.'

It was a weary, plodding journey back, along the deserted road, under the cruel moonlight which revealed only dust and desolation. Father Salvatore had forgotten how much he hated his boots; now he hated his whole exhausted body, from the top of his aching head to his bone-tired legs and blistered feet.

He had been awake since before dawn; now he seemed to have been walking since before dawn, and talking, and worrying, and doing his flesh-and-blood best in a world which had suddenly decreed that only iron men could survive. His cherished altar weighed heavy in his arms. He was light-headed, and leaden-footed. He had seen too many fearful things that day.

But he was on his way to seek out and comfort people who might have seen worse, who must have suffered more, who had been driven to panic and despair without any spark or spirit to sustain them. At least he must tell them to be brave.

As, guided by Rafel, they neared the bastions of the Cottonera Lines, he heard the tolling of the last bell of the day, from some faithful wayside church which had surrendered nothing of its faith. It was the bell called *Tal-Imwiet*, the bell of the dead, the request to the living to remember the dead in their prayers.

He saw Rafel cross himself, and heard him mutter something. He did the same, but his inner voice was clear. God help them. God help us all. God help me. God help me to do more than *remember* the dead. *Per Christum Dominum Nostrum.*

The great wall of rock which formed the bastions rose above their heads. It was lit here and there, at its base, by flickering lights, lights never seen before, nor ever kindled since the last little brother was laid to rest. The pierced rock must be alive with people.

Rafel said: 'I know the best way in. There, by the big shadow.' They began to pick a pathway round and over a mountain of ruined masonry, which made the rubble they had left behind them seem like a fistful of pebbles scattered by the way.

A yellow light gleamed from within, and grew stronger. A woman's voice, astonished, called out: 'Dun Salv!' and his name was repeated, in a ghostly hissing murmur, from all over the wall of rock. Cooking smells met him: grosser human smells: ancient smells of burial and dry bones: comforting smells of wood-fires and glowing embers. A child cried, and it was as if the grey bastion of the Cottonera Lines, long the abode of death, had miraculously given birth to infant life and hope.

Bearing his church with him, Father Salvatore entered into this new kingdom.

HEXAMERON ONE

1500 BC. The Fore-Runners

'Let us now praise famous men,' he began immediately, as soon
as he had finished his brief prayers, and it was the accustomed
time for the homily. He sought to catch them unawares, between silence and tears, tears and sleep. 'Let us now praise
famous men, and our forefathers which begat us.'

The words were from the Book of Ecclesiasticus, which
other, separated brethren dismissed as part of the Apocrypha,
one of the doubtful books of God. How sad... But even if
the noble phrases had been suspect, they might still have
risen to his lips. So much else was thundering in his brain that
he was at ease to use whatever weapons came to hand, in his
quest for certainty and truth.

Indeed, scarcely had he begun to hear his own voice echoing
round the great shadowy vault of their refuge, flowing over the
spaces packed with men and women and children in every
stage of tumult and misery, flowing past the carved niches
where the bones and the brown dust of the little brothers lay

in peace, than he was possessed with tongues, and other powers took command.

With a pious madness, he began to stab with words and phrases, words never recorded, never to be recalled by himself. It was other people, weeks and months afterwards, who remembered and marvelled and told him what he had said.

We have lived through a terrible day, full of blood and slaughter and weeping.

We end it hiding in the rocks among the dead, as if forgotten by God, as if we were nobody.

We MUST NOT hide tomorrow.

We are NOT dead.

We are NOT forgotten.

We are NOT nobody.

We have a thousand ancestors to be proud of. Bravery and adventure is in our blood and bone.

We have been conquered before. But NOT for ever. We have always survived, and overcome. We are Maltese.

We have a shining, glittering history. We MUST earn it again, and live it again.

We MUST know, and remember, what that history is.

Long ago, this island was not an island, but—

Only an up-thrust of high ground, a sort of pylon in the vast land-bridge joining Italy with Africa. The Mediterranean Sea was no sea at all, at that moment of time; it was a part of the main, where wild animals roamed the forest and men, outnumbered, camped and herded together for their own safety.

It had valleys, and freshwater lakes, and rivers to feed them. It had good earth. Then, under the hand of God, or the weight of aeons of time, the good earth sank and the Atlantic Ocean began to roar in through the western sluice-gate, the Pillars of Hercules, now named Gibraltar and Ceuta.

Gradually the land-bridge was breached, was rejoined, was breached again. When it collapsed for ever, millions of animals, in uneasy wandering flight from arctic Europe to warm Africa, were cut off, and began to die.

Malta was left, the last refuge on a journey which changed from a puzzle to a rout with terrible swiftness. Lucky were the animals which, on this colossal stampede southwards, shook

their hide or their fur free of briny, engulfing sea-water, and
reached its haven.

They were lucky to begin with, then less lucky, then doomed
as their ancestors had been doomed. In a few years, as time
must be reckoned on this unimaginable scale, Malta, a green
island, turned pale grey, then burnt-out yellow. Very soon, it
could no longer support the animals which had taken refuge
on its high ground.

After they had ravaged every tree, every leaf, every blade
of grass, they fought each other with murderous savagery for
what remained. They turned carnivore, and cannibal; they ate
the stinking bones of fish, also trapped and stranded in this
huge calamity. They grew fewer, and smaller, and then they
began to die in their turn.

They left their bones behind them. Five million years later,
fish still emerged from the quarried rock of Malta: rock up-
thrust from the sea as Malta itself was up-thrust, fish fossilized
but still delicately boned, delicately etched in blue and pink
and yellow, as they were when they first swam into this
sandy trap, and gasped, and panicked, and died.

Mammoths, driven out of frozen Europe, lingering too long
on the way, there left their monstrous skeletons. In forests
stripped down to tattered bark, wild boars shed their tusks
for the last time. Wolves, with no softer prey to tear to pieces,
turned upon their own pack, and then on their young. Giant
tortoises, graceful swans, lumbering hippopotami, and leaping
red deer, all longing for Africa, found slow agony and then
eternal rest in Malta.

Among the last to die were the dwarf elephants, starved
and stunted – and *their* bones were gnawed by ravening polar
bears, who left their teeth to prove it.

Even the children, weary-eyed, wakeful, fractious, hushed and
listened as they saw the poor little elephants, hungry and afraid,
with no mother or father, lie down and die.

Then, when it was safe, man came to Malta: Neolithic man,
untraceable man, man perhaps from Europe, or from Africa,
or from somewhere which could not be classed by name or
race or even exact humanity. They lived, and built, and died,
and were swallowed up, like the mammoths and the swans
and the leaping deer. Then there was a pause, a missed heart-

K.M.—6

beat, a thousand-year catching of the breath. Then we came, and our name was Phoenician.

It was the proudest name in all the known world. A man was then as happy to say, 'I am Phoenician', as he was, 800 years later, to say, 'I am Greek', or later still, with even more satisfaction, 'I am a Roman citizen'. The Phoenicians were the masters of the civilized world, and they deserved it.

They were Semites, and their cradle was Lebanon. From this tiny base of power, they swiftly made themselves supreme as ship-builders, navigators, and merchants. Their reputation as the world's bravest sailors was never questioned, even by the most envious of stay-at-homes.

From their thriving seaports of Tyre and Sidon they set out in search of all the ocean deeps, and even here their cradle was still Lebanon. The fabled cedars of Lebanon furnished the great curved planks, made secure with resin and pitch, from which their hulls were fashioned.

These ships had a high stem with a horse's head emblem, and a matching high stern-post for the pilot to stand on. (A *luzzu* from Gozo, 4,000 years later, was an exact copy, with the eye of Osiris replacing the horse's head.) Behind this high stem, which could ride and top and surmount any wave, were the ritual places for the amphoras of wine and water.

The big square sail was set on two huge yards; sometimes it was dyed a proud purple, so that any watcher, spying any purple sail on the horizon, could say, in admiration or envy, 'That one is Phoenician.'

Such a ship was good for a three-year voyage, and such watchers were legion; they were to be found on any coast, from nearby Greece to the distant Baltic. Phoenicians took their ships and their trade from the Red Sea to India and Ceylon, or round the Horn of Africa and then the Cape, four thousand miles to the south; from the Mediterranean to Cornwall, where they mined the tin, or to townships not yet named Oslo or Copenhagen.

In a three-year voyage round Africa, their crews would go ashore each autumn, build a camp, sow a crop of corn, wait to reap it, and then sail on. Herodotus told this story, in amazement. The Phoenicians lived it.

They did not only sail; sometimes, when they stepped ashore, they stayed ashore, and set the commercial pattern for a quarter of the world. Their coastal settlements stretched from the land of Israel to Gibraltar, from Sardinia to southern Spain, from Tunis to Morocco.

They became masters of 300 towns, linked and maintained by all the intricacies of maritime intercourse. They founded Marseilles. They employed 40,000 men in the silver mines of Spain alone. They set up cargo depots and bonded stores. They had their own insurance business, for ships and cargoes. Their word was also their bond.

These our most famous forefathers first came to Malta, as traders, some 1,500 years before Our Saviour's birth. They called it Malet, meaning shelter; it was the same shelter as Ulysses, another matchless sailor, had found when he was wrecked on Gozo, and there spent seven years in seclusion with the nymph Calypso. But being proud Phoenicians, they were sure that they must be the first important callers for a very long time, and when they came ashore they came as townsfolk visiting country cousins. Being Phoenicians, however, they also brought one or two things to sell. There must be *some* inhabitants.

They were small men, as tough as their ships, with dark eyes, black hair gleaming like metal, and the hooked noses which were already the sign-manual of the eastern Mediterranean. They wore woollen clothes to absorb their sweat, and long baggy trousers to outwit mosquitoes. In fact, they were the most astonishing tourists ever seen in these parts.

As soon as they stepped ashore from their strong, well-built ships, they attracted crowds to the beaches. The newcomers were smiling and friendly, and they certainly had some beautiful things to offer, imported lines never before seen in Malta.

They brought cargoes of incense, glassware, and jewellery; since they excelled in gold and silver filigree work, this was a taste and a skill which they left behind them for ever when they moved on. They brought a marvellous new range of fabrics, cunningly dyed from plants and fish. Their finest colour was that same purple which the richer merchants used for their sails. It came from the little murex shellfish of Tyre, their home port; they called it Tyrian purple – very exclusive, and very reasonably priced, considering that it was the first choice of emperors and kings.

We say now that a man 'is raised to the purple' when he is made a cardinal. This is the purple he is raised to.

They traded with any coin that had the ring of truth: silver shekels and demi-shekels, coins of gold and brass, coins of electrum, their own alloy of silver and gold which gave, perhaps, a certain opportunity for sharp practice. But the Phoenicians were never too sharp. They wanted to come back next year, and it was bad for business.

They made certain discoveries about their country cousins. As they poked about the island, seeing what was what, keeping an eye open for a bargain, they found that they were not the first sophisticates to be found hereabouts. Someone, some people with a lot of sense and skill, had been here long before they themselves landed – perhaps a couple of thousand years before.

It was not a specially good tonic for national pride, but one could always learn, even from the funny little natives of Malet... They learned that these people, whoever they were (and it was comforting to think that they could have been Phoenicians of a sort, their own long-ago forefathers, just as well as northern wanderers from Sicily or Sardinia), had been farmers and hunters, making the best of an arid, stripped-down island, somehow scratching a living before the export–import trade became an alternative to hard work.

They had lived in caves, and that was still the smart thing to do. As well as flint blades and farm tools, they had used copper daggers, and arrows tipped with obsidian, the dark lava which could be cut and polished till it shone like bottle-glass. Already they had learned to make bronze, by fusing copper and tin. (So nothing was new, on the face of the earth!) They stored their grain and oil in huge jars; they spun their cloth on wheels not very different from the brand-new model of 1500 BC.

They had built temples, and catacombs hollowed from living rock like this one, and they buried their dead in rock-tombs, or stored their dust in cremation urns lovingly ornamented. They could handle enormous blocks of stone without benefit of modern tackle; one *upright* stone at the place known as Ggantija measured twelve feet broad by seventeen feet high.

They honoured their dead, as we do now, and as the Phoenicians did then: besides the most ancient of bones, the rock-tombs always contained furniture of alabaster, glass, terra-cotta, and marble: figures of clay for the amusement of the dead:

cooking utensils: meat and drink for the long journey.

Since women would wish to please, even in death, they were buried with their necklaces, rings, bracelets, ear-rings, metal mirrors, and little 'vanity boxes' of cosmetics and perfumes.

There were seven thousand of these long-ago people buried in one place, the inquisitive Phoenicians found. They had been laid to rest in a vast, three-tiered, underground vault which, apart from superb architectural skill, must literally have taken ages to construct. How death had struck on such a scale, one could only guess. But whether it was a war, or a plague, or a single tribal burial-place, the dead had been duly honoured, and the living had gone back to living, and to work.

There was one curious aspect of this work which puzzled even the up-to-date Phoenicians, who prided themselves on knowing everything about anything. All over the two islands, Malet itself and its little sister to the north-west, there was a pattern of deeply rutted cart-tracks: something more than roads (both Tyre and Sidon had plenty of first-class, stone-paved roads), more like a system of movement and communication for a single purpose.

So deeply and exactly were these tracks scored into the hard yellow stone that they must have been in continuous use for a thousand years or more, and their pattern enforced by authority. Sometimes, at important junctions, they ran double or even triple, so that a cart (if it was a cart) or a train of carts going in one direction could give way to traffic coming from the other.

What was it all about? Why didn't anybody *know*? Naturally, it was no good talking to the people of Malet. Every last one of them had a different story.

Some said it was for the huge loads of stone used for temple building. Some said it was for carrying corn and fruit to market. Some said it was for chariot-racing, and that the driver whose horse (or camel, or even team of galloping slaves) caught and touched the chariot in front was the winner. Some had even wilder notions.

They would take you down to the seashore, and point out where the tracks disappeared under the waves. It was certainly true that some tracks went northwards, and some went south. Old men with nothing to do but dream and gossip said that these tracks continued all the way along the sea-bed, and came up again over *there* (they pointed to the line of their shadows) and over *there* (they pointed behind them at the burning sun).

It was a very old road, they said, joining Africa to the other land which some now called Sicily. The island of Malet was a sort of meeting-point in the middle. People used to talk of 'riding to Africa'. Who would want to know more than that?

The Phoenicians always wanted to know more. They were questing people, the best kind of people to be. For one reason or another, they came to like Malet very much; quite apart from the dreaming old men and their tale of a cart-road between Africa and Europe, the island had become a trade-link for ships, an established way-station between east and west, and a most welcome harbour in this troubled sea.

Many Phoenicians settled there. When their homeland to the east came under attack from the Israelites, and waned in power, Cathage was founded, a thriving town only two hundred miles away on the African mainland, and Malet became even more handy, even more important. It was a secure haven for ships, not to be matched in the whole of the Mediterranean; it was even a good place for a holiday. It also became a new spring-board for that questing spirit.

Some of them stayed, and settled contentedly; for others, the sea and the horizon – any horizon – still called. From Malet, Malta, they voyaged yet further.

They voyaged even to America. On one of the islands of the Azores, in mid-Atlantic, later travellers found a huge statue carved on the westernmost cliff. It was the statue of a horse-man – the figurehead of the Phoenicians – pointing the way still farther westwards. He was saying, either 'I have been there,' or 'I am going there,' or '*That* is the way for a man to go.'

On his breast was carved a great letter 'K' – K for Karthago, Carthage.

Even the men, shocked and exhausted, dreading the thought of another day of blood and terror like the day they had just survived, came to new life and hope as they saw the giant Phoenician horseman, the man from Malta, standing on a cliff-top in the middle of an ocean, proclaiming his faith and manhood before all the world.

One of the last boats out of Carthage, before the Roman legions moved in for the kill, carried a man called Joseph Saadi, and his wife, and his three children, and the maternal grandfather, and their furniture, and some money saved from his military pension, and a few sheep and goats which did not survive a very rough voyage.

But the family survived, and under the lead of Joseph Saadi, a strong and self-reliant man who, as a soldier under General Hannibal, had seen far worse things than this, they quickly regained their spirits, as soon as they put foot on the good firm earth of Malet.

Anything was better than that terrible boat in a storm, and anything was better than Carthage, in its present peril and chaos, which could only have one end.

It had been a wrench to leave their homeland, but it was high time. The city had grown impossibly overcrowded, and dirty, and diseased; civil order had broken down; there was looting, there was casual murder under the cloak of night, there was the vindictive paying-off of old scores. What did such things matter? The Romans would wipe the slate clean again, as soon as they stormed the last gate, and took possession.

The people of Carthage had lived for a long time under the threat of this disaster. Now that it was at hand, now that two great wars had worn them down, and no rescue seemed possible, it was every man for himself.

Of course, every man had a choice. He could stay, and starve, or be killed or enslaved. Or he could leave, and try again somewhere else. But, after a certain fatal point was passed, though a soldier could lay down his life – and Joseph Saadi had never shirked that final offer – a family man could not actually win. He must therefore survive, with his own weapons and his own cunning.

It was the old story: the story of anyone who opposed the Romans.

Carthage had grown strong and proud; Rome had grown strong and proud; the adversaries glared at each other across the Middle Sea, making faces, bawling threats. Carthage had shouted: 'No Roman shall dip his finger in the Mediterranean without our permission!' Rome had shouted back: 'Carthage must be destroyed!'

This challenge – 'Delenda est Carthago' – was the phrase which even such a hidebound old conservative as Cato the Elder used, to round off every speech he made in the Senate, after he had visited Carthage and seen its might and splendour. It had slowly advanced from a windy threat to a poised sword.

Carthage *was* about to be destroyed, though it had taken a hundred and twenty years to do it, and they had had a good run for their money and their blood. Indeed, they very nearly won – this was what Joseph Saadi always maintained, ever since he had taken part, as a young foot-soldier, in the last spectacular throw of the Carthaginian army under Hannibal.

Together they had conquered southern Spain, crossed all France, scaled the Alps in fifteen days (who else but Hannibal would have thought of using elephants to haul the baggage-train over those fearful Alpine passes?), and marched all the way down Italy to Cannae on the Adriatic, thrashing the Roman legions at three set-piece battles as they went. It could be done, it could be done...

But then, while they were away, other Roman legions had attacked them in their own back-yard. Hannibal had hurried home, but it was too late. The balance tipped; over the years the city-state was ringed, and gently, inexorably throttled. Though Carthage had proved that the Romans could be beaten, it did not always happen. It was the man who won the last battle who laughed over the spoils. However, one could, with luck, live to fight another day.

Perhaps in Malet... For Joseph Saadi, it was a sad retreat, from a city which was part of his man's pride and his heart's blood. He had served his country honourably. He had made the great three-year march with Hannibal, surviving the burning summer sun, the brutal winter snows. He had earned his pension and his peace. Now it had all gone for nothing.

He had brooded on these matters during the voyage, when all his family were sick as dogs, and he could brood alone. It was enough to make a man vomit, without any help from the sea. It was enough to make a man give up, and turn pimp or thief or Grecian love-boy instead of a soldier. It was so unfair... But by the time they had sighted the island, smoky-yellow under a sky now calm and blue, and shortened sail to make for the

narrows of the anchorage, he felt that he had come to terms
with the future.

It was not true that the past had all gone for nothing. A man
was a man. In victory, he held his back proud and straight.
In defeat he did exactly the same. He did not wait for the luck
to turn. He did not wait for the Carthage City Council to
come to his rescue. He came to his own rescue.

Himself, he had his health and his strength and his wife
and his children and a little money saved from the robbers and
thieves who battened on disaster. All that was needed was a
new start in a new land. A new start at forty? Why not, for
the love of God? He had heard a lot of good things about
Malet. It could be done. Indeed, it must be done, and he was
in the mood to do it.

The newcomers set up house on the slopes of a hill overlooking
the deep-water harbour. It was now the principal settlement
on the island, and was taking shape as the newest Carthaginian
colony, full of people with tales of bad luck and bad manage-
ment in the old country, but determined also, like Joseph
Saadi, to start up again somehow.

They had to contend with a frosty welcome from some of
the 'first families', who traced their pedigrees, five and six
generations back, to what they called the 'real' old country,
Phoenicia, and made it very clear that Malet was theirs, by
right, and that any new settlers had better accept the fact,
and keep their distance and their place.

To Joseph Saadi, this sort of thing did not matter at all. He
had cut loose from the past, he was eager for the future, and
he had enough companions in misfortune to give him a sense
of community. He wanted to buy a farm, somewhere inland,
but with all the new people flocking in the price of land was
terrible.

Meanwhile, he turned his hand to anything: first making
their stone shanty fit to live in, then helping out with odd jobs
down in the harbour – there was always a ship to be loaded
or unloaded, a fisherman who needed a hand with his nets or
his sails, a night-watchman's job, a painting job, a rust-chipping
job, a rope-coiling job, a fish-gutting job.

The wife, who was a fiercely proud housekeeper, worked
hard and kept her silence. The children loved every moment

of life; there was always something new in a new country, and down by the seashore the chances of novelty were doubled. The eldest boy, sixteen-year-old Hannibal (what else would a soldier's first-born son be called?), helped his father, and watched him carefully, and copied his straight back and determined pace.

When Joseph smiled, he smiled. When Joseph looked grim, Hannibal's cheerful face became a positive thunder-cloud.

Only the *nannu*, the grandfather, could not come to terms with any of this. He was nearly seventy; he had rheumatism, like many old sailors; he had been uprooted, at the very time of life when a man wanted to sit back, and doze in the sun, and gossip with neighbours who shared the same sort of past, and knew what he was talking about, and respected his opinions. He had grown dirty in his habits. He was always complaining about the children's noise and clatter. He grumbled. He grumbled all the time.

'What sort of life is this? What sort of an *end* to life? Haven't I deserved better? When I was a young man I sailed all round Africa! I've seen black men with long tails! It's true, I tell you. We used to put ashore, when winter was coming on, and plant a whole field of corn...' He droned on, while no one listened. They knew the story, and all his other stories. 'A man who has sailed all round Africa, to finish up in this *shed*, in a country no one's ever heard of, without so much as a cup of wine to warm his bones.'

'We can't afford wine. You know that.'

'Why not? What has happened? We were smarter in the old days, you can be sure of that! And as for the old forefathers... Did I ever tell you how they founded Carthage? They went ashore, and bargained for a piece of land. The other folk thought they were smart. 'For a thousand shekels,' they said, 'you can have as much land as can be covered by an ox-hide.' An ox-hide? Such robbery! But we were smarter still. We cut the ox-hide into strips, and marked out a piece of land big enough for the whole city of Carthage. Heh, heh, heh!' He crowed with laughter, and coughed, and spat copiously on the stone floor. 'Big enough for the whole of Carthage. How's that for brains?'

They knew this story too. Every last man, woman, and child in Carthage knew the story.

'Why didn't you think of something like that, Joseph?' the *nannu* whined. 'Instead, we live in this misery. Where will it end? No real money coming in. Not so much as a cup of wine at sundown. The children running all over the place. If young Hannibal messes up my things again—'

'Leave the children alone,' Joseph Saadi commanded suddenly.

'Eh? What's that?'

'You heard what I said. Stop complaining. We're all in this trouble together. At the moment it's the best I can do. *These are hard times!* We're lucky to have a roof over our heads. You must just put up with it.'

'I didn't mean anything,' the *nannu* faltered, and then recovered. 'You can speak to me like that because I'm old! When I was a young man, I'd have taken an ox whip to you, for saying such things!'

'Well, you're not a young man.' Joseph Saadi had been driven beyond his patience. 'Come to that, I'm not a young man either. But I'm doing my best, and that's got to be good enough for all of us. Think yourself lucky... Now be silent.'

Like many an old man, the *nannu* could shed tears easily, and at will. He shed them now. 'That I should come to this,' he sobbed brokenly. 'But I'll be a burden no more... You'll be sorry when they fish me out of the harbour... You can have my box of sea-shells. It's all I have to leave...' He tottered out of the stone shed, limping and gasping, a very moving sight.

After ten minutes he returned, glaring at them all. 'I forgot my cap,' he said. 'But I'm prepared to accept an apology.'

In the deep dark of the night, behind the ragged curtain separating them from the children, and from the old grandfather who coughed and hawked continuously, the wife rebuked her husband.

'How can you speak to an old man like that?'

Joseph Saadi was already ashamed. But he was not quite ready to be repentant. 'Well, why does he grumble so much? Why can't he keep silence? It's like I told him, these are hard times! We all have our troubles.'

'*Your* father used to grumble enough.'

'Not like this one.'

'*Nannu* feels out of it.'

I wish he was, Joseph Saadi nearly said, but he forebore. It would not have been true, in any case. He liked the old man well enough. It was just that this was a bad time to have to listen to other people complaining. 'All those old stories,' he muttered. 'We must have heard them a hundred times. Does he think he's the only one who's sailed round Africa?'

'We heard enough about your father and the time he saved General Hamilcar's life. Come to think of it, we hear enough of you and Hannibal crossing the Alps on an elephant.'

'That will do,' Joseph Saadi said. 'I want to sleep. I've got to get up before sunrise to help with the grain bags.'

'We should have our own grain,' his wife said. 'And a flock of goats. A cow maybe. Joseph, we *must* get out of here. Find a little place of our own. Somewhere in the country. The children are growing up wild, hanging about the quays all day. They're using words I couldn't even repeat... When are you going to look for a farm? Or a field, even?'

'I'm always looking.'

'You weren't looking today.'

'I had work to do! I have to earn something every day, just to keep going. I'm not going to spend our savings on food. The money saved is for the house and the farm.'

'What farm?'

'Why doesn't your father look round for something, while I'm working?'

'*What*? At his age? You know it's as much as he can do, to walk out into the street. The very idea!'

'He'd walk down to the wine shop quick enough, if he had the money... All right, all right. I'll take the time off somehow, and have another look tomorrow. Now let's have some peace, for God's sake!'

As he drifted into sleep, Joseph heard his wife say: 'You never liked my family, did you?'

On the morrow Joseph Saadi was as good as his word, partly because this was a habit with him, partly because he was ashamed of what he had said to the *nannu* and wanted to make it up to his wife. He loved her dearly; he still found her fair, after nearly twenty years; and he knew, only too well, that she was the rock on which all this family enterprise was founded. If she was defeated, then they were all defeated.

Before the sun was high he left young Hannibal to finish the job of stacking the grain bags, and spent the whole day wandering about inland, near the old walled capital which the Greeks, who built it, had called Melita. In fact, they had called the whole island Melita, because the word Malet meant nothing to them, and Melita, it was said, meant honey, and sweet honey abounded here. (Or was it because of the honey-coloured stone? Who could tell, after all these years?) Either way, Joseph Saadi liked the sound of it. A land of honey. Would that it would prove so!

There were still some Greek families hereabouts who had stayed behind when the Carthaginians took over the rule. They were quiet folk, like all conquered people, keeping themselves to themselves. But they would make good neighbours, if neighbours they were to be. They had been through the mill-stones themselves.

When he came back Joseph was greatly excited. 'I saw lots more of those old cart-tracks,' he told his wife. 'Running all over the place. But they really are a puzzle. I don't think they were made by wheels at all. They're too deep, and too smooth. It's my belief the old people used a sort of sledge with runners, like the ones we used going across the snows in Italy. Come to think of it, they could have put their boats up on skids. Made a sort of land-galley. The way the wind screams here, they could even wait for it to blow their way, and then hoist sail. But I'm only guessing. If you had a horse or a camel pulling a kind of slide-car—'

His wife, who had been listening in silence, suddenly exploded. She almost screamed at him: 'Cart-tracks! Land-galleys! Slide-cars! What's all this nonsense, for the love of God? Who's asking about cart-tracks? I thought you were going out to look for some land! Will cart-tracks buy the children their winter clothes?'

'But I was just going to tell you,' Joseph Saadi began. 'I saw—'

'You saw cart-tracks!' She really was in a flaming rage, and for the very first time in their life together, she showed it. 'I'll give you cart-tracks! I'll give you cart-tracks up your backside, if you don't stop this nonsense and start thinking about your family!'

Even the women, burdened with their cares, near to weeping with fear for their children, heart-sick at the thought of the

*morrow, cackled with laughter as they listened to the wife
having her say at last. So he thought he was the head of the
house, did he? Ah, but it took a woman to make a man see
sense, when times were hard.*

Terrible news came from Carthage. The remnants of its defending army had been routed by 30,000 Roman legionaries
under General Scipio, who had been lying in wait for so long.
A shameful peace had been signed. The city lay at the mercy
of anyone with a sword or a dagger. Scipio, it was said, was
to be called '*Africanus*' for ever afterwards, and might be made
Roman dictator for life.

'I reckon he deserves it,' said Joseph Saadi, when he heard
the news, which filtered through slowly from fishermen and
coastal traders. 'That Scipio! The old fox! We beat him on the
road to Rome. We beat him at Cannae. We had him on the
run! Who'd have thought it would come to this?'

The *nannu* was contemptuous, as usual. 'It wouldn't have
come to this, in the old days.'

'Now this really is our home,' the wife said. 'There's nowhere else to go.'

'We don't need anywhere else,' said Joseph Saadi stoutly.
'We've found the place we want. Another ten days, and we'll
be moving in.'

'A hundred paces square,' the *nannu* said. 'About the size of
my best mainsail. Who can live on that? You should have
taken an ox-hide with you.'

The wife, staring at the guttering wick of the oil lamp, asked:
'But what happens if the Romans come here? Not just a raid
now and then. People don't seem to mind that. But to live.'

'We'll see about that when they sail into the harbour. They've
got to make a new province out of Carthage, first. Mark you,
I don't mind the Romans, when they're not trying to kill me.
They're a tough lot. But they make good soldiers. Did you
know, if a Roman regiment ever ran away, or lost its eagles,
the general ordered: "Survivors! Fall in!" and then they killed
every tenth man on parade. Shoved a little stabbing-sword
right through his gizzard. That's the way to get discipline!'

His wife knew this story too. 'But suppose they do come
here, just when we've got the farm going and the crops planted.
It's not worth the trouble of moving in.'

'I'll take care of that.' For a homeless man, Joseph Saadi was very confident. 'I tell you, I can get on with them, as long as they don't want to make a slave out of me. If they try *that*, there'll be trouble. This isn't the sort of island you can just march in and take over. It could be made into a fortress! I'd like the chance of defending it myself!' He coaxed her. 'Come on, Mother. You like the little farm. You know you want to settle down there. We could do a lot worse. At least there are no taxes to pay. And I think young Hannibal has his eye on a girl.'

The wife was startled. 'A girl from *here*? It's the first I've heard of it. What girl is this?'

'Oh, just someone next door to us. I mean, out at Melita. Pretty girl with fair hair.'

'But what *sort* of girl?'

'A Greek, I suppose. Well, she *was* Greek. Now she belongs to Malet, like the rest of us.'

'A *foreign* girl? How will they ever talk to each other?'

Joseph grinned. 'They'll find a way... Come on, Mother,' he said again, 'In a few years we'll be laughing at all this. I tell you, it's a good place. A hard place, but none the worse for that. All we have to do is work till we drop, and we'll make something out of it.'

The Fearful Day
of Father Salvatore

16 January 1941

'Don't you bother any more, Dun Salv,' Nero Cassar said. He was pushing a mountain of filthy rubbish, almost as high as himself, towards the nearest outlet into the fresh air. 'We'll soon finish cleaning up here. Won't we, Rafel?'

Rafel Vella, grumpy as usual in the early morning, straightened his enormous back. His task was also menial – to carry buckets of water, slung on a wooden yoke across his shoulders, from the water-cart outside to the underground cistern within the catacombs of the Cottonera Lines. 'I suppose so,' he agreed, without much spirit. 'But I wish more people would help us keep this place tidy. After all, it's *their* home! Why can't they treat it decently?'

Nero grinned up at him. He was used to Rafel's ill-humour, which was part of the way of the world in 1941. 'Because they have a few other things to think about. Like the bombs and the food. Because they're a lot of jelly-fish, and we are not. That's why!'

The bombs and the food, Father Salvatore thought, as he dusted off his cassock, which nowadays was never clean for more than a few hours. These were the twin elements to which life had been reduced, in the short seven months of the war. The first of them was terrifying, the second a nagging problem which could only grow worse. But he could still never understand why one man, like little Nero, was able to surmount these things with laughing energy, and another such as Rafel was ground down to dull indifference by the same ordeal. Simple humans should never develop such a wild mutation.

They were all God's children, fashioned in the same sacred mould. So he had been taught, and so he taught in his turn. Yet it could not be denied that these, God's children, began to differ from their very birth; some raced, others lagged; death was indeed the only leveller. Father Salvatore remembered a line from a song or a film of long ago : *I got wings, you got wings, all God's children got wings.* It was not true! A few had wings, and soared at will. The rest began to moult their feathers at the first unfriendly blast.

Another long-ago couplet from *English Literature*, Part One, came to mind – 'Two men looked through prison bars, The one saw mud, the other stars' – followed by that formidable word '*Discuss*'. It would have been easy to *discuss* the mud of their lives for ever; even Father Salvatore did not like the early mornings in the Cottonera Lines, when pale light filtered into their shelter through a dozen eastern openings, and another night's safety had to be weighed against the sordid and smelly prison which had ensured it.

Ever since that first night, he had toiled endlessly to make something of their refuge : organizing food and water and sleep, settling quarrels, calming fears, rebuking flagrant sin, and always proclaiming, against all the evidence, that God's watchful and loving mercy still held them secure.

Even when another such shelter, no worse protected, received a direct hit, and everyone in it was killed outright, except for a luckless handful who could be heard whimpering and moaning three days later, and who died licking moisture from the walls under the torture of thirst – even so, his message was still : 'We are safe here, under the canopy of God.' There was no other way to make their nightly vigil tolerable.

The citizenship of the catacombs had grown swiftly, since the first night of the war; now they could count on as many as six hundred souls using this refuge every night, or returning to it to be reunited with their families. It had won a reputation for solid safety, and a fair and firm hand in control; it boasted Father Salvatore, the working priest who was so much loved; and the story of that first night, and Dun Salv's astonishing contribution to it, still lingered, and was talked about, and admired.

The people he cared for were those he had hoped would come, the people most in need : the ravaged poor of Cospicua, the homeless, the frightened, the crying, the hungry; the men in fear of their lives who must soon face a new day.

As he moved among them, and ministered to them, and prayed with them, Father Salvatore thought always of the throngs of persecuted, terrorized early Christians, huddling together in the catacombs of Rome; and his text was the same as it must have been, two thousand years before: 'Comfort ye, comfort ye my people, saith your God.' These Christians of 1941 even behaved in the same way, somehow making homes for themselves in this hollow wasteland, carving out small wall-niches which were shrines to Christ and the Blessed Virgin, building together a brotherhood, a communion, which made the weak and lonely feel that together they might be strong and safe.

Little Nero Cassar, who had found his own way to the cata-combs within a week of their first meeting, and had instantly turned his hand to the first urgent task – a primitive form of sewage disposal – had proved a tower of strength. While Rafel was the plodder, Nero was the spark. It was he who had some-how fixed up a system of radio reception, so that all within could listen to the daily and nightly bulletins of news and government directives in the Rediffusion Service.

He had extended this to a microphone and a link of Tannoy loudspeakers, by which Father Salvatore's prayers and words could be heard anywhere within this vast and gloomy warren. The frequent broadcasts of the Governor of Malta, General Dobbie, always stressing that religious note which came as naturally to him as to the Maltese themselves ('Profound faith in the justice of our cause, and the certainty of Divine assist-ance') rang loud and clear and comforting, all over the cata-combs.

When permission came for the removal of the mortal re-mains of the little dead brothers who surrounded them, it was Rafel Vella who was the sexton. But Nero somehow managed to turn this grisly task into a labour of love, and thus of joy. He could be heard talking cheerfully to them, even as he dis-turbed their eternal rest. 'Come along, my little friar,' he would say, as he scooped the bones and the dust and the sentinel skull into a basket. 'You have slept here long enough. *We have a much better room for you, just round the corner.*'

It seemed hardly necessary for Father Salvatore to say a prayer. The blessing, from a devout heart, had been given already.

Sometimes Nero would ask: 'When are you going to speak to us again, Dun Salv?' and when Father Salvatore answered that he spoke every day, Nero would say: 'No, I mean really *speak*, like the first time, I wasn't there, but they say it was really something! It changed the whole night! Don't you think the people need another dose? Some of them are just like jelly-fish!' It had become his favourite word.

Another dose... Allowing for the crude slang, Father Salvatore could agree with Nero's verdict. But he still could not make up his mind, nor fully comprehend what had possessed him, on that first night in the catacombs. He had spoken of matters which he scarcely understood, which he scarcely *knew*; more strangely still, he had even juggled with certain dates (though only by fifteen years, out of fifteen hundred!) in order to make history more tidy, and also more dramatic, than it could ever be in fact...

He had been inspired, or sparked, or compelled by so many things: by the terrible day, by the weight of human misery which bore down on them all, by the stunning blow to his head during the last air-raid. Then there had been the thin, lonely cry of the child which had greeted him as he neared the shelter of the Cottonera Lines.

Someone, some French or German statesman with fear or pity in his heart, had once said, when he read the crushing terms of the Treaty of Versailles after the First World War: 'I seem to hear a child crying.' Father Salvatore had never fully understood what the man had meant.

But whether, because of these seeds sown by history, this man of compassion foresaw that the crying child of 1918 would be the dead soldier of 1940, or that today's weeping, fruit of brutality or bereavement, was already borne on the winds of long ago – that the fatherless were doomed a generation in advance – both answers yielded the same tears, and were equally pitiful.

Had it been this which had finally set the strange pattern of the night? Father Salvatore could not tell. But he had never 'spoken' again; there had been too much humdrum detail to take care of, in the daily and nightly running of the great shelter. For all who were drawn to it, things had settled down; after seven months, they had grown old in war, and a little better able to cope with it.

Some drew comfort from belonging to the family of the catacombs; some had grown lethargic or selfish; some saw it as a quick-profit market, others as their first and only chance to share and serve; some took, others gave. There had also been some misbehaviour, as Monsignor Scholti, who 'kept his ear to the ground', had not failed to point out, though in the kindliest spirit imaginable.

He had heard rumours, he said, of 'goings-on' in the catacombs. The bishop had once or twice expressed concern. What was the truth? *Was* there drunkenness, among those who took refuge there? *Was* there singing, loud argument, rowdiness, dancing, gluttony? Were there worse things, as men and women sought to exclude the horrors of the war? He only wanted to know...

What were these 'worse things'? Well, let us say manifest love-making between married couples, even fornication... Father Salvatore sometimes wondered how to assess the scale of these sins. Drunkenness or fornication? Which was the winner? The swinish toper against the fumbling boy? Both must be measured against the immeasurable cruelty of man to man, which now resounded and thundered all round them, every night of their lives.

He could only answer Scholti that he was doing his best, like hundreds of other people. Solace came in many forms. The lust of one was the tender release of another. Was this an official message from the bishop?

Well, no... 'But I think I know his Lordship's mind,' said Monsignor Scholti.

I know a lot of people's minds, Father Salvatore had thought, instantly rebellious, even though he realized that this was unjust. But his people were not bishops. They were men in fear, women in misery and want, children in hopeless tears. They were the urgent young, seizing their first and last chance of love, or what they thought to be love; the middle-aged, turning to each other's embrace though they lay within six feet of their neighbours; and the old, resigned to the hammer-blows of a monstrous world, not even hoping beyond the next dawn.

They were all God's children, winged and wingless. Christ would have forgiven them before they even conceived their pitiful sins... But he could not say this to Scholti, who might cry Disobedience! or even Heresy! or, worse still, might make kindly excuses for Father Salvatore's own confusion.

Instead, he had said: 'We must try to understand what the war is doing to these people' – and these were, by chance, the

very words he used to Nero Cassar, on this later morning when
the cheerful little dwarf seemed to be deriding all lesser
men.

'We must try to understand what the war is doing to these
people,' Father Salvatore said. He straightened up from his
own task, which was to collect and stack the empty bottles of
the night – not all wine, and not all milk either – out of harm's
way. 'Certainly there are jelly-fish. There are one or two sharks,
too! But there are plenty of brave people. Those are the ones
we should remember.'

Yet it could be true, as Nero sometimes hinted, that the time
had come for another recollection of the splendid past, to
balance the present. The bombing alone of the last few months
had been fearful; the worries about food, about separation,
about invasion and defeat, the eternal queueing and contriving,
had all become monsters; the terrors by day, and the crude
discomforts of the night, were almost unendurable. In this, his
only church, he must strive and strive again to give them back
their spirit and their hope.

A child, filthy and nearly naked, wandered out of one of
the murky side passages. When he saw Father Salvatore, he
stared; when he saw Nero, his face, which was covered in sores,
broke into an enormous grin.

'Come here, little one,' Nero said, putting his broom aside.
'It's Wenzu, isn't it? Where are your manners this morning,
Wenzu? What do you say to Dun Salv?'

The child, staring again, muttered 'Bongu,' then turned and
scampered away, whooping as if propelled from behind by
Nero's own broom. The familiar, strident 'Ejja!' of a woman's
voice echoed from the darkness inside, to greet him.

'Well, that one's no jelly-fish, anyway,' Nero laughed. And
then: 'Won't you be on your way, Dun Salv? I know this is
your visiting day. I'll see to those bottles. Some of them are
worth a penny each – we'll put it in the fund. One day we'll be
rich!'

'One day we'll all have our toes cut off, unless people are
more careful about broken glass.' But Father Salvatore knew
that Nero would deal faithfully with the task, as he did with
everything else. 'Very well, Nero. I'll leave the rest to you.
Remember about the kerosene coupons, when the man comes.
And Gianni Calleja promised us a big load of fire-wood from

the bomb dump. That was five days ago. Better remind him. These nights are getting really cold.'

'He will hear from me,' said Nero. 'Or I'll marry his sister!'

'Now, Nero.'

Rafel Vella, who had been listening, unhitched the big wooden yoke from his shoulders. 'May I walk a little way with you, Dun Salv?' he asked. His tone was slightly foreboding. 'I have something important to ask you.'

On the cold and windy walk from the Cottonera Lines towards Senglea, the 'something important' turned out to be Rafel's eternal problem, stated all over again with up-to-date embellishments. His poor old mother in Gozo needed him. His formidable wife in Valletta did not. Could he not go home? There would be no shame or scandal. It would just be the sensible thing to do.

Father Salvatore had difficulty in controlling his impatience, which made a very bad start for the day. Here was the whole world always threatening to fall about their ears, and Rafel still had domestic troubles which loomed larger than Mussolini and the German Luftwaffe in Sicily and the menace of defeat by bombing or starvation, all put together.

He found himself answering sharply, which was another bad beginning.

'Rafel, it would *not* be the sensible thing to do! It would be wrong. It would break up your home. I've told you a hundred times, your first duty is to your wife, *not* your mother. What has made you think of all this again?'

It became clear that Rafel had never stopped thinking about it. 'Because she sends me letters when I don't come to see her. She sent me a *postcard* last week! It was such a disgrace. You know how people read postcards. And when I do go home, she is always in bed. She is old and ill. She has a new pain in her hip. She says it is a scandal in the village, that she should be left all alone.' Rafel spread his enormous hands, in a gesture of despair. 'I never get a moment's peace, from one week to the next. You know how she is, Dun Salv. You have met her.'

Father Salvatore had indeed met the mother of Rafel. He had made a special journey to Gozo and the village of San Lawrenz a few months earlier, when this same crisis seemed once again to be coming to a head. In a squat stone farmhouse, huddled against the ground as if determined to give nothing to the elements or to the world around it, he had found a watchful, malevolent old woman : tough, enduring, and unapproachable, like the prickly-pear bushes which leaned and crowded against the back door, as though they wished to invade and throttle the house itself.

She had made it clear, in a word, in a look, that she regarded Father Salvatore as the enemy, one of the people conspiring to come between son and mother, and to keep a lonely old widow in fear and want. She made him feel very uncharitable, very irreligious. The trouble was that old Mrs Vella was extremely religious herself.

Sewn to her rusty black dress she wore the two strips of cloth, one over her breast, one down her back, which symbolized the scapular, the monastic short cloak of the Carmelites, and proclaimed her a devotee of the cult of Our Lady of Mount Carmel.

It was their belief (Father Salvatore would privately have called it a boast) that they had the Blessed Virgin Mary's assurance on a most important point : that if they wore this scapular, and abstained from eating meat on Wednesdays as well as Fridays, they would be freed from Purgatory on the first Saturday after their death.

It was difficult to quarrel with this creed, which was a matter of innocent faith and should never come under attack. But Father Salvatore found it easy to quarrel with some of its faithful, who could become a self-elevated nuisance, and in particular with this one, whose devotion had made her proud, censorious, mean and (she clearly thought) a match for any priest who withstood her holy intention.

He had not stayed long in the house. He could not. Old Mrs Vella, crouched in her stone cell, with many a plaster statuette on guard in its wall-niche, many a pious blue picture of Our Lady staring down, but only turd-encrusted goats for company, and not even a chair for a weary man, was adamant. She concealed nothing of an implacable will. Why should she have to? God, and Our Lady of Mount Carmel, and public opinion, were ranged irrefutably on her side.

Rafel's place was with her, not with *that woman*. It was his mother who needed him. It was he who needed his mother, the only one to understand him. Who could possibly argue about it? And apart from all else, Rafel would surely be safer in Gozo, where scarcely a bomb had fallen, and the war did not come.

Rafel repeated one of these very phrases now, on the road to Senglea, so that Father Salvatore found himself wondering if this – a form of prudence, or an aspect of cowardice – had now assumed a much greater importance at the core of the sacristan's troubles. It was true that sleepy Gozo had become very popular of late, and the reason was not far to seek. It had no 'targets' in the military sense. It was thought of as a market-garden and a 'rest-centre' for the weary. Was this what Rafel was really seeking?

'She says I would be safer in Gozo, Dun Salv. I can believe it, after these awful days and nights... And she always calls my wife nasty names. Well, *I* call my wife nasty names sometimes, but this is terrible! And she says, what am I doing in Malta anyway? There is no proper church for us – and one can't deny that. So she says, what is the use of a sacristan if there is no proper church?'

She would! Father Salvatore thought. It was extraordinary how un-Christian Rafel's Christian mother could make him feel. He reacted vigorously once again.

'We *have* a church! It is blessed by God, and its little altar is sacred, and it does important work, and you are its sacristan. I need you, Rafel. There is so much to be done, every night and every day. You know that.'

For the first time Rafel, the giant who was also humble and pliable, betrayed his rebellious thoughts. 'Little Nero can do my work, Dun Salv.' But he did not sound at all admiring, or grateful. 'Isn't that what people say? It is Nero this, Nero that, these days. Sometimes I think he is the sacristan, and I am just another pair of hands.'

'That's not true at all.'

'He was not even there at the beginning. Only you and I were there. Now he does everything, and people go to him when they want an answer.'

'But Rafel, this is ridiculous! Of course you are my sacristan. Nero is just a helper. He's very good, very useful. But it is you I depend on.'

'Then why did you put him in charge of collecting the empty bottles?' There was extraordinary bitterness in Rafel's voice:

it was as startling as when a child, thought to be loving and contented, betrayed a spiteful hatred. 'I can take care of the bottles. It is my job. Am I too stupid to count the money? Or am I not trusted? Why is it always Nero, and not me?'

Father Salvatore stopped, and turned to face him. They stood on a windswept corner of the road, near the first houses of Senglea. The dockyard lay beyond, the dockyard which had taken such terrible punishment, which was never free of fires and wrecks and the smell of death. But there were small things as well as great to trouble the spirits of men.

He spoke with care. 'Rafel, you really must stop thinking like this. I told Nero to see to the bottles because he spoke about them first. It does *not* mean that anything is changed. You are my sacristan. I cannot spare you, to go to Gozo. And your wife cannot spare you either.'

'You would be surprised how she can spare me, Dun Salv!'

Once again, the note of bitterness, of hurt pride, brought a fresh shock. Was *all* the world coming to an end? ... At seven o'clock, before sunrise on a cold winter morning, with all the demanding day ahead, there was only one thing to be done.

'I don't want to hear any more of this, Rafel,' Father Salvatore commanded. 'I have work to do, and so have you. Go back to the catacombs, and make sure that the water tank is full. Then get some of the women, and sweep out the galleries on the left-hand side. They are full of rubbish. Burn it. And they say that Carmel Caruana is keeping a pig in one of the upper grottoes. Climb up and find out if it's true, and let me know. Chickens we can have, and rabbits, and goats for milk. But pigs, no!'

'Are you angry with me, Dun Salv?'

'Yes, I'm a little angry. But it will pass. I love you, Rafel, and God loves you. Never forget that. *Tkun imbierek.*'

Rafel Vella, subdued again, bent his head. 'Thank you, Dun Salv. I will try to remember. Please give my respects to the Baroness.'

'I will do that.'

'And give my respects to the big ship, too, when you go past. May God keep her safe!'

2

The big ship lay alongside Parlatorio Wharf in French Creek; a ship reduced to a fearful wreck, within and without, after an ordeal such as no other vessel had ever lived through. Father Salvatore, passing close by in old Angelo's *dghajsa*, looked up at her, and was amazed to see that she still floated.

Even Angelo the *barklor*, a man not given to sympathy with the troubles of others, was silent as they glided past the towering, stricken hull. He did not sneer, he did not even spit; he only shook his head at the wonders and terrors of the world. One could tell, even at the first glance, that this was a ship which must have suffered the tortures of the damned, before she reached her safe haven.

She was, or had been, a giant aircraft carrier, though it was difficult to imagine that she would ever be one again, or could even survive a last voyage to the scrapyard. Now her flight-deck, as big as a football field, was smashed and rent, and deformed by great jagged hummocks of steel, as if it had been ploughed up by a hundred mad farmers with tractors as strong as the clawed fingers of God. She was deep down at the stern, and tilted over to one side. Wooden pegs protruded from her punctured hull, in rough-and-ready carpentry against the sea.

There was a gaping hole in one side where, it was said, a bomb had passed right through. Over most of her length, the steel sides were blistered and streaked and blackened by the raging fires within. Guns, wrenched off their mountings, had been flung against the tall 'island' in the middle, gashing it fatally.

Here, on a burnished plate, was still inscribed her famous name : HMS *Illustrious*.

An army of ants, which were men driven by hope or fear, now toiled all over her. She was festooned with repair-stages, pumps, fire-hoses, scaffolding. Filthy water cascaded from her side as she was pumped out. She looked different, in another way, from when Father Salvatore had first seen her; and presently he discovered what it was.

Much of her upper works had been roughly daubed with cream and yellow paint, to match the surrounding houses, and to ward off further attacks from the air – attacks which must inevitably come. But this was the strange, the incredible thing about *Illustrious*. Ever since her desperate arrival at dusk, pursued and harried, bombed and battered until the very last moment, nothing else had happened to her.

She had lain at her quayside berth, unmolested, for five precious days and nights, while the ants toiled, first to save her from sinking and then to make her ready for sea again; and this in spite of an immediate broadcast by the Germans who, baulked of their prey at sea, had snarled a promise : 'Malta Harbour will be her graveyard!'

It had sounded as menacing as anything ever heard from the same source. But was it, after all, a futile boast, as foolish as that other broadcast which had set all Malta laughing, earlier in the year, when they had heard the same doomful accents proclaim : 'The British Naval Base in Malta has been annihilated!' (It was working at full stretch.) 'HMS *St Angelo* has been sunk!' (*St Angelo* was a building, from whose walls the Turkish galleys had first been sighted in 1565.) 'The Maltese coal-mines have been destroyed!' (There were none, in the entire island.)

The old *barklor*, bending to his oars again, summed it up : 'I don't understand it. One more little bomb would tip her over and send her straight to the bottom, as if she was this *dghajsa*!'

Father Salvatore knew, better than most, how true this was. Old Angelo was only going by what he could see of the ship, from outside. Father Salvatore had seen her full desolation at first hand. He had been wandering, appalled, and then working on board *Illustrious*, within a few minutes of her arrival.

She had been the last to reach harbour, a survivor of what must have been an epic sea battle. Even now, five days later, the guarded news bulletins and the endless word-of-mouth gossip had not established exactly what had happened. The people of Valletta only knew what they had seen with their own eyes. It had been enough to terrify and to enthral them.

First, soon after dawn on that day, there had arrived, like children of the storm, certain deep-laden merchant ships, proud and unscathed, steaming up the swept channel towards Grand Harbour. The noise of distant explosions, borne on the wind, told what they must have survived, to bring home their precious cargoes. Then a destroyer, known to be called the *Gallant*, with her bows blown off and a terrible air of ruin about her, had been nursed into safety by harbour tugs.

Then there was a long lull, and then the battle noises were renewed, louder and much closer to the island: the cacophony of huge explosions and the scream of diving planes seemed endless, and murderous in their ferocity.

From the bastions, black with crowds, the people of Valletta had seen swarms of planes, ignoring Malta, swooping westwards towards some target of which they still knew nothing. But gradually the thunder drew nearer, the whining shriek of engines became brutal; then the fall of bombs could be seen, a tossing grey-white plumage which to the innocent eye was beautiful, and then this final straggler came out of the dusk, creeping towards safety, with smoke and flames to mark the last few miles of her tormented passage.

A vast sigh rose from the onlookers, and then a burst of cheering, when this terrible wreck came at last under the guns of Malta, to find peace, pitiful peace as she joined the merchant convoy she had been protecting, the convoy for which she might have given her life. Nourished by the same tugs, *Illustrious* berthed with agonizing slowness, in the ten o'clock winter darkness, and slid into French Creek as if to her grave.

It was here that Father Salvatore, drawn by the noise and the wild reports, had his first sight of her.

He had never seen such a colossal ship, nor such a hideous piece of wreckage afloat. She was still on fire: great gulps of smoke, smelling of oil and scorched metal and boiling paint, wafted towards the quayside as she drew near. When at last she was secured, and the gangways came down from cavernous holes amidships, a stream of jerking stretchers, each with its blanketed burden, began a slow progress ashore.

He waited for a lull in this dismal traffic, and then worked his way on board. Who would stop a priest? Who would want to? Not any of the sailors he met, on whose faces, in whose bloodshot eyes, could be read a desperate weariness, and whose clothes – oil-soaked, fire-scorched, snatched up from ruined messdecks – had lost the name of uniform.

He smiled often, but since smiling back required a tiny remnant of strength, and there was scarcely any to spare, he met only blank and pallid masks. He began to walk at random, his thick boots setting up a mourning echo in this iron desola-

tion. Soon he lost track of where he was. 'I wouldn't go that
way, mate,' a tall sailor standing amid a tangle of hose-pipes
told him. 'That bulkhead's red hot.' Father Salvatore turned,
and walked down another twisted alleyway, and then another,
amid chasms of torn and blackened steel such as he could
never have imagined.

It was horrible. He was appalled to his very heart. Riven
decks, shattered hangars, aircraft smashed like the toys of a
very rich and evil child, lift-shafts bent as if by some drunken
blacksmith a hundred feet tall, all assaulted the eye.

He was afraid. If bombs could do this to such a steel mountain, what could they do to men? Presently he found out.

He emerged into a shadowy open space. He could not have
told where he was – whether on one side of the ship, whether
on another : whether high above the water, or deep down
within the entrails of this groaning animal. He found out one
thing – that he was alone among the dead.

There were long lines of them, stretched out in their immortal rest. There were oily men, burnt men, ripped-up men,
men unmarked and at peace. He counted, and then lost count.
There must have been fifty, there could have been a hundred.
He dropped on his knees, and lost count of his prayers also
as he strove to speed each shattered human being towards or
past eternity.

The smell of death was nothing. He was used to it, after all
these months. The ugliness of death was not for him to judge.
A man, whole but crushed out of mortal shape, and a man unmarked but cold and stiff as a day-old fish, and half a man
whose open, surprised eyes seemed to be asking : 'What happened to my feet? Where's my other leg? The skin off my
chest? My manhood? My arm, my arm?' – they must all be
the same in the sight of God, under whose gaze they now rested
for ever.

They all seemed so touchingly young, though this could not
have been true. He prayed : Oh God, take them, be merciful,
give them peace! But he had the desolate feeling that he was
no longer needed here. The sword of death had swept and
fallen, as cruelly as he could ever have imagined. A man alive,
even a priest alive, was a boastful intruder who should have
stayed away.

As he knelt for the last time, there was a movement which

for a moment surprised and terrified him, at the end of the passageway. He looked up. Two sailors, as matter-of-fact as barmen stacking the empties, were carrying in a third: the odd man out, the dead duck. When they had laid him down with the rest, and straightened him in a seaman-like manner, and stood upright again, one of them said:

'Sir, are you a priest?'

With a mad kind of amusement, Father Salvatore realized that he had never been asked this exact question before.

'Yes, I am.'

'Then, could you come to the sick-bay? There's one of our lads asking for a priest.'

It was not worse than he had imagined, as a man who had so often seen suffering and death, both in simple and lately in exaggerated forms; but it was dreadful enough. The sailors in the sick-bay who were still alive, or just alive, or giving up life as the only offering left to give, were mostly burned cases; though tenderly treated, their agony was in the very air.

It did not need sounds to show this, though there were sounds enough for the most minute record of pain. Sight was enough, under the naked bulbs of the emergency lighting: the sight of flaying alive, the sight of a winding-sheet of bandages which made a living mummy out of a dead man: the sight of eyes so bright with futile hope, so dulled by the cloudy onrush of death, that they could not be met with anything except tears.

The 'one of our lads asking for a priest' turned out to be a dying man of about forty, a veteran of much booze and brawling – if his face was anything to go by – as well as of the Navy. But now, his face was nothing much to go by; the scars of sin and self-indulgence, perilous to the soul, had been overlaid by other scars which were likely to prove mortal to the body.

He could only croak, through blistered bright red lips which made a horrid contrast with the greenish pallor of his face. But he croaked with the ultimate determination, he croaked to good purpose, from the point of view of someone to whom his soul was precious.

'Thank God, Father!' he said, as soon as he had taken in the fact that the doctor had been replaced by the longed-for priest. 'Help me. Give it to me.'

Father Salvatore took his hand. 'What is it you want, my son?'

'The rites.' The sailor was almost petulant. It was clear to Father Salvatore that he had been a long time absent from the confessional, from the sacrament, and thus from God. 'I'm sorry for what I done.'

'What have you done?'

'A bit of everything.' But it was his last boast; the onset of pain suddenly wiped the look of impudence from his eyes, leaving only fear. Muttering and gasping, he launched into a confession of murder.

Perhaps it was fantasy: something he had wanted to do, or feared he had done, or had read about, or dreamed about, or heard from a friend or an enemy. Hong Kong, ten years ago. A girl under the lamplight, and then the same girl in the darkness. 'She must have been drunk, like me. She bit me, Father. You know, where it hurts most. So I picked up the candlestick, and smashed her head in. There was blood all over.' Blood and silence, in some unspeakable house. 'I washed it off somehow. Then I got dressed and ran. We sailed next morning. I never heard nothing more about it.'

The hoarse words ceased. Father Salvatore, still holding the man's cold hand, asked: 'Is this true, my son?'

'Of course it's true!' The petulant note had returned. 'But I'm sorry. I said I'm sorry, didn't I?'

'What else are you sorry for?'

'Christ, isn't that enough? ... You mean, like a general confession?'

'Yes. And contrition. True contrition.'

Now the fear was back again. 'Help me, Father. I forget the words.'

When it was done, Father Salvatore anointed, as tenderly as he could, the ruined face, the hands which must have been wicked, the feet which had strayed. The sailor was now gasping, but he seemed comforted, and at peace.

'Am I all right then, Father?'

'Yes, my son.' God would judge, God would correct all mistakes, his own and this other sinner's, with the mercy and knowledge denied to mortal man. He grasped the sweaty hand again. 'But you are *not* going to die.'

When he had been proved wrong, as he knew he must, and

an orderly had curled the sheet back over the man's face, with
a flick of the wrist so expert that it was painful to watch,
Father Salvatore lingered in prayer. But then someone reaching across to the next cot stumbled against his feet. He awoke
to urgency and need. There was so much to do besides pray...
He rose from his knees and, after looking round him, quietly
joined in the work of mercy.

He became one of a moving, bending, fetching-and-carrying
throng of grey and tired men : hard-pressed doctors, sick-berth
attendants, ambulance men from ashore, stretcher-bearers from
other ships in harbour. He fetched glasses of water. He sat
and comforted and consoled. He bathed sweating foreheads. He
eased bandages too tight for the raw wounds they covered.
He brought bed-pans, and disposed of them. He held on to
men's hands until he could feel that, out of two sets of clasped
fingers, only one retained its grip.

He noticed, now and again, a servant like himself, a naval
padre in tattered uniform surmounted by a blood-streaked dog-
collar, busy at the same work. Once they passed each other
in a passageway. They were both carrying vase-shaped urinals,
one full, one empty. The Englishman grinned, and spread his
hands ruefully, and passed on. It seemed to Father Salvatore
that the brotherhood of Christ had never been better expressed.

Then, while he was busy holding, under careful instruction,
the tube of a bottle of blood dripping gently into the arm of
a restless man who needed it but did not want it, he became
aware of a stir at the far end of the sick-bay. It was a visitor
of some consequence : the four gold rings on the sleeve proclaimed him a captain of the Royal Navy – by now Father
Salvatore, like most Maltese, could recognize the rank-badges
of all the services.

Soon he realized, from the demeanour of everyone round
him, from the special alertness which the captain's presence
produced, that this was in fact *the* captain – the captain of
Illustrious herself.

Restraining the fretting man who was trying to push the
rubber tube away, Father Salvatore watched the new arrival.
He looked something like Salvatore's own father, though without the beard which George V, the Sailor King, had made
popular in the old days. He had the same height, the same set
to his head, the same air of cool authority.

He was going all round the sick-bay, with a word or a laugh or a touch for every one of his crew who lay there. Father Salvatore had never seen a more exhausted man. But he still had time for his wounded, as he must have had time for his ship.

Presently the captain stood beside him, and smiled, and said: 'Good evening, Father. Thank you for helping us.'

It was almost the same voice, too: clipped, precise, absolutely unruffled, conveying only one message – confidence, command, minute attention to all that was in his charge.

Father Salvatore smiled back. 'It is nothing. I'm glad to be here.'

The man he was attending suddenly tried to wrench the tube away from his arm, and the captain said sharply: 'Briggs!'

The sailor opened his eyes, astonished: 'Sir?'

'You won't get well unless you do exactly what the doctors tell you. Leave that tube alone, and lie back.'

'Aye aye, sir.'

It was done, just like that. The wounded sailor subsided, and indeed seemed much improved, even by this curt encounter. If only a parish priest could command such obedience... Father Salvatore adjusted the tube; the life-giving blood flowed gently and easily. The captain of *Illustrious* lingered, watching. Then he put his hand up to his lined face, and rubbed his eyes.

'You must be very tired,' Father Salvatore said.

'I'm hungry,' the captain said unexpectedly. 'In fact, very hungry, like everyone else on board. "The hungry sheep look up, and are not fed."' John Milton, Father Salvatore thought, in wonderment: how could such a man quote Milton at such a moment? 'They're sending us some hot soup from ashore, bless them, but it's taking a little time.' He added: 'I'm afraid all our cooks were killed,' and somehow these were the saddest words Father Salvatore had heard, in the whole seven months of war.

The Captain nodded, said, 'Thank you again, father,' and drew back a few paces. Then, with no discernible effort of concentration, he spoke to the signalman at his elbow.

'Take this down, while I remember. Following reports are necessary by eight AM. Fuel remaining. Ammunition remaining. Fresh stores required. Medical stores required. Draught fore and aft, increasing or decreasing. Number of wounded sent ashore. Burial arrangements for how many. Minimum crew replacements. Damage, rough outline. Number of aircraft, damaged and serviceable. *Estimated time to make ready for sea.*'

By the end of that night, and of his hours of patient mortuary service, Father Salvatore felt that he had had his fill of carnage, for the rest of his life. But at least there was something added – knowledge of other men, an enlargement of understanding. He knew at last what sailors might have to go through, in the task of bringing food and weapons to an island under siege.

What he did not know was what the ship herself had actually endured, to reach her state of ruin. Even a man who had seen her, and smelled her, and slipped on her blood-stained iron deck, and mourned the dead and watched the faces of the living, could not guess the half of her story.

HMS *Illustrious* (Captain D. W. Boyd) could be proud that she had long been a hunted and hated ship. She was something special : the first aircraft-carrier in the world with an armour-plated flight deck, able to withstand anything up to a 500-pound bomb. She had revolutionized fleet protection, and Admiral Cunningham, the Commander-in-Chief of the Mediterranean, took her with him everywhere he could. She had thus acquired a reputation as a tremendous convoy work-horse, and the hardest-driven ship in the fleet; and in her five months of active service under a resolute captain she had become, in enemy eyes, the most desirable prize afloat.

Her most spectacular strike had been a torpedo-bomber attack on the Italian fleet lying at anchor at Taranto in the heel of Italy, when two Italian battleships had been sunk, another wrecked and beached, and three cruisers put out of action, all in the space of two hours. For the loss of two Fleet Air Arm planes shot down, *Illustrious* had disabled half the Italian navy, substantially altered the balance of sea-power in the Mediterranean, and inflicted more damage than the German Battle Fleet had sustained during the two days of Jutland in 1916.

Her latest job, at the end of a long list, was to provide air-cover for two fast convoys converging on Greece and on Malta from east and west simultaneously. She was there to protect both the convoys and the fleets guarding them (and these were certainly worth protecting : four battleships, nine cruisers, and twenty-three destroyers in all, the entire British naval strength in the Mediterranean), and to bring in a consignment of Fulmar and Swordfish aircraft vital to Malta's defences.

But these convoys, and *Illustrious* herself, had to face, for the first time, a new hazard. With the declared aim of 'neutralizing Malta' (a horrid phrase, a cloak for wholesale murder, reminiscent of 'the final settlement of the Jewish question' as used by the same speaker), the German Air Force had now elbowed out the Italians and moved a whole *Fliegerkorps* to Sicily, sixty miles away.

There they waited, in overwhelming strength, for any ship or any plane which might try to succour the island.

General Geissler's Fliegerkorps X, which specialized in attacks on shipping and had proved the fact brilliantly in Norway, added up to 150 long-range bombers, 150 Stukas devoted to the brand-new technique of 'dive-bombing', 50 Messerschmitt 109s, and some reconnaissance planes – more than 350 aircraft altogether.

By way of opposition to this potent air armada, Malta at that time had its two surviving Gladiators, one of them so hybrid, so patched up, so Christmas-treed with extra machine-guns mounted on top of its wings, in the fashion of World War One, that it was nicknamed 'The Bloodiator', and fifteen Hurricane fighters.

It was no wonder that Fliegerkorps X, at midday on 10 January 1941, could afford to by-pass Malta and to pounce on the latest convoy, and especially on *Illustrious*, its chief guardian, with rare appetite and a confidence to match.

They made their strike when the convoy and the ships escorting it were past the narrows of the Skerki Channel between Sicily and Tunisia, past Pantelleria, and – at eighty-five miles west of Malta – very nearly home. Almost from the beginning, they ignored the mass of shipping below them, and concentrated on the carrier, the prize.

It was no spur-of-the-moment decision, by a bunch of planes looking for likely targets. This attack had been patiently rehearsed, with a dummy aircraft-carrier, in sheltered waters off Sicily, over and over again, until every last pilot and navigator and bomb-aimer knew exactly what to do. When it came to the real thing, it was carried out with extreme efficiency, perfect timing, and undoubted bravery.

Forty Stukas were involved, in successive waves which gave

no respite to the defence. They circled overhead at 12,000 feet for the minimum time required to establish the pattern of their attack; they watched the Fleet Air Arm Fulmars taking off from *Illustrious*'s flight-deck at panic speed; and then they struck.

With precision timing, they peeled off from a dozen different heights and angles in quick succession; they dropped their bombs, came down to deck level to press home the attack with machine-gun fire, and soared up and away almost before the living could react or the dead could surrender.

At the end of six minutes of flaming violence, *Illustrious* had been smothered by six direct hits and three crippling near-misses. The bombs, unfortunately, were not the 500-pound weapons, guessed at when her keel was laid in April 1937, the kind she was built to withstand; they were 1,000-pounders, and they ripped through the armoured flight-deck like a bayonet through a paper parasol.

A squadron of Fulmars had just taken off when the water began to boil all round *Illustrious*. The last two planes somehow made themselves airborne through a hanging curtain of spray and smoke, leaving behind them a flight-deck completely wrecked, and presently, from the deep fires within, too hot to walk on.

Under the eyes of the fleet, *Illustrious* hauled out of line, and began to go in circles, like a dog with its brains bashed out in a road accident. Her hoisted signal, '*I am not under control*', politely excused a writhing agony.

Her flight-deck no longer existed; it could be shored up, like a crazy thatched roof, but it could not be of significance except as a relic of the serviceable past. Half her guns were knocked out; her steering-gear was in ruins. Her main hangar, and all the planes inside, were a mass of roaring fire. The two lifts serving it, steel platforms each weighing 300 tons, were first punched out of any recognizable shape and then welded into meaningless blobs by great tongues of white-hot flame.

Steel splinters from this fearful holocaust ripped and tore at anything that lay in their path: at men strapped into cockpits, men fighting fires, men serving guns, men warming soup in the galleys, men at the plotting-table, men trying desperately to keep calm, to think, and then to act, while all the time *Illustrious*, with thousands of tons of octane fuel and ammunition briskly cooking below decks, could have disintegrated at a single stroke.

What could be done, with a ship in this condition? Captain Boyd did not have to look at his rule-book to find the answer. He had to control the damage, keep his ship fighting, and above all keep her steaming towards safety. Crippled, and advertising the fact from fifty miles away, she was wide open to attack, and there were still seven perilous hours of daylight left.

Fire was the chief enemy on board : fire in the main hangar, fire in what was left of the lift-shafts, searing flames and acrid poisonous smoke issuing from a bombed paint store. The teams of men in asbestos suits went to work, but it was a slow, exhausting job with constant setbacks.

Once, all electric power was lost, and everything – pressure, suction fans, even light itself – was lost with it. Vital equipment kept jamming in the intense heat; broken petrol pipes stoked up the flames with liquid fire; water from the hoses dissolved into steam, and vanished for ever, as foolishly as a single drop of rain in the Sahara.

When the enemy planes returned for what must be the *coup-de-grâce*, and swooped on *Illustrious* again, she could only muster half her guns and the surviving men to man them. But the rest of the fleet closed up round her, concentrating a massive barrage which was almost too tough to penetrate; and *Illustrious*'s own Fulmars, which could not land on the useless deck, circled and fought as long as they could, flew off to Malta to re-fuel and re-ammunition, and then streaked back to protect their mother-ship.

Twice they intervened at a crucial moment and – sometimes nearly ramming the diving Stukas in a wild determination to drive them off – broke up their attacks. They shot down five Stukas each time, with the result that *Illustrious* was not hit again until the late afternoon.

By this time she was forty miles from Malta instead of eighty-five – for, miraculously, her main engines were still untouched and could give her a speed of up to twenty knots. The trouble was in the boiler-room, which near-by fires had roasted to a hellish heat. Smoke and chemical fumes from the fire-extinguishers poured down the ventilators in choking clouds; stokers, working in temperatures up to 130°, could not stay on their feet for more than a few minutes before they fainted.

But somehow, for hour after hour, they maintained enough pressure to keep the engines turning; and *Illustrious*, yawing wildly about as she steered first with one engine and then another, listing from the tons of water on board (a shell splinter had jammed the sprinkler system full on), with smoke and flames billowing from the huge jagged holes all over her hull – *Illustrious* had, by 5 PM, made forty-five precious miles nearer home.

Then the Stukas and Messerschmitts came back, and hit her again, with another 1,000-pound bomb.

There were twenty of these latest bombers, and once more their main attack was broken up or frustrated by the faithful Fulmars from Malta. But one of their brave or cunning pilots did get through, and his bomb, like some monstrous homing bird, plunged straight down the same ruined lift-shaft into the heart of the ship, and started all the fires again.

Illustrious still did not sink, nor stop her agonizing progress. Men in the last stages of exhaustion, from Captain Boyd downwards, went through all the things they had done before, four hours earlier: the ferocious fire-fighting, the damage-control, the shoring-up, the rescue of the wounded: a rerun of the same sickening horror-film, with no guarantee that they would ever see its end.

It took the ship another five hours to make the last forty miles. She entered the Malta swept channel by moonlight, an unearthly and terrible sight: glowing red within, trailing a pall of smoke behind her, listing, faltering, yet somehow grinding onwards. It did not seem that she could ever fight again, nor even float for much longer; and her eighty-three dead had made the price of admiralty unbearably high.

Though her marvellous construction, and the steel heart of man, had saved this much of the ship, by the time she reached French Creek in Grand Harbour she had been reduced, inside and out, to a fiery, bloody shambles.

3

Many times, as his *dghajsa* made its slow passage across the harbour, Father Salvatore looked back longingly at the great ship. Already he was conscious of a bond between himself and this brave survivor; *Illustrious* was now *his* ship, as the catacombs were his parish and Malta his motherland. The sight of hundreds of men toiling all over the upper deck was enough to rejoice the heart. But could these rescuers really do anything? Would the ship ever sail again? And why had not the Germans come back to finish her off? When in fact *would* they come, as come they must, if they had any sense and any determined purpose?

He was hardly aware at all of the old *barklor's* monologue, on the price of this and the shortage of that. Of course, it was all true, and they all had troubles which never ceased to nag and to frustrate. But food, in the end, did not cost money; it cost ships, ships like *Illustrious*, and the lives of the men in her. All else was, by comparison, petty nonsense.

Not until he landed at the Customs House steps did he cease his backward glances, and his yearning for her good fortune. But after that, as always, Valletta claimed him again.

The city, after seven months of war, had come to look rather like *Illustrious*, though not in terms of such concentrated ruin. It had been battered about, flattened, torn up, and wrecked, by successive air-raids which rarely ceased to take their daily or nightly toll. Many streets were now impassable, and must remain so until happier days; whole blocks had been gutted, and showed only roofless buildings gaping at the sky.

Perhaps it was not yet the worst bombing in the world: there had been terrible stories and pictures from London and the other ports of Britain, from Amsterdam and Warsaw and many another hapless target. But for the small capital of a small island, what Valletta had suffered was brutal enough for any appetite. He saw and felt the desolation, as he stumped up the street of steps towards his mother's house; and he saw another kind of desolation, much more sad, in people's faces – the fading of hope before the prospect of a new day, the limbo of faith betrayed.

How could he pass on his own feeling, which had slowly become one of pride: pride that Valletta had been singled out for this punishment because Malta, a tiny island in the cauldron of war, had grown so important that she could not be ignored?

This importance was concerned with things – strategic matters – which only a strategist could comprehend: the ebb and flow of the battle in the North African desert, the need for Malta as a supply-base in the centre of the Mediterranean, the absolute insistence that such an island in such a place must be denied to the enemy, at whatever cost.

But there were other things which even the man in the street – the man in *this* street, which led so slowly upwards past wreckage towards the heights – could understand, and talk about, and feel proud of, even in adversity, because it meant that Malta was not just lying there, waiting to be over-whelmed, but standing up and showing the clenched fist of resistance.

It was clear that Malta was already fighting back. Those first dear saviours of the island, the three Gloster Gladiators which had passed into common speech as Faith, Hope, and Charity, were not what they were: one had been shot down, and its pilot killed; and the others had been replaced by newer, better planes with the now magic name of 'Hurricane', which were at last a real match for the enemy.

The Hurricanes had been able to break up countless bomb-ing raids; in one, made by nineteen Italian bombers, all but six of the bombs had fallen into the sea – and the rush to collect the stunned fish had developed into such a hilarious picnic that fishing-boats were now forbidden to indulge in the practice.

But already Malta was a base for bombers as well, which meant attack, not defence: Wellington bombers which harassed Italian shipping, and had now struck at Taranto, Corfu, Tripoli, Palermo, and Naples, turning these hated enemy names into 'targets', which was something quite different.

It was difficult, even for a priest, not to feel bloodthirsty when one read and witnessed such things. . . Remembering one's own dead, it was difficult not to accept such counter-murder as a satisfactory answer. Indeed, now that the Germans had moved into Sicily, sixty miles away, and were poised and avid for devastating action, it was difficult not to applaud any such stroke of war.

Germany, glorying in ferocious strength, had already over-run Belgium, Holland, France, Norway, Poland, Austria, Den-mark, and Czechoslovakia. If North Africa was now in the balance, and Malta lay directly in her path, the choice was no choice at all. The dogs of war were loose all round them.

Malta *must* be more than a bloody bone, to be thrown to such a ravening pack.

Malta *must* resist, and fight, and win at any price. Yet the price, evidenced all round him in the streets of Valletta, had already proved cruelly high, like the price of *Illustrious*, the price of admiralty.

The bombing had swiftly grown concentrated, and vicious, yet strangely routine. Day bombing, night bombing, *Sunday* bombing – which was held to be sacrilegious indeed : bombing by massed flight, bombing by the single sneak raider which swooped in from Gozo, unloaded, and was up and away before anyone realized what was happening : all this had become part of life, to be borne, to be endured.

The bombs were now all high explosive; incendiaries had been tried, but there was nothing much to burn in Malta's simple houses, where even the shelving was likely to be of stone. The ready-made shelters, the miles of ancient tunnelling with which Valletta was honey-combed, were, with luck, impenetrable; it was the people trying out another kind of luck, from laziness or bravado, and staying where they were even at the height of a raid, who were killed, and killed by the hundred.

Though the night-time searchlights were numerous and heartening, the morning after always showed the same inevitable destruction and death. The anti-aircraft batteries which ringed the harbour and the town allowed little sleep to anyone; it was the worst preparation for facing the aftermath of a raid.

At such a time, there were terrible things to be seen and heard, things which debased and denied the sanctity of life : people with fading voices trapped for ever beneath ruined houses, a sewer bursting open and drowning in slimy black muck a shelter full of women and children : a leg-amputation on the pavement : grey dust settling on corpses, on severed limbs, on a lone head presently covered – but too late – by a towel.

Sometimes, very rarely, there were happier stories. Families had been found alive after being buried under rubble for three or even four days. There was the tale which had enthralled and cheered all Malta, of the two naughty children who, left alone in the house, had taken refuge in the massive family *senduq* when the warning sounded. They had been told *never* to touch it. . . Their home was utterly destroyed; but two whole days later, after frantic digging, they were discovered safe and well under the closed lid of the chest, and no worse than hungry.

But one such happy ending could not efface the ghastly total of horrors. People had seen and heard terrible things. How were the people?

There was a man coming towards Father Salvatore now who might be called typical, and could give the answer. This was Manwel Azzopardi, a stonemason of skill and cunning who had recently spent three weeks restoring one of the balustrades in the courtyard of the Palazzo Santo-Nobile, which had been dislodged by near-by bombing. It had been a joy to watch him at work, bringing down the twelve-pound *mannaret*, the razor-sharp steel axe, on to the swelling curves of a pillar with such delicacy, such a sure touch and eye, that he could have been peeling a grape just as well as cutting stone to a hair's breadth.

Manwel Azzopardi had six children and a house in Pieta, about two miles down the hill from the main gate of Valletta. After the shock-bombing of the first day, he had gone to ground, like one of the hedgehogs Father Salvatore had been thinking of: staying home from work so as to be with his family, along with most of his neighbours, and surrounded by closed shops and offices, and streets deserted even by the public transport.

Then he had drawn all his money out of the bank, following a rumour, widely believed, that if a particular branch was hit, the depositors would lose every penny standing to their credit, and had taken off for the country. Then, after a series of morale-raising broadcasts by Governor William Dobbie, on the familiar theme which promised them deliverance in God's good time, he had followed the drift back to town. Just as men went back to fishing or to the fields, and the dockyard picked up its routine again, so Manwel built himself a shelter under his backyard, and became once more a citizen of Pieta.

He had not been there a month before a violent air-raid struck the street on which he lived, and plastered it with misery. His mother, and one of his children, had been killed; his wife, distraught, had first rushed into the nearest church and tried to drape herself with the altar-cloth, then threatened to leave him unless he quit Pieta and went back to the village where they had been billeted. For the second time, Manwel Azzopardi packed up and left his home.

Now, it seemed, he had returned once more. It was silly and endearing at the same time; it was true Maltese – the veering from one extreme to another, from happy-go-lucky confidence to despair, and then back again; as outside pressure eased or tightened. No hedgehog could be so stupid, or so resigned to fate. . . A small man with shoulders like the statue of Hercules, Manwel was coming down the street towards Father Salvatore, frowning at his thoughts, and then forgetting the cares of the world as he greeted someone he knew. His little flat tweed cap sat on his head like an English muffin on a plate.

They met in the cold morning sunlight on a corner of Old Bakery Street – or what had been Old Bakery Street before the Germans began to dismantle it. Now it was hardly a street any more, just successive rubbish-heaps of stone and wood and dust, the haunt of the flourishing rats and the savage hungry dogs which were another familiar feature of Valletta at war. On the opposite corner, a restless queue was forming, waiting for one of the five staples of life : bread, milk, pasta, olive oil, or kerosene.

An earlier anti-hoarding order, broadcast by General Dobbie, had not worked at all : given this hint, everyone had rushed out to buy as much as they could afford of anything still on offer. Now rationing was upon them all, and the usual start to every day was a lengthening queue in chill winter weather. It was just preferable to a crying child or a grumbling mother-in-law, but the margin must have been slight.

Manwel Azzopardi caught sight of him, and touched his little cap with a grin, suddenly cheerful, 'Bonġornu, Dun Salv !'

'Bonġornu, Leli.' Every man in Malta who was called Manwel was also called Leli. It was as immutable as Gigi for Lewis or Koli for Nicholas. 'What are you doing here? Have you come back again?'

'No, no. Just for the work. I get the first bus in. When the bus runs, which isn't every day.' Now Manwel sounded tired and dispirited, like so many other people : the black mourning bands on his grey shirt suddenly seemed close and real and significant. 'But what's the answer, Dun Salv? You can't earn a living in Siġġiewi !'

Siġġiewi was a village about six miles from Valletta. Manwel made it sound as if it were China or Peru.

'What work is that, Leli?'

'Down at the docks. Just patching things up. Heaven knows there's plenty of *that*! But it's not easy, living so far out. I'd like to come back to Pieta.'

Father Salvatore shook his head. 'You shouldn't do that. It's not safe.'

'Plenty of people are coming back.'

'But the Government doesn't want a lot of people in one place.'

Manwel Azzopardi shrugged his shoulders. 'Government says one thing. People do another. . . I tell you, Dun Salv, it's no joke being billeted with a lot of strangers. Take the place we're living in. They don't want us, and we don't want them. They're such a *dirty* family.' He caught the look on Father Salvatore's face. 'I'm sorry, Dun Salv, but some people *are* dirty, and it's no good pretending.'

'Perhaps they cannot help it.'

'They can help keeping the place like a pig-sty! They can help hanging out the washing in the front passage, so you run your face into a wet pair of knickers every time you come through the door! They can help frying up a lot of rabbit's guts in the middle of the night!' Father Salvatore, hearing undertones of Manwel Azzopardi's wife in full recrimination, almost smiled. But Manwel had not finished. 'And their children! They're like a lot of little animals! I tell you, they do it in a corner of the front room! Not even in a bucket!'

'You must make allowances, Leli. Other people have their troubles, as well as you.'

'But they don't have to make it worse, behaving like a flock of dirty goats. We might as well be living in the leper hospital!' Father Salvatore frowned, and Manwell saw that he had gone too far. 'I'm sorry, Dun Salv,' he said again. 'I'm in a bad mood this morning. I had to leave the house at five, without a bite to eat. They say there's no more cooking-oil till next week. . . Are you going to visit your mother?'

'Yes.'

'Please give her my respects.'

'I'll do that. She often speaks of the work you did on the balcony. It was really beautiful.'

'It's a beautiful house to work in. And don't forget, I'm going to build the altar for you when the time comes. . . Well, I must get on, Dun Salv. You wouldn't think that talking to you could cost money, but it does! There's a time-keeper down at the docks who counts every minute. If you're late, he makes a little mark on a sheet of paper' – Manwel mimed a meticulous old clerk, bent and mean, scratching away with a pen – 'and at the end of the week, when you hold out your hand, you find there's a shilling missing from your wages, and the man says' – his voice now changed to a miserable whine, ' "Don't you remember, Azzopardi? You were two minutes late on Tuesday." '

Father Salvatore laughed. 'All right. I won't keep you any longer.' He touched the other man on the shoulder. 'Bless you, Leli. And life's not really so terrible, is it?'

Manwel Azzopardi grinned back. 'If we can't grumble when we feel like it, what's the use of living at all? *Sahha!*'

A few minutes later, cheered for no reason at all except his thankfulness for the huge and loving variety of life, Father Salvatore was in his other world, the world of Santo-Nobile.

The Most Noble the Baroness Celeste Emilia Santo-Nobile had permitted no change, either in herself or in her great house. If the past months of war had been an ordeal, she did not admit it; if the bombs falling near by had disturbed her, they were now forgotten, and the damage speedily made good, as it had been on other disgraceful occasions of violence.

A *palazzo* which could, for example, withstand a company of musketeers from the French line-of-battle ship *L'Orient*, trying to take it by storm in the hope of slaking Napoleon's greed for loot, could certainly ignore Mr Hitler's later intrusions.

At seventy-four, under the burden of war, Baroness Santo-Nobile might have felt older than she should, but this was another fact she would never acknowledge, and thus it did not exist. The folded hands, the black silk dress, the feet neatly crossed on the tapestried footstool – all were just as they had always been: a signal to the present that the past still ruled.

Straight-backed, calm, and regally composed, she entertained her son to morning coffee punctually at seven forty-five. There had been no compromise with that grim mid-winter hour, either. Once one relaxed a single standard of the past, all such rules might be broken. This was *not* to happen.

When the servants had gone, she said: 'I'm afraid Gregory is getting old, Salvatore. Did you notice how he closed the door? I believe he actually *stumbled*!'

'We're all getting old, Mother.' Father Salvatore sipped his fragrant coffee – that had not changed, either – and wished for a moment that everything in life could be as delicious, as calm, and as assured as at this moment. 'We must just accept it.'

'Nonsense.' The word, quietly used, still had its note of command. '*You* are not getting old. Are you suggesting that *I* am?'

He smiled. 'I would never dare.'

'I should hope not!'

'But all the same. . .' He looked round the high ceilinged salon, listened to the deep peace of the courtyard which shut out all the rest of bustling Valletta, before he went on: 'What I really meant was, the things that are happening to Malta are enough to disturb anyone. Even old Gregory. Even you.'

'Then one has a duty not to be disturbed.'

The absolute certainty of her answer was somehow depressing. Life, true life, was not to be measured on this scale of disengagement. Would she have been disturbed by wet underclothes hanging in the entrance hall below? By the smell of fried rabbit invading her drawing-room? By incontinent children fouling this most beautiful salon? By the crude freedoms of the catacomb? The contrast was so unthinkable that he could never have expressed it openly. Instead he said:

'You are lucky to be able to remain so – detached. I wish I could.'

As if catching his thought, she answered: 'Salvatore, I am *not* stupid. I am not *detached*, either. I know what is going on. It is simply a question of whether one gives in to it, or does one's best to continue living a normal life. Would you want me to go into hysterics every time a bomb falls on Valletta?'

'No. Of course not. You would never do that, anyway.'

'Well, then. . . Tell me, how is the *Illustrious* getting on?'

He could still be astonished about his honoured mother. 'You know about the *Illustrious*?'

'Salvatore, really! Of course I know about the *Illustrious*. Was it very terrible?'

'How do you mean?'

'When you went on board.'

He gave up. All he could do was love her, and acknowledge her quality. 'Yes. She is horribly damaged. I don't know how she is still afloat. I only hope she can get away somehow, before they try to bomb her again.'

'Of course she will get away! Admiral Cunningham needs her. He told me so himself. I wish you could have met him.'

He held out his cup for more coffee. 'I don't know very many admirals.'

'That's your own fault. Your father would have been an admiral if he'd not been killed.' She busied herself with the coffee and the cream and the honey-coloured crystals of sugar. 'Did you know that his flag-lieutenant was called Walter Starkie?'

'Father's flag-lieutenant?'

'No, no! How could a captain have a flag-lieutenant? Admiral Cunningham.'

'I'm sorry. I still don't understand.'

'Starkie. Only he spelled it differently. I went to his wedding nearly a year ago, at the Anglican Cathedral. He married Cunningham's niece.'

For the first time, he wondered if her wits were wandering. 'Starkie,' he repeated, temporizing.

'Well, doesn't it strike you as extraordinary? In 1940, Admiral Cunningham, who's really in charge of defending Malta, had a flag-lieutenant called Walter Starkie. Who was in charge at the Great Siege, 400 years ago? La Vallette. And who was his principal aide? Oliver Starkey! They say he's a direct ancestor of Starkie the flag-lieutenant!'

Father Salvatore emerged into daylight, with great pleasure. Starkey. . . He had been reading his name only a few weeks ago, on the tomb in St John's Co-Cathedral. He had also been reading his words, carved on a second tomb in the crypt, a moment afterwards: 'Here lies Valette, worthy of eternal honour. He who was formerly the scourge of Asia and Africa ...' – for it was Sir Oliver Starkey, the only English Knight at the Great Siege of 1565, who, as La Valette's secretary, had composed his general's epitaph, and now lay beside him in eternal rest.

'How extraordinary!' Father Salvatore would have queried the phrase 'direct ancestor', since the Knights of St John were meant to be celibate, but there could have been a brother, and thus a common father, and such delights of history were too precious for quibbling... 'How extraordinary,' he repeated. 'Why didn't you tell me before?'

'I'm sure I did. You know you never listen.'

It was not true – neither sentence was true – but in face of this remarkable gift from the past he could forgive her anything. He said: 'You've no idea how happy that makes me feel! La Valette and Cunningham, with their two English secretaries from the same family... It's as if history has always come to our rescue.'

'Dear Salvatore, you are *so* detached.'

They were friends again.

They were also mother and son. 'You're looking pale,' the Baroness presently announced. It recalled a hundred, a thousand times in the past, when she had said: 'You have a cold,' or 'You have grey circles under your eyes,' or 'You are not looking after that cut finger properly,' or 'It is time you went to the dentist,' or even 'Do you need a laxative?' But it was still an expression of love, impertinent and intrusive though it sometimes seemed. Now she asked: 'Are you getting enough sleep, Salvatore? Are you getting *proper* food?'

'Yes, Mother.'

'In those awful catacombs?'

'They're not awful. They are the blessing of my life.' The strange words came out unawares, before he had time to check them, but he did not want them recalled. They had begun to be true, even in a short seven months. 'Of course there's a lot to do, and a lot of disturbances all the time. But we sleep pretty well, and we eat – well, we eat.'

In his mother's face, stern and gentle at the same time, there was now an alert look. 'What do you mean, disturbances? What sort of disturbances?'

He spread his hands. 'You know how it is with a lot of people, all crowded together at night.' They exchanged glances, and then smiles. 'That was a silly start, wasn't it? You *don't* know how it is with a lot of people, all crowded together at night.'

'I should hope not!'

'It's like it must be in a ship,' he said, and hoped he had caught her serious attention again. 'Some people want to sleep. Some people can't sleep, so they need to talk, or even sing.

Some people want to eat. Some people are sad, some are happy, some are even afraid, because the ship might catch fire or be wrecked. So – there's always something going on, even in the middle of the night.'

'And some people want to drink? Or to make love?'

'Well, yes.' It was, from her, an astonishing remark: 'love' was a word he had heard from her lips countless times, but 'make love', never. He had not even realized that she could know what such an expression meant... He was about to acknowledge the absurdity of this when she went on:

'Salvatore, don't look so shocked! I have had three children of my own – remember? Do you think they were brought by the doctor?'

It must be the war, he decided. But he could still match her mood. 'That's what you once told me.'

'I once told you that Father Christmas could be angry with you, and that naughty boys didn't get new bicycles.'

'And I believed you.'

'Well, believe me now... When you said "disturbances", I thought you meant – that sort of behaviour, bad behaviour.'

'But why did you think so?'

'There has been some talk about it. And about you.'

'Who from?' He knew the answer, and he knew also that she was not going to give it.

'How can I remember? I meet a dozen people every day.'

It was a time for honesty. 'People behave in the catacomb as they do in their own home. It is their own home, quite often. Their only home. But there is always fear, Mother. Terrible fear of the war. So they—' He did not know how to phrase it, and it was very important. 'So they seize on life, before death seizes on them. The good people are better, the bad people are worse. The drunkards drink more. The people in love are more in love. Those who hate find their hatred turned into loathing.' He was almost pleading with her, it was so important. 'But they are all God's children. What is in their souls, good or bad, was planted there by God, and it grows by His will and His mercy. I pray all the time that *all things*, even the wickedness of war, may be turned to good. But am I to say, Do not drink, when drink is the only thing that gives a man courage? Am I to say, Do not make love where others can see you? *They may never make love again!* Am I to tell a boy,

Do not kiss so fiercely, it can lead to mortal sin? *It is his first kiss, but it may be his last!* Am I to tell a child, Be polite, say please and thank you, don't make a noise, Jesus tells you to be gentle and good? What does the child see and hear when he walks into the world outside? – blood and horror and enough noise to deafen him, and as much gentleness as he would find in hell! So where is Jesus Christ, his gentle Saviour? ... I beg your pardon, Mother,' he said, seeing her startled face, even as he wondered in his very soul: Did the child ask that terrible question, or did I? 'I did not mean to be so – emphatic. But when people talk of bad behaviour, I wonder where they spend their nights. I wonder where is their charity, their compassion... Let me assure you, I have seen *nothing* in the catacomb which God would not forgive.'

Now there was silence in the handsome room, the silence of astonishment and deep feeling on both sides. Father Salvatore passed his hand over his face, and felt it leave his forehead wet as well as trembling. It was true, that he had not meant to be so forceful. Especially not with her, never with her.

It must be the big ship, or the war, or something in the jagged patchwork of his possession – if it was true, as he sometimes felt, that he was becoming possessed by a *daemon* of determination, where the catacomb was concerned. God grant that it was only a small demon, one that a small priest could wrestle with... From a long way, from the ordered world of Santo-Nobile, he heard her voice:

'I think I am beginning to understand... Is there anything I can do to help, Salvatore? Do you need money for the shelter?'

'You have been generous enough already.' But he was a practical priest, as well as a priest in doubt. 'Well, we always need money. I want to buy more beds. Those wicked beds... And material for curtains between them. And a reserve of oil. And powdered milk, if we can find powdered milk. And – but you mustn't laugh – scrubbing-brushes.'

'Why should I laugh?' The Baroness Santo-Nobile, whose acquaintance with scrubbing-brushes could only have been limited, passed them swiftly by. 'Very well. You can spend up to £500 on your beds and your scrubbing-brushes and whatever else you need, and have the bills sent to me.'

'How good of you.' It was a magnificent gift, one that he had

prayed for. 'I can't tell you what a difference this will make...
I love you, Mother.'

'Five hundred pounds' worth?'

Her mischievous eyes recalled a shared memory, as she in-
tended. Once, long ago, when she had rescued him from some
appalling schoolboy dilemma with a covert transfer of five
shillings, and he had said, dutifully but sincerely, 'I love you,
Mother,' she had asked: 'Five shillings' worth?'

Now he could answer: 'Oh, much more!' and smile his
thanks. It was exactly the same answer as thirty years ago, and
not less heartfelt. Indeed, gratitude had grown with the years.
Just like the money, he thought, and knew that if he had said
this out loud, she would have been the first to find it funny, and,
with equal spirit, the last to admit it.

It was Francis, the young footman, who escorted him to the
postern door, instead of old Gregory; and he could not help
noticing that something had changed in Francis. Father Salvatore puzzled over it for a few moments, and then he found
the answer. Francis was walking like a soldier, one of the
soldiers now daily crowding the streets of Valletta. The straight
back and the firm footfall, the swinging arms and the click of
the heel as he turned, were all authentic. Even his green-and-
gold livery seemed to have taken on a martial cut. Francis
the footman had privately gone to war.

He had gained stature in another way, also; in the realm of
confidence.

'Mr Gregory asks to be excused,' he said, as they crossed the
courtyard. It was really a very odd remark, as if from a play
not quite geared to reality, only to the artifice of stage-direction.
His lean face with its high cheek-bones was almost aristocratic
in its authority. 'He is lying down. Sometimes he gets dizzy,
and he has to rest for a while.'

Father Salvatore was concerned. 'I'm sorry to hear that. Perhaps I should see him again before I leave.'

'I don't think so, Dun Salv. May I say something?' It was
clear that Francis was going to say something anyway. 'When
it happens, he likes to be alone. He feels ashamed, though
there is no need for that. Did you know he was eighty-two
last birthday? So' – Francis turned back towards Father Salvatore, because his determined military stride had outpaced the

priest's by several paces, 'it would be better to let him rest.'

'Has he seen a doctor?'

'Yes, Dun Salv. The Baroness was very insistent. But the doctor said, it is just that he is old and must take it easy.'

Alas, poor Yorick. He hath bore me on his back a thousand times, and would do so no more...

'Very well. I won't bother him now... Tell me, does the Baroness still go downstairs when the air-raid warning sounds?'

'Oh yes. She does not like it. She says it is only because she promised you. But we have made the armoury comfortable, with a bed and tables and chairs. She has even slept there sometimes.'

'Excellent. I hope you'll always encourage her to do that, when the raids start again.'

A slightly puzzled look came over Francis's face. How did a footman encourage a Baroness to do anything? His confidence had not yet aspired to such dizzy heights. He murmured: 'I will do my best, Dun Salv. And so will Mr Gregory.'

'I mean, make it easy for her. Remind her. You could even pretend to be afraid yourselves.'

'It would not need much pretending.' But Francis was smiling; a man could admit to fear, and still conquer it in his own fashion. They were across the courtyard now, and near the street door. Francis slowed his military step. 'There is something special I wanted to ask you, Dun Salv. But I did not wish to bother you. I know how busy you are.'

'What is it?'

Francis came to attention by the postern door. 'I want to join the army. The Royal Malta Artillery.'

Well, why not? ... One had only to spend an hour (or, in Father Salvatore's case, a succession of joyful hours extending over twenty years or more) in the musty old library which formed an entire wing of this house, to be able to answer, Why not? There was enough of war and fighting in the mouldering family journals to satisfy King Henry V himself.

It was the footmen of the Palazzo Santo-Nobile, given muskets and the promise of all the wine they could drink, on every feast day for the rest of their lives, who had withstood Napoleon's ruffians and put them to ignoble flight. Salvatore's own grandfather, one of the Maltese contingent which went off to fight the Russians in the Crimean War of 1854, had taken with him as his body-servant one Bernardo Galea, an under-butler who had saved his life before Sevastopol.

History did not recall what such men might have done at the Great Siege, but one thing was sure: a Santo-Nobile foot-man, then as now, would have been as good as a Turk any day, as good as five Turks... All that Father Salvatore needed to say was to echo his own thoughts, with the single phrase:

'Well, why not? I think it's an excellent idea.'

'Do you really, Dun Salv?' On the instant, Francis's eyes were shining: suddenly he was less a soldier than a small boy, given *carte blanche* to do exactly as he pleased for a magic day. 'I was afraid that... I mean, how can I leave the Baroness, now that Mr Gregory is like this? I owe her so much. I owe this house so much. She might think—'

'I am sure that she would not stand in your way, if it is something you really want. But you have made inquiries? Do they need recruits?'

'Yes. I know all about it already. My cousin is a lance-bombadier, a gun-layer in the Hal-Far battery. They shot down a Savoia bomber last week!'

So that was it. 'Well, that's the way the war must be won. Of course, you will be missed here, Francis. But it's not as if you would be leaving the place empty. There are still three footmen, are there not? And Gregory is really wonderful for his age. It's even possible that the Baroness might close part of the Palazzo, until the war is over.' There had been an im-mediate and fiery response to this suggestion of his, but he was not yet done with it. 'If you like, I will talk to the Baroness about it first. Then it will be easier.'

'If you could, Dun Salv.'

'I could, and I will.'

'Thank you very much.' Francis the footman struggled with Francis the gun-layer, and both of them with Francis the young man in need of help and wise counsel. 'You are such a good man.'

With this blessing, unearned in the sight of God, precious to the human heart, Father Salvatore emerged from the postern door and into the streets of Valletta again. It was only another small problem... His back was broad... It would hurt his mother a little, yet please enormously a simple man of admir-able upright spirit. Francis a gun-layer? ... He was almost envious. Why could not a priest be a gun-layer, and shoot all the forces of evil down from the sky in flaming ruins, *and go back to the worship of Christ the lover of peace?*

Perhaps it was too early in the morning to be anything but confused about the ethics of legal murder, and their conflict with treasonable surrender, with turning-the-other-cheek until the cheek was torn to the bone in ragged strips of humility ... But at least, for the third week in succession, he had paid his duty call, found pleasure and peace with a dear human being, and escaped without meeting that indefatigable churchman, courtier, and gossip, Monsignor Scholti.

He had not.

Bruno Scholti was an element in the urban landscape from quite a long way away. He was advancing up the street towards the Palazzo Santo-Nobile on a wave of ecclesiastical consequence, answering salutes from shopkeepers, pausing briefly to speak to someone on the pavement, bending to pat a child's head, even smiling at dogs.

It was a royal progress and (Father Salvatore had to admit) it was very well done indeed. The fact that it made him want to turn down a side-street, or hide in a doorway, or (the wildest idea of all) start running in the opposite direction as if he had heard the sirens, was a measure of its success.

It was a measure of other things as well, and it was these which made Father Salvatore plod manfully forward, in spite of leaden feet. Avoidance was cowardice: flight was unworthy of his cassock : the dislike he felt, even at this distant view of the enemy, was so un-Christian that it was disgraceful as well as ludicrous. It would be better for his soul, better by far, if their meeting took place naturally, and he emerged from it without rancour.

Monsignor Scholti saw him quite clearly from about twenty yards away. Their eyes met; and it was mortifying in the extreme when Scholti, without a sign of recognition, turned back to the old woman he was talking to, and went on with his conversation. Father Salvatore, his irritation now fully restored, decided that two could play at that silly game, and crossed the street to hurry by.

It was only then that Monsignor Scholti, with an exaggerated start, a widening of the eyes such as he might have accorded a vision of holy grace, called out his name :

'Salvu! How nice! I was hoping our paths would meet to-day!'

What could one do? ... Father Salvatore stopped, and waited for the other man to cross the street towards him. The cordial handshake which followed seemed to set the seal on the day's most fortunate encounter.

Monsignor Scholti was another man who, like Francis the footman, had increased in stature with the war. In his case, as well as growing fatter (which was already a difficult thing to achieve, in these straitened days), he had somehow managed to acquire an air of outstanding competence and busyness. *Fear nothing*, his whole face, body, and bearing seemed to say: *things may be difficult, things may be going badly, things may even appear hopeless – but I, Scholti, the valiant soldier of Christ, am here at your side!*

'And how did you find your mother?' he now asked, as if Father Salvatore could not, literally, have found his mother without the manly guidance always so ready, so unstinting. 'I was telling her, only the other day, that she was looking younger than ever! Between you and me, she was worried about a little domestic matter, something to do with – well, it's not important, but I was able to give her the benefit of my own experience. She was like a new woman!'

'That was very kind of you,' Father Salvatore answered. The day when his mother needed Monsignor Scholti to advise her on any aspect of any 'domestic matter' would be a catastrophic dawn indeed, but to say so would conflict with his good intentions. 'I'm sure you have so many other things to do.'

'My dear Salvu, you have no idea how busy I am!' He gave a benign wave to a couple of passing sailors, who appeared startled – though not too startled to salute. They must have been told: You're in Malta now. Catholic. Priests are like officers. If they look at you, salute... But Bruno Scholti was in full flood. 'I spent nearly all yesterday at the palace. Just one committee after another. Then there was the Scicluna party in the evening. Not much of a party, when you have to go from one group to another, simply to reassure people that all is well. This morning I have to take a message to His Excellency the Governor. I won't bore you with the details, but it's something highly confidential and important. And after that, guess what? – a working lunch at the palace again! We have to

settle, *in detail*, the seating arrangements for the diplomatic
and services' Solemn High Mass, next Sunday week. Such protocol! You really have no idea.'

'I'm afraid that I haven't,' said Father Salvatore.

'Dear Salvu! You are *so* direct!' But at least Scholti was
checked for a moment, and lured a few steps away from his
main preoccupation. 'Let me see ... I suppose you're on your
way to the Debrincats?'

'Eventually. The usual lunchtime meeting. But I have three
or four calls to make before that.'

'Oh, *really*?' It was clear, for the hundredth time, that Monsignor Scholti had no idea how condescending and offensive he
could sound. 'Now what could those be?'

'I have to buy candles,' Father Salvatore answered. 'And about
200 beds. And gallons of disinfectant for our chemical toilets.
Then I hope to find someone who might let me have some curtain material cheap. Even calico would do. I need' – he had
done a rough sum already – 'at least a thousand yards of it. I
suppose you don't know anyone?'

'My dear Salvu, I don't even know about *expensive* curtain
material... I was going to say, I haven't seen Lewis Debrincat
for some time. But I hear that, for various reasons, he should be
extremely grateful to the Baroness.'

Father Salvatore waited. Monsignor Scholti was going to tell
him why, whether he was prompted or not.

Scholti blessed a passing child, and gave a courtly salute to
a certain Mr Hazin, a black-suited, white-tied, fleshy business-
man who was creeping up one side of the shadowed street like
a slug avoiding the sun. 'A really splendid fellow,' Scholti murmured, out of the corner of his mouth. Father Salvatore could
scarcely believe his ears.

Surely he, Salvatore, could not be the only one to know that
Hazin was already so deeply involved in the black market that
his arrest and imprisonment must only be a matter of ... Ah,
well ... Pockets of innocence were always welcome in a
naughty world... He awoke from a confused daydream to hear
Bruno Scholti say:

'Lewis Debrincat. Yes... He is very *quiet* these days, isn't
he? It is certainly the wisest thing he could do. There was a
time – I think we both know this – when his future was a
little – shall we say, in the balance?' Scholti moved his palms

gently up and down as if he were in truth weighing something – but the something looked far more like a *ratal* of scrap-
meat than a man's life and reputation. 'The way that the
Baroness used her influence was really splendid, from a family
point of view. And of course she was right! Lewis seems to
have learned his lesson! Ah, what it is to have a great
name!'

Father Salvatore, sickened by a dozen aspects of this sly
version of the truth, decided he would have none of it. 'I am
sure,' he said, 'that my mother's influence would have counted
for *nothing*, if the authorities thought that Lewis had presented
any kind of security risk.'

'Why, Salvu! How up to date you are. Security risk! I didn't
know you have ever heard the phrase. And please don't mis-
understand me. Of course I didn't mean *undue* influence. I
mean' – and his fat hands had become balance-scales again, 'I
mean, a *little* help. The benefit of the doubt, isn't that what
we should call it? One man can be interned for his political
views, another man can be left free. The authorities, one hopes,
looks at them side by side. One man is a nobody, but he could
also be dangerous. The other is a Santo-Nobile son-in-law. Surely
he would not be so stupid! So – that is what I mean by influence.'

'I must go,' said Father Salvatore. 'Otherwise I shall be late
for lunch with Lewis Debrincat, the son-in-law.'

'Oh dear, I've annoyed you again.' Monsignor Scholti fetched
a most convincing sigh. 'I was trying so hard to be diplomatic.
Let's forget all about it, shall we? Did I hear you say you were
buying two hundred beds? *What* a good idea! That must mean
that your *catacomb*' – he pronounced the word as if it were
halfway between a Rabelaisian joke and a serious civic blemish
– 'is full to bursting.'

'We often have as many as six hundred people there. More,
on bad nights.'

'Really? *Now* I understand why it's so difficult to – well, to
supervise them.'

'It isn't difficult at all.'

'I mean, you can't be everywhere, can you?'

'I don't want to be everywhere.' Father Salvatore knew that
he was failing the test he had set himself; he had promised,
before God, to endure Monsignor Scholti, and anything he

might say, with all the grace due to a superior, and already his promise was in tatters. 'It isn't a matter of supervision. We are all there together, for shelter and for worship. They are grown-up men and women, most of them. Of course there are boys and girls too. But they – we – all have one thing in common. Fear. So I try to give us all another thing to share. God's help. God's hope.'

On a cold morning, on a street corner in Valletta, it sounded too dramatic, too intrusive, too raw in faith; and it only needed Monsignor Scholti's patiently neutral look to make the fact plain. There was silence between them; then Scholti said:

'Well, of course, if you are satisfied... Perhaps I should pay you a visit some time. I *would* like to see what it's like in practice.'

Father Salvatore was capable only of the minimum answer. 'Of course. You will be welcome. You will find it very simple. And rough, I suppose. And humble.'

'My dear Salvu, you don't have to tell me anything about humility.' The falsity of this was positively choking. But there was worse to come, a little worse. Scholti's lips moistened and slid into a confederate smile. 'I would particularly like to be there when you give your next *performance*.'

It was enough. Burning resentment overcame him. He said, abruptly: 'Bruno, I really think I am beginning to hate you,' and turned on his heel, and left the other man staring.

Stupid fool! he raged, as he began to walk downtown again; idiot, characterless man, silly child... But it was himself he was raging at. His mortification and grief at failing in his resolve knew no bounds. To allow himself to be provoked was bad enough; but his schoolboy cry of resentment at the end had been utterly shameful. If this was the best he could do under trial, then he might as well exchange his cassock for a clown's pantaloon rig.

God give me strength, he prayed, even as his eyes were searching for the wholesale cloth-merchant's shop he had heard spoken of. God give me humility, and a soul free from pride and pettiness. God give me the sense to see the worth of others, even if I cannot love them. God keep me from making fresh enemies, when there is so much peril in the world already.

God give me the pure joy of finding disinfectant for the toilet buckets.

4

'It's not a question of believing what they put on Rediffusion,' Lewis Debrincat said, from his position at the head of the family lunch-table. His voice, like his face, was sour. 'I suppose the daily situation report, or whatever it's called, is *some* use to *some* people. But frankly, I'd rather just be given the facts, as far as there are any facts these days, and make up my own mind about them. Then at least I'd know whose judgement to trust. And whose honesty.'

Grudging though the words were, they comprised his most positive statement so far. For much of the time – and this was not just today at lunch, but on most other days also, as Father Salvatore had learned from his sister Giovanna – Lewis Debrincat seemed sunk in apathy, only coming to the surface for occasional flashes of what could best be described as sneers against the huge stupidity of the world.

He was now neutral, he kept insisting, by look and word and inflexion and even silence. *They* had a war on their hands? Let *them* get on with it. Himself, he was content to watch, content to see all his prophecies of ruin come true. If they'd wanted his help, they should have asked him for it earlier, instead of treating him like a leper or a criminal... Even as he sat there now, fat, sullen, sloppily dressed in a stained grey pullover, collapsed into his high armchair like a bag of assorted *pasta*, his whole bearing could still proclaim: *I am right. You are wrong. I will win. You will see.*

It was quite true, what Monsignor Scholti had said of him, and it troubled Father Salvatore even to think of it. Without his mother's influence, or intervention, or pressure, or pleading, or whatever else one might call it, Lewis Debrincat would today be languishing in gaol – unjustly, perhaps, but necessarily within the context of war – in common with dozens of other Maltese notables who had declared their hand too early, too forcefully, and too publicly to be overlooked.

As a generous compromise, he had been told to keep quiet. His conduct would be carefully noted. If at any time... It was the best that authority could do for him, and he was lucky. But, being Lewis Debrincat, he was not prepared to accept such luck gracefully. He still had to exhibit a continuing air of what the British Army called 'dumb insolence'. It could still get him into trouble, and he was contemptuous about that also.

It was almost as depressing to see how his family reacted to this bitter spirit. Occasionally they could be embarrassed, and show it; more often they were indifferent, or pretended that Lewis had said nothing out of the ordinary, or even pretended that he, the head of the family, was not there. The latter was the case now, as he concluded a conventional diatribe about war-time propaganda with his innuendo about the 'honesty' of the Maltese radio service.

His wife was murmuring something to Carmelina the maid – the fatherless Carmelina, whose seven-months-old bereavement had now, helped by the blessed resilience of youth, vanished into the background. Marija, her beautiful face turned inwards towards what might well have been beautiful thoughts, seemed hardly present at the table at all. Pietru, just past his fourteenth birthday, outgrowing the magic of a bicycle, beginning to set covetous eyes on the motorcycle which lay a long two years ahead, had also gone blank.

Father Salvatore, from sad practice over the last few months, could read the thoughts in the small averted head. *The way my father talks is awful, but I don't have to say so. I don't have to say anything. I am not a grown-up, though when I am, and it is my turn to sit at the head of the table and say something, I won't say anything like he said. Meanwhile, I am eating.*

Only Salvatore, a little distance away from this family absorption, felt that he had to make his contribution, even though some inner protest was involved. Was this his day for being trapped into talking to people he did not like? No, there had been Nero, and Rafel, and Manwel Azzopardi, and his mother, and Francis, to balance the account. The good far outnumbered the bad. Let him then accept the bad, with a good grace.

'I don't think we should blame Rediffusion for trying to keep us cheerful,' he said, as mildly as he could. 'You can hardly expect them to concentrate on the bad news, when there's so much of it. And as for making up one's own mind – well, it's still a free country, isn't it? There's still a free Press. The *Times of Malta* has never missed an issue since the war began—'

'That rag!' Lewis Debrincat interrupted. 'I don't mind if they never publish another issue, from here until doomsday! You won't get any truth from that quarter!' His eyes, darting this way and that, suddenly fixed themselves on the nearest object, which was his wine-glass. He began to address it, in a long, rambling, grumbling monologue which could not be ignored. 'Is this a free country? I doubt it! ... Can you go out at night? No, there's a curfew. Can you buy what you want? No, there's this ridiculous rationing. If you ask for an extra pound of butter, people look as if they want to call the police! What happens if you go for a drive in the country, *if* you can get the petrol? There's barbed-wire strung all over the place: hideous concrete pillboxes round every corner: tank-traps and mines on the beaches. St Paul's Bay *evacuated* because they say there might be an invasion! And if you drive back in the dark, you can't see a thing because you have to have those stupid cardboard masks on your headlights. If that's a free country, then give me—' he paused, and they all knew why, because they knew what he was going to say; he was going to say 'Italy', and it would have been disastrous. But instead he let his chin drop on his chest, and mumbled: 'Then give me *anything*. It couldn't be worse.'

Silence fell, and persisted. Carmelina cleared away the plates, and brought in, with a smile, the Charlotte Russe she had promised Father Salvatore earlier. But what a blight his brotherin-law had become... The uncharitable thought prompted him to try to find excuses for Lewis Debrincat, and he did his very best. A man under suspicion, a man on probation, a man who found his strong views not only out of fashion, but almost out of lawful licence, might well be forgiven for retreating into sulky non-cooperation. All his known world had turned against him. What else was left, to someone as vain and greedy for public esteem as Lewis? Of course his reaction was weak and foolish. But so were many people, and many things.

Perhaps lunch would have been gloomy anyway, without Lewis Debrincat to cast a morbid, guilty shadow over it. Even in this strong and elegant house, they were living in fear, just as they did in the Cottonera Lines. Fear had been given an added power, an extra surge, just before they went into lunch, when a strange warning had been broadcast urgently on Rediffusion.

It had been a curt 'instruction for all civilians' to take cover

immediately they heard the air-raid sirens, as 'special tactics'
were to be used.

There had been no elaboration. What did it mean? Special
tactics? Whose special tactics? The Germans'? Their own?
Father Salvatore, at a loss for a subject, returned to this one,
as he tried to bridge the gap between the embarrassment of
dead silence and a reasonable ending to their meal.

'I still wonder what they meant by that warning,' he said,
to the world at large, to anyone who would listen. 'It sounded
so mysterious. I hope it's not some horrible new weapon.'

'Let them play their silly games,' Lewis snapped back. From
talking to his wine-glass, he seemed to have struck up a friendship with it; it was now cradled in his hand, and the deep and
noisy gulp he took from it was a pledge far more intimate
than he would have given to any human being. 'No doubt
they'll tell us when it's all over, and the damage has been
done.'

Pietru suddenly came to life. But it was his Uncle Salvu
whom he addressed directly.

'Do you think it means that we've got some new Hurricanes?
That they'll be flying all over the place, and the bullets will
go smashing into people unless they stay indoors?'

Giovanna protested: 'Pietru dear, don't be so blood-thirsty!'

'Oh, I don't *want* it to happen,' Pietru answered. 'But it
could, couldn't it? I mean, now that the Gladiators are so
slow, we *do* need Hurricanes, and they *are* marvellous!'

It was already a subject of family teasing that Pietru had so
swiftly transferred his allegiance from his shrunken heroes,
Faith, Hope, and Charity, to the new darlings of Malta, the
squadrons of Hurricane fighters which could at last out-fly and
out-gun the opposition, and had scored success after success.
It was now the Hurricanes which could do no wrong. As for
those old Gladiators. . .

Father Salvatore smiled at him. 'Does that mean that you've
finally taken down your photograph of *Il Ferocio*?' This was
the universal nickname of the Gladiator pilot, Wing-Commander
Burges, who had won the DFC for his exploits and who was
acclaimed all over Malta. 'Have you forgotten him so soon?'

'Of course not!' Pietru's bright eyes were scandalized. 'He
shot down six planes! He *saved* Malta, in the beginning! But
now—' he wanted to share his expert knowledge with anyone

who would listen. 'You see, Faith, Hope, and Charity were absolutely *worn out*. They couldn't even *boost* the engines. Hurricanes can fly more than seventy miles an hour faster. It's the only way they can intercept.' He sighed, as if he were looking at an operations-map of the skies above Malta, and saw the fearful gaps and holes in their defences. 'I do hope it means more Hurricanes. Hundreds of them! I hope the pilots walk up and down the street, so I can get their autographs and talk to them. There was a pilot yesterday with a *huge* moustache. I'm sure he was a Hurricane pilot. But there were so many people, I couldn't get near enough to ask him.'

His father swallowed another gulp of wine, and then roused himself again. 'I hope you'll never do any such thing!' he said tartly. 'If they really are pilots, and not just office-boys and clerks, they ought to have better things to do than parade up and down the Strada Reale, showing off. All I hope is, if we do get hundreds more of these heroes crowding into Valletta, they behave better than the sailors do.'

Pietru opened his mouth to speak, and then subsided. Another embarrassing silence fell. It was clear what Lewis Debrincat was referring to: the frequent drunken forays, the undoubted rowdiness and vulgarity, especially where women were concerned, which could be expected whenever the Royal Navy liberty-boats discharged their nightly cargoes. There had been one or two guarded references to this in the newspapers, and quite a lot of cases which had ended up in court, before the naval shore-patrols reclaimed their stray lambs and hauled them off for punishment.

Father Salvatore, though he despised drunkenness and abhorred sexuality, felt that he must say a word for the other side. He had long ago learned at first hand that, in human terms, such sins were not always so awful as their public labels. A man could be driven to drink: a man could be provoked to lust.

Of course these things were wrong, but so was human condemnation, human contempt for the transgressor, delivered so long in advance of the final accounting. There would be a lot of surprises in heaven... It was his turn to look at his own wine-glass, as he said:

'I don't think one should blame all the sailors for what a few of them do when they come ashore. It's difficult for us to realize what they may have been going through, a few hours before. I don't believe I told you, I went on board the *Illustrious* as soon as she came into harbour.' He noticed that Marija, sitting opposite him, came to sudden attention as he spoke, though he thought nothing of it at the time. 'I've never seen a ship in such a horrible mess, or men so exhausted by what they had to do to get her to Malta. That's quite apart from the wounded, and the – well, I'm afraid a lot of men had been killed. That's what you have to remember, when you see sailors walking about in Valletta. They've come ashore to forget. And the things they want to forget are often more terrible than any of us can imagine.'

'Well, of course, if you're going to make excuses ...' Lewis Debrincat mumbled, taken aback by the opposition.

Father Salvatore decided he had made his point strongly enough, certainly for family consumption. He was aware that Marija, of all people – the gentle, beautiful Marija who could scarcely know what he was talking about – was staring at him as if what he was saying was Divine, revealed truth. He altered his ground gently:

'But I still can't understand why the Germans haven't come back to bomb the *Illustrious*. She's in such an awful state. Even one more bomb could sink her. Yet they've left her alone for five days! It doesn't make sense.'

'What does?' Lewis interjected. 'It was probably fixed up years ago. War is just an international racket.'

'I hope she gets away all right.' He ignored Lewis Debrincat, out of anger, out of pity. He looked across the table, at Pietru who was listening with solemn, almost strategic concentration, and then at Marija, in whose glowing eyes there was now a transparent warmth and sympathy. What could he have said, to spark such interest, such comradeship? ... 'It's a funny thing about the *Illustrious*. Even after a few hours on board, I've come to think of her as *my* ship.'

Darling Uncle Salvu, Marija thought, in loving astonishment: what a sweet thing to say... Because the *Illustrious* is my ship as well... Of course, I don't mind sharing her with someone like you... If only ... She closed her mind, dutifully, to all family comparisons. But all the same, Uncle Salvu *was* wonderful, and the ship was *her* ship also.

The *Illustrious* had been Marija's ship since the morning after her arrival in French Creek, for the best of all possible reasons. It was the morning when she had met, actually met, someone who belonged to the ship. Uncle Salvu would probably call him her 'knight in shining armour'. She would not mind if he did, because already, in a silly, sentimental, terribly important way, it was true. Even if his shining armour was just a blue uniform with so little gold braid that it was positively unfair.

It had happened five magic days ago. She had been shopping for her mother in Floriana; sometimes one had to go rather far afield nowadays, to find even the simplest things, which in this case were real olive oil, chipolata sausages for which her father had developed a greedy passion, the sandalwood soap without which she could never really enjoy a bath, new potatoes for Pietru's ravenous palate, Stilton cheese, egg-noodles in the shape of sea-shells, and the gooey chocolate-bars made by Toblerone of Switzerland.

She had got them all! She was winning the war already! In a happy mood, she had crossed the bastions to have a look at the ship which everyone was talking about. She had only to follow the crowds, drawn in huge numbers to this magnet of the sea. But what she saw was more splendid, and more awful, than anything she could have imagined.

Was this *Illustrious* really a ship? She looked more like a ruined old factory, torn by terrible winds, by an earthquake, by furious mobs of thieves and rioters. Mingling with the crowds, she shared their admiration and their horror. Across Grand Harbour, under a haze of dirty, drifting smoke, the thing they had come to see now lay at rest, looking as if it would never move again except to settle into its grave under the troubled surface of the water.

Then, being a girl, with no cares in the world except the silly cares of being a girl, she had looked round at the people, and found, close by her, the most wonderful, the most beautiful young man she had ever seen in seventeen long years of life.

He was tall, and fair, and proud: he was young, and slim, and alive. He was in naval uniform which did not seem to fit him very well – or perhaps it was because it was rumpled, as if he had put it on too quickly or worn it too long without giving it a chance to recover. He was staring at the ship, like everyone else, yet somehow in a special way, a hungry way.

But almost immediately – such was the mysterious telegraphy which made the wonderful world go round – he was staring at her instead.

She was very glad, secretly overjoyed, that she just happened to be wearing the new blue dress, the one which made her look – well, it really was the prettiest dress she had ever bought. Her father, seeing it for the first time, had asked grumpily: '*How* old did you say you are?' By mistake, it was the nicest thing he had said for a very long time.

She let the young man stare at her for a reasonable number of minutes. Then, without hurrying, she moved away from the thickest of the crowd, and made for a quiet corner of the bastions. Presently he moved also – ah, how brave he was, as well as beautiful! – and came directly towards her. It was only a moment before he was standing at her side. It would have been rude not to turn, to see who it was. When she looked up, he was smiling at her, and she was trembling.

He pointed towards *Illustrious*, just visible round the corner, and spoke in a voice so full of happiness that she was almost jealous:

'Doesn't she look marvellous!'

'Marvellous' was certainly the very last word she had expected to hear, but she was so glad he had spoken to her that she could almost agree.

'Yes... Doesn't she? ... But ...' The pauses were well-bred gulps for breath: she had wanted to make some grown-up, sophisticated, and witty comment, but it could hardly be said to have come out that way. She felt as if she had just run a hundred yards up the slope of Mount Sceberras, and that the words she spoke could have been spoken by anyone: especially anyone as stupid and breathless as she must have seemed. She tried again, and tried also, to sound intelligent and sensible 'But she looks terrible as well, don't you think? And sad.'

He considered this. Perhaps he was really as nervous as she was: only he was a man, and it didn't show much. 'No, what I meant was, the fact that she got into harbour at all.' He had a funny, jerky way of speaking, as if he was out of practice, or as if wasting words on someone who did not understand made him impatient. 'Did you see her come in last night?'

'No, I didn't. What time was that?'

'Ten o'clock.'

How could she have been on the bastions of Valletta at ten o'clock at night? 'No, of course I didn't. It's much too late.'

'Oh.' He smiled at her, and at her tone of voice, which — she could hear its echo herself — sounded like an outraged school-girl's, offered a cigarette or a strong whisky-and-soda. 'Sorry . . . Well, I saw her come in, and it was the best sight I ever clapped eyes on.' There was something else he had to tell her, to tell anyone, and it came out with a rush. 'You see, she's my ship.'

After that, it was much easier, and wonderfully so.

'You mean, you're one of the officers?'

'One of the pilots. Fleet Air Arm.' He reached out his arm, and pointed to the little letter A in his sleeve ring. 'A is for Air.' He saw that she was looking at his uniform as well, and he added: 'I'm sorry about the rest of the suit. But it's not mine, thank God. I'm just wearing it for a friend.'

'How do you mean?'

'I lost all my kit. It was perfectly all right when I flew off, but when I went back on board this morning, there wasn't a darned thing left. Everything was either burned to a crisp or soaked in oil! I tell you, this means total war!'

'But what happened?' It was sad that she had to ask so many questions, instead of making wise and fascinating re-marks which would capture his interest immediately, but she was still feeling her way in an astonishing new world. 'When did you fly off?'

'Just before the bed fell on Father.' She must have looked puzzled, because he apologized. 'Sorry. I mean, just before we were bombed. I think I was the last plane to take off. Me and my faithful Fulmar were half-way down the flight-deck when they dropped a bomb just in front of the sharp end. Dirty great clouds of spray, falling all over us. Such bad manners. . . So there we were, surrounded by sea-water! I didn't know whether I was meant to fly, or swim, or sit still and drink it.' He grinned, as if he could scarcely take it seriously, even now. 'Anyway, I diced with death for a bit, and then made for your hospitable little island, and then came back to help. But by the time we got there, poor old *Illustrious* was shot full of holes. So here I am, in somebody's third-best suit, and no plane to call my own, because *that* ran into a horse-tram stuffed with blocks of con-crete as soon as it landed. Talk about a wizard prang! But what I always say is, there's a first time for everything. And anyhow – look!' He pointed again, this time at *Illustrious*, still masked here and there by drifts of smoke. 'She got in! And if I know anything about our electric skipper, she'll get out again.'

There was silence between them for a moment. In the peace of the Malta bastions, on a sunlit morning, it was almost impossible to realize that what he was saying was true – that it had all happened to him, a few short hours ago, and that he could joke about it, even in that jerky way, and look at her with such lively admiration, such *naughtiness*, all at the same time. Were there really young men like this in the world, and it had taken her so long to meet one? Had her father ever been like this? Had anyone?

After his long outpouring of words, it was her turn to speak. It was important to know every single thing about him.

'But what are you doing now?'

'Talking to the most beautiful girl I've ever seen since Cleopatra snuggled up to the asp.'

She frowned. She did not want him to be like this – silly and flirtatious. She wanted the real young man, whose name she did not even know. 'I meant, why are you over here?'

'For the same reason.' But he realized he was not talking the language she wished to hear, and he swiftly changed it. 'I wanted to have another look at the ship,' he said, much more seriously. 'As a matter of fact, I can hardly take my eyes off her. I had to go to Mtarfa' – he pronounced it all wrong, 'to see someone in hospital there. But on the way back, I thought I'd make sure that *Illustrious* was still all in one piece. What's left of her.'

'Was he a friend, in hospital?'

'Best friend a boy ever had. One of our top maintenance chaps.'

'Is he all right?'

'No. He died.' But he said it in the same tone of voice as he had used earlier: as if death were just something that happened on an average day, like the clouds of spray at the end of the flightdeck, like ruined uniforms, like crashing his plane on landing. 'It was probably just as well.'

'Why?'

'He was in a bit of a mess. Like that poor old mess down there. Do you know, there's a whole hangar full of—' he checked himself. 'Well, anyway, Jerry did a slap-up job. Very worthy cause. You can put my name down for two guineas.'

Out of the strange, almost incomprehensible slang, she managed to find the sense. 'The Germans must be absolutely awful!'

'Oh, I don't know. You've got to see their point of view. Heil Hitler, guns before butter, do unto thy neighbour before he does it unto you. They've got bags of guts, anyway. That pattern-bombing yesterday was something to watch. Pressing on regardless! But I just wish they wouldn't machine-gun our chaps coming down in parachutes. Damme, sir, a sitting bird!'

'Do they really do that?'

'With great regularity.' But he wasn't really serious, even about such a terrible thing. 'We had to work out some jolly smart evasive action.'

'How do you mean?'

'It's called Operation Peter Pan. We slip out of our parachutes' – he made an absurd wriggling motion, like a woman squeezing out of a tight dress, 'and they float off into the blue, and while the Germans are shooting them down in flames, we just tiptoe away.'

It was so ridiculous that she had to laugh.

'That's better,' he said instantly. His face took on that alarming look of admiration again. 'You're real pretty when you smile. You're real pretty anyway.'

It was still too early, and he ought to realize it. Unskilled in such manoeuvres, she only knew one way of telling him, which was to change the subject.

'Do you think they'll come back to bomb the ship again?'

'Bound to.' He looked down at *Illustrious*. 'Poor old girl – as if she hadn't had enough already. But if we can rustle up a few extra planes in expendable Malta, we'll do the best we can. Leave it to the intrepid birdmen.'

He had slipped in a very strange word, which she hardly knew how to pronounce. 'Expendable?'

He assumed a pompous tone of voice. 'Since it cannot conceivably be defended against air-attacks from a land-based enemy sixty miles away, Malta must be regarded as expendable.'

'Who said that?'

'Some clot.' He sighed. 'All our best thinking was done in the Boer War. Of course they've changed their minds about

Malta *now* – someone must have found a new map – but it
makes things a bit dicy just at the moment. It would be awful
to lose *Illustrious* after what she's been through, but you can't
do miracles on a bow-and-arrow run. There's that one, too.' He
pointed to a different part of the harbour, where a merchant
ship, moored to a buoy, was surrounded by a feverish flurry
of barges and lighters. 'That's an old chum called the *Essex*.
She's got x thousand tons of ammunition for you. But if she
goes up, so does the whole dockyard, and half Malta as well.'
He turned back again, and saw her troubled face. 'Oh, let's
forget it. Not to worry, my poppet. Come and have a drink.'

The frank approach of the invitation was matched by his
face, his lean and alive face, which once again alarmed her.
Her heart had performed such a total somersault at the word
'poppet', which must mean something special and intimate, that
she could scarcely answer. She managed to shake her head.
'I'm afraid I can't.'

'I meant it about being beautiful,' he said, in an adroit change
of mood which was much harder to resist. 'But I'm really very
respectable. I won't – I won't even *look* at you, if you don't
want me to. Just a little drink? Twenty minutes? Ten minutes?
They tell me there are all sorts of good places.' He reeled off
a list, with astonishing readiness. 'Do you know the Moulin
Rouge? Maxim's? Rexford's in the Strada Reale? Captain Caruana's Bar? The British Empire Snug? – I like the sound of that
one. Or Auntie's – surely you'd feel safe at Auntie's?'

'I feel perfectly safe anywhere,' she answered severely. It
was not true, but she really must take charge of herself, and
of him. Some of the places he mentioned were already notorious. Auntie's was scarcely whispered about. 'But I've been
shopping, and I must get home.'

'Where's home?'

'In Sliema.'

'That's down there,' he said helpfully. 'Can I walk along with
you? My name's Michael Ainslie. Mike.'

She said : 'I'm Marija Debrincat.'

'That's a bit more dicy. Marija Debrincat.' But this time his
pronunciation was perfect, and a joy to hear. 'I'll carry that
large shopping bag for you, and I won't make a single remark
about a beautiful name for a beautiful girl.'

Even if she had said No, it would have sounded like Yes.

He walked with her nearly all the way home. Their strides could not possibly match, but they seemed to be in step from the very first moment. The nearness of his tall figure was intoxicating. Though he behaved as well as he had promised, his eyes whenever he turned to look at her face were almost glowing with frank attraction.

There was one moment of glorious silliness, and another of magic excitement. As they turned a street corner, he suddenly said, out of the side of his mouth: 'Oh God! Take the shopping bag!' and thrust it into her hands. A wizened old naval captain approached along the pavement, rolling towards them like a bad-tempered barrel. As he passed, Michael Ainslie whipped his hand up in an immaculate salute. It was acknowledged with the minimum of attention.

'The old bastard!' Michael Ainslie said, when the captain was safely past. 'He was looking at you!'

There was such mortal injury in his tone that, in spite of the terrible language, Marija burst out laughing. Warm happiness was in the very air as she asked: 'Won't you please explain? What was all that about?'

'You may not believe this,' he answered, 'but naval officers aren't allowed to carry parcels in the street. At least, that's what they told me when I was going through routine. At my age, you believe *anything*.' He turned round swiftly, to make sure of the captain's retreating back. 'All right, give me the loot again... I knew that war would be hell, but this is ridiculous!'

The exciting, the overwhelming moment had been at the street corner on the Sliema sea-front, just short of her house. She had stopped, to say goodbye with a margin of safety. She could not possibly be seen with an escort – particularly such a noticeable one – on her own front doorstep. But already, after a short hour of talking sense and nonsense with Michael Ainslie, she was much better equipped to deal with the moment.

'This is it,' she told him. 'Give me the parcels. I must hurry. Thank you so much.'

He did not argue, even though they were standing outside a broken-down old coach-house ('A blot on the neighbourhood!' her father called it, at least once a month) which could not possibly have been 'it'. Accepting her decision, he surrendered the shopping bag, stood back a pace, and looked down at her.

K.M.—9

'What are my chances of seeing you again?'

'Do you really want to?'

He was almost annoyed, or pretended to be. 'Marija, I don't think you quite realize what an absolutely lovely girl you are. But you will, as soon as I've given you the short course.' He smiled. 'No, the long course... Can I ring you up?'

'It's in the telephone book.' Heaven only knew how that could be explained to a listening family. 'Early in the morning would be best.'

'Roger... There's a sweet old character in Dickens,' he went on, with scarcely a pause, and she thought it was going to be someone called Roger, whoever Roger was, until he finished his sentence, 'by the name of Captain Cuttle. All he does is to keep on muttering: "When found, make a note of"... I'm bound to say, Marija De-Brin-Cat, that that's how I feel. Not about the telephone. About you.'

He took a step forward, until he was standing almost touching her. His grey-blue eyes, gentle and hungry, flickered over her face, then her breasts, then her face again, and she could only think, Why not? Why not? He half-raised his hand. What terrible, wonderful thing was going to happen? But suddenly he shook his head, and said: 'No. Next time,' and the hand dropped away, and he turned, with a gorgeous smile, and was gone.

Next time.

'Marija, *dear*!'

'M'm?'

But it was her mother's voice. 'Uncle Salvu is speaking to you!'

'Oh!' Marija came to herself, blushing scarlet with embarrassment. She had not heard a word for the last five minutes; the contrast between the dreamy secrecy of her thoughts, and the close, inquisitive inspection which her whole family was now giving her, was the most mortifying thing which had ever happened to her.

She knew already, from much less important ordeals, that there was no way of controlling a blush... As wave after wave of colour mounted to her face, she had no choice but to endure: conscious of her mother's watchful gaze, Uncle Salvu's amused look, Pietru's brotherly glee. Only her father, sour and morose at the head of the table, was outside their circle. That was particularly unfair... Nobody paid any attention to him when he lapsed into private daydreams... It was Pietru who broke the silence.

'What's the matter? Have you swallowed a beetrot?'

She ignored him loftily. 'I'm so sorry,' she said to Uncle Salvu. 'I must have been miles away. I was thinking of something else.'

'And I know *what*,' Pietru said, switching his role to that of a sinister police inspector. 'Denial is useless. Escape is out of the question. You have been *observed*.'

Marija looked at him warily. It might be true. Pietru could have been watching from the roof, his favourite retreat. She must have been mad to let Michael Ainslie come so near the house. On the other hand, her brother did not look *quite* confident, just beastly and teasing... She decided to be brave.

'Tell us, Sherlock Holmes. What *do* you know?'

'I would prefer not to make a statement. Not just at the moment. But I know your vile secret. When the time is ripe—'

His mother intervened. 'Pietru, I don't know what you've been reading lately, but if there's a secret, we don't want to hear it.'

'It's all right,' Marija said. 'He doesn't know anything.'

'Ho, don't I?' Pietru's character-changes could be baffling. 'Ho, ho, ho! Well, I do know. In fact, I know all. But I will be generous. I will give you a clue. Initials C.Z.'

'But of *course*!' C.Z. was obviously Charlie Zammit, one of her fringe suitors, a pale young man of such paralysing shyness that he almost had to be helped over the doorstep, both coming and going. Marija's relief was so enormous that she could have kissed her odious little brother. But he deserved something else; he deserved a dose of sarcasm at least, for giving her such a scare. 'How stupid of me! C.Z. Darling Charlie Zammit! I dream about him day and night!'

Pietru, deflated, turned his attention to the last of the Charlotte Russe. 'I said you had a secret,' he muttered into his plate. 'Why are girls so sloppy?'

'That will do,' his mother said briskly. 'We've heard quite enough about secrets today.'

Father Salvatore caught Marija's eye, and smiled. There was

something going on – he could tell that, from the complicated
look on her face, a mixture of relief and guarded secrecy. The
faint traces of that scarlet blush still betrayed a moment of
crisis. Could it be love? He hoped so. He hoped for many
things, including a wise choice. It was time to smooth over
the awkward corner.

'What I was trying to do, before Peter Paul took over—'

'Well, I like that!' But Pietru's was only a subdued chirp
of protest. He was outnumbered, and must live to fight another
day.

'—was to ask if you had seen any of those American drums
of egg-powder, on your various shopping trips.'

Marija shook her head, but gratefully. The question and the
topic were both so banal, so gloriously normal, that she could
have kissed her uncle as well. (But what was all this kissing? ...) 'No, they seem to have disappeared lately. I wanted
some for the nuns' Christmas cake. But Uncle Salvu, what do
you want egg-powder for?'

He smiled. 'If you ever tasted my herb omelette for fifty
people – egg-powder, goat's milk, clover leaves, and the tops
of turnips, cooked in the lid of a dustbin which Nero Cassar
has turned into a huge frying-pan – you wouldn't ask such
a question.'

His sister shuddered. 'Salvu, you don't really eat it yourself,
do you?'

'Oh yes! Well – when I am *very* hungry. But of course I
serve myself last, and sometimes there is none left.'

Lewis Debrincat came to the surface again, after the latest
of his long silences. 'I think you will find,' he said disagree-
ably, 'that your egg-powder will be back in the shops just as
soon as there's a fat enough profit to be made out of selling it.'
His face matched his tone – sneering and self-satisfied at the
same time. 'War is like that. You can forget the heroes in
their silly little suits. The real battles are fought round a pad-
locked garage full of egg-powder and tinned ham and Scotch
whisky, and the medals are money.' He stood up, reasonably
steady. 'I think that, delicious as it was, this lunch has gone
on long enough.'

Giovanna Debrincat said goodbye to her brother in the hall. As
usual, there was little need for explicit words or explanations.

'Is there anything I can do to help?' Father Salvatore asked her, as he had asked so many times already.

'No. Really no, Salvu. It just goes on. I've become used to it.'

'How's the drinking?'

'Not too awful. It's mostly at night, which at least solves one problem. But it's so destructive, such a waste of a man.' The fact that she did not say 'Waste of a woman' was a shining virtue, beyond price. 'Oh Salvu, what's the answer? Don't tell me it's prayer, or I shall scream!'

'That's a nice thing to say to a priest.'

'It's a specially nice thing to be able to say to a brother... All right, Dun Salv, I'll be good. Do you think Marija is in love with someone?'

'I hope so.'

'So do I. We need it here.'

From a beautiful woman, a wife and a mother, they were sad words indeed. He touched her arm gently. 'You mustn't think like that, Giovanna. You *have* love here. So much of it. The house is full of it. The past years have been full of it. The best will come again.'

'The best has twenty years to catch up... If it wasn't for the children... You and the children ... and Mother—'

'You see – the list gets longer and longer!'

'I suppose I mustn't forget Prince, either.'

By an agreeable miracle of timing, the dog wandered into the hall at that moment, its claws tick-tacking like knitting needles on the terrazzo tiling, and wagged its tail furiously at the sound of its name.

They both burst out laughing, and on that healing note, with a sisterly caution – 'Do take care, Salvu: remember the warning, and don't be silly about it' – they said goodbye, and parted. She was still the rock on which this house was founded, and he thanked God for it, even as he prayed God for her strength to endure.

5

It was just after half past one: lunch had been punctual, and Lewis Debrincat's closure of it had come promptly on the hour. Father Salvatore, standing in the thin January sunshine on the steps of the Casa Debrincat, surveyed the Sliema seafront, which was almost deserted, and wondered exactly what to do next.

He still had various shopping errands, which his mother's magnificent gift had made possible, but this was the dead hour of commerce, when the shutters went up for the afternoon siesta, and a man could starve before he was sold as much as a crust of bread. In fact, Father Salvatore found himself with time to spare, something so unusual that, like the slave who lost his shackles, he hardly knew how to walk free.

What a stupid, fanciful thought for a perfectly ordinary afternoon... He took out his breviary, and, as he strolled slowly along the pavement towards Sliema Creek, began to read the Office of the Day. Discipline, the great gift of the Church, re-asserted itself, coming to his rescue as it had done a thousand times in twenty years of priesthood. But in spite of this accustomed duty, and the precious pattern of its enforcement, and the comfortable words enshrined in it, he could not help feeling uneasy.

There was something brooding and dangerous about this silent mid-day hour. It could have been due to the urgent broadcast from Rediffusion, and Giovanna's reminder of it; or the sad denial of life and love which he had left behind him at the Casa Debrincat; or the barred stillness of the siesta hour – for who could tell what fear and anxiety it masked? – or to the simple fact that all Malta was now waiting, as it had already waited a hundred times before, for the next hammer-blow from the poised fist of the enemy.

It could have been the presence of *Illustrious*, of which every-one was conscious : *Illustrious* the target, *Illustrious* the hunted refugee, *Illustrious* the unwanted hostage which might seal the fate of all around her... He decided, on a sudden impulse, that he must go and take a look at the ship again : just to make sure that she was still safe, or had somehow miraculously made her escape : just to bear witness by his attendance that, perilous bait or not, she was welcome to the haven of Grand Harbour for as long as she chose.

A stroke of luck assisted him. He looked up from his breviary to see a small ferry boat about to cast off from one of the quays in Sliema Creek. He knew the man in charge, a roly-poly character with a jolly name to match – Koli Apap : a distant cousin of the very man who ran the water-cart which brought water to the catacombs in the Cottonera Lines. It was this Koli Apap, his jaunty gold-crested cap proclaiming him at least an admiral of the Valletta waterfront, who now hailed him:

'Eh! Dun Salv! Are you coming with us?'

For a moment Father Salvatore could not remember where the ferry would take him. 'Where is it you land, Koli?'

Koli Apap clapped his hand to the side of his head, in theatrical despair. 'How can a man forget his own landing-place? The San Salvatore Bastion, in Marsa Muscetto Harbour, that's where we land! Your own bastion, Dun Salv! What more could you ask?'

'I was going to walk,' Father Salvatore said.

'Walk? Walking is for goats!' Koli had clearly taken a glass or two with his midday meal. 'It must be more than a mile. You know our motto. We may sink, but we save our feet!'

Everybody on board the little wooden ferry boat was grinning, enjoying the encounter. Father Salvatore could only join in the spirit of the moment.

'How much is the fare, Koli?'

'To anyone else in the world, one shilling. To you, Dun Salv' – Koli made a great show of frowning calculation, 'one shilling also. Otherwise I lose my licence.'

'What licence is that?' a voice came from behind him.

'Dog licence.'

There was a cackle of laughter. Koli Apap, standing in the stern, ignored it. He extended a courtly arm. 'Welcome aboard, *sur kappillan*. I always feel safe with a priest.'

'But does the priest feel safe with you?'

Thus they set out, with gusts of earthy laughter, with great good humour. Father Salvatore, sitting in the stern-sheets, squeezed between a man with a vast bundle of wicker fish-traps and a bulging woman hugging a fractious child, marvelled once again at the resilient spirit of the Maltese. People had already been killed, crossing Grand Harbour on just such a ferry boat as this. People would doubtless be killed again. This might be the very day appointed for it. But rough humour was enough to calm all such fears.

The humour had not mocked his priesthood. It was only meant to show that a priest, with one foot in heaven, was still a man of their world. He could not have asked for more generous acceptance – nor a better epitaph.

Koli Apap's boat, though named *Ferdinando* after the patron saint of engineers, was powered by machinery so ancient and asthmatic that it often seemed to miss a vital heartbeat between one moment and the next, like an old man climbing a punishing flight of steps; and their progress across the sunny blue water of the harbour was slow. But such slowness was a gain rather than a loss. They were plying their way past the history of Malta, bloody and triumphant at the same time, and the names, like the stones, cried out for recognition.

They chugged manfully past Dragut Point, where the eighty-year-old corsair Dragut Rais, Pasha of Tripoli, of evil yet heroic memory, fresh from his gory sacking of the Citadel of Gozo, had set up a battery of culverins during the great siege in order to pound the fortress of St Elmo into submission. In this endeavour he had forfeited his own life, being sliced through the head by a stone splinter from one of his own cannonballs.

They passed Manoel Island, first fortified by one of the greatest Grand Masters, Antonio Manoel de Vilhena, the pale, refined, aesthetic Portuguese whose fourteen-year reign was splendidly marked by buildings which still survived – much of the walled city of Mdina, the Manoel Theatre, erected in 1731 and now the oldest theatre of Europe, the once-exquisite Banca Giuratale in Gozo : a Grand Master who had tired, as La Valette had tired, of keeping his rebellious young Knights in order, who must have finally dismissed them with the later epitaph of Edward Gibbon – that they were prepared to die, but neglected to live, in the service of Christ.

(But why was he, Dun Salv, a faithful parish priest, thinking of that old villain Gibbon, so ludicrously anti-Papist, so prominent in the *Index Librorum Prohibitorum*? Was he composing his own forlorn epitaph, on this foreboding day? It would have been better by far if he had continued to plod along the Sliema road, his eyes firmly fixed on his breviary, instead of sowing and reaping yet another crop of fanciful thoughts, on a slothful journey across the harbour.)

They passed the mouth of Lazzaretto Creek, where in former days some the galleys of the Knights (which all carried the Blessed Sacrament into battle, for fear of untimely death) were moored : where now the baleful black submarines, which might still prove to be Malta's present succour, were ranged in tiers.

They drew near to their goal of Marsa Muscetto, a bastion of the island for 400 years.

It was across this harbour that the Knights, made furious by the death and decapitation of four of their comrades, whose bodies were then sent floating in on the sluggish tide, had taken their vengeance by butchering their most convenient victims, and firing back upon the opposing guns the most gruesome cannonade in the annals of war, the still-warm skulls of their Turkish captives.

There must be small droplets, tiny skeins of ancient blood, still suspended in this innocent clear water... The ferry *Ferdinando* was indeed sailing past history; and the moment it landed, a new page of that history began, as bloody as anything in the past.

The air-raid warning sounded: the great green-and-white pennant rose swiftly to the top of its staff on the Palace Tower, the highest point in Valletta; and as Koli Apap's passengers scurried to safety without a word of farewell, the noise of approaching aircraft triggered off a new and frightful sound.

Malta, and especially Valletta, and the Three Cities across the harbour, had by now grown used to fearful noises; they lived with noise, as they lived with food-rationing, and family upheaval, and death. But what they heard on that day was something scarcely to be imagined. Later it was to be described, officially, as the Box Barrage, a lethal and murderous cube of anti-aircraft shells exploding just above their heads, flung upwards by every shore gun which could fire, and orchestrated by the guns of *Illustrious* herself.

But on this, their first baptism of desperate defence, it was a sound so shattering that men could only tremble, and crouch close to the ground, as the curtain of steel burst upon the still air like the crack of doom. If their own guns could inflict such punishment, what could the enemy do?

The enemy did very well. They had come back for *Illustrious*, and in spite of this iron shield they hit her again.

Father Salvatore, stepping ashore from the *Ferdinando* and running for shelter as soon as the ferocious uproar began, experienced his first moment of stark terror. He had known that the attempt, and the punishment it was bound to inflict, would be awful; but this shattering assault was beyond imagination. Yet he was still driven to climb the heights of Valletta, and to watch: to make his way somehow towards the Floriana bastions, creeping onwards and upwards like a terrified cat, street by street, corner by corner, shelter by shelter, until *Illustrious*, and the harbour, and the savage slaughter beyond, came into his view.

By then he was trembling uncontrollably. Constantly he had to wipe the sweat from his eyes, in order to see what was happening. But presently his sweat was freely mingling with his tears, as he was forced to witness the punishment raining down upon the twin targets of the enemy: his own big ship, and his own small people.

The Stuka dive-bombers, about a hundred of them, were coming in very high from the south-east, circling their target, and then plummeting down upon it. In spite of the 'box-barrage', so terrifying to the earthbound, so perilous to the airborne, the Stukas plunged through it and then continued on downwards, as straight as rails.

The successive waves, piloted by young men of superb courage – who could deny that? – dived with an eerie whine, increasing to a monstrous scream as they neared ground level. This could be heard as far away as Gozo, so Rafel Vella reported later. 'Even my poor mother was forced to listen to the noise!' he told Dun Salv, as if this were some special affront to the faithful. Perhaps it was. Closer to the source, it was an affront to every sense which could be called human.

At the moment when the diving noise became unbearable, the bombs began to fall, and the earth began to shake.

Amid great bursts of spray, the *Illustrious* was directly hit, by a huge bomb which went down the same lift-shaft as had almost proved mortal to her before. Father Salvatore watched, fascinated, horrified, and shaking with fear, as other bombs crashed down on the dockyard, on the water boiling all round the ship, and on the houses and shops of the Three Cities, swiftly pulverized into a great cloud of evil yellow smoke.

The statistics were to come later: 900 homes shattered, 500 people killed or injured, in the first hour of the attack; for the watcher from the shore, all that could be perceived was a relentless, merciless rain of death.

The shock-waves roared and pounded across the Floriana Heights in an engulfing storm. What must it be like, to live or to die in the eye of that hurricane? ... *Illustrious* was hit again, and seemed to stagger under the scourge of pain. Fierce fires enveloped a merchant ship unloading near by, a ship which weeks later was known to be the *Essex*, crammed with ammunition which miraculously did not explode. (But even if it had been known *then*, was there any terror which could have been added to the terror before one's eyes?) The harbour, taking its fearful punishment, became a cauldron of smoke and flame and columns of erupting water. Beyond it, the near-misses and the over-spill of bombs were falling upon Cospicua, and the Cottonera Lines, and his own people.

The smell and then the smoke billowed up, spreading a death-like pall across the harbour, blotting out the sun, hiding God's eyes. Nothing which had happened so far, in all the pitiless misery of their war, could compare with what was happening now.

It took him a long time to reach the Cottonera Lines. He began his weary pilgrimage, which could only end in grief and horror, on foot; there was no other way, nor, on this day of terror, would he have expected any. An absurd and blasphemous thought – that as he trudged along he was matching the footsteps of another Man on the way to Calvary – was quickly quelled. The crucified dead were already waiting for him; and the road was downhill.

He made first for Hamrun, the town which lay between Floriana and the Three Cities. Hamrun, he saw, with preliminary misgiving, had itself been bombed; and he found himself, as so often before, caught up in its miserable tide of refugees, moving mindlessly away in any direction which would take them from certain shock to supposed peace.

The fact that the people he met were fleeing *towards* Valletta, a prime centre of peril, was part of the same evil dream; the fact that his own way led him past certain sad evidences of corruption – not the bombed houses, but the shops hurriedly boarded up, and the troops standing by in case of looting – completed the small nightmare of debasement.

Then he began to meet the real overflow of pain and fear: the people streaming out of the Three Cities, pale, haggard, and seemingly stupefied by what they had seen and suffered: young and old alike all terrified in the same degree, except that while the children cried, the women shrieked their recital of the Rosary and the men cursed and fought anything which stood in their way.

By now he had secured a lift, in a flat-boarded, high-wheeled Maltese cart drawn by one of the smallest, ugliest donkeys he had ever seen: a plodding pigmy of a donkey, which once again reminded him of a blasphemous parallel – that Christ Himself had been borne into Jerusalem on just such a patient animal, on a Palm Sunday two thousand years ago: and that a poet had blessed the ennobled beast with all the necessary words of the humble and the despised:

> The tattered outlaw of the earth,
> Of ancient crooked will;
> Starve, scourge, deride me: I am dumb,
> I keep my secret still.

> Fools! For I also had my hour;
> One far fierce hour and sweet:
> There was a shout about my ears,
> And palms before my feet.

But he found a ready antidote to such wild and whirling thoughts: the man who drove the donkey-cart, a sour-faced, spitting, rebellious old farmer who had hesitated a long time, and then demanded passage-money, before giving Father Salvatore his lift. They had only exchanged a couple of sentences, as they rumbled along the coast road round the Marsa, the lower end of Grand Harbour.

The opposing flood of refugees who barred their way – it had happened to him before, on the very first day of war: one either walked with grief, or tried to stem its tide – prompted Father Salvatore to ask the farmer why he was going in this direction at this particular time.

'God knows!' the man replied, with extraordinary venom. 'I've made two trips already. More than four hours on this cursed road!' He whipped up the donkey, with a vicious flailing of his arm. 'Took all the sheep and rabbits to my brother's place, out at Qormi.'

'But now you're going back again?'

'Got to fetch the wife.'

After that, Father Salvatore sat with his aching feet hanging over the tail-board, leaving the man to curse and spit and lash his wretched donkey as he wished. It was a relief when they stopped at a crossroads on the outskirts of Paola, and the farmer snarled 'That's as far as I'm taking you,' and Father Salvatore said 'God bless you.' He was really speaking to the donkey.

It was a much greater relief to get another lift in a British Army ambulance, manned by cheerful and determined young men who said 'Hop up, Father!' and 'Hold on tight! Fares, please!' and even sang, astonishingly: 'We're off to see the wizard, the wonderful wizard of Oz!' as they rocked along the pitted road. When presently he asked where they were going, the driver, who had blood on his hands and sleeves, answered: 'Senglea again. There's been an incident.'

In Senglea, an earlier 'incident' – that strangely insufficient word out of the Air Raid Precautions Manual – had partly destroyed the beautiful baroque church of Our Lady of Victories, built by La Valette himself at the founding of the city, and had stopped its clock on the instant of destruction, at twenty minutes past two on that January day. For years afterwards, passers-by were to be reminded by it of the exact moment when life, for the church and many of its faithful, had ceased to be.

The toll of mutilation and death all around had been brought up to date, within the last hour, by another monstrous blow from the sky; and it was this which Father Salvatore, and the ambulance crew who now lost their merry humour, began to salvage, amid the familiar rubbish-tip of shattered glass, corpses, broken beams, spent shells, dead dogs, cats, and poultry, choking layers of dust, and the faint chance of surviving life.

Perhaps the worst thing about it was that it *was* familiar. Six months earlier, Father Salvatore would still have been astonished and appalled to see himself as a crouching, blood-stained figure, elbow-deep in dust and dirt and crushed humanity and pain and the ebbing tide of life. He would have found unbearable the living victims of this violence: the people who now crept out of their shelters like ancient cave-dwellers whom some cataclysm of the earth's crust had rendered homeless, shocked, deafened, and bleeding.

He would have found pitiful beyond endurance the people

scratching with their bare hands to rescue those trapped, or believed to be trapped, underneath the ruined buildings, while now and then the rescue squads sounded a whistle for silence, so that they could listen for any sign of hope. He would have found insupportable the number of dead and dying, and the fact that his little gold phial of holy oil was, within an hour, empty.

But now all this was normal.

As he worked on, in company with scores of others, the excruciating noise of the box barrage exploded again, hammering upon their bowed heads, cancelling any puny efforts to listen for signs of life below ground. While a new air-raid started, the rescuers still toiled on, their knees and feet often in pools of blood. Father Salvatore was giving all his shocked attention to yet another dying man, under whose shredded clothes was a body so racked with pain that it was like one great open mouth, screaming with agony, when the sound of two gun-shots near by disturbed him.

Momentarily he looked round, to see a policeman standing over a dead dog, its bloody muzzle still half-buried in flesh torn from a corpse.

Father Salvatore wept. Then, a few seconds later, he found that he was humming a tune. Was he mad, was he mad? ... It was an aria from the first opera he had ever seen, in Rome as a boy: its name, *La Forza del Destino*, and the song, the heart-rending *Madre, Madre pietosa Vergine*, with which Leonora de Vargas acknowledged at last her utter despair. Near the end of life, she had given away to railing curses – *Maledizion! Maledizion!* – at some vile intruder; and Father Salvatore could have echoed them from his heart, as the man beneath his hands also achieved death, through the most terrible gateway he had ever witnessed.

When it was over he sat back on his haunches, sick unto dying himself. Then he heard his name called – '*Dun Salv! Dun Salv! Have a swig of whisky!*' – and he laughed aloud through bitter tears to see beside him a man even madder than himself, little Nero Cassar.

Nero presented a really extraordinary figure, even on that day of violent surprises. He had managed to equip himself with something which looked like a tiny blue RAF battledress, topped by a tin hat fashioned from a hammered-out saucepan.

Slung across his shoulders was a gas-mask haversack: from his leather waist-belt hung a regulation Army water-bottle. He had a sheath knife tucked into the top of one boot, and a swagger-cane in the other. A bottle of whisky and a tin cup completed his equipment.

As he hopped about among the rubble and the dead and the dying, his beaked nose swivelling this way and that, he looked for all the world like a little mad clown pretending to be a pirate. But the stains on his hands and cuffs could only have been blood.

'Nero!' Father Salvatore exclaimed. He was so glad to see this lunatic apparition, bouncing out of the flame-flickering darkness like the dwarf Alberich in *Götterdämmerung*, that he could have wept again. 'What on earth are you doing here?'

'Looking for you, Dun Salv. And helping, helping. When the bombs began to fall, I elected to join the ARP. There's no use just sitting still, is there? And how do you like my uniform?' Without waiting for an answer he glanced down at the tortured figure lying at Father Salvatore's feet. 'Well, we can save the whisky on that one, can't we?'

'He is on his way to heaven, Nero,' Father Salvatore said reprovingly. Half-deafened, they were both shouting at each other, even though there was a lull in the uproar. 'Think of his soul. Pray for it.'

A curious look – half cynical, half sad – came over Nero's face. 'God must be busy listening tonight.'

'But He is never *too* busy.'

'I hope not.' There was a mutter of distant guns, and then the hideous sound of the box barrage erupted over their heads once more, so that it was scarcely possible for them to hear each other. 'Here they come again!' Nero shouted. His sweating face, turned to the sky, was alerted to danger like a hunting dog's. 'We'd be better off in the catacomb, Dun Salv. And they need you there. That's why I wanted to find you. It's time to speak to them again. There are people half-mad with worry, all screaming at each other.'

Father Salvatore looked round him. There was certainly little more to be done here: the wounds had all been bound up, and the dead speeded towards eternity. Then another bomb fell in the harbour near by, and the moonlight glistened on

the giant water-spout thrown up, and on the curtain of spray
as it drifted downwards again. He was reminded of another
target, another orphan in their care.

'We must try to be brave,' he shouted back. 'We must bear
all the pain we have to, while they're making the big ship
ready to go to sea again.'

'To hell with the big ship!' It was a wicked and blasphemous
thing to say, but little Nero, now jumping up and down, waving
his bottle of whisky, seemed past caring about such things.
Perhaps the whisky bottle was the clue... 'We still have our
own people to think of, Dun Salv. *Please* come to the catacombs,
and speak to them! Show them how to bear the pain. Before
they all die of fright!'

The noise coming from within the catacombs was almost as
frightening as the noise without. As they passed beneath the
great stone and rock face of the Cottonera Lines, and through
the screened doorway, they could hear a high-pitched sound,
wild and wailing, like a herd of baby cattle in stampede; closer
to, it could be defined more certainly, though the translation
was not comforting.

It was made up of shouting and screaming and weeping: of
dogs barking, sheep bleating, children crying, women beseeching help, men calling for silence on a note of strident alarm.
Father Salvatore could also hear prayers amid the clamour.

Prayers had always been welcome to his ears, but not these
prayers, which were infected with a desperate fear. There was
even the smell of fear, wafting along the tunnels to supply
odious confirmation of the chaos within, to prove that these
sounds came from the throats of God's creatures, animal and
human, in a sweat of terror.

He walked out of the shadows as briskly as he could, flogging
a tired body and a confused mind to make the best entrance at
his command. He was greeted with sudden silence, and then
a gasp of horror. Dishevelled, blood-stained, and exhausted, he
must have seemed a living proof that Death lay in wait for all
who ventured outside, and could even reach them here with
one careless stroke of his scythe.

Father Salvatore blessed them, with an uplifted hand, and
made the sign of the cross, as if to prove his credentials. He
bent his knee to the altar, with its magnificent gold crucifix

and gleaming altar-cloth – both of them his mother's gift. Then he climbed the steps to the stone pulpit which Rafel Vella had built for him, and spread his hands on either side of the microphone which was Nero Cassar's contribution, and looked down upon his people.

It could have been a scene from the Inferno, brought up to date by the evil devices of man. Under the vaulted ceiling, smoky and filled with shadows, men and women, children and dogs, were all huddled together in what seemed the last stage of misery and desperation. Some were propped up in their beds, watching him. Some were quarrelling, some drinking, some singing; some were on their knees, some on their wives. Others peered fearfully out of the narrow rock fissures which lined the main concourse, like goatherds affrighted by a meteorite, an eclipse of the moon, a prowling lion.

Somewhere, he knew, all the little dead friars must be looking down from their carved niches, horrified and ashamed at this desecration.

The crash of a bomb near by, and the shudder of the earth under their feet and loins, released fresh screams, fresh panic. He saw the huge Rafel wrestling with a man who insanely tried to fight another. He saw Nero hugging a tormented child to his narrow chest. He recalled Nero saying, a few dark minutes ago: 'You *must* speak to them, Dun Salv.'

It was true. He, Father Salvatore, must also play his part. This was the night for it, the second terrible night. But what should he speak of?

The men and events of a thousand years before the Blessed Saviour were too far away, too remote from the terrors of reality. It must be someone, or something, nearer to their present ordeal.

It should be someone who had seen Him, and could humbly pass on His message of peace. Someone in danger, someone tortured, insulted, and betrayed in the same way.

Someone who knew the fear of death, yet had conquered death, the last enemy. Someone who had survived shipwreck and misery and fury from the skies.

Someone who had brought hope and faith to this very island.

Father Salvatore bent down and blew fiercely through the microphone, as he had watched and heard sailors and airmen and air-raid wardens do. Mutinous silence at last surrendered to

the crude blast of his breath. Then his voice rang clearly through
the loudspeakers, and echoed through the caverns beyond:

'*Uliedi!* Children! God bless you! God love you and keep you
safe. The Mother of God protect you from harm... Let us now
praise famous men.'

HEXAMERON TWO

In the Year of Our Lord, 60
An Illustrious Gift from the Sea

He began with a string of texts, which did not sound too promising; it meant that this could be just an ordinary sermon, in spite of 'Let us now praise famous men', which they remembered as a prelude to delight, and they did not want sermons on a night like this. Father Salvatore detected a familiar 'settling down' atmosphere – settling down to be bored, or at least dutifully neutral towards admonishment – when he announced:

'There was once a man who told us: "Comfort ye, comfort ye my people, saith your God," and I have repeated this to you many times.

'The same man, knowing that we were to be puzzled and afraid, said to us: "For now we see through a glass, darkly; but then face to face."

'He also said: "We brought nothing into this world, and it is certain that we can carry nothing out."

'He also said – and we should be proud to say it too: "I have fought a good fight, I have finished my course, I have kept the faith."

'He also said: "O death, where is thy sting? O grave, where is thy victory?"

'He also said – to us, tonight. "Behold, I show you a mystery: we shall not all sleep, but we shall all be changed." '

There was a stirring among the listeners at this, because the words did seem to be directly spoken to themselves, the sleepless; and another when Father Salvatore went on:

'This man said, and you have heard it from me a thousand times: "The peace of God, which passeth all understanding, shall keep your hearts and minds through Christ Jesus." For many of you, that is probably your favourite text,' he continued, in a different tone of voice, 'because it is the end of the homily, the dismissal, and you can all go home.'

There was subdued laughter at this, laughter and a feeling of hope. The *kappillan* did not make such jokes in church. There must be something special coming. The feeling was confirmed when Father Salvatore went on:

'The man of whom I speak also said words which have echoed down to us today, for quite a different reason: "Now abideth faith, hope, charity, these three; but the greatest of these is charity." '

The aeroplanes, the three little planes which had saved them! ... There *must* be a story coming, a story of Malta, a story for themselves alone. They knew for certain what was in store when Father Salvatore added, with that special inflexion which heralded one of his small, off-duty jokes:

'He, the man I am quoting, was the most *illustrious* man ever to arrive in Malta, though it cost the wreck of a fine ship to bring him here.'

Illustrious... Of course! ... They now knew that they were safe, and swiftly they settled down, in quite a different way, to enjoy his words, and to hear him begin:

'Saint Paul – and there are *no* prizes for guessing Saint Paul – was a little man, like me, and he was seasick. Four weeks from today we celebrate the shipwreck which threw him up on to the rocks in our own St Paul's Bay. He came ashore ...'

He came ashore, bruised, half-drowned, shivering with deadly ague, after the most fearful voyage in a life which had sub-

jected him to many such ordeals. He gave thanks to his dear
friend and dead master, Jesus, for the fact that he had escaped
death, though he knew in his hammering heart that death still
lay in store for him, within a few weeks or months.

If it was not to be the sea, then the hangman or the heads-
man, the strangler or the poisoner, the gladiator or the lion,
were waiting for him in Rome; and to Rome he must go, as a
bound prisoner who had appealed for final trial before Caesar
himself.

It had been a long, cruel, and glorious journey, this life of
his. Since death, on the harsh winter coast of Malta, had
stayed its hand, a little of that life must be set aside for him.
Since he had been spared, it was for the mysterious purposes
of God. He whispered aloud, through chattering teeth: 'Thanks
be to that God. Thank You, Jesus. I live for You. I die for You.
I love You.' Then painfully he crawled across the rocks towards
safety and warmth.

What had brought him to Malta, at the end of life, was
strange to him, though crystal clear to God because God had
sketched the plan. Paul accepted all things, and regretted
nothing except the evil days before he saw the light.

He was then a fiery little Jew, a Pharisee and a bigot, who
had excelled in hunting down, rooting out, and wreaking vengeance on all Christian souls, whether professed or suspect, for
their filthy crime of accepting Christ as the Messiah. There had
been enough consuming hatred in his heart to drive him to promote a charge of blasphemy against Stephen, and then to watch
this, the first Christian saint and martyr, stoned to death in
his presence.

But that was before Damascus, the division of his life between
hate and love, the sudden light from heaven which changed
him in so many ways – from a hawk to a dove, from a hyaena
for Satan to a lion for the Lord, and (though he did not know
it, and would have grimly derided it if he had) from a sinner
to a saint.

It was Saint Luke, telling the story, who called it 'a light
from heaven' bursting upon Paul on the road to Damascus
(where he had a choice piece of Christian witch-hunting
arranged), a light which struck him blind for the next three
days, while a voice demanded: 'Why persecutest thou Me?' It

was a fantastic story, and not all who heard it would accept it.

Some said that it was a trick, to gain the confidence and then the secrets of his Christian prey. Some said he had had a fit, or had been struck by lightning for his sins. Some, more charitable or more hopeful, said that he had seen a vision of the crucifixion at the moment it occurred, when Christ and Paul were both thirty-three years old, and only Paul lived on.

If this was so, he was lucky, and the world was lucky. For whatever it was, it turned this little monster of darkness into an apostle of light. It made him the most potent missionary the world had ever seen, and a tireless traveller for Christ.

Sometimes alone, sometimes with Barnabas, or John Mark, or Luke himself, he crossed and recrossed the whole Mediterranean seaboard, from Corinth to Athens, from Antioch to Palestine, from here to there and back again. He preached the gospel, he persuaded, he wrestled with men's souls; he was loved by many, he was mobbed by many more, and spat upon, and scourged by Roman lictors, and thrown into prison.

When, sadly, he quarrelled with Barnabas, his best friend, and the first man to persuade other Christians that Paul's conversion on the Damascus road was no confidence trick, but a miracle from heaven, Paul went on alone, until he made new friends to bear him company. It was not always easy.

Paul was never well fitted for such fierce ordeals, nor for the close human contacts on which so much depended. He was small and ugly, with bushy eyebrows joined together above a big hooked nose; he was nearly bald, and his short crooked legs carried him awkwardly. He had what he himself called a thorn or stake in the flesh, which 'buffeted' him, and humiliated him every day of his life.

The exact nature of this humiliating thorn – or stake – has remained doubtful for ever afterwards; somewhere between scholarship and forensic medicine, guesswork always takes over, and gives a dozen answers. 'Humiliation' implies some affliction which could be heard or seen : a persistent stammer, or those embarrassing blotches of red colour on the skin, nicknamed St Anthony's Fire and later called erysipelas.

Recurrent epilepsy must surely have seemed a 'buffeting' adversary. A thorn in the flesh could describe daily headaches, or some diseases aggravated by the fierce Mediterranean sun. Pos-

sibly Paul had malaria; its spasms could prostrate him at any
time, and leave him with no feeling stronger than self-disgust
at his own incapacity.

On the other hand, a migraine, that shattering pain which
seems to divide the skull in half, leaving one side, and one eye,
as blank and useless as a shrivelled claw, could certainly feel
like a stake in the head.

Ecce homo – here was the man, anyway: small, ugly, awkward, ashamed, never knowing when he was going to stammer,
or come out in blotches, or fall in a fit, or run at the eyes, or
shake with fever, or scream for the mercy of darkness when
his head was split; and as such he was committed to work and
travel, speak and argue, in the service of his Lord, for as long
as he lived. What was truly marvellous was that he did so
with such tireless energy and devotion.

Yet there was something else. There was always something
else with Saint Paul. Persistently, it was said that 'sometimes
he had the face of an angel'. *This man?* Yes, this man, this
magical man. Perhaps it was such angelic glimpses of glory,
and his sweet reason, and his burning faith, which began to
bring in the converts. Also, in spite of his physical drawbacks
and embarrassments, he was a good mixer; he had knocked
about the world more than most, and though it was the small
world of the Mediterranean, it then loomed as large and as
various as the whole globe. In this world, he had learned to
talk to anyone he met.

His reputation as a woman-hater was a twisted version of
what he really felt and preached. Wherever he travelled in
Asia, he found sex-cults which no true Christian could sub-
scribe to. The idea of a woman as the plaything of man was
anathema to him. If he became over-protective in this regard,
or disciplinarian, it was in a good cause – the cause of chastity.

A man might be the lord of creation – under the Lord – but
a woman *was* creation. She *must* have the final say. She must
be honoured, and set apart. She must be allowed, encouraged,
ordered to say No if she felt like it. If part of that No was to
conceal a beautiful head of hair in the company of men, then
she must be encouraged to that also.

What Paul really loathed, among a great category of sin,
was the degradation of women in the pagan world. What he
really loved was Christ. 'For me to live is Christ,' he said

constantly. No one who talked to him, whether friend or foe, mocker or martyr, could be in any doubt of it.

So, as he travelled, he made many converts, men and women, Jew and Gentile. With this success came an avalanche of anger from his enemies, which made him the target for a hatred just as virulent as his own had ever been.

The Jews could not forgive him two things: for being a turncoat who knew too much for anyone's comfort – he had been briefed to *persecute* Christians, not to change sides, cherish them, and propagate their odious faith; and for preaching the Messiah, not to the elect, the chosen, but to any Gentile dog or pagan rascal who would listen.

What was the good, the Jews asked – and they often asked it in screaming rage, sparked by that violent pride of race which, after all their travail, one could understand, if not forgive – what was the good of telling *everyone* that Jesus Christ was the longed-for Messiah?

If it was true, then He was the Jews' Messiah, not the public property of any unbeliever, any infidel who happened to be passing through the market-place. If it was not true, then the man who proclaimed it was a vile blasphemer, and it was a duty and a pleasure to slake the thirsty earth with his blood.

The pagan rascals could not forgive Paul because they were quite happy with their own forms of worship, and wanted none of them changed, especially by some wandering trouble-maker who had nothing to lose. When Paul described all other gods, and in particular Roman deities like Juno, or Apollo, or Proserpine, as myths, it was offensive for a whole variety of reasons. It was also bad for trade.

One of the most memorable riots which Saint Paul could recall, in a lifetime of such tumults, was set off by one Demetrius, a silversmith of Ephesus, who made his living from selling statues and shrines of the goddess Diana. Demetrius saw his business sagging, and blamed it on Paul. He called together his fellow trade-unionists, told them most eloquently that if things went on like this they would all be ruined, and set them on to Paul like a pack of hungry dogs.

For the space of two hours he was surrounded by a murderous, mindless mob who would not hear him, but screeched, again and again, the same slogan: '*Great is Diana of the Ephesians!*' as they lashed themselves towards the final violence. Paul was rescued at last by a brave town-clerk, who must have been at least as eloquent as Demetrius. He told the furious accusers: 'The law is open. If you have a complaint, make it in the courts. This is *not* the way to do it. Now go home.' Amazingly, they went. But it was a very near thing.

Yet the Jews were always the worst, the most threatening, the most strident in their calls for vengeance, as perhaps they had a right to be. Paul's new doctrine, after years of preaching to the Jews and being rejected and harassed in the process, that only by freeing Christianity from its tie with Judaism could it become a world faith, had all the weight of total insult, and they responded in kind.

They hounded him wherever he travelled; they spied on him, and sent secret intelligence of where he was going, so that a mob, or a riot, or a ferocious inquisition was always waiting for him, to explode its fury in his face. These were tempestuous and frightening years; often he must have wondered why he ever left Tarsus, where he was born to all the privileges of Roman citizenship, where he had a good trade – tent-making in summer, sail-making in winter, and solid security at all times.

He was uplifted only by his faith in Christ, solaced only by the converts he made, and their abounding love which found expression in ways so deeply moving that they could readily bring him to tears. Whenever he had to say farewell – and his tireless travelling involved more farewells than any man could count – the local Christians, full of foreboding that Paul must always be going to his death, first begged him not to leave, and then came down to the seashore in a body to see him off.

Sometimes they knelt in the sand, pricked with purple murex shells, as they said their desperate goodbye. The children, affected by grown-up emotion, solemnly staring at this funny old man with the bow legs who could make their mothers and fathers so happy and then so sad, added the final touch of tender distraction.

'What mean ye to weep, and break my heart?' Saint Paul would ask, in gentle chiding, only to be overcome by weeping himself. Then he would set sail: ever further, ever onwards, towards his final appointment.

Presently the Jews booked that final appointment. They engineered his downfall, and his world began to crack.

It could have been no more than another murderous riot in the life of this besieged man, but this time it went too far, and Roman authority, with its preference for the quiet life, was at last forced to act. Now Paul was in Jerusalem, in the very footsteps of his Master; now the orthodox Jews, driven to frenzy by his presence on such hallowed territory, closed in for what they hoped would be another kill.

They staged a gigantic riot to coincide with one of his public appearances with Luke, his faithful companion in adversity. They milled about in tumultuous crowds; at the word of command, a well-drilled, hard-core mob tore their clothes in unison, threw dust in the air, and shrieked: 'Away with such a fellow from the earth! Kill him! kill him!'

Roman Governor Claudius Lysias, with a reputation to keep up, did not want this sort of thing on his own front doorstep, and he took the simple way out, which was to arrest Paul as the cause of this disgraceful uproar, and threaten him with scourging if he did not clear out. Paul pleaded his Roman citizenship, which meant that such treatment was illegal; he had disdained to claim this protection, once before in the early days, and the memory of those cruel stripes must have lingered with him ever afterwards.

But the continuing cry of 'Kill him!' was real; it rang in Lysias's ears just as loudly as in Paul's, and Lysias knew from his intelligence corps that a lynching party of forty Jews was lying in wait for Paul, bound by a most solemn oath neither to eat nor drink until they had done him to death. They would surely pounce as soon as he was released. It would look *very* bad in the half-yearly dispatches to Rome... Lysias once again took the simplest course, to rid himself of a dangerous nuisance before Christian blood stained the clean white sheets of his command.

Since it was impossible to smuggle out such a rare prize, he gave Paul an armed escort tough and disciplined enough to hack a pathway through any opposition, however brutal or cunning – 200 soldiers, seventy horsemen, 200 spearmen – and drove this awkward little hostage through the raging mob to the care of the Procurator Antonius Felix of Caesarea, sixty-two miles away up the coast.

If Claudius Lysias was a prudent career-soldier with hopes of other comfortable governorships in the future, Antonius

Felix, on whom Paul had been palmed off, was a venal, jumped-up coward with two contemptible mottoes – 'Safety first', and 'What's in it for me?'. On him, Tacitus the historian passed an acid judgement: 'He wielded the power of a monarch with the disposition of a slave,' and he was to give ample proof of both segments of activity in the immediate future.

He kept Paul in prison for the next two years, officially 'deferring his verdict', though the suspicion that he was hoping for a bribe in return for Paul's release was common gossip, sustained both by his reputation and by the fact that he frequently sent for Paul and talked of this and that with engaging optimism.

When the time came for Felix to be relieved as governor, he remembered 'Safety first' and, 'being willing to show the Jews a pleasure', pocketed the spoils of office and left the prisoner still in custody.

As sometimes happens when appointments change hands, whether it concerns a proconsul, or the captain of a ship, or even a bishop, the man who took over as Procurator of Judaea was in total contrast with his predecessor. He was Porcius Festus, an upright and honest man, who would as soon have thought of soiling his hands with loot as he would have considered running naked through the streets at high noon. He came in to clean up the stables; and one of his cleansing jobs was to deal with the matter of Saint Paul.

As soon as he had time he sent for Paul. He examined him, and his accusers, in great detail; he listened for truth and for lies, he weighed the man against his enemies, and all of them against the eternally tricky situation of ruling a province which had its own Jewish king, under a military occupation which had its own ideas of decency and order.

In the face of a threatened Jewish revolt, he decided that Paul was, after all, the trouble-maker who must be punished, or at least sent back to a seething Jerusalem to be tried. When this dire verdict was announced Paul again pleaded his Roman citizenship. This guaranteed that he could never be scourged; he could not be crucified; and he had the right to appeal to his emperor against any provincial law. He appealed to Caesar, and thus he had to be remanded, and sent to Rome by the first available ship.

One curious happening distinguished those last few days in Caesarea. That Jewish king, Herod Agrippa, expressed a wish to meet Paul; to see him and to hear him. Once more, Paul was brought out from his cell to face an enemy. Herod's sister, Berenice, was an interested spectator. So was Governor Festus.

King Herod Agrippa was the last of a cruel line, great-grandson of the Herod who had ordered the slaughter of the Holy Innocents – all the children to be found in Bethlehem under two years of age – in order to catch the infant Jesus in his murderous net. Agrippa was in fact the current 'King of the Jews', whose dynasty Jesus had been accused of supplanting.

Saint Paul, with hopes of freedom, might well have been daunted. Instead, he launched into an impassioned plea, not for his own skin, but for Jesus Christ.

He made it with such force, such candour, and such shattering eloquence that Porcius Festus, well disposed towards his prisoner, was appalled, and tried to halt him in mid-flow. He called out – he shouted: 'Paul, thou art beside thyself! Much learning hath made thee mad!'

'I am not mad, most noble Festus,' the answer came gently and firmly. 'I speak the words of truth and soberness.'

He went on to speak such words, and Herod Agrippa heard him out. At the end, the King of the Jews could only say to Festus: 'This man might have been set at liberty, if he had not appealed to Caesar,' and to Paul himself: 'Almost thou persuadest me to be a Christian.'

In the circumstances, coming from such a man, such a black-browed autocrat whose blood ran hot at the very whisper of Christ, the words – and particularly the word 'almost' – might have been a good Herodian joke, and nothing more. But if they were truly meant, then they were Paul's greatest triumph of persuasion. Perhaps it was one of the days when he had, beyond compare, the face of an angel.

But he *had* appealed to Caesar, and to Caesar he must go. Nothing now stood between him and his last voyage. Ageing, tired, battered by fate and his enemies, always in fear, sustained only by faith, he must embark for Rome, where he would be on trial for his life: where he was to lose that life, indeed, at the hands of a demented tyrant whose name alone was a byword for all things bloodthirsty, and wicked, and cruel. The name was Nero.

Though the story was really too terrible for laughter, there

*were a few sniggers here, and some sidelong glances at little
Nero Cassar, who had now given the sleeping child back to
its mother and was standing sentinel under Father Salvatore's
pulpit. So that was where Nero got his name! A mad tyrant,
eh? No wonder he jumped about like a jack-in-a-box, and
would not let them play the gramophone when they wanted
to. Such a little emperor!*

Paul began his journey in a small coasting vessel which carried
him from Caesarea, under the lee of Cyprus, to Myra on the
south coast of Turkey. The party was in the command of one
Julius, a centurion of the Augustan Cohort, whose word was
law. He was in charge of the prisoners, and of his own soldiers,
and of the crew, who were mostly Phoenicians, and of the
master of the vessel. When they all transferred to a new ship
for the main part of their journey, this precedence was un-
altered.

Julius's new command, and Paul's new prison, was an Alexandrian corn-ship, the largest and finest of the century, the
equivalent of a crack transatlantic liner, bound direct for Rome.
By modern standards she was tiny – less than a hundred feet
long; but at that time she was the very best that could be built
for the deep-water carrying trade. Such ships of the Roman
grain fleet had an importance political as well as maritime; they
brought in the corn ration which, distributed freely to needy
plebeians, kept them happy – or, by its non-arrival, made them
unhappy and therefore mutinous.

On sailing-day, the ship's complement was set down as:
sailors, one hundred: soldiers, one hundred: prisoners, seventy-
six. They embarked on a sea and a voyage as stormy and
perilous as anything in Paul's own perilous life.

Bleak winter was well advanced, and the Mediterranean, by
tradition and by hard experience, was greatly feared, at any
time between mid-November and the tenth day of March. Any
merchant captain, not under pressure, kept his ship snug in
harbour; any fisherman with sense in his head hauled up his
boat and wintered with his wife and children, mending his nets
against the day when he could ply his trade without fear of
leaving a widow and a draggle-tail of orphans to gaze seaward
in hopeless grief.

Even the birds soared up and away, flying south in search of

warmth and calm airs; even the fish dived deep and stayed out
of sight. Better for Julius and his *centuria* of soldiers, better for
the ship-master and his crew, better for Paul and his fellow-
prisoners, if they had followed the birds instead of risking a
rendezvous with the fish.

But a Roman grain-ship had a timetable to follow, and a
Roman centurion had his orders. They sailed from Myra in
accordance with both; traditional fears proved well-founded;
they plunged straightway into desperate trouble.

A foul wind forced them northwards, to another Turkish
port which they had not planned to visit; when they dared
to leave harbour again, they were turned inexorably south,
and their next landfall was Crete, which was not on their
charted course either. There they took refuge under the shelter
of the Cretan hills, in a south-coast port called Fair Havens,
and here, while they waited for the wind to change, they held
a council.

Paul, though the most notorious of the captives, was invited
to that council, which says much for his formidable personality
and more still for the common sense of Centurion Julius, who
recognized that while a prisoner was always a prisoner, a world
traveller such as Paul, with great experience of the sea, was
someone worth listening to.

They had to decide whether to stay where they were, and
see the winter out; or to shift berth to some better harbour
on the island; or to continue the voyage, come what may. Paul's
advice – and it was *possibly* the advice of a man who was in
no hurry to get to Rome, where his life might be quickly
forfeit – Paul's advice was to stay where they were in Fair
Havens. He prophesied, in Luke's words, 'hurt and much damage
if they moved, not only of the lading and the ship, but also
of our lives'.

The centurion, less of a sailor than a soldier with orders to
proceed forthwith from Point A to Point B, wanted to hoist
sail and get on with it. But he had, in this one respect, to defer
to the master of the ship, who knew, in this alien world, what
was probable, what was possible, and what was stupid.

The master's advice, which Julius accepted, was that they
should move from Fair Havens to a better harbour, farther
along the Cretan coast, where they could lie up till the spring.
He had his eye on Phenice, on the western side of the island.

'Very well,' said Julius the centurion, after long discussion. 'Phenice it is. But if the weather gets better, we'll carry on as planned.' Every day of this voyage cost public money; though prisoners were dirt-cheap – cheaper than rats, which *stole* the grain – soldiers had to be paid by the day, and the vessel itself was on government charter which, since there were Egyptian shipbrokers involved, was sheer daylight robbery. He did not look at Paul, whom he liked, whom he had talked to, whom he now had to overrule. 'But for Jupiter's sake, let's do it *now*!'

They did it now; and scarcely had they let go the mooring-lines than everything, as Paul had foretold, began to go wrong.

After a brief, treacherous hour of calm, they were struck by a ferocious *gregale*, the north-easterly 'Greek Wind' against which no ship could make an inch of headway. They could not round up to get back into Fair Havens; they could not even turn north to make for Phenice; they could only bear away and, as Luke put it, 'let her drive'. There then began a nightmare of two weeks – fourteen days, 336 hours – when they were trapped in this howling wilderness, and could do nothing but crouch under its fury, and stagger down-wind into unknown hazards.

They used every trick of seamanship, in grey days and evil black nights, to ward off the blows of this fearful sea. They reduced sail to a patch of canvas, just enough to keep the ship from slewing broadside on to the waves, and lowered all the unused spars. They lightened her as much as possible, by throwing most of the spare gear overboard, and half the cargo. When the tortured frame began to loosen, and the planks started to gape, they bound them round with ropes, and tightened them on the windlass, to try to hold the hull together. They kept pace with the leaks by furious baling.

All the time, they were in terror of the unknown. The ship, even under bare poles and a kerchief of sailcloth, was surging westwards down the Mediterranean, helpless and half water-logged. Ahead lay rocks and islands on which they might strike before they realized the peril under their bows. Ahead were the shoals and quicksands of North Africa, or even the un-speakable void of – who could tell? – the great ocean beyond the Pillars of Hercules.

No glimpse of the sun or the stars reached them for many days. Weak from hunger and cold, their clothes soaked through, they tossed about on tempestuous seas, wallowed in the bottomless troughs between the waves. When the bare mast was outlined by St Elmo's Fire – the terrifying glow which devout believers were later to call the corposant or *Corpo Santo* – they all resigned themselves to miserable death.

All except Paul. He rose to this occasion as he had risen to so many others, with courage, love, and above all, faith. Though he could not resist the temptation of saying 'I told you so – we should never have left Fair Havens', he told them other things as well. The ship was *not* going to sink. They were *not* going to drown. But they *must* eat, to conserve their strength. Soon this ordeal would be over and they would be safe and sound on dry land. *He had been told so by the Lord.* He believed it, and they must believe it also.

He moved among them, this little man with the headaches and the trembling fevers, like a giant. At that moment, and for ever afterwards, he *was* a giant.

Not one – not even the experienced master of the ship – knew where they were. They had not had a sight of the sun, nor of a single star, for two weeks. When sailors' ears picked up the dreadful sound of breakers ahead, crashing down on some unknown shore, the shore might have been Sicily, or North Africa, or Spain, or some territory not yet named.

They took soundings. Twenty fathoms. They took soundings again. Fifteen fathoms. The sea-bed was shelving upwards, the boiling water below their keel becoming shallow. Soon it must end in shoals and rocks, on which their ship would be split.

It was night, pitch-dark night, screaming night. They put out four stern anchors, to slow their onward rushing, and prayed for daylight.

Trapped by the *gregale* on a lee shore, they spent that night in the sort of torment which had been familiar to Maltese sailors and fishermen for centuries, and would doubtless always be so. In black darkness, with sheets of rain flailing down on them, there was nothing to be seen but streaming decks and curling wave-tops: nothing to be heard but the wailing wind and the timbers groaning as they worked loose again: nothing to be felt but the shudder and jerk of the anchor cables as they fought the seas crashing down on the stern-post.

The long night ground slowly onwards. Just after six o'clock, a faint lifting of the gloom to the eastwards, far behind them, told them that dawn was at hand. It was not much of an improvement, but at least they could glimpse, through the murk, a line of wicked-looking breakers smashing against the coastline of a land they did not know.

As daylight gained, they saw that they had almost been cast upon a tiny island; then they noted a point, a shallow patch at the meeting of two seas, between the island and the mainland beyond, where it might be possible to drive the ship ashore. There was no hope of saving her now; they must run her aground, and trust to luck, or the gods, or Paul's own god, to bring them safely to land.

Paul still continued to move up and down the heaving deck, comforting his friends and enemies, all half-dead with cold and fear, telling them to keep up their spirits, to trust in the Lord, and to eat something for their strength's sake, for without strength they could not hope to survive the last ordeal of jumping overboard from a wrecked hull, and swimming for their lives, and struggling ashore through those hungry breakers and up on to the rocks.

It was a time – perhaps the last time – for the sailors to act. They threw overboard the rest of the cargo of wheat. 'There goes the dole!' one of them shouted, tipping a sack over the side, and he did not sound too unhappy about it. Why should honest sailors risk their lives to bring home a government hand-out for a work-shy Roman mob? Then they hoisted the tiny foresail, and cut the anchor cables, and drove straight for the beach.

As the stem, with a rending crash, struck the sand bar, the whole ship quivered. The crippled timbers cracked and splintered, the stern towered above the waves, and she began to break up.

It was a time – perhaps the last time – for the soldiers to act. They drew their swords, since there was an army drill laid down even for such a moment as this, and shouted 'Kill the prisoners!' and advanced on the men huddled high in the stern. According to the rule-book, they were right. If the ship was breaking up, then the prisoners were about to leave her. They were escaping. Escaping prisoners could be killed – must be killed – on sight.

It was a time for Julius the centurion to act. He drew his own sword – and he was a good man with a sword, none better

– and stood in their way, and told them *'No!'* He did it, Luke said, *because he wished to save Paul's life.*

As his soldiers fell back, confused, he ordered: 'No killing! Everybody overboard! Jump for your lives, and swim!'

One by one, sailors and soldiers and prisoners, they left the ruined ship: some jumping bravely, some sliding down the shattered bulwarks as they shrieked their prayers, some waiting in terror to be washed off by the mountainous waves. Struggling in the raging surf, clinging to loose boards, clutching broken barrels and boxes, they slowly fought their way to land. The wind howled as it plucked at their hair, the rain lashed down on their bobbing heads. At last they reached the rocks, and clambered up, bruised, bleeding, near death, but alive!

Every last soul was saved, as the saint had told them.

In the shelter of the cliffs, a marvellous peace descended.

The bare silent land, from which all living things seemed to have been swept by the gale, stared back at the castaways for a long time. Then, as Paul rose from his knees and his prayers, and set about comforting his groaning companions, the inhabitants of Malta came out fearfully to greet them, and to discover what the raging sea had brought.

Luke, in his later account, called them 'the barbarians', meaning that they were neither Greek nor Roman. Barbarians or not, they gave the shivering mariners a kindly welcome. Their first thought, the most sensible one of all, was to light a fire from the plentiful driftwood now piling up on the beach.

Paul helped them, with his usual compassion and energy. As he was adding a bundle of sticks to the flames, a snake jumped out and fastened on his hand. The 'barbarians' were aghast, and then suddenly superstitious and threatening. 'Undoubtedly this man is a murderer,' they muttered among themselves – and Paul could understand that muttering, because his speech was Aramaic, the 'speech of Canaan', which was a sister tongue to the Arabic of the Maltese. 'Though he has escaped the sea, yet vengeance suffereth him not to live.'

Paul was not a murderer, and had no time for such far-fetched deductions. He shook the snake off, and it dropped into the fire and was lost for ever. As soon as they saw that Paul did not swell up and die, the Maltese changed their tune, and, in Luke's words, 'said that he was a god'.

Paul had no time for that sort of veneration either, though

at least it turned an uncertain moment into a happy one. But if indeed the snake was poisonous, then it was the last poisonous one ever to be seen on the island. Where all its wicked sting disappeared to, what man would dare to say?

> *The old jokes are best, Father Salvatore thought, as he paused for the gale of laughter which greeted his words. The laughter was half a release from intolerable tension, half an acknowledgement of a hallowed jest. By tradition, it was agreed that the venom in the snake's fangs had reappeared, without undue delay, in the tongues of women.*

Julius the centurion, reporting formally to Publius, the Roman governor of Malta, told a spare soldier's tale. The ship had been wrecked, but all had been saved. His hundred soldiers would be quartered for the winter with the island's garrison; the sailors had already made themselves comfortable, as sailors do, in various lodging places round the harbour.

The prisoners were likewise held in reasonable security in barracks; they were under open arrest, but it was quite safe – it would take a clever prisoner to quit this island in winter, and the word had been passed round the fishermen that if anyone aided an escape, his boat would be forfeited and he himself installed in the prisoner's place. Julius was satisfied that the message had gone home. But there was one prisoner...

'*Paul of Tarsus!*' Governor Publius was taken aback, and he showed it, with patrician emphasis. 'Receive him *here*, in my palace? That trouble-maker? We've heard more than enough about Paul! What an extraordinary idea!' He looked at Julius with a frosty eye. 'He's a *prisoner*, isn't he? What makes him different from all the other riff-raff?'

But Julius had had to deal with patricians before. Governors, consuls, senators, generals, maybe even emperors – they were all the same. They just needed a nudge in the right direction. You had to catch them before they made up their minds. You had to find the right word.

'Sir, he's a bit more than a prisoner. Or a trouble-maker, either. He's been a great help to me, during the last few weeks. He kept everyone cheerful. Quite a character. Very persuasive. They say he had King Herod sitting there with his mouth open... I think you'd like to talk to him.'

'What on earth would we talk about?'

The centurion grinned: 'I think you'll find, sir, that Paul will take care of that.' The governor's eye was turning upper-class again, and Julius produced a more formal argument. 'We're likely to be here for two or three months. I think that head-quarters would be grateful if you kept a special eye on him. He might say something worth reporting.'

'Oh... Intelligence, eh? Political?'

'Just so, sir. Political and religious.'

'All right...' Perhaps it might be interesting, after all. Life in Malta was comfortable and pleasant, but one did feel out of things. If this fellow Paul had one or two good stories to tell, confidential stuff about Judaea, it might make them sit up in Rome. 'You'd better bring him to see me... As a matter of fact,' he said, with the faint surprise of many governors in the same situation, 'I've really got very little to do this morning.'

Thus it was that Paul made himself known to 'the chief man of the island', as Luke described him. By now, it should not seem astonishing that within the three allotted months of his stay, Paul had lodged with Governor Publius, talked with him, con-verted him to Christianity, and, just before he left, consecrated him as the first Christian bishop of Malta.

In Melita, the ancient capital which the Romans had inherited from the Carthaginians, and they from the Greeks, Governor Publius lived in some style, as did most of the Roman settlers who now called the island their own. In 300 years of rule, the Romans had transformed Malta from a rough mariners' refuge to a sophisticated community; they had built small yet magnificent palaces, dedicated rich temples to many of their gods, brought in theatrical troupes to fill the new theatres, and secured any im-portant point with massive earthworks and fortifications.

That strange device, the hot bath, was commonplace among the rich on the island; so were imported works of art, which made them feel at home and advertised their superiority over the dull barbarians. It was the smart thing, particularly among Sicilians, who could sail there comfortably in half a day, to have a summer villa in Malta, and pass several months there in agreeable ease. But even in Melita, the palace of Publius was, by general agreement, the show-off place above all others.

'I'm glad you like it,' the governor answered his guest, when

Paul commented on their truly palatial surroundings. They were taking their ease in the *atrium*, the pillared courtyard where they could enjoy the afternoon sun without baring themselves to the wind; the mosaic paving, the fishpond in the centre, the jars of honey stored for coolness under marble shelving, the spreading candelabra behind them, the little statues at the four corners, the cushioned sofas on which they sat – all were elegant, graceful, comforting. 'People have been kind enough to say that they enjoy it here. Of course, one has to import almost everything. But this cloth' – he patted the brown-and-yellow cushion under his arm – 'is local. Genuine Maltese weave. Not bad for people who can't even tell the time, eh?'

'Is such a thing important?' Paul, lost in dreamy indolence, guilty about his magnificent surroundings, yet enjoying every moment of them, knew that the question was unworthy. Time was the most precious gift of God, to be used by all humans to His greater glory. But not today, or not yet today, when the whole world was at peace in warmth and comfort and love, and his battered body and the salt-inflamed wounds on his arms and legs could be forgotten.

'I suppose not. Just as long as *we* can tell them the time.' Publius looked at Paul's goblet, saw that it was empty, and clapped his hands. A slave brought a small serving jar, and poured out more of the rich Falernian, and added water. 'You must tell me if that's too strong. Two parts to one is my mixture, but then I'm an old soldier.'

Publius was one of the people – like Porcius Festus, like the centurion Julius, like a thousand converts, even like Herod Agrippa – who after instinctive suspicion had taken to Paul straight away, and he was troubled by his plight. He admired, and could recognize, a brave man. He was also deeply grateful for something which Paul had done for him that very morning – or rather, had done for his honoured father, who had been near death with a fever and a persistent haemorrhage.

Now the old man seemed at ease, after a simple laying-on of hands and a prayer to this fellow's new god. He might possibly be cured... Paul had made light of it; he had even said: 'You should thank my doctor friend, Luke' – and it was true that Luke had been hovering somewhere in the background, brewing up some mysterious medicine from herbs and poppy-seeds. But Publius preferred to accept it as a miracle, as did the rest of his household, and the enormous, unrepayable debt remained in his mind.

Now he said, in the sententious, rather prosy way which Paul already recognized as masking a generous heart and an acute mind: 'The trouble with time is, it goes so quickly. It seems only yesterday I arrived here, and yet I've nearly finished my term... They're cutting down on these governorships nowadays. *And* keeping a sharp eye on the accounts. Not like old Verres,' he added, with a meaning smile which Paul did not understand.

'Verres?' he asked.

'What? You haven't heard of Gaius Verres? Well, thank heaven for that! He made himself quite a reputation in these parts. Long before my time, of course, more than a hundred years ago. But it gave us all a bad name, I can tell you. Verres was the governor of Sicily, and that included Malta, in old Pompey's day. He didn't even set foot in Malta, but he stripped the island bare! Taxes, extortion, robbing the temples, carrying off food and clothing – there wasn't anything he wouldn't do. He had four hundred jars of honey shipped out in a single month! He even stole all the cushions – *cushions!* The place was ruined for generations... Of course, you can't get away with that sort of thing nowadays. Even if you wanted to, which personally I don't. Roman governors have to be a different type altogether.'

'Have you heard of Antonius Felix of Judaea?'

Publius gave him a sharp glance. 'Well, of course there's always *Felix*. But generally speaking...'

Paul roused himself. Informed gossip was pleasant, particularly in such surroundings, but the time spent was God's, and God deserved better from man. The brief holiday from care must be brought to an end. He began to feel his way gently towards something which had come to him, the apostle of the Gentiles, in the night watches.

'May I ask after your father?'

'Oh, he's much better. No pain, and that infernal bleeding has stopped. I must say I couldn't be more grateful. It really is a miracle... If there's anything I can do for you, while you're here' – he coughed, unwilling to introduce the subject of Paul's captivity, 'just say the word.'

'I would like to preach.'

'Preach? Who to?'

'Any soul who will listen. Slaves. Freemen. Patricians. Carthaginians. Greeks.'

'Well, now,' Publius began cautiously, and then changed his mind. Surely a man of Paul's quality would never play him any tricks. 'Why not? We're always glad to hear some new ideas. One gets so out of touch... I take it you don't want to stir up any political trouble. Not like Jerusalem, or wherever it was.'

'I want to preach Jesus Christ, the son of God.'

'The son of which god?' Publius took another sip of his wine – there were so many gods, everyone had their own favourite, the shrines here were as thick as fleas on a Maltese hound – and then curiosity got the better of him. This fellow had such force, such shining character, behind his funny looks. 'What is it *exactly* that you want to tell them?'

'Let me tell you first.'

Paul spent three full months on the island. Though he kept up his warm friendship with Governor Publius, and built upon it, he moved out of the aura of palace luxury within a few days, and into a cave-grotto hollowed out of the sandstone hill, just below Melita. Here was a place more suitable to humble thought and earnest striving, a place where his friends would be in awe only of Christ.

With Luke as his companion, he trudged to and fro across the island, talking, answering questions, preaching the word of God, and securing many followers. Naxxar, three miles away from Melita, could claim the first converts; indeed, it was named for them – the word 'nassar' still means 'made into a Christian'. The fame of his miraculous cure of Publius's father, who still lived, had also spread; there were many other such demands on him.

To see such faith in Christ was a joy; a greater joy was to have the living word, rather than some drama of the flesh, acclaimed. Paul made this his first care; and his ministry, even on this tiny island, prospered wonderfully.

Perhaps it was the last happiness of his life, and he found it in Malta. The happiest moment of all was to receive Publius as a Christian, and baptize him in his own palace, which had now become a church.

When Paul said: 'I want you to be the first bishop of this island,' and Publius answered: 'If I am worthy, in the Lord Jesus

Christ,' it seemed as astounding and then as inevitable as any other miracle.

Julius the centurion, rounding up his prisoners, reported that it was time to go. Another Alexandrian corn-ship, named *Castor and Pollux*, which had wintered in the island, was due to sail. They must all be on their way.

Paul's new Christian friends loaded him with provisions for the voyage, and came down to the harbour to see him off. Once again, it was a desolate farewell; once again, he had to say: 'Why are you crying? Do you want to break my heart?' But this time he did not weep. His last goodbye, his last journey, must show a steadfast face.

There could have been no one at the harbour who did not believe that Paul was going to his death.

The church of Saint Paul Shipwrecked, in Valletta, remained forever afterwards the guardian of two relics of their own apostle: a piece of his arm-bone in a hallowed ossuary, and, from a place called Three Fountains in Rome, a splinter of the stone pillar on which he was beheaded.

His faith also remained, centuries after he died for it. He brought to Malta the first news of Jesus Christ its Saviour; and his bravery, his resilience, his capacity to resist earthly torments, gave the island its most priceless example.

Though few on earth could be saints, yet all could be men.

They had hardly been aware of the thunder outside. Then a breathless bloodstained man burst into the catacomb, and panted for help. There were people buried alive near by. They were calling out pitifully. The rescue workers could not get through. The bombs were still falling.

At the words, more than fifty men rose to their feet, and crowded towards the exit tunnel. It was these brave volunteers, with Father Salvatore at their head, who went out into the fearsome darkness once more, and so continued steadfast in the faith of their forefathers.

The Hopeful Day
of Father Salvatore

26 July 1941

Father Salvatore loved his little cell, which had become his home, his heart-beat, his rock-womb: where night after night he drifted into exhausted sleep, where morning after morning he woke to the sounds and smells of the catacombs towering and pressing all round him, and to a new day of tears and terrors and happiness and the love of God for man.

The cell was ten feet by six, and bare to a degree which would have horrified his mother. He made his bed on top of a stone slab which had once roofed the immortal home of one of the long-dead brothers. The floor was worn smooth by countless pious feet; the walls were dank stone. A crucifix guarded his head: an oil-lamp gave him smoky light at night: through the open archway of the door, pale daylight filtered through, and fell on two human faces: his own, and the picture of St Barnabas carrying a rake, the symbol of the harvest which the saint always blessed.

Two pegs furnished Father Salvatore's wardrobe, and a stone pot his wash-basin. That was all. But it was never his prison. It was his cradle, in which, by God's grace, he had been newly born to guardian priesthood.

Today he awoke early, before the first thin bell, the best that authority would allow, sounded the call for Mass. In the whirling, light-headed moment between sleeping and waking, he thought – or was it the end of a vanished dream? – 'I have just found out! I am one of the little dead brothers!' He strove to pierce a veil, and discover whether he was in heaven or not.

Then the dormant blood flowed to his brain, or whatever alchemy it was which sounded 'Sleepers, awake!' to all mankind, and he knew the truth: 'No, I am a little live father, and the time is a quarter to four, and I thank God for it, and for the promise of a new day.'

Already he could feel, from the prickly discomfort under his worn blanket, that this would be another day of blinding heat.

Of course, the new day could only be like yesterday, and the four hundred yesterdays since their war began: a four-hundredth part of the same endless story. It was truly astonishing to think that they had lived for more than a year in the catacombs, and had seen them grow from a tomb ripped open to a refuge made secure: had seen themselves – or many of them – grow in the same degree.

By now they were better men, better women, even better children. Any collection of humans, subjected to three or four air-raids a day for the best or worst part of a year, must inevitably change; they would either rise or fall, like a thermometer, like Adam and Eve. His people, his Maltese, had risen.

They had risen above blows which especially wounded. Apart from the damage to be seen all over Valletta, all over Malta, there were particular hurts which drove home the fact of total war. There were the big blows which could put a small nation in fear: foremost was the bomb-damage to the dockyard, the life-line of their island, which cut its working efficiency by more than a half, and reduced the dry-dock itself to laborious hand-operation.

Part of this fear was the fear of the unknown, fear even of words which, though common talk for fighting men, were mysterious and terrifying to all the rest. What exactly were 'magnetic mines', what were 'acoustic mines', which dropped by parachute into Grand Harbour and Marsa Scirocco Bay? How could men and women, going about their business in broad daylight, be machine-gunned on the streets of St Paul's Bay? How could a mine be nine feet long, like the one which destroyed sixty houses in Zebbug? How could actual roads be set on fire by flaming kerosene, and burn for three days?

Gradually the questioners had risen above such things. But it hurt, intimately, when the little church of St Publius in Floriana had been half-ruined at a single stroke. It hurt when a local cinema was hit, and a hundred people died in the midst of their innocent enjoyment. It hurt when the 'Chapel of the Bones', walled and ceilinged with relics of an ancient burial-ground, was demolished, and the skulls of men long dead mingled with the flesh and blood of their descendants. It hurt when church bells could not be rung except to sound an alarm, and village *festas* were banned.

It hurt to see their peaceful and pretty countryside so disciplined by the government and so mucked about by the soldiery. It hurt to see all signposts and milestones erased, and open spaces which might be used for invasion landing-grounds defiled by concrete blocks and iron spikes. It hurt when they were ordered to leave their homes, and to follow signposts with arrows pointing the way to safety, with barbed wire to ensure that they did not stray from this cattle-track.

But *still* they had risen above such things. They had even absorbed, or at least come to grumbling terms with, the dreary rationing system, which made every day a secondary battlefield for the housewife, a belt-tightening worry for the husband, and a potent source of quarrelling for both. But what could a woman do, to promote the joy of family life, when sugar, coffee, matches, and soap were all strictly rationed: when butter, cheese, milk, chocolate, and pasta were often unobtainable: when vegetables and fruit were scarce, and horribly expensive: when the bread ration was down to ten ounces a head per day – less than a third of pre-war consumption: when a lot of rubbish like potato *purée* was mixed into that bread to make up a reasonably sized loaf?

What could a woman do about the robbers from Gozo who priced their eggs at half a crown each, take it or leave it, and exchanged potatoes only for gold ornaments? *Gesu Marija*, the next thing one knew, these rascals, these *brikkuni*, would be snatching the very gold from their teeth!

But it was all part of the war, the wretched, nagging, frustrating part which had to be endured. It was explained, time and again, that the convoys could not get through; and anyone wandering round the desolation of Grand Harbour did not need to have any such explanation. The harbour, like the cupboard, was bare.

Malta lay open to all the ferocious elements of war. To the north, Greece and Crete had fallen: to the south, the Italians were back in Libya, completing the encirclement: east and west, the nearest helping hands, Alexandria and Gibraltar, were each a thousand miles out of range. Stuck like the bait in some enormous fishtrap between Sicily and Tunis, the island could scarcely be reached by any succouring hand. When ships did manage to get through, more often than not they were bombed and sunk before they could unload.

The only question was, how long could this last? They were all a year older already. How *was* the war going?

There were no answers: only rumours, and pins jabbed into the map of the Middle Sea's littoral, and the general knowledge that there were always 250 German bombers in Sicily, sixty miles away, waiting to pounce on anything that moved, anything that brought them the shadow of hope. Apart from that, it was just stories of tanks racing up and down the northern coast of Africa, now winning, now losing; of a new name, Rommel, and a new enemy, the Afrika Korps, both seemingly invincible: of all Europe crushed under the heel of Germany, of slaughter in the North Atlantic and terrible damage to the heart of London: and finally, of the threat of invasion to their very own homeland.

Yet against all such fear, there was still hope. If, in spite of frenzied efforts to destroy her, the *Illustrious* could get safely away from their besieged island, then anything could happen.

Malta itself had saved *Illustrious*, to live and fight again. Though it was six months ago now, the story still shone with pride, and it deserved to. Maltese dockworkers by the thousand – shipwrights, electricians, fitters, stevedores – had toiled all round the clock, for fourteen solid days and nights, to get the poor wreck ready for sea; and this in spite of a continuous rain of bombs which not only hit the ship, or fell close to her, exploding on the sea-bed and acting like mines, but which plastered the dock area and the Three Cities with a lethal carpet of destruction.

They left behind them acres of wasteland where not a single building survived, nor one stone upon another.

It became at one point so bad that all the Three Cities were evacuated, and the poor refugees, shocked and penniless, streamed out once again to the countryside. That was the night when the Cottonera catacombs housed more than two thousand people. But still the work went on, even though two near-misses lifted the *Illustrious* bodily out of the water and bashed her against the quay, fracturing a turbine and flooding the boiler-room for the third time.

The dockers toiled, and the gunners toiled in their support. Mr Winston Churchill, broadcasting a few weeks later, had recorded that 'in this effort to beat the harbour to pieces', the German airforce lost ninety planes. Tension rose unbearably all over Valletta as the ship, in spite of all, grew ready to sail. Finally, on the fourteenth night, *Illustrious* steamed out of Grand Harbour under her own power.

She made a most secret exit, cloaked by darkness, and in so great haste that she was still festooned with repair stages and scaffolding and dangling ropes and even fishing lines, none of which could be jettisoned until she reached deep water. But she sailed to such purpose, with her hull and machinery so valiantly patched up, that she outstripped the destroyer escort, and a later rendezvous with a cruiser force was cancelled.

Illustrious, romping along at an unbelievable twenty-five knots, was then too near home to bother, and it was the cruisers themselves, panting to catch up, which were attacked, while the rare prize reached Alexandria, on a happy dawn, two days later.

Father Salvatore, not less exhausted than the men who had worked so faithfully to repair the ship, was one of the few hundreds who watched her leave, in the dead of night. It seemed like a miracle, or the biggest conjuring trick in the world. One moment she was there, towering upwards like a castle which ruled all their lives and took all their sweating labour; and then, with a few softly called orders, the great black shadow moved away into deeper darkness, and there was not a trace to be seen: only swirling grimy water, and a pale void in the skyline which, after fourteen days, was the most astonishing thing of all.

But it was the proudest, most gulping, most wet-eyed moment he could ever remember. He hoped, he prayed, that the sleepless and hungry captain, and the survivors of his crew, and every skilled shipwright, and the humblest man with a hammer, were all happy in the same degree... With such triumphs for the human spirit, how could Malta lose the war?

The tinny bell, warning all within their small world that they might wake, and dress, and be ready to attend the first Mass at half past four, sounded near by. It was Rafel Vella, as usual, Father Salvatore thought, gratefully stretching his legs at the knowledge of an earlier riser already at work. It was a fine thing to have a dependable sacristan – even though, this morning, Rafel semed to be ringing awkwardly, and the ragged sound was more like a child playing with a new Christmas toy than a solemn call to worship.

Father Salvatore stretched again, willing himself to conquer the deadly sin of sloth. He had the good excuse of a bare four hours' sleep, but God did not accept excuses, only duty and obedience... He felt his sore toes aching as they uncurled, and he thought: it is time, more than time, for a new pair of boots, but how can I find the boots I need, now that Vincenzu the old cobbler is dead, and his son, working down at the docks, prefers welding steel to stitching leather, and will never change his mind or his trade again?

At the thought of steel, the hard element of life, he overcame sloth, and physical infirmity as well, and got down from his high stone bed, thanking the dead brother with whom he had shared a short night, on the way. Then he dressed, and left his cell, and mingled with the waking throng.

He felt bound to admit that his mother, whom he would see within a few hours, would once more have been shocked at what he, another scion of the Santo-Nobiles, now accepted as part of the fabric of their wartime life. He loved all these people, these better people, but love could not blind the eye nor muffle the ear to the sights and sounds of cramped humanity facing the burden of the day, after yet another night in the Cottonera Lines.

Love could not plug the nose either. The first thing one noticed about the catacombs was, unfortunately, the smell of them. In the hot July weather which had now descended on all Malta, it had become a most noisome mixture: of heated unwashed bodies, paraffin, cats, goats, cooking odours, the dregs of beer and wine, the particular smell of feet: and, inescapably, urine and excrement.

There was a Latin phrase which Father Salvatore had always especially hated, because of its crudity: *Inter urinam et faeces nascimur* – Between urine and excrement are we born. It had been coined (though it might be heresy to say so) to express a churchman's contempt for women, or his fear of their private parts, or a certain gleeful satisfaction that the holy act of childbirth took place between two other passages which the prelate found disgusting.

The idea, and the coarse expression of it, defiled and degraded womanhood. Father Salvatore thought of it now, as he inhaled an early morning sample of the catacomb smell. Both elements were there, in full measure; yet surely the hopeful word was *nascimur* – we are born!

They were born anew, every day of their lives, and there were two ways of seeing, feeling, and speaking of that birth. One was gross, the other hopeful and joyful. Even the cock on the dunghill praised the Saviour as he saluted the dawn. Let them all do likewise.

His practical mind dwelt on the smell, and as usual turned away again. There was nothing to be done about it. The motionless, loaded air must always bear down on them. The heat made it worse, and that was insoluble also. The catacombs could not be ventilated, without weakening the shelter they provided.

Better to pant, and suffer, and live, than breathe the open air and die. It must be appreciated that their shelter smelled like a giant hen-coop. Indeed, why should it not? It had hen-coops by the hundred : the *gallinari* which supplied their breakfast eggs were among their most envied possessions.

After the smell, the noise and the people... The chorus of hawking and spitting from the old barely rose above the blaring wireless sets and the raucous gramophones with which the young saluted the day. Little children were crying, older children were quarrelling already, or clamouring for something to eat – anything, a raw onion, a rib of rabbit still fit to be chewed, a loaf-end hollowed out and stuffed with tomato paste, *anything* to stay the pangs !

There were arguments about cooking pots, curses because a drunkard had been sick over the next man's pillow, bellowing laughter round a couple who delayed too long under a heaving blanket.

Yawning and scratching, people peered out from behind curtains of laundry to see what the new day promised, or menaced. The laundry-line itself provoked a distant, injured cry of 'Who's taken our dish-cloths?' and Father Salvatore hoped that the dish-cloths were only mislaid. There had been a case of theft, just a few days earlier, and he did not want such a thing repeated; the pair of working trousers spirited away in the night, and next sighted on the shameless culprit's loins, had threatened communal chaos.

Father Salvatore had applied his own rough justice, before the inevitable vendetta started. He had remembered his father once saying that the worst crime on board ship was 'stealing from a shipmate', because the crew's close quarters, as well as their equal poverty, made mutual trust essential. Thus, they must all be shipmates here, in their huge craft which was their only life-boat; otherwise the fate of the strongest man, or the poorest beggar, would be the same : a hateful jungle savagery.

His sentence had been expulsion from the catacombs, with no arguments and no delay.

Now he approached his altar, for his private devotions before he began the Mass. Then came a surprise. He was met, not by Rafel Vella, but little Nero; and in his hand Nero held the bell he had been ringing, the bell-of-office of the sacristan.

'*Bongu*, Dun Salv.' Nero greeted him cheerfully enough, but there was hesitation in his face. He looked down at the bell, firmly muffled by his thumb. 'I'm sorry about the rotten noise I made. I'll try to do better in future.'

'But what's happened, Nero? Where is Rafel?'

Nero avoided his eye again. 'He's not feeling well, Dun Salv. So I took over his job.'

'What's the matter with him?'

'Just a headache.'

There were people watching them, with more than the usual interest, as if curious to gauge his reaction to the news. Though 'just a headache' might mean one of Rafel's rare yet recurrent drinking bouts, it did not exactly fit the circumstances. And there was another puzzle as well.

'What did you mean, you'll do better *in future*?'

'Nothing, Dun Salv. I meant, during the Mass.'

With that, Father Salvatore had to be content. Gradually the concourse became quiet, and the customary discipline made itself felt. He became absorbed, first in the formality and then in the joy of the Mass. Nero tolled his little bell at the right moment for the commencement and, at the elevation of the Host, produced a creditable salute. The faithful supported them both; it became, as usual, a purge for the spirit and a brief glimpse of glory. All was well, between God and man.

All was not well. As soon as it was over, and Father Salvatore had gone back to his cell, Nero Cassar sidled in.

'Dun Salv?'

'Yes? What is it?' He did not like to be interrupted, between the miracle of supreme communion and his re-engagement with humanity, until he gave the sign himself. A priest should be able to shed such fervour in utter privacy, otherwise it became a matter of play-acting, and that was never to be true. He looked at Nero, and saw in his face the same secrecy and embarrassment as before: at that moment, he was not the man he had become, but the little penitent boy whose size his body matched. There was something here to be cleared up. 'What's the matter?'

'I told you a lie, Dun Salv. I did not want to make you sad.'

'What lie?'

Nero's mouth was actually trembling, as if he feared what he had to say, what he had to do to someone he loved. 'Rafel is not ill. He has gone. He has left.'

'I don't understand.' But Father Salvatore did understand, with a bitter pang of bereavement. 'How do you know?'

'He left me a letter.' The dwarf seemed almost to be grovelling on the stone floor, he was so sad, so ashamed. 'It was a silly letter. I tore it up. But then I stayed awake all night, thinking about it.'

'What was in the letter?'

'Just that Rafel had to go back home, to Gozo. That he had to be with his mother. That he was afraid, that he didn't believe in the catacombs any more. That he had met a man who told him that what you were doing was forbidden.'

'Forbidden? What man is this?'

'I thought you would know.' And then, seeing Father Salvatore's face, which was just as stricken as his own, Nero cried out: 'It doesn't matter, Dun Salv! Let him go! I can do everything!'

Without warning, guns began to yell and bark and scream, almost over their heads, and the terrible moment, the Judas stroke, became lost in something more awful still, the brazen voice of war. Father Salvatore, with a coward's readiness, said: 'Later, Nero. Something is happening,' and snatching his satchel he almost ran out to see what it was.

2

It was very difficult to decide what in fact had happened, or was happening, or would happen next. A burning sunrise brought nothing but confusion and doubt; the listening ear heard only different stories from different people. The sound of gun-fire, which had started just after the Mass, at a quarter to five, continued for about half an hour and then abruptly ceased. But it was not the end of an air-raid; no bombs had fallen, no sulphurous blobs of black and yellow stained the pale blue sky.

There seemed plenty of fighter aircraft about, and the sharp rattle of their cannon occasionally cracked the silence. But whose aircraft they were, and what they were doing, no one knew. While the wildest rumours filled the town, there were no answers, only questions: no facts, only guesses.

Father Salvatore, waiting at French Creek for a ferry-boat which did not come, heard a dozen stories from the people milling about on the quay. He could credit none of them.

'It was the invasion from Sicily. Thousands of ships! They say there were landing-craft as big as houses.'

'How can that be? Where are the landing-craft?'

'All sunk!'

'No, no! It was an air-raid. They were after the big convoy that just got in.'

'But they didn't drop any bombs.'

'These were torpedo bombers. They came in low, making straight for the ships. *I saw them!* But they were all smashed up by our guns.'

'They say the end of the breakwater blew up. Whoosh! Just like that.'

'Who blew it up?'

'Sabotage.'

'The guns at St Elmo must have been firing at something.'

'Perhaps they were practising.'

'*Gesu!* Sorry, Dun Salv. But who needs practice, these days?'

'It must have been *something*. All the sirens sounded.'

'And the searchlights were turned on.'

'But they shone the searchlights along the water! Why should they do that?'

'Perhaps they were looking for this cursed ferry-boat.'

'I think they dropped one big bomb on the breakwater, to close the harbour.'

'Don't you believe it. It was just a false alarm. To keep up morale.'

Then old Angelo the *barklor* arrived, urging his *dghajsa* towards the quay like a mad rocking horse. As usual, he had the whole story.

'I saw it all,' he told his audience. 'I was just starting out from the Customs House. You wouldn't believe what I saw!'

'That's the first true word today.'

Angelo ignored the jibe, and the laughter which followed it. 'You can laugh. But *I know*! It was hundreds of little boats coming in from the sea. They say it was the invasion, but I think they were after the convoy. Anyway, they were all blown up. First by the guns, and then by the fighters. I tell you, I was right in the middle of it! I thought I would be sunk myself. You could have *trodden* on the bullets!' His whiskers bristled fiercely. 'But it's all over now. Those stupid Italians! We beat them off!'

Astonishingly, old Angelo's story, and his pride in it, was somewhere near the truth.

It was a good try, a very good try indeed: the kind of lunatic exercise which a nation not very accomplished at war-in-the-mass wisely delegated to a handful of brave and daring volunteers, who might just bring it off. The fact that it was doomed from the start did not make it any the less admirable – or inspired. In such mad enterprises did the warrior's spirit in man often come to full flower.

The target of the Italian navy was a convoy of six ships, of immense value to hard-pressed Malta, which had just reached harbour after a ferocious fight stretching half across the Mediterranean. This convoy-operation was code-named 'Substance' – a dull-as-ditch-water label for a perilous undertaking; and it had involved, initially, an armada of those six merchant ships, plus the troop-transport *Leinster* carrying 5,000 men, plus an escort of the battleship *Nelson*, three cruisers, eighteen destroyers, and the mixed striking force called Force 'H', headed by the carrier *Ark Royal*.

Together they were to run the blockade of an island which had not received any worthwhile supplies for nearly three months.

They set out from the Clyde on the 11th of July, and reached Gibraltar on the 19th. Shortly afterwards the *Leinster* ran aground, and had to put back into harbour. The rest continued onwards, towards the certain battlefield.

It now became a familiar story, save in one particular. The cruiser *Manchester* was torpedoed and heavily damaged: the destroyer *Fearless* was sunk : the destroyer *Firedrake* was put out of action. But only one of the six store-ships, the *Sydney Star*, was hit; and even she managed to make Malta along with the other five. A vital convoy had thus got through, its ships triumphant and its supplies intact.

Perhaps a little touch of Italian–German rivalry crept into history at this point. The great German Air Force might have knocked off a few of the escorts, but they had let six crucial cargoes slip through. The Italians decided on a bold stroke by way of highlighting this failure, and rectifying it.

This was nothing less than to nail and destroy those six ships where they lay, in the farthest corner, and under the guns, of a harbour which, ringed by protection nets, had become one of the hardest in the world to crack.

The British convoy had reached Malta on the 24th. Two days later a curious kind of mother-ship, called *Diana* after the moon-goddess, set sail from the port of Augusta, just north of Syracuse in Sicily. She was playing mother to eighteen Italian craft of an even more curious breed. To call them suicide-boats was, to say the least, an Italian understatement.

They were one-man jobs : small motor launches, very reasonably christened *maiali* – pigs – with a torpedo-head as a bow, an engine in the middle, and a brave sailor in the stern whose job it was to aim the boat at its target, activate the torpedo, and then jump overboard before the impact. That was all.

The choice of these death-or-glory boys, whose gallantry was beyond dispute, was thus death by their own torpedoes, death by drowning, death by pot-shot from the shore, or capture and imprisonment for the rest of the war.

As she neared Malta the *Diana*, with her load of valiant mischief, was tracked by radar to a point nine miles north of Fort St Elmo. There, just at daybreak, she launched her eighteen turbulent children, turned round, and made for home again. She was radar-tracked doing this as well. But the lethal little Pigs were too small to be picked up on the defence screen.

As the *Diana* faded, and the radar watchers scratched their heads and wondered what it was all about, the eighteen torpedo-boats sped towards Grand Harbour.

Perhaps they would have done better if they had made their

approach shortly *before* dawn; but perhaps, equally, without light of any kind, they could never have steered towards their target. In any event, from the first moment it all went wrong. An alert gunner, one Sergeant Zammit of the Royal Malta Artillery, heard their snarling engines and then spotted one of them, coming towards his battery on Fort St Elmo in the pale eastern glow between night and day.

He could not believe his eyes, but wisely he decided to do so. The crash-alarm sounded, and the big and small coastal guns, manned by bored gunners who had shot at nothing since the war began, now jumped into delighted action.

The watchers on the roof-tops and bastions of Valletta had a grandstand view of the opening, and closing, of Malta's very first marine shooting season.

The leading torpedo-boat hit the bridge between the two arms of the breakwater – perhaps on purpose – and blew up with a huge explosion which partially blocked the entrance. As the shore searchlights came on, the second boat was hit and blown up; then the next, at a hundred yards range. After that the rest of the flotilla, zigzagging wildly in a sea now floodlit from a dozen angles, were picked off one by one, as the guns thundered, the red-and-green tracer bullets bounced off the water, and the spectators cheered what was undoubtedly a skilful piece of targetry.

The harbour was never breached, and out of eighteen starters in this killing steeplechase there were no survivors. Hurricane fighters, alerted when daylight gained, disposed of the last four as they retreated – they had nowhere to retreat to, anyway. One boat was captured, and towed into Malta as a war trophy. Three prisoners were taken.

The spectators on the bastions had good reason – far better reason than they knew – to cheer their side of a brave action. The rich prize which had escaped this attack was, after all, well named 'Substance'. Besides the thousands of fighting men transferred to other ships when the *Leinster* ran aground, the six-vessel convoy carried a massive amount of supplies to relieve the straitened island.

Frozen meat (2,000 tons), edible oils (2,000 tons), three months' supply of sugar, coffee, fats, and tea: 10,000 tons of ammunition: spare submarine propellers, spare Hurricane engines, hundreds of anti-aircraft guns – such was Malta's desperate shopping list, and it had been delivered just on time. In all its odd variety, it had totalled 65,000 tons.

Of the brave effort to deny it, only splinters of wood, oil patches, three prisoners, thirteen dead sailors, and a slightly damaged breakwater were left to tell the tale, as the fierce July sunlight began to beat down on the city, and the audience, deliriously happy, went home to a hearty breakfast.

Among those who found themselves going home, though without the advantage of having watched the fun from the bastions, was Father Salvatore. He was late for his morning visit to his mother, and he walked swiftly up hill from the Customs House steps where old Angelo, who had rowed so slowly because he talked so much, had finally put him ashore. But he picked up plenty of gossip, on his way to the Palazzo Santo-Nobile.

Everyone wanted to talk to everyone else, on that triumphant morning; a priest in haste was not excepted from the universal need for happy human contact. There was a wonderful lightness and good humour in the air, the first true expression of pride and hope which he could remember, since the war began.

The glorious defeat of the massed torpedo-boat attack − for this was the general consensus of rumour and boasting − had been a tonic, and the tonic was a potent stimulation, on every street corner, in every shuffling queue, on doorsteps and shop entrances from Lascaris Wharf to the heights of the Strada Reale.

He felt cheered himself, as he exchanged greetings and collected bits of news which, true or false, were all part of the same pattern of rejoicing. A man, a stranger, said: 'You must have been praying hard, *sur kappillan*!' Another man, a shopkeeper, stepped out of his doorway and thrust a great fruitcake into Father Salvatore's hands. 'Give that to the orphans!' he shouted. 'To celebrate!'

A market woman called out: 'Is it true they sank fifty ships?' and before he could answer, a chorus round her, nodding delightedly, chimed in: 'Yes! Absolutely true! Everyone says so!' Yet another man, whom Father Salvatore only knew as a persistent nuisance in the catacombs − he hung about the women when their husbands had gone to work, giving household advice which was sometimes too intimate for the taste of the returning breadwinners – this domestic hero proclaimed: 'So much for the Italian navy! Now for the Germans!'

Only one sadness nagged him, in all this celebration: the desertion of Rafel. He had known that this must come, but it was still a shock – not least the cowardly manner of its climax – and it would remain so for a long time. That being so, he could logically put it aside, to consider and to mourn later.

He entered the Palazzo through the postern gate, ready for another sadness, of a more intimate kind: the shrinkage of this great house under the pressure of war. A tottering old Gregory let him in, after a long wait – and this was the first reminder of decay. The major-domo should not really be answering the door; and an old man, past eighty-three and ailing, should not do so in any case.

But Francis had gone, with the Baroness's blessing, to join the army, and another footman had also left, to help a widowed mother in the fields. There had been a necessary scaling-down of the house in every respect. Formal entertaining, in the old style, was out of place. Two whole wings had been closed and shuttered; and when, for the first time, Father Salvatore had peered into these twilight caverns, and seen them dust-sheeted and silent, he had felt truly bereft, as if the end of an era had been signalled.

But it was not for himself that he was sad, only for his mother. Houses such as the Palazzo Santo-Nobile might not endure in any case; in war, they must certainly have a low priority. Yet it was still *her* house, and *her* years of care, and *her* pride in tradition, which were suffering the blows and the pain; she had given much of her life to it, much of her love, and now life and love and the Palazzo itself might all be ebbing away on the same tide.

Beyond doubt, two things only were important in war: the winning of it, and the death which it cost. The high quality of life, enshrined in this house, could not be listed among the real dead. Death was bloodshed, not dust-sheets, or empty spaces where proud portraits had hung, or the lack of servants, or the end of dinner parties for sixty guests. Yet in the midst of global uproar, one might still spare a thought for such small areas of mourning.

He could spare a thought also for Gregory the major-domo,

as the old man first peeped sideways out of the postern door-way, and then gave him a wavering bow.

'Dun Salv!' Gregory's voice was a throaty croak. 'I knew it must be you. *Bonġornu, bonġornu!*'

Father Salvatore touched the old man on the shoulder. '*Tkun imbierek*. . . Gregory, you should *not* be answering the door. One of the girls could do it.'

'What? A girl to answer the door at the Palazzo? Suppose they saw it from the street!' Gregory was horrified – or was he only pretending to be horrified, and thus acknowledging, ruefully, the decay of the house? One of the difficulties with talking to the very old was that one always underestimated their awareness – and their sense of humour. The mind so often out-lasted the body: he had seen it on a hundred death-beds: one could accept it as a blessing of God, or a cruel jest, or as some absolute guarantee that the soul would outlive the flesh, if only for a few heartbeats, which meant for eternity.

He had always remembered, for ever afterwards, his very first death – that was how he had phrased it, as with trembling hands and the great doubt of the novice he had anointed the lips of an old woman slipping away from life as if from a family party which had gone on long enough. He knew her to be eighty-five years old, and himself exactly sixty years younger.

He had thought that she was already dead, so calm was the grey-white face, so peaceful and relaxed the wasted body after months of pain. Then the anointed lips had opened, and he bent his head to hear what she might say. Some holy thought? – some last confession? – some confused memory of a life of travail? Not so . . .

Her eyes remained shut, but her lips were smiling. 'You did that very well . . . for a young chap . . .'

On which brave and blessed farewell, she had died.

At that moment he knew that he had lost a friend, and gained an advocate in heaven. After twenty years, he still prayed for the soul of one Anna Caruana, of the village of Santa Lucia beyond Tarxien: mother of eight, daughter of God, teacher of courage to the very threshold.

Old Gregory, another survivor of the same quality, was still mumbling on, as they moved slowly across the central court-yard.

'A man should answer the door here, if he is the last man left in the Palazzo... I do not like the way things are going, Dun Salv, but I know my job... After fifty-seven years, who should know it better? ... Last winter we couldn't even get enough oil to heat the house properly. Those rooms we've closed up, there's damp there already, you can smell it... I was telling the Baroness only last week, the next thing will be dry rot in the roof timbers... And do you know what she said, God bless her and keep her? ... She said: "We had dry rot in the stables when Grand Master Lascaris was a little boy! As soon as we win the war, we'll see about the dry rot!" What a spirit! ... But when will we win the war, Dun Salv?'

As he turned to ask the question, Gregory stumbled on the stone flags, and Father Salvatore put out a hand to steady him. They were in the harsh sunlight of a very hot morning, and gently he guided the old man into the shade of the patio.

'I don't know about the war, Gregory. But I do know that you've walked quite far enough. Now go back to your room, and have a little rest.'

'But I must conduct you to the Baroness,' Gregory protested feebly. 'It is the way things are done here.'

'I am the only visitor you need not conduct... Now, will you be good, or must a priest order you?'

'If you say so, Dun Salv.' But he passed his hand over his forehead, as if fretful. 'Wait... There was something I wanted to tell you.'

Father Salvatore took this for a childish delaying tactic. He smiled, and shook his head. 'Now Gregory...' He waited until the old man walked away, obedient at last, and then made for the staircase leading to his mother's apartments.

The first thing he heard, as he paused outside the door, was a man's voice. The sonorous, fruity accents were unmistakable. It was the first time he had ever been forestalled, on his traditional visiting day, and he felt as he used to feel long ago, when some promised treat was, for a good reason, denied. Now there was no good reason except his own delay, and he had been supplanted by the last man in the world he would have chosen.

With such foolish, rebellious thoughts still unconquered, he turned the door handle and entered.

His mother was sitting in her accustomed chair, upright and

severe in her black dress, with Monsignor Scholti standing beside her, bending over with benign solicitude as he listened to what she was saying. Father Salvatore found it unacceptable to find them in such intimacy, and instantly annoying that they stopped talking as soon as he had made his appearance. Theirs was not quite a guilty silence, but once more it brought childhood recollections : this was the silence of grown-ups when children entered the room, it was the guarding of adult 'secrets' again, the line drawn between free conversation and the version which must be edited for little pitchers with long ears. It was really intolerable.

His mother, facing the door, at least smiled at his entrance; whereas Monsignor Scholti turned with an affected start, as if some important business had been interrupted in spite of strict orders to the contrary. When Father Salvatore advanced to greet his mother, Scholti did not even give ground, but remained where he was at the side of the chair, disdaining common politeness in favour of a privileged nearness.

'You are so late, Salvatore,' the Baroness complained, as soon as he had kissed her. 'And Monsignor Scholti came early.'

'So I see... I'm very sorry. There were all sorts of excitements down at the harbour, but no boat to take me across.' He nodded to the other man. 'Good morning, Bruno. I hope you're well.'

Scholt gave him a curt, almost disciplinary nod. 'Oh yes, oh yes. As well as one can be, with a load of work which would kill a donkey!'

'I'm sure no one compares you with a donkey.'

'I should hope not!'

His mother interrupted. 'Well, sit down, now that you are here. The coffee is still hot, though it tastes perfectly terrible. These girls haven't the faintest idea how to make it properly.'

She sounded so unlike her normal self that he looked at her more closely. She had become a little frail during the past few months, and her face had that inner pallor, that fragile tautness, which he had come to associate with the first margins of mortality. The changes in the household, dictated not by herself but by forces she could not control, had annoyed her, and thus tired her more than they should.

Though she sat as straight as ever, it was now the straightness of stern self-discipline, not of natural habit. She was in her seventy-fifth year, and at long last the sad fact must be faced that time was taking its toll. This morning, the pettish voice, inclined to shrillness, was the deepest mark of decay he had ever noticed.

'I'm sure coffee will be excellent, as usual,' he said. 'You must cheer up, Mother. We have so much to be thankful for.'

'It's easy to say that.' Monsignor Scholti's tone was reproving, in a way which revived all Father Salvatore's rebellious mood. 'But your mother has a great deal to worry her. She has had a letter from Paris, with some very bad news.'

Father Salvatore forced himself to turn towards Scholti. The other man's protective air was almost impossible to endure. This was *his* mother, *his* mother... 'A letter from Paris? How can that be? Was it smuggled out? I don't understand.'

Scholti made an impatient gesture. 'Well, to be exact, a letter from England, with some news from Paris which came from a neutral diplomat there. Really, Salvu, what a time to ask such questions! It is the news that matters, not how it reached Malta!'

Father Salvatore turned back again, without answering this rebuke, and gave all his attention to his mother.

'Was the news from Benedict?'

'It was *about* Benedict,' the Baroness answered sharply. She was really very agitated – an astonishing departure from all that he knew of her. 'Your dear brother had been distinguishing himself on a truly magnificent scale!'

'Please tell me. What has he been doing?'

'Only *collaborating*! Only entertaining Field-Marshal Göring and half his staff at Maxim's!'

Father Salvatore felt like laughing. Of course it was disgraceful that the heir of the Santo-Nobiles should do such a thing, but the heir of the Santo-Nobiles had been misbehaving, in the full glare of publicity, for over twenty years, and there was scarcely anything he could now do which would seem in any way extraordinary.

Father Salvatore loved his elder brother for his kinship, as he was enjoined to do, and despised him for his myriad weaknesses, because he made no discernible effort to resist them, and forgave him, because if gentle Jesus could understand, and forgive, a notorious whore, then gentle Salvatore could do the same for a wastrel and a sinner. Benedict dining with Göring at Maxim's? One could almost be jealous. The food must have been *marvellous*! ...

The Baroness had no such indulgent thoughts. 'I have it in mind to disinherit him! Instantly!'

Monsignor Scholti had no such thoughts either. 'I can assure you, everyone would understand. There would be no question of that.'

Father Salvatore could only add: 'Legally, it would be almost impossible.' But he could scarcely suppress his private amusement at Scholti's backing for such an idea. What a fearsome choice it must have been! If Brother Benedict was disinherited, then the next Baron Santo-Nobile would be Salvatore himself.

The Baroness seemed to detect the fact that her son was not taking this very seriously. 'Salvatore, have you no pride?'

'I try not to have. It is a sin.'

Scholti said stiffly: 'We are not talking of *sins*. Of course, your mother means ancestral pride, the pride which compels one to uphold the honour of a family such as yours. There is absolutely no harm in that. Very much the reverse!'

Father Salvatore had had enough of Scholti. 'That sounds like a very interesting Maltese heresy.'

Monsignor Scholti glared at him, not without reason. The remark had been injudicious and, since he had made it on purpose, undeniably impudent. What had prompted it was more than an irritation with Scholti. Indeed, such irritation had largely vanished, between his entering the room and hearing about his brother in Paris. Father Salvatore was now aware of a strange light-heartedness, by contrast with his first ill-humour: it was as if he had suddenly decided that nothing could make him unhappy on this happy day. It must be the little Italian motor-boats, and their bravery, and their utter rout at the hands of the Maltese gunners.

For the first time in many months, he felt supremely careless. The vision of the slim and elegant Benedict, the product of first-class tailoring and second-class morality, plying Hermann Göring with vintage Champagne, while the fat Field-Marshal ogled the pretty girls (or the pretty *commis* waiters, so it was said) in the plush opulence of Maxim's, was really hilarious, compared with Malta's stringency, Malta's doleful rationing.

The fact that they should be worrying so much about it,

wringing their hands at such social iniquity, while Malta revelled in its own good news at last, was also ridiculous.

His mother was speaking, 'Whether it is *almost impossible* or not, to disinherit him, I shall certainly consider it.'

He knew that he owed her more than a light-hearted verdict. 'Of course it is sad that Benedict is making a fool of himself again. And I am truly sorry that you should be worried about it. But we shouldn't be too surprised, should we? I imagine that the situation in Paris, under the occupation, is very difficult indeed.'

Scholti said grandly : 'That is no excuse!'

'Even so, we should try to find excuses. We should put ourselves in the same position, and try to guess at the result. I wonder how certain of the Maltese would react, if the Germans were installed in San Anton Palace. If it was likely that they would be there for years, if not for ever. I wonder how *you* would react, if a German general invited you to dine at the Palace, and the alternative was dismissal from the Bishop's staff, or demotion to simple priest. Or just plain hunger.'

Scholti was all fiery resolution. 'I hope that I would reject such an invitation with contempt!'

'Oh, so do I. But we are not all made of the same stern fibre.'

'Are you making excuses for your brother's treachery?'

'Yes.'

His mother, who had been watching them, turning from one to the other like a bird seeking sanctuary, broke in. Her voice was almost plaintive.

'But *why*, Salvatore? I thought you would be as shocked as I am. And think of the disgrace!'

'The disgrace is Benedict's, not ours. Benedict can no longer shock me. Can he shock you?'

'He can go too far.'

'Not at Maxim's... Surely there are worse things than accepting social flattery, social bribery, even from the German High Command. I am quite certain that he has *gone too far* already, on the only path which really matters, that he has committed all the sins... This last one is mere feebleness, mere vanity. I doubt if Benedict could appreciate the difference between entertaining Göring, the arch-enemy of France, and entertaining Joan of Arc. He has a weakness for celebrities, that is all. They give him a warm feeling of achievement... There is nothing we can do about it, anyway. It is no use hissing our disgust, far away in Malta. It is something for God ...' He leaned over, and clasped his mother's hand, so wasted, so white and bony. It made his own feel like a peasant's paw. 'The only bad thing is the way it has hurt you.'

'You believe that I should forgive him?'

'I believe that you should understand him, and show compassion.'

'Well! ...' Scholti began, on a scandalized note.

'It is also a family matter.' What was prompting him to such *bravado*? It must be the little Italian boats again. 'So we must cheer up, and look on the bright side. Did you hear about the torpedo-boat raid?'

They had heard about the torpedo-boat raid. Monsignor Scholti had heard *all* about it.

'It was of course the beginning of the invasion,' he declared, ready to take the centre of this stage also. 'But I am told that they will think twice before trying again. Their fleet was utterly smashed! We have probably taken thousands of prisoners!'

Father Salvatore let him talk on. The change of subject was all that he wanted; the wild suppositions, the pretence of inside information, did not matter. Even when, at the end, Monsignor Scholti said 'I am sure your mother is tired,' and rose to go, clearly intending to take Salvatore with him at the same time, such presumption did not seem important. He made his farewell as if it were nothing out of the ordinary, glad to see that his mother now seemed more relaxed, more reconciled to her dire news from Paris.

He said: 'If I may, I will telephone you from Giovanna's,' and left their proper intimacy till later.

Monsignor Scholti, however, had not finished with his side of things. He had only been controlling his displeasure.

'I did not wish to speak of it before your mother,' he said, with a formidable change of manner, as soon as they were outside the postern door. 'She has suffered enough already. But your remark about heresy was really unforgiveable.'

'It was a joke, Bruno.'

'It was not a joke to me. You seem to forget that I am your superior.'

'Only in rank.' It was hopeless: he could not take things

seriously today. 'No, no, I withdraw that. You are my superior in every way. In rank, in looks, in social graces, in access to official secrets. You have the ear of his Lordship—'

'*Salvu*—' Scholti began furiously.

'You also have the ear of my sacristan.'

For once, Monsignor Scholti was taken aback. 'What do you mean by that?'

'I think you know. You have been talking to Rafel, haven't you?'

'We met by chance in the street. That is all.'

'It seems to have been enough. Was it you who made him go back to Gozo?'

'I certainly did nothing to dissuade him.'

'Did you tell him that what I was doing was wrong?'

'He told *me*!' Scholti suddenly launched into violent speech, which showed not only a guilty mind but also that poor simple Rafel had been lured into all kinds of indiscretion, ambiguous and damning alike. There were accounts of 'gross defilements' in the catacombs : of Father Salvatore's permissive attitude to sexual misbehaviour – he had actually laughed when a flagrant case of self-abuse was reported, and said : 'At eleven, he is too young to marry' : his tolerance of noise and wild parties : his carelessness over money matters : his laxity in religious observance : his ridiculous 'performances' which took the place of a proper homily, and showed that the catacomb was not a real church at all.

He had called St Paul 'an ugly old man with bow legs'. He had made fun of the blessed St Publius. He had curtailed the Mass on the pretext of so-called rescue work which should have been left to the proper authorities. He had questioned miracles which had been certified by Holy Church... 'Apparently I cannot save you from corruption, Salvu,' Monsignor Scholti ended, on a note of doom. 'But at least I can rescue an innocent like Rafel Vella from being contaminated!'

It was ridiculous and pathetic at the same time. Father Salvatore could not even bear to answer back. The main charges were baseless, in the context of the catacombs. There had been no 'performances' for more than six months. But with heaven's help, and such provocation as this, there very soon would be! ...

'Which way are you going, Bruno?'

'*What?* Is that all you have to say?'

'Yes. I forgive you... Which way are you going?'

Scholti gestured with an uncertain hand. 'Down there, I suppose.'

'Then I am going up here. Goodbye. God bless you.'

Presently he found himself back on the bastions again, free as the air under the warm sunshine. But now came a surprise of a different sort. The first person he recognized, among a throng of chattering cheerful people still engrossed in the morning's victory, was his niece Marija.

She was alone with two tall young men in uniform, a sailor and a soldier. They all stood close together, and they were laughing. But when she turned to look up at the sailor, Marija's face was so utterly blissful that its beauty gained tenfold, transformed as if by magic.

As he walked towards them – both as an uncle and a priest, he must look into this – Father Salvatore realized that there was in fact true magic in the air. Indeed, he had never before seen Marija like this: never observed such shining eyes, such happy freedom, such an open avowal of life and love, in the days since she was born.

3

Pietru Pawl had asked, for the third time: 'What are we waiting here for? There's nothing to see,' before Marija decided on desperate remedies. She had to stay on the bastions, and Pietru had to stay with her, for family reasons which were too complicated to be denied. Finally she said: 'Can you keep a secret?'

Pietru, though wild about secrets, knew that keeping them was another matter. 'That depends. Not if it's something silly.'

'It's not silly. It's terribly important.'

'And it's terribly important for me to have an ice-cream before I die of thirst. And some *pasti* before I die of hunger.' But he was forced to add: 'What sort of secret?'

'Promise you won't tell anyone.' While she spoke, Marija's eyes were still searching the bastions, and the long approach to them. 'Not anyone in the whole world.'

'That depends.'

'Oh, *Pietru*!'

'It's no good saying "Oh Pietru" like that. We have our pride, the male line of the Santo-Nobiles. The last secret I kept for you was about selling your stamp collection, and I heard *Carmelina* talking about it, the very next day. You'd better tell me first, and I'll decide if it's a worthwhile secret.'

'That's just blackmail.'

'My speciality.'

She saw that this line was no good. Simple avarice might be the answer as so often before. 'I've got a better idea. Stay with me for another quarter of an hour, and I'll give you – I'll give you—'

'You'll give me what? And why are you looking all over the place like a mad old woman?'

'It's the female line of the Santo-Nobiles.' Her voice had suddenly changed, from desperation to a triumphant happiness, and before he could quite take it in, she said: 'I'll give you absolutely *nothing*!' and raised her hand to wave.

It was Michael Ainslie, splendid in uniform, beautiful as this day and a hundred days like it... He smiled as he caught sight of her, and strode swiftly past the people who separated them. He trod the bastions like their newest conqueror. Pietru Pawl, turning to find out the cause of action, could think of nothing to say but 'Ho, ho! What have we here?'

'Pietru! Please behave.'

'*Me* behave? You were *waving*!'

Then his time ran out, and two became three, and Michael Ainslie was the blessed, the fabulous third.

He saluted. What did girls do when they were saluted? As far as Marija was concerned, their insides turned over and all they could manage was a silly, joyous smile. Pietru, immensely impressed, saluted back, his hand ripping up to his golden forelock as if it bore all the brass insignia in the whole world of rank. Then his mouth dropped open, and stayed open and, for a happy change, absolutely speechless.

'I'm terribly sorry I'm late,' Michael Ainslie said. 'But I've got quite a good excuse.'

'It doesn't matter,' Marija answered, and indeed it now mattered less than anything else in all her life so far. 'Oh – this is my brother, Pietru.'

Michael held out his hand. 'That means Peter.' He was excited, keyed up, and the fact was apparent in every move he made and every inflexion of his voice. 'I'm Michael Ainslie, just in case your sister forgot.'

Pietru, still wordless, shook hands. His avid eyes were taking in every detail of the uniform : the beautiful doe-skin cloth, the two gold stripes with the little A in the circle, the gold buttons, the peaked cap with the gleaming white cover, the glossy black half-boots. He had never been so near to such gorgeous perfection.

'I didn't forget,' Marija said. 'Well, of course I *forgot*...' It was without doubt the silliest sentence any girl had ever uttered, and she strove to improve on it, to catch up with reality. 'What did you mean when you said you had a good excuse?'

He turned towards her, and his pleasure in doing so was obvious. 'Well, as a matter of fact – and do stop me if you've heard this one before – I was sinking an Italian E-boat.'

'Michael!'

'True as I stand before you.' He meant 'stand near to you', and they both knew it, and were delighted. 'Believe it or not, a man woke me up and said "Get dressed, Ainslie, get into that Hurricane, get airborne, and *get weaving*! There's a funny-looking boat with a red-white-and-green flag, due north of your bedstead. It's running away. Sink it!" You know, the man was right!'

'But did you really sink it?'

'Subject to confirmation, as they say when they may be telling lies, the score in Ainslie versus Mussolini is now one-nil.'

'But that's wonderful!'

'Personally I think the Italians were nuts to wake me up.' Suddenly he stretched out his arms, embracing the sunlit world and everyone in it. 'Oh, it was such a lovely morning! Fancy coming all the way from Sicily, just to try and spoil it.'

'They deserved everything they got!'

'Those chaps deserved a lot more, if you ask me. I wouldn't have made that trip in an underwater battle-wagon. But that's a long and subversive story. You can put me down for two guineas.' He smiled at Marija. 'I've said that to you before, haven't I? That's the trouble with living with the Raff. There was I, surrounded by pale-blue catch-phrases. I'll be more careful in future.'

There was a future already.

Pietru, his sparkling brown eyes now looking as if they grew on stalks, came to the surface breathlessly.

'Did you say a *Hurricane*?'

'Yes. Mark Two.' Michael checked himself. 'You are now in possession of a military secret known only to the enemy.' He bent down, and whispered fiercely in Pietru's ear: *'Don't leave the country!'*

Pietru, utterly captivated, lost no time in consolidating this marvellous friendship. 'But aren't you a sailor?'

'A flying sailor. That's rather like a tame duck. As soon as we get scared enough, we take to the air and, flying round in ever-decreasing circles—' but he did not want to finish it. 'I'm shore-based now, anyway. Are you interested in flying?'

'Oh yes! Specially the Fleet Air Arm!' The questions flooded over. What was the difference between a Hurricane and one of the new *Seafires*? What was it like to take off from an aircraft-carrier? And landing – what happened if the hooks didn't work? Where was *Illustrious* now? Would she be coming back again? How long had Michael Ainslie been in the Navy? Was it easy to get in? How did one find out if one was colour-blind? Did you learn to fly first, and then join the Navy, or join the Navy and learn to fly? What did 'vectoring' really mean? How could you possibly hit a ship with a shell at thirteen miles, like the *Warspite* had hit the *Cesare*?

'Bless your little cotton socks,' said Michael, after ten minutes of this. 'You know more than I do.'

'My grandfather was killed at the Battle of Jutland.'

'Well, good for him... That wasn't very well put, was it? I mean' – he turned to Marija, comically baffled. 'What did I mean?'

She could rescue him! It was a partnership again, after dan-derous diversions and great waste of time.

'Pietru, *hanini*,' she said. 'Don't you want to go and buy that ice-cream?'

'What, *now*?'

'You said you were dying of thirst.'

'That was ages ago...' Pietru turned back to Michael. 'Is it true that—'

'Pietru,' Michael said, with a reasonable air of authority.

'Yes, sir?'

'A word in your ear.'

It was very adroitly done, out of earshot and almost out of sight. When Michael returned, after a couple of sentences and what looked like a handshake, he was alone.

'Where did he go?' Marija asked.

'Shopping.'

'But it was so quick.'

'We're both realists.'

'Michael! Explain.' But suddenly it didn't need much explanation. 'Did you give him some money? How much?'

'Half a crown.'

'Half a crown!' Now she was really shocked. 'Sixpence would have been plenty. But what did you tell him?'

He was standing very close to her, his hand on her arm. 'I just told him, man to man, that I wanted to smother you with kisses.'

'You didn't!'

'No. That's a secret. Actually I said I wanted to talk to you alone, and here was half a crown to prove it.'

'What did he say?'

Michael laughed. 'He said: "I am baffled, Watson, baffled. But thank you all the same." Then he took the money, and charged off... That's quite a lad. I must say, you're a handsome lot, the Debrincats. How old is he?'

'Fourteen.'

'Good lord! When I was fourteen I'd only just given up knitting.' He stretched out his arms again. He was becoming marvellously relaxed, and so was she. It did not matter what they said to each other, nor how silly and vulnerable they were. 'I had two older sisters. Great knitters. When I was nine, I decided if they could knit, so could I.'

'What did you knit?'

'Grey scarves for old-age pensioners. Only my sisters had to cast on for me. Then I did the middle bit. Then they had to cast off at the end. If they were both away, or we had a row, that scarf could be nine feet long.'

'Did you often have rows?'

'Oh yes. Big sisters can give you hell. Do you give Pietru hell?'

'That's not an expression we use.'

'Are you religious?'

'Well, of course.'

K.M.—12

'I'm not. But I've got some saints I rely on.'

'So have I. Which are yours?'

'Saint Michael and all Ainslies.'

It was a moment before she could take it in. 'That's not a nice thing to say.'

'I thought it was rather clever... Oh, you're so beautiful when you're shocked.' Now he had taken hold of her hand instead of her arm, and an important frontier had been crossed. There was another, almost immediately ahead. 'Do you smother easily?'

This was a serious question. 'I don't know yet.'

'That's *very* good news.'

It was incredible to think that they were, at last, alone. It was only the third time in six awful months.

She could have recited them all by heart, along with her prayers, with places faithfully described and precious hours measured by the minute-hand of joy.

The first time didn't count as a *time*; it was just the fantastic beginning, never to be forgotten, and special for ever afterwards. It was the second meeting which, in her loving private mind, started the sequence.

Michael had rung her up early next morning, as they had planned (she had waited by the telephone, in dressing-gown and slippers, from half past five till nearly seven); and somehow, by juggling with a shopping trip and a vague appointment with a girl cousin, she had managed to meet him in Floriana, and have coffee in an obscure café called, adorably, the Benevolent. But it was not as good as they had hoped.

He was still terribly worried about his ship, and didn't know when she was going to sail, or where, or how long he might be away. For some stupid, disjointed reason, it was almost as if he didn't know why he was sitting talking to her. They parted in secret despair which neither could yet admit, because nothing important in this tender area had been spoken aloud. It had set the sad, heart-rending pattern of love in wartime.

He had sailed away without warning, breaking another appointment with no word of goodbye; harsh security dictated *that* piece of the pattern, as it dictated so many others. She knew now that he had been on the swift critical journey to Alexandria. There followed a miserable separation of two whole months. He wrote ambiguous, cheerful, indecisive notes

– he was better with spoken words than on paper, and his handwriting was disgraceful – and presently the notes were headed 'HMS *Ark Royal*', and after that she never knew where he was, to the nearest five thousand miles.

Suddenly he came back to Malta – and this was the second remembered time – in another aircraft-carrier, the ancient 1917 veteran *Argus*. But it was only for half a day, between convoys, and it was a horrible meeting, somewhere in the 'Ditch' below the bastions of Valletta. He had been strung up to the point of insanity, and rather drunk as well. He had tried to kiss her almost straight away, and she had been silly about it.

It had all been dreadful, and she had cried for days and nights afterwards. But tears could not bring him back, nor the lost kisses either. Another long separation, of nearly four months, star-crossed their lives again, dividing them fatally, rationing the priceless chances on the same sordid scale as butter or olive oil. Though he had written 'There's no one like you in the world', she was sure that he was with horrid, *easy* girls all the time.

She was also sure that he would be killed (she knew this could happen at any moment, because of a story he told her) before she could explain that she had changed her mind. Though what she had changed her mind about was almost impossible to say, or to write.

Then, fantastically, he had rung up last night. He telephoned from the RAF base at Hal Far, and though he talked guardedly, the news was overwhelming enough. He was ashore in Malta! Land-based! He was flying different aircraft. He ought to be free next morning, 'unless there's a flap'. Could they meet at that point on the bastions where they had first seen each other?

What other answer could there be but Yes, though a hundred problems stood in the way? She spent a sleepless night in delirious joy, ecstatically glad to know that he was here, planning *exactly* what she would say and do this time, thanking God and the compassionate Virgin that Michael was not in an aircraft-carrier any more. There was a special reason for this.

At the beginning of the awful *Argus* meeting, he had told her, because it was so long afterwards and the secret was known, a terrible story about the *Argus* herself. It was the story of how some of its planes, flown off for Malta, had, in a slang phrase which masked a desolate fate, 'run out of air'.

The *Argus*, venerable and stately, creaking like many another old lady of the same vintage, was not a real aircraft-carrier at all, in the operational sense, but a converted merchantman now largely used to ferry aircraft towards the point where they were needed, fly them off, and head for home again before such a lumbering target could be discovered by the enemy.

She carried, on this November 1940 journey, a squadron of twelve new Hurricane fighters, with two Skuas to guide them, destined for Malta and needed there as no other planes had ever been needed before. With her delivery to make, she approached the island from the west.

This was not a dramatic operation; it was a problem in mathematics rather than a death-or-glory dash. The farther eastwards she ventured towards Malta, the greater the danger to herself from an Italian fleet known to be at sea. She must therefore carry the planes only as far as necessary. It was an equation, quite simple by slide-rule standards, involving two factors: the fuel-consumption of the aircraft, and the weather they might encounter on the way.

Tail winds would give them a few extra miles in range; head-winds meant that a margin-of-safety allowance must be made. *Argus*, having done the necessary sums, released her flock of fourteen doves, shortly to become hawks, at dawn just south of Sardinia, in what seemed like ideal conditions. They had 420 miles to go, a wind blowing steadily and comfortably behind them – west-south-west at 16–20 knots, and a known endurance of 520 miles in still air. They could thus over-fly Malta by a clear 100 miles.

Of course it might be a close-run thing; so were countless other calculations of war. But *Argus* herself, with a thousand men on board, was also important... Thus she flew off her Hurricanes with a good conscience, unable to forecast that, within a few hours, the close-run thing would become a disastrous treachery.

The squadron had flown 250 miles, with 170 to go, when the guiding Skuas, and the Hurricanes behind them, noticed something serious on the surface of the sea below. It was the wave-formation. This, which had been ruffled in their favour, was now ruffled against them. There was only one explanation. It meant that the Mediterranean wind, which had become the despair of weather prophets centuries before St Paul was trapped by its malice, had suddenly changed. It had whipped round from that safe forecast of 'westerly', almost 180 degrees to east-south-east. The creaming wave-tops showed that it was increasing steadily. The build-up of mist and cloud promised a severe storm ahead.

Presently the beleaguered Hurricanes were flying blind. Presently it became clear that they could *not* overfly Malta by a 100 miles. Or ten miles. Or any miles. They were not going to make it. The easterly gale was dead against them, and they were dead against it.

The pilots did their best, in the only way they could. They had nowhere else to go but Malta, a hundred miles ahead in the teeth of the weather. They throttled back to their best-known 'economical speed', and juggled with the mixture-control, to get the last ounce of performance out of their engines. But pre-war parsimony had cut short the training of these new pilots. *They did not really know how best to economize with fuel on these planes.*

Fifty miles short of Malta, their engines began to splutter, and then to cut out. Urgent calls for help filled the turbulent air, and could not be answered, and faded abruptly. One by one they plummeted down, uttering the faint cries of exhausted birds as they dropped to sea-level, and lost their wings for ever.

Nine out of the fourteen made this first and last plunge, and were abandoned. Only five survivors landed in Malta, struggling home with three gallons of petrol to spare, with two, with none. They left behind them, with the sick hearts of survivors, the nine who could never be rescued, whose wild graves were unmarked after the first few seconds of committal.

Marija could shed bitter tears, and had done so, every time she thought of that story. But she did not think of it now, on this bright morning. Michael was not dead, lolling upright in his sodden Mae West, broiled black and then bleached by the sun above and the fish below. He was wonderfully alive, and next to her, and within reach at last.

He was asking: 'Why did you bring your brother along? Not that I mind.'

'Mother said I wasn't to wander about town alone. So I promised not to.'

'That's going to make it difficult.'

'Make what difficult.'

'Marija!' he said immediately. 'Please don't look at me like that. Do you want to drive a man mad?'

'That depends.'

He drew a deep breath. 'Am I glad to be still alive... Tell me, what was that you called him?'

'Pietru?'

'No. The word after.'

She thought back. 'Oh yes. Hanini?'

'That's it. What does it mean?'

'It means – well, "darling" is the nearest.'

Their eyes were very busy. 'Can I call you hanini?'

'Of course not!'

'I think that I will.'

A most intrusive voice, much too near to them, broke a magic moment. 'What ho!' it said. 'Is this how the flying Jack Tars relax? I think I'll swap uniforms!'

They turned from each other, not without an effort, and faced the invasion. A tall young soldier was standing in front of them, grinning all over a freckled face. He had red hair, and a sharp pointed nose, inquisitive and aristocratic at the same time. He was almost overwhelmingly smart: he shone all over, from the strap of his beret to the elegant pointed toe-caps of his shoes. His uniform was enhanced by the gold-tasselled aiguillettes of an aide-de-camp.

'Ian,' Michael Ainslie said, without enthusiasm.

'Hallo, Mike! I hear you distinguished yourself this morning.' He was staring at Marija. 'But not half as much as now. Who's this absolutely ravishing girl?'

Michael introduced them, in a voice so grumpy that Marija could have laughed, if she had not felt the same about the intrusion. Captain Ian Ross had roving eyes and a very knowing smile indeed, and he used them all most effectively during the next few minutes; it was clear that their presence on the bastions, close together, obviously enjoying each other's company, was for him something between a ripe scandal and a welcome invitation to indulge his particular sense of humour. This ranged adroitly from the barracks to the barnyard.

Michael grew progressively more bad-tempered. Finally, when Ross said something about all the nice girls loving a sailor, and a sailor loving *all* the nice girls, tra la la, with the same sly inflexion as before, he broke in with a cool change of subject:

'What are you doing up here, Ian? Or is it the army's day off?'

'We never sleep,' Ian Ross answered. 'Very moral lot...' But at least he showed some sort of reaction to Michael's tone. 'As a matter of fact I've been touring all the gun-sites with my master.'

'Who is your master?' Marija asked. She did not really want to know; she was only glad that he had one.

'The Reverend Dobbie. No, I mustn't call him that. His Ex, our gallant Governor. He wanted to say a hearty "Well done" to the chaps. I must say they deserved it. There was some mighty shooting this morning. I've never seen gunners so pleased with themselves.' But he could not leave Marija for long. 'Did I hear Debrincat, when your sailor friend introduced us? Any relation of Lewis of that ilk?'

'I beg your pardon?'

'Lewis Debrincat. You know, the—' but he bit off whatever he was going to say.

'My father,' Marija said.

'Oh.' A wary look came into Ross's face. 'Then the esteemed Baroness must be your grandmother.'

'Yes.'

'Well, well. No wonder Mike's in such an uproar. Personally I'd settle just for those big grey eyes, any time.'

She turned away, embarrassed. It was not the sort of conversation she had ever been involved in before. And he wasn't looking at her eyes at all... Behind her she heard Michael mutter, with the utmost savagery: *'Cut it out, Ian!'* and the other man answer: 'Sorry, old boy. I didn't realize.' (Later, Michael was to tell her: 'I like Ian. But I don't like Ian and you. In fact, I don't like *anyone* and you.') It was a great relief to find, when she turned back again, that Ian Ross was suddenly much better in every way.

'Forgive a rough soldier,' he said. In his faultless uniform and splendid accoutrements, he looked about as rough as the young Duke of Wellington, and they all laughed. Their talk grew easier. Marija searched Michael's face for good-humour again, and was rewarded. Then Ian Ross, glancing over her shoulder, spoke of something new. 'Don't look now,' he cautioned. 'But that funny little black beetle seems to know you.'

Marija turned again, and felt her heart sink. 'He's my uncle,' she said. It was a pleasure to see Ross, for a change, totally embarrassed. But it was, otherwise, not at all a comfortable moment.

She introduced them coolly and efficiently, though it was far from her true mood. Uncle Salvu was looking very guarded and watchful... Then Captain Ross, who had not recovered from his *gaffe*, took himself off with the minimum of delay, and the three of them were left. She prayed that there would not be too many questions just yet. It was going to take hours to think of the answers.

The first question was easy enough.

'Are you here alone, Marija?'

'No, no.' Her reply came, perhaps, a little too quickly. 'Pietru is with me. He just went off to buy something.'

'H'm.' It explained nothing, and Father Salvatore felt bound to pursue the subject. 'So you met—' he had forgotten the young man's name already, and he could only repeat, rather awkwardly: 'So you met.'

'We've met before,' Marija said bravely. It was all going to come out: there were endless hazards ahead: better to face them. 'Two or three times, in fact. Michael is stationed in Malta now.'

Michael... In spite of lawful suspicions, Father Salvatore found himself irresistibly drawn towards the splendid young man with the alarmingly attractive smile, who was looking down at him so intently. Was this the knight in shining armour? 'So you're in the Navy?' he said, for want of a better probe.

'Fleet Air Arm, sir,' Michael answered. 'I was here in *Illustrious*, originally.'

'O-o-oh...' Things fell neatly into place: Marija's confused look and heightened colour supplied the links. '*Illustrious*... She isn't back here, surely?'

'No. Still being repaired, I'm afraid.'

'I'm not surprised about that. I went on board, the first night she arrived.'

'Yes, I know, sir.'

How did he know? That could be found out later. The young man looked honest and open : not dangerous, except in the way that all the explosive young were dangerous. Father Salvatore decided to relax his role of inquisitor; the crowds round them, and the ring of dancing water, were too happy a setting, the sun too hot for persistence. He said : 'It was really amazing that the ship went away so quickly, from what I saw of her.'

To Marija's relief, Michael and Uncle Salvu now got on very well. Michael was polite and deferential : the word 'sir' reappeared every few moments. They talked about the ship, and convoys, and rationing in Malta. Then, for no reason at all, the subject was boots.

'If you really want a new pair, sir, I could fix it with the RAF. The erks — I mean the aircraftmen wear the kind you like.' Michael looked down, politely yet dubiously, at Father Salvatore's feet, and their deplorable covering. 'If that's what you really want. I know they've got about a million pairs in stock. But they're a bit *bulbous*. Are you sure you wouldn't prefer—' and he raised his trouser leg to display the slim half-Wellingtons of a dressy junior officer.

'No, I want the ordinary kind,' Father Salvatore answered. 'Big toecaps, and laces that go round those little metal clips, and good thick soles. I've seen them. They would be just right.'

'What size do you take?'

Father Salvatore did not know. Maltese boot-makers in this particular line did not make sizes, only big, medium, and small. He and Michael, linking arms, measured their feet side by side, Marija delighting in the absurd picture, and decided that size nine would be the likely answer. While they were still smiling at their ingenuity, Pietru Pawl reappeared.

'Uncle Salvu! Are you *dancing*?'

'No, Peter Paul, I am not dancing.' Father Salvatore straightened up, and smoothed his ruffled cassock. 'But I see you have been eating.' Crumbs and a ring of milky white round his mouth betrayed the gluttonous boy. 'You know it will spoil your lunch.'

'Not mine. I only had two *pasti* and some ice-cream.'

Father Salvatore sighed. 'I don't know where you get your money from.' For some reason this seemed to amuse everyone else inordinately, and looking from one smiling face to another he felt so close to youthful happiness, so much at one with the guileless joy of the world, that he could only see it as a privilege. Details must certainly come later; in the meantime, innocence and laughter supplied and deserved their own passport. He looked at his watch. 'It's nearly time we were on our way. Peter Paul, will you go and find us a *karrozzin*, and we'll ride home in style.'

'But I wanted to ask about bomb-sights.'

Michael said : 'I'll tell you all about them next time.'

'Is it true there's one that has a spider's web inside, to make the . . .' he did not know the right word.

'The cross-bars? Well it was partly true, at the experimental stage.' He smiled. 'Next time. All right?'

'But when's next time?'

Both Michael and Marija being wordless, Father Salvatore supplied the answer : 'That depends. Now go and choose us the best *karrozzin* in Floriana.'

When Pietru was gone, rebellious but sustained by promises, Father Salvatore shook his head. 'Spider's webs? Bomb-sights? I don't know where that young man picks up all his information. . . I'm sorry to cut short this meeting,' he told Michael, 'but today is our family lunch day.'

'Yes, I know.'

There was a lot this young man seemed to know. Perhaps that was as it should be : it gave whatever was going on – and he was still a long way from discovering even the rudiments of this – a certain honesty, a certain respectable frame. He looked from Marija to Michael Ainslie, and back again. What he saw, in their nervous, electric, private entrancement made his next move easy to determine.

'I think I'll just make sure that Peter Paul is doing what I want.' He pointed to the lower street-level behind them. 'Meet us down there. Shall we say, in two minutes?'

They joined him again in five, which was a reasonable extension, Pietru had picked a really fine *karrozzin*, a splendid turn-out of polished brasswork, gleaming leather, tossing plumes, and intricately studded harness. The driver, whom Father Salvatore knew by sight, said : 'Hey, Dun Salv! What about all those Italians we sunk!' and flourished his feathered whip as if he were asserting, against all comers, the freedom of the seas.

Marija and Michael walked down from the bastion, studiously apart, looking sad and secret and happy and expectant, all at the same time. Young lovers could do this, old priests could not. Father Salvatore held out his hand.

'Goodbye, and good luck.'

'Thank you, sir. I hope we meet again some time.'

'I wouldn't be at all surprised.'

'Goodbye, Pietru. Remind me to tell you about the Royal Navy dolphins some time.' Michael saluted them all, smiled in the vague direction of Marija, and was gone almost before they realized it.

'*Dolphins?* I bet that's something to do with submarine detection!' But Pietru was very impressed with something else. 'Uncle Salvu! He called you "sir".'

'That's because I'm older.'

'Well, of course. But still... He's a Hurricane pilot !... Can I ride on the front seat with the driver?'

'I think that's a very good idea.'

To the clip-clop of the hooves as they went downhill, Father Salvatore, sitting beside his niece, and out of earshot of anyone else in the world, said :

'*Now.* What is all *this* about?'

'Dear Uncle Salvu' – Marija was at her most appealing, '*please* don't be angry with me.'

'Why should I be angry, Marija? Is it something sinful?'

The startled look in her face was a joy to see. 'No, no! How could it be?'

'Deceit is sinful. Have you told your mother about this meeting?'

'Well, no ... I didn't want to worry her. Not that there's anything to worry about... You won't say anything to her, will you? Not just yet.'

'Deceit is sinful,' he said again. 'I need to know more. How many times have you met him?'

'Only three. Three times, in six months and ten days.'

'Tell me more about these other times. Tell me about the beginning.'

She told him. It was another sort of joy, as their *karrozzin* wound its way onwards at a gallant pace, to listen to her meticulous accounting, to hear the why and wherefore of chance meetings which became milestones of excitement and awakening. Father Salvatore had heard many such stories, within the confessional and outside it; usually they were cheap and shoddy stuff, often dishonourable, sometimes revolting.

What distinguished Marija's account was the purity which shone out of it. She wished to obey, she wished to love and give, she wished to know. It rejoiced him, as it would have rejoiced her mother, his dearest sister Giovanna.

Marija returned, at the end, to the violent preoccupation of the young. 'But I *do* want it to be a secret. Uncle Salvu, *please* trust me.'

'I trust you, if you trust yourself. Do you love Michael?'

'I don't know. We don't know. Not yet. But it feels like it. It isn't wrong, is it?'

It feels like it... Is it wrong? ... Here she had given him a glimpse of unknown, disputed territory, forsworn by a priest, forbidden by decree and then by life-long habit. What it felt like, to be in love, he had never known and, after the first few turbulent years, had never wished to discover. If marriage was, as the Church enjoined, a great mystery, then love itself was the final enigma, to which the simple and the lucky might find a key, the greedy and the lustful never. And here was little Marija already voyaging on these perilous seas...

All the music of their movement – the creaking of the carriage, the clopping of the horse's hooves, the cool breeze under the tasselled canopy of the *karrozzin*, the sunlight of Msida Creek and the foreshore of Ta'-Xbiex – all supplied a dreamy, faraway background to his thoughts. If he had not been a priest, would a love such as this have come his way, and all the doubts which went with it? Would it have been a turmoil or a blessing? Would it have seemed clean and reputable, or the loathsome reverse? How did engulfing desire for another's body become seemly, sanctioned love – not within the law, but within the chaste soul?

What could he tell Marija, so fresh and beautiful, so tempting and tempted, trembling with such delight on the verge of divine discovery – what could he tell such a girl, when he did not know himself?

He woke to hear her say: 'Did you like him? He liked you *terribly*. He said you were absolutely wizard!'

'Good gracious!'

'But *did* you like him?' Her lovely *eyes* beseeched him; for her, there could be nothing more important.

'Well, it was only a short meeting, wasn't it?'

'But still. . .'

'He's very tall.'

'Six feet and one inch. But what else?'

'I liked his uniform.'

'But—'

'His feet are smaller than mine.'

'Oh, *Uncle Salvu*!'

Enough was enough. He put his hand firmly on hers. 'I'm bound to say that I thought he was a very fine young man. Perhaps *just* good enough for you.'

Her answering eyes were so joyous that, moved suddenly by emotions unknown and never to be shared, he had to turn away to hide his own.

4

Family lunch was as much fun as it should always have been. To begin with, there was a signal blessing, announced by Giovanna Debrincat as soon as she greeted her brother in the hall.

'Gigi is so sorry he can't be here. He had to go to the club for a meeting.'

Unworthily pleased, Father Salvatore said that he was sorry to miss his brother-in-law. After that, he settled down, alone with Giovanna and the children, to enjoy himself. Underlying all their happiness was the morning's news of the Italian 'defeat' : and within this framework of hope, each had a private source of satisfaction which multiplied by sharing and ordained a memorable day.

Giovanna was composed and contented; with the head of the family absent, the mother assumed an honourable, loving role on which no shadow need fall and no harsh injunction could trespass. Marija was silly with happiness, and surfaced only to advertise the fact; Pietru was bursting with news, and presently with food. It was certainly true, as he had forecast earlier, that a couple of *pasti* and some ice-cream only sharpened an appetite which could now deal with the serious business of melon and Parma ham, *cannelloni*, and strawberries snared in whipped cream.

No one, Father Salvatore thought, need feel guilty about wartime rationing on a day such as this.

'The *karrozzin* driver told me,' Pietru announced, between bites and gulps, 'that it might be the end of the war. He said he would give his horse *oats* tonight. What do you think he gives it ordinarily?'

'Why didn't you ask him?' Marija said.

'Oh, I did! He said: "Only what God allows." What does God allow for horses, Uncle Salvu?'

'Clover stalks,' Father Salvatore answered, drawing on his memory of the horses he knew personally.

'Is that all?'

Giovanna said: 'Darling, *not* with your mouth full.'

'I'm sorry... But *clover stalks*!'

'You eat them yourself,' Marija said. 'I've seen you, crossing a field.'

'That's only *between* meals. Mother?'

'Yes, dear?'

'We met a Hurricane pilot this morning. Only he was in the Navy.'

'That's nice, dear.'

'He was terrific. He told me all about landing on an aircraft-carrier. And he's going to give Uncle Salvu some boots.'

'Boots?'

'We were talking,' Father Salvatore interposed, 'and I just happened to mention boots, and he said he could get me a new pair from the RAF. I don't know whether he'll remember.'

'What a nice man.'

'I'm sure he'll remember,' Marija said.

'I'm sure he'll remember you,' Pietru muttered.

'Now, Pietru.'

Giovanna looked from one to the other. 'Am I supposed to understand all this?'

'Of course not,' Father Salvatore assured her. 'These are but wild and whirling words.'

'Who said that?'

'Hamlet.'

'Oh, him. We did him at school. "Get thee to a nunnery!"' Pietru looked across the table at his sister. 'Have you ever thought of being a nun?'

'Pietru, really!'

Marija smiled dreamily at her mother's protest. 'Oh, let him ask. The answer is, Yes.'

'What happened?'

'The answer was No.'

'Surprise, surprise!'

'I think,' said their mother, 'that's quite enough silliness for today.'

'Hamlet also said,' Father Salvatore smoothed the way, ' "Oh that this too too solid flesh would melt", and that's exactly how I shall feel at the end of this wonderful lunch.'

'How do you know so much, Uncle Salvu?'

'I listened very carefully until I was twenty-five.'

'Oh...'

They were enjoying their coffee out on the patio when Carmelina appeared, full of important news.

'Excuse me, Dun Salv. There's a man on a motor-cycle to see you. He's in uniform. He says he has a present for you.'

They all trooped out into the hall, Marija noticeably in the van of an unusual procession. But it was an RAF dispatch rider in a blue-and-white-striped crash helmet, grinning all over his face as he proffered Father Salvatore a brown paper parcel.

He seemed to know all about it, or to have been very carefully drilled. After a tremendous curving open-handed salute he announced: 'Sir! Boots, one pair, aircraftmen, for the use of. Compliments of Mr Ainslie.'

'Well, thank you very much,' said Father Salvatore. 'Er...'

'No charge,' said the dispatch rider. 'Goodbye, all.' He executed another impressive salute, and a foot-slamming about-turn which rang through the tiled hall like a stroke upon a gong. Then he marched out again. He must have winked at Carmelina as he passed, since she dissolved into helpless giggles long before his motor-cycle roared into action.

It was like Christmas. Unwrapped and displayed on the patio table, the boots held the centre of the stage. They were everything which had been promised: gleaming black, with bulging toe-caps, a veritable ladder of metal clips, and soles like seasoned planks.

Surrounded by admiring helpers, Father Salvatore tried them on, and essayed a few steps. 'They're perfect,' he said. 'They should last for years.'

Giovanna looked round her family, aware of all sorts of mysterious undertones. But she knew them to be benevolent, and therefore acceptable.

'Well ... You must have made quite a hit with this pilot.'

'Oh, I think we did...' Father Salvatore was sitting down again, but he was not going to take the boots off. 'What a happy day. You know, I think I shall go for a walk.'

He had already decided exactly the walk he wanted to take.

The one and only railway system which Malta had ever known, running eight and a half miles from Valletta to the old capital of Mdina, opened in 1883 and closed for ever in the mortal year of 1931. It was first known as *il-Vapurtal-Art*, the Land Steamer, and colloquially as *Xmundifer*. It was many years before Father Salvatore connected the strange word *Xmundifer* with the phrase imported by Maltese who had been working in French-speaking Tunis and Algeria, and had thus seen other lands and other railways. *Xmundifer* was the Maltese version of *chemin de fer*.

Malta's *Xmundifer*, at its peak, boasted ten steam-engines (two to each train, because of the gradient), first- and second-class carriages, and a few goods wagons. It ran seven times a day on a single line from Valletta, through the Floriana Tunnel which was now their life-saviour in air-raids, past a flower-chain of little wayside stations which he could have recited by heart – Hamrun, Msida, Santa Venera, Birkirkara, Balzan, San Anton, Attard, San Salvatore (his own station already! Why did it have to be subtitled 'Hospital for Mental Diseases'?) – and after rising to 600 feet with the aid of sand-boxes and those two puffing engines, ended its journey in a tunnel under the hill-top citadel of Mdina, which senior generations still called Citta Vecchia, the Old City.

Father Salvatore had always loved that railway. Today, for no special reason except that he wanted to weave the happiness of the past into the contentment of the present, to link the child he had been with the children he loved and shared at second-hand – today he wanted to retrace on foot a journey, the most exciting of his young life, which he had taken, as a special family treat, with his mother and father on *Xmundifer's* twenty-first birthday in 1904, when he was nine years old.

Today, according to its promise, had become very hot: too hot for plodding along hard city pavements, even in beautiful new boots which hardly squeaked at all. Father Salvatore got a lift in a returning *karrozzin*, from Sliema as far as Msida Creek, and thence for another dull urban mile to the outskirts of Santa Venera, in an army lorry full of rowdy gunners boasting of their part in that morning's exercise.

He could share their enthusiasm and their triumph. But the real pleasure started when he had set out on foot again, and found the disused railway track he was looking for, running beside a country road, and began his pastoral journey, slowly and gently uphill to distant Mdina. His mind was at peace, his spirit buoyant, and his boots seven-league.

Now it was the other journey he wanted to recall, the train journey of thirty-seven years ago, with his beloved father and mother, with elder brother Benedict and four-year-old sister Giovanna, when the world was young and peaceful, and his only worry was that something awful would happen and they would miss the train.

They did not miss the train. He should have known that Commander Hugo Westgate-Saul, Royal Navy, and his beautiful and noble wife Emilia, did not miss trains; trains would if necessary wait for such as they, and for the other distinguished company sharing in this same birthday journey. He should have known that when they arrived at the station, they would find a reserved carriage ready for them.

His father, a magnificent figure in dress white uniform, his reddish-gold beard matching the proud insignia on the peak of his cap, waited while their mother folded her parasol, then handed her up as if she were the Queen herself.

Indeed, they both looked regal. The ages of mothers and fathers were then an unmentionable secret. Salvatore knew now that they had both been thirty-seven years old, at a certain peak of looks, bearing, and confidence. On that day, they were simply mother and father, beyond compare as people, just and loving and strict as parents, a joy to be with, and – in some mysterious way which was the happiest part of home – a joy to each other.

Their father lifted up his three children with less ceremony, though with the same strong competence. To Giovanna he said: 'Up you go, old lady!' and to the boys: 'Marry the falls! Hoist and away!' It was something in the Navy. Their carriage, decorated outside with flags and streamers, had leather-covered benches, and a carpet on the floor, and brass lanterns with the new electric light bulbs inside, and a strange notice reading: 'BEWARE OF CARD-SHARPERS!'

Salvatore, still proud that he could read, spelled out the words with moving lips and then asked: 'Father, what's a card-sharper?'

His father, who had a wonderfully precise and confident way of answering all questions, unless he dismissed them with the phrase 'You will understand when you are older', which always marked the end of that particular conversation – his father answered:

'A card-sharper is a man who plays cards for money with strangers, and cheats, and takes all their money away from them.'

'How does he cheat?'

His brother Benedict, who was twelve years old and therefore knew all answers to all questions, though not in such a nice way, chipped in:

'He puts cards up his sleeve, like a conjurer, and brings them out, and then he wins.'

'Why can't you tell him to stop?'

'Because you don't see him doing it, stupid!'

'Benedict,' his father said.

'Yes, sir?'

'I do not think we will use the word "stupid".'

'I'm sorry, Father.'

Their father always honoured this phrase. 'Very well... Giovanna, are you comfortable?'

Giovanna, starched and sun-bonneted, who always whispered, whispered now: 'Yes, thank you, Father.'

'Hugo,' their mother said. How important one had to be, to call father 'Hugo'!

'Yes, my darling?'

'Have you got the tickets?'

'Well, God bless my soul,' he said, and began to pat his pockets, look in his wallet, even take off his cap and peer inside it. 'I could have sworn... Now where in thunder did I—' They were all appalled. Suddenly he held up his open palm, which was bare, snapped it shut, and opened it again. There were the tickets, pink and safe.

'Hugo, *really*!'

'I thought it would amuse the children.'

'Sometimes I'm not sure how many children I have.'

This was mysterious grown-up talk. She knew very well that

she had *three* children, and they were all here, their legs swinging and dangling over the edge of the benches.

'Father.' This was Giovanna, whispering again.

'Yes, dear?'

'How much do tickets cost?'

'More than all your pocket-money.'

But Benedict had to know. 'More than *my* pocket-money, father?'

They were not at all surprised that their father could quote the exact prices, without hesitation. 'Tickets cost a penny a mile first class, and a halfpenny a mile second class. But if you are a workman you can buy a ticket from Valletta to Rabat, which is eight miles, for twopence.'

'*Workmen!*' said Benedict, who already had pretensions to a withering snobbery. 'Who cares about them?'

'I do,' said his father rather coldly. 'And your mother. And God.'

Benedict subsided, scarlet and embarrassed. Their father was always more strict with Benedict than with Salvatore or Giovana. Gregory the head footman, appealed to on this point, had once answered: 'It's because he's the eldest son.' That seemed to be that.

'Hugo,' their mother said again.

'Yes, my darling?'

'God first, I think.'

'Whatever you say, dear.'

Mother pursed her lips. But it was easy to see that she was laughing inside.

Salvatore had another question. He loved asking his father things, because his father always knew the answers. 'How do the electric lights work? There can't be any wires going to the train when it's moving.'

'There's a new invention called an accumulator. We carry it along with us. It has electricity inside it. They put a new one in when it runs down.'

Giovanna whispered: 'How does it run down? Where does it run down to?'

For some reason their father thought this very funny. 'It picks up its little skirts,' he answered, between saying 'Ha ha' and snorting, 'and gallops off down the railway line.'

'Hugo, you'll only confuse the child.'

'Then it will be mutual.' But of course he could not leave it like this. He reached over and pinched Giovanna's cheek gently. ' "Run down" means something different, when we're talking about accumulators. It means the electricity inside is all finished.'

'Thank you, Father.'

Salvatore was looking out of the window. It was already understood that one could only do this when the train was standing still. The crowds on the platform were growing thinner as the passengers took their places. He could see the first engine, just two carriages ahead: a wonderful snorting monster with a dark green boiler, a black funnel where the smoke and the steam came out, vermilion beams called 'buffers' to stop it running into things, and a shining brass dome on top.

When they had walked by it, he had also seen that on this special day it was decked out with flags and branches of trees as well, and that the driver, a splendid figure of authority, had little sprigs of evergreen stuck into his cap. There were *eight* carriages altogether.

'Father, what happens if the engines aren't strong enough?'

'We have to stop until they get their breath back.' Typically, he had an excellent story about the engines too. 'Do you see how one engine is pointing forwards, and the other backwards?'

'Yes, Father.'

'That's the way they have to stay for the rest of their lives. There's no way of turning them round. Once they're put on to the railway line, they either face Mdina, or Valletta. There are ten 'engines' – how *did* he know these things? – 'and two of them point towards Valletta, and eight towards Mdina.'

Salvatore said: 'So the ones that look towards Mdina never see the sunrise.'

His father was suddenly staring at him, with alert, speculative eyes. 'True. And that is a *very* interesting remark.'

Salvatore never knew why. But his father was quite serious, which was gloriously enough on this glorious day.

The engine's whistle blew, with a startling shriek. Excitement and tension rose. The conductor walked slowly down the platform, an imposing personage in blue uniform with a stiff white-winged collar, formal black tie, peaked cap, and gold-embossed buttons. When he saw their father he saluted.

'Good afternoon, sir. Good afternoon, madam.'

'Good afternoon, Abela.' (Later father was to explain: 'His son is one of our stewards at St Angelo. Very promising lad.') 'Time to go, what?'

The conductor drew out his watch, at the end of a long chain. 'Exactly time, sir.' It was now his turn to blow his whistle. Further up the platform, a handbell started to ring. There was a hiss of steam, a clanking jerk, and they were off.

There had never been a journey like this one. The train plunged straight into the Floriana Tunnel, a thousand yards long, cut through the solid rock underneath the old bastions. Then it was suddenly cheerful daylight again, and they were running through the middle of Hamrun, looking into people's backyards, into their very windows, seeing them eating, examining their washing on the clothes-lines, everything. They made their first stop here, to pick up lots more passengers who wanted to join the exciting trip; and soon afterwards they were out into the fresh countryside.

The little stations were bright with flower-beds, and palm trees and carobs, and orange and lemon blossom; more people came out to board the train, or to wave to them as they passed. They were *famous*, and the birthday train was famous too... Here and there along the track, tar-streaked barrels stood like fat sentinels. 'That's to collect the lumps of coal we drop as we go along,' their father explained, and their mother said: 'Waste not, want not.'

Mother had her own stories, told in a different way from father's, as if nothing in the world was really worthwhile except seeing things and enjoying them. When they crept through the pitch-dark Floriana Tunnel, she had said: 'Once the train broke down here, and stayed for *hours*. They say lots of people got frightened, and wouldn't use the railway at all after that. But I wouldn't have minded.' Yet most of her stories concerned her special claim to distinction. Long ago, she told them, with her own father and mother, she had been one of the passengers on the very first journey, the actual day that the Malta Railway was opened.

'I was still just a girl,' she explained. 'You can imagine how exciting it was.'

'Were you married to Father then?' Giovanna asked, in her conspiratorial whisper which somehow suited the question.

'Good gracious, no! That was two years before we met. I was going to marry someone quite different!'

'Mother! What do you mean?'

'I mean, someone else was planning to ask me.'

Their father said, in a sinister way which must have been meant to be funny, because they both laughed: 'I soon put paid to him!'

But he would not say how.

The two journeys, the first one of all and the twenty-first birthday, became intermingled. As they rumbled and puffed along the curling stretch leading to San Anton station – a special stop for the Palace! – their mother recalled the rare quality of the opening day.

'It was very smart. I had a new silk dress, and a ridiculous hat which nearly blew away. We were going so fast! But there were plenty of priests and monsignori, so we all felt safe. The Archbishop, Count Scicluna, brought sixty of them in his party, and the Reverend Mother of Sliema Convent as well. He blessed every station, and the bits in between! Then when we got to Mdina – only it was called Notabile then – we all had tea at the Inguanez palazzo, just like we're going to do today.'

They paused at San Salvatore station, with its rather ominous air, because it was really only for lunatics, and their families who might also be lunatics, and the people who had to guard them. This was the last stop before the end of the journey. The gradient grew steeper; the engines strained and roared as the train struggled upwards. Then they all got out, and laughed and chattered in the sunshine, congratulating each other on a safe and splendid voyage.

Giovanna asked: 'Do we say thank you?' and was scoffed at by Benedict – until their father put him hopelessly out of countenance by actually going up and thanking the engine-driver. After that, they began to walk in a vast concourse up the last slope which led to the gates and towers of the old city. A few special guests, the Santo-Nobiles among them, made for the Inguanez palace, and the promised tea.

Though behaviour here, particularly for children, had to be of the highest order of nobility, the meal was so sumptuous that it was worth it, a hundred times over.

The pleasures of the small years persisted, as Father Salvatore –

now forty-six instead of nine, black-cassocked instead of wearing his dazzling sailor suit, heavily booted by the RAF instead of shod at long range by the Children's Department of the Army & Navy Stores – retraced the dusty overgrown path which had once boasted a highway of shining rails and rough-hewn sleepers.

There were traces of the vanished railroad still : successive hummocks of earth which rippled away into the distance, discarded rails and the rusted iron ties which had once bolted them down : the stone chippings which had made their firm bed : and at one point the ruins of an ancient barrel, from which the coal dust had spilled out to make a black circle among the weeds.

As he walked, he could only enjoy. It was a peerless day; overhead, the blue arc of the sky was a perfect frame for the citadel of Mdina far ahead, crowning a hill-top which could be seen from Valletta itself. It was a view which had enthralled him, on that magical train-ride of long ago; now it was a delight to find how the two journeys – the three journeys, counting his mother's reminiscence of her own voyage of discovery – were closely interwoven.

All the people were closely interwoven also, even after thirty-seven years. He could recall now, with all the bright spirit of youth, how much he had loved and admired his father, and how wonderful it had been to have him there on such a day. The remote and mysterious figure, always magnificently dressed, was so often away; from time to time their mother was away as well, leaving the nursery bereaved.

Many times they had wept to see her go, and she had wept also. But : 'I married a sailor,' she would tell them, and for her, as well as for her children, it was the last word. Then she would kiss them goodbye, and disappear to join their father in far-off, fine-sounding places : the Indian Ocean, the South Atlantic, Portsmouth where the Home Fleet stood watch-dog over the Channel, and that corner of the world which could conjure up such images of fantasy and romance – the China Station!

But by the day of their train journey, he had been posted at last to Malta. He would be there for two whole years! It was no wonder how happy and content they had all been. All families should have such fathers.

All families did not. The little Giovanna, who had progressed from a whispering four-year-old to a wife and mother of forty-one, did not have so splendid a husband, and her children would never count such a person in their young lives. Why could not Giovanna have found the same happiness as had shone out of her mother's eyes on that day, and on so many other days? She had been blessed with the same beauty, the same lively mind, and the same love to give. But she had given all to Lewis Debrincat.

'Look here, upon this picture, and on this,' Hamlet had said, comparing his father's portrait with that of his usurping, incestuous uncle. 'Hyperion to a satyr', he had called the contrast of the Titan god with the base animal: citing Hyperion as 'so loving to my mother' that he would not allow the winds of heaven to visit her face too roughly. The latter-day contrast was indeed appalling: Lewis Debrincat would not have minded if the winds of heaven had ripped and torn through his whole household, as long as he himself could lie in slothful ease.

So the years had turned, and brought Lewis as the father-figure to Marija and Pietru. Now Marija was woven into the pattern of his journey, Marija the young and vulnerable, with all the tearing passions of love and life still before her. *Somehow she must be helped*, towards the happiness which had so swiftly drained away from her mother's span of hope.

It was a new thought, but not less compelling for that. Father Salvatore had liked that young man instantly. He must tell Giovanna about him *in the right way*. That still left Lewis, the head of the family whose word was law, the jealous father who, he suspected, would never be satisfied, nor reconciled to a suitor from the camp of the enemy.

He was passing now a small landmark of the railway, one of the stone-built sheds known as 'Railway Guards' Huts' which had been placed along the line to house the guardians of the track. This one was No 12, as a flaking painted sign still proclaimed, and the last one before the end of the journey; it had been kept in good repair, though now doing duty as what the Maltese charmingly called a 'rural room' – a shelter for farm implements and for men caught in rain-storms.

It could also shelter lovers, according to local legend, but he did not want to dwell on that. On such a day as this, he could even admit that many homeless lovers deserved their happi-

ness, and must find it where they could. For he was still wondering who, among his family portrait gallery, was happy, in
the sum of today and yesterday. It was not a comforting
tally.

Their father lay at peace in his sailor's grave. Their mother
was old and troubled. Giovanna was not happy. Lewis was not
happy. Inconstant Benedict, far away in Paris, perhaps was.
Marija, yes and no. Pietru, yes. Himself, yes. *Yes*, he was happy,
in spite of all.

It was on this note of cautious gladness that he was now
topping the crest of the hill, passing one of the essential sand-
boxes, reaching the end of the line as the railway itself had
reached the end of its life, in that 'mortal year' of 1931. For
his harassed *Xmundifer* had not been able to survive a succession of crises, ranging from a rise in the price of coal to a trade
recession which meant that the poor and the not-so-poor were
forced to walk instead of ride : from debts which could never
be paid off, as takings fell from £60 a day to £13, to tough
competition from two new enemies – the electric tram and
the motor-bus.

Among the latter, a 36-seat double-decker, boldly labelled
'John I. Thorneycroft', seemed to set the seal on the railway's
defeat. Buses could stop every few yards, if need be, to pick
up passengers; trains, clinging to a more lordly schedule, could
not compete. Soon they did not try, and the government, running out of money and patience, suspended their service for
ever.

It had been a sad and sick year when his cherished railway
closed down, in a sad and sick year when Malta was not only
desperately poor but tormented by political and religious strife
as well. He had always thought of that year of 1931 as 'mortal',
when more things had died than the railway : it was the un-
happiest year of his priesthood, which he had embraced with
such fervour and hope.

The year before was, or should have been, election year.
He could remember, even now, reading out the pastoral letter
which had forbidden the faithful to vote for one of the parties,
as a grave sin, and instructing himself to refuse the sacraments
even to its party workers. The turmoil which followed was
especially awful to a priest whose only love was the peace of
God. A British protest to the Holy See had received an in-

flexible reply: the election had been cancelled, and the constitution suspended; and Malta returned to a long paternal servitude, under the colonial power of Britain.

Religion and politics... He prayed that so gross a conflict would never happen again. This was not why he had become a priest, to drag his soiled feet through a muddy temporal stream, to serve a policy which (however politely one phrased it) planned to tie Malta closer to Italy than to an older ally and friend. He had become a priest, against all the wishes and hopes of his family, because . . . because . . .

He tried to be honest here, as he had always tried. He had become a priest, instead of a sailor like his father or a law-giving judge like his great-uncle, for reasons which even now were infamous, and grounded only in shame and anguish.

He had become a priest because, at the age of sixteen, he had taken a tremulous, agonized vow to do so, if a certain girl did not find herself with child, as they both feared in their mutual terror. He would be chaste for ever afterwards, if only, if only . . .

God had spared her, and him, and thus enrolled him in His ministry. By the time that the girl, released from her fearful burden of guilt, had married someone else, he had already kept his vow. He could tell no one about it, not even his astonished family; only his confessor. For himself, there had been nothing but silence, and the humility and glory of service.

There were many paths to God. His had been sin, and re-demption, and faithful dedication, for ever afterwards.

He had thought, even as he stood in the pulpit, and read out that pastoral letter as he must, that he would not be standing there, and proclaiming, with a sick heart, something he did not believe, if he had not embraced, for a few frantic moments twenty years earlier, a willing wanton who knew more things about the rampant secrets of his body, and her own, than he had yet even dreamed of.

Now it was another ten years later, and matters of policy at least had come full circle, though the days were not less cruel and tormented. Then, Malta was inclined to be anti-British, pro-Italian; now she was bound to Britain by ties of blood and tears, and the Italians had become their Anti-christ. Could it ever be reversed, yet once more? Men, following as sheep, could also devour as wolves... He almost cried aloud: *'Where is truth?'* as he climbed the last slope towards the bastions of Mdina.

Then his peace returned.

Walking with wary eyes past the noisy bars and flagrant whorehouses which disfigured the hill-top of Rabat, he passed through the great and timeless gate of the Citadel (Mdina, Notabile, Citta Vecchia, Medina, Melita – the banners of the years proudly proclaimed an ancient lineage). He had always loved this silent city, with its aristocratic aloofness seemingly preserved intact through successive ages of turmoil; and never more than now, when, after a day of twentieth-century surprises, he found himself received into the contentment of the past.

Gently, taking refuge from the broiling sun within the cool caverns of the street, he penetrated deeper into peace. Often, as he walked, there was no more than a slit of sky to be seen, above streets so narrow that it was possible to reach out from the upper floors of one house and touch the hand of someone dwelling opposite. Among these palaces, courtyards, splendid houses of weathered stone, coats of arms which had withstood the centuries, pious retreats, churches, all contained within the cincture of the bastions, the silence was all pervading, the seclusion absolute.

In the whole of this sleepy hour, he met no one except a single mendicant friar, a Carmelite, dusty and sandalled, burdened with a sack into which he had just thrust a loaf of bread before turning away from a door. Passing him, Father Salvatore raised his hand in blessing, and the friar, a spare and shabby man whose white cloak was threadbare, smiled in answer. It could be said that they were both engaged in God's business, though Father Salvatore had to admit that his was the more enjoyable branch of it.

A walk through Mdina started, not with aristocratic reserve but with a pious virginity, just as difficult to pierce: with the 500-year-old convent of St Benedict, behind whose forbidding walls lived nuns of an order so strict that it could not be matched anywhere in the world. None of the female inmates was ever allowed out; no one with any taint of the male world was allowed in, save only the doctor and, by tradition, the white-washer, whose stock-in-trade was a substitute for disinfectant, unknown when these austere rules were set.

Such determined piety, Father Salvatore thought, skirting the edge of the faceless building, must command respect. Perhaps even a priest should here avert his eyes.

But he need not avert his eyes from the next great land-mark of Mdina, the Casa Inguanez, where the handsomely barred windows – looking outwards, yet adamant against strangers – set the true pattern of the whole city. Even before the coming of the Knights, the Inguanez family had been ack-nowledged as the hereditary governors of Mdina; the sprawling mansion, which had once meant no more than a satisfactory tea for a ravenous schoolboy, should more properly be saluted as the seat of the most noble Maltese family of all – Sceberras-D'Amico-Inguanez, Barons of Diar-il-Bniet and Bucana since 1350, and of Castel Cicciano for a mere 250 years.

He could have wished that the Casa Inguanez promised a cup of tea today for a thirsty priest. But to arrive unannounced, even in time of war, would have been something which his mother – not lagging far behind in her quarterings of nobility – would have been the first to find unforgiveable.

The prospect now opened out again, to include the impressive palace of the Testaferrata family, another great name in Maltese history, and then to the cathedral, built on the site of that Roman villa where Governor Publius had listened to St Paul, and become, inevitably, a saint himself. Such a shrine, such a hallowed realm for miracles, set all doubts at rest. In war or peace, there could be no turmoil here.

It had not always been so. Within a few moments he was standing outside a house from which, long ago, a body with its head crushed in by a stone had come plummeting down from the first-floor balcony, to be rapturously welcomed by the mob below and to give them the signal for revolt against a rapacious overlord – the invader Napoleon Bonaparte. The house had been the abode of one Notary Bezzina: the corpse, the bloody remains of Citizen-Colonel Masson, commander of the French troops: the year, 1798: and the occasion, a day of fury and rebellion against an enemy who had at last gone too far.

It was a matter for pride that this rebellion had been sparked by a small number of priests, mourning their looted churches and defiled sanctuaries, and then taken up by a Maltese people goaded past endurance, to whom the ringing of church bells, for hour after hour, all over the island, meant not a call to worship but a summons to arms.

It started with one officer, one tyrant corpse tossed into the street where Father Salvatore stood; continued with the slaughter of the French garrison, man after man, until the last hapless grenadier was cornered by a howling populace; and ended with a simple stage directive on the platform of history: Exit Napoleon, Enter Nelson and Britannia in Arms.

It was a story, he thought, which he must tell some time, because it was a particularly Maltese story, of fiery patriotism at last flaming into revolt: suitable for the citizens of his catacombs, who would one day also have their hour of triumph. But it was not a story for a day like this. There was a little too much blood in it.

As he walked slowly back to the main gate, past the Casa Inguanez again, feeling his new boots beginning to pinch at last, longing for tea, the remembrance of the catacombs reminded him also of Rafel Vella. He had scarcely thought of his sacristan since this morning when, hearing the news of his desertion, he had thought of him as a traitor.

Thereafter, he had put the matter out of his mind; in fact, for a large part of the day he had forgotten it, except to realize, from time to time, that there was something worrying him, and then to find that it was the problem of Rafel, which must inevitably be faced. But always he had decided that later would do.

Later was *now*; and now, when he was really prepared to face it, he discovered to his astonishment that it did not matter at all.

There were many reasons, none of them cynical or cowardly. On the practical side, little Nero could cope with the work; he could do it as well as Rafel, perhaps better, spurred by boundless energy, freed from such worries as beset Rafel all the time – his mother, his discontented wife and loveless marriage, his occasional jealousy of Nero himself.

For the rest, it was sad, but it was not the end of the world – of anyone's world. All sorts of things could happen. Perhaps Rafel's wife would follow him to Gozo. Perhaps Rafel, after a brief experiment, would change his mind. Perhaps the old lady would die. Perhaps it was, after all, best as it was.

He was only sorry because Rafel, to begin with, would feel so ashamed.

But even that would not last. The giant was simple, and

simple men forgot more easily than the introspective or the vain. His conscience would not be nagged for long. Only when they met, as they were sure to do, would Rafel come face to face with guilt at the same time.

He must find some way of convincing the other man that all was well between them.

Father Salvatore sighed, and smiled, and walked on down the hill towards the plains of Attard where, of all unlikely things, roses bloomed. If roses could bloom in the parched soil of Malta, then so could charity and hope, and acceptance of all things fearful and strange.

It really did not matter any more. The happy day, and the peace of Mdina, had won.

5

It was a lucky day for lifts, as well as a happy one. He had scarcely gone a quarter of a mile, on feet which now seemed to be under a private inquisition from the pinching-irons of new leather, when he was given a lift by a farmer taking the last of his onion-crop to the storage place at Attard.

This was a most cheerful man, brown as a wine-barrel, full of his many blessings. All was well with his world : the onion-bags which pressed against Father Salvatore's back were bulging, the price was good, the Italians were on the run, his wife had been safely delivered of their first son, after four girls in a row, his mare was in foal, *horse-meat was fetching good prices too*, the war would soon be over and then Malta would be run by the farmers and the Labour Party. It was all planned.

'Planned by God,' he added piously, with a side glance at Father Salvatore's dusty cassock. Even as an after-thought, that seemed to be good news too.

The farmer set him down, with a hearty farewell, at the end of the avenue of huge trees which led to San Anton Palace. Once again, fortune was on his side. Opposite the gateway, a car swept by him and turned into the entrance. He had a glimpse of a Union Jack on a small flag-staff, of a compact grey man sitting in the back, and a young man also in uniform by his side. Then the young soldier looked back, and after a moment the car stopped.

A trim figure walked back towards him, his gold tassels swinging in perfect tempo. It was Captain Ross the aide-de-camp, who had seemed so unaccountably ill-at-ease when they had met that morning.

Ross saluted. 'Sir,' he said formally, 'His Excellency would be delighted if you would come in for a cup of tea.'

Father Salvatore knew the great house well, and honoured it as a focus of Maltese history which had housed sixteen Grand Masters and twenty-seven Governors. But he could scarcely honour the man who had built it and named it: the French Grand Master Antoine de Paule, who had grown old in luxury, self-indulgence, and duplicity, and who, dying at eighty-four, was a sad monument to the decay of the Knights of Malta since their crowning glory at the Great Siege of 1565, only seventy years earlier.

His household, in this very house, had been absurdly, disgracefully ostentatious and affluent. It had included a Grand Vizier, a covey of chaplains and physicians, liveried servants by the score, and a long tail of gamekeepers, falconers, drummers, trumpeters, valets, grooms, pages, wig-makers, clock-winders, a rat-catcher, and a man whose sole task it was to bake bread for the San Anton pack of hounds. Its style had been set, in 1623, by a house-warming party for 600 guests.

But Grand Master de Paule might perhaps be forgiven for the house he had warmed and left behind him: basically a huge country house, yet noble in proportion and set amid orange groves which remained, after 300 years, the very signature of pastoral ease and elegance. Now this magnificence was occupied by an austere, markedly non-indulgent Governor, whose deep religious sense, though of a different faith, might have shamed Grand Master Antoine de Paule – or perhaps only made him smile.

General Sir William Dobbie received Father Salvatore, at tea-time, in a small salon, under the portrait of another admired warrior, Alexander Ball, Nelson's most trusted captain and the first Civil Commissioner of Malta after the British succeeded the French – taking the place, among others, of the unfortunate Citizen-Colonel Masson whose blood had briefly fouled the main street of Mdina.

Dobbie was a grey man, grey all over, with a grey bristle on top; between his truly enormous ears was a lined face, on which a terrible exhaustion had begun to carve its mark for ever. But he was politeness itself to his guest : politeness, with overtones of a religious rectitude which was not going to pass unnoticed for want of a word in season.

'You may or may not know that I belong to the Plymouth Brethren.' Father Salvatore did know. 'Their *principal* article of faith—' and he expounded briefly and cogently the faith of a Plymouth Brother, which seemed to reject Church government and Church hierarchy of any kind, any 'chaps like bishops', any 'showy ornaments', any drinking, smoking, dancing, or using 'that rouge stuff' : yet allowed anyone to get up and expound the faith as long as he was inspired by zeal, piety, Calvinism, rejection of worldly pleasures, and a taste for 'household baptism'.

'This may seem rather strange to you,' General Dobbie concluded.

Father Salvatore was enjoying his third cup of tea, and could not possibly be ungrateful. He said that it was always interesting to hear a different point of view.

'I'm glad you said that,' the Governor interrupted him. His grey face was almost lively. 'It means that we're on the same team.' This very large assumption slipped by, and was lost for ever. 'It means that with God's help, the rightness of our cause ...'

He dealt with the rightness of their cause. Father Salvatore listened, and nodded, and wiggled his toes which were now comfortably at ease, and stared up at the handsome portrait of Sir Alexander Ball, who stared back as if to say : 'I was a man of few words. I can recommend it.' General Dobbie reminded him of another stern soldier of Christ in history, Oliver Cromwell : it would be unfair to dismiss him as a bigot, accurate to call him a devout bulldog for his faith – which was unquestionably the only true gospel.

Cromwell had once admonished some unruly parliamentarians : 'I beseech you, in the bowels of Christ, think that you may be wrong!' There was no record that he had ever said it to himself. Yet Cromwell had also said : 'Put your trust in God, but keep your powder dry!' – an endearing gloss on Holy Scripture. General Dobbie was endearing in the same way. Manifestly he was always right, and his battles inevitably just and commendable to God; but he was not hesitating to work himself to death to prove it, and the lively realism of 'Keep your powder dry!' was present all the time.

'We put up a splendid show this morning,' he said, and once more the battered, weary face awoke to pleasure and pride. 'Absolutely splendid! The chaps were right on their toes, and we hit them for six! I believe it will happen again and again, until in God's good time...'

God's good time passed in a steady flow of facts and figures. The line of thought was methodical, the exposition fascinating. One plan slotted neatly into the next, until the whole grand design was marching irresistibly onwards. When necessary, a wall-map was referred to. An attack *here*, a holding operation *there*. England's own defences placed beyond doubt. Scandinavia neutralized. North Africa cleared of the enemy – this was where Malta was so important. Then for the final attack, when under God's Providence...

Father Salvatore listened, deeply impressed. Captain Ross stared out of the windows at the avenues of oleander, now blazing pink and white and red in the last brave display of summer.

Presently the Governor grew overwhelmingly tired, and his face, which had always been grey, took on a sheen of pallor, of final exhaustion. It was time to go, and General Dobbie handled it with the dispatch of a man who *must* take a rest before the next task.

'Ian, arrange for a car, will you please? We can't have Father Salvatore tiring himself out... Goodbye, Father. It was delightful to talk to you. Please remember me to your mother. We do not meet as often as we should, but' – he pointed for the last time at the wall-maps of Europe and the Mediterranean – 'God disposes, as you know.'

Outside, under the massive pillared portico, Captain Ross saw him into the official car. The young soldier was all salutes and smiles and shining efficiency; it was the only time he had come to the surface during the past hour.

Father Salvatore thanked him. 'I enjoyed that very much. The Governor was so *inspiring*, wasn't he?'

'He has that effect,' Captain Ross answered.

Then Father Salvatore, in the big black car with the soldier-driver at the wheel, rode in style down town, and round the harbour, and back to the catacombs of the Cottonera Lines.

* * *

The catacombs, at seven o'clock on that hot summer evening, were in a boisterous ferment, which had spilled over outside so that joining the throng was like being engulfed in a huge country picnic, where one was an honoured guest. As soon as his imposing car drew up, Father Salvatore was surrounded by a laughing, whooping mob which almost carried him into the cool twilight within. Obviously wine had been circulating freely, for many hours, but something more than wine had prompted this joyful explosion of good humour.

It was hope, hope long deferred by the months and years of their ordeal: hope now expectant, electric, gloriously alive.

There was music from a dozen gramophones and radios: family parties loud with talk and laughter: food and drink being shared with anyone near by: couples dancing, others trying to listen to the Rediffusion loudspeakers, others arguing as to exactly what they had seen and heard on this historic day. It was all geared to that morning's rout of the Italian 'fleet', and what it meant to Malta, and what it might mean in the future.

Excited questions greeted him wherever he went. He was asked, a dozen times: 'Is the war really over?'

It was some moments before he found Nero. The little dwarf, also in high spirits, came trotting out from a dark passageway with a sack of rubbish on his back, which he tipped on to the main pile, ready for next morning's collection. Then he straightened up, and laughed as he caught sight of Father Salvatore.

'I wish I had a shilling for every load! I wish I had a *penny*! ... I'm sorry I didn't meet you, Dun Salv. But that Rafel! He left everything! Even his own room was like a pig-sty!'

'He had a lot of things to think of, Nero.'

'Then why didn't he think of them, instead of running off like an Italian? Deserting us! And on a day like this. I'll give him a piece of my mind when I see him next!'

'You must forgive him.'

'I'll forgive him *after* I've told him what I think. Useless old elephant!'

'Nero, you mustn't say things like that.'

'Perhaps not to you, Dun Salv. But to Rafel ...' Yet Nero could not be angry for long. 'Did you hear about all the little boats that blew up and sank?'

'Yes, indeed.'

'That's the way to deal with that lot! Make a spaghetti soup, with meat balls! Sorry, Dun Salv – it's only something I heard.' Suddenly he jumped in the air and capered round their rock grotto, as he did when he was really excited. People watching and listening to them laughed: one called out: 'Steady, Nero! Save your strength for the wedding.' Then Nero burst out with his news: 'Dun Salv, I think I've found a girl!'

'But that's excellent.' The beaming face crowning the shrunken body was irresistible. 'Who is she?'

'Oh, just a girl. But she says she'll marry me. Only she's not from anywhere near here, I'm afraid. She lives in Mellieha.'

Mellieha was a full twelve miles away. 'That doesn't matter at all, Nero. As long as she's a good girl.'

'I'm sure she is. She's not very pretty.'

'That doesn't matter either. How old is she?'

'Perhaps twenty-seven.'

'Have you spoken to her family?'

'Not yet.' For a moment the dwarf looked sad. 'They don't think much of me. You know how it is. Can I bring her to see you, Dun Salv?'

'As soon as you like.'

'Then you could speak for me. Tell them I'm all right. Because she *does* want to marry me.'

'I'll do everything I can to help.'

'That's wonderful!' The small despised cripple of nineteen became the confident lover again, and his rare bride an attainable prize. 'Do you remember I once said – when I was talking about finding a girl—'

'I remember everything you said, Nero.'

'Well, she's more than five feet tall!' With that vital item of news, he had told enough of his triumph, and swiftly he turned the conversation. 'Everything's ready for Mass, Dun Salv. As soon as we get some of these' – he gestured, 'these noisy jokers out of the way.'

'Splendid. I knew I could trust you.'

'Will you speak tonight?'

'Yes.'

'Have you got a happy story for us?'

'A very happy story.'

HEXAMERON THREE

AD 1090.
Count Roger, of Blessed Memory

Such was the mood of joy and excitement that it took them nearly an hour to settle down. Even the Mass was disturbed, for the first time since the church of the catacombs had begun its ministry; he could see Nero moving about from group to group, hear him hissing for silence as whispers and even subdued laughter echoed round the great rock cavern of their refuge. But Father Salvatore could not find it in his heart to rebuke them. On such a night as this, after such a day, even the little dead brothers in their niches must be smiling down on the lively world which enjoyed such good fortune.

When the time came to speak, he disdained formality – except for his first word – and entered into their mood as closely as he could.

'*Uliedi* – children – I do not wonder that you feel like children tonight. I feel like a child myself – a child of God, as we all are, and a child of happiness as well. Today has been a wonderful day, and it would be silly to forget it, even in church, even if we could. It would be ungrateful as well. Such wonderful days come from God, and from our own strong arms. This one has come after many terrible months. Terrible months are the gift of God also, but that is a great mystery, and I have spoken about it often.

'We should never forget that the wonderful days and the terrible days have all happened before. They are new to us, but as old as man himself in Malta. There was a time when Malta was miserable and afraid, not for days or months but for whole centuries. After the time of St Paul and the Romans, we suffered under many conquerors. Their very names are enough to frighten us, and to make us glad that after the black hours and the black ages, the dawn came again.

'It was a dawn like the dawn of today, but it was so slow to arrive! When the Romans were driven out, and their empire destroyed by the Vandals and the Goths, the longest night in the world came down. Rome itself, with all its treasures, was pillaged by the Vandals for fourteen wicked days. Soon Malta had its share of this pillaging, and after that, only barbarians governed our island. For centuries, there was no one within reach of Malta but the Vandals and the Ostrogoths. If they have a bad name to us, a merciless name, it is not by accident.

'Then the Saracens came here, and stayed two hundred and twenty years. They were Moslem Arabs, under their prophet Mohammed, and they ruled all the known world from Persia to Spain, and wandered farther still. You have heard of Stonehenge, in England? The huge stones there are called Sarsen stones, and the word is the same. The Saracens ruled all North Africa. They ruled Malta, but used it only as a garrison town, despising us, and reduced it to ruin and neglect.

'The faith, our faith, almost disappeared. Since Christians were taxed, and Moslems were not, it was enough to say: "I am a Moslem" to escape the tax-collector. The faith of destitute people came near to dying, and Malta with it. The dark age grew darker, and more cruel.

'Then at last a man came, a Christian soldier, to change our history for ever. The sky brightened like magic, as soon as he set foot here; and we have said a Mass for that man's soul, in the cathedral church of Mdina, on every fourth day of November since the year 1090.

'This Christian soldier arrived from Sicily...'

*   *   *

Fresh from ridding the whole of Southern Italy and Sicily of the Arab invader, he had a reputation as a fierce, invincible conqueror. But he had no need to conquer Malta. He had long been expected, and hoped for, and (by a few) prayed for. As soon as his sails were sighted, and his strange flag – a square banner, quartered red and white – made out, boats put off to meet him, dipping their oars gently, keeping their distance, with the men in them continually spreading their arms to signify : 'No weapons.'

Then some of them came speeding back, with the joyful news which confirmed seaborne rumour. The red and white flag was indeed the flag of the Hautevilles, and the general on board the last and greatest of that line. This was the man for whom they had been waiting.

From the moment that Roger the Norman, Count of Sicily, set foot on a dry beach in northern Malta, he was welcomed as its saviour.

As its saviour, this Christian soldier looked the part. He marched through the shallows and up on to the foreshore as if he owned every foot of the ground. He was attended, and screened, by thirteen knights and many other men – all equipped like himself in chain-mail the like of which had never been seen on the island : some of them with swords, some with cross-bows, some with daggers and clubs. But there was no doubt who was their leader and their chief. It did not need the Hauteville quartered flag on his breast-plate to distinguish him.

The people who were gathered on the shore, and the others who now came flocking up, leaving the cover of rocks and boulders, gazed at this tall man in armour. He wore the same intricately worked chain-mail, from breast-bone to knee : above it a massive shoulder-piece which glinted in the sun : above that an iron helmet guarding the top of the head to the brow, with a meshed chain curtain to cover his face. Chain leggings, a long shield shaped like a kite, and a great two-edged sword, completed a massive armament.

Where the sea met the land, Count Roger stopped and looked about him, while his knights and his other soldiers spread out on either side, their weapons at the ready. But nothing stirred. Who could attack such an iron-clad man? Who would wish to? Finally he made the gesture they had been hoping for. He reached up his hand, and swept off his helmet.

A murmur went up from the crowd. This was a new face altogether, cheerful and ruddy. The sunlight glistened on his fair hair, and on his red-gold beard. Though he was fifty-nine, he looked younger, and full of life, fresh life. This was the man for them.

When he smiled broadly, it seemed more than ever certain that this was the man for them.

But he was not the man for all of them. At the back of the crowd, a single figure began to edge away and then to walk swiftly, perhaps to prepare an ambush, perhaps to take news of the landing to the feeble Moslem garrison inland. Count Roger, whose eyes were sharp and roving in spite of his merry face, pointed at him and growled an order.

Out on his flank, a soldier whipped up his cross-bow, cocked it with a jerk on a leather thong, took aim and let fly. The iron-tipped arrow whistled through the air and found its mark, straight between the shoulder blades of the retreating spy. The man dropped like a stone. A short scream became a cough, and the cough a torrent of blood on the sand.

That was all. Count Roger was still smiling. He was even laughing, if the kind of harsh barking noise which came from his lips could be called laughter. He nodded to the beaming marksman, and then once more he waited. After a prudent and necessary pause, a man from the crowd came forward.

It was the head man of the village, one Joseph Bin-Said. Bin-Said was accustomed to rule his small kingdom, but not to govern such a moment as this. He made gestures of peace and humility, once again spreading out his hands to show that he was not armed.

He said, in the Arabic tongue: 'You are welcome, Lord. We will not fight you.'

Count Roger turned to the man at his elbow, the only un-armoured man in his company. He had the bearing of a priest, though he carried a club and looked as if he could use it. They conferred briefly. Then the priest said: 'We do not mind if you fight or not.'

He spoke sternly, echoing Count Roger's tone, and some of his contempt. From long experience, he knew that the first man to come forward was not always the best man.

Bin-Said spread out his hands again. 'Lord, believe us. You are welcome here.'

Count Roger threw back his head, thrusting his red beard forward so that it caught the sun again. He spoke a single phrase, and the priest translated it:

'I take possession of this land.'

In ones and twos, led by Bin-Said, the crowd came forward to kneel in homage and to accept their ruler.

That was the very *last* time that it was so easy and so simple, to take Malta from the sea.

The congregation of the catacombs, who had been listening enthralled to this strange story, now broke out into smiles and nods and murmuring. They realized that Dun Salv had been talking of today, when he spoke of taking Malta from the sea. Today it had not been easy and simple at all; in fact it had been impossible. But there were still many questions. Why was Count Roger so welcome? Where was the enemy he had come to fight? Who was the man who walked swiftly away, and, at the word of command, had been killed by an arrow? And why was a Mass still said for so blood-thirsty a fellow as Roger the Norman, Count of Sicily?

Count Roger had taken possession of many lands, like all the rest of his eleven brothers. Of the father, the progenitor of this clan, little was known except his name – Tancred d'Hauteville – and the fact that he married twice and produced five sons by his first wife and seven by his second. There were daughters as well.

Tancred d'Hauteville may thus rest secure in his chosen niche, while the light turns on those two of his sons who made their mark on Maltese history – Robert Guiscard ('Guiscard' meant 'cunning') and Roger the Norman.

Robert Guiscard was more than cunning; he was brutal, determined, and lustful for conquest. It was often noted that Tancred's second batch of sons were the ones that counted. Robert was son number six, that is, the first son by the second wife, and Count Roger was son number twelve, the Benjamin of all this brood.

Of the other older sons, only four names survived the fall of the leaf called history: William of the Iron Arm, Humphrey, Drogo, and Behemond. As names, and as men, they were only minor conquerors. Their merit was that they acted as a spur to the other two.

Father Tancred, who must have had problems of family precedence, domestic jealousy, and even plain house-keeping, sent all
his sons 'to seek their fortunes in Italy', which in honest terms
meant that they were dispatched with a modest purse and a pat
on the back to steal, plunder, and generally to make their way
in a world of robber barons, warring popes, and humble, per-
suadable people.

It was not very long before Robert Guiscard, taking his turn
on this wheel of fortune, rose to prosperity, plundering and robbing better than all the rest combined. With his particular
appetites, he had no other choice and no surer destiny. When he
arrived in southern Italy to join his elder brothers, he was given
a cold shoulder (their profession was becoming overcrowded)
and a meagre portion of their lands. It was not enough, especially for a half-brother whom fraternal purists equated with
a bastard.

Before long he had outstripped all his disdainful family, and
progressed from simple cattle-thief to marauding general. By the
time that he invited his youngest brother Roger to join him, he
had already challenged the temporal power of the papacy, in
pursuit of the spoils of war; he went on to imprison two popes,
and to be excommunicated three times : to subdue southern
Italy, sack and burn Rome with scars still apparent, invade
Sicily, and make his name feared and detested wherever he
advanced.

Guiscard had all the worst characteristics of a Norman baron:
insensate cruelty, consuming greed, and a total contempt for
moral standards. His brother Roger was different. They quarrelled freely in the course of their joint adventures, and though
the quarrels often concerned the division of their plunder, when
they strove to outwit each other, the split went far deeper than
this. It was a matter of morality, a matter of faith.

Many of the Norman barons had originally been welcomed
wherever they went in Italy, as papal allies against the infidel,
since their prime object had seemed to be the expulsion of the
Moslem Saracens from Catholic territory. They came to be
hated for their rapacity, their malice, their flint-hearted
butchery, and their forgotten vows.

Roger the Norman was not such a man. He kept his dream of
the crusade in view all the time, while his brother had long
abandoned even the pretence of it. Guiscard stole anything from

K.M.—14

anyone, used any treachery, sealed and then betrayed any bargain, allied himself as easily with Satan as with the angels, and
customarily cheated both.

It was no wonder that the brothers quarrelled. The wonder
was that they could endure each other's company, even for
profit.

But presently Robert Guiscard died, in the odour of infamy,
and brother Roger, now named Count of Sicily and Calabria,
Protector of the Holy See, was free to pick and choose his
course. It was this freedom which brought him at last to the
shores of Malta, where a remnant of Arab rule was ripe for
overthrow.

He did not especially want the island. Why should he, when
he had spent nineteen years in conquering all Sicily, which was
fertile and could be immensely prosperous? He wanted Malta,
dry and poor Malta, to be restored to the faith. That was all,
and that was absolute.

Now, while the small waves lapped at the heels of his escort,
and the crowd waited fearfully in the sun, Count Roger spoke
to Bin-Said again, through the priest:

'You have seen what can happen when I am opposed, or
betrayed, or even threatened. It will happen again, the moment
I give the word. I am here with a message of peace. Christ our
Saviour said, "I come not to bring peace, but a sword." Well, *I
bring both*!' He was smiling still, but the red-gold beard jutted
out like a rock as he spoke. 'And I will use both, if need be. But
I have peace in my heart, not war.'

Bin-Said, already under the spell of this man, answered: 'Lord,
no one in this village will oppose you.'

'Do you swear?'

'Yes, Lord, I swear.'

'We have a special death for those who break their oaths. It is
one of the slower deaths...' He pointed up the beach, where the
retreating man, having coughed up the last of his life's blood,
lay like a piece of driftwood. 'Who was that man?'

'A stranger.'

Count Roger suddenly glared at him. 'There can be no strangers on a small island. Tell me the truth!'

Bin-Said swallowed. 'Lord, I spoke the truth. He is not from
this village. I do not know his name.'

'And now we will never know. Too bad, too bad...' Count

Roger could change from anger to a jest very swiftly, the sign of a sure man. 'Well, where was he going, then?'

'Perhaps to the citadel.'

'Why?'

'Perhaps to warn them.'

'How many are in this citadel?'

'They say two hundred.'

'And well-equipped?'

Bin-Said at last essayed his own small joke. 'Not with manhood.'

Count Roger gave his short, barking laugh. 'Well said... We will put it to the test, in any case...' Over his shoulder, he called out an order, and his soldiers began to assemble, a handful to each of his thirteen knights, all led by a standard-bearer with the red-and-white quartered flag. 'We march to the citadel. How far is it away?'

'Some four miles.' Bin-Said took the wisest decision of his life. 'Lord, can we march with you? I have nearly a hundred men fit to bear arms.'

'You can march behind us,' Count Roger answered. 'At a distance. And behind *you* will be my friend with the cross-bow. Do you understand?'

'Yes, lord.'

But Bin-Said's face was downcast, and Count Roger took it for an honest look. He said, more kindly :

'If I need help, I will remember you... Now, collect your men and be ready to march. What arms have they?'

'Only clubs.'

'A club will crack a skull, as well as any sword.' Count Roger gestured towards the priest at his side. 'My chaplain carries "only a club", but I have seen him – well, no matter. Let him do his own boasting.'

Bin-Said, puzzled but respectful, glanced at the priest and then back again. 'Lord, we have heard it said that holy men are forbidden to shed blood.'

The priest answered, of his own accord : 'That is why I use a club,' and the laughter which rang round the beach transformed the landing-ground into a happy meeting-place.

'Collect your men,' Count Roger ordered again. 'The sooner we march the better.'

Bin-Said's eyes were on the flag of the Hautevilles, gleaming proudly in the sunshine. 'If only we had a banner to march with...'

'I will give you a banner,' Count Roger answered promptly. 'Your very own banner,' He beckoned, and the standard-bearer brought the flag to his side. Count Roger reached up, took the standard with its squares of red and white, and tore it down the middle. Then he handed the strip of cloth, now reduced to one red square and one white, to Bin-Said. 'Here is your flag, and I charge you, never stain it save with your own blood. Now hoist it up, and march!'[1]

> Suddenly the catacombs were buzzing with the story of the flag. This was no old chapter from some musty history book! This was the flag of today, the red and white flag which flew all over the island, from the heights of Valletta to the police-station at St Paul's Bay. So that was how they had first won it! It seemed as if everything in the world suddenly had a real reason behind it, and as if everything in Malta, sprung from the past, was still important today.

A dispirited garrison, doing nothing in Mdina for years on end, sitting there waiting for their pensions, was no match for Count Roger, his knights, his swordsmen and cross-bowmen, and his fiery spirit. He took the citadel without stratagem; he simply arrived before its ramparts, sent the priest in as an envoy under a flag of truce, declared that he would put every man to the sword who did not surrender before sundown, and presently marched in with the Hauteville banner flying.

He was compelled to kill four men, stupid fellows with some wild idea of resistance; and at the next dawn he had to execute, publicly, a fifth man who had tried to stab his chaplain under the very folds of the white flag, and had been clubbed senseless by this doughty soldier of Christ.

The execution was swiftly done. The Saracen crowd gasped as a single stroke from the two-handed sword smote off the treacherous head. But since a Norman two-handed swordsman would have been deeply chagrined if he could not have be-headed a *horse* with one stroke, they might have saved their breath to salute the conqueror.

The conqueror set up his headquarters within the citadel, and consolidated his position with rare efficiency. He stood no nonsense from anyone. But there was little opposition. The story of the execution spread far and wide, convincing any doubters that they had better join the winning side, because there was not going to be any other. As for the majority, they decided before the first week was out that Roger the Norman was the sort of ruler they wanted.

It was clear from certain things he said, clear from his first actions, clear from his reputation, that he would be just. He was also amiable (until he was crossed), good-looking, and industrious. They had never had a ruler with red hair, a ruddy complexion like a Viking (or what they imagined a Viking to be), and a persuasive tongue. He was also a Christian, and he proceeded to make clear – more than anything else – that if there was to be any big difference, it was this.

He found the church of Publius, their earliest and most renowned Roman ruler, in sad decay. Half of it had fallen down; the rest was a ruin where the rats warred with the cats and seemed likely to win; there were no worshippers, because the faith, persecuted and derided, was now only a faint trace-memory from the distant past.

The church was his first care. 'Build it again,' he told Joseph Bin-Said, who had become a trusted ally and a hard-working foreman of public works. Bin-Said had his own reputation; he also had villagers skilled in stone work, friends who had worked in the quarries since they were limping barefoot children, even relatives who were glass-blowers, silversmiths, carpenters, and lamp-makers. His own sisters could sew an altar-cloth like a band of angels... He went to his task with a will.

The cathedral church of St Publius rose from the ruins like a declaration of faith, strong, handsome, unambiguous, eternal. Count Roger finished it off with a pair of carved gates made of Irish bog-oak, black and solid as a ship's timbers, which he had picked up on his wanderings as a young man and now installed in their last home.

The church, and the newly ordained bishopric, crowned an act of apostleship which Malta had been awaiting a long dark time. For this reason alone was the Mass said for Roger's soul, a Mass which outlived his rule by at least 800 years.

But he did far more than this. He rescued a desolate and wasted island from the worst kind of overlord – the kind which did nothing with its prize except occupy it and tax it to death.

From the sloth of centuries, Malta woke to enterprise and activity. Though Count Roger ruled from Messina in Sicily, his own base of power, and his rule ended with his death eleven years later, he set his mark on Malta for ever.

He proved what he had always wanted to prove: that one could be a tough soldier like his brother Guiscard, yet not a cruel brigand: a conqueror but not a plunderer: a lord and not a tyrant. He smiled even as he pronounced firm laws, and enforced them. He also prayed, and the people prayed with him.

There was only one attempt, by an invading force of Barbary corsairs, to overthrow him, and he drove this off with disdainful ease. He could not have done so if he had not been trusted, and respected, and even loved by the islanders he had come to rule.

The invasion, if one could use such a word of a pirate raid which hoped for greater things, was led by one Ibrahim Hakkim, self-styled Lord of the Waves, who had a small fleet of ten ships and a lair in Tripoli. Owning allegiance to no man, Ibrahim had long been a thorn in the flesh to the island; at one time he had even set up a camp on Comino, the island of cummin seed, between Malta and Gozo, until the supine Saracen garrison roused itself to protest and then to prudent action.

They smoked him out – literally – with a ring of fire which burned all the underbrush and reduced Comino to a smouldering desert of ash and blackened boulders; and Ibrahim, Lord of the Waves, took to his boats just in time.

After that, he bided his moment for revenge. But meanwhile he listened to many false reports of Malta, which spoke of a foreign count and a mere thirteen knights in occupation, and did not mention their quality. Presently, after long talks under the desert stars, and much wine to aid the spirit, he decided that he was strong enough to take Malta by storm from the sea. If a red-headed usurper could do it in a day, the Lord of the Waves could finish the business in an hour.

But the Lord of the Waves was a boaster. He and his corsair captains talked too much of their plans, and all became known: gossip flew as swiftly by sea as by land, and gossip reached the ears of Count Roger, who had spies ringing his whole domain, almost as soon as it was uttered. When Ibrahim Hakkim sailed, Malta was ready for him.

It was forecast that Ibrahim, as a matter of bravado, would land on the same beach as Count Roger had used, three years earlier. This could have been a false rumour, a feint, but knowing his man Roger believed it to be true, and made his dispositions accordingly. He set Joseph Bin-Said, who knew every inch, every rock and shoal of his bay, to prepare the defences.

On many dark nights Bin-Said and his people toiled. But what they set up was no massive earthwork or watch-tower. Instead, about fifty feet out from the shore, where the bay began to shelve, they planted boulders, and between them wedged a long line of upright stakes. To the stakes, which just broke the surface of the water, they fastened that simplest of all island snares, a net.

A man in a hurry would take it to be some fishing device, used by plain and probably stupid islanders. It was.

Daylight came, and with it the enemy, a squadron of ten galleys speeding towards the shore. Behind their cover of rocks, the defenders watched them. The boats fanned out on a broad front, which was all that could be desired. The rowers cheered themselves on with shouts and cries. Men at the stern-posts beat gongs and cracked whips, while soldiers in strange garb, but no armour, stood ready to jump and wade ashore. Then, still moving at their best speed, the line of galleys reached the line of the stakes.

Chaos came. At almost the same moment, the leading rowers in each boat found their oars trapped in the underwater net. They lost their stroke, and fell in writhing heaps, while their companions in the stern rowed bravely on, until they themselves were caught.

The fleet came to a stop. Cries of Saracen rage filled the air. The defenders left their cover, and walked out to watch the fun. Boats were milling about, turning vain circles, crashing into each other: men with whips lashed at the tumbled slaves: others cursed the steersmen who had led them into this trap. It was like some drunken holiday frolic.

The defenders laughed, and then began to shoot.

It was all planned. First a volley of stones from a corps of expert slingmen, who could toss a ten-pound boulder into a well a hundred feet away, came crashing down on the boats and the men in them. Next a shower of cross-bow arrows flighted towards the *mêlée*, and found flesh and turned it into

meat. Then another volley of stones, launched into the bloody
water, stirred it into a cauldron of smashed wood, broken oars,
and despairing swimmers. Then there was a pause, filled with
much thought and anguish.

Count Roger's men, and Bin-Said's own small band of club-
wielding villagers, were ready to charge. But there was nothing
left for them to repel. The wrecked boats stayed where they
were, hopelessly entangled; the last gasping swimmer was
picked off by marksmen who had not had such a day since they
took Palermo. It was a merry rout. No war-galley grounded on
the beach, and any man who set foot on the shores of Malta
only did so in cold bedraggled death.

It was barely noon when the first bodies, pushed in by a
ruffling wind, began to drift ashore. But by that time, Count
Roger and his men were breaking their fast, with many flagons
to wash the victuals down, many toasts to the Lord of the
Waves now drying out in another place, and many tales of
what the day had brought to a rash enemy.

*There was no need to say what this story was. First they had
been told of the flag, the living flag, and now it was the little
boats of the enemy, destroyed and driven off that very morning. The catacomb erupted into wild rejoicing. Best of all
was the thought that they were not less valiant than their
fathers, nor less cunning, nor, for that matter, less ready to
give a party to celebrate.*

When Count Roger died, full of years and honours, Malta was
still ruled from Sicily, for the next 400 years. After the Normans came many other nations, Germans and French and
Spaniards, who coveted the island for their several needs. Sometimes its faith wavered, but, like the Mass for Roger's soul, it
was never forgotten.

Nor were these other nations there to stay. Only one people
was there to stay, the Maltese: who could be as proud and
happy, on a latter day, as when Count Roger first gave them
their flag, and restored their church and put the imprint of lusty
manhood, the pride of a nation, on a people who had long
despaired of either.

The Christmas Day
of Father Salvatore

25 December 1941

I

Marija Debrincat awoke in a strange bed, and was for a moment
terrified. She awoke saying 'Michael' out loud, just as she had
gone to sleep saying 'Michael'. The bed, which had been warm,
was now cold; her nightdress had slipped above her waist; her
dream, which had been so urgent, so sensually perfect, now
seemed disgraceful. Had she sinned? Had it happened? Had
she now done what she longed for?

She awoke properly, and saw the gilded ceiling and tapestried
curtains of her room, and remembered, and thanked God for
His safe keeping, even as a small rebellious part of her mind
wondered: Well, would it have been so terrible? And then
again: Well, what *would* it have been like?

What thoughts, on the holiest morning of the year! ... She
realized that she was cold because the gorgeous eiderdown had
slipped to the floor; and that her nightdress was in disarray
because that was the way of nightdresses. Nothing else was
wrong; she was in a strange bed only because she was spending
the night with her grandmother at the Palazzo Santo-Nobile, to
help (just as Carmelina had come with her to help) in preparation for the grand family lunch-party at noon on Christmas
Day.

She retrieved the eiderdown, and pulled it up to her chin;
arranged her nightdress more modestly (how awful it must be,
to belong to that order of nuns who were not even allowed to
see their own bodies when they were undressing, and had to
keep their eyes shut): then she looked at the ceiling again, and
went back to a more decorous daydream-version of her sleeping vision. It had been about Michael, of course; Michael in all
his young and loving manhood. Waking, it was still about
Michael, but in a way she could control, if she wished.

He was becoming so *naughty*... They had progressed a long

way since the first days of their shy loving; now it was an acknowledged love, and an acknowledged tempest in the blood also. He was often away, in ships or on missions which cancelled their plans without warning; whenever he came back, they always contrived to fly into each other's arms, with a readiness which made it terribly difficult to remember the rules. It had never actually *happened* yet, of course; that would have been unthinkable. But they both knew that it must, that it was all nonsense to pretend otherwise.

In imagination, all things had happened already; in reality, more than enough for a quiet mind. Loving was wanting, wanting more and more. And when one thing was allowed, how difficult it was to deny it the next time. She remembered – and how easy it was to remember such things, lying in a wide bed on Christmas morning, with her dreams still vivid – she remembered the first time they had confessed the urgent hunger between them.

Michael had made a joke of it, of course; he always did. But the joke was part of love, a precious part, and the most dangerous.

It was dark, on a walk home after a decorous evening, and they were alone. He had drawn her into the shadows under the trees, and began to tell her things she had been longing and fearing to hear. She was the most beautiful girl he had ever seen, or ever put his arms around. She had a beautiful face, and beautiful lips – he kissed them. She was beautiful up here – and he fondled her breast, so gently and lovingly that she could not have protested even if she had wanted to. She had beautiful legs – and he pressed against them, through the thin silk of her dress. She was beautiful – and he pressed again, with such obvious determination that she had broken away, scandalized and afraid.

After a panting moment, the storm had turned to laughter as he said : 'Well, that's all I know about beautiful you.'

'I should hope so!'

He could turn anything to laughter. But it did not answer any questions at all, nor solve any problems. She could still blush scarlet at the memory of his hands on her breasts, though it had happened many times since that first night. Often now – such was the insidious progress of love – when she felt his body becoming urgent, as on that first time, she could feel her own answering: she wanted, wanted, *wanted* him to have every-thing, to take everything and give her everything – whatever 'everything' meant.

But always she pushed him away, or asked him to unclasp his hands, or told him 'No'. What else could she do? Since he had not even mentioned marriage, beyond the fondling and the pressing there could only be fornication, that fearful sin. How could she even be imagining such things? What had happened to St Agatha, and her special devotion to a saint who had died rather than submit? What had happened to all she had been taught, all that she had vowed?

Already there had been impure thoughts. Impure actions, too. She wanted to talk to somebody about it, really talk. Not to other girls, who were either prim or silly or with bad minds. Not to her mother, who could know nothing of love. What she wanted to know was, how could a man propose marriage – if marriage was in his mind – or a girl say 'Yes' to it, without impure thoughts?

She had talked about this, finally, to the only person she could trust, her Uncle Salvu. But it was so difficult. He had been sweet, and reassuring, yet not very helpful. There were certain rules, he insisted – she must know this already, from her con-fessor. If she was falling in love with Michael, and he with her, and all things were properly arranged, then they might marry. Marriage sprang from pure love. Only pure love was permissible before marriage. Afterwards, love itself – making love – was sanctified.

'But Uncle Salvu,' she had almost wailed, 'how do you find out?'

Astonishingly, he said that he did not know.

So, apart from a thudding heart and occasional surges of wild delight, there only remained confusion and a little shame, great longing and great fear. It was something she had to solve by herself, like all other secret temptations. Michael was naughty because he was a man, and couldn't help it. She must be good, because she was a girl, the shrine of purity. It was dull, being a shrine. Perhaps she was just a bad girl after all...
She had been to Midnight Mass, a few hours earlier, but it had been a woeful performance.

All the time her thoughts had strayed. Try as she would, she could only think of him. He was up there, flying somewhere in the black night: nearer to the Star of Bethlehem than any-one in the church. Nearer to the Birth, nearer to death.

It was love in war. Michael was going to telephone, as he always did: not immediately he got back, which was what they both wanted, but as early as he could interrupt a great household. It was love in war, uncertain and beset by unmen-tionable fears. Marriage was not yet even a word between them. The family was aware of him, but only on a careful plane of non-involvement.

It was accepted that she had met a young lieutenant in the Navy. Uncle Salvu had met him also, and liked him very much. Pietru had met him, and was full of technical praise. However, there was plenty of time – an absurd and cruel idea, but a basic, comfortable, family idea. It was love in war.

But he was coming to lunch. It was the least they could do, her darling mother had announced, with the straightest of faces, to entertain a British serviceman at Christmas, when he was lonely and far from home.

Cold morning light was slipping through the curtains. It was seven o'clock, and Christmas at last. A punctual knock on the door brought Carmelina, with hot chocolate and a cheerful greeting.

'*Bon ġornu, Sinjurina Marija. Il-Milied it-tajjeb!*'

A happy Christmas! Carmelina looked like a happy Christ-mas herself, pretty and bubbling with life. Marija knew why. Francis the footman, home for the holiday, was giving up the whole of his time off to help at the Palazzo. Francis the foot-man looked really sensational in his Royal Malta Artillery uniform, with the brand-new lance-bombardier's stripes. There was an understanding – or a hint of an understanding, presently to be declared – between them. Carmelina was on top of the world. It was love in war.

'Good morning, Carmelina. Happy Christmas.'

The smell of the hot chocolate was enough to re-christen the day. They *never* had hot chocolate at home... She took a first sip, while Carmelina drew back the curtains, letting in light which, to judge by a glimpse of pale clear sky, would shortly turn to sunshine.

Then she noticed that there were two little parcels, flanked by scarlet poinsettia leaves, on her tray.

'Presents already?'

'It's only mine, *sinjurina*,' Carmelina answered. 'And another one that a man brought last night. I thought you'd like it now.'

'A man? What man?'

'That man on his motor-cycle.' Carmelina tossed her head, and sniffed: evidently some Christmas Eve skylarking had taken a dramatic turn. Francis to the rescue? What could it matter, compared with the wonderful fact of arrival? Michael must have arranged it all, just before he flew off into that black night. She hugged her dear secret, which was not a secret at all within this room; Carmelina knew all about Michael, just as Marija knew all about Francis, without a word being spoken.

But there were other priorities, on Christmas morning. 'Which one is yours, Carmelina?'

'The one with the ribbon, *sinjurina*.'

'It looks beautiful.'

It was a little silk scarf, bright as flame, chosen with care, costing all sorts of hoarded pennies from modest wages. She gave Carmelina her own present, which was a dress-length of flowered yellow chiffon, just right for a pretty girl who could sew a fine seam, and there were mutual expressions of delight. Marija licked the last drops of chocolate as Carmelina tidied up the room. Then she said:

'I'm expecting a telephone call at half past eight, Carmelina. But I don't want to disturb the house. If I don't hear it, could you listen for it, and tell me?'

'Yes, *sinjurina*. Will you answer it in the armoury?'

'I think that would be best... Is the Baroness awake yet, do you know?'

'Oh yes, *sinjurina*. She's been wandering about – I mean, she's been up and dressed, seeing that everything's all right, since five o'clock.'

'Heavens! I must go and help her.'

The Baroness Santo-Nobile had indeed been up and about, since before dawn on a cold winter morning. Disdaining to wake anyone so early, she had put an end to fitful sleep by making up her mind to get up and dress herself: a simple exercise which would have been simpler if she had not been plagued by one of the terrors of old age, rheumatism. The deep wells under the Palazzo Santo-Nobile brought more than water; between dusk and dawn they brought creeping moistures, foggy airs, which invaded old bones and stiff joints as if recognizing that here was their natural home.

'After all, I am seventy-five,' she said aloud, and crossly, struggling into her high-necked black dress with the regiment of buttons which defied fingers no longer nimble. It was not quite true; she was seventy-four and three months. But 'seventy-five' had a certain ring about it, whereas 'seventy-four' was nothing more (as her husband had once explained, when she joined him on the South Atlantic Station) than the name of a fried fish served in the Cape Province. She was seventy-five.

This Christmas morning was a day she had been secretly dreading, yet proudly announcing as 'the usual family lunch'. Lunch for twenty-six people at the Palazzo had once been a simple matter of giving certain orders, and making a five-minute tour of inspection to see that every detail was exactly as it should be. This time, it had taken the best part of an exhausting month to organize.

There were so many things, so many worries, so much that could no longer be taken for granted. She had reopened both the closed wings of the house, because one of them contained the formal dining-room and the other a salon where Christmas morning had always been inaugurated, as far back as she could remember, first with a family gathering round the Christmas tree and later with a reception to which anyone of consequence might come.

There was no general reception this year. But there would be other guests at lunch. Thus the wings must be opened. It was a task for fifteen servants, and she had only four, and one of them, old Gregory the major-domo, was, to his infinite shame, ill and confined to his bed.

'But I shall get up for the lunch, Madame,' he assured her, time and again. 'You can count on me.'

She counted on herself. Though she now seemed to tire easily, she was still firm as a rock, and adamant in her determination to have her Christmas lunch-party according to the old scale. The roms were opened up, cleaned, dusted, polished, and set to rights after their long sleep. Her chef brought in his family to help: a menu was planned: tradesmen's old aunts, gardeners' second cousins, the twin daughters of Manwel Azzopardi the stone-mason – all were co-opted and set to their tasks, which ranged from unwinding the silver place-settings from their green baize cocoons to pounding the brandy-butter sauce to the perfect creamy consistency of her grandmother's recipe.

She drove all these helpers with a steely will, and herself most harshly of all. It was thus that her granddaughter Marija found her, at half-past seven on Christmas morning, surveying her half-set lunch table, moving place-cards on the embossed leather table plan, and also moving heavy chairs.

'Grandmother!' Marija said, shocked. 'You shouldn't be doing that.'

'And why not, pray?'

'Because I'm here!'

Marija spoke more sharply than she had ever done before; the sight of the little old woman, encased in her severe black dress, straining at an armchair with paper-thin hands, was almost shameful. Her grandmother rounded on her, and seemed about to explode into anger, or at least into a cutting dismissal of this interference; then, just as suddenly, she smiled, and sat down in the chair at the head of her empty table, and said:

'You're a dear girl, Marija. A happy Christmas. Come and kiss me.'

When Marija touched the parchment cheek, she found that the Baroness was trembling. She sat down by her side, and for a moment they were composed in silence: the old woman and the young, at the head of a long vista of polished mahogany and crested silver platters, crowned by a huge branched *épergne*, exquisitely fashioned, on which the first shafts of sunlight were now falling.

I shall never have a table like this, Marija thought. It did not matter. It only mattered that she would never have another grandmother like this.

'Have you had your tea?' she asked, after a moment of silence had stretched into a peaceful harmony. 'Can I get you anything?'

It was the signal for the most memorable conversation of her life.

'Not tea,' the Baroness answered. 'Not coffee, either. On Christmas morning, I would like something a little *stronger*. If you would please open that corner cupboard' – she nodded towards a walnut cabinet, 'you will find a decanter of brandy, and some glasses. Bring me one.'

The glasses were tiny, all of different colours, small jewels of polished crystal. Marija chose a green one, filled it with brandy, and brought it back to her grandmother. She consoled her uneasiness with the thought that it was really only medicine.

Between sips, her grandmother asked: 'How old are you, Marija?'

'Eighteen.'

'I am seventy-five... When I was your age, the gentlemen often used to have a glass of brandy and soda before breakfast. The soda-water was called *seltzer*, until German became unfashionable.'

'Goodness!' Michael, she knew, sometimes had a bottle of beer, but it was not a good moment to announce the fact. 'Seventy-five' had been daunting enough already.

'Just as the waltz became the *valse*, in polite society... When I was your age,' her grandmother repeated, her voice beautifully calm and measured, 'I had just met your grandfather.'

Marija waited.

'My family did not like him,' the Baroness went on, 'or rather, they liked him very much – everybody liked him – but they did not like the idea of my marrying an English sailor. So we did not get married until I was twenty-three.'

'But that was five years!'

'Five years.' The emerging sunshine flickered on the branched silver *épergne*, as if counting out the months, the very hours, of all those five years. 'But we were quite sure of ourselves, so it did not really matter.' She took another sip of her brandy. 'Of course, it *mattered* tremendously, but in those days it was natural to do exactly as one was told, so we did not think it was so terrible.'

'But what did you *do*?'

'We loved each other, and we waited.' The Baroness, normally so stiff and upright, leant against the high back of her chair. She was almost lounging, if so absurd a word could be applied to the head of the house of Santo-Nobile. 'Now – tell me about this young man who is coming to lunch.'

Marija, confused by the sudden change of subject, decided to take the easiest course.

'Mother thought it would be nice if we asked a soldier or a sailor to lunch on Christmas Day.'

'How very interesting... And how pretty you look, Marija...' Her voice sharpened alarmingly. 'Tell me about the young man who is coming to lunch.'

Marija told her. At the start it was terrifying, and embarrassing, yet once she was launched it was easy. She said exactly what had happened, and how, and why, and what the future held, or might hold, or could hold. She kept nothing back. There was no need to. The gulf of the years proved to be no gulf at all. It dissolved, melted away, in tender trust and huge relief.

Her grandmother listened in silence. It was impossible to tell what she was thinking; her face was as calm and controlled as it always was. Sometimes she nodded, as if recognizing a part of the story which she had been expecting. Once she smiled, when Marija was telling of the spell cast over Pietru by this glamorous suitor. But for the most part she had a judge's look: the look of wisdom and maturity which waits for all the facts before considering a verdict.

At the end, silence fell like a graceful curtain: all had been told, the only thing which could follow was the applause, or the polite neutrality, or the hissing of a disappointed audience. Finally the Baroness said:

'I think I would like a little more brandy... Just half a glass, there's a dear girl.' And as Marija busied herself at the walnut cabinet, she went on: 'Your Uncle Salvatore says that Michael is very good-looking.'

'Oh, yes!' Marija brought the glass back, and set it down on the table. 'But he doesn't – I mean, it isn't really important to him. He doesn't *use* it, like lots of men try to do. Even though he knows—'

'What does he know?'

'That he can drive me right round the bend.'

'Marija, *what* an expression!' But her grandmother was not angry, or shocked: she was even smiling slightly. Emboldened by this, and by the relief of shedding her secret burden, Marija said: 'Can I tell you a secret story?'

'If you wish.'

'In the Royal Air Force, when they want to say, "He's right round the bend," they say: "He's Harpic".'

'I don't understand.'

'Harpic is – well, it's a lavatory cleaner. The advertisements always say : "Harpic goes right round the bend".'

'Marija, *really*!'

But, on this unusual Christmas morning, even this was permissible. The Baroness sipped her brandy, not at all put out. However, she brought the conversation firmly back to its proper sphere when she said :

'You say that he has never proposed marriage?'

'Not really. Well, not at all.'

'But he wants to – to love you.'

'Yes. At least, I think so. But when I say no, of course not, it's impossible, he doesn't seem to want to any more.'

'Ah... Then I think he will propose... Has he given you a Christmas present?'

Marija smiled. 'Yes. I just opened it. It was a pot of strawberry jam. I know it sounds silly. But you can't *get* strawberry jam!'

'Silly presents are the best... Hugo – your grandfather – once gave me a litle bunch of carrots, tied up with navy-blue ribbon.'

'*Carrots?*'

'Certainly. He wanted me to be able to see him in the dark.'

'Did you love him very much, Grandmother?'

A change came over the Baroness, one of the swift changes of old age. True feeling flooded in, affecting her face and her manner most movingly; memory became real, memory became *today*, replacing the brittleness, the light-fingered nonsense of the last few moments.

'We loved each other equally from the moment we met. I adored him always, and he felt the same. He was a fine-looking man... And I was a great beauty. Why should I not say so? You would be a great beauty too, if you would only eat properly. Skin and bone! However, I suppose that's the modern taste... As I told you, we had to wait five years to get married. When my turn came, I made your mother wait four years, but there were other reasons for that... Now, I suppose, like all young people, *you* want to get married tomorrow.'

In a heart-stopping moment of realization, Marija understood what her grandmother was really saying.

'*Grandmother!* Do you mean you don't mind?'

'Not so fast. We will have to have a look at him first.'

'But even the *idea*—'

In a strangely small voice, the Baroness answered: 'Do you really think I would object to your marrying an English sailor?' Then, to top all the surprises of the morning, her frail face seemed to crumble, and she was in tears.

It was a brief weakness, but enough to bring Marija near to weeping herself. She had never seen her grandmother like this, nor even imagined that it could be possible. She wanted to say: 'Grandmother! You're crying!' and take the old woman in her arms, but she knew that this would have been utterly wrong. The pride of privacy must be respected, even at this unbelievable moment.

She got up, with a word of apology, and occupied herself at the corner cupboard, rearranging the glasses, taking out the brandy decanter and fiddling with its crystal stopper before she replaced it. Not until she heard, behind her, a sound of delicate nose-blowing did she turn round and approach the table again.

It was as if it had never happened. 'Well, we must be sensible,' the Baroness said. But 'sensible' was to mean something much more than the recovery of composure. 'And *you* must be sensible. Marriage is a family matter – nothing can change that. Love is between two people – *only*.' The extraordinary emphasis she placed on the last word had strange undertones of complicity. 'I will have a look at your young man this morning, and if all you tell me is true ... It may be that you cannot be married for quite a long time. Michael might be sent away. Sailors are always being sent away, sometimes to the other side of the world. Perhaps your father will object. He has a right to do so, as the head of your family. We will deal with that when the time comes... What I want to tell you now is how to deal with love – love before marriage. *Wanting* before marriage. There is such a thing. You will find it surprising, not only that I speak of such matters, but that I even know about them. But I do. I was not always seventy-five. You must realize something which perhaps seems incredible – that I was once eighteen, and deeply in love with someone I could not marry for five years.'

Marija was listening in astonishment, almost in disbelief. Could this really be her grandmother, the old lady with the straight back and stern eye, the guardian of behaviour and

convention, the head of the Santo-Nobile family and its un-
questioned ruler? Who or what was really speaking? The
Baroness? The brandy? The strain of the Christmas gathering
on a frail old woman? The longer strain of war? The memory
of love denied or frustrated which – greatest of rarities – she
did not want to deny to others? Marija felt that she would
never know. She also knew that the moment was precious,
and could never happen again.

As her grandmother paused, she said: 'When I asked Uncle
Salvu, he said that there could be no love like that, no thoughts
like that, before marriage.'

'That is the correct answer,' the Baroness answered, without
sarcasm. 'I would never deny it. It is the ideal, the perfect
answer. After that, we must take advantage – *you* must take
advantage – of the fact that human beings are not ideal, not
perfect, and are expected to make mistakes.' The amazing
liberality of this, coming from such a person, was all part of
the same early morning Christmas fantasy. 'Men are sensual
animals, with sensual urges. So are we, though we are not
allowed to say so... I want to tell you now how to get through
this very difficult time... Because *I know*... Perhaps I should
say that I never talked to my own daughter, your mother, like
this, because there were many reasons why I did not want her
to get through it. I wanted to prevent it altogether... There, I
have said it... But the things I never told her, I will tell you
now.'

The sunlight, already strong, fell on the polished table and
the gleaming *épergne*. The Baroness's brandy glass was empty,
but she did not want brandy any more. She wanted her own
particular moment of truth and communication.

'People, men and women, boys and girls, hunger for each
other, long before marriage. If they are lucky, they do the
same, long after marriage... As soon as we were sure, honourably sure, that we would marry, we found ways of assuaging
that hunger.' What ways, what ways? Marija dared not ask,
but her astounding grandmother was going to dare to tell. 'I do
not mean that we became lovers, in the vulgar sense: I always
thought that this would be wrong, and so did your grandfather
– or at least—' and she smiled a delightful, secret, tender smile,
'he agreed to respect my point of view. When that question
was settled, we thought of what we *could* do, rather than what

we could not. It did not happen quickly, because we were learning, learning together, a very precious time for both of us... But
this is what we used to do, after a while, to make wanting –
wild wanting – bearable.'

She told her story, tendered her advice, dictated ways and
means, as explicitly as if she had been reciting the alphabet.
Marija had never heard such words from any human being
before; the fact that they came from her grandmother should
have been shaming and embarrassing, but it was not – it was,
on the contrary, as warm and comforting as a caress between
friends. The word 'release' occurred many times; only now was
its meaning made clear, and its reality frankly pictured, as
something accessible to loving hands and hearts.

Only now did she understand, really understand, that the
ache of love need not persist. It could be tamed, against the
day and the night when it need not be.

At the end, Marija had nothing to say, and nothing more to
hear: she felt as if she had grown up, had been admitted to
some special circle of initiation, all within the space of half
an hour. When her grandmother said: 'Is there anything you
would like to ask me?' she could not think of a single question,
except one which came from a loyal heart:

'But isn't it sinful?'

'Yes.' The answer was admirably prompt. 'Or so the religious
say, and we must believe them. Though they do not know all
that they pretend, and it is tempting to forbid the unknown...
There are worse sins than giving comfort to someone you love,
and receiving it... Let us call it a small sin, to avoid a greater
one.'

Now the Baroness was sitting back in her high chair, more
at ease than at any time since Marija entered the room. A task
had been done, a blessing conferred. What else could a girl
with a whirling brain say, except 'thank you'.

But when she tried to put it into words, she found that her
grandmother had one more point to make.

'You sound surprised that I should talk to you like this. You
should not be. You know that we have a proverb here: "There
is a time to fish, and a time to dry the nets." What I have told
you has been waiting a long time to be said. But it was always
waiting for you. Try to believe that nothing in the world is
new, except the words we use. The things we did in 1885 are

exactly the same as the things of today, except that we did not talk about them so much in public. Beautiful, hungry bodies were just as normal then as now, thank God. And I mean "Thank God" literally, because they are His bodies and His hunger... And now, let us go back to Christmas Day, and our troublesome lunch party. There really must be a limit to – now let me see how you young people would phrase it – to sex before breakfast.'

There was a curious fumbling knock on the door of the dining-room, and then it swung open. Old Gregory the major-domo, a figure of shrunken magnificence in his green-and-gold livery, advanced with a profound bow.

'At your service, Baroness!'

It was a difficult moment. Gregory, pale and shambling, should clearly not have left his bed, and might have difficulty in regaining it. The Baroness took charge, with practised economy of words and the discipline of complete authority. Gregory, assured of gratitude and a happy Christmas, was to rest until he was called for. He was to rest *now*. Nothing was required of him until noon at the earliest. And yes, his Lord-ship the Bishop would visit the servants' hall as usual, bestow his blessing, and take a small glass of wine.

When old Gregory had made a halting exit, the Barones sighed. 'I hoped he would sleep until much later.' Then she and Marija happened to catch each other's eye, and feminine irrever-ence took over. ' "*At my service*", indeed!' the Baroness mimicked, with sly emphasis, and the eldest and the youngest of the female line of Santo-Nobile dissolved into helpless laugh-ter.

As it subsided, the Baroness stretched out her arms – and Marija had never seen her make this undisciplined gesture. 'Oh, how I wish my dearest son were here, to listen to all this non-sense!'

2

In the cold and draughty tenement which was the catacomb of the Cottonera Lines, her dearest son was putting in an ordinary morning's work. Christmas Day made no difference to this; there were things to be done, as soon as the four-thirty Mass was celebrated, whether the calendar announced the day of their Saviour's birth or the day of their delivery from the Turks. After his customary private pause, to separate communion with God from all other contacts, Father Salvatore went soberly to his tasks.

It was just another day, and that was the strangest thing about it. This, the second Christmas of their war, was a Christmas under siege, and the siege, with its attendant miseries, ruled all their lives; the day was simply the twenty-fifth of December, and, for the first time that he could ever remember, no one was really bothering about it.

There were no Christmas decorations, no strings of coloured lights – who had money for that? Presents? – well, presents were for happier days. A special meal? – a lucky few might kill a chicken or a rabbit, under envious eyes, but the special meal was likely to be Father Salvatore's *soppa ta' l'armla*, Widow's Soup, the soup for the poor, which he had promised to serve sometime during the evening, if Nero could find some fresh sheep's cheese to add to the brew. Wine? – a man was lucky to get a cup of clean water in this smelly old ruin!

Money was short. Food was short. Bells could not ring, nor lights glow. There would probably be air-raids again. Thus had Christmas shrivelled, copying life itself.

Father Salvatore made his rounds. 'Prowling', they called it, but with affectionate meaning. If Dun Salv did not prowl, God knows what certain people would be up to. He approved a neat piece of workmanship, when he came upon a gang of youths repairing a crumbling staircase with a section of dry-stone steps. He scolded some children for getting in the way of the rubbish collection, even though he knew their urgent concern: they were avid for any eatable scraps which might be carted away before a hungry boy or girl could snatch them from the refuse bins.

He settled a raging quarrel about an egg. 'It is mine!' one of the women screamed: 'Laid in my own kitchen.' 'It is mine!' her opponent screeched. 'Only I have hens in this corridor.' They went to it like a pair of harpies looking for promotion.

'Then keep your cursed hens out of my kitchen.'

'Then do not entice them in with scraps of bread. I've seen you!'

'The egg is mine. I found it.'

'The egg is mine. My own hen laid it.'

'Then take it. Take it if you dare!'

'I'll take the egg, and half your hair too, unless you give it to me.'

'I'm not surprised you want my hair. Old baldy!'

'Thief!'

'Hen woman! I can smell you a mile off.'

'With a beak like that, you could smell a bomber in Sicily. Give me that egg!'

'Never!'

They appealed to Father Salvatore, who gradually sorted out a tortuous story. In law, there must be an exact answer, though he did not know what it was: in law, it must long ago have been laid down, just like the egg, that finders were keepers, an egg being abandoned property: or that the owner of a hen was the owner of its egg, *contra mundum*: or that a hen, if trespassing on private property, lost its civil rights: or that a hen, deliberately enticed away at such a crucial moment, became a ward of the court, and its egg was no longer in the private domain at all... He felt weary already, and Christmas Day was still as young as the Christ Child. He said mildly:

'If I can keep the egg for the *soppa* tonight, then you would both have a share of it.'

They simmered fiercely, and then grumbled, but that was the way it was settled.

He helped an old man, shivering in a bitterly cold room, to get some warmth and blood back into his legs, chafing and rubbing them until they turned from faint blue to pale yellow. He told another man, *No*, he could *not* store boxes of straw and rabbit dung inside the catacombs. The air was foul enough already. There was a place for such things by the bastion walls. 'But Dun Salv! I want to keep an eye on it!' 'And we want to keep our health.'

He praised, with warm words and a full heart, a little girl who was patiently fashioning a Christmas crib – stable, manger, Virgin Mother, tiny child, wise men, ox, ass, and sheep, winged angels, shining star of Bethlehem – all from matchsticks and bits of torn paper.

Then he heard a long-drawn-out cry, from a corner of the catacombs he had visited many times during the past twenty-four hours. He had hoped that he would hear the cry of a child, but after all this time, it was still the cry of a woman.

Up in one of the high galleries, to which he now climbed, a girl was in labour, as she had been since the dawn of yesterday. She lay in a stained and tumbled bed, surrounded by old women in black, who crouched like a ring of crows round a dying sheep: by staring children, constantly shooed out of the room and as constantly filtering back again: by a distracted husband, calling on heaven to witness that they need never make love again, if only this one was safely delivered: by a calm and competent nun who was the girl's sister: by a head-shaking mother-in-law whose complaint never varied – she had always said the girl's hips were too narrow, and no one had paid any attention; and now by Father Salvatore, who sidled into the room like any fearful child, and privately wished that someone would shoo him out again.

He could never be at ease, in such a rank female world of torment and suffering. The pious pictures of Christ in the manger had *this* foundation, and no other.

Silence fell as he approached the bed. 'Help her, Dun Salv!' someone whispered, as if he had a miracle at his command: as if he could lay on hands, and bring calm and peace to this racked and wrenching body. He knelt, and prayed, and took the girl's hand, taut with pain, burning with fever.

'Concetta. Can you hear me?'

The cloudy eyes opened wide, and then closed again. Even the flickering oil lamp was too strong to be borne.

'Is it coming yet, Dun Salv?'

'Not yet. But only a little longer.'

'It must be a big one.'

'Big and strong. A child you can be proud of... It's not too late to go to hospital.'

'Never!' Concetta was actually smiling, in the midst of her torture. 'I want to have it in the catacombs. That's where it started!'

She had never wavered from this resolve.

He stayed for twenty minutes, while gradually the desperate straining ceased, and calm returned. Her hour was not yet... When he came down again, he found himself wondering, fancifully, if the child, in spite of the pain it was inflicting, was not right after all. This was a poor time to be born in Malta.

Their war, in its short life of nineteen months, had already grown old in sin and misery. Nothing now was new; it was only worse. There had been a short respite in the bombing, while Germany turned her fury on Russia, but it had all started again on 2 December, and they had suffered 175 raids – nearly six a day – during the month. Two good convoys, one of them numbering eighteen ships, had got safely through to Malta in September; now, because of ferocious reaction to this success, there was nothing more planned, and nothing hoped for, and rationing was harsher than ever.

Hope was what they all needed: hope that this cruel siege would be lifted: hope that the war was going well, and would soon be won. In all honesty, it was impossible for authority to tell them this, or to believe it if they did so.

Meanwhile, their nearest land-battle raged up and down North Africa. The desert war had become somewhat unreal: it was just names on the map, hackneyed labels which were triumphantly 'Ours', and then swiftly ripped off and changed to 'Theirs', as the tide of war ebbed and flowed. There was no further explanation of this, beyond the cant phrases of the *communiqués* – 'magnificent advances' alternating with 'strategic withdrawals to prepared positions', or the bland 'adjustment of uneven sections in our defence line', which turned out to be the same thing.

One thing was certain. Malta was contributing vitally to this battle, and was being punished for it.

She was punished for her big build-up of Hurricanes and Spitfires, and for maintaining a striking force of the new Blenheim bombers, which harassed enemy shipping at a crucial moment in the North African campaign. The bombing 'holiday' had followed the German onslaught on Russia, with whom Germany had a solemn treaty of friendship; now that the Russian front was immobilized by winter – 'frozen to death' would be more accurate – the German air force swung back to Malta.

The pounding started again, and continued mercilessly, accelerating up to Christmas as if to some obscene pagan festival. When the *Times of Malta*, its pages sometimes charred by fire, reported, as it did nearly every day, 'slight damage to Government and civilian property', it meant that Malta's airfields were being steadily pulverized, and the surrounding towns and villages flattened by the overspill.

Malta was punished just for being *there*, astride the Axis

supply lines from Europe to Africa, and able to cut these supplies by anything up to seventy per cent. She was punished by ruined convoys which were driven back before they could complete their own task of supply; and by rumoured naval losses, across the length and breadth of the Mediterranean, which had now reached such a peak that convoys of any substance – that blessed, almost forgotten word – were now under the interdict of war.

When single ships ran the blockade and made harbour, it was no wonder that Maltese stevedores, immediately beset by pin-point attacks on the dockyard, grew dispirited, and slow at the job of unloading. What was the good of starting to unload, when a man could be killed, or a ship sunk at the quayside, almost before the first cargo sling was rigged?

Malta was being punished for simply trying to stay alive. A Government grant of nearly half a million pounds kept the price of essential food down. But one could not eat money, and where was the food anyway? The rationing scale sank steadily downwards, and the spirits of the men with it.

There was one ray of hope, just before Christmas, though it came from a long way away. The Japanese attack on Pearl Harbor – the Day of Infamy of 7 December – had brought the Americans into the war at last. They *must* be allies worth having, even though the day of infamy had clearly been a day of disaster also.

But in the meantime, an egg cost God-knows-what: a sheep or a cow seemed to be made of gold: there were queues for everything, from bread to paraffin; and petrol was so scarce that horse-drawn trams had reappeared on the run between Valletta and Hamrun.

What would come next? Swapping a sheep for a house? Queueing for coffins? *Camel-trains?*

Even the cheerful, energetic, bouncing little Nero was looking depressed and out of sorts, when Father Salvatore met him near the entrance to the catacombs. Nero had gone out at first light, shortly after six o'clock, to scour the shops of the Three Cities for something worthwhile to put into the promised *soppa ta' l'armla.* 'Leave it to me, Dun Salv!' he had said, by way of farewell, and added: 'I'll get something, if I have to dress up as a Carmelite and beg!'

But the estimated 600 people who would attend this Christmas feast needed seventy-five gallons of soup at one pint a head (Father Salvatore was becoming used to such monstrous sums); and seventy-five gallons, even if watered down as thin as a widow's wedding ring, and thickened with mountainous crusts of bread, demanded its own mountain of other ingredients. Nero, from the look on his face, had procured no more than a mole-hill.

'I've done the best I can, Dun Salv,' he reported, as soon as he saw the *kappillan*. But he was empty-handed, save for a fistful of grimy lettuces, and noticing Father Salvatore's expression he hastened to reassure him. 'It's all right – my cousin's collecting the stuff at his garage, and he'll deliver it somehow – he promised. He's never let us down yet.'

'Ninu is a good boy.'

'I wish his van was as good... First, I got some cheese. It's mostly *rikotta* – I know people don't like it as much as sheep's cheese, but they don't have to pay for it. So – fifty cottage cheeses, quite big ones, and about a dozen sheep's. Plenty of rabbit bones, to make a bit of juice. But only thirty eggs. I tell you, I could have gone bankrupt buying eggs!'

'Thirty eggs,' Father Salvatore repeated, doubtfully. Thirty eggs between 600 people was not a recipe that sounded very much like Christmas.

'We can make them look more, Dun Salv. I'll boil them hard, and then slice them up into rings. They'll float on top of the drums, and there you are – eggs for everyone.'

'I suppose that will have to do.'

'I'm sorry, Dun Salv.'

Nero was looking so sad that Father Salvatore immediately reassured him: 'Of course it's not your fault, Nero. You've done very well. Did you manage to get anything else?'

'Lettuces, as you see. They look a bit tired, but who doesn't, these days? A big bundle of herbs – well, they're weeds really, but they must taste of *something*. Plenty of bread, if you can call it bread – I call it sawdust and potato mush, myself. But' – there was something important coming – 'I bought a whole sack of dried beans. Well, it wasn't quite full; the rats got there first. But it was cheap, and it'll go well in the soup. Give it a bit of body.'

'You've done very well,' Father Salvatore repeated, and it

was true. Against the background of their lives, Nero's assorted wares were riches indeed. If only this wasn't their entire Christmas feast... I'm sure we'll manage to make a fine soup... Everyone realizes how difficult it is... What a pity your fiancée can't be here tonight.'

Nero shrugged his small strong shoulders. 'You know how it is, Dun Salv. Her mother doesn't trust me after dark. I suppose it's a compliment really. I'd rather have a few insults... But it's taking such a long time! Do you think we'll *ever* get this wedding settled?'

It was a difficult question to answer, with any degree of honesty which would allow for hope. Father Salvatore had met the big ugly girl, Teresa Grima, who was Nero's chosen bride, when she visited the catacombs. Throughout her stay she had observed everything with a dull indifference which contrasted sadly with Nero's bursting pride – in her, in this place where he worked and lived, in the fact of their love and their engaged status.

Teresa Grima, at twenty-seven, was a thickset, black-browed peasant girl, bulging of limb, vacant of face, to whom the word 'love' seemed as remote as the words 'elegance' or 'tenderness'. She towered above Nero, whose delight in this, as in everything else about her, was pathetically fierce. But if she was in love with him, it had never been publicly advertised by a single glance, gesture, or word that anyone could recall.

'She has a good heart, I know,' Father Salvatore had assured the prospective bridegroom. He hoped, in spite of all appearances, that this was true. It was certain that Teresa seemed to have nothing else, and that her parents in Mellieha, whom he had visited three times, had not even this commendation. They were stubborn, selfish, and mean, and relentlessly engaged in giving poor Nero the most miserable time of his life.

Teresa was the last of their seven children to be unmarried and to live at home; and they were going to preserve this status against all hazards. The father worked his fields hard enough, but he had only Teresa to help him, and thus she laboured half the day at hoeing, planting, gathering, watering, milking the goats and sheep, making cheese, cleaning out the barns, and feeding the rabbits and chickens.

The mother, strong as an ox, was yet given to fainting fits and bad spells; upon Teresa therefore devolved much of the cooking, bed-making, cleaning, and sweeping which kept the household going. The bare idea of Teresa taking a day off to visit one of her married brothers or sisters was enough to give old Mrs Grima a very bad spell indeed.

It was sad to see how the emancipated brothers and sisters connived at keeping Teresa in this servitude. Father Salvatore had spoken to some of them about Nero, and the reaction was always the same. Marriage? For Teresa? Out of the question! – and there followed the inevitable catch-phrase: 'She is so close to her mother.' Having all made their happy escape – all except Teresa, who had been trapped before she had time to fly the nest – they were only concerned to see that she stayed trapped for ever.

But it was the old folks who were the most adamant. They had four lines of defence against the threat of change: Teresa was perfectly content as she was: she could not be spared, however delighted they would be to see her married: Nero Cassar was 'not good enough': and they could not afford the dowry. They had been ringing the changes on this malevolent strategy for the past five months, without the slightest sign of weakening.

They had tradition and morality on their side: a twisted morality, but authentic none the less. It was true that Teresa had a duty towards her ageing parents, when they needed her help. The law laid down that they could not object to a prospective son-in-law save on one ground alone: his *public* behaviour, which must be shown to be scandalous or criminal. Since there could be nothing against Nero on this score, they made the most of his physical shortcomings.

Did Father Salvatore want their daughter to be a laughing-stock, marrying a little man half her size? What about children, the holy purpose of such a union? There must be bad blood involved somewhere – otherwise, why was Nero a dwarf? – and the Church could not give approval to its continuance. Did he want Malta to be peopled by such miserable, stunted stock?

Finally, there was the matter of the dowry, the last ditch of resistance. Once again, the law decreed that Teresa was entitled to a marriage dowry, even though it was only a double-bed: if her parents were not alive, she could demand it from the grandparents. But demanding was one thing, delivery was another. A *dowry*? Mr and Mrs Grima repeated the word as if Father Salvatore had said: 'One million pounds, cash on the nail.'

How could poor people such as they afford yet another dowry, the fourth in a dreadful draining of their resources imposed by the blessing of having four daughters? With the best will in the world, they had nothing left to give. So – no dowry, no marriage. They were so *ashamed*. But life was life. These were hard times. Did not Father Salvatore agree?

Father Salvatore could willingly have bashed their stupid, mulish heads together, and told them: *'Let her go!'* But a priest could not do so, and a stranger could not interfere in the sacred area of family and marriage ties. So the matter remained, after five weary months. They agreed that there could be an engagement – of a sort. They had grudgingly admitted that *if* Mr Grima could get some full-time help on the farm, and *if* Mrs Grima could afford a cook and a maid, and *if* her delicate health improved, and *if* the matter of the dowry was waived, then there might be a chance of marriage.

They could have added: And *if* Nero Cassar grew another eighteen inches, and turned out to be a millionaire. It was a complete deadlock, and poor little Nero was the frustrated loser in the middle of it.

But Father Salvatore could not possibly tell him this. It would have been cruelty, and Nero was the least deserving of it. Now he said:

'You mustn't give up hope, Nero. These difficulties often happen. Marriage is a very serious business.'

'Dun Salv, I know!' Nero sounded as though he were ready to cry, which might have been near the truth. '*I* am serious about it. Teresa is serious about it – at least, she would be, if she was given half a chance. My father is serious about it; he'll give us his consent as soon as they offer something – anything – as a dowry. But are *they* serious? No! They don't like me, and they won't give Teresa a penny. But I tell you, they're rich! They just bought a field in Ghadira for two hundred pounds! And now they argue about a double-bed and a set of saucepans! And do you know what one of the brothers – Guzepp, that fat pig who lives in Mosta – said to me? He said: "What does Teresa want with a double-bed? She has her own bed. She could tuck you under the pillow!" What sort of a thing is that to say?'

It was such a horrid remark that Father Salvatore steered away from it, and took an easier course. 'Nero, you should not call Guzepp Grima a fat pig.'

'Well, all I know is, I wish we had him for the soup...' Nero stretched out his arms in a gesture of despair, which made the wilting lettuces look like a flag of truce. 'Oh, I'm so sick of all this talking and arguing. And I'm afraid Teresa will cool off, if it goes on much longer. It's not as if she was so – so...' he searched for a word, and did not find it. He moved nearer to Father Salvatore, and dropped his voice. 'Dun Salv, what can I do to make her more interested?'

'How do you mean, interested?'

'In love. Kissing, if you like. When I try to kiss her, she always makes some excuse. Either it's too light, or it's too dark, or someone will see us, or that sort of thing will have to wait till we're married. But what's wrong with kissing?'

There were all sorts of answers, all sorts of wounds to be inflicted, all sorts of careless insults to a dwarf who wanted to marry a girl of normal size – a girl who might once have dreamed of something different, and was now resigned to nothing at all. Once again, he gave a feeble reply:

'There can be too much kissing.'

'But there's none at all! Three times, in five months! A monk could do better! I'm sorry, Dun Salv, but you know what I mean.' He moved even closer, lowering his voice again, so that Father Salvatore had to bend his head to stay in communication. 'You understand these things. People tell you their troubles, and you give them advice. Everyone says you know so much about – about everything.' He drew a deep breath, the breath of despair and intimate longing. 'How can I make Teresa really want to marry me?'

Father Salvatore wished he could have answered: 'Buy her a love potion and see that she takes it,' and left it at that. It would have saved him a lot of trouble; it might also be no more futile than any other advice he could give. Not for the first time, he found himself full of misgiving at the topic of their conversation. Sex was not of his world; it could not be, it must not be; he should be able to say, to any inquirer: 'Do not ask me that – I am a priest.'

Yet, absurdly, it was *because* he was a priest that people plagued and swamped him with such questions, questions so intimate that if he had taken a doctorate in sexual technique, *magna cum laude*, he would still have found his qualifications tested to the limit.

There was something ridiculous, even indecent, about a celibate giving advice to married couples, even seeking to regulate their cycle of sexual intercourse; or instructing engaged lovers in the permissible limits of a caress. Nero had just said: 'You know so much about everything,' and by 'everything' he had meant, quite frankly, the teasing of female desire until only marriage could slake it. *It was not true.* He did not know so much, and he did not wish to. He was a servant of God, not a marriage broker or a gynaecologist.

He knew a little about the human heart, a lot about the holy communion of the Mass, almost everything about running a parish, and – once again – a little, a tiny part, of the glorious mystery which was Man crucified and made God. Was this not enough, for a working priest?

He recalled, almost with shame, dear little Marija, and her problems, and her dewy desires, and her humble appeal for help. To her, as to Nero, he had wanted to say, in honest despair: 'Don't ask me. I know nothing of love.' He had felt entitled to do so. Just as, long ago, the Blessed Virgin, told the fearful news that she was to bear a child, had said: 'How can this be, seeing that I know not a man?' why could he himself not say, with the same amazement: 'How can you seek my help, seeing that I know not a woman?'

Would there come a day when men themselves, in their turmoil of the flesh, would ask of the Church: 'What is it to do with you?' – when even priests would ask it?

Now he could only dismiss Nero with: 'Love will grow between you. It does not need any tricks. Have faith.'

It was a dusty answer, a cowardly answer. It was no answer at all. When Father Salvatore added: 'Let's see about the cooking-drums and the stove. Then I must go, or I shall be late,' he knew in his melancholy heart that he had just celebrated this, the first and dearest morning of every Christian year, with that most un-Christian of all human acts – passing by on the other side.

3

Though it was never like the great occasions of the past, the Christmas lunch-party at the Palazzo Santo-Nobile was, to begin with, a cheerful and rather moving occasion. It was good to see the splendid house restored to something like its past magnificence, to know that it stood like a rock against war, and an elegant refuge against the dismal drabness of their siege. Though by the end the party had become a disaster, its start was memorable.

Father Salvatore, in his best black cassock and still-handsome boots, arrived late, to find a distinguished and traditional company already assembled. The Governor, General Dobbie, and his aide-de-camp, Captain Ian Ross, led the field, as far as temporal power was concerned; his Lordship the Bishop of Malta, flanked by Monsignor Scholti, stood surety for the spiritual arm; the admiral who commanded the dockyard, and the Air Vice-Marshal who held an umbrella over it, were matched by the Mother Superior of the Baroness's favourite convent, and the best-behaved orphan from the home which the Santo-Nobiles had maintained since its founding in the days of Charles II, when the problem of bastardy attracted fashionable attention.

Lewis Debrincat and his family of three headed a sprinkling of Debrincat relatives, all on their social mettle in this superior gathering; among them was the children's prime choice, Cousin Lawrence, a jovial old rogue who ran a garage for a living, dabbled mysteriously in politics for pleasure, was a ready supplier of the most delicious, jaw-cracking, tooth-pulling nougat (he had a small nougat factory at the back of the garage), and, best of all, took snuff, a fact advertised by recurrent trumpetings which made a normal, conventional sneeze sound like a funereal whisper.

The numbers were made up by some members of Malta's shrunken diplomatic corps; by the governor of Malta gaol, whose inclusion in this assembly was lost in the mists of antiquity; and by Michael Ainslie who, desperately tired after a night's flying and slightly bemused by all the 'hot brass', as he termed anyone above the rank of commander, clung to Marija's side like a home-sick limpet. He was never in danger of being prised away.

By the time that Father Salvatore arrived, they were all gathered round the crib, a family heirloom which had enthralled at least ten generations of Santo-Nobile children. All the figures were of silver, but silver of a marvellous vitality: the bending Madonna, the infant Christ, the withdrawn Joseph, Balthazar with a beaming black face, the tiny animals surveying the intruders with munching respect – all were touchable, breathing creatures, telling their once-a-year story under the glow of minute branched candlesticks which lit the stable scene with a miraculous, living warmth.

After this had been duly admired, the company moved to the near-by Christmas tree, under which were presents for all; and Father Salvatore took the opportunity to greet his mother.

'You are so late, Salvatore,' she told him as he kissed her. 'What have you been doing?'

'Making soup.'

'You will get better soup here!'

'I don't doubt it.' He stood back, still holding her wafer-light hand. 'A happy Christmas, Mother. You're looking wonderful.'

But it was not true. In successive weeks and months he had been forced to notice how worn she had become, and what an effort it was for her to maintain her straight back and proud carriage. She now walked with a stick: 'My odious crutch', she called it, but odious or not, she had come to depend on its ebony strength for the simplest of movements from room to room. He realized that he had been foolish to think, or hope, that she, alone of all people, could remain untouched by war: war was taking its toll – even Christmas had taken its toll – and no degree of pride or courage could disguise the fact.

'I hope you haven't been doing too much, getting ready for the party,' he told her.

'Don't fuss, Salvatore,' she said immediately. 'Of course there was a good deal to do, but I'm not a helpless old woman yet.' She looked round the great salon, her eyes in the pale face full of a fierce satisfaction. 'It does look nice, doesn't it?'

'It looks perfect.'

'Wait till you see the lunch table. All the old Waterford goblets – I don't think we've used them since the jubilee!' What jubilee was this? Queen Victoria's Diamond Jubilee of 1897? George III's, in 1809? Either was quite possible, in a palazzo where the courtyard clock chimed away the centuries as some common time-piece might tick away the minutes. 'Have you spoken to the bishop yet?'

'No. You first, everyone else afterwards.'

'That is *not* the way to get preferment.' But she sounded pleased. Her hand reached out for the polished black stick, propped against the arm of her chair. 'Help me up, Salvatore.' He could not recall ever having heard her say this before. 'I must see that my guests have everything they want... Lunch is in fifteen minutes... That young man of Marija's is really extraordinarily handsome... Please find yourself a glass of sherry, and go and speak to the bishop *now*. I know that he wants to talk to you.'

She moved away, leaning unobtrusively on her stick, halting but still upright. He heard her say, to the lowliest of the Debrincat aunts: 'My dear, you look *charming* – that fur collar really suits you!' and knew that he need have no fears for her spirit, on this morning at least. She was in her element... So Michael Ainslie had already become 'Marija's young man'... And the bishop wanted to speak to him... It sounded like one of those bulletins which spoke of excellent progress on all fronts. They did not have to be believed... He took a glass of sherry from the vast silver salver with which Francis was slowly circling the room, greeted him warmly, and set off in the direction of the Bishop of Malta.

It was inevitable that he should be intercepted by Monsignor Scholti.

They had not met for nearly a month, since Scholti had paid his memorable visit to the catacombs. It had been one of those nights when everything had been at its most earthy. There had been four different birthday parties, presently combining into one ribald, song-singing, dancing, rip-roaring celebration. Nero, who could walk on his hands, walked on his hands the whole length of one of the upper galleries – all very well for a muscular dwarf whose party tricks were much admired, less appropriate to a sacristan in the presence of his superiors.

Monsignor Scholti, who began his visit with portly good-humour, had become perceptibly more withdrawn; his smile grew thinner and thiner, and presently vanished altogether, as bursts of laughter alternated with cursing-matches: as the sirens sounded, and each faraway thud of bombs was cheered – it had fallen somewhere else, it had missed them! as shadowy young figures were seen to be intertwined, in shameless display: as a chicken was chased and cornered within sight of the altar: as rats crossed and recrossed the littered floor: as a chorus of groans greeted the news that one of the toilets was overflowing *again*: as he was offered the first swig at a newly opened bottle of best Cospicua wedding wine: and especially as Father Salvatore, rising to make an announcement about next morning's early Mass (first Sunday in Advent, very important), was cheered as if he were a visiting filmstar.

When, rather sooner than planned, he had escorted Monsignor Scholti to his car, Father Salvatore said: 'I'm sorry. They were a bit out of hand tonight.'

'I agree.'

'But at least they are not afraid.'

'Perhaps they should be...' Scholti glanced back at the grey cliff which was the outpost of the Cottonera Lines. The robust voices of the laity could still be heard. 'Do you really say Mass *there*?'

On this Christmas morning, however, Scholti had regained all the poise and presence which had been menaced by such vulgar surroundings. He greeted Father Salvatore with full-scale aplomb, sure of his place on his own ground, with a bishop to prove it.

'Salvu! At last! I was afraid you were not going to join us.'

'Good morning, Bruno. A happy Christmas.'

'What? Oh yes, of course. And what a happy Christmas it is! What a pleasure to see this house as it ought to be. At least you must agree to that.'

Father Salvatore sipped his sherry, eyeing the other man over the brim of the glass. Scholti's proprietary air was not less offensive than usual, but this was Christmas morning, after all, and it was indeed true that the palazzo, restored to its traditional style, was a heart-warming sight. 'Why should I not agree?'

Scholti smiled, without calling on his eyes for help. 'Well, you must admit that when we last met it was in rather different circumstances. I thought perhaps that your tastes might have changed.'

'I am more at home in the catacombs, if that's what you mean.'

'But how *can* you be? Oh, I admit there is pastoral work to be done there. A great deal, if I may say so, judging by some of the behaviour I saw. But the *prestige* of the Church is also important. The need to set certain standards, and maintain them. The *quality* of priesthood. The dignity. The—'

'The privileges?'

'I do not think one need lay special emphasis on them,' Scholti said tartly. 'Do I detect a note of envy?'

'I can truly say that I am not envious of—' he was about to say, 'of you,' but he changed his mind. It would have been too pointed, and their conversation was arid and stupid enough already. Instead he finished: '– of anyone, in or out of the Church. I am able to do exactly the work I want, and no one can be happier than a man who is allowed to do that.'

'That is rather the point, isn't it?' Scholti still sounded affronted, as if Father Salvatore had touched a tender nerve. The idea that Scholti was blessed with any such vulnerability was a novel one, enlarging the whole area of man's capacity for redemption. But Scholti was continuing, with the same edge in his voice: 'At the moment, you are *allowed* to conduct this rather extraordinary assembly, this *circus*. But it is somewhat irregular, don't you think?'

'War is somewhat irregular.'

'Then one should not make it worse than it is.'

'Oh come, Bruno!' Now it was Father Salvatore's turn to grow irritated, in spite of noble Christmas resolutions. 'The catacomb is not a circus, as you put it. It's simply a large air-raid shelter where I try to take care of people, and celebrate Mass twice a day. Why should that not be allowed? In fact' – he looked at the other man sharply, 'why did you use the word "allowed" at all? Are you trying to—' he could not quite put it into words: the idea that his work might be curtailed was too appalling to contemplate. 'What are you trying to tell me?'

'Two things,' Scholti answered promptly – so promptly that he might well have rehearsed his answer. 'First, that some of the behaviour I was forced to witness the other night was disgraceful, and it is my duty to say so.'

'To whom?'

'Why, to you, of course. Who else?'

'I don't know... What was the second thing you wanted to say?'

'It follows naturally from the first.' Scholti was in full control again, as bland and confident as if he were delivering an end-of-term seminary lecture. Perhaps he was... 'It is this. *If* the catacomb project is getting beyond your control, and *if* it is doing harm rather than good, then you should consider seriously whether the whole scheme should not be modified.'

'But neither of those things is true.'

'Then of course there is no more to be said.'

'And how do you mean, modified?'

'Obviously that point does not arise.'

Father Salvatore decided that he must force this issue, at whatever cost. 'What are you trying to do, Bruno?'

'*I* trying?' Scholti's large brown eyes opened very wide indeed. 'Nothing at all, except to help you to the best of my small ability. The question is, what are *you* trying to do?'

'The best I can. With my small ability.'

'No man can do more... Would you like me to take you to the bishop?'

'No.'

It was Scholti's turn to insist. 'But you must pay your respects!'

'I am going to. When the bishop is a guest in the house where I was born, I do not need any passport.'

He had grown furious, and sick with fear also, as he turned on his heel and made for the other side of the room. Now he did not know what to expect. Was this why the bishop wanted to speak to him? Had Scholti laid his plans thus, before he even knew there was to be a battle? It was a fearful prospect, a fearful truth, that small men of small authority, *who knew how to use it*, could destroy an innocent dream and trample it into the mud. Was it in the house where he was born that he was to die?

He was destined for a swift surprise.

The much-loved old man, Monsignor Dom Maurus Caruana, who had been Bishop of Malta for the last twenty-six years, had a gentle dignity in marked contrast with Bruno Scholti's florid self-importance. It was plainly evident, and came as an immediate balm to Father Salvatore's troubled spirit, from the moment that he made himself known, and bent to kiss the bishop's ring.

In the confused cross-current of voices which now filled the room, his welcome was as clear, concise, and personal as the blessing which preceded it.

'My dear Salvu!' the bishop said. 'How good it is to see you again! I have been watching you ever since you came in.'

'Watching me?' Father Salvatore was confused. Whatever he had been expecting, it was not this.

'Certainly. You look so well. From something that Bruno Scholti said, I thought you had been over-tiring yourself, and needed a rest.'

There were many tempting answers to be made, but Father Salvatore resisted all of them. 'I would like a rest,' he admitted. 'I think we all would. But that doesn't mean that we shall take one.'

'Well said.' The bishop, who was in his seventy-fifth year, and whose face was as craggy and lined as a small-scale model of Malta itself, smiled his approval. 'War is the greatest test of man. Perhaps it is meant to be. Perhaps it is a test we set ourselves, against God's will. But one cannot deny the ordeal, in either case.' He noticed Father Salvatore's puzzled expression, and smiled again. 'Am I being too serious, for such a pleasant occasion as this? I can't help recalling that I became bishop in the middle of another war, in 1915, and that even then there were three more years of weariness before we had peace and rest again. It was about that time that I first met you. Do you remember?'

'Yes, *Eccellenza.*'

'You were still at seminary, but you came back from Rome for a holiday. What year was that?'

'Nineteen-seventeen.' Already Father Salvatore felt marvellously healed by this contact. Was this what was meant by 'a good shepherd'? He could almost feel the abundance of grace and kindliness flowing from one soul to another. 'I was twenty-two.'

'And I was fifty… But only two years old, as a bishop.' The old man was musing, recalling the past with pleasure and good humour. 'I will tell you one thing. I was very nervous of your mother, when I first met her. She was such a great lady, such a devout friend of the Church. And she seemed to know so much more of the world than I did.' He smiled. 'Perhaps I am still a little nervous, just as she is still a great lady. But that young seminarian became a parish priest.'

'And still is.'

'Some regrets, my son?'

'Never!'

The old man nodded. 'It is comforting to be certain... But even certainty has its pitfalls... There is one thing I want to say to you, and Christmas morning is a good time to say it. I gave my permission for your church in the catacombs... From the reports I have had of it – some good reports, some not so good – it has grown in a way I did not expect... Do something for me, Salvu. Search your conscience, and see if it has not enlarged *you* rather than the Church and the faith. You understand?'

'Yes, my Lord.' He might have felt afraid again, but when a bishop of this quality said 'Do something for me', with such infinite kindness, how could a priest take any other course but steel his heart, and agree? 'If I have made mistakes—' he did not know how to finish.

'Then I trust you to discover them.' The old man, whose sharp eyes had been on Salvatore's face, turned away, apparently satisfied. 'I spoke to you like this,' he went on, even as he looked round the room, 'in your own house, on Christmas morning, because I wanted to mark the difference between a talk with a friend and an interview in my palace. You understand that too?'

'Yes, *Eċċellenza*. Thank you.'

'Then the homily is ended.' What extraordinary things he could say. The bishop's eyes, moving from person to person, from group to group, were caught by something which amused him. He nodded: 'Whatever we may feel about the troubles and the weariness of war, there's one young man at least who is having a happy Christmas.'

For a moment Father Salvatore thought that he must be referring to Michael Ainslie, the young man of the party with the likeliest claim on happiness; but when he followed the bishop's glance he saw that the young man was younger still, and more exuberantly joyful than any Fleet Air Arm lieutenant could possibly be in public. It was Pietru, who had fallen wildly in love with one of his Christmas presents, and wanted the whole world to admire and to share it.

He was going all round the room, beaming and chattering, to demonstrate from every angle what had come to him under the Christmas tree. This was a very large model, some three feet in wingspan, of a Hurricane fighter plane, complete to the last detail, with propellers which turned, wing-elevators which moved up and down, wheels which spun, and guns with miniature ammunition-belts feeding into their mechanism. It was a triumph of the model-maker's art, gleaming with polished metal and freshly painted roundels. No other Christmas present in the world, not even a motor-cycle, could stand a chance against it.

Other eyes besides the bishop's were following Pietru's progress as he swooped from guest to guest, explaining everything in highly-charged detail.

'You are a darling,' Marija said to Michael. 'I don't think Pietru will ever recover. I'm sure he'll sleep with it tonight.'

'He's still young.'

'That will do... But how did you ever find such a thing?'

'It took two of our armourers the best part of a month to produce that little item. The war came to a total stop – didn't you notice?'

'You mean it was specially made?'

'Rivet by rivet. I'm trying very hard with this...' He was not even glancing in her direction, but he said: 'You look different today.'

'How different?'

'More beautiful. *Most* beautiful. But more alive. Are you more alive?'

'Now... You look rather tired.'

'I was dicing all night.' 'Dicing' meant dicing with death, the silly RAF slang which made a joke of the truth. 'But I told you that on the phone... Thank you again for my present.'

'If you can knit a long scarf, I can knit a long scarf.'

'Just what I wanted. Whoever said that Malta was warm in winter was a bloody liar.'

'Michael! Really!'

'Sorry. This sherry's terribly strong... Tell me,' he glanced swiftly at her, and then away again, with a jerk of his head, 'who's the smoothie over there?'

'The what?'

'The priest, or whatever he is, with the big pussy-cat style.'

'That's Monsignor Scholti!'

'Oh, him. You mentioned him before. Grandma's pet.'

'He's nothing of the sort! Well, I mean, you shouldn't say that about a monsignor.'

'Money for old rope... Do you remember when you asked me what I wanted for Christmas?'

'Yes, I certainly do. You said, "Well, my *second* choice is," and then you just laughed. Why do you ask?'

'I just thought I'd keep the subject alive. But it's a very beautiful scarf. For some reason it seemed to amuse your grandmother very much. She said: "I did not know Marija was so domesticated. Wonders will never cease."'

'How did you get on with her?'

'Like a house on fire. She's a real old charmer. But her language!'

'Language?'

'My dear, *who* has she been mixing with? She said something about the Japanese and the Russians, and then she said: "Would you say that the whole world was Harpic?" What sort of talk is that?'

'Very up to date.'

'Well, I hope she doesn't try it on old man Dobbie. He'll rupture his halo. Never mind, she's an absolute sweetie, and I love her already. That only leaves your mother... At the end she gave me a real old-fashioned gleam, and said: "Don't let me keep you from my granddaughter." What's been going on?'

'Nothing. I just mentioned you.'

'Well, I wish you'd mention me to a few admirals. I need the money. In fact,' and now at last he turned back again, and looked directly at her, 'I wish you'd mention me to you.'

'Michael Ainslie.'

'*That's* better!'

With the expert connivance of the young they submerged, as far as they could, into a private world of delight, while all round them, as the trays of drinks circulated, the sound of conversation rose and fell in a steady rhythm. The hour of the *apéritif* seemed unusually long, but at the moment it did not matter: the occasion was happy, the surroundings magnificent, and the delay acceptable.

The Air Vice-Marshal, with flailing arms, was describing how his fighters had completely broken up the first raid of Christmas Day, while the admiral, in whose dockyard the bombs had actually fallen, listened with all the courteous scepticism of a solid sailor for a romantic airman. General Sir William Dobbie wrestled in vain with Monsignor Scholti on the question of divine revelation : if it had not been granted to the Plymouth Brethren, then it must equally be denied to the Roman Catholic Church. Their collision course, terminating at a marker-buoy labelled 'Papal Infallibility', was for the moment delicately adjusted.

Captain Ian Ross was flirting manfully with the best-behaved orphan, probably the most bashful human being he had ever encountered. The governor of Malta gaol was explaining the remedial aspects of total withdrawal from the outside world – to the Mother Superior of the convent. An occasional brazen roar from Cousin Lawrence indicated that he was taking a little snuff while waiting.

Lewis Debrincat had already become a centre of embarrassment and irritation to almost everyone in the room.

He now looked so terrible that it was difficult to avoid telling him so. Somehow he had achieved a feat rare in Malta during wartime, which was to put on weight, grossly and continuously. None of his clothes fitted, none of his buttons fastened easily; above a slack, shambling body his face, jowly and ill-shaven, was balanced like a malevolent egg. Only his eyes seemed alive; they darted to and fro through little creased pig-slits of flesh, in search of something wrong, something insulting, something to fight. He had become grotesque, and he knew it, and he challenged the world to dare to say so.

He had tripped once on entering the room, and again when he tried to greet the bishop in the fashion to which a bishop, within the circle of the faithful, was entitled. It was clear that the glass of sherry offered him was not the first drink of the day, nor the fifth. Then he had settled down, installed like a sack of potatoes in a large gilded armchair : the only person in the room to be sitting down, and the only person whom everyone, after a brief conversation, now avoided as if he were a source of the plague.

'Gigi Debrincat is in a bad mood,' was the most generous

comment among a wide variety, accompanied by the shrugs
and head-shakings which indicated that no one would very
much care if Gigi Debrincat sank without trace in the depths
of the courtyard well. It seemed to be established that he
could not bear the sight of anyone in uniform. He was not
interested in any of his relatives: he had made good, they had
not. He had been curtly formal with the Governor, and de-
risive with Father Salvatore – 'Your holier-than-thou brother,'
he commented to his wife, and added: 'That takes a bit of
doing, I can tell you,' for all to hear.

The governor of Malta gaol had been sent briskly about his
business. 'What are you doing here? Looking for customers?'
had been Lewis Debrincat's offensive greeting. Any well-
conducted popular poll would have him nominated at Customer No. One.

It was the ever-loyal Giovanna who bore the brunt of all this
boorish impudence. She never left his side for a moment, though
there was a large number of people whom she wanted to talk
to, and to greet on Christmas morning. But she was trapped
by this monster who was still her husband, and so they remained isolated, like Beauty and the Beast, with only the beast
enthroned. Continually on the defensive, she softened such
casual insults as she could with a smile and a turned phrase.
It was the public role of devoted wife, and the private one of
nurse-companion to a sick nuisance.

Time passed. The drink trays went round again. The noise-
level in the room still maintained a satisfactory pitch, but it
faltered now and then as people glanced at their watches, or
looked towards the double doors which *must* open before long
to summon them to lunch, or decided they had had enough
salted peanuts, and savoury croutons dipped in *fondu*, and dates
stuffed with cream cheese, and biscuits topped with caviar
and chopped white of egg, or ran out of conversation and did
not know how, with politeness, to change places and partners
and topics.

Pietru Pawl, ending his personal tour of the rom, bearing
the gleaming model Hurricane like a precious Olympic torch,
hesitated as he suddenly came face to face with his father.
But it was impossible to alter course, and he advanced bravely.

'Isn't it *super*?' he exclaimed, and held the model closer,
under Lewis Debrincat's inclined head.

Lewis, who had been watching his son when he might have been thought to be dozing, gave an irritated start.

'Don't poke that thing at me!' he snarled. 'If you can't behave yourself properly, you won't come to these parties in future.'

'I'm sorry, Father,' Pietru said, shocked and stricken, 'I thought you'd like to see.'

'He didn't mean to startle you, Gigi,' Giovanna intervened.

'He didn't *startle* me,' Lewis snapped back. 'He nearly stabbed me with the damn thing! What is it, anyway?'

'It's a Hurricane,' said Pietru, regaining confidence. 'Specially made. Look – everything works. Even the canopy slides backwards and forwards.'

'Very pretty.' But he somehow contrived to make it sound stupid and worthless. 'Where did you get this – whatever it is?'

'Michael gave it me for Christmas.'

'Who?'

'Michael Ainslie. You know, the Fleet Air Arm pilot that Marija met.'

'I *don't* know,' Lewis Debrincat said brusquely.

Giovanna bent over him. 'I did mention him, dear. Marija met him at the Sciclunas.' This was evasive, in terms of chronology, but still technically true. 'He's here this morning.'

'You mean, your mother knows him as well?'

'Of course.'

'Well, *I* don't know him. I don't know a lot of things, it seems.' He glared at Pietru, under creased eyebrows. 'Why should he give you this – this super present?'

'He's a friend,' Pietru answered, subdued again. It did not sound too convincing, in grown-up terms, and he had his own astonishment and delight to contend with.

'He must be.'

'Wasn't it kind of him?' Giovanna said.

'Maybe it was just clever.' His eyes began to dart about the room. 'Which one is he?'

'Over there.' Giovanna pointed discreetly. 'The tall boy by the big mirror.'

'Oh, him. Looks like a dancing teacher.'

'He's not!' Pietru said rebelliously. 'He's a Hurricane pilot!'

'When I want your opinion,' his father told him, with menacing clarity, 'I'll ask for it.'

'Wouldn't you like to meet Michael?' Giovanna asked.

'No. I've seen more than enough tailors' dummies in uniform for today.' With a swift change of mood, more alarming than any dead-level of ill-humour, he addressed Pietru again : 'What's that you're chewing?'

'Nougat, Father. Cousin Lawrence gave me a box.'

'Nougat, *and* a Hurricane plane, *and* money from your grandmother? Quite a Christmas.'

'But that was a super chemistry set you gave me. Thank you awfully.'

'If I'd known about the competition, perhaps I wouldn't have bothered... And if you're going to blow anyone up, start with – well, never mind... I wish Lawrence would give *me* a box of nougat. *I'm hungry!*'

He was not the only one to feel so, but the only one to say so out loud, with such savagery. Heads were turned in his direction; there was even laughter, in a swift decay of good manners. They were all hungry... The Baroness herself heard it, and signalled vexedly to Francis the footman. They conferred for a moment, and then Francis turned and left the room. The trays of drinks circulated yet again, and a tired drone of conversation picked up once more.

Lunch was not, as the Baroness had promised Marija, in fifteen minutes. It was not in twenty-five, nor thirty-five; it hovered mysteriously out of reach, in spite of messages to Gregory, urgent conferences between the Baroness and Francis, and pangs of public hunger so acute that they could almost be felt.

Finally, at ten minutes to two – fifty minutes late – when even Governor Dobbie was consulting Ian Ross about his next appointment, an orphanage tea, and Father Salvatore was considering a personal foray to the kitchens to find out what was going on, the double doors at the end of the salon were flung open, and Gregory the major-domo appeared.

All eyes turned on him; to many of those present, he was a life-long friend, and for everybody else a respected institution. Though neatly and handsomely dressed, from buckled shoes to high winged collar, he looked undeniably old and mad; his eyes glittered in a face hectically flushed, and when he took two stumbling steps into the room he peered about him as if he had no notion where he was.

Finally he caught sight of the Baroness, and bowed low. Then he said, in a weird cracked voice :

'Dinner is served, your Royal Highness.'

Emilia Santo-Nobile was not a royal highness, and this was lunch, not dinner; the twin *gaffes* had a sad effect of dissolution on the company. A few laughed nervously; most pretended not to have heard, even not to be able to see; then total silence fell. In any other household, the unearthly pause might have stretched to infinity. But the Baroness had been born for such moments as these. If her knuckles turned white as they clenched over her stick, there were few to see and none to comment. All she said was :

'Thank you, Gregory...' Then she turned to the Governor. 'Your Excellency ... shall we go in ?'

On Sir William Dobbie's arm she led the way forward, as erect and proud as if she were in truth royal, and took her seat at a table of such splendid elegance that it could well have restored all things to their accustomed state.

Yet there were worse crises to come than an unreasonable delay and a painful mistake by Gregory. Though planned with great care over several weeks it was, by the standards of the palazzo, a simple lunch of six courses : avocado pear, *gazpacho* soup, a baked fish, the traditional turkey, a *relève* of iced *sorbet*, and a vintage Christmas pudding so pregnant with sixpences and other silver trinkets that no one receiving a slice could possibly miss a prize.

When the Baroness took her place at the head of the table, and the bishop on her left hand had pronounced grace, and Sir William Dobbie had added a sonorous 'Amen!' she might well have expected that the next hour, at least, would go smoothly.

But terrible things were to happen – terrible by Santo-Nobile custom – which were to reduce the lunch party to a shambles and herself to trembling rage and bitter disappointment. Gregory, who should have continuously waved his wand over the service, made no further appearance. Francis, though immensely efficient in a military fashion, had not the style of a butler; and he was supported by strange-visaged footmen whose ill-fitting liveries only advertised the fact that they did not belong to the household, and by maids whose energy and cheerfulness was only a minor substitute for skill.

Father Salvatore, whose devotion to opera had given him certain standards of comparison, began to liken it to a very bad amateur production of the banquet scene in *La Traviata*. By the time it had degenerated into *opera buffa*, with undertones of *Macbeth*, he was beyond all feeling save shame and pity for the affront to his mother.

A loud crash had signalled the entrance of the Hollandaise sauce which was to be served with the avocado, itself a rarity with a complicated history of local shipwreck. As all eyes turned in the direction of the sound, the whispered '*Gesu Marija!*' of the girl responsible diverted attention back again to the bishop, in whose department this mishap had suddenly been placed. The moment passed, since His Lordship was magnificent in diplomatic deafness, and there were three other sauceboats borne by three other girls, equally sprightly, more adroit; and the dropped dish was only Sèvres. But the sauce itself, succumbing to long delay, had curdled fatally. It set the pattern and the quality of all that was to follow.

There was now a very long pause. Some wine *en carafe* was brought in, but at a signal from the Baroness was taken out again : it was red, which could not be acceptable either with the avocado now being politely abandoned by the guests, nor the soup, nor the fish which was to follow. The soup proved intolerably sour, though blandished by an occasional homely thumb as it was served; and when the fish-course finally arrived, after lengthy delays, there was not enough to go round, and those at the bottom end of the table were left with empty plates.

The giant turkey which replaced it, after yet another long interval, was, though beautifully carved, so overcooked and dried up that the white meat was scarcely distinguishable from the dark.

There was no longer any room for pretence that the lunch party was even a normal occasion, far less a superior one; and for the Baroness, flanked by the Governor and the bishop, it was impossible to maintain the appearance of composure. She was reduced by impotent rage nearly to tears. After all the planning and preparation... Her two table companions both talked, compassionately, to the people on their other side. For the first time within memory, Christmas lunch at the Palazzo

Santo-Nobile had ceased to be under the control of their hostess.

The iced sherbert, when it finally arrived, was a warm and watery disaster. The champagne which should have accompanied it was served just as everyone had finished. They then waited for the Christmas pudding. They continued to wait, almost in silence – social conventions had been eroded by time and impatience – for an unconscionable quarter-hour, while vague sounds of commotion came from the kitchens. Experienced housewives deduced either that the pudding would not leave its vast bowl in one piece, or that it was proving impossible to set alight.

At last the double doors swung open again, and Francis appeared, bearing the flaming offering on a fluted silver salver. Its entrance happened to coincide with yet another almighty blast from Cousin Lawrence. The force of this *seemed* to blow out both the brandy flames and all the candles surrounding the dish, though it must have been due to the slight draught from the open doorway; and this instant fire-extinguisher was too much for the company. As Francis, coughing and spluttering through wreaths of candle-smoke, struggled to maintain both his composure and the salver, which was unbearably hot, the room dissolved into helpless laughter. It was not the laughter of friends.

The excellence of the pudding itself, of which there was plenty for all, and the *richesse* of silver trinkets accompanying it, went some way towards restoring calm; and by the time the port had gone round the table – *one* glass for the ladies, after which they would withdraw – the Baroness had reasonable hope that lunch would end without further embarrassment. There would have to be a lengthy *post mortem*, but that was a private matter.

But she was doomed, like the lunch party, to yet another lamentable breakdown of decorum. This time it was her son-in-law who transgressed all custom with a disgraceful scene, and set the seal of disaster on a happy Christmas.

Lewis Debrincat had been drinking his way through lunch, with a determination which resisted all attempts to interest him in food. 'I'm doing your mother a favour,' he said loudly to Giovanna at one moment, as he waved away the meagre remains of the fish-course, and the pointed insult was not lost on those around him. Instead, he drank whatever was placed before him, and on occasion even snapped his fingers for more wine. Sinking lower and lower in his chair, he was, by the time the port was going round, almost incapably drunk, and vile-tempered as well.

He drank thirstily of the port, which was several years older than himself, as soon as he filled his glass; and then – a monstrous breach of etiquette – reached across for the decanter as it passed down the other side of the table, and poured himself a second glass. No one remarked on this: it was only Gigi Debrincat doing as he liked. Then he sat back, bored with himself, bored with his company, a likely prey to the crippling fate of the outcast – to be ignored. He sought a target, and found it in Cousin Lawrence sitting opposite.

He did not like Cousin Lawrence, because everyone else seemed to do so. He was ashamed of Cousin Lawrence, and contemptuous, and envious. Surveying the other man under lowering brows, he picked on the first soft spot he could observe.

'Do you always take snuff with port?'

Cousin Lawrence a jolly bald sausage of a man who preferred friends to enemies, and an easy life above everything else, absorbed the insulting tone. With his hand halfway to his nostril, he answered cheerfully:

'I take snuff with everything. You know that.'

'No accounting for tastes... All I can say is, I wouldn't like to be married to you.'

'Ah, but you're not, are you?'

'No. I've got troubles enough as it is.' The silence spreading round them began to engulf the rest of the table. It was obvious that Lewis Debrincat's offensive crudity must find an outlet, and that no soft answers would deter him. 'How's that garage of yours getting on?'

'Busy, busy.'

'Doing all right for petrol?'

'Well, you know how difficult it is.' Cousin Lawrence still had not taken his snuff, and was hoping to do so unmolested.

'I don't know anything of the sort,' Lewis said contemptuously. 'All I know is, you can get anything you like these days, if you know the right people.' He waited, but there was no

answer from the good-tempered, wary man opposite. He pressed
further: 'You know the right people, don't you?'

'Not in the way you mean.'

'Oh, come on! All those crooked politicians with their fingers
stuck in the till! I don't mean *these* right people' – he gestured
round the table, as if he were indicating rubbish ready for disposal. 'They're too damned *moral* for the likes of you and me...
But rationing's a lot of nonsense. It's the biggest joke of the
whole stupid war! ... You want some petrol coupons?'

'No, thank you.'

Cousin Lawrence's tone continued to be good-humoured; he
was still trying for a quiet disengagement. Having answered,
he lifted the pinch of snuff balanced on his index finger towards
his nose. The dismissive gesture seemed to infuriate Lewis
Debrincat, and he finally lost all patience and control. In the
total silence of the whole table, he shouted coarsely:

'Why don't you stick some of that stuff up your bottom?
Then we'd really hear something!'

The worst thing was that, in that total silence, somebody
laughed. Yet within a few seconds, this was no longer the worst
thing. Lewis Debrincat acknowledged the compliment of laughter with a fat grin, which suddenly changed to a painful grimace.
Under all their eyes, his face turned pale and sweaty, and he
levered himself up and made a stumbling rush for the door.
The crashing slam of this could not mask the gross sound of
retching, nor the splash of vomit on the tiled floor outside.

An urgent whisperer at Father Salvatore's side broke into the
most painful reverie of his life. To see his mother so shocked,
his sister in tears, the children scarlet with shame and embarrassment... He turned quickly. It was Francis.

'Dun Salv! Dun Salv! Can you come, please!'

'What's the matter, Francis?' He was sure that it was Lewis,
who must need help, who might have collapsed before he
reached the lavatory. It might even be the necessity of organizing a cleaning operation, before the guests could pass through
the defiled doorway... But he was wrong.

'It's Mr Gregory, Dun Salv. Please come and see him. But
quickly!'

Father Salvatore rose instantly. 'Is he ill? Have you called
a doctor?'

'The doctor has been here for an hour.' Astonishingly, movingly, the eyes of Francis, the competent soldier, the only true stalwart in the house, were bright with tears. 'It is for you now.'

4

Safely at peace, far away from the awful adult world, Marija Debrincat and Michael Ainslie lay in a fold of the hills above the cliffs of Dingli, on the south-west coast of the island. Between them they had chosen, as if to solace all the wounds of the day, the most superb view of the whole of Malta.

Behind them towered the battlements of the Verdala Palace, vast, square, moated by the quarries which had supplied its own cream-coloured stone, and fringed by the green woods of the Boschetto, the only standing forest between Africa and Sicily.

Beyond *that* were the misty outlines of Mdina; and at their feet the sheer 800-feet drop of the cliffs, and a breathtaking view of the island's other battlement, its rampant western coastline, and the tiny islet of Filfla where the birds took refuge, and another green fringe – of wreck-buoys – marking the sunken hulks of ships, the faraway refuse of war.

In the evening sun, it had all the magic of longed-for tranquility.

They were there because they had to be there. Fugitives from the terrible Christmas gathering, they had found themselves standing together on the steps of the palazzo. Michael, looking at her stricken face, had taken charge.

'Come for a drive,' he said. 'I've got Ian's car for the day,' and Marija, distraught, had answered: 'Yes. Anything.'

But the desperate wish to escape, to wipe their feet clean of an ignoble swill, had melted quickly into tender contentment. Only on the bumpy drive westwards, had they talked of it.

'Oh, that awful, *awful* lunch!' Marija kept repeating, huddling down inside her coat. 'I'm so sorry. I'm so *ashamed*.'

'It wasn't so bad...' Michael, looking straight to his front, concentrated on the rutted road leading towards Zebbug. 'We don't get turkey and plum-pudding at the NAAFI every day...

Do you know what avocado pear is called in the Navy? Midshipman's butter.'

She was forced to laugh. 'Now why should that be?'

'None of the smart boys know. I suppose when it goes bad you can spread it on bread, and that's how the poor live.'

'Ours looked so beautiful when I saw them in the kitchen... I was so sorry for Grandmother...' She settled her neck deep into her collar again; Ian's car was a draughty relic of the 'Open Tourer' days, and it's cracked side-curtains flapped like mangy feathers. Then she said, bravely: 'I didn't really mean the food, anyway.'

'I know. But let's forget it.'

'You can't forget things like that. How can I forget my father? He was disgusting!'

'You should have met mine.'

There was such strange bitterness in Michael's voice that she turned to look at him. He was coatless ('I'm not a he-man – I've got a Norwegian string-vest under all this lot') and his head was bare; above the cocoon of his scarf – her scarf – his face was set in a most determined scowl. Wondering at his swift change of mood, she prompted him:

'How do you mean?'

'We all have fathers, Marija... Mine was a drunk as well.' It was the truth game, and he was not going to spare either of them. 'That's my mother's story, anyway, but I can remember some of the evidence, even as a little boy... He walked out years ago, with a selection of jewellery. I haven't seen him since. My mother brought me up on the proceeds of a dress shop... That takes some doing in Cornwall, I can tell you... We haven't seen him for years,' he began again. 'But I know where he is.'

'Where?'

'In prison. In the Isle of Man.' He turned for an instant to look at her. 'You know about the Isle of Man?'

'No.'

' "*Kelly from the Isle of Man*," ' he sang, in a sudden harsh falsetto. 'That's an old music-hall song. Now it's Ainslie from the Isle of Man – but not for a few years. He's a political prisoner, interned there since 1939. We have a thing called 18 B. Ever heard of that?'

'No.' Absurdly she added: 'I'm sorry, Michael.'

His hand dropped on hers. 'Don't be. Innocence is all...
Regulation 18 B is something they brought in at the beginning
of the war. If you were a fascist, or likely to be a traitor, they
nabbed you on that, and put you away without trial. My
father was quite high up in the British Union of Fascists.'

'But that's awful!'

'Oh, I don't suppose he knew anything about it, really. It
was probably a jolly good boozing club when it started... And
he's in very superior company. There's Sir Oswald Mosley, down
in Brixton Prison... They've even got an admiral locked up
in Brixton. His son's just been killed in action. Now there's a
stinking world for you...' But he laughed all the same. 'When
I applied for a commission, and told them about it, the man
said : "You'll just have to be twice as bright, that's all" ... Good
old England. They knew all about it, anyway...' Then he expelled his breath in a single sound of dismissal. 'Well, anyway,
that's *my* father, safe behind bars for the duration. So we might
as well shut the family album, and just worry about ourselves.'

'Thank you for telling me.' She knew why, and loved him all
the more for it.

'We are *us*,' he said, with complete certainty. 'They are
them... Never forget that.' He took a grip of the shuddering
wheel, and set the car at the next slope. 'But now we'll forget
everything else. I must say,' he said, looking round at the unfolding view of the plains before Verdala, 'you have a nice little
place here.'

They *had* forgotten everything else, and now they were at
peace again – complete and loving peace. But even here, in pastoral paradise, doubts and mysteries returned to confuse them
both.

There was some kissing at first : not as much as she had expected, or hoped, or was prepared for. On such a day, after such
an introduction, she was even ready to practise some of her
new arts, if that was what he wanted. But strangely, it was
not what he wanted.

After a first hungry embrace when they got out of the car,
and another when they chose their sheltered spot, safe from
all eyes, he had drawn back, and turned his attention to the
view, to some minesweepers below them probing among the
wreck-buoys, to the coming sunset – to everything but herself. When would she ever understand men? ... Of course she

was contented, if he was. But why, why, why, on this day of all days? Was he angry? Was he bored? Was he sorry he had come all this way? Was he having second thoughts about that shameful lunch party?

It seemed that he was only tired.

'I'm sorry, *hanini*,' he said presently. He was lying back, a little apart from her, sucking a dry blade of grass and staring up at the pale sky. 'I'm not much good today... I was doing some horrid things last night – and you don't have to be jealous... Maybe I drank too much at lunch.' It was not a question to be pursued. 'Anyway, I seem to have used up all the juice.'

'It doesn't matter.'

'It matters if you're sad. Are you sad?' Suddenly he came to the alert, and sat up. A drone of aircraft passed overhead, and disappeared to the south-eastwards. 'It's all right,' he assured her. 'They're ours.' When, even as they watched, some lazy puffs of smoke and dust erupted in the direction of Valletta, followed by the thud of bombs borne on the wind, he only said: 'Sorry again. I meant, *theirs*. Same thing.'

His head fell back, and this time it lay securely in her lap. He snuggled down, apparently satisfied.

'How can it be the same thing?' Though she was blissfully happy to have him so close and seemingly so relaxed, the question still could not be denied.

'Oh, the war...' She had to bend over him to hear what he said: he was muttering indistinctly, almost talking in his sleep. 'I must have killed some people last night. Now it's their turn. Fair's fair... It's just arithmetic, with a bit of blood on it... I can tell you one thing, though' – and his voice sounded far away, and near at the same time – 'too many sailors are being killed. Unless we're very careful, we might lose this contest.'

Then he fell asleep.

In the annals of naval slaughter, the last half of that year was indeed proving memorable; and nowhere more cruelly than in the middle sea round Malta – Malta the fatal magnet of disaster, whose support was now more costly in blood and treasure than the building of the Pyramids. It had become a death-trap for ships and men; and many of the latest victims were the old faithfuls of this harassed supply-line.

Returning from a ferrying job to Malta, the aircraft-carrier *Ark Royal*, so long a prime target of this battlefield, had been torpedoed and sunk within a few miles of Gibraltar. Shortly afterwards, the old battleship *Barham* was also sunk: cost, three torpedoes, elapsed time, three minutes, and the *other* cost, 862 men drowned out of a ship's company of 1312. Then two other valuable battleships, *Queen Elizabeth* and *Valiant*, were limpet-mined in Alexandria Harbour, and put out of action for months. Then the cruiser *Galatea* was torpedoed and sunk in the same area.

Lastly, the fleet known as 'Force K' was virtually wiped out at one stroke; it ran into some newly laid mines off Tripoli shortly after it left Malta, and the bill for that was two cruisers, *Penelope* and *Aurora* (sisters of *Galatea*), damaged near to sinking, the destroyer *Kandahar* blown in half, and the cruiser *Neptune* left for dead in the centre of the minefield, with *one* survivor (four days on a raft) remaining out of its entire crew.

Thus the whole top *échelon* of the Eastern Fleet had been eliminated, within the space of two months, at the lowest ebb of fortune in the Mediterranean war. But this cumulative disaster was no more than a segment of a crudely dissolving picture. In the Atlantic and other oceans, merchant ships were being sunk like toys in a bubble-bath: three a day, six a day, *nine* a day, for a total, in the worst month of all, December, of 285.

Far far away in the China Seas, the two battleships *Prince of Wales* and *Repulse* were both bombed to oblivion in one short action, a Japanese Christmas present which toppled down upon Allied hopes like a thousand tons of Maltese stone.

For those who had to tot up this grisly global arithmetic, it was a debit sum beyond belief; and for Malta itself, with prospects of survival modestly improved, the most desperate setback of all time.

It was early evening dusk when Michael fell asleep, and the moment of sunset when he woke again. During all that brief half-hour, Marija, cradling his head in her lap, gazed down at him, and thought, and loved, and finally wept.

She had started, when she knew he was asleep, by examining his face inch by inch. He was so beautiful, but so desperately tired, like all the airmen, all the sailors. It was the Michael she knew, but Michael with his guard let down: it had become the face of an exhausted child, too thin for happiness, lined where it should not yet be lined, fragile when he was really so strong. If this was what war did to men, even young and loving men, then war was wicked beyond anything else in the world.

Most wicked of all, war might mean that she would lose him, before – before anything. He had said, a little time ago: 'Too many sailors are being killed,' and the unspoken thought behind all such foreboding was that one of these doomed sailors would be himself. There were so many ways in which it could happen: all the sad stories she had heard, some that he had told her himself, rose up like haunting ghosts.

Planes could be shot down: ruined aircraft struggling home could crash and take fire on landing: planes could collide in mid-air: planes could lose their way, and fly on into the blue until the blue turned to grey, and then to black. Pilots could be hit and killed: pilots could be wounded and bleed to death: pilots could land in the sea, and live in the sea until their lease ran out: pilots could faint, or die of exhaustion, or even go mad.

All the sad and aching hazards of war were pressing in on them, all the time.

She wanted to touch his face, but dared not; he needed sleep more than any caress known to man or woman. She thought of his story of those lost Hurricanes from the *Argus* which had 'run out of air', and dropped one by one into the sea like crippled birds.

It was then that she began to cry, and a tear fell on his face, and he woke. He woke swiftly, as he must often do in these urgent, troubled times. He sat up, and looked about him, and then at her, and then at the fiery red globe of the sun, dropping below the west horizon as if commanded to dowse the daylight at one stroke.

His face had changed instantly as he woke, gaining strength marvellously. He was not an exhausted child at all; he was a rarely handsome young pilot who had been taking a nap.

'Isn't that beautiful?' he said, nodding towards the last half of the vanishing sun. 'I'm thirty-four shillings richer than I was yesterday... And aren't you beautiful, too? Will you marry me?'

Her little heart turned over, stopped, and started again.

'What?'

'You heard...' He leant over and kissed her tenderly. 'Marija, don't look so surprised. It's not very flattering... Yes, of course I was going to try to make love to you, but this seems a better idea. It *is* a better idea, isn't it? Will you?'

Regaining control, she said solemnly: '*Iva*.'

'Well, thank you very much...' He searched her face, and saw that it had now changed to a mischievous, teasing entice-ment. 'Marija! Was that yes or no?'

' "No" is "*le*". I've told you.'

'Well, thank God for that! And please don't do that again!'

'Why should I have to?'

They embraced joyously, tenderly, hungrily. Soon they were talking of a thousand future plans, and then they returned to kissing again. It grew darker as the sky surrendered all claim to the day. When he said: 'It's getting cold,' she only answered: 'Come closer.' In the precious twilight she practised, shyly, the beginnings of what her grandmother had told her.

They lay together in the bliss of mutual rapture: her shapely body had never been so frank in its response, nor moved so cunningly. He seemed to know the rules – her rules – and to accept them. When at one moment she whispered: 'Use me,' he understood that too, and did so without trespass.

He was astonished, and then he ceased to be, and forgot every-thing in a wild climax of ecstasy. Afterwards his overwhelming gratitude had room for guilt.

'Darling, what about you? It seems so selfish.'

'It won't be.'

'What's happened to us?'

'Nearly everything, I hope.'

5

Trudging wearily towards the Cottonera Lines as night fell, Father Salvatore had time to think, and time to mourn as well. He could even make a private list of his dolours, which were three: old Gregory, the dreadful palazzo lunch-party, and the desolate Christmas Day itself. Though these, he thought, with a rare spark of rebellion which came near to blasphemy, could not match the Seven Sorrows of Our Lady, they were still enough burden for a man and a priest.

Gregory had died that afternoon, in the dull oblivion which was the true mercy of God, and he had closed the old man's eyes with a painful feeling that his own span of life would never be quite the same again. He had lost an old friend – indeed, his oldest friend – and to see the wasted body at peace could only bring a flood of memories.

His recollections, even during the last anointment, were of Gregory the small boy's steed: Gregory the benevolent money-lender when times were hard: Gregory the stern adviser on deportment, Gregory the mainstay of a magnificent household: and especially of that Gregory who had been the first to kiss his hand, with undreamt-of humility, when Father Salvatore had returned to the Palazzo Santo-Nobile as an ordained priest.

Had it been enough to think, on this final day: 'Well done, thou good and faithful servant,' as he rose from his knees by the death-bed? In the Parable of the Talents, that mystifying story of successful stewardship, it had served as a word of praise for a man who had doubled a sum of money entrusted to him. But old Gregory had multiplied more than money; he had transformed service into friendship and trust.

The life-long enterprise, immeasurably more worthwhile, multiplied also the sadness of bereavement.

It would fall hardest on his mother (Gregory had no other family save the one he served): on his mother the Baroness, whose day had been wretched enough already. Father Salvatore could not think, without fearful embarrassment, of the course of the lunch-party, which had become a sick joke, and would doubtless grow into a legend. To have the last wound inflicted by Lewis Debrincat, in such odious circumstances, was all that was needed for a shameful family defeat.

But where did such things come on the true scale of misery? The wounds, which seemed mortal, were only the faint shadow of a thousand other wounds, more terrible than a thousand lunch-parties gone wrong. A drunken guest? A dried-up turkey? Some avocado spoiled? A social fiasco, even at the highest level? This was not Malta's war, nor even the smallest part of its real ordeal.

On dusty tired feet he was now passing something which *was* part of Malta's war, a wound more fresh and bloody than Lewis Debrincat's puerile thrust. On the edge of the Marsa Harbour a bomb had fallen – was anyone still counting the bombs of this cascading war? – and had hit a winter boat-house full to the roof of *luzzus*, fishing-gear, *dghajsas*, ropes and cordage, oil drums, oars, outboard-motors, barrels of caulking pitch, marker-buoys : all the necessaries of fishermen and ferrymen, stored for the season of waiting.

The inflammable mass was burning briskly, surrounded by a smoky ring of sad-faced men whose livelihood had been lost, and women who would have to bear the brunt of this disaster. But more had been lost than the chance of gaining a bare living next year. Another small circle of people, with bowed heads, stood round the dead laid out on the ground. There were five of them, neatly ranged on the quay-side, waiting for their last transport. Malta had grown very orderly in such disposal.

Since there was a young priest kneeling among them, and all else was still, Father Salvatore knew that he could not be of service. There must be a reasonable division of labour, even among the ushers of the dead. He passed on, with a prayer, and breasted the next slope of the road.

Then he heard footsteps behind him, and turned. A man emerged from the fiery, smoke-fouled shadows, a small fat man who panted, 'Dun Salv! Wait for me!' while he was still un-recognized. But the voice was enough, and the figure, when close to, confirmed it. It was Koli Apap, the Sliema ferry captain, the jolliest inhabitant of all the waterfront.

But Koli Apap was not jolly tonight. He was mumbling, and near to tears. Was this the end of another world?

It was. 'I thought it was you when you passed, Dun Salv,' the fat little man said. 'I've had enough of it down there... Bless me, for God's sake!'

'Tkun imbierek.' He put out his hand to steady the swaying body in front of him. 'What's the matter, Koli? What has happened?'

'The worst thing of all my life.' Koli drew a deep shuddering breath. 'My boat, the Ferdinando – it's gone! And the lad who helps on deck – there's nothing left of him but a lot of—' he gulped, and swayed again. 'My God, on Christmas night!'

'Walk with me.' It was better to put some distance between the man and his shock. 'And tell me how it happened.'

'One bomb. Not even a big one, they say. But big enough for me. My boat was in the middle of the boat-house. They told me it was safer there than out on the Sliema quay. Safer! It's burning like a lot of old rubbish!'

Father Salvatore put his hand across Koli Apap's shoulder.

'I'm so sorry... And that boy – what was his name?'

'Ganni. Fifteen years old. He was always hanging about the boat-house, even in winter. He loved the boat! He spent all the day polishing and cleaning... What do I tell his mother?'

Father Salvatore could feel a sob shake the thick shoulders. 'Would you like me to tell her?'

He saw the other man hesitate in mid-stride, and then Koli answered:

'No. It's my job. I suppose it's my fault, too. But thank you... And how do I live next year? I wish someone would tell *me* that!' He exclaimed again: 'On Christmas night, too! My God!'

Presently, near the dimmed lights of Senglea, they said good-bye. Father Salvatore plodded on alone, his spirits lower than ever. This was the war – nothing else, and nothing less: blood-shed and destruction, heartbreak and death. Could it really be Christmas night, the birthday of the Saviour of the world? Could God give so marvellously, and then take away again with such cruel change of mind?

Christmas night... There would never be a worse one, nor a birthday more desolate: no bells of promise, no decorations, no little shrines beckoning the passer-by: no lights to uplift the heart. It was just the end of the second year, another weary Christmas under siege, with a murderous air-raid to mark the date in the calendar of the saints.

He came within sight of the looming bastion of the Cottonera Lines, and found, for the first time, that he was dreading this return. He had promised himself that he would 'speak' again tonight, but what could he speak of? And was it wise to do so? The bishop had given him a kindly but clear warning: not to exceed his province, which was the care of souls: not to exalt his own role: not to play God, nor his prophet.

What *could* he speak of, anyway, on such a wicked Witches' Sabbath as this?

As soon as he had passed through the masked portals of the catacomb, and found the comforting warmth and light within, he was greeted – as had happened on the very first night – by the cry of a child. For a moment he was confused, unable to relate it to anything he had been expecting. Then he remembered. It must be Concetta's new baby, Concetta whom he had left in such agony that same morning. Her travail must be over.

Glory be to God for another safe delivery, on Christmas Day itself.

It was little Nero who confirmed the news. 'It's a boy, Dun Salv! Huge! Nineteen pounds!'

'Nero, it *cannot* be nineteen pounds.'

'Well, nine pounds. Fat as butter, and nearly as big as me, anyway. They're going to call it Salvatore.'

An old man died, a child was born. It was as if the day had been saved after all. He was suddenly overjoyed.

'That's wonderful news, Nero. I must go and see Concetta. How is she?'

'Full of life! She wants to have another one!'

'What does her husband say to that?'

'He's willing.'

There was a throng of people pushing about all round them, securing their places for the evening, and a savoury smell of cooking. 'How is the soup, Nero?'

'Going well. I found a bit more stuff to put in it. That old skinflint Tony Mizzi came through with two dozen eggs at the last minute. And I got some more cheese from the canteen down at the docks.'

'I didn't know they had any to spare.'

Nero tossed his head irritably. 'I could have stolen a whole ship if I'd wanted to! There was hardly anyone there except a few sailors. Do you know, there was nearly a strike when the air-raid warning went? They stopped unloading, and half of them never came back after the all-clear. They said it wasn't safe.' He made the up-throat gesture which signified the ultimate in contempt. 'Safe! What do they want? – a feather-bed with a concrete roof on top? We'll never win the war this way.'

'People are tired, Nero. It's gone on for so long.'

'If we all feel like that it will last for ever. There were some old chaps down here this evening, looking at the soup and say-ing, "What's the good? What's the good? We eat it today, but what do we eat tomorrow?" They didn't offer to help, by the way. Just kept on moaning about the war going on till we were all dead.' Nero cocked a cheerful, inquisitive eye at Father Salvatore. 'That can't be true, can it?'

'No.'

Concetta's baby, the newest citizen of the catacombs, wailed again, on a note of command. An old man died, a child was born... Father Salvatore knew now that, come what may, he must speak tonight of hope: hope, and beyond hope, self-help. However deadly or depressing the evidence to the contrary, there was one certain truth – that no siege could last for ever.

It must never be forgotten – and he was now determined to remind them – that another siege of long ago, on this very same ground, *because it had been valiantly withstood*, had ended so suddenly that the men and women of Malta found themselves laughing for joy almost before they ceased to cry.

HEXAMERON FOUR

AD 1565. The Greatest Siege

When he faced his flock, meagrely fed and resigned to the end
of Christmas without great hopes of the next dawn, Father
Salvatore doubted his power to do anything to raise their spirits.
The trouble was novelty, or the lack of it.

They knew all about the Great Siege, from their earliest
schooldays. It was something which had happened a long time
ago: the Knights had won, the Turks had been kicked out (on 8
September, a national holiday ever afterwards), and the Maltese
had gone on living until the next time. It would seem to have
little to do with *now*, with the bombs raining down on Christmas Day, and eggs as rare as hens' teeth.

Did they know, could they imagine, what the greatest siege of
all had really been like? Did they realize what the Maltese themselves had done? Did they understand why the Turks gave up, in
face of a nut too hard to crack? Could they comprehend the golden age of peace and splendour which the victory had brought?

Perhaps if he could start with the men, the fabulous men...

The most fabulous man of all, at that moment of history, and
the most feared, was Suleiman the Magnificent, Sultan of Turkey: conqueror of Belgrade, of Rhodes, of Aden and Algiers, of
Hungary and Baghdad: scourge of the Mediterranean seaboard,
and enemy of all things Christian. Though his other, more ful-
some titles included 'Possessor of Men's Necks', 'Allah's Deputy
on Earth', and 'Shadow of the Almighty', he had not been called
'the Magnificent' by fawning courtiers, but by reluctant admirers who had felt either the bite of his sword, or the cutting
edge of his genius for law-making and law-keeping.

He was now an old man, but still ferociously determined that his rule and his faith should prevail, wherever his warriors could march or his war-galleys could sail. Of all the men barring his way in the Middle Sea, the most capable and the most hated were those other warriors called the Knights Hospitallers of St John of Jerusalem. Sultan Suleiman had been twenty-nine when, long ago, he had expelled this Order from its base in Rhodes, where it had ruled for more than 200 years; he was seventy-one when he took his final oath to expel them from Malta also.

Impressed by their bravery, he had allowed the Knights to leave Rhodes with generous honours of war, bearing their arms and embarking in thirty vessels led by the legendary Great Carrack of Rhodes. But he would not make that mistake again. This time, his vindictive resolve was that there would be no living Knights left to embark.

Against Suleiman was another man of exactly the same age, the French Grand Master Jean Parisot de la Valette, the sixth to rule the Order since the Knights began their wanderings in search of a refuge to replace the lost island of Rhodes. He was head of a brotherhood of men who, from strange and humble beginnings, had grown to power and magnificence as the greatest fighting sailors of their time.

The Order had started, in the long-ago of five centuries, as a small company of stretcher-bearers, caring for those Christian pilgrims who, dying of fatigue or poverty, had managed to drag their wretched limbs to that unimaginable shrine, the Holy Sepulchre of Jerusalem. Presently it became necessary to found a hospital for these sick waifs; the hospital was dedicated to St John the Baptist, and the staff – the Hospitaller Brothers of St John of Jerusalem – to vows of chastity, poverty, and obedience.

From hospitallers they perforce became fighting men, pledged to defend the pilgrims on their journey (a nightmare of violence and theft as soon as they neared the Holy Land), and to succour the Faith at all times; and Mediterranean fighting men were inevitably sailors. In their wanderings after the sack of Jerusalem by Saladin they ranged the whole Phoenician coast : poor homeless mariners again, their coffers empty after ransoming all the prisoners they could afford.

First they tried Cyprus, and were driven out; then they took Rhodes from the Saracens, and kept it for 221 years.

Expelled by Suleiman after a bloody six-months' siege, they

wandered another seven years before the Emperor Charles V of Spain gave them the island of Malta, in exchange for a single falcon payable yearly to the Viceroy of Sicily on All Saints' Day. They arrived in their flagship the *Mograbine*, 'Queen of the Sea', that fabulous carrack captured from the Prince of Egypt. She towered to seven decks above the waterline, with bows forty-five feet high; and presently the Knights themselves began to tower again, policing the Mediterranean and denying to Suleiman or any other infidel dog-of-a-Turk a mile of sea-room west of Venice.

This was to be the frontier of Christendom. Not for nothing had they brought to Malta a burning faith, and one of the hands of John the Baptist.

They made of Malta a naval base, impregnable, proud, and sustained by their own unstinting efforts. In 1549, when every single ship of their navy, though snugged down in Marsa Scirocco Harbour, was wrecked by a huge storm, and cast ashore in splinters, they lived on beans until they had rebuilt their fleet.

Such were the men commanded by La Valette when, in the seventy-second year of his life, the Turkish battle-squadrons – 31,000 men in 180 ships – forced a landing on Malta and began their assault. It was enough to daunt, without shame, a garrison whose fighting élite numbered 641 Knights. But if the Grand Master had a single doubt, a single qualm about the outcome of this mighty thrust by his oldest enemy, it did not show in his bearing.

Beneath the blood-red emblem of the Order, the four barbed arrowheads whose points met in the middle to form the Maltese Cross, his heart, like his valiant sword, was already worthy of eternal honour.

Against La Valette there was also ranged a splendid and subtle rogue, the Corsair Dragut Rais, Pasha of Tripoli.

Dragut was the sort of man much admired in the Saracen–Arab world: a born nuisance, a talented murderer, and a most cunning tactician ashore and afloat. He was even older than the two principal commanders, being eighty years of age when he joined the siege. But age did not count, where this remarkable character was concerned. Trained as a gunner, matchless as a pilot, surpassing even his former captain, the fabled pirate Barbarossa, in all the skills of sea warfare, he was an ally beyond price.

Moreover, he knew these waters, and these islands, as he knew his own main-deck. Already, fourteen years earlier, he had raided and sacked the sister isle of Gozo, and carried off every able man, every usable woman, and every walking child, to the number of 6,000, into slavery. It was said that he did this to avenge the death of his brother, whose corpse was publicly burned in the main street of the capital. It was said, by others, that he would have stormed Gozo anyway, for the professional pleasure of the exercise.

When his fleet of fifteen war galleys, 1,500 men, and an array of monstrous siege guns, joined the assault, Suleiman welcomed him, and ordered his commanders to take the old man's advice in everything. La Valette, whatever he thought, kept his counsel. Once, when he was forty-seven, the Grand Master had survived capture, and a year in the Turkish galleys as a slave chained to a bench. But at seventy-one?

Such was the glittering array of the supreme commanders: Suleiman, Dragut, and La Valette, whose worth as fighting men was pure gold, and whose combined age at the time of battle was 222 years.

They had been silent up to now, listening to the beginnings of the half-remembered, half-forgotten struggle. But when he mentioned again the great age of the captains, there was a stir and some whispering among the older men. Seventy-one, and seventy-one, and eighty! So war and pride of strength was not reserved for the strutting young. War need not leave a middle-aged man behind, forgotten and despised, a 'useless mouth' as some said. If old Valette, as they all knew, could give these intruders the thrashing of a lifetime at the age of seventy-one, why then, why then...

Against Suleiman the Magnificent, and Dragut the wily corsair, were the Knights of the Order of St John: 641 of them, with about 8,000 troops of varied quality to furnish their regiments – volunteers from Italy and Sicily, slaves who could be trusted to fetch and carry, and to row the galleys under the scourge of the lash: and some Maltese, slowly coming forward as their island was threatened. But the Knights, drawn from the eight 'Langues' overseas, were the spearhead of resistance. If their spirit failed, then any other weight of numbers would be futile.

To begin with, the Knights of St John had not liked Malta at
all, and Malta had not liked them. They found the local nobles
snobbish, and the common people apathetic and (to their way
of thinking) barbarous, speaking 'a sort of Moorish' they would
never understand. They thought the island itself was awful : a
barren rock, stripped of vegetation, scant of soil, short of water:
gale-ridden without warning, scorched in summer and drowned
in winter, and continually raided by Barbary pirates. Inland, an
old deserted town by the name of Mdina ruled over a waste of
brown nothingness.

The contrast with the island of Rhodes – dear Rhodes, where
they had lived at ease among the pleasant hillsides, smiling valleys, luxurious crops and flowers, and matchless views of green
and blue – was too appalling to contemplate. Malta's marvellous
harbour was the only bait.

But for wandering sailors a safe haven was bound to be the
crucial magnet of their lives, no matter what the other drawbacks. So Malta it was; and in Malta, after a look at the bare
rock of Mount Sceberras, they had settled in the fishing village
of Birgu, which later ages were to call Vittoriosa.

Time passed. The Knights still did not like Malta. But now,
threatened with yet another eviction after thirty-five years, not-
liking had been overtaken by a kind of love. This was their only
home, and they were not going to give it up.

Those thirty-five years in one dependable stronghold had revived all their sophisticated life-style and many of their ancient
disciplines. They were not all saints, but under certain Grand
Masters, and now under La Valette, they had become, at least,
aristocratic sinners redeemed by their devotion to an unbreakable code of courage, endurance, and military honour.

They were organized in the eight *langues* or tongues of their
various fatherlands : three of these were French – Auvergne,
Provence, and France itself – and thus numerically superior. The
rest came from Aragon, Castile, Italy, Germany, and England.
The lone English Knight, Sir Oliver Starkey, was the gifted
'Latin secretary' and closest confidant of Grand Master La
Valette.

Drawn from the noblest families of Europe, volunteers either
for Christ or for a Foreign Legion type of life well-suited to
young men of spirit with their youth to burn, the Knights were
quartered separately, and often luxuriously, in the various

auberges which they had built in the narrow streets of Birgu and Senglea. They were kept apart, by *langues*, to avoid quarrelling, and it proved an effective safeguard.

It was a fact that, in Malta, Knights belonging to nations on terms of traditional and ferocious hatred towards each other somehow managed to live in perfect concord on their shared island. The common purpose softened their differences; familiarity bred tolerance; as young nobles, they achieved an 'epitome of all Europe' on a scale of amity which Europe itself never knew. All that was left of barred frontiers and warring princes was a kind of regimental rivalry which did wonders for morale.

Within the *auberge* where they lived and ate, life under the 'Pillar' – the head of the *langue* – was strictly disciplined. The Knights were bound to celibacy, though their men-at-arms and servants were not; for this rumbustious gathering of youth, eating and drinking and sleeping and violent physical exercise took precedence over all other appetites. They were commanded to 'dine in' on four nights a week, as in a well-run university. There was a curious rule of 'No Dogs Allowed', at variance with the normal sporting tradition of bachelor life.

When errors of deportment or morality were noticed, punishment was swift and harsh. The penalty even for a minor transgression was a seven days' fast, including two days on bread and water in solitude, and two floggings (Wednesdays and Fridays). Four years' service in the galleys was the sharp rebuke for wearing embroidered stockings. But there was within the fortress of St Angelo, where the Grand Master had his headquarters, a dungeon known as the '*oubliette*' – a sort of underground cistern, eleven feet below floor level, airless, windowless, as forlorn a prison-cage as could be devised; and this was where the heaviest stripes were felt.

It was reserved for errant knights guilty of serious crimes; and here the luckless sinner, be he ever so noble, served out a sentence which might be for the term of his life.

He might spend two months in this dank and mortuary cell, never more than five paces wide, for quarrelling in church. Three months was the sentence for a fiercer quarrel in which beards were torn off; and a full year the punishment for 'disobedience'. For robbery and sacrilege, or for murder, even in hot blood, the guilty wretch waited below, indefinitely, until his formal sentence was pronounced.

Then, on a day decreed, he would be expelled from the Order as 'a putrid and stinking member', hauled up, and either drowned in a weighted sack or strangled. In the latter case, his body was then tossed into the gutter for the dogs to eat.

Ironically, this fearsome dungeon, to the respectable, was known as the *guva* – the bird-cage. But no birds sang here. A man condemned had nothing to do but broil in summer and freeze in winter: nothing to do, whether drenched with sweat or shaking with cold, but carve his name and his proud armorial bearings on the stone shroud of his grave. Sometimes he added an expression of his hope, or his humour, or his despair, to show that certain sparks in the human spirit never died.

A man in this torment could still spend months painfully depicting a hearse carrying a coffin, or a full-sized lute with strings and frets complete – for solitary silent finger-practice. He could incise, boldly and elegantly: 'The ruination of just men' or 'Imprisoned in this living grave where evil triumphs over good'. In a more resigned mood, he could carve a pious '*Ad meliores*' – 'Towards better things' – as he waited for whatever choice of death would release him.

Such was the discipline of the Knights, for the greater glory of Christ and the preservation of a superbly dedicated code of conduct. But even the well-behaved were, in their daily lives, put through a mill of comparable severity.

The Order had never forgotten its origins, nor their mainspring in human pity. The first of its cares, on reaching Malta, was to build a hospital; the first of its rules was that *all* young Knights, of whatever degree, must perform their share of nursing the sick – a menial and unpleasant task as far from the normal life of a nobleman as cleaning out his own stables.

Its parallel task was to maintain the cult of physical excellence, essential for fighting-men who must be tough sailors as well.

The Knights underwent a ruthless regime of training, designed to root out weakness and to refine every last skill of weaponry. It was no accident that Grand Master de L'Isle Adam, who had maintained their spirit on the heartbreaking odyssey from Rhodes to Malta, was hailed by Pope Hadrian VI as 'The Great Athlete of Christ', a title at least as bizarre as any of Sultan Suleiman's.

This was their whole tradition: strength, speed, tenacity, and a nimble cunning; and every day of their lives was devoted to it. They even exercised in heavy armour, yet fought in light, to gain extra agility when it came to the test of blood.

Even to qualify for knighthood, young boys had to perform four 'caravans' (cruises) of six months' war service in the galleys. This was their hardest work of all. Though the slaves rowed, sometimes for twenty hours a day, and could die a dog's death doing so, the young Knights were the steel battering-ram when it came to battle: they had to navigate, ship-handle, stand to arms at all times, man the monstrous guns, and leap on board the enemy as soon as their vessels touched.

The speed of that armed leap, or the angle of it, might win or lose a ship, or an action, or even the fortress of Malta itself. It must be perfect, like all the rest.

So trained, and armed, and inspired, the Knights had settled down to police their half of the Mediterranean, and to ravage, sting, and discomfort the other half, Suleiman's half. The provocation was intolerable, and now they were preparing for what must be the answer, the assault on an island which Suleiman, dreaming and waking, loathed as a nest of impudent vipers.

He planned a final breakthrough to the west. The Knights stood in his path. Malta was his key, and their lock. They had come to acknowledge it also as their home, and under God and La Valette they were *not* going to give it up.

Against La Valette, and his 641 Knights, and his 8,000 auxiliaries, were the Turks: more than 30,000 of them altogether, including 6,000 Janissaries, men of the Sultan's own guard, whose huge mustachios and leopard-skin bonnets marked them out as the core of the élite. As well as these disciplined hordes, their fleets carried cavalry horses, barrels of gunpowder, tents for a long siege, and a great battery of sixty-three guns, capable of discharging volleys of stone cannon-balls weighing more than 150 pounds each.

When Dragut Rais arrived, with his 1,500 seasoned pirates, a special gunnery skill and a bloody element of plunder were added.

All that need be said of the Turks was that they matched the Knights in bravery, in their ferocious determination to overthrow their enemy, and in their devotion to their faith. To this must be joined a capricious brutality which had made them feared and hated throughout the Mediterranean world, and which guaranteed that a man would fight to the death rather than fall into their hands alive.

Against all these visitors, to a greater or lesser degree, were the people of Malta. They had hardly swallowed the Knights, being unable to spit them out, when yet another tyrant was on his way to conquer and enslave their island. When in heaven's name would it end? To the very last man, whether noble or humble, they had heard this song before, and they were chokingly sick of it.

After the Normans, there had been the Angevins, a sort of French–English cross-breed. After the Angevins came the Aragonese, and after them the Castilians – both Spanish, and as cruel and proud as Lucifer himself. Then the citizens of Malta had woken up one morning to find that some foreign emperor, without a word to anyone, had presented their island to the Knights of St John.

The first they knew about it was when the Knights arrived in the biggest ship anyone had ever seen, and announced that Malta was theirs. Here, they said, were all the new laws. Anyone disobeying them would be breaking God's command, and the only judge of that, and the executioner, would be the Order, because the Order had been thus authorized, by divine grace, and any argument was blasphemy.

This breathtaking impudence was deeply resented. With the Maltese nobility, it was a matter of injured pride. They could not endure the patrician arrogance of the newcomers. 'We were noble, 200 years before these *apothecaries* arrived,' a Santo-Nobile had once been heard to say; and though this was an extreme view, it was not an unusual one.

Why should such ancient families as the Murinas, the Sceberras, the Inguanez, the Santo-Nobiles, or the Manducas, whose lineage was the equal of any seaborne Knight alive, suddenly find themselves excluded from society, treated like country cousins, robbed of their privileges, and ordered about like lackeys?

It was not to be endured. Before long, the noble families turned their backs on these upstart usurpers, withdrew to their crumbling palaces in Mdina or anywhere else where they might find privacy, and shrugged their shoulders of the whole vulgar business. It was a relief to find that the Knights preferred to settle round the harbour, like common sailors. What else could one expect?

Even the news that the Turks might attack was not taken very seriously. If the Turks were coming, it was because the Knights had arrived already. It was *their* quarrel. Let them sort it out for themselves, and not bother important people.

It might even teach them a lesson.

The noble Maltese were not to know, at that moment of time, how these Knights of St John, whatever the arrogant crudity of their incursion, would pay their full entrance-fee in blood and sweat, ten times over, and then go on to endow a small, impoverished, and backward island with all the graces of civilization, and all the strength to resist a barbarous alternative.

For the common people the view was different, and would always be so. They were used to arrogance, and to servitude also: it was the penalty, the condition, of not having noble blood, not marrying money, not owning enough land, not knowing friends in high places, not being born in the right bed. They had been born instead to a lifetime of sweat and toil: counting themselves lucky if, at the end of life, a man had enough to pay for his burial.

They were resigned to taking orders, kneeling to great men, trusting to God for the fish and the harvest, and, if they could, escaping notice. The only riches for them were the rain when it fell, the goats and sheep when they increased, and plenty of sons to grow up and help keep starvation at bay. All they wanted, all they ever looked for, was peace, and from time to time a little stroke of luck.

But they still did not like what their new masters, the Knights, were doing to their island and their home. They did not like the loss of certain small liberties, the petty interference. There were so many new rules: life was so organized, people were so fussy. And they resented, fiercely, what the foreign emperor had written when he gave Malta to the Knights: that he was granting them 'the power of the knife over the men and women living therein'.

Who said so? It was *their* land, *their* life, *their* freedom! Who said that strangers could come in from nowhere, and dictate their whole future at the point of a sword?

Now, to top everything, they were told that another band of brigands were on their way to steal the country yet again;

and that the Knights would see it torn into bloody strips before they gave it up. Not for the first time, nor for the tenth, the Maltese people were involved in a quarrel not of their making, a quarrel which could crucify their island, and enslave its survivors for ever.

As poor men without any strength of their own, they could do nothing. They could only resent, and retreat into a sullen hatred of all masters, old and new. As if at a signal, the Maltese went to ground, rolling up in a ball like the hedgehog, playing dead until the storm was over. They had not been consulted? Then they would do *nothing*! Since they had no palaces like the rich to hide in, any hole must serve.

Then suddenly the climate changed, just as suddenly as the fierce western *sirocco* whipped round to become the *gregale*, the rain-bearing Greek wind from the east. It might indeed have been that detested *gregale*, such was its effect as the breath of rumour stirred, and became something like a hurricane. This was no ordinary foe whose sails were now soiling the horizon. It was the Turk! The baby-killing, woman-raping, man-castrating Turk!

Stories of the vast and ravening fleet on its way to attack them multiplied, and grew into the blackest cloud ever seen in any quarter of the heavens. People began to ask each other what would happen if the Turks won. It was said that they would take every last man, woman, and child into slavery. It was said that they practised loathsome tortures, not for gain, not for information, but for simple pleasure.

It was said that a Turk in a rage was not half so much to be feared as a Turk with a smile on his face. It was said that they played hand-ball with the heads of their prisoners, and 'Turkish bowls' with more bestial trophies still. It was said that their hatred of Malta was so devouring that, once they had taken it, they would burn every living thing showing above the face of the ground, and then plough up the cities and the plains with salt, as the Romans had done to Carthage in the terrible days of long ago.

What would happen if these cruel wolves from the north and the east became their new lords? No Knight, however strict or overbearing, could be as bad as such monsters!

On a certain morning, the Maltese began to come forward, and to help. They begged to do so: they begged to be allowed to do anything – anything which would prepare the island for its ordeal. No matter if their betters had gone to earth; they would not copy cowards – they would stand, and resist. The terror of what might befall them, if Grand Master La Valette lost the battle, struck home, and overrode everything else.

Before a week was out, they were working side by side with the Knights, labouring fiercely to fortify their homeland and make it ready for the attack. After that – this was the unspoken thought in every breast – the prospect of *fighting* side by side would not be such a wild dream after all.

With a giant's strength and a tireless will, La Valette was hurrying to make his moat secure. Forts and watch-towers were completed, including one, St Elmo, on Mount Sceberras itself; walls and barricades soaring to thirty feet were thrown up, with huge blocks of stone pushed and pulled and coaxed into shape; gun-emplacements, with slits cunningly designed for cross-fire and enfilade, were fashioned as fast as men could run from one vantage-point to another. Behind the fort of St Angelo, where the Grand Master had set up his command post, a great ditch was dug, and reinforced with retaining walls, cutting it off from assault on the landward side.

Nature had given Malta a superb harbour; men now strove to turn it into a sea-girt fortress. In all these feverish efforts, the Maltese, who knew more than anyone about the working of their native rock into manageable shapes and sizes, were the first to give strength and sinew to this dream of an impregnable stronghold.

Behind these mounting ramparts the armourers worked like madmen, with hammer and cutting edge, mould and crucible, to produce all the weapons of war, whether they were culverins to fire a searing iron ball or saw-edged daggers for close combat. They laid in supplies of all that might be needed; mounds of shot for the cannon, barrels of powder, ropes and axes to repel the scaling ladders, cauldrons of hot oil to be poured down on the attackers.

It was said that the Turks advanced into battle in foolish flapping garments which only needed a gentle sprinkling and a single spark to turn them into whirling torches. Excellent!

But it was the Maltese fishermen of Birgu who put the finishing touch to the harbour defences. Across the mouth of the deepest creek, between Senglea and St Angelo, it was planned to place a chain-boom which could be raised or lowered at will, allowing the galleys of the Order to pass in and out of their anchorage, barring the way to all others. It needed great skill and strength: it needed floats fastened across the whole length of the chain, to take its enormous weight: it needed swimmers to attend to this, and to the final placing. Who better than willing Maltese sailors could make a proper job of this one?

The massive main anchor from the Great Carrack, embedded deep in the rock, made one end of the boom secure on the Senglea side. Slowly, link by link, the chain – hand-forged in Venice, more than 200 yards long – was fed out across the harbour mouth, and married to a giant capstan on St Angelo Fort. It lay on the sea-bed until all the fleet of galleys had come to their final berths, where they must stay until the siege was over.

Then a thousand slaves, in relays, bent their backs to the capstan-bars, tautening the chain, raising it to water-level. Underneath it, the Maltese swimmers and boatmen threaded more than forty pontoons and rafts, and made them fast: completing a floating iron rampart, the cunning of which could not be matched in all the Middle Sea.

Now the inner harbour was secure. The forts were as strong as they would ever be. The granaries were bulging with grain, the underground cisterns with clay water-jars, and the stables with animals driven in. Outside the fortress, the land had been stripped bare of its last peacetime crops, and the wells poisoned with dung and flax. All had been done that could be done; now a man could only wait, and receive the comfort of the sacraments, and perfect his weapons, and pray.

Thus it was that on the fifteenth day of May Malta awoke to thunder, and all the gods – the true God in the sky, the false Allah in his den of thieves below, the Christ and the Antichrist alike – gave the order:

'Bid the soldiers shoot!'

It was wonderful to hear the names again, and to remember that they were old in glory as well as new in strength. St Angelo still stood like an everlasting rock on the point of Birgu. Senglea meant home to many who sat and listened tonight. Some of the streets where the first auberges were still landmarks – those of France and Italy, of Auvergne and

Provence, of England in Majjistral Street – had been bombed that very morning.

La Valette's chain-boom – what an old fox he must have been! – had stretched across their own Dockyard Creek; and there was another one of the very same design today, protecting Lazzaretto Creek, where the submarines, like the ancient galleys, lay in their guarded tiers.

Best of all, this had been a siege which, terrible as it was to endure, terrible as the present onslaught, had been fought to a standstill. Perhaps it was still true that the death-struggle of 1941 was not their own quarrel. But once again, what would happen if they lost it? . . . Once more, once and for ever, the siege of Malta must be made to fail.

It failed because its valiant garrison would not give it up, no matter what was done to them or to their fortress. No desperate assault ever broke their spirit; it only destroyed their bodies, and at the end there were still enough of these to send the enemy fleeing from the field like beaten dogs. No land attack took the strong-points from behind – except tiny St Elmo on the tip of Mount Sceberras, and this held out until the programme of the siege was ruined.

No sea-assault prevailed; the harbour forts were too strong, and the Great Chain too formidable. No merciless pounding by artillery succeeded; brazen machines might crush stone to powder, but they could not crush men. In the loneliest bravery of all, even captured prisoners would not tell the truth about the defences, though the Turkish *bastinado*, the beating on the soles of the feet, continued until screaming death silenced a steadfast mouth for ever.

The garrisons would not surrender, though wave after wave of furious attackers stormed the walls, treading the corpses of their drugged holy men who had died in the belief that they would meet that night in paradise. This bridge of bodies was not enough foothold for the shrieking, surging regiments of Janissaries; but a carpet of their own dead was platform enough for the beleaguered Knights.

In four months of gory chaos, with cruelty unmatched, tricks unimaginable, and bravery supreme, 35,000 men could not beat 9,000, nor steal their home, nor destroy it.

* * *

It failed because the brutal and cunning plan of the corsair Dragut Rais failed. When the old pirate arrived, two weeks late, and saw what was being done by the Turkish commanders, he spoke his mind without delay.

'You are wrong, and all your plans are wrong,' he told them, and even at eighty years of age he was the sort of man who could say this, and still be heard with respect. 'You will never take St Elmo, nor any of the other forts, by a simple land-attack.' This was what Pasha Mustapha, the Turkish Commander-in-Chief, was trying to do, by advancing along the spine of Mount Sceberras. 'Don't waste your men – not yet. These forts are too strong. Bring up heavy guns, and bash them to pieces first! *Then* make your advance, and they will fall like rotten, half-eaten fruit. *I know!* I have done it before.'

This was true, and all who listened knew it; it would take a foolhardy man to argue with the old corsair about his own reputation as an invincible artilleryman. And had they not been told by the great Suleiman himself to believe Dragut, and to take his advice in all things? ... The battle plan was altered, after a single meeting of the council.

Under Dragut's expert eye, the Turks put batteries of their largest cannon, culverins, and basilisks, on Tigné Point, a mere five hundred yards from St Elmo : and another on the slopes of Mount Sceberras : and a third on Gallows Point on the south-east side. From there they began to smash the fort to pieces, while Dragut settled down to watch. Like many old men, he was sleepless; like very few old men of his age, he was tough and enduring as one of his own oak galleys.

No silken tents or cool evening sherbert or plump grapes for him. He shared his soldiers' rations, and at night slept briefly by the guns, under the stars, on a stone bed, and was the first to wake and sight the culverins for the dawn cannonade.

From three points of the compass – north-west, south-west, south-east – the guns roared and pounded and hammered away, for hour after hour, day after day, at the small fort with the hastily built walls and the handful of defenders inside. One special mark was selected each day, and on this the avalanche of shot crashed without ceasing, until stone became powder, and bastions were reduced to shapeless rubble.

A man inside, a Maltese who lived to tell the tale, counted more than 6,000 cannonballs – of iron, of stone, even of marble

– which found their mark on the defences between the dawn of one day and the dusk of the same evening.

Time and again, Dragut judged that the moment had come for an attack, and Mustapha, the field commander, sent in his hordes to throw themselves up and over the walls. Time and again the Turkish Janissaries – those curious stable-bred warriors for Islam, Christian by birth, military by ferocious training, Moslem by conversion – led the tempest of troops against the bastions of St Elmo.

Time and again they were thrown back, and Mustapha, surveying moats and ditches full of the corpses of his irreplaceable élite, said that it could not yet be done, and Dragut, growling curses and orders in the same breath, set up his guns and resumed the fiery weight of the cannonade.

There came a day when the Knights inside St Elmo, which was no longer a fort but a heap of stones trembling at each fresh fall of shot, believed that they could do no more. Their defences were gone. Their numbers had been decimated. They scarcely had strength enough to stay awake, much less to throw back the endless waves of the attackers.

The wounded lay and suffered agonies in their own blood. Heat, thirst, and bloated flies tortured every one of them. Threatened starvation could not be relieved by a piece of bread soaked in wine, which was now the staple ration. Outside the walls – if mounds of shuddering, blood-soaked rubbish could be called walls – the stench of decaying bodies, of the sandwiched heaps of Turkish dead, was almost suffocating.

After a prolonged argument, and some mutterings of mutiny, they sent a respectful message to La Valette across the harbour. St Elmo, they told him, was now useless. Life there was insupportable, and death futile. They had once numbered 118; they were now sixty, most of them wounded, all exhausted. Since they were unlikely to last out another day, could they not make a final sally, and try to fight their way out?

It was not cowardice; it was brave common sense. But the Grand Master had his own time-table, and his own stern code of discipline. He was waiting for promised reinforcements from the lacklustre Viceroy of Sicily, and every day, every hour, that St Elmo could survive was a golden hope for all Malta. He sent back a message by a Maltese swimmer who made a perilous moonlight crossing, swimming most of the way under water to escape the sharp-shooters at the Turkish gun-points; and it was an icy answer indeed.

The garrison, under its vow of obedience and valour, was *not* to make any attempt to leave the fort. They were to stay where they were, and St Elmo was to be held to the last Knight. However, if this order was not to their taste, he would arrange to replace them with braver men.

It was said that there were other messages from brother Knights, couched in less formal language. With humble apologies, the defenders returned to their duty, Dragut Rais to his smoking guns, and Pasha Mustapha to unleash, once more, his demented legions.

The final days were terrible; but they *were* days, not hours: the valiant Knights of St Elmo, whose last commander was the Aragonese Melchior de Monserrat, held onto their fort with matchless bravery for an incredible thirteen days more. Melchior had seen his brother Antonio de Monserrat killed by an arrow a few days earlier; it may have been this, as much as his knightly devotion, which drove him to such fury of resistance before he forfeited his own life to a musket-shot, in the last hour of St Elmo's ghastly twilight.

It came – it was bound to come – to a bloody end. The handful of survivors were now only fearful spectres : maimed, half starved, stumbling about, nearly out of their wits. But they had sworn to stand fast, and they did so. As the last attack, which continued for six hours, rose to its climax, even the wounded were carried to their battle stations, and set down like bloodstained dummies.

All were confessed, and received absolution; then they waited for death. But some still fought, with a maniac, steely will, and if a man propped up in a crumbling corner of a wall could manage to swing a broad-sword for the last time, that was what he did.

Dragut Rais did not see that last assault, nor its triumph; he was slowly dying of a fearful wound – killed by his own fools, as he may have had time to say before he lapsed into mortal stupor. Five days earlier he had been directing his guns for a final cannonade.

'Aim lower,' he signalled to the battery behind him. 'You are overshooting the walls.' The fault was corrected, but not enough. 'Lower still!' he signalled, and they took him at his word. A Turkish cannonball crashed into the trench where he stood, and a sliver of stone sliced into his skull so that (to quote the man standing by him) 'his brains spilled out from his mouth and nostrils', and he fell.

So Dragut, battling for his own life, could not witness the victory which, after the long-drawn-out turmoil, was a brief and bloody carnage. A last wall was breached, and suddenly there were no more men left to stand and bear arms; a raging sea of white and green broke over St Elmo, and it was lost. But Dragut's corsairs, in whom the lust for loot was ingrained, managed to snatch nine live prisoners for ransom, and five Maltese soldiers dived off St Elmo Point and swam for their lives towards Birgu, before the Janissaries topped the citadel. Within moments, the rest of the garrison was dead to a man.

Dragut Rais also breathed his last as the fort was taken; the news of triumph only reached his ears in time to speed his stubborn, cunning, wicked old soul to its eternity. If he had given his counsel earlier, or if the fort had fallen a few days before, or if he had been standing an inch to the right or left, perhaps he would have lived, and perhaps conquered all Malta.

As it was, St Elmo lost was the key to Maltese victory. Though the fort was rubble, and all inside were dead, the delay in taking it was fatal to the Turkish plan. Eight thousand of them had been been killed, in exchange for 1,500 soldiers and 109 Knights; and instead of the promised four or five days' siege, St Elmo had held out for thirty-one days. Neither the time lost, nor the men thrown away, were ever made good.

When he entered the ruins of St Elmo, Mustapha Pasha found 1,300 corpses of the defenders, and all the dead Knights. But as he mourned the monstrous total of his own dead, he could only say : 'If the daughter cost us so much, what will be the price of the mother?'

The mother was St Angelo.

The siege failed because when St Angelo's turn came, on the morrow of St Elmo, it withstood everything that the savage wit of man could devise. Attacked with the same fury, it replied with the same courage; and its courage was just enough to out-last the worst that the Turks could do. The Knights of St Angelo, having watched St Elmo die, took a fresh oath that their fortress would live, and they kept it.

A foretaste of what the Turkish 'worst' might be was given them on the sullen evening of St Elmo's defeat. Borne forward by the evening breeze, four ghastly cargoes were launched from across the water, and presently drifted ashore at Birgu. They were the bodies of four dead Knights, all headless, with the mark of the Cross gashed into their Christian breasts, lashed to wooden crucifixes for their last caravan.

Raising their eyes from this foul jetsam, the Knights of St Angelo saw a bristling row of pikes being raised on St Elmo Point, each topped by the head of a Knight, with his armour beneath to supply his name and rank.

La Valette's answer – to kill all his Turkish prisoners and fire their heads back across the harbour – was only the reply of a grief-stricken man who wished to show his contempt and defiance. After that grisly bombardment, his fury turned cold-blooded, and calculating, and utterly determined.

He had two frontiers to guard: the ditch behind St Angelo fort, and the harbour defences themselves. The first was held against every device of attack, whether it was bombardment, or fiery hoops launched against the walls, or men massed in their thousands who threw their bodies at the ramparts, content to form a bridge of the dead which would serve for the last assault by living comrades.

The harbour side remained impregnable, even though the Turks brought up some eighty galleys dragged on rollers nearly a mile overland, by slaves and oxen, from Mount Sceberras to the Marsa Creek. The Great Chain kept them out of the inner harbour, and all other attacks came to naught. They might range the waterfront impotently, or seek the back way into Senglea, now protected by yet another chain-boom, threaded through stakes driven into the sea-bed by the same band of Maltese boatmen and swimmers; but men in galleys could not take this fortress, any more than men on foot or men on ladders. It failed because when the Turks, armed with hatchets and knives, tried to cut a way through this new palisade, the weakest point of the defences, they were routed by a body of the only accomplished swimmers on the island, Maltese fishermen.

The attack came as a surprise: the first warning that Admiral de Monte, the commander of Senglea, received was when he saw the turbanned heads of some swimmers moving steadily, in broad daylight, across the four hundred feet between the Corradino Heights and his own command.

He waited, not knowing what to make of it. Even the mad Turks would not swim against a fortress . . . Perhaps they were deserters . . . He waited a little too long. The next thing he saw was these same invaders close inshore, hacking away at his palisade. The flash of hatchets and axes in the sunshine was enough to bring him to full alert.

He sent a captain running down to the foreshore, with orders to collect volunteers to repel this impudence. He needed that palisade, just as much as Grand Master la Valette needed the bastions of St Angelo; it was the only seaward defence of Senglea. The captain, panting downhill, presently found that he was surrounded by other runners, and that they were being joined by still more of them, coming out from Senglea lower town.

They were all Maltese, villainously armed : and the Senglea band was led by a man known to the captain, one Ben Sayid, who had already achieved fame in the siege, and seemed ready for more.

This Ben Sayid, at the head of his gang, had worked on the Great Chain, and proved himself a fine swimmer as well as a good shipwright; then he had volunteered for the St Elmo garrison, and was indeed one of its tiny group of survivors. He had seen his commander, Melchior de Monserrat, killed, his head torn apart by a musket shot at close range, and had judged that to be the signal to leave. Better a live Maltese than a dead Knight... But he had been the last to dive off at St Elmo Point, and had swum back like a weaving dolphin to tell the story.

Now he saluted the captain with a grin, and said : 'Look at that! They're cutting down our palisade!' He had played a part in securing this defence also, and it was just as much *his* palisade as it was the captain's, or the Grand Master's either, for that matter. He spoke in rough French, having worked on the building of the *Auberge* of Provence, and this was the captain's own tongue. 'What shall we do, *capitaine*? Swim out and ask them to stop?'

The captain, who for all the ardour of the siege was exquisitely dressed, with a burnished breastplate adorned by a trio of pale-blue running greyhounds, looked at Ben Sayid. He

saw a small brown man, with a chest like a barrel and arms
like branches of a Provençal oak : nearly naked, with a mass of
filthy yellow hair, the colour of an olive tree in a parching
summer, above a face chiselled from Maltese rock. His weapon
was a Turkish scimitar, gold-handled, honed thin like a rapier
blade, fit to shave an egg, of which he had said : 'I took it
from a dead dog.'

There was talk that Sayid was a Greek, or had been a Greek,
or had a Greek ancestor somewhere in his family. But when
he was asked about this fair hair of his – though it had been said
in jest – he replied, with a cutting indifference : 'Who cares
what my granny did ? I am Maltese !'

There was no doubt of his spirit, or his courage either.

The captain said : 'You must drive them off !' He looked
round the men crowding about Ben Sayid : they had the same
rough cast, the same eager faces, and the same weapons at the
ready. 'Can you do it ?'

'Easy ! But we must be quick ! They are spoiling all our best
work.' He clapped his hands for attention, and spoke to his
men, pointing once at the Turks bobbing up and down along
the palisade, once at the length of the creek between Senglea
and Corradino, and once at the point of his razor-scimitar,
with a wicked up-swing motion.

He finished by saying something which brought a roar of
laughter; and the Provençal captain, who loved a joke like all
his compatriots, asked :

'What was it you said at the end ?'

'I was telling them exactly how and where to strike . . . Have
you ever played ball-in-the-water, *capitaine* ?'

'I don't think so.'

'It is how we learn our swimming. And some of our tricks. I
said we would give it a different meaning today.'

'Well, go with God.'

'Oh, always . . .' Ben Sayid swept his hand upwards, making
the scimitar sparkle in the morning sun, and gave his last command, which was to put their weapons between their teeth.
Then, followed by his cohort – perhaps a hundred men by now
– he took five short steps, plunged into the waters of the creek,
and struck out for the palisade.

It was then that the watchers on the shore, and the men
thronging the bastions above, saw and acclaimed one of the

bloodiest battles of all the siege. It was brief, because no attack of such thrashing fury could last very long. Some of the Turks, astride the palisade, slipped into the water as they saw the enemy coming, and heard their angry cries; others continued their axe-work until the last moment, until a leg or an arm was caught, and they were toppled downward. But there was little difference in the way they died.

The water round the palisade boiled and frothed as the Maltese, superbly skilful in their native element, darted to and fro like ravening fish. Axes swung at them, and missed; dripping knives flashed upwards or flailed down; shouts changed to screams as the ball-in-the-water game became a hideous affray.

The Turkish ranks thinned: soon it was a matter of hide-and-seek for the last survivors among the cables and the woodwork of the palisade. The water in the creek darkened in a great spreading circle: bubbles and God-knew-what danced on the surface: wavelets of blood began to reach the shore.

With sudden silence, it was over.

The Maltese swam back more slowly from this gruelling match. Some were talking and laughing, others laboured and gasped. The sunshine gleamed on glistening red forearms as they drew near the shore, and heard the full-throated cheers for their victory. Ben Sayid, stumbling up the beach, was seen to have a gross axe wound in his shoulder, from which one arm hung limp as a piece of frayed rope. He was shivering from shock and loss of blood, but like all his band he was exultant. He panted, through clenched teeth:

'That'll teach them to swim in our creek!'

The captain from Provence, who had not seen such a gory fight, nor such furious courage, for many a day, greeted and embraced him as a comrade.

'But staunch that wound quickly,' he warned. 'It's deep. And we need blood like yours.'

'Don't worry,' Ben Sayid croaked. He had swallowed a lot of foul water, the salt in his wound was now agony, and his head was whirling from all he had endured. 'You'll see me again, whatever happens ... I have five sons!'

They were delighted with the story of Ben Sayid, and showed it in their faces and their voices as the tale of the palisade came

*to an end. What a man! What a swimmer! And it was true –
water-polo was a dirty game . . . The awful battle had been in
French Creek, where the old Illustrious had taken refuge: four
hundred years, and three minutes' walk, from the catacombs
where they lay. And this time, the Maltese had done it by
themselves . . . With guts like that, no wonder that old siege
had come to nothing.*

It failed for ever because one breed of the human spirit out-
lasted another. There were other attacks on the palisade – once
the Turks tried to pluck it away with grappling hooks from
the opposite shore, and once they charged it with a line of
galleys, which came to a dead stop and stuck there like fish
gaping in a net – but they were all beaten off. There were other
attacks, outreaching St Elmo in fury and bloodshed, on all the
remaining forts. These held also, because the defenders were,
when necessary, more enduring than stone.

La Valette, the grave and handsome old warrior with the
weight of the whole island on his shoulders, showed his true
metal as a man at one crucial hour of the siege, among countless others which had never ceased to plague him for four long
months.

On a certain day a gigantic mine, planted after weeks of
tunnelling by Turkish gunners under the 'Post of Castile', a
part of the defences of Birgu, went up with a roar, bringing
down a great section of the ramparts and leaving a gaping hole
in the defences. Through this the attackers immediately began
to pour, while the defenders were still dazed and deafened by
the explosion.

It was the moment when Birgu, and St Angelo with it, came
nearest to ruin, but La Valette was ready for it. As with all
great captains, there was nothing he asked his men to do which
he would not do himself; he could also recognize a fatal hour,
when the nettle danger had to be grasped, before the strength
for grasping failed for ever. He advanced into the breach himself, at the head of a small band of men which presently
swelled to hundreds as his heroic figure was identified.

Under the lash of their furious energy, the ramparts were
swept clear of the enemy, the breach sealed, and the city saved;
and La Valette returned at nightfall to have his wounds dressed,
and to mourn the loss of Henri de La Valette, a beloved young

nephew specially entrusted to his care, now to be numbered among the dead.

It was such exploits as these which ensured the blind loyalty with which he was followed, even in the darkest hour. If the old Grand Master could do it, then shame on the man who did not try! . . . This feeling had spread beyond the Knights, who had taken vows to this effect, and possessed the whole garrison, down to the slum-dwellers of Senglea and Birgu, the fishermen of the waterfront, and the women who had to share all the horrors of siege.

Throughout the long ordeal, Maltese men, women, and children toiled to repair the walls; they hurled stones at the attackers, carried away the dead, tended the wounded, brought food and drink to the fighting men, and had the pleasure of pouring cauldrons of boiling water over the ramparts to scald infidel heads. Many were fighting men themselves: many were faithful unto death; and no single Maltese ever deserted to the enemy.

Suddenly, like a shaft of sunlight in a lowering sky, the rumours of help coming from the slow-moving, prudent Viceroy of Sicily became joyful fact. A relieving force of some 9,000 men landed at Mellieha Bay, and marched southwards. For the Turks, it was the last straw. Exhaustion and disease had spread their wings across the heavens, like monstrous spectres; the remorseless toll of their dead could no longer be endured. Just as suddenly, fear took hold of their ranks.

Now they could never win . . . They faltered, and lowered their arms; then they turned away from the impossible task, and began to run helter-skelter for the ships, and to sail away, in utter rout, as fast as the sailors could embark them.

Perhaps it was true that the Turks were all mad. In the last hours, there was a fantastic story, witnessed by many, of a Turkish officer, a proud and invincible man, who mounted his restive horse and was promptly thrown, thus shaming himself before the world. He rose to his feet, drew his scimitar, ran back to the horse, and slashed off its legs before he took to his heels.

What happened to him? What could happen, to a man on foot beset by a dozen others aflame for his cursed blood? He should have trusted his horse . . . The defenders, now the

attackers, returned to the main Turkish rabble, the confusion
and terror of their retreat, and to the agreeable task of chasing
the last of the fugitives into the shallows of Mellieha Bay, and
a harbour now bare of ships to carry them away.

Suddenly there were no invincible Turks left in Malta. The
gates of St Angelo, of Birgu and Senglea, of the forts of St
Michael and Castile, were pushed open, and the inhabitants, in
the sweet silence of release, streamed out into the dayspring
of freedom.

Though they must mourn their dead bitterly – 250 Knights
and 7,000 others killed, leaving only 600 men fit to bear arms
out of a garrison of 9,000 – they could turn to rejoicing at what
they and their warriors had done to the enemy.

A bare ten thousand Turks were left alive, fleeing for home
to face the wrath of their Sultan and the laughter of the
world; and there remained Malta, unbroken, unchained, where
they need only remember glory, and the words of the blessed St
Francis of Assisi, who would greet everyone he met with the
words:

'My dear brother, God give thee peace.'

The Worst Day
of Father Salvatore

10 May 1942

That morning, Father Salvatore came with a heavy heart to visit his mother. He came straight from the prison – the crisply named Ta' Kordin – where his brother-in-law, stripped of his civil rights for the duration, had been under lock and key since the previous night. It was, to his family, an inconceivable blow, but it had happened none the less. Lewis Debrincat, at last, had gone too far.

The story was a remarkably silly one, even by Lewis's own standards of furtive enmity towards the war effort. He and certain of his friends had formed a club to send food parcels and other creature comforts to German and Italian prisoners of war – all airmen – captured and imprisoned in Malta. In theory, it was not such a terrible idea; it could even be seen as admirable, or at least as humane and charitable. But the club was called the Friends of Enemies, and before very long it took a wrong turning.

The evidence was uncertain, and would probably remain so for ever. But it was a fact, established by authority, that one food parcel, subjected to routine inspection, was found to contain some items which were not charitable at all, but were treasonable: notably a pocket compass, a sketch-map of the island, a sum of money, and an all-purpose 'escape tool' equally suitable for sawing prison bars and digging tunnels.

Responsibility was hotly denied. It was a police plant, the Friends of Enemies maintained. This was not credible, though it was *just* possible that the 'plot' was one stupid man's aberration, unknown to the rest of the club. The Friends were warned to stop it, anyway: to stop everything. While the dust of this was still settling, something happened which authority could not ignore or excuse.

An Italian pilot, baling out from an aircraft in flames, disappeared altogether. He was seen to land in a remote part of the island, but when the police and the military arrived, he was not to be found.

What was to be found, during the next few days, was a buried parachute, and a trail of gossip, speculation, and reliable evidence leading to a fishing-boat missing from Marfa harbour. The enemy pilot, in fact, had been hidden, and then helped to escape. The farm where the parachute was discovered belonged to one club member: the boat had probably been hired by another; and a news item in a Sicilian paper which presently found its way back to Malta cited, somewhat uncharitably, 'our thousands of true friends in Malta, with their headquarters in a certain house in Sliema.'

When the Debrincat home in Sliema was raided, nothing was found. But Lewis himself, under questioning, made one unwise answer and one revealing slip. Asked about his part in the affair, he denied all knowledge of it, but added: 'Would it be such a crime, to help a man who was only doing his duty for his country?' Questioned about the possible motives of those now proved to have been involved, he made a jaunty joke: 'I suppose they did it for the Chianti!'

A grim-faced security man interjected: 'What Chianti?'

'I mean, for Chianti. Like an Italian bribe.'

'But you said, *the* Chianti.'

'What difference does that make?'

It made a great deal. The buried parachute had been wrapped round a Chianti bottle, now empty, which the Italian pilot, a young man of spirit, had grabbed just before he baled out. Nothing about it had been mentioned before.

Though this was not hanging evidence, it was enough. Lewis had been warned about his conduct, long ago: the Friends of Enemies had been given the most explicit orders to close down all their operations, however innocent; they had all, obviously, persisted in their activities. They were promptly arrested, and interned; it was the first order of its kind signed by the new Governor of Malta, Lord Gort.

Lewis himself might be facing something worse than internment. It was small comfort to his friends and his family that, under another system, he would already have been shot or hanged. The disgrace was so hideous that nothing which happened to him now could make it worse.

Within the grim and grimy walls of the Corradino prison,

Father Salvatore had found a strangely contented man. Lewis Debrincat no longer cared about anything. In thought, he had long ago crossed the fatal frontier of treason; now he had done it in fact. As a result he was on the cross, doomed beyond doubt to crucifixion of one kind or another. Perhaps this was what he had always wanted, and if it needed a lunatic enterprise to bring it about, then he was ready for that also.

Having cast his vote, he now had nothing more to say except that he was *not* sorry.

When Father Salvatore, by privileged permission hard to obtain, entered the prison cell, he had found Lewis Debrincat still asleep. He lay on the stone shelf which was his bed, covered by a coarse grey blanket like the poorest shroud in the world : all that could be seen of him was a pallid, puffy, dawn face, a fringe of straggling hair, and the little pointed beard which he had never abandoned, even though the fashion had long been violently out of favour.

One could only feel sorry for such derelict humanity, and appalled by all the evidence of disrepute – the dank cell, the foul-smelling bucket in the corner, the door which a visitor had been ordered to leave open, the staring sentry on the alert for further signs of guilt. No man, however evil or foolish, should be brought so low. . . He advanced a few steps into the narrow slit of the room, and touched Lewis Debrincat on the chest.

Perhaps Lewis, weary of intrusion, had only been feigning sleep, for he opened his eyes immediately, without blinking at the light. He hunched his shoulders, and the threadbare blanket fell away, to reveal a sweat-stained under-shirt. Then he swung his legs, and sat up on the stone bed.

'*Bonġornu, sur kappillan.*' His voice was low, and his face indifferent. 'Have you come to see the condemned man? . . . I said that to you, two years ago. Remember?'

'Yes, I remember. And I said : "No one has condemned you".'

'You would hardly say that now.'

'How are you, Lewis?'

'Worse than yesterday, better than tomorrow.' But he did not sound sad about it, nor self-pitying : these were facts, not complaints.

'I'm terribly sorry this has happened.'

'Such a family disgrace!' But even this was not a sneer. The disgrace was a self-inflicted wound, and therefore private, not designed to cause trouble to anyone else.

'Is there anything you want?'

'No.'

Within the shadow of the doorway, the sentry coughed and shuffled his feet, as if to remind them that he – the man with the gun – was the man who would decide what Lewis Debrincat wanted, and what he would get.

'Can I take any messages for you?'

'No.' Lewis Debrincat, staring down at his feet, was a picture of polite resignation rather than despair. 'Just say that you saw me, and that I am – as you see me.'

'You must try not to worry.'

'Why should I worry? *They* have to worry, deciding what to do with me.' He raised his eyes for the first time, and they were astonishingly gentle. 'What would you do with me, Salvu?'

'I don't know.'

'Am I so hopeless?'

'You must have been very foolish.'

'I have been true to what I believe.' Suddenly Lewis drew the blanket round his shoulders, and lay down again. 'I'm sorry, Salvu. I don't want to talk to anyone any more.'

'I understand. I'll say goodbye. God bless you.'

'*Grazzi.*'

Whether it was thanks for the blessing of God, or thanks for coming, Father Salvatore did not know. With a last glance at what had now become a formless grey sack again, he backed out of the cell; and the guard, a stolid young policeman with a job to do, slammed the door shut as if glad to be quit of one offensive part of it. With the clang of the cell door echoing behind them, and their footsteps falling heavily on worn stone, they walked down the long corridor towards the free world of decent citizens.

Father Salvatore thought: How strange – I liked him more today than I ever did before. But as he left the prison, his heart grew weary again. A moment of private sympathy was no counterweight to the scandalized world outside.

2

The part of that world which was his mother's house had shrunk down until it was a shadow of all it had ever been. The Palazzo Santo-Nobile had (as Father Salvatore phrased it to himself) gone small again, after the brief glory and catastrophe of the Christmas party. Rooms which had been opened up with such generous hope had been dust-sheeted and closed off; the two larger wings of the house were now locked and barred, against the outside world, against their owner.

Old Gregory was gone, never to return to the living earth; Francis rejoined his regiment, never to return as long as there was a need for soldiers; two maids, a chef, and an ancient gardener who could not keep pace with spring, were all that was left of an establishment which had formerly numbered sixteen.

The baroness lived and slept downstairs in the armoury, where her cherished four-poster, canopied like Cleopatra's barge, had been reassembled after a week's painstaking carpentry. ('I wish to die where I was born' was all the reason required for this.) The sandbagged postern door was now the only entrance. Hens scratched a living in one corner of the coach-house. The shape of the great house, a lying shell, and the sunny courtyard within, remained as the sole witness of four centuries of merit and magnificence.

As with the house, so with the noble occupant. Father Salvatore, who in former days had never ceased to wonder at his mother's spirit and strength, with the same admiration as in boyhood, could only mourn to see what had befallen her. Even at seventy-two, she had still been the watch-tower to which all the Santo-Nobile family looked for guidance; the warranty that all was well. Now, at seventy-five, she was a little old woman who fretted because coffee was so hard to find, and derided the stupid doctors who knew nothing about rheumatism.

When he greeted her in the armoury, which was now no more than a lavishly appointed bed-sitting room, she seemed possessed by a single woe.

'This coffee!' she exclaimed pettishly, as she sipped it. Though poured from the same silver pot into the same blue-

and-gold fluted cups, it was indeed tasteless and gritty, like all the coffee in Malta. 'It's horrible! Do you know, we have to buy it in *packets*! Salvatore, surely there must be some way of getting coffee beans?'

'I'm afraid they're not importing them any more.'

'But do you *know* that? Who decides these things? When I think of the old days, when one only had to mention something like that to one of the equerries . . .'

He essayed a joke. 'I suppose father would have sent a warship to Colombia.'

'He would have done something!' She sipped again, and made a wry face. 'How I miss Gregory!'

'We all do that. . . But how are you, mother, apart from the coffee?'

Looking at her, as she sat in the tall-backed chair which was too big for the room, he really had no need to ask. She had shrunk with the house; she was old, and in poor health; the ebony stick which she had once despised as an enemy was now an essential friend. This pale, brittle, almost transparent woman whom he loved so much was beginning to lose her last race. . . The disgrace of the Christmas party had, he knew, dealt her a blow so raw that its brutality still lingered; and the bombing which now ravaged the city had ravaged her also.

Above all, she could not reconcile herself to the fall of the house of Santo-Nobile. She was ashamed of her state : shocked by many other things : and beginning to be afraid also.

Her next few words made this pitifully clear.

'I am as well as one can expect. . . If only there could be an end to this dreadful noise. . . Tell me, how is my famous son-in-law?'

It was a matter to be faced. 'I've just come from seeing him. Lewis is quite' – the absurd word could not be changed, 'quite happy.'

'In prison! How can that be?'

'I suppose he expected it – even wanted it – and now that it's happened he is resigned to everything.'

'Resigned to disgrace? What about his family?'

'I think he feels that he is alone.'

'He is *not* alone! He has dragged us all down with him! A traitor! He is worse than Benedict, with all his nonsense in Paris. What a generation!'

'You mustn't distress yourself, mother.'

'I am not *distressed*.' Her trembling hand was making the coffee cup rattle in the saucer, and she put it down with a final clatter. 'I am *very angry*.' How sad that the words, which once could have made the hearer, whether high or low, stand in fear of what might come next, were now only sounds, as empty and futile as if she had whispered them against the winds of heaven. So the Baroness was angry? Well, she must just lump it. . . 'It should have been hushed up, anyway. This would never have happened if Sir William Dobbie were still here.'

The voice of privilege was equally futile, and he could not ignore it. 'I'm afraid that's not true, mother. Lewis went much too far. Helping the enemy in wartime is – is the most serious crime. It couldn't be hushed up.'

'Then Lewis must be mad! I always knew it. I knew it when he made that disgusting scene at Christmas. And he always *looks* so terrible... What will happen to him, Salvatore?'

He had already worked this out, from his modest knowledge of the law.

'At the best, he will be interned for the rest of the war. At the worst – if he is brought to trial and found guilty – he might spend fifteen years in prison.'

'Nothing worse?'

'What could be worse than that?'

'I do not wish to give Lewis Debrincat a welcome-home party when I am ninety ...' She had recovered a little of her spirit, though the reason was not commendable; she had resented her son-in-law for at least twenty years, and the total of that should be included in the sentence. 'Well, I can do nothing for him now, even if I wanted to. I have not even met this Lord Gort.'

'I expect he's busy, like everyone else.'

'But he must hold some sort of reception. There was always a *levée* for a new Governor. When Field-Marshal Lord Plumer arrived—'

Father Salvatore put his hand up to his face, in an involuntary gesture of weariness. With all the love in the world, he could only feel that his mother's complaints were trivial and selfish. People were *hungry* in Malta; people – particularly the old – were *dying*, of poor food, of rotten food, of no food at all; people were fading out of life, giving up hope, not because coffee now came in cheap packets, not because the new Governor had failed to hold a *levée*, but under merciless twin pressures which could no longer be endured – the bombing which was beating their brains out, and the hunt for scraps of food which sickened all appetite.

That was Malta, 1942. Nothing else. Not even Lewis Debrincat and his crass, mean treachery. People did not die of disgrace. They died because they could no longer live.

Something of this sad despair must have shown in his face or manner, for the Baroness suddenly paused in her nostalgic description of the martial elegance of Lord Plumer's swearing-in, and asked:

'Is anything the matter, Salvatore? Are you feeling unwell?'

'No, no.' He collected himself, and sat up straight in his chair. 'I'm sorry. I was thinking of something else.'

'You've been looking so tired lately. Are you getting enough sleep? Enough to eat?'

'Oh yes.'

'You really need a proper rest. And I'm not the only one who thinks so.'

He smiled. 'Who else thinks so?'

'The bishop. He is quite sure that you are wearing yourself out.'

'Not more than anyone else. There's so much to do, and it must be done. Otherwise ...' But there was no 'otherwise' in war. It must be done. 'Do you know, we have had eight funerals from the catacombs in the last few weeks?'

'The bombing?'

'No. The bombing is extra, I'm afraid. This was just – giving up. Exhaustion, I suppose. And we've had some food-poisoning, too. When people are hungry, they'll eat anything.' Then he queried something which, uneasily, had caught his attention. 'Why should the bishop think I am wearing myself out? He really can't know much about me.'

'I can assure you, he knows a great deal. You are becoming quite famous, you know.'

'At last?'

'It is not a joke, Salvatore. Sooner or later you will—' she stopped suddenly. It was clear that she had been going to quote a certain remark, a certain form of words, and had then

decided against it. Instead she finished: 'Sooner or later you
must have a real rest.'

He was not going to venture further. Whatever the bishop
thought or said about him, whatever the bishop had been told
about him, must somehow be kept at bay; and the best way of
doing that was to know nothing, and thus to avoid worrying
about the answers.

He said: 'I don't want to rest before we can all rest,' and
stood up, more promptly than good manners would have dictated. 'I'm afraid I must go, mother. There are quite a lot of
things to do. And we have our first wedding this afternoon.
Remember? They are so grateful for your generous present.'

'What a time to get married!' she answered, and it was, at
last, the simple Maltese truth. Then she seemed, in a brief
instant, to gather her strength, to become real again. As he bent
to kiss and bless her, she said: 'Give my dearest love to
Giovanna and the children. You will know what to say to
them – better than I do, perhaps.' Her frail, lined face had a
kind of beseeching look which he had never seen before. 'I'm
silly sometimes, aren't I? You must forgive me.'

He was deeply moved. 'There is nothing to forgive.'

'There is something every day. But Salvatore—'

'What?'

'If you *are* going shopping – and if you *do* hear of any coffee
beans—'

It was a brave joke, and a brave acknowledgement: so much
so that, even as he left the armoury and walked across the
courtyard, he found himself wondering: Now where *could*
there be coffee beans? How wonderful if somewhere in Valletta,
somewhere in the island, some huge forgotten sack of this
rarity was only waiting to be liberated.

Lewis would have known.

3

He spent the rest of the morning in shopping – scavenging
would have been a better word – not for fragrant Colombian
coffee beans, which in sober consideration could not be high
on his list, but for some of the meagre necessities of life in the
catacombs: for the powdered milk which the children must

have, for olive oil – or anything resembling olive oil – which would make dry food eatable, for pasta however coarse or mouldy, for fish that was not positively foul-feeding. Had even honest fish deserted Malta? One could hardly blame them. Who would wish to swim in this direction, if they could swim in any other?

The food situation on the island had now become so desperate that it had overtaken even the bombing as the worst misery of their lives.

During the last few days the newspapers had been full of the arrival of a new Governor, to succeed Sir William Dobbie. Dobbie, the 'Cromwellian soldier' as Churchill called him when speeding his departure, had worn himself out in the defence of his island; he was also losing heart about the result, as his last dispatches showed. These spoke of his distress at 'Malta's critical position', and gave warning that 'the very worst may happen if we cannot replenish our vital needs, especially flour and ammunition, and that very soon... It is a question of survival.'

Churchill's judgement was that the man, if not the island, was headed for a total breakdown, and he replaced him with Lord Gort. Gort arrived from Gibraltar in a flying boat, which landed off Kalafrana at the height of an air-raid. He met General Dobbie in a hut ashore – a hut already ruined by bombing, its windows covered with flattened petrol tins – and there the oath of office was administered, by a Chief Justice bleeding from a near-miss. Gort and Dobbie then shook hands, and the exhausted ex-Governor took off in the same plane.

Lord Gort, arriving in such heightened drama, had considerable personal *panache* as well. He was a Field-Marshal, and a lord. He had a string of names – John Standish Surtees Prendergast Vereker, sixth Viscount Gort – and a string of magnificent medals to match: the Victoria Cross (from 1918), the Distinguished Service Order, the Military Cross, and nine Mentions in Dispatches. In addition, he brought to what must have seemed a doomed island a medal of its own: the insignia of the George Cross, awarded to the whole of Malta three weeks earlier, with a citation from King George VI which did not overstate the case:

To honour her brave people I award the George Cross to the

*island fortress of Malta, to bear witness to a heroism and
devotion that will long be famous in history.*

Even the Russians, not given to praising their allies, sent their
congratulations at the same time. But when Lord Gort made
his first tour of Valletta, he was greeted, on certain street
corners, by men who stood in silence and rubbed their bellies
with a circular motion. They were giving him a message: not
an insult, not a threat, not a prayer: just a message:

'We cannot eat the George Cross.'

It was a fact – stated and suffered by Dobbie, confirmed by
Gort – that Malta was now within a few weeks of starvation
and defeat. There was already talk, official talk, of a 'target
date', beyond which the island could not possibly survive without fresh supplies of food and weapons. What was this date?

No one could say except the men wrestling with the dwindling stock-lists, and they were forced to keep silence, and to
hope. The man in the street could only confirm, like the new
Governor, that there was, in Malta, no longer enough to eat.

What was to be had in the shops? Nothing much. The things
that were not rationed disappeared into the limbo of the unobtainable: the things that were quickly shrank down to contemptible levels. There was almost no sugar, cooking-oil, soap,
or flour. There was no butter, no jam, and no potatoes until
the next harvest. Since there were no cows, there was no fresh
milk, and Malta's 35,000 goats had to fill the gap.

Even bread – plain bread, the staple of life – was now a
luxury; from the three loaves a day, scooped out and refilled
with a stiffening of garlic and tomato paste, which were a
working man's natural expectation, the allowance was now half
a loaf, and that half-loaf had a perceptible content of potato
peelings mixed with its reclaimed flour dust.

By an inevitable process of strangulation, one shortage led to
another, and so on down the line. There was no more coal, so
the power-stations faltered and electricity was cut off. People
turned to kerosene, and presently there was none of that either.
After that it was wood and candles, until these in turn ran out;
and then it was cold food, and bed at sunset.

Certain treasures commanded a price which would have
made an angel weep. If it could ever be found, meat, real meat,
cost £1 a *ratal* (about 1¾ lbs). Rabbits and chickens were another

2*s* each. An honest loaf, made from honest black-market flour, cost 10*s*. There was a time when snails became popular, and then they too disappeared. The joke-question: 'How do they run so fast?' was a sour joke indeed.

Stranger things than snails had a habit of disappearing. When a bomb fell near a man driving a horse-and-cart through Kalkara, the horse was killed by stray splinters. The man, after taking shelter, went off to get help; and when he came back, the horse was not to be seen. An eatable horse was worth a princely £40.

What was being done about this civil famine, which hardly gave a man the strength to work next day? The best that could be, with the best that could be found. Since supplies from outside were no longer reaching Malta, except in small packets by submarine and small cargoes from the occasional ship which passed the blockade: since even food-boats from Gozo – *luzzus* and schooners – were mined or sunk by low-flying planes: since little more could be grown on an island which had not been self-supporting since Napoleon, like the Knights before him, had dismissed it as a barren rock, every scrap of food had to be hoarded, and fairly shared out.

Rationing was rigidly enforced: bread every day, kerosene every fortnight – though only enough for four hot meals during the next fourteen days. Then communal 'Victory Kitchens' were established – 'So that we can all starve equally', as the grim saying went – and with the help of the Army (itself on half-rations) these fed a regular 200,000 people a day.

The kitchens provided one square meal, at 6*d* a time plus ration-points, to be collected at noon or at 5 PM; as early as nine every morning, a long queue of saucepans and pots were placed on the pavement outside, to stand sentinel for the hungry owners. Often the meal could hardly be called square; a sample would be three thin sausages, and fifteen peas, to be divided between three people; or soup with beans, or a slice of corned beef, or a hunk of goat in pasta, or tinned fish.

On one day, a band of infuriated or despairing housewives picked up their day's 'meal', and marched in a body to Government House to protest. What they were protesting was a hand-out, costing precious points on the rationing system, of some squares of greenish liver floating in watered gravy. But on that particular day of national housekeeping, it was all that was available.

How did people really live, in their wrecked and beleaguered island? They lived very small. They grew thinner and weaker from lack of food; starved of essential calories, they suffered from scabies, and the pangs of hunger within were matched by the maddening itch of flaking skin. Throughout that summer there was a widespread typhoid epidemic, a product of broken sewage pipes, contaminated reservoirs, and the use of raw excrement to irrigate fields during a 'Grow More Food' campaign.

Shelter-life bred verminous children. The crash of bombs led to ruined eardrums. The use of cotton-wool ear-plugs made for a brooding family despair.

Even when they found something to cook, many bombed-out families had nothing better than rough stoves carved out of stone, and with these they made the most of that dwindling kerosene ration, which had sunk to the rate of one quarter of a gallon per week for two people. They made the most also of the water allowance – eight gallons a day, which sounded a lot but was not: a flushed toilet used two gallons, and a bath was beyond the dreams of any normal household.

They made the most of the sun, putting tins of water on the roof and letting the heat bring it half-way to boiling-point. A bootlace or a piece of string stuck in a kerosene bottle furnished a light of sorts, when the wavering electricity finally died.

They queued for everything, and more often than not came away disappointed, with half a day wasted for nothing. Hundreds of people waited for hours to pick up the weekly ration of one packet of cigarettes. But these were luxuries; now, even the things taken for granted during a whole lifetime were rationed like gold-dust.

As the 'target date' approached, this was a weary woman's hope, for a week of such queueing:

Bread: 73 oz.
Fats: 3½ oz.
Cheese: 1¾ oz.
Coffee: 1¾ oz.
Milk (goat): 3 pints
Tomatoes: 3 lbs
Potatoes: 1½ lbs

Matches: 1 box
Sugar, rice, flour, tea, oil, butter, soap, jam, and
meat: NIL.

The rations for Senglea and the Three Cities were brought
across Grand Harbour from Valletta by *dghajsa*, and often, on
the return journey, the *dghajsas* carried corpses for burial
inland. The obscenity of this grisly trade seemed, after a
while, as normal as any other bargain. 'What was that target
date again?' 'When the bread runs out.' Or would it be the
dead?

Father Salvatore, touring the shops and store-rooms of Valletta
for the hundredth time, was feeling something less than human.
It always happened. As with thousands of others, it was brought
home to him once again that he was now only a troublesome
statistic, a unit of consumption caught up in this dreary web,
serving only to crowd and tangle it beyond endurance. It would
be better if he disappeared off the face of the island.

He had a shopping-list – of things that Nero said they *must*
have, things that other people had begged him to try for, things
he had thought of himself. But he might as well have let the
slips of paper blow away on the wind, and sink in Grand Harbour with the rest of the rubbish, for all the use they were to
him.

There was always the same answer, from harassed shop-
keepers who, because he was a priest, and a friend, did not
give him the rough side of a professional tongue. No, there was
no pasta to be had. No, there was no flour to make it – had he
not heard the man on the wireless say so? No, no one had seen
a bar of chocolate since – oh, since the last Christmas rush
cleaned out the shelves. There was no spare soap; soap was on
the ration, and now it was off the ration, and God knew when
it would appear again. He wanted milk powder? He must be
joking!

There was only one good thing, in the whole of that morning,
and that was the weather, which was hot, sunny, and (compared with the past) perfect. They had had an atrocious winter;
cold, with torrents of rain; now at last the merry month of
May had relented, and a man could stand on a street corner –
or what could vaguely be remembered as a street corner, two

years ago when the world was young and innocent – and enjoy a breath of warm air.

Considering what they were going through, they were astonishingly cheerful, the crowds which thronged Valletta's tumbled streets. The mood of 'We cannot eat the George Cross' must have been there, and occasionally it could be glimpsed in a sullen face, or an argument between neighbours, or a quarrel about a kerosene tin which had been spirited to the top of the queue while no one was looking. But there was still good nature to be seen, and friendly greetings to be heard, and courage in adversity, and humour among hungry men as they compared the number of holes remaining to be tightened in their belts.

It was enough to make Father Salvatore praise God, and to persist in his forlorn search. He was determined to find something which he had promised Nero: something special for the wedding feast. They had the cake already, saved and scrimped for, built up almost piece by piece from hoarded flour, eggs begged one by one from every hen-owner he could trace, sugar wrung and even hammered from empty bags which could still surrender a grain or two.

They had the wine also, a magnificent 140-gallon butt of it, brewed from the sweet muscat grapes in the Santo-Nobile vineyards near Mdina, and sent by the Baroness as an extra gift 'to bless the marriage'.

But 'Please find something special for us!' Nero had repeated, as they said goodbye at dawn. 'Even if it's only enough for two. We can't get married on Widow's Soup!' So he kept on with his search, acknowledging secretly that part of this persistence was a cowardly wish to delay his next appointment. Lunch at the Casa Debrincat was not, on this particular morning, something one hurried to.

In the end he succeeded. Picking his way, on aching feet, down lower town, through the mean slit of St Nicholas Street which had at its end that enchanting glimpse of blue water, he came upon a young man he knew. This was Wenzu Tonna, the son of old Angelo, the *barklor*, who was now so busy with his cross-harbour *dghajsa* that he did not bother with passengers.

Angelo had a contract with the Food Office, for the delivery of rations, and perhaps another sort of contract for the return journey. He was one of the affluent heirs of this war. His son Wenzu, who ran a general shop, was probably another.

Wenzu Tonna was a fat, sharp-eyed, greasy young man in stained overalls. He stood outside the flapping bamboo curtain of his shop door – one of a thousand such curtains masking the thousand holes-in-the-wall which housed Valletta's retail trade – and smiled equally at all passers-by. He did not look like an angel, but he proved to be one.

'Dun Salv!' Wenzu greeted him as a friend, which was within limits true, and as a man with family connections. The sister of old Angelo was an inmate of the catacombs: not one of the best inmates – she complained too much, she was mean like her brother, and she put on airs because Angelo had a better trade than most of her neighbours. But she had lived there since the beginning, which was a compliment of sorts, and certainly a connection. 'How good to see you on a morning like this! How's my auntie?'

'Well enough,' Father Salvatore answered. 'She has a bad leg, as you know.'

'She is lucky to have a leg at all,' Wenzu said uncharitably. 'Did you hear about the man in Old Bakery Street who was trapped by a girder? They had to take off both legs with a saw, right there on the pavement! They say there was blood—'

'I know,' Father Salvatore interrupted. He had had enough of horrors; there was no story of bombing in Malta which could not be capped by a worse one. He looked beyond Wenzu at the bamboo curtain. 'Well, what have you got for me today?'

Wenzu's eyes, wide with the pleasures of tale-telling, quickly narrowed down to bargain-size again. 'It depends what you want, Dun Salv. But if I said "Nothing", I wouldn't be telling a lie.'

Father Salvatore went through his list once more. For rationed goods he had the coupons, collected from all over the catacombs; for anything else, he had hope. But the answer, like all the earlier answers of the day, never varied. Wenzu Tonna had nothing, on or off the ration, which had not gone to his customers already.

He kept spreading his hands, in the familiar gesture of despair. Times were hard. Food was short. This cursed war... Sometimes he could cry at the stories people told him. But he could not *make* food. He could not even make a decent living.

The priest, as one Maltese to another, persisted. There was something in Wenzu's manner which indicated an area of negotiation. There was also something in his reputation.

'Well, have you anything *special*? I want it for the wedding.'

Wenzu's eyes opened wide again. 'A wedding? What wedding is this?'

'My sacristan is getting married this afternoon. Your auntie must have mentioned it. Nero Cassar.'

'Oh, the little fellow. Yes, I did hear something. Let's see – who is it he's marrying?'

'Teresa Grima. From Mellieha.'

'Mellieha? Why aren't they getting married there?'

'Family reasons. It's more convenient in the catacombs, so that's how it's been arranged.'

'Ah, well.' Wenzu smelled a rat of some kind, but he also heard something in Father Salvatore's tone which halted further questioning. 'I hope they'll be happy. As happy as anyone can be, these days. A wedding in the catacombs, eh? I wish I could do something for them.'

'I'm sure you could, if you tried.'

'It would need a miracle! Like Cana in Galilee!' Father Salvatore let the joke go; if it was blasphemy, at least it was appropriate. 'All I've got is a tin of biscuits.'

'Well, that's something.' It might be everything. 'What sort of biscuits?'

'They're called dog-biscuits. Little round ones. It's a special import: you don't often see them here.' He noted Father Salvatore's face, and spread his hands again. 'Yes, I know it sounds funny, Dun Salv. But if you chopped them in half, and put a bit of jam on top—'

'Have you any jam?'

'Not a spoonful.'

'Then it's no use.' It would have been no use anyway. Dog-biscuits... But even now he would not give up, and he had a card left to play, a good card for the right man. He turned as if to go, and then turned back. 'Do you still make wine, Wenzu?'

As soon as he said it, he knew that he had been right. It *was* a good card, a genuine Maltese bargaining card, the kind that opened a crack in a closing door. He knew this because Wenzu Tonna, who had been looking straight at him, and smiling from time to time, now looked sideways up the street as if some strange curiosity had caught his attention. Then his head came round again, and he was grave, and wary.

'I make a little wine,' Wenzu answered. 'Just for the family, and a few friends. But I've none left to sell. Last year was a bad year, even for wine.'

'I don't want to buy wine. We have plenty.'

'You're lucky... They say it's going to be a bad year, even for *barrels*. That's why I don't think I'll bother. People are burning them for firewood! I suppose you can't blame them, but it's such a waste.'

'Tomorrow, or the next day, I might have an empty barrel.'

'Is that so? An old barrel?'

'No. A new one. And a huge one too. A hundred-and-forty gallons. It has the Santo-Nobile arms on it.' There were possibilities here that he did not wish to think about. 'Would that be any use to you?'

Wenzu Tonna considered the matter. 'I suppose I could take it off your hands.'

'It's worth a bit more than that.'

'Maybe, maybe. A barrel like that takes up a lot of money.' It was a curious slip, which delighted Father Salvatore, and Wenzu corrected it swiftly. 'I mean, a lot of room.' He backed away towards the bamboo blind, motioning with his head for the priest to follow him. 'Come inside, Dun Salv. It's too hot out here. And I've just thought of something.'

Inside, there was the deep gloom of a windowless room, and a smell of musty sacks. Then shelves, mostly bare, could be made out, and two tables for coffee-drinking customers, and grubby cases of empty bottles, and buzzing flies, and a counter with a pair of battered scales. But on the counter was something else, hidden by a muslin cover; and over this a small child was bending, a boy with his hand outstretched.

'*Ejja!*' Wenzu shouted. 'Get away from that!'

'I was just looking,' the boy whined.

'Then go and look somewhere else. I've got business.'

As the boy ran through the door at the back, Wenzu's expression altered. The bad-tempered father became the good-hearted business man again.

'I've just thought of something,' he said again. 'It's only just been made. That's why I forgot it.' He pointed towards the muslin cloth. 'What would you say to a nice veal loaf?'

There were a lot of things Father Salvatore could have said to a nice veal loaf, which was an unheard-of luxury these days, but he contented himself with:

'It sounds wonderful.'

'It *is* wonderful!' Wenzu Tonna removed the cover gently, almost reverently, exposing a large object which polite society would have called a galantine of veal. Even in the murky light, it shone with richness: the glazed surface was decorated with sprigs of parsley, and beneath the pale golden gelatine shell could be seen quite large pieces of meat, real meat.

It was at least two feet long, and it looked succulent beyond the dreams of hungry man.

Father Salvatore sighed, and swallowed. 'It's just what we want.'

'I'll say it is. The finest ingredients! It must weigh fifteen *ir-ratal.*'

Father Salvatore peered again, more carefully. 'But what's in it? A lot of the meat is white. But veal? You can't get veal these days.'

'You can't get anything these days. That's the best goat in Malta. As good as veal, any day. As good as lamb.'

'Then what's the dark meat?'

'What dark meat?'

Father Salvatore pointed. 'There seem to be bits of—'

'It's only the shadow.' Wenzu sounded rather hurt. 'You've got to admit, it's a splendid veal loaf.'

'Would it be horse, Wenzu?'

The other man shrugged his shoulders. 'Perhaps. Just for colouring. These are difficult times. But taken as a whole—'

'Oh, I agree.' He watched while Wenzu put back the muslin cloth, as carefully as if he were covering the face of the dear departed. 'Well, thank you very much. It will make a wonderful wedding feast. God will bless you, Wenzu.'

But God was not quite ready to bless either of them.

'I'm glad it suits you, Dun Salv.' Wenzu rubbed his hands. 'What shall we say? Sixteen pounds?'

'*What?*'

Father Salvatore was genuinely taken aback. He had thought that this was to be a straight exchange, the veal loaf for the barrel – the barrel which he was sure Wenzu had somehow heard about, and had coveted. *Sixteen pounds?* It was a ridiculous price, even without the barrel; and dearly as he wanted this 'something special' for the wedding feast, there were limits to such wild extravagance. There were limits also to submission – submission to sharp practice. But before he could speak Wenzu forestalled him, very adroitly.

'Oh, I know it sounds a lot, Dun Salv. But look at the size of it. If I sold it by the slice, I could make twenty pounds. Maybe more. People would be round like vultures!'

'That's not what I meant,' Father Salvatore answered sharply. 'What about the barrel?'

'Oh, I'll take care of the barrel for you. Don't you worry about that.'

'That's not what I meant,' he repeated. 'And you know that perfectly well. The barrel is worth a great deal of money.'

'Is it?' Wenzu's eyes widened. 'I thought you wanted it carted away.'

'And sixteen pounds is far too much, anyway.'

'Not for a veal loaf as big as this.'

The real bargaining began.

But even this was more formal than real, like the end of a dance in which pattern was all, and feeling almost excluded. There was a certain price, Father Salvatore now knew, which Wenzu would take: it might not be quite as high as sixteen pounds, but it would be very close to it. The Maltese did not bargain like Arabs, or like Indians, or like Jews in a Lebanese bazaar; they had their own style.

Not for them the inflated demand, and then the acceptance of half what they asked. They set a good price, a fighting price; and from that, if they chose to retreat, it would be a single step backwards – and it would not be taken at all if they were treated rudely, or roughly, or with the contempt of the tourist for the seller of trinkets.

This feeling, this understanding, was in Father Salvatore's blood as well as Wenzu's. He knew that if his counter-offer was too low, or too brusque, that would be the end of the matter. Wenzu would not sell the veal loaf at all; he would rather have it rot on the shelves before he agreed. If Father Salvatore said: 'Ten pounds – take it or leave it,' Wenzu would turn his head aside, and that would be that.

It did not happen. 'For you, and for the wedding, fourteen

pounds,' Wenzu said, not more than three minutes later. They shook hands, and the small fever abated. 'For that, I'll have it delivered. My dad can take it across on his last trip, and the boy will bring it out to the catacombs. And thank you for the barrel.'

The barrel was worth at least another ten pounds, but not to Father Salvatore. He only wanted the veal loaf, and he had got it. Not for the first time, he wondered at the persistent appetite of men; he wondered that, in the midst of war, the blind-worm of commerce could still wriggle and thrust and bore its way onwards, with such greedy devotion.

It was not only Wenzu Tonna: it was himself, it was Malta in both of them... The prizes were an empty barrel, and some money, and a veal loaf made of chopped goat and horsemeat. But they were as real, and as precious, as victory.

'There's just one more thing,' Wenzu said as they parted.

'Now, Wenzu!'

'No, it's not for me. But you'll see my auntie gets a good slice, won't you?'

'I promise.'

He went on his way rejoicing, in a glow of triumph. A veal loaf... It would be the wedding of the year... Fourteen pounds was a terrible price to pay, even for such a rarity; but no man who had secured exactly what he wanted need feel that he had been duped.

As he walked towards Sliema he made the most of his foolish happiness. The non-fool in him knew that it was likely to be the last of the day.

4

There was a police guard on the Debrincat house: a fact so shameful and senseless that it could hardly be reconciled with the world of sanity at all. What was the purpose of a policeman with a gun, standing at the foot of the steps of a house on the Sliema sea-front? Was he keeping watch on the inmates? Was he scrutinizing their visitors? Was he there to protect them all from infuriated patriots, who might storm the building and black their treacherous eyes?

Was he perhaps a departmental artefact, a thing that happened when certain security files came to the boil and threw off a physical manifestation – in this case a man in blue?

Perhaps it did not matter. The man in blue was there anyway. Lunch with a shamed family included this particular decoration; and it was a small embarrassment, compared with what the family itself must be enduring... With a guarded politeness – he was a priest, he was neutral, he was beyond suspicion in a world of vigilance – Father Salvatore nodded to the policeman, rang the bell, and was presently admitted by Carmelina.

Carmelina had been crying, and looked ready to do so again. It seemed that he was always meeting Carmelina in tears; once, long ago, it had been for the war itself, then for her father, then for old Gregory, now for the master of the house. But she had more spirit today, in the midst of sorrow. She was eighteen, she was engaged to a soldier, she was no small part of the war herself. Before she closed the door she glared at the policeman, whose wary back seemed to proclaim that he had endured this scrutiny before; then she shut it so firmly that the action could be called a slam.

But, alone with the priest in the silent hall, she became Carmelina again, simple, dependent, and out of her depth. Her pretty eyes beseeched him as she said:

'Oh, Dun Salv, isn't it awful? They took him away in a big black car!'

There was nothing profitable to be said about that. 'You mustn't worry too much, Carmelina. These things happen. Pray for him. That is all.'

'But what has he done?' Her clasped hands indicated all sorts of imagined horrors, and now she put them into words. 'Is it true the master will be hanged?'

'Carmelina! Of course not! You mustn't talk like that. Where did you get such an idea?'

'Francis said he was a traitor.'

It was a difficult point. 'He did something very stupid. I'm afraid we must admit that. But to talk of hanging is silly. When I saw him this morning—'

'Do you mean one can still *see* him?'

'Of course.'

'You are so brave, Dun Salv!'

The picture was confused, and it was not getting any better. Father Salvatore took refuge in a traditional formula. 'What's for lunch, Carmelina?'

'I think it's fish pie.'

'But that's wonderful!' He had to make up for Carmelina's notable lack of enthusiasm. 'Fish is very hard to get.'

'We've had it all this week, Dun Salv. Miss Marija's friend brought a whole basket.'

'I didn't know he was a fisherman.'

'He said they were killed by a bomb.'

It was possible. But before Father Salvatore had time to explore this further, there was a step behind him, and when he turned it was his sister Giovanna, crossing the hall from the patio. The moment he had been dreading was at hand.

She seemed composed, though pale, and dressed in black, which gave her a sad air of bereavement. She said, in a normal tone: 'I thought I heard your voice, Salvu,' and kissed him in welcome. But as soon as Carmelina withdrew, her face and manner altered. She became, indeed, more like Carmelina: puzzled, bewildered, barely able to cope with a shocking array of facts and happenings. She asked immediately: 'Have you seen Gigi?'

'Yes. I went there early this morning.' It was difficult to avoid the terrible word 'prison', but he was determined to do so. 'He had a good night, and he is quite comfortable.'

'You are so wonderful, Salvu... Did he send any message?'

A priest could not lie. 'No.'

'Does he want anything?'

'No.'

Her control showed signs of failing. 'But what does he expect us to *do*? You say he had a good night? Does he think *we* had a good night? It's so disgusting, the whole thing!'

He put his hand on her arm. 'You must be brave, Gio. What's done is done. Lewis took a chance. He knew quite well what he was doing, and he was caught. That's all there is. Now he must be punished, and we must go on without him.'

'But what will happen to him?'

'I don't know.'

'Will he stay in prison?'

'Yes, I'm sure of that.'

'Well, that's one good thing.' And as he looked at her, sad and surprised, she burst out uncontrollably: 'He was making our lives hateful! You must know that. I'm *glad* he was caught! Why should I pretend? Why should the children pretend? Now he's disgraced us all, but there are worse things than that. He *destroyed* everything, long ago.'

'But he's your husband.'

'Not any more... It's no good looking at me like that, Salvu. I don't care what the Church says. Let him stay in his prison. We are free! And we are going to stay free. I will never live with him again.'

Her high voice ceased, choked with feeling, and he could not answer. There were things he ought to say, but the moment for saying them was not now, and might never be. Beyond doubt, this was the end of contentment, of reputation, and of love. What could a priest, a stranger to such turmoils, a stranger to love and hate, marriage and the end of marriage, really contribute to such a moment?

He might talk of duty and sacrifice, but they would be false words, because he would not have to live them himself, in such intimate misery.

He had never felt so ineffectual, nor so confused. All he knew was that, this morning, in this house, he could no longer be a priest. He could only be a brother.

'Giovanna?'

'Yes?'

'Where are the children? What are they doing?'

'Crying, I expect.' But already she was calmer, because he had allowed her so much, because he was not going to argue or lecture. 'I don't know where they are, Salvu. We're all separate today... But they'll be hungry in half an hour, bless them.'

'Fish pie, I'm told.'

'It may not be too popular. All they dream about is sausages and mashed potatoes... But thank goodness Michael is coming to lunch.'

The girl for whom Michael's coming to lunch was the most important thing in the world sat in her bedroom, staring at the mirror. Though the clear sunshine was revealing, it did not bother her; the full glare of daylight, falling on the nineteen-year-old face of Marija Debrincat, could search and search again before it found a flaw. It seemed that cruel starvation suited her, whatever her dear grandmother had forecast.

On this particular morning she was secretly pleased – but only because Michael would be pleased – that she had not 'lost her looks' (that daunting phrase from some forgotten Victorian novel) during the last horrid twenty-four hours. It was no longer possible to tell that she had been crying, and had gone to bed in shattering, red-eyed misery.

She had shed no tears for her father: only for her mother, the worst sufferer from all the humiliation and disgrace. To watch her father crossing the hall on his way to the front door, flanked by two plain-clothes policemen, carrying a silly little bag with his 'night things', had not really been moving: she had seen it so many times before, in films – it was only James Cagney or George Raft, on their several ways to the courthouse or the condemned cell.

But to have to cling to her mother after the front door shut, because her mother was clinging to her: to feel a dear body racked with sobs, to dry someone else's tears before she dried her own – that was the wickedness, the only part that mattered, or would ever be remembered again.

Waking next morning, she had been at first appalled, then rebellious at the destruction wrought by love, then strong once more. All she needed to do was to recall Michael, on another wretched day also smirched by her father, telling her: 'Never forget – they are *them*. We are *us*.' At the time it had sounded selfish, and contrary to all accepted teachings; now it seemed the only thing to believe.

The new alliance was herself and Michael, with all spare support given to her mother. Thank God that Michael, the rock of her new life, would soon come back from that perilous sky-world he never talked about, and they would be hand-in-hand again.

She looked once more at her face, at her eyes which hid thoughts and then betrayed them, at her bare shoulders which for some reason were his delight, at all the rest which a loosely tied bathrobe revealed. There was very little of her body that he did not know, and after a shy start she had matched that knowledge with her own. She gloried in the fact that she could excite him to such splendid manhood, and need no longer leave him dissatisfied save in the last thing of all.

He could still call her 'my virgin', as he often did, without complaint, without wanting to persuade her otherwise. She could still be content with the touch of his hands, not less skilful than her own in exciting, cresting, and releasing the

tormented urges of her body. They could talk of this without
fear or shame. 'We don't do so badly, do we?' he had once
asked, when they were both spent in ecstasy at exactly the
same moment.

She had been trembling and gasping in his arms, cradled in a
wild rocking paradise. It was some moments before she had
been calm enough to answer: 'We do very well. But don't stop
wanting to marry me.'

'I don't think that's my problem.' As usual at such moments,
his voice had gone husky, deep in his throat. 'Is it yours?'

She shook her head, against the rough facing of his tunic. 'I
want it a little more each time.'

'How long, Marija?'

'As long as the war, I suppose. Not a moment longer.'

'Oh well, if *that's* all. . .' He suddenly released her, and sprang
to his feet, with that renewed vigour which, at such moments,
always astonished her.

'What *are* you doing?'

'I'm off to finish it.'

How wonderful that he was coming to lunch.

The boy to whom Michael's coming to lunch was an agonizing
embarrassment and shame was lying on the roof, playing with
the model Hurricane which was still his dearest possession.
Pietru Pawl had come racing home from school, tears on his
face, rage and fear in his heart. He had brushed past his mother
in the hall, wild for solitude. 'Everyone knows!' he called out,
and ran upstairs in stumbling misery.

School had been a torment. Though there had been nothing
yet in the newspapers, everyone had heard already: everyone
whispered, or laughed, or looked sideways at him. The worst of
the masters, an old brute of a priest who taught them Latin
grammar, had purposely ignored him all through the lesson,
even though his hand had often gone up first with the answer;
and one of the boys had walked out behind him, whistling
'*Giovinezza*' and giving the fascist salute.

His father was in prison, and everyone knew it, and it was
the end of the world. Now he had stationed himself on the roof,
because if there was an air-raid, and a bomb fell on the house,
as he prayed would happen, he wanted it to kill him first.

He was almost ashamed to touch the Hurricane, even as he

stroked its smooth fuselage and turned its propellers. *What would Michael think?*

Raising his head above the stone parapet, he watched his uncle Salvu come up the steps, past the awful policeman who was the badge of disgrace, the plague sign on the whole house. How could Michael bring himself to pass the same guard? Why should he have to? Uncle Salvu was a priest, and an uncle. He had come to comfort them, and he would say that it was all for the best, or that they mustn't pass judgement on their father, or even that a man was entitled to his own opinions.

Michael was a fighter pilot, and he wouldn't think like that at all. He would think the whole thing was disgusting, and he would be right, and perhaps he would never come back again.

The sun was hot, the sky clear and blue, the water in Sliema Creek sparkling. There was a drone of aircraft overhead, but no warning signal to match it. So it must be one of their own... Perhaps it was Michael himself, winging back from some terrific dog-fight over Sicily, shooting down the Italians, the Italians whom his father wanted to win.

Michael would land at Kalafrana, and someone would say: 'Did you hear about the Debrincats? They've been found out! The father's been put in prison! Better not waste your time with that lot.' Or perhaps no one would tell him anything, because they were too decent, and Michael would come along the street and see the policeman, and as soon as he got inside he would ask: 'What's that copper doing on the front steps?' and it would all have to come out.

It would be too awful, because he'd still have to stay for lunch, since he'd been invited, and what could they possibly talk about? Winning the war?

He heard his mother call from below, and for a moment refused to answer. But that wasn't fair... There was even the fantastic thought that he was now the only man in the house... Cradling the Hurricane in his arms, he walked to the head of the spiral staircase, and called out: 'Coming!'

Then he went down to his bedroom, washed his face and hands without prompting, and – sick and hungry at the same time – prepared to join his family downstairs. But he *wouldn't* go back to school. Not that afternoon. Uncle Salvu would understand, and make everyone else understand as well.

At lunch he would talk about all sorts of things.

Out on the patio, that traditional family rendezvous, they waited a long time for Michael, sipping their drinks and talking of nothing at all. They waited so long, in fact, and their conversation grew so trivial and awkward, that Father Salvatore knew that he must speak of what was in the forefront of his mind, and in theirs. The evidence of sorrow and guilt sat in all their faces. To ignore it was cowardice. It was also futile.

'Before Michael comes,' he said, breaking into Pietru Pawl's imitation of an unpopular boy at school who could not tie his shoelaces properly, and excited widespread contempt on that account, 'I want to say something about your father.' It was strange how such an innocent and honoured word could have the effect of a deliberate shock, but it was so, and all their reaction proved it. 'I went to see him early this morning, at Corradino... You must accept the fact that he will be there for a long time.'

No one said anything. Their startled faces only grew wary. It was something they had already accepted, in their different ways.

'I don't want to say anything, *anything*, about what he has done.' Try as he would, Father Salvatore could not help feeling that he was delivering a church homily, to an audience which would sit and listen – which *must* sit and listen – without answering back. Perhaps it was the best way: the family became the congregation, and his task was thus pastoral, almost disciplinary. At such a remove, it was less embarrassing for all of them. 'What we have to deal with is *now*... There will be a lot of talk, a lot of gossip, perhaps a lot of publicity. But after that has settled down, you will go on as before. People will not think of you as different. There will just be three of you – three Debrincats – instead of four.' He prayed that all this would be true. 'That doesn't mean that you should forget there is such a man as your father. That would be wrong. But you should remember him in private, and pray for him in private. If you are careful about that, then everyone else will be careful, and things will come back to normal again.'

He was cutting several corners, he knew. With the Debrincats, things would never be quite normal again: socially it might become true, as time passed, but as a matter of interior self-repute, never. He was clinging to what he wanted to do: to take them past this horrible day, and the horrible days that were to come, and lead them beside the still waters, as the dear Psalmist said.

One particular point he was suppressing was that this father of theirs, Lewis Debrincat, wanted nothing more to do with them. His solitary confinement was self-chosen, self-inflicted, self-enjoyed... Pity must spare them that. It was only a matter of time before their own solitude brought them into line with the facts.

He wondered who would be the first to speak, and it was the talkative Pietru, too long silent on a day cursed with more new topics than he could cope with.

'Uncle Salvu?'

'Yes, Peter Paul.'

'You said it would be a long time.' He did not want to use particular phrases of shame. 'But how long?'

'I don't know. I'll find out as soon as I can. At the moment—' he was as unwilling as Pietru to bring in the awful words like prison and trial and sentence, 'your father has only been detained for inquiries.'

'But he was *arrested*.'

'Yes, he was arrested.'

'So it's the same thing.'

'In a way.'

'And he'll be found *guilty*.'

From the depths of her armchair Marija said, with gentleness: 'Don't make it worse, Pietru. It's the same for all of us.'

'It's *not*! You don't have to go to school.'

This was one area where Father Salvatore felt he could take charge. 'Were they talking about it at school?'

Pietru's face grew sulky, but it was only the sulkiness of despair. 'Not exactly. But they all know.'

His mother said: 'But you have so many friends there.'

'It's not fair to make them – to expect them to be on my side.'

'I think you might be surprised—' Father Salvatore began, and then broke off. Bold words were all very well for adults who did not have to sweat them out. Noble resolution, dictated at second hand, was the cheapest coin in any realm. It was cruel to involve a boy of fifteen in such a miserable conflict, such a test of loyalty, when it could be avoided. 'Do you want to stay away for a few days?'

Pietru looked at his mother, and then back again. He was very tense, on the verge of saying something violent or stupid, and breaking the barrier of behaviour for ever. What he said was violent enough. 'I don't want to go back *ever*!'

'Well, we'll see about that. One thing at a time. Do you remember, I said "We have to deal with *now*"? This is what I meant.' He leant towards Pietru, and felt his heart going out at the same time. 'I can ring up the principal, and say it would be better if you didn't come back till next week. Would you like that?'

Pietru nodded, wordless. He was so near to tears again that no one could look at him.

'Then that's settled!' Father Salvatore declared, with a false heartiness which he hoped would be forgiven him. He winked at Pietru, who immediately got up and walked to the far end of the patio, his back resolutely turned. It was a moment when each one of them could see and feel, sharp as a thorn, the exact meaning of disgrace. But at least a single step into the future had been taken, one painful corner turned. Giovanna, sitting next to her brother, put her hand over his.

'Thank you, Salvu. You think of everything.' Then she glanced down at her watch, and became a hostess again. 'Good gracious, it's nearly half past one! We really should be sensible, and go into lunch. I'm sorry about Michael, but even fish pie can be spoilt.'

Marija came to the alert. 'We *must* wait for him. I'm sure he hasn't forgotten, or – or anything.'

'Well ...'

Father Salvatore took charge again. 'I don't think he'd mind, Marija. Perhaps he tried to send a message. You know – extra duty or something.' He rubbed his hands together. 'Well – who's hungry?'

'I am,' said Pietru, turning swiftly. He had most things under control again. No school until next week, and he had guessed right about Michael – he must have heard the story, and was too ashamed to come. There were all sorts of reasons to be glad.

'I'm hungry too,' his mother joined in, 'and poor Uncle Salvu must be starving. Ring the bell, will you, Pietru?'

'I'm *not* hungry,' Marija persisted, and in truth she was not. Suddenly she was feeling mortally sick and afraid. What was happening didn't make sense. Michael *would* have got a message through, if he couldn't come. It was the sort of thing he could always do. So... So he wasn't even in Malta. So he hadn't come to lunch for that other reason, the reason which could, now and at any other moment, waking or dreaming, clutch at her throat and squeeze her heart dry.

'Three to one,' Pietru said cheerfully. 'Democracy wins.' His hand, hovering over the bell, plunged firmly down in a triple ring: 'Three to *one – means – lunch!*'

They had progressed past the soup – 'It's just soup, I'm afraid,' Giovanna told them. 'The little grey things ought to be barley, but they're Government lentils' – and had taken their first helping of the iron-crusted fish pie when Pietru, who had been full of high spirits, cocked his head on one side. 'I thought I heard the front door,' he said, and he sounded suddenly crestfallen.

The rest of them brightened, and then listened. Footsteps could be heard, and then voices – particularly a man's voice – and then the closing of a solid door. The omens seemed very good.

'Better late than never,' Father Salvatore declared.

'He's only missed the soup,' Giovanna said, 'and it wasn't the best soup in the world, was it?' She smiled at her daughter. 'Will you go, Marija? Just explain that we had to start.'

Marija stood up, slim and beautiful as a girl could be. But her face, which had taken on a rare look of happiness, was now troubled. 'I don't think that was Michael,' she said, and left the dining-room.

It was not Michael. The man in the hall, crossing towards her with Carmelina alongside, was in khaki, and was Captain Ian Ross.

'Hallo, Ian,' she said uncertainly. She liked the smart and soldierly aide-de-camp much better than in the old days; he had lost all the 'silliness' of sexual gallantry, or had surrendered it to the facts, and had proved himself a good friend in all sorts of ways. But she could not guess why he should be there. Was it something to do with her father? – he would have telephoned her mother. Was it just a chance call? – no, he would never call in the middle of lunch. Some news?

It was some news.

His handsome face, so unlike Michael's, yet solid and honest in the same way, was as troubled as hers had been, a moment ago.

'Marija,' he said, and touched her shoulder as a brother might, 'I've got a message for you.' He looked round the wide hall. 'Can we go somewhere?'

'Is it Michael?' Her heart had dropped like a stone, and she was trembling already.

'Yes, it's Michael.' Seeing her stricken air, he added quickly : 'No, it's *not* the worst news.'

'Come out to the patio.'

Alone in the deserted room, he began immediately : 'I'm not sure how to say this, so I'll bash straight ahead. Michael's missing in action – that's the official bit. He was on a fighter-bomber thing last night, over Sicily, and his plane was shot down.'

Her hand went up to her mouth. 'Did anyone see—'

'No. It was pitch-dark, and there was a hell of an uproar going on.' He touched her shoulder again. 'But darling, for all anyone knows he baled out, and he may be perfectly all right. But – well, you're listed as his next-of-kin, as well as his mother, so—'

'Oh God.'

He looked away, as desperately sad as she was. 'Oh God, indeed... They rang me up, because they know the – the situation, and I said I'd tell you.'

She nodded her thanks, totally unable to speak.

'Well, that's all so far. Just "missing". There's no—' he found he could not add the cold official words, 'Presumed killed'. 'There's nothing beyond that. Don't forget it happens all the time, and then the chaps turn up safe and sound, and you get a nice postcard from the Red Cross to prove it.'

She found her voice again, though it was no more than a whisper. 'Was it over the sea?'

'No. Somewhere inland. I tell you, there are all sorts of chances... Is there anything I can do, at the moment?'

'I don't think so. No, thank you.'

'Then I'll move on. But as soon as they hear anything, I'll let you know straight away. All right?'

'Thank you, Ian.'
'Oh yes— His Ex asked me to say, he's terribly sorry.'
Marija nodded, wordless again.
'About everything.'

5

Father Salvatore left the house in unbearable sadness. To re-
count the fate of Lewis Debrincat, and to see its effect on the
family, had been bad enough; but to leave them faced with
another terrible question-mark – the life or death of Michael
Ainslie – was refined torture. It had been made more dreadful
still by a tender introduction.

They had waited quite a long time for Marija to return from
the front door. The silence was not astonishing. The lovers had,
perhaps, something to tell each other, beyond the fact that fish
pie was now available. 'What *can* they be doing?' Giovanna
had asked, with a gentle smile, and did not demand an answer.
But after five minutes of this, it seemed that enough was
enough.

Giovanna called to her daughter, and received no reply. Then,
coming out from the dining-room, with the stage-cough which
circumstances indicated, she had discovered Marija, in helpless
misery, crouched in a corner of the patio. Father Salvatore,
following swiftly, was only in time to witness a collapse into
desperate sobbing, and the choking whisper which told them
why.

Now, as he went down the front steps of Casa Debrincat, past
the policeman who, impressed by the arrival and departure of a
Government House car and a gold-decked equerry, was ready to
admit kinship with inmates no longer beyond the pale, he had
the feeling that people were staring at the house. Well they
might be. It must now enshrine more heartbreak and suffering
than any other building in the whole of Malta.

He secured a lift to Valletta, from yet another army lorry
returning empty from some outlying task, and then began to
walk downtown, from the heights of the Auberge de Castile,
through the wreckage of the city. It suited his forlorn mood, it
suited the malevolent day, to start his descent from the very
spot where, for him, this wicked war had begun, and to pick
his way laboriously past the ruins of its flailing punishment.

The real reason for the award of that George Cross lay before him, and all round him, to be seen and smelled and mourned at every turn. What Valletta had suffered during the last five months of the war was already past belief.

In so far as anything so horrible came from the mind of one man, their ferocious ordeal was the misbegotten brain-child of Field-Marshal Kesselring, the German commander in Sicily, who had decreed that the island of Malta was now too great a nuisance to be allowed to live. It was to be first smashed to a heap of builder's rubbish, silent and uninhabited, and then invaded. The idea had been thought of before, and even tried before, but for some reason the executioners' hands had faltered. Now it would be done.

The prospect of invasion had been foreseen; as early as January of that fatal year, an official broadcast had told people what to do when the 'imminent threat' became a fact. 'Stay in your village or town,' was the order, 'and take cover. Keep off the streets. As from now, the ringing of church bells means that an invasion has started.' What could *not* be foreseen was the loving detail of the prelude, which was to leave thousands of dead in its wake, and one and a half million tons of assorted masonry spread over Valletta and Floriana alone.

A terrible exhaustion began to grip the island as the raids multiplied; it was impossible to rest, to move about, to work, to live anything which could be called a life, under the thunder of the bombs and the desperate answer of the guns. There were never less than four raids a day, which might last two hours each; an 'alert' could continue for thirteen hours, disrupting all normal behaviour. In one of the worst months, March, Malta stood to arms for a total of 372 hours – fifteen days out of the thirty-one.

Like other invaders before them, the enemy planned to select one point, and pound away at it until it was pulped out of existence. But now the day-and-night target was not a single fort; it was a circle two miles across, with, as its centre, the fouled waters of Grand Harbour. The result, and the bloody rubble remaining, were identical.

Bombs fell by the ton : by the hundred tons : by the thousand. In April, an average of 190 bombers raided Malta every day, and dropped 6,730 tons of bombs (the city of Coventry itself, that tortured monument to the Battle of Britain, only had to endure 200 tons). Bombs came in sizes big and small : bombs weighing 500 lbs, bombs weighing a thousand : huge land-mines which floated down by parachute, like spectral bats against the moon : incendiary bombs, delayed-action bombs, whistling bombs, butterfly bombs, plain bombs for a plain, quick, service-able death.

Sometimes they arrived as strings of bombs chained together, which fell, and bounced, and tumbled over each other like little dogs at play. Sometimes they were 'anti-personnel' bombs, shaped like Thermos flasks, seeking no heavier target than flesh. They lay, innocent and silent, until they were touched. Then they killed the inquisitive.

With such raw pleasantries did the days and nights pass.

While the people crouched and bled and suffered – for the bravest man in Malta could not stop a bomb falling, nor catch it with his bare hands, and thus he was best out of the way – the professionals did what they could to ward off the blows. Yet there came a time when the defences, mercilessly swamped, had to bear these attacks as helplessly as any mother and child holed up in a cellar. Guns, blazing away with barrels red-hot, ran out of ammunition, and had to be rationed to ten rounds a day – scarcely enough to find a range. Squadrons of precious Spitfires, brought in by the American aircraft-carrier *Wasp*, went up in smoke before they could even get airborne again.

Forty-eight of them were flown off the carrier, forty-six arrived in Malta – and within seventy-two hours every single one of them had been destroyed on the ground, by German bombers which, maintaining a constant patrol over the island, pounced on them within a few minutes of touch-down. There was no cure for so baleful a vigilance.

Yet, at a time of such ill-success, such importance, it was moving to see how the Maltese still trusted and admired their defenders. The flying men, especially, were regarded as heroes, even if their planes seemed useless, and their pilots as helpless as a baby strapped in a pram and beset by a swarm of insects. Any serviceman with wings on his uniform was always followed by crowds of children shouting 'Speetfire!', clapping their idol, saluting him, and furtively pulling at his crested buttons in the hope of the proudest possible souvenir.

The Debrincat household came to know this better than most. Michael Ainslie, a frequent visitor, was often nearly mobbed as he mounted the steps, and besieged again by faithful followers when he left the house. Once he arrived for dinner, not only deplorably late, but dishevelled and harassed as well. What had happened?

'Everything!... I'm awfully sorry, Mrs Debrincat,' he apologized. 'Those kids cornered me again. I was just passing the orphanage when the whole lot came rushing out. A couple of them actually jumped out of a window and landed on my shoulders. Even the nuns couldn't stop them!'

'But what have you been doing?' Marija had asked him fondly.

He was delightfully embarrassed. 'Signing autographs.'

There were other heroes, who did not get mobbed – except by the enemy. These were the ground-crews and the maintenance men, Maltese and imported, whose job it was to protect the planes, to keep them flying, to cobble them together if they were still worth the effort, and to patch up the ruined, pitted airfields which were also a prime target of the attack. They lived in caves and concrete holes, like the people they were shielding; and each time the storm passed, they sallied out manfully to repair the damage before the next one broke.

To shelter those precious aircraft they built makeshift garages out of the only material available – empty five-gallon petrol tins, filled with earth and sand, and lashed together with wire. In fact they assembled small villages of these cubicles: each with three walls, ninety feet long and fourteen feet high, and twelve tins wide at the base. Every such crazy honeycomb used 60,000 tins, 3,500 tons of earth, nearly three miles of wire, and such uncounted man-hours, such laborious scooping and shovelling, such fetching and carrying, such sweat and strain, that they challenged the Pyramids for ant-like, inch-by-inch construction.

But they could never keep pace with those flying ants who plagued and plundered Malta all the time, who destroyed a day's work in a few seconds, who began to seem invincible. These struck as they pleased, and for every one shot down, ten more came winging in from Sicily to take their place and complete their work. Before long, the airfields of Luqa, and Ta' Kali, and Hal Far were cratered like the surface of the moon: pock-marked by deep wounds, strewn with mounds of earth and rock, condemned to desolation.

As fast as they were hit, they were repaired: as fast as they were repaired, they were ruined again. There was a time when, for eleven days on end, not a single fighter aircraft could leave the ground to challenge the assault. Exhausted men could do no more than dump a few tons of rubble and sand into a bomb-crater, and then run for cover as the enemy returned to gouge it all out, with a little extra blood to cement the pact between earth and sky.

With the defenders thus occupied, thus fooled and frustrated, countless other iron fists and claws beat and ripped at the places where people lived, steadily tearing out all the old and new heart of Malta. Father Salvatore, now plodding and stumbling downtown, was traversing the aftermath of this frenzied punishment.

This above all was George Cross territory, the condemned cell without reprieve.

It started, at the crown of Valletta, with one of the proudest assets of a proud capital: the Opera House – more accurately the *late* Opera House – before a chance bomb reduced it to tawdry make-believe. A few of its elegant arches still stood, but now they ended in midair, like crippled wings: underneath, the dusty rubble made a tidemark, the low ebb of everything that mattered, everything that lived and sang.

Here men must go into mourning for the death of beauty, and after that, they were in mourning for almost everything useful, or habitable, or familiar. Father Salvatore, descending with a sick heart into this sprawling hell of destruction, was only one of a thousand such pall-bearers, carrying their little coffins of dead hope through a graveyard city.

Theirs was the only traffic, in a once-thriving town brought to a standstill by pressures of torment which had reduced its population from 21,000 to 6,000, most of them cave-dwellers or dispossessed migrants. Whole streets had now been permanently closed off, choked by heaps of fallen masonry impossible to tackle, deserts of muck and rubbish which must be left to moulder till a brighter day, if such a day ever dawned. Blocked intersections forced Father Salvatore into a dozen detours; sometimes he stood on a street-corner which he could not recognize, lost in his own city which had become a hopeless maze.

The land-marks gone, or cruelly defaced, were almost too precious to count: the list, starting with the Opera House, now included the *auberges* of Auvergne, of Castile, and of Italy: the

Great Market; and the Governor's Palace, from which the Governor had been bombed out, like any other citizen. These were the most recent wounds; to them must be added the merciless inventory of the last two years, which so muddled the memory that a man could ask: 'Did you hear about the Chapel of the Bones?' forgetting that he had known of its ruin for half the war.

The Strada Reale, to which Father Salvatore kept returning as his best-known point of reference, was a vista of more humble desolation. Great gaps in its line of shops now offered only a crazy façade of doors and lintels: behind these, there was nothing but dusty chaos; and in front, on the pavement, were placed a few tables where hopeful men, undefeated, set out their wares.

Even in this last-ditch endeavour, such a man had to maintain a watchful eye. Flies and huge rats abounded, feeding on human desperation and disorder. Even *humans* fed on such foul fare. Looting and stealing had lately threatened to get out of hand; while a man mourned his own dead, and his eyes were blurred, his wrecked house might be stripped of everything movable, everything which could be wrenched away by greedy hands: doors, cupboards, window frames, shelves, mirrors, clothing, bathroom taps; the food from the kitchen, the blankets from the bereaved bed.

This cannibal lust, which should have been the greatest shame and sadness of all, was now a commonplace evil. It did not call for public censure, only for troops.

Halfway down the hill which had once been handsome Valletta, and before that the noble eminence of Mount Sceberras, still trudging through the rubble, and broken glass, and splintered wood which made up a springtime walk in Malta, Father Salvatore came upon a *vignette* of a different quality: the badge of self-reliant courage in anguish.

Under a tattered tarpaulin, in front of a shop which no longer existed, was set one of these hopeful tables of commerce; and behind it sat a small boy, not more than eight or nine years old, guarding his capital investment, a basketful of shrunken lemons.

Father Salvatore smiled, and blessed him with all the inward fervour at his command, and bought six of his stock. Lemons were the last thing he wanted, but the exchange involved the first thing of all, the *most* wanted, which was compassion. It did not demand a single word, because it could not. The little boy, wizened and watchful, totally suspicious of a horrid world and all its horrid people, was a routine casualty of his time. Orphaned for six months, he had been, and would for ever be, dumb from birth and stone deaf by later arrangement.

He had been christened, by trusting parents now rewarded, Amadeus – beloved of God.

Father Salvatore blessed him again, and passed on down the hill. Rage against heaven was not for a priest. Only pity was allowable. The hungry eight-year-old was not even from Valletta; he was one of the migrant squatters, driven from an area harsher still, across the harbour where the Three Cities had virtually ceased to be : where, on certain unspeakable days in April, priest and sacristan, Dun Salv and Nero Cassar, had collected shreds and rags of human bodies, and stuffed them into empty cement bags, for their Christian disposal.

Presently he reached the harbour water-level at the Customs House, and found a place in a navy store-boat returning to French Creek. He knew a lot of these sailors by now, and never ceased to rejoice in their cheerful readiness to help anyone, whether it was a pretty girl or a battered old *kappillan*.

For the hundredth or the thousandth time, he began his crossing of Grand Harbour.

Grand Harbour had become, in the last few months, the watery twin of ruined Valletta. It had taken the overspill of bombs, the bad shots, as well as the concentrated fury of dockyard attack. It was full of wrecks, still showing their wounds above water, and the winking green buoys which marked the shallow graves of total losers; it was fouled by scum, and broken timber, and dead fish, and the slow seepage of oil which was the life-blood of lost ships.

It was ringed by docks which were little more than junkyards of smashed and crumbled stone, and toppled cranes, and concrete shelters which gaped at the sky as if astonished by its treachery. It had been brought very close to a standstill, and, since it was the heartbeat of Malta at war, it had also come close to making a corpse of its mother island.

Some of its wrecks were famous, or infamous, or familiar as rotten teeth, ulcered gut. The Navy store-boat, under the command of a large bearded coxswain with more tattoos than bare

skin on his arms, made a wide, prudent circle round the best-
known wreck of all, the hulk of the Norwegian ship *Talabot*.
The *Talabot*'s notoriety lay in the fact that she was still
smouldering, six weeks after she had been half sunk, half
beached; that she carried ammunition in unknown quantities;
and that she had brought the whole of Grand Harbour to the
verge of a one-second, one-blow, total destruction.

She was part of the last convoy to get through to Malta,
viciously fought, cruelly expensive. But owing to the fury of the
air-raids when she reached harbour, she had lain for twelve
hours at anchor without any activity, or any effort to deliver
her precious supplies; and she had unloaded no more than a
few hundred tons of these when she was dive-bombed, and hit,
and set on fire.

Huge mounting tongues of flame advertised her coming death.
Though it was not publicly known, she carried enough ex-
plosives to lift the whole harbour, and half Valletta, and all the
Three Cities out of existence.

On a certain morning, all these areas had been evacuated,
without explanation, and then a handful of brave men went on
board the *Talabot* as soon as this was possible, to try to flood
her holds and sink her – *with explosives* – before the raging
fires touched off her ammunition. It was enough to say that
they succeeded in this hair-raising exercise. Now the *Talabot*
was just another wreck, much respected, gently going off the
boil below the bastions, with her remaining cargo neutralized –
to the best of official belief.

As the store-boat left the *Talabot* safely astern, the tattooed
coxswain caught Father Salvatore's eye, and jerked his head
back with a smile.

'Always glad to see the last of that one.'

'Is she still dangerous, do you think?'

'All I know is, I don't want to find out.' The coxswain had a
rough gruff voice, with abundant individual life and strength in
it. He smiled again. 'I feel safer with you on board, Father.'

Someone else had said that, in the long-ago of the war. Father
Salvatore searched his memory, and recalled it. It had been
another ferry captain, jolly Koli Apap of the *Ferdinando*, when
they were crossing from Sliema Creek to the Salvatore Bastion.
'I always feel safe with a priest,' he had said. Now the *Ferdinando* was a burnt-out wreck, and even the boy who had cast

off their mooring-lines had been dead for five months. But at least they had survived the harbour crossing itself.

There was something curious about their passage today, and presently Father Salvatore discovered what it was. It was the light. In spite of a brilliant sunny day, the best of a longed-for spring, the harbour was overcast. It was not only the drifting black smoke from a fierce series of raids that same morning, which seemed to have been concentrating on French Creek, where they were bound; there was smoke of another sort – luminous pale smoke, the colour of a saintly halo, pungent to the nostrils, which was putting a uniform blanket of nothingness above their heads. Puzzled, he asked the coxswain.

'It's chemical, Father.' The man was preoccupied with passing close under the stern of a minesweeper on its way out of harbour, and that was all he said for a few moments. Then, relaxing, he explained: 'It's a smoke screen. There's a ship in French Creek unloading in a hurry, and they want to cover her up. So they've touched off a few tins of Tickler's best.'

'What?' It was all very well to be puzzled, but one should not be completely nonplussed, as if by verbal hieroglyphics.

The coxswain grinned again. 'Sorry, Father. Tickler's is navy tobacco, but it's not really that, of course. It's like a big canister, and when you turn the knob, out comes this chemical fog. All you see from the air is a patch of snow, so you go away and have another think. At least, that's the idea. I would have thought—' he broke off.

Father Salvatore, intrigued, asked: 'What would you have thought?'

A loyal service discretion intervened. 'I don't know enough about it, Father. But if you're in a bomber, and you see a smoke screen, there must be something underneath it. Right? So all you need do is bomb the smoke – plaster it all over.' The coxswain flexed his forearms, making the blue tattoo marks ripple; then he eased his hand off the wheel, and pointed ahead. 'Anyway, that's where we're going, and that's where the ship is.'

'What ship is that?'

'Just a ship. The *Welshman*. Minelayer or something. But they say she's full of good stuff.'

When presently they drew near French Creek, and slowed for their landing, the dead harbour at last seemed to come alive again. The dockside scene was familiar enough: a bone-yard of wood and concrete, stone and steelwork, all torn out of context and left to find its own desolate level. There was a ship sunk at her berth, criss-crossed by iron girders tossed on to the foredeck by a giant, murderous hand. There was another hulk, high out of the water, empty, derelict, from which the smell of burnt paint, scorched and buckled steel, wafted across like the incense of hell.

There were buildings flattened, and trucks sitting squat and forlorn on rimless wheels, and twisted pipes, like a plumber's nightmare, which would never carry oil or water again. There was an awful air of defeat and surrender, a silent cry of 'No more! No more!' which only the pitiless would question.

But there was also another sort of ship to be seen, a newcomer, hale and hearty, a thriving centre of activity and noise – the noise of feet hurrying down gangways, and donkey-engines going full blast, and the hiss of wire hoists sliding through iron blocks. It was a grey ship, a Navy ship with three funnels, and manned guns pointing at the sky, and signal flags drying off after a wet voyage; a ship on which something was happening, a ship which was *making* things happen all round her, like a master at a school picnic or a queen on her coronation day.

She was the mainspring of the most heartening, bustling diligence which had been seen in Grand Harbour for many a weary day and night.

HMS *Welshman* signalled a romantic revival of an ancient and honourable tradition – the lone blockade-runner coming to the rescue of a hard-pressed fortress under siege. Since it was now a harsh fact of life that convoys, or any small clutch of supply ships, however well escorted, could no longer get through to Malta, and that the island was starving as well as bleeding to death, something else must take their place.

The something else was the *Welshman*, which, following a bitter series of defeats and fiascos, *had* to plug the perilous gap in supplies, or see the island lost.

It had been the most melancholy tale of the war. With the Mediterranean, east and west, beset by U-boats, E-boats, mines, dive-bombers, torpedo-bombers, and the spirited Italian navy, no big convoy had been able to fight its way through for eight months. Three ships from Alexandria had managed to make it in January. A convoy in mid-February had been stopped in its tracks, and had retreated. In March, the *Talabot* and her three comrades had tried again; of the quartet, two had been sunk a few miles short of the island, and the other two in harbour; only one-fifth of their combined cargoes had been unloaded.

By May, mining and bombing had made Grand Harbour such a shambles, with eighteen sunken wrecks, and twenty-seven damaged ships lying about waiting for the men from the scrapyard, that it was hardly worth a visit. The May convoy had to be cancelled.

It had been cruelly expensive to find out that the only possible link with the outside world was now by submarine. These did their valiant best. But they could only deliver in penny packets, at 200 tons a time; and, of necessity, most of their load was octane spirit for the fighter planes. Malta *must* get more.

For her blockade run, *Welshman* was romantically disguised as well as re-invented. A 2,600-ton minelayer with a speed — 35 knots — which made her one of the fastest ships in the navy, she happened to look rather like a French destroyer of the *Léopard* class. This gave some bright spark in the Admiralty a bright idea. All she needed was a little more bulk on the bridge and the quarterdeck, an enlarged third funnel, and a good big tricolour ensign, and she could pass for a Vichy-French warship on her lawful Axis business, perhaps making a run for Algeria just inside territorial waters.

All that the crew needed were some blue-and-white striped singlets, and a different kind of cap, which they must have thought foolish, with a red pom-pom on the top, and they were in business: *ooh-là-là* by day, bangers-and-mash at night, and full ahead at all times.

The theatrical deeds were done. *Welshman* loaded certain essential stores and people, and perfected her disguise with five-ply wood, at Gibraltar, and then ran hell-bent for Malta, like a French poodle with its bottom on fire.

A combination of iron-nerved bluff and superb navigation brought her through. First she closed the Algerian coast, and weaved in and out of the territorial limits as she sped eastwards. Challenged by shore stations, she fooled around with bad signalling and ambiguous answers until she got out of range.

Twice she was visited by patrolling German aircraft, which made low-level passes overhead. They could not really figure her out. She looked all right, but she was not on anyone's list: though they did not dare to bomb, yet they must somehow put her to the test.

Welshman, sweating under this scrutiny, did not even man her guns as the most determined of the German bombers swept overhead at masthead level. All that the fancy-dress crew did was to wave. The bomber finally waggled its wings in salute, and went off home again. By the time a report could be filed, and checked, and found ridiculous, night had fallen and *Welshman* was well into her last full-speed dash.

Eight hours of pitch-black, truly remarkable coastal navigation took her, at over thirty knots, in and out of the minefields and over the shoals of the Tunisian Channel. Nothing went a foot wrong. When she arrived off Malta, spot on time at two minutes after sunrise, she left behind her a trail of anguished question marks, but never a cross word.

She got into Grand Harbour at 6 AM, and unloaded her entire cargo in seven hours, in spite of bombing which cost the resentful enemy forty planes. Then she topped up with oil and passengers, and sailed again at dusk. As she cleared harbour she was cheered from the bastions of Valletta by a singing, shouting crowd which – using the magic of wildfire gossip – already knew her story. Well she might be.

The rusty iron ladder leading up from water-level to the lip of the dock was not only steep; it was bent outwards, like a bow, and some of its rungs were loose. A young man might have climbed it with agile appetite; a middle-aged priest in a flapping cassock had to take it slowly and carefully, aware of aching feet and short breath. When Father Salvatore arrived at the top, he would have preferred to sit down on the nearest bench, and give himself up to meditation, or what might seem to be meditation. But as soon as he arrived, and turned to look at the grey ship, he was caught up in the thrusting activity of which she was the centre.

With hardly a pause, he found himself one of a line of men who were passing small wooden crates from hand to hand: a human chain – only they were more like ants – connecting the ship's side with a big Army truck thirty feet away. By his very presence on the dock, it seemed that he was a volunteer for whatever had to be done next.

There were many like him. One could recognize a stevedore easily enough; but the meagre dock-gangs were outnumbered by all sorts of other people: men in business suits, children who should have been in school, soldiers, Capuchin friars, people whom he knew, by sight, to be farmers, stall-holders, *dghajsa*-men, loafers: all banded together in a furious effort to empty the *Welshman* and get her on her way again.

How had it happened? What call had been made, and answered? When he asked the man next in line to him, a brawny fisherman in a stained smock, the reply was a shrug.

'They say there was something on the wireless, but I didn't hear it. I was sitting on the edge of the dock when that man' – he pointed across the quay – 'said: "Come on, you. Give a hand." So I did.'

Father Salvatore looked at 'that man'. He was a soldier, in khaki trousers and a shirt with the sleeves rolled up: a man of middle age, energetic and straight-shouldered, with a ruddy face and a clipped military moustache, unloading cardboard cartons from a cargo-sling as it descended out of the white smoke above their heads. There was something about him which was familiar: Father Salvatore had seen his face some-where, or had passed him in the street. The air of authority was unmistakable. People round him were doing what he told them to.

As Father Salvatore stared and wondered, the fisherman nudged him, without ceremony, and thrust another small crate into his hands. 'Come on, Father! We must be nearly done.'

Father Salvatore gave another hitch to his cassock, and fell to again.

They worked for half an hour, under the lowering smoke, amid the noise and bustle, and then the pace slackened and died. The loaded trucks were all gone; the single crane which was still working fell silent: the cargo-hoists on board the *Welshman* produced nothing more. The 'human chain' dissolved again, as an officer came on to the upper deck and gave the crossed-wrists signal which meant 'All wrapped up'. After that there was nothing but the stretching of weary arms and aching backs, and an exchange of cigarettes, and, for Father Salvatore, an astonishing encounter.

He was sitting on a bollard, moving his cramped feet inside his boots, staring at the ship which seemed, like him, to have done her job, when a shadow fell between him and the pale sun. He turned, to find the commanding military man at his side.

Close to, he was daunting indeed: a tough and soldierly figure with a brusque, no-nonsense look in his eyes. But his words could not have been more friendly.

'Thank you for helping us, Father. Jolly fine show all round. Set a good example. What? What?'

He spoke in a voice as clipped as his moustache, and the 'What? What?' seemed to need an answer. Father Salvatore got to his feet. All he wanted to know was, who are you? But he could not think how to phrase it.

'I was glad to be able to help.'

'We need every scrap of help we can find. This ship has been through all sorts of nonsense to get to Malta. Now it's our turn to see that the trip isn't wasted. What would the navy think if a few Jerry bombers destroyed all their hard work before she was unloaded. What? What?'

Perhaps, after all, he always said 'What? What?' and never expected a reply. But it still seemed necessary to make a contribution. Silence, or even inattention, might have been construed as mutiny.

'It's so good to see a ship coming in at last. Do you know what she's brought?'

'Certainly! I can tell you *exactly*!' All the authority was back again, so that Father Salvatore was almost ashamed of his question. 'There's no need to make a secret of it, because she's got here safely, and the stuff has been unloaded. What? What? Apart from some ground-crew for the RAF—'

But he was interrupted. Another, much younger soldier approached, carrying a uniform tunic which was, astoundingly, neatly balanced on a coat-hanger. I would never have thought of that, Father Salvatore told himself, as the great man took it and put it on. And he *was* a great man: the tunic had scarlet facings, and all sorts of gleaming emblems on the epaulettes, and such an array of medal ribbons that they seemed about to overflow the breast-pocket. It was now impossible not to recognize him.

Father Salvatore had seen his picture in the *Times of Malta*, that very morning. It was the man with all the names: John

Standish Surtees Prendergast Vereker, Viscount Gort. A lord, a Field-Marshal, and the new Governor of Malta.

Lord Gort pulled his glittering tunic down, and straightened his shoulders. The medal ribbons expanded, as if a brightly coloured balloon had been blown up. Father Salvatore, in his shabby black cassock, was almost childishly elated. How could they lose the war now?

'Now what was I saying?' the Governor went on. 'Yes, the cargo... I can tell you *exactly*! What? What?' The silliness of 'What? What?' could not cloak an astute, all-competent intelligence, and a rat-trap memory as well. 'Over a hundred RAF ground-crew. Ninety-six spare engines for the new Spitfires – that's the lads that gave Jerry such a rough run this morning. Torpedoes for the submarines. Thousands of rounds of Bofors ammo – anti-aircraft stuff. Smoke cannisters – and it didn't take long to get them cracking, did it? What? Then, three hundred tons of flour. Powdered milk and tinned milk. Olive oil. Canned meat. Seed potatoes. They had to strike a balance, you understand? Something to eat, and something to fight with. I know it doesn't sound a lot, but it was the best we can do, at the moment. The important thing was to get it here, and get it off the ship. And it was done! All ticketty-boo! Tell your people that, will you, Father?'

'Yes, I will.' But tell them what, exactly?

Lord Gort knew the answer to a puzzled subordinate face. 'Tell them, A—' he ticked the items off, with a stubby forefinger on the palm of his hand, 'that some fresh supplies have arrived. Enough to keep us going till next time. Tell them, B, that there *will* be a next time. Another ship like this, or another convoy. Tell them, C, that when ships do get to Malta, they have to be unloaded. *Forthwith!* We don't want another *Talabot*.' Suddenly he seemed rather bad-tempered, and the world, which had been hopeful and happy, turned a little sour again. 'Self-help! Self-reliance! Don't you agree? What? What?'

'Yes,' said Father Salvatore.

'Then tell your people.'

6

To reach the catacombs of the Cottonera Lines, Father Salvatore had to retrace his morning steps past the grey-black fortress,

Ta' Kordin, where Lewis Debrincat, now his nearest neighbour, lay hidden in his cell for the second night of hundreds or even thousands more to come. The sad, foreboding thought seemed a natural ending to a terrible day already stretching back more than seventeen hours.

Lewis, now trapped in another catacomb as an infected, putrid member, must be kept apart from the world which had condemned him. Soon he, Father Salvatore, would return to his own cell: a sort of refuge, a sort of prison also. But no prison could shut out what the world had done to him, and others dear, today.

Lewis in his odious disgrace: Michael Ainslie vanished into doubtful territory, somewhere between life and death: Marija distraught, Giovanna possessed by shame and a mutinous hatred which would kill love for ever: it was an endless recital of grief, without a spark of redemption. And in spite of the *Welshman* and her cargo of hope, the Governor's farewell had not sounded a happy note. His call for 'Self-help!', his air of admonishment, his command to 'Tell your people!', now seemed harsh, almost contemptuous.

We are doing our little best in Malta, Father Salvatore thought. Are we so hopeless a people? Are we doomed?

His aching feet carried a weary body and a sore heart through the twilight and into the catacombs – and into what seemed like drunken chaos.

The dwarf Nero, as usual, was the first to greet him, as a sacristan should. But tonight he was Nero the centre of interest, taking a certain licence which soon became obvious. He was also Nero the bridegroom, dressed with a miniature elegance which was somehow pitiful, in a tiny suit of evening tails, white tie, white waistcoat, glittering patent-leather pumps, and a top hat.

Where had such finery come from? From some theatrical costumiers? From a circus? Surely there could be no wedding outfitters who had a pair of tails to fit a body three feet and nine inches high.

The strange figure skipped and capered towards him through the gloom of the catacombs. 'Dun Salv! Dun Salv!' Nero had to shout to make himself heard. 'Welcome to the wedding! Thank God you've arrived! We can't do without you tonight!'

'I'm late, I'm afraid,' Father Salvatore answered. But he made his voice sound reproving. Nero had obviously drunk more than a glass or two already: his voice was high-pitched and slurred, his small swarthy face was sweating, and his beaked nose, in the shadow of the top hat, rode up and down like the bouncing bow of a *luzzu*. Granted that this was his wedding day, his long-delayed day-of-all-days, it was still impossible not to wish that he had kept himself in hand.

There were worse things to be regretted. Father Salvatore, looking beyond his sacristan to the depths of the catacomb, was forced to ask: 'But Nero! What on earth is happening?'

He might well wonder. In the flickering yellow light which gave shape to the great concourse of their cavern, there was nothing but disorder, nothing but shameless abandon. The noise was appalling: an uproar which could only be drunken, a constant movement which seemed as mindless and destructive as sin itself. A hundred people were bawling out different songs: a hundred people were lurching about, dancing or wrestling, quarrelling or embracing, playing the mandolin or fighting for its possession.

Children were racing to and fro, tripping over prone figures and being cuffed and kicked for their intrusion. A goat bleated on the altar steps, and then released a stream of excrement, to bellowing laughter which drowned even the blast of the loud-speaker music. It was the worst surrender of virtue Father Salvatore had ever witnessed: as if Antichrist had invaded their only refuge:

He said again: 'Nero! This is terrible! What has happened?'

Nero reacted to the shocked tone, but even he seemed to be resigned to such mischief, and was thus an accomplice. He shrugged his shoulders.

'I know it's getting a bit rough, Dun Salv. But what can I do? They opened the wine cask, about an hour ago.'

'They shouldn't have done that. It was for the feast afterwards. Why did you allow it?'

'I couldn't stop them. And you know how it is these days. Everyone's so miserable. Then they heard about the ship coming in, and they wanted to celebrate. You can't blame them. They say it brought in three months' supplies!'

'Not nearly as much as that.'

'Well, *anything* is better than nothing. So they started cele-

brating. I even had a glass myself. Just for the nerves ...' Nero
no longer seemed concerned. He straightened his back, and
squared his little shoulders, preening himself. 'How do you like
my suit, Dun Salv?'

It was better to leave things as they were, until he could
move about and establish control again. 'It's very smart indeed,
Nero. It looks just right. Where is Teresa? Has she arrived?'

'Hours ago. But she's still getting dressed.' Nero giggled. 'I
wish I could watch.'

'Now, Nero... Was the veal loaf delivered?'

'Yes!' The dwarf's eyes shone afresh. 'It's *beautiful*! You
have been so good, Dun Salv. And so clever!'

'I hope no one has started eating *that*.'

'Over my dead body! I hid it in your room, anyway. Behind
the best cassock. Who would dare?' Nero stretched out his
small muscular arms, and tossed his head back. The shiny top
hat slipped, baring a scarlet weal on his forehead. 'What a day,
what a day! To think that it has all come true at last!'

It had not come true without great trouble, and a ferocious tug
of wills, and perhaps gross deceit.

The parents of Teresa Grima had been obstructive to the
last. Pleading abject poverty, they had steadfastly refused their
daughter a dowry. As soon as the Baroness offered a handsome
sum of money to solve the problem, they had retreated into
shock. How could Teresa take her dowry from a stranger? It
would shame them before all the world...

When the Baroness replied, through her priestly son, that she
was *not* to be described as a stranger, anywhere in Malta, and
that if she wished to endow *ten* brides she would do so, without permission from anyone, they had retired in haste before
such patrician rebuke. But they still would not give their
consent. All the other difficulties remained, and were not to be
endured.

Teresa could not be spared from the farm. Her father was
always desperately short-handed. Within the house, her
mother's health was pitiful – and she took to her bed to
prove it. And besides, there was still Nero himself. How could
their daughter, in the prime of life and beauty, a catch for
any man in Malta, throw herself away on this – this little
clown?

Then, amazingly, the girl herself took a hand. For the first and perhaps the last time, she showed herself not only a spirited human being but a cunning strategist as well. Her private reasons for this were hidden. Perhaps, at last, she had come to accept the fact that she was over thirty-two (instead of the official twenty-seven), and ill-favoured, and by now firmly installed on a shelf from which no ordinary suitor would ever rescue her. Nero would have to do... But her public reason – public within her family – was much more dramatic.

Without preamble, Teresa told her mother that she had missed her last period, and already feared the worst. Mrs Grima screamed her wrath, beat her breast in woe, denounced Nero as a lascivious monster who should be locked up, preferably after castration, fainted dead away, and then took to her bed again. But the shameful facts were far beyond what could be resisted, by any Maltese mother or father.

Father Salvatore, alerted to this terrible crisis, did not believe the story. It had been tried before, as, within the confessional, he knew at first hand. He believed it even less when he learned that both Teresa and her mother had refused to allow a medical examination. (Their reasons differed: Mrs Grima had croaked, from her proclaimed death-bed: 'A *doctor*? It will be all over Mellieha!' and Teresa had announced that she did not need a doctor. She *knew*.) He disbelieved it, finally, when he had talked to Nero.

Taxed with the crime, Nero had denied it absolutely. There had been nothing like that at all. It must be a mistake. Girls sometimes got this sort of thing wrong, didn't they? Well, Teresa must have got it wrong. On his sacred word, he had *not* done anything like that with her.

He added, mutinously: 'I only wish I had!'

'You mustn't say that, Nero. It would be a mortal sin. It is fornication. An engagement is no excuse. You have heard me say so a hundred times.' But Father Salvatore's mood was changing, in the face of a firm denial and an honest look which never wavered. Stern for several minutes, he relaxed at last to compassion.

'Nero, I'm going to ask you once more.' They were sitting opposite each other in the confined cell, within touching distance, and the *kappillan* suddenly reached out. 'Put your hands in mine... Remember, for every sin of man there can be for-

giveness... Now tell me, on your honour and on your friendship. Have you made love to Teresa?'

He felt the dwarf's hands tremble within his grasp, but it was
no betrayal of anything except deep emotion. The emotion was
echoed in Nero's voice as he answered:

'No! I swear it, Dun Salv!' His tone was anguished. 'She
never lets me come near her. I've told you that, often.'

'Then what has happened?'

'I don't know. Either it's a mistake, or it's some kind of a
trick?'

'What trick?'

'To get round her parents.' Briefly the slack hands tightened.
'Perhaps she *really* wants to marry me.'

'What does she say to you?'

'She won't say anything. She says it's rude to talk about
such things.'

'And you have nothing more to tell me?'

'Not a word. Dun Salv, *please* believe me. I've never touched
her.'

'Very well.' Father Salvatore relaxed his grasp, and the
dwarf's hands, which had grown sweaty, slipped downwards
and away. 'I believe you, Nero... But now there's something
else. I don't want to hurt you. But could it be another man?'

'There could always be another man, I suppose.' Nero, with-
drawing from a close communion which had perhaps exhausted
him, was looking down at the rough stone floor. He shook his
head from side to side, despairing and bewildered. 'But it's not
very likely, is it?' After a long silence, the death of a question
unanswerable, he added: 'I can say this only to you, Dun Salv.
I would not mind.'

After that, the dubious matter ran its course, in a last flurry
of complication. Mr and Mrs Grima gave their permission, in
the ungenerous sense that they washed their hands of their
daughter. She could marry or not, as she pleased. But they
would not tolerate such a wedding in their own village. It
would be ridiculous, as well as shameful.

If the parish priest of Mellieha agreed, and if Father Salvatore
wanted to arrange it himself, and if the bishop gave a licence for
a wedding in the catacombs, then that was the end of it. But
the family would not attend, wherever it was held. Mrs Grima
had added, with a final flourish of Christian malevolence:

'When the first child is seven months, and the wrong size, we'll know the truth, won't we?'

The noise and the rough behaviour abated slowly as Father Salvatore's presence was observed. He found, as usual, that it was enough for him to move about, to talk to some people, to frown at others, to peer through the smoke into cooking-pots, to catch and caution a boisterous child, in order to restore the missing element of harmony. Even a small priest, with a small allotment of God's blessed authority, had power beyond his stature, especially among known friends... There were no more furtive trips to the wine barrel, which sat enthroned on its trestle, the Santo-Nobile arms gleaming splendidly. Soon the catacombs would be worthy of the sacred hour.

When he returned from his long, slow circuit, it was to find Nero still elated, but less with wine than with a very strange piece of news. He clutched Father Salvatore's arm.

'Dun Salv! Have you seen the monsignor?'

'Who?'

'Monsignor Scholti! Your great friend. He's sitting with two other priests.' Nero seemed ready to jump up and down with excitement. 'It's quite a society wedding!'

Father Salvatore, surprised and uneasy, checked him. 'Just a moment, Nero. Where are they?'

'Over there.' Nero pointed to the left, and well above the level of the floor. 'They're looking this way, too.'

It needed only a moment for Father Salvatore to discover his visitors. In a small upper gallery sat Bruno Scholti, flanked by two younger priests whom he knew by sight as assistants on the bishop's staff. Scholti was indeed looking his way; the whole watchful trio was staring at him, across a space which, though quieter, was still confused and restless.

Against his better judgement – for the visit was inexplicable – Father Salvatore waved and smiled. No flicker of feeling crossed any of the opposing faces. Monsignor Scholti inclined his head in the smallest possible acknowledgement; then he looked away again, towards a corner behind the altar where some of the faithful were still rowdy. It could not have been a more studied rebuke if Scholti had stood up and turned his back on the whole degrading scene.

Very well... If that was the way he wanted it... Father

Salvatore found himself, first shocked, then angry, then rebellious. This was his own catacomb. Guests were welcome. But
guests were also lucky to be there. They must not find fault.
This was a special occasion. It was not to be spoiled by sour
faces, by a small censorious inquisition sitting in judgement up
there in the gallery. He had done nothing wrong, and as for his
people – well, they had behaved badly, for a short season, and
now they would behave well again.

That was the pattern of the fabric of life, and this was the
catacomb of the Cottonera Lines, a poor untidy squalid refuge
from the hurt of war: *not* the cathedral on a high day of
ceremonial, with the Diplomatic Corps ranged like expensive
puppets cased in gilded cottonwool. Very well... Let us wait till
Christ comes to judge the just and the unjust... In the meantime...

He staggered slightly, losing his balance, and knew that he
was unspeakably tired as well as foolish, and too quick to anger,
and prone to hatred, and unworthy of grace... All sins, all
sins... Nero, who had been looking at him with concern, asked:
'Are you all right, Dun Salv? You're so pale.'

'I'm just tired, Nero. But it will pass. We must get ready for
the wedding.'

'Would you like a glass of wine before we start?'

There was only a moment of hesitation before he answered:
'Yes. I believe that I would.'

The bride was late, and the company grew restive again, and
the humour rough. A man called out, to Nero waiting near the
altar in his doll-like splendour: 'What's happened, little man?
Did you frighten her?' and another voice answered: 'He must
have shown her his big top hat.' But presently Teresa Grima
made her entrance, at a peasant's plod: a bulging figure advancing like a veritable tent of white satin, topped by an
impenetrable gauzy veil.

The accordion band struck up; people craned their necks;
some even clapped. Nero, who had been calm, began to shake.

Just before he called for God's blessing, and began the nuptial
mass, Father Salvatore realized with a fearful pang that in the
midst of all the turmoil of the past few weeks he had forgotten,
unbelievably, to obtain the bishop's licence for a wedding in the
catacombs.

*   *   *

An hour later the wedding feast was in full swing. The wine barrel gurgled incessantly; the food, to which all had contributed something, even if it was only a spoon or two of tomato paste, was being handed round and wolfed down throughout the catacombs; the noise and the movement had again grown overwhelming.

At the high table, Nero Cassar and his chosen wife, with Father Salvatore on her other side, sat perched above the company, along with a dozen of the bridegroom's relatives, and two or three others who had ignored Mrs Grima's vindictive family boycott to support the bride.

Unveiled, Teresa Grima's face was as they all remembered it: heavy-featured, black-browed, sullen, expressionless. To this the summer heat and foetid air of the catacombs had added a flaming colour and a light sweat. There were audible comments about this from round about; the free-and-easy atmosphere of their surroundings, coupled with the communal lechery inspired by a wedding, provoked the ribald tongue to a certain peak of malice.

Father Salvatore could not help overhearing a near-by exchange : 'She should have kept her veil on.' 'Never mind – he can put the pillow over it.' Teresa must have heard it also. But nothing changed in her face or manner : a cow-like – indeed, a bull-like – indifference was all that showed. Perhaps it was all that mattered, Father Salvatore thought, covertly observing his neighbour, who was now munching a huge slice of the baked macaroni pie called *timpana* as if life was a one-thing-at-a-time matter, and the one thing at this time was a solid, stolid intake of food.

She knows she is ugly, he thought. She lives with it. She knows that this marriage is a kind of a joke. She lives with that also. Blessed are the meek – or better still, blessed are the humble brave.

Raucous cheers greeted the arrival of the golden-cased veal loaf, the most elegant item of food seen in the catacombs for many a long month. People crowded round as it was ceremonially cut : a slice to the bride, a slice to the groom, a slice to the *kappillan* : smaller helpings for the rest of the wedding party; and a very large wedge for the aunt of Wenzu Tonna, the author of this prize, who elbowed her way through the throng to demand her rights and stayed to dictate their exact dimensions. The rest of the loaf disappeared as if melted by the fiercest of suns, and the guests went back to the wine barrel.

Even this monster was growing hollow, as its legacy of merriment and unbuttoned liberty multiplied. Jokes which once would only have been whispered behind a cupped hand were now directly addressed. 'Eh, Nero!' a tipsy shambling man shouted at the bridegroom: 'Have you got your step-ladder ready?' The roar of laughter at this sally was such that even Father Salvatore let its grossness go by, and joined in.

He knew that he had drunk too much; the wine, strong, subtle, and delicious, had wooed him from continence, and his exhaustion had welcomed it as an ally. Ill-humour and rebellion were gone. The cares of today could become the cares of tomorrow, leaving a space for simple enjoyment. The thought of the unlicensed wedding still nagged him, but it was not the first time this had happened, nor would it be the last, and it could be put right without serious trouble, though the foolish fault remained his own.

To obey the letter of canon law, the ceremony would have to be repeated, later and in private if necessary, to regularize a wedding taking place outside the bride's parish and after the hour of darkness. The Maltese, he knew, were not quite so finicky about it as their spiritual mentors. There was a saying, a lewd joke, which covered this lapse from convention. 'So they're not married properly? Try putting it all back!'

Of course, he would be rebuked... The thought, by natural transfer, made him look up to the galleries again, towards Monsignor Scholti and his friends. Since they had shown no wish to come down and join the feast, Father Salvatore had done nothing about inviting them. It would only have needed a sign from Scholti, and none had come. A glance upwards made it crystal clear that none would come now.

They sat in their same position, withdrawn yet watchful: Scholti brooding heavily upon the scene, his young companions as prim-faced as nuns at a tea-dance. A hanging jury, Father Salvatore thought, and then changed his mind. Suddenly the black-cassocked trio seemed absurd in their isolation; not a jury at all, simply the skeletons at the feast. What did one do with skeletons? Give them a Christian burial? No – a Christian welcome.

On an impulse, he took up a bottle of wine, perhaps the last to be poured from the failing barrel, and went upstairs to meet them.

Though he came in good heart, bearing gifts, he had a glacial reception. Monsignor Scholti barely acknowledged his arrival, while the young priests stared at him as if *he* were the intruder, not they. But he did his best.

'Bruno! How nice of you to come to our wedding! But why didn't you let me know? You could have joined us at the top table.'

'We are perfectly comfortable here.' Monsignor Scholti's voice sounded as comfortable as a cactus bush. His cold glance rested on Father Salvatore for a moment, taking in all he wished to see, and then turned aside.

'Well, have some wine to drink to the happy pair.' The *kappillan* advanced the glowing bottle, and the three glasses he had brought as well. 'I think you'll like this. It's very good.'

'Thank you, no.'

'Not even my mother's wine?'

Scholti's eyes, now baleful, rested on him again. 'Not even that. I will leave it for you.'

'But I've had my share.'

'Evidently. And so, I must say, has everyone else here.'

'But it's a wedding!'

Monsignor Scholti pursed his lips. Indeed, they all three pursed their lips in concert, like well-drilled puppets miming 'Disapproval'. No answer was made.

It had been a mistake to come, but Father Salvatore did not regret it. He said: 'What a pity,' and turned to leave again.

He heard Scholti's voice behind him. 'It is indeed a pity.' And then, with special emphasis on the final word: 'This has all been most irregular.'

Downstairs once more, he found that it was time for the bridal pair to leave. There was a truck outside the main entrance, waiting to bear them away to a cousin's house. He went with them to the doorway. Under a starry sky, in the cool of a May night, he blessed them, and said farewell.

Nero hung back after Teresa had climbed up. He seemed suddenly depressed, and his face was grim.

'What's the matter, Nero?'

'All these jokes... You'd think people would have better manners.'

'They were the jokes of friends.'

'*They weren't!* Everyone was making fun of me. I know what they think. They think I won't be any use.'

Father Salvatore stooped, and put his arm round the dwarf's shoulders. 'Forget about it. Forget everyone but Teresa. Be happy tonight, and all the rest of your life.' He sought for further words of comfort, and unexpectedly found them. 'There's one more thing I want to say, Nero. As a friend. Treat Teresa gently. Remember how strong you are.'

I'm glad I said that, he thought, as the noise of the truck died away and he began to grope his way back into the catacombs. The look of sudden pride, sudden confidence, on Nero's face had been a joy to see... Standing within the close-packed concourse again, his head slightly muzzy, he was assailed by something most surprising – an almost complete silence. The people had been waiting for him to come back, and for some reason they were watching to see what he would do next.

He walked up to the high table, and found it deserted. As he faced the main body of the room, a voice called out:

'Tell us a story, Dun Salv! The wine's finished, and we can't all take the bride to bed!'

A strange impulse made him look up to the side gallery again; and there, as if by appointment, he met the disapproving eyes of Monsignor Scholti. As their glances locked Scholti began to shake his head from side to side.

It was enough. Not all his rebellious thoughts returned, but sufficient to clinch a resolve. Lord Gort, the Governor, had talked of self-help for the Maltese, in a way which could have been disdainful. Scholti was only there to spy on him. *He must have known about the missing wedding licence*, yet he had never uttered a word of warning. Was this the act of a man of God?

Very well... He would show the world, tell the world, what *real* priests had done, and *real* people, in days just as fearful as these... He took up the last glass of wine, and drained it defiantly, and began to speak with tongues.

HEXAMERON FIVE

AD 1798.
Tyrant, Priest, and Frigate Captain

'I have not spoken to you for two hundred and thirty years,'
he began. It was an extraordinary start, and it caught their
attention instantly; not least the attention of Monsignor Scholti,
who exchanged meaning glances with his companion priests
before bending forward to listen. 'During those two hundred
and thirty years, from the time of La Valette to the time of
Napoleon, Malta grew and prospered. Great names have come
down to us, in an unbroken chain; names which are still part
of our heritage, still part of our daily life.

'Many of them are the names of Grand Masters; from La
Valette who raised our capital city to another Frenchman,
Verdalle, who fortified Gozo, planted our Boschetto Gardens,
and built his own splendid palace: from de Wignacourt who
beat off the Barbary pirates and then the Turks, and gave
Valletta its first water-supply by the aqueduct from Dingli, to
Antoine de Paule who left us San Anton Palace; and then to
Grand Master Lascaris, who revived our navy and even bought

and ruled St Kitts and three other islands in the Caribbean, but who was so stern and severe, so churlish and forbidding' – here he looked up at Monsignor Scholti, in a manner direct and certainly imprudent, so that many other eyes followed his – 'that even today we say *wiċċ Laskri* – the face of Lascaris – to describe a man who took a bite off a lemon when he was young, and chewed it for the rest of his life.'

There was laughter at the homely words, and the forthright way they were spoken. They had never known Father Sal- vatore in such a mood. Of course, the Santo-Nobile wine- barrel might have something to do with it... And the way he looked at the priests – those other priests who sat there like stone dummies in a whore-house – could not be ignored. There was something going on. There was also the prospect of a good story. Either way, it was not yet time for sleep.

'Last in a great tapestry were Raphael and Nicholas Cotoner, who built the Lines where we lie in peace tonight. But after that...'

After that there was only the Portuguese Manoel de Vilhena, the elegant, worldly-wise, and gifted builder of 1730 – builder of Floriana, of the Manoel Island fort, of the Manoel Theatre; and after him the Grand Masters, and their Knights with them, decayed fatally. They had nothing to do, except bicker about fancied insults and quarrel over minuscule points of precedence. It was a life of white-gloved ceremonial, of disgraceful show, of sport and soft living and endless parties, of the worst of murders – the killing of time. Napoleon, an interested party, summed up the once-splendid Order with plebeian contempt: 'An institution to support in idleness the younger sons of certain privileged families.'

It was true. Insolent yet gutless, disciplined in protocol but aimless in purpose, the Knighthood of Malta had run its course, and was ripe for the scrapyard of history. As was usual in his- tory, all the necessary characters for this tragi-comedy were ready and waiting. Only the last act turned out to be a total surprise.

The villain, the heavy lead, was Napoleon Bonaparte; the pantaloon-clown was Hompesch, last of the resident Grand Masters; the heroine was the fair land of Malta, due to be ravished; the band of brigands, the Forty Thieves within, was a French fifth column; the story-book heroes, Horatio Nelson and his favourite captain, Alexander Ball; and the true stalwarts of the cast – the priest and the people!

Napoleon, at the age of twenty-nine, had really done very well. He had already been a general for five years, and had won a string of battles, principally against Austria and her allies, which had made himself and France the masters of most of Europe. But, as a man of questing, relentless ambition, he had even now dismissed Europe as 'a mole-hill'.

His was the dream of Alexander the Great, of the mastership of half the world, and in particular of a vast Asiatic empire, stretching eastwards from the Mediterranean to the limits of any known military communication. He had active plans for a deep-water canal in the Suez area, to take his transports on their way.

For a start, he must conquer Egypt and then India. But at the moment the island of Malta, in the narrows of the Middle Sea, stood in his way. He wanted it made secure, to round off a tidy tactical triangle with Sardinia and Corfu; and above all he wanted to deny it to his arch-enemy, Admiral Nelson and the British Fleet. 'I would rather see the British in the Faubourg St Honoré,' he declared, and embarked on vast naval preparations at Toulon, involving more than 400 ships, to make sure that this did not happen. It should not take long.

One of his reasons for this optimism was the man in command of the island, the Bavarian Grand Master Ferdinand von Hompesch, the 28th, the last, and the feeblest of the line. Flabby, irresolute, and unpopular, plagued by his quarrelsome Knights, he dithered while others acted. The peril to Malta was apparent to every discerning eye; but the best he could do at a moment of acute crisis was to hope that it would go away, and to refuse to arm the Maltese or to concentrate them in Valletta. 'They will turn against me,' Hompesch told his advisers, and retreated into lethargy again. He was a man ready-made for Napoleon to topple.

But it was not the Maltese who would turn against him. There was a worse pollution among his Knights than unemployment. There was treason.

The French Revolution, eight years earlier, had turned Europe upside down; and the Order of the Knights, who looked to

Europe for money, moral and political support, and the latest
fashion in modish clothes, had been up-ended with it. The very
survival of the Maltese Order, as its protective world collapsed,
was now in question; and the French *langue*, the strongest of
all, was the hardest hit.

These privileged aristocrats woke up one morning to find
their titles and rights abolished. As they waited, thunderstruck,
the harsh decrees multiplied. Any Frenchman belonging to an
order of knighthood automatically ceased to be a citizen of
France. Presently, all the property of the Order, in France and
in Italy, was confiscated, and the Order declared extinct. Suddenly they were orphans.

This bad news was brought, in relays, by a flood of refugees
who now found their way to Malta. Though they were made
welcome, and quartered with the various *langues*, it could not
be forgotten that they were bankrupt, and would no more pay
for this hospitality than the *auberges* could afford to give it.
They only contributed an infection, which was doubt.

The steady process of defeat brought other visitors who could
afford to pay their way. Certain odious agents of despair filtered
in, along with the refugees: certain intriguers, certain spies and
informers. Within months they had formed inside the citadel a
fifth column of collaborators who, in the person of the French
Secretary of the Treasury, penetrated to the very heart of the
Order.

Their message, slipped into every conversation, hammered
home in every argument, was simple, persuasive, and disabling.
Things, in France and elsewhere, would never be the same again.
Times had changed; men, even knightly aristocrats, must change
with them. The penniless vagrants, lately lords and ladies, now
overcrowding their city and running up bills they would never
honour, were proof of this.

There would be no more money coming in, no more backing
from men of influence in Europe, no more political accommoda-
tion, no more arms, unless... 'Unless' could be summed up in a
few crisp sentences:

'Make a deal with the French revolutionaries. Make a deal
with Napoleon. He is coming to take your island anyway. Resist
him, and you will lose all, including your lives.'

There were even moral pressures, to supplement this appeal
to self-interest and the instinct for survival. Many of the

Knights, being young, were idealistic, and hopeful of a new and better world. The novel doctrine of the Rights of Man made a strong appeal to youngsters who had nothing much to cede except their elders' treasure-on-earth. But if this was a true doctrine, worthy of support, where did it leave their aristocratic, privileged Order? *It could only declare them all guilty.*

In Valletta and elsewhere, certain revolutionary clubs were formed, where such things were discussed, and pacts of action and inaction sworn. Among the Knights, the talk grew free, and the ideas daring. The more they talked, the less they wished to withstand the great fraternity of progress.

Napoleon presently judged, from the reports of his professionals, that he had enough friends within Malta to weaken its defences, dilute its honour, and poison its courage. The island, like Grand Master Hompesch, was ripe for what must happen next. It was time for the invader to sail.

Another voyager, more seamanlike than Napoleon or any man in the world, stood in his way. Nelson, at forty, was older, physically more battered, emotionally less stable; but he could match a land-career with a sea-career, and never shirk the comparison. The admiral with 'one eye, one arm, and one ambition', as superb a tactician in battle as he was a brooding genius when faced with a chart of the sea world, also had a string of victories and brave endeavours to his credit.

They stretched from Corsica to Cape St Vincent, from Toulon to Santa Cruz; and they could be etched as big upon the blue sea as were Napoleon's campaigns on the brown earth of Europe.

There was one striking difference between these two men. General Bonaparte, so far as the history books could establish, had never been known to alter one hour of one day's programme, much less delay or avoid decisive action in the field, in favour of racing home to embrace his mistress. Admiral Nelson could not positively claim such a clean bill of behaviour.

How unfair, how scandalous, that the stern man of duty died in exiled defeat and ignominy, while the sinner triumphed, even in death.

A buzz of comment greeted these last words, spoken so strangely. People even looked again at the monsignor and his friends, seeking their reaction. What was Dun Salv trying to

*tell them? That a sinner could deserve success? That there
were worse things in the world than adultery? It was puzzling.
It was also exciting. There were so many strands to this story
that a man could only listen, and hope to sort them out
afterwards.*

Nelson might stand in the way of Napoleon, but he was finding
it hard to bring him to the clinch. To deny Malta to the French
was crucial, and remained so to the end. 'Malta is in our
thoughts, day and night,' he declared; and again, later: 'I am in
desperation about Malta – we shall lose it, I am afraid, past
redemption.' At sea with his fleet, his flag hoisted in the *Vanguard*, he scoured huge tracts of the Mediterranean, looking for
the French armada, now known to have sailed from Toulon.

In this endeavour he had one stroke of bad luck: *Vanguard*
was dismasted in a violent gale, and had to put into Sardinia for
time-wasting repairs. In this endeavour he made one bad guess,
relying on false news – that Napoleon had by-passed Malta and
was making for Alexandria. In this endeavour he chased a
phantom fleet across the thousand miles between Toulon and
the Isles of Greece; crossed their track at night, missed them,
carried on too long, and then doubled back in search of the
quarry.

But he had turned too late. He was still holding the weather
gauge on an enemy who was not there when a look-out frigate
relayed some news from a Sicilian coaster.

Napoleon was not in the eastern Mediterranean at all. He was
anchored in Grand Harbour, and his troops were already ashore.

Even given the cunning preparation, it had been shamefully
easy. The forest of masts and sails which appeared off Malta on
the afternoon of 9 June struck terror into many hearts, particularly the hearts that really mattered. Look-out men, posted
on all the eastern heights of the island, presently reported a total
of 472 sail, including fifteen men-of-war led by Napoleon's flagship, *L'Orient*, spread out just north of Valletta. Secret Intelligence, not necessarily alarmist, had already spoken of a force
of 40,000 troops on board this foreboding fleet.

A French pinnace sped ashore, making for the heart of the
island, Grand Harbour. It carried a request from Napoleon to
the Grand Master, couched in peremptory terms, for permission

to enter the harbour and take on water. Hompesch chose the only course of valour; he called a committee meeting.

With one eye on the enemy fleet and the other on their own unmanned defences, they laboured to produce the soft answer which the Grand Master insisted was all that could be done. 'With the greatest sorrow', the French request was refused, on the grounds of neutrality. They ventured to remind Napoleon that the Treaty of Utrecht had declared Malta a neutral port, and that the statutes of their Order did not allow them to admit more than four belligerent ships at any one time.

In reply, Napoleon exercised the tyrant's traditional gambit of flying into a rage when frustrated. 'They refused me water!' he shouted, as if he were some pitiful parched child in the middle of the Sahara. 'Such barbarians! This means war!'

It meant war, and no one could not say that he was not ready for it. That same night, his troops landed simultaneously at four different, well-calculated points: Marsa Scirocco to the south, St Julian's on the east coast, Mellieha Bay up north, and Ramla Bay on the north-east coast of Gozo.

There was hardly any opposition, because there were no concise orders and, in most cases, no men. By 8 AM the whole coastline was occupied; by noon the old capital, Mdina, was in enemy hands. Gozo took a little longer, until Fort Chambray succumbed to bombardment by battleship. There was also some stalwart resistance from the Cottonera Lines, where certain Knights suspected of treachery were murdered by more deter- mined men, and gunpowder which failed to ignite at a Cospicua battery was taken as proof positive of treason, with the same swift verdict.

But within twenty-four hours the Grand Master had sent a deputation to the flagship *L'Orient*, asking for the French attacks to cease, and at midday on 11 June General Junot, Napoleon's senior aide-de-camp, was riding up the road to Valletta to dictate to Hompesch the terms of surrender.

Eleven hours later the same deputation, after a murky boat- trip during which they were all sea-sick, returned to *L'Orient* to put their signatures to 'an act of capitulation'. Napoleon himself handed them the pen with which they signed away every vestige of their sovereignty, and the ownership of Malta, Comino, and Gozo, together with all their fortifications.

They might retain their religion, and their private possessions.

Grand Master Hompesch, whether he left the island or not, could enjoy his 'military honours', together with a notably golden handshake: an annual pension of 300,000 francs, plus two years' pension in advance to compensate for loss of property.

The deed was done, and signed, at dawn. Just after sunrise, three bristling warships entered Grand Harbour: at mid-morning, with French troops lining the whole of Valletta, Napoleon walked up Merchants Street towards the Parisio Palace, off Castile Square; and that was that. It was the morning of 12 June 1798: one of his shorter campaigns – fifty hours.

Napoleon, ever in a hurry amid the profusion of his mounting dreams, seemed in a hurry to make himself first feared and then loathed. Though he quit the island seven days later, he managed in that short space of time to leave behind him more petty tyranny, more insults, more harsh decrees, more examples of barbaric theft, and more trouble laid up for the future, than any man since Cromwell in Ireland or Attila the Hun on a ravage-tour of Europe.

He set up his headquarters in the Parisio Palace; the fact that this splendid edifice later became the General Post Office was a good example of how even a building could aspire to virtue by casting off its former sins and embracing a life of humble service. From the Parisio, he set to work, in his six days of creation, to turn Malta into an orderly department of the French Republic.

French was declared the official language. The population must sport red-white-and-blue cockades. The Palace Square became the *Place de la Liberté*. All armorial bearings were torn down, and all Maltese declared 'equal in rights'. Malta and Gozo were to be administered, under a brand-new constitution, by a commission of nine persons concerned with food, taxation, sanitary regulations, public order, and 'respect for established institutions'. Scurrilous posters were forbidden. Windmills were nationalized. The university was abolished, in favour of a Central School, which (with fifteen others) would teach mathematics, stereometry, astronomy, physics, chemistry, navigation, geography, oriental languages, anatomy, and medicine, together with French reading, writing, arithmetic, pilotage, political principles, and morality.

By the time the Maltese had caught their breath, they knew at least one thing. Napoleon was fussy. With a few days still to go, he then became brutal.

Grand Master Hompesch, and such of his militant Knights as might be dangerous, were given three days to leave, and then kicked out, without ceremony. Every town and village was garrisoned, by 3,000 troops who knew from long experience how to make their personal mark on a conquered nation, and how to make them pay for it as well. Taxes were laid on every common commodity, from bread to candles, to meet the cost of this occupation.

Maltese sailors were press-ganged into the French fleet, and their families left to starve. Religious marriages were declared illegal; and when this was protested, further stern rules were laid on all ecclesiastics. The bishop was ordered to call a meeting of Maltese parish priests and clergy, and Napoleon himself addressed them, with a nice blend of ironic courtesy and blatant threat :

'Reverend gentlemen, preach the gospel, respect the constituted authorities, and recommend submission and obedience to your people. If you are good priests, I shall protect you; if you are bad priests, I shall punish you.'

Napoleon hardly gave them time to digest this homily before he began a systematic plundering of all church and civic property in Malta. A sharp-eyed commission made a whirlwind tour of churches, cathedrals, the *auberges* of the Knights, and any municipal building which might house anything saleable, convertible, movable, or stealable. Then the official looting began.

Gold, silver, and precious stones were all scooped up and borne away to a gigantic thieves' kitchen of stolen goods. The most exquisite silver plate, two hundred years old, was melted down into bullion. Gold chalices and candlesticks became portable ingots; pictures and tapestries were folded, rolled up, and packed like stage properties; jewels were poured piecemeal into a huge 'Army chest'.

The whole of the plunder, topped by the gates of Valletta cathedral, was then loaded on board the giant three-decker ship-of-the-line, the flagship *L'Orient*, in time for Napoleon to keep his next appointment, which was with Egypt.

At the head of his enormous fleet he sailed before Nelson

could catch him. As a final calculated blasphemy, he allowed the church to keep its most revered relic, the right hand of St John the Baptist, brought from Rhodes nearly three hundred years earlier. But before returning it he pulled off its precious ring, and slipped it on to his own finger, crowning his brief tyranny with an atrocious tyrant's joke:

'The hand is yours. But the ring suits mine much better!'

Though the story of cowardice and defeat had been disgraceful, there had earlier been laughter when Dun Salv had called Napoleon 'fussy'. It was a favourite word for any character too zealous for the public taste. There were fussy policemen, fussy politicians, even fussy priests. So, a fussy emperor? – at that moment it had seemed just the word. But now there was a swift revulsion. A gasp of horror went up, a great catch of breath like a missed heart-beat which filled the whole catacomb, as the kappillan's words – Napoleon's words – found their mark. Could there be, in the whole of the world, a worse thing to do and to say? Surely such a fiend must be punished instantly, struck dead or dumb or blind, for so monstrous a sacrilege? If there was any justice under God...

There was justice under God, and it struck the tyrant as swiftly and surely as a bolt of lightning under a tall tree in a meadow. The French fleet, with its hundred of transports, reached Egypt undetected, and there it disembarked Napoleon and his army, who marched away to attack and take Alexandria. Then his warships – thirteen battleships and four frigates – sailed farther east up the coast and anchored in Aboukir Bay, near the Rosetta mouth of the Nile.

They formed a line of majestic, concentrated strength, and they thought themselves further protected by the rocks and shoals guarding the entrance. They were thus relaxed, their decks covered with newly arrived stores and half their crews ashore filling water-barrels, when Nelson came upon them. It was the evening of the first day of August.

Either his luck had changed, or an admiral's skill had sharpened. He led his squadron of twelve ships, without charts and near nightfall, straight into the bay. Plans for this sort of encounter had already been laid and meticulously rehearsed. The only signal his captains needed was 'Enemy in sight'. In the course of the night action, fought with the greatest courage on both sides, the British fleet sank, crippled, or captured thirteen out of the seventeen French, without a single loss to themselves.

The last ship to clinch this, the greatest sea-victory in the course of the war, was *L'Orient*, the 120-gun pride of the fleet. She had spent the day painting ship; thus she was readily set on fire, and served as a torch for the whole battlefield. Towards midnight, under an August moon, she blew up, with a shattering roar heard twenty miles away in Alexandria.

Disintegrating at one stroke, she took to the bottom every scrap of her Maltese loot, from priceless ornaments and pictures to the melted gold and silver. Though the loss to Malta had been terrible, the swift punishment had matched it.

At the end of August, the survivors of this Battle of the Nile limped back into Grand Harbour: one battleship, the *Guillaume Tell*, and two frigates (the fourth French ship to escape had sailed elsewhere). The Maltese watchers on the bastions looked at them in amazement, and then in contempt, and then in mutinous speculation. This was all that was left of that ferocious fleet? These three torn ships? This was the invincible French armada?

Within hours, it was the signal for the flaming revolt, which had been brewing ever since the tyrant left the island.

During the ten weeks' interval, General Vaubois, whom Napoleon had installed as Commander-in-Chief of Malta, had continued his master's rule. Vaubois was 'affable', and a diplomatic phrase-maker of some note; when the three French ships returned to harbour, he announced that Napoleon had scored a tremendous series of triumphs in Egypt, 'only marred by a slight mishap to the fleet'. But the smooth tongue could not mask the repressive acts. Malta was under the yoke, and was made to feel it every day.

The occupying troops were rough and ready visitors, like all soldiers in the same position; even if they had behaved like uniformed angels, it was enough that they were *there* – billeted in private houses, or living in barracks at Maltese expense, skimming off the best of the crops, the best of the cattle, the best of the girls. There was no compensation for any damage they might do to private property. The families of Maltese soldiers and sailors who had followed Napoleon to Egypt were still penniless.

The French were always mean. In the face of mutinous acts, they now became ruthless.

A system of forced loans was proclaimed, to swell the dwindling coffers. Vaubois, whose style was sharpening, announced it thus:

'*Liberté! Egalité!* The atrocious crimes committed by your country people compel me to have recourse to a loan to pay the troops... It is imperative that the soldier should be punctually paid, to calm his just resentment...

'I have therefore put you down for the loan of 200 *scudi*, to be paid within 24 hours from the moment you receive this letter... As I have been informed of your means, your refusal will be considered with suspicion... Health and Fraternity! Vaubois.'

Discontent grew rife throughout the island. A man could scarcely eat. Malta was dead. Nothing was happening, and nothing would happen until these vultures were chased away. But who could act, who could lead? The nobility, never reconciled to the Knights and the troubles they had brought, remained in close seclusion. The Knights were scattered. Hompesch had retired to Trieste, and would never return.

On the day that the bruised rump of the French fleet returned, there was a further proclamation. All remaining church property was to be auctioned off. The process would start with a sale of tapestry and valuables in the Carmelite convent church of Mdina, on 2 September – a Sunday.

Something must be done. But who could act, who could lead? The answer was no one – no one but themselves.

On the morning of the auction, of which people and priests had talked far into the night, and lamented, and raged against, huge crowds began to converge upon Mdina and the Carmelite church. They could not all be buyers... Those who were able to push their way into the church found it transformed into a disgraceful circus: a cheap market-place of stolen goods, or goods about to be stolen.

The church plate, the chalices, the candlesticks, were laid out on the altar, as if on a shop counter. A carpenter, a man from outside the city, a man with a look of shame on his face, was unhooking the red damask hangings which lined the walls, and piling them on the floor.

Two officials seemed to be in charge: two auctioneers, men

of some position, known to the people. These were Notary Alessandro Spiteri and Giuseppe Farrugia. The crowd began to growl in protest as the carpenter completed his task, his display-for-sale. Notary Spiteri, aware of the contempt he aroused, stepped forward and put upon this charade the best face he could.

'By order of General Vaubois, Commander-in-Chief of the occupation forces...' He read the French proclamation, in a matter-of-fact voice, as if there were nothing in it which good citizens need worry about. Then he said: 'Now... A number of red curtains... What am I offered?'

A priest standing in the forefront of the crowd called out loudly: '*No!*'

Notary Spiteri, doing his duty as he saw it, persisted: 'I am asking for bids for these curtains.'

The priest repeated, in the same voice of shock and disgust: 'No!... It is sacrilege! Let no one offer money.'

Suddenly, above their heads, the bells began to peal, and the crowd moved forward menacingly. As space was made at the back of the church, more people pushed in. They were growling and shouting, and shaking their fists. It was clear that they were not going to have this: not at the price of shame, not at any price.

Spiteri, when he was not a notary, was a comfortable family man with a good heart. In the face of bitter resentment which he could understand, he fell silent. His companion Giuseppe Farrugia, who had hoped to record the bids and the prices, tried to intervene.

'Keep silence... Let us have order... This is an official sale...'

He was interrupted by the sheer pressure of bodies, forcing their way up to the altar which had become a common auctioneer's rostrum, a place of no account. The priest who had first spoken, spoke again: 'Stop this! Stop speaking! There will be no sale.'

The noise of the crowd, which had been a low-pitched growl, rose to a howl of angry agreement. The church was now so packed and so tumultuous that those in front were standing on the damask curtains. No one could see anything; they could only hear the mounting hatred, and the furious determination to bring this to an end. Notary Spiteri gave up.

'The auction is postponed,' he shouted, and dived for the side door. Though both he and Farrugia were roughed up by the crowd, they managed to make their escape. They escaped to the headquarters of Citizen-Colonel Masson, commandant of the Mdina garrison, and told him their scandalous story. It cost the colonel his life.

That night, the bells never ceased to toll, a tocsin of alarm which spread outwards from the churches of Mdina like a fiery ring. 'We are celebrating a little feast,' was the smooth answer to a protest from authority, and with that, authority had to be content. But success had given the Maltese a taste of triumph, perhaps a taste for blood. When, next morning, Colonel Masson rode out, he rode headlong into disaster.

It was thought that he planned to summon reinforcements from the Valletta garrison, to disperse the crowds and force the auction through; and this, in the general mood of riot and rebellion, was not to anyone's taste. Masson and his escort were followed downhill from Mdina by a crowd, howling insults and pressing in on the soldiers. But it was a small boy who triggered the final explosion – a small boy with a well-aimed pebble.

Sailing through the air from behind a wall, it hit Colonel Masson on the bridge of his prominent nose. While the crowd roared their delight, Masson drew his sword, waved it furiously, and made as if to jump the wall and ride the boy down.

As the spectators screamed in anger, Masson lost his nerve, whipped his horse round, and galloped back to the citadel. But he had made too many enemies. On foot, chased by a howling mob, he ran through the narrow streets for the house of Notary Bezzina and there, panting, took refuge. Within minutes, the doors were battered down, and the mob surged in; within minutes, a balcony window above was flung open, and Colonel Masson's body, sailing through the air like the pebble, landed with a crash on the cobbled street. The priest who ran forward and knelt beside him was too late to catch his soul.

In the next twenty-four hours the entire garrison of Mdina was hunted down and slaughtered, and their corpses burned in public. It was the end of the auction, and the beginning of everything else.

There could be no turning back now: the people knew that they had gone too far, and that Vaubois would rightly be merciless if any of them were caught. The bells began to ring again, and now they rang all over the island, from St Paul's Bay to the Three Cities. The priests called, the people answered; and their courage flowered like a blood-red clover-field under the surge of spring.

First, they elected their own 'revolutionary council' which, with courage and confidence, became the Provisional Civil Government. At its head was Notary Emmanuele Vitale (the notaries had the brains, the priests the divine spark, and the people the guts to follow both). Another cleric, Canon Francesco Caruana, also played a leading part; and with them, three noblemen of Malta's most ancient lineage – Count Manduca, Marquis Depiro, and Count Castelletti – abandoned their posture of neutrality and, to their eternal honour, declared themselves for this desperate fight.

The rebellion spread like the wild fire which it was. Armouries at Zebbug and Attard were broken into, and precious guns seized. There was hard fighting at Cospicua – unhappily suppressed, with the leaders executed. There was better luck, and the same shining courage, in half a dozen other villages – Siġġiewi, Hamrun, Birkirkara, Mosta, Zabbar, and Corradino, whence long ago the Turkish swimmers had swum towards their watery graves.

Gradually a ring closed round Valletta, as the French were driven into the city, or pushed out into the sea, or killed in flight. Presently the ring was tight, the countryside cleansed, and the invaders, reversing history, were penned up in the capital with the Maltese patriots screaming for their blood before the bastions.

General Vaubois, as hard-pressed as any man could be, summed it up in words which were a thousand miles away from Napoleon's crude contempt of four months earlier. He was now pleading, like a runaway boy, for help from home.

'For forty days we have been blockaded ashore by all the inhabitants of the island, and afloat by the Portuguese fleet. We have no meat, no wine, no brandy, no victuals except corn. We have no ammunition and no clothes... We have lost many brave soldiers, and we have none to lose... Fanaticism and hatred have raised the Maltese courage to an extraordinary level. Help us with men and food.'

The facts were correct, with one exception. It was not exactly the Portuguese navy which had put this throttling grip on the sea approaches to Malta. They had been replaced by a particular friend of Nelson's, one of the gifted and daring 'band of brothers' who so brilliantly commanded the ships of his fleet: Captain Alexander Ball of the 74-gun *Alexander*.

Ball, who had been a frigate captain before he achieved a ship of the line, combined the swift initiative bred in a small ship with the solid, all-capable strength of command necessary for a battleship. He had undoubtedly saved Nelson's life, a few months earlier, when the *Vanguard*, dismasted in a hideous gale, was drifting towards the rocks of Sardinia; somehow he had got a towing-hawser on board the crippled ship, and hung on to it in the teeth of the storm, and refused to let go when even his admiral had advised him to cut the tow and leave the *Vanguard* to her fate.

'Better one wreck than two' had been Nelson's line of thought, as he watched the hungry breakers under his lee sucking him nearer and nearer to disaster. 'Better no wreck at all', Ball decided, and clawed them both out of danger and into the blessed haven of calm water. Later, with the same fortitude, the *Alexander* had been the last ship directly opposed to the *L'Orient*, a monster of nearly twice her fire-power, in the final hour of the Battle of the Nile, and had lived to see her adversary sink in fiery ruin.

Now Captain Ball in his brave 74, with two frigates, a sloop, and a fire-ship, had arrived to take over from the Portuguese force, and to support from seawards what the Maltese were doing on land: strangling the French.

It took a long time. Vaubois, the affable Frenchman who had been left out on this long and lonely limb, was also brave and determined. He refused two demands for surrender, one from Captain Ball, one from Nelson himself. He was always polite; once, even when he was at the last extreme, he replied: 'You would no more expect me to dishonour my country by surrender, than I would expect you to fail in your own duty. I do not understand your request, and I lament your language.' He was, under the furnace heat of proof, a steel-hearted foe who would not give in.

The sea-blockade continued, for month after month. Nelson, though fevered and sick from a brutal head-wound sustained at the Nile, came to have a look. He could only tell Alexander Ball to keep going, to confirm him as the commandant ashore as well as afloat, and to take back with him the French flags captured on Gozo when Ball's marines stormed and overran Fort Chambray.

Ball, now free to move anywhere in Malta except near the fortress of Valletta, gave the land-fighters great encouragement, and made many friends: so many, indeed, that the Maltese civil government sent constant appeals to have him named as their 'protector', under the British flag.

It was something for the hopeful future. But there was always Valletta the fortress, and Vaubois the valiant defender, standing in the way of hope. There was also malignant fever and famine in the land, enough to break the heart of a people who did *not* have to rid themselves of a foreign tyrant. Nothing was happening, of which a man could say: '*Now* we are winning!'

Five British ships could not maintain a cast-iron blockade. Four thousand British and Maltese soldiers – Maltese by nearly three to one – commanded by General Graham, could not storm the bastions nor tempt the enemy to a pitched battle.

Presently another Maltese patriot, another priest, tried something else.

It was a plot, a daring plot: nothing less than that certain Maltese penned up within the citadel should, at an agreed moment, ring the church bells, open the gates, and let the attackers into Valletta. Like all the best and bravest plots, like any hare-brained scheme devised by desperate or loving men, it had almost no chance of success. But it was planned, and when the hour struck it was put into operation, and it failed because of the most common human frailty of all. There was too much talk about it.

Three men were involved as leaders. Outside the city, Canon Caruana of the Provisional Civil Government laid careful plans which the attackers must follow. Inside Valletta, the man who had conceived this valiant stroke, Father Michael Xerri, whom his faithful friends knew as Dun Mikiel, undertook the task of ringing the alarm and seeing that the guards on the gate were overcome. The two were in constant touch by secret letters.

The third conspirator was a strange bedfellow, who made his brief appearance on this single page of history, and vanished as suddenly as he had arrived: Guglielmo Lorenzi, a 'Russian corsair, who was to trigger the attack and, at a precise hour, unlock the city gates. Captain Alexander Ball knew of the scheme, and gave it a sailor's blessing. He was in favour of *anything* which would break a mortal stalemate.

There was a gala performance at the Manoel Theatre that night. A gala performance during a cruel siege? – *mais naturellement!* Why not? No Frenchman worth the name would tolerate a life which was *all* misery, *all* bloodshed, *all* starvation and disease and despair. The bright lights beckoned, and the bright eyes also, and death could take at least an evening's holiday.

But there had been too much plot-talk already. Not every man-at-arms was at the Manoel Theatre that night; important commanders remained on the alert. Movements inside and outside the city were noted. Certain curfew-breakers on their way to a mysterious rendezvous were detained. At the appointed hour, the bells did not ring, the guards were not surprised and overcome, the gates were not opened, and the enterprise collapsed before a single blow could be struck. In the cold dawn, a terrible *post mortem* began.

Lorenzi, the Russian corsair with the dubious name and proven spirit, refused to betray his accomplices, and died in that defiance. But mute courage was no shield for men whose names had been whispered for week after week in cellars, on street corners, behind doors thought to be closed. Forty-five conspirators were rounded up, among them Dun Mikiel, and after a brief court-martial they were condemned to be shot in the Palace Square.

A moment of glory lightened a desolate scene. Dun Mikiel, who felt the guilt of a leader whose followers now had to pay the supreme penalty, did not beg for life or mercy. Instead, he spoke to the commander of the execution squad.

'Shoot me last of all.' He was calm and compassionate, beyond fear and beyond death already. His only wish was to comfort his companions. 'Grant us a few moments of prayer. I will give you the order to fire.'

The French officer, who had been a devout son of the Church before history made him an atheist, agreed. On such a bleak morning, who could have a stomach for this task, who could ram home the last harsh word of the rule-book? Dun Mikiel moved among his friends, comforting, confessing, absolving, loving. When his fortitude, bright as flame, had become theirs, he walked forward, and gave his silver watch to the French commander.

'In memory of today,' he said. 'You may fire now.'

When the echo of the volley ceased, Dun Mikiel walked back, and stood among the ring of forty-four bloody corpses. Then he nodded, and embraced his own death with the last heart-beat of courage. He fell forward on the gory stones of the Palace Square, that *Place de la Liberté* which thus deserved, for a single moment, its new, immortal name.

> With such pride had Dun Salv told his story, the story of the brave and loving priest, that he was forced to stop speaking. For the first time in the history of the catacombs, he was brought to a halt by a roar of applause. It echoed round the hollow concourse in a burst of emotion and release; the forest of clapping hands waved and fluttered like tiny banners, many of the eyes which had been dull with wine were now glistening with tears. Even the little dead brothers in their dusty niches must hear, and add a ghostly rustling tribute from the grave. Dun Mikiel, Dun Mikiel... What a man, what a priest...
>
> Only Scholti and his companions held aloof. The young priests were staring straight ahead of them, as if such talk of blood and fire might adulterate their faith or stain their cassocks. The monsignor, of all things in the world to do, was writing in a notebook. But nothing, nothing in the same world, could put a shadow on the story. For now, after all the heartbreak, the end could only be triumph.

Though the brave plot failed, Vaubois was also failing, by the day, by the hour. There was a limit to endurance, even for such a resolute commander, and he had almost reached it. No food, no men, could now come to the aid of the citadel, following two great sea victories which removed from the scene the last two French battleships in the Mediterranean – the *Généreux* which tried to run the blockade, and the *Guillaume Tell*, interned in Grand Harbour since the Battle of the Nile, which sought to break out.

These last survivors of the Nile were fought to a standstill by the British fleet, with Alexander Ball and Horatio Nelson taking turnabout for the honours. With their disappearance, Valletta was at last isolated.

The Maltese and British troops closed in. Batteries of guns were set up on an ancient vantage-point, the same spit of land used by Dragut Rais to batter the walls of St Elmo. Starvation and disease finally closed the book, after more than two years. Broken at last, reduced to bread and water, refusing to eat rats even for the honour of French arms, Vaubois marched out of his citadel, and Captain Alexander Ball marched in.

It was now his turn to walk up Merchants Street: a tall and handsome man with the look of action joined to intellect, taking longer strides than Napoleon could ever have managed, two years earlier. The cry of the Maltese was still: 'Give us British rule! Give us Captain Ball as our leader!', and he was in fact confirmed as Civil Commissioner of Malta, in 1802, and set up house and home in San Anton Palace.

There, in old Antoine de Paule's house, amid the orange groves and the terraced gardens, the honey-yellow stone and the brick-red bougainvillea, he worked for eight devoted years; and there he died. The frigate captain who came ashore as a baronet was buried in a position of the greatest honour, the Abercrombie Curtain of St Elmo Fort.

He would have been the first to say that he had only built on what the Maltese themselves began.

In Limbo

Into his borrowed cell, the dawn crept like a thief, like a nagging woman whose voice could not be denied. High up, a shaft of pale light came through the missing stone which was the only ventilation; under the cell door which gave on to the courtyard, a longer slit of daylight changed from dark grey to white, then to white with a yellowish tinge.

Father Salvatore, turning in his cot, stared at it for a moment, and made his calculation. After two weeks, he could at least do this sum right. He could tell the early morning time exactly.

Try me. Go on – try me. I say that it is half past four on a summer morning in Gozo. Perhaps just before half past, since the bell has not yet rung. No – that would be cheating. I will say half past.

The single muffled bell across the courtyard tolled. It was half past four. He relaxed, and lay back, and stared at the ceiling, or where the ceiling would be when the light gained a little. Shuffling sandalled feet outside told him that the brothers were assembling for their walk to Mass. He was excused from this. He was excused from everything. He was a guest, and the world – even the monastery world – let him go by without comment.

The world might stare at him a little, and speculate, and perhaps criticize or even condemn. But it did not say anything out loud. He was a guest of the Capuchins. He was important. He was nothing. He was two weeks old, or dead for a thousand years. He was Father Salvatore, the famed *il-kappillan tal-katakombi*. He was known only to God, like the Unknown Soldier of an older war.

Two weeks ago, for a single day, he had started to keep a diary, a foolish, pompous assertion of self. It began:

'I, Father Salvatore, born Santo-Nobile, disgraced and sent away, have decided to keep a journal during my exile in this wilderness. But a time so terrible can only be borne if one stands aside, and views oneself as another person. When "I" becomes "That man", the wounds are not so fearful, since they pierce the flesh of another, and pain is swallowed by pity. I now become "That man".'

There, thanks be to God, the arid exercise in self-pity ended. But some of its mood returned, on every morning of every day, to add that day to all the other days of sour, sad, and futile banishment.

The interview with his Lordship had been short and, for so gentle an old man, sharp. The bishop wished him to leave the catacombs 'for a while', and go into retreat in Gozo. He would be notified when he might return.

Father Salvatore, sitting upright on what must be the hardest chair in the palace, a chair of true penitence, might pretend to be surprised, but he was not. He was not even surprised that Dom Maurus Caruana seemed to have made up his mind – a steely mind, when it came to decision – before the interview. When he asked 'Why?' with due respect, he knew the answer – all the answers.

The bishop was gentle, as usual, but he was not yielding.

'I spoke to you before about this, Salvu.' They were still father and son, but the son had erred, and the father was telling him so. 'Quite apart from the unlicensed wedding, which was a silly mistake, and the bad behaviour on the night in question, which was perhaps understandable, there is your own role. I warned you that this should not enlarge *you*, rather than the Church and the faith. A priest is not to be applauded when he speaks to his people... He is not to make himself a popular hero, poking fun at authority... Above all, he is not to take pride in war, in the military activities of other priests, however brave. Our faith is the faith of the Prince of Peace...' The old man's face was grave; already, there would be no appeal from what was to come. 'When we last met, I said: "Search your conscience." I do not believe you have done so.'

Father Salvatore said nothing. It was all too true to be denied: unfair, biased in a certain measure, as the Church itself was biased towards strict observance of the faith, but true. He could only wait for the blow to fall.

It fell, with all sufficient strokes of authority. 'I have come to the conclusion,' said the kind, stern old man, 'that you are tired, overstrained. You have taken on too much, and it has grown too big for you. I may say that your mother feels the same... Please understand that we are your friends. One might even say, admirers, in a certain sense. But there comes a time when friends must speak out, and admirers must examine what they are admiring. After that, the Church which we both love and serve demands one thing more – obedience.'

There followed the sentence of exile.

He asked for time – time to settle his affairs, time to instruct people like Nero Cassar how to carry on in his absence – and time was granted. But it was time under a strict edict. There were to be no more speeches, no more performances: *nothing* except the simple service of Christ and his Church.

He agreed, and kissed the ring, and withdrew from audience. Monsignor Scholti did not make an appearance.

Father Salvatore had kissed the ring in true humility, but he could have wept, he could have raged. What happened to him was nothing; what happened to his Church and his people, everything. It was a fearful time to leave Malta, and the Cottonera Lines. Cruel hunger, wicked bombing, now ruled their lives again. Was it pride which made him think: How can they survive without me? Or was it plain fact? He could not stay to find out.

In farewell, his small despairing mother said: 'I am sorry, Salvatore. Don't blame me. Don't be bitter. You *are* tired, exhausted. You *have* been doing too much, you *do* need rest... If you go on like this, you will kill yourself!... What could I do but agree?' He left her wordless, as he had left the bishop. Like his beloved St Barnabas, he had quarrelled fatally, he had fallen at strife with St Paul, and it was St Paul, nearest to the throne of God, who now sent him into limbo.

He dressed, and waited for the knock on his cell door; and the knock came at six o'clock, as punctual as the sun, as predictable as the bell for the first Mass. It was Brother Ninu, the friar who served him, and seemed to love him; a man whose simple heart would have put any rebellious priest to shame.

Brother Ninu was small, and rather fat – all the brothers seemed fat, on a diet of bread and *pasta* which never varied, from one January day till the next. He was also earnest and enthusiastic, gullible and kind, ready to laugh at the joys of the world, apt to weep for its cruelty. He ran many of the monastery's errands; he was a loving and expert gardener, he was undoubtedly one of God's children. Now he put his head round the door, and smiled his good-morning, and brought in breakfast.

Breakfast was coffee – of a sort – and bread which they baked for themselves, and a little dab of precious jam, and a peach from Brother Ninu's own small orchard. While Father Salvatore ate, Brother Ninu tidied the cell, and carried out the basin which served for washing, and brought in a fresh pitcher of water. Moving about, going in and out, he talked, and seemed to enjoy all the answers as if they were pearls of revelation.

'Are you rested, Dun Salv? Did you have a good sleep?'

'A very good sleep, thank you.'

'That's wonderful! When you first came here, and slept so long, I said to myself: "There is a man who is *really* tired. He must have a proper rest." Isn't that true?'

'I was tired, yes.'

'But a few more days or weeks, and you will be well again. Better than ever!' Brother Ninu was looking at something on the shelf at the head of the bed, just below the crucifix, and Father Salvatore thought he was going to ask again, but he delayed for a moment. Instead he said: 'There was lots more bombing last night. Did you hear it?'

'No. Do you mean bombing in Gozo?'

'No, no. Across the water. They say it was Mosta. Why should they bomb Mosta, Dun Salv?'

'There's no reason, really.' Father Salvatore drank the last of the bitter coffee, and set down the mug. 'But when a bomber is attacked, sometimes it lets all its bombs go, wherever it is, and flies off home.'

'What a thing to do!' But Brother Ninu's eyes had gone back to the shelf again. He even reached out his hand, as if to touch something, and then thought better of it. 'Dun Salv? Can I ask a favour?'

'You want to see the relics, Ninu?'

'*Yes!*' The friar's eyes brightened wonderfully: he looked just as ready to laugh as to cry, and both for joy. 'You did say you would show me one day. Is this a good time?'

'I think so... Will you take them down for me?'

'Can I *really*?'

With the most reverent hands Father Salvatore could ever remember watching, Ninu lifted the shabby old case from the shelf, and put it gently down on the cot. Then he laced his fingers together as if in prayer, and waited.

'Sit down, Ninu.'

The case lay between them on the blanket. With a whisper of devotion which he must have uttered a thousand times, Father Salvatore raised the polished mahogany lid, to show the relics which he had brought from his cell in the catacombs. They were the garnering, the prizes, of a lifetime's faith, belief, and adoration.

They were under a glass cover, not to be touched by profane or holy hands; but he could point to each one, as it rested in its small compartment, and explain it to Brother Ninu, and tell where he had bought it or been given it – sometimes in Rome, sometimes in Malta, in Rhodes, in Crete, once on the never-to-be-forgotten pilgrimage to Jerusalem. Brother Ninu listened, and stared, and sighed, and exclaimed, as if miracles were unfolding under his very eyes.

Perhaps they were. Father Salvatore could show him – *was* showing him – such treasures as a simple friar could scarcely imagine. All were reverently housed; some were set in exquisite medallions which bore witness to their holy repute.

There was a tiny fragment of cloth labelled *Ex Velo S. Veronicae de Judaea* – the very veil of Saint Veronica, with which she had wiped the sweat from Christ's face on the road to Calvary. There was a sliver of grey-black wood, *Ex Vero Ligno* – from the True Cross. There were pin-points of bone, the remnants of holy saints now in the bosom of Christ. There was another thread of cloth, *Ex Birreto Sancti Philippi Neri* – the sacred cap of that St Philip who founded the Congregation of the Oratory in the very year of the Great Siege.

There was a faded grey speck upon a piece of parchment, on which was written *Latte della Beatissima Vergine* – the Milk of the Blessed Virgin. There was the greatest prize, the holiest relic of all: another splinter of wood, with the world's most awesome title: *Cunis Dom. Nost. Jesu Christi* – the Cradle of our Lord Jesus Christ.

Father Salvatore sat back, while Brother Ninu continued his rapturous examination of these treasures. He sat back, and the

earth turned under him, like a rock made to tremble and tip by
a fearsome wave. Suddenly, in an awful avalanche of doubt
and shame, he found that he did not believe a word of what
he had said and shown.

Carrion vultures of derision pecked and clawed at his head.
Cynical and shameful thoughts flooded in like a sewage tide. A
veil that had wiped off the sweat of Christ? Who could possibly
believe that? Had St Veronica sold it to a junk-man? To a
pawn-broker? The only true Veronica of this century was the
veronica of the matador – the classic slow swing of the cape
before the bull's face, imitating that holy wiping, mocking
it.

A piece of the True Cross? There must be enough of these for
all the standing timber on the Mount of Olives. The Virgin's
milk? – what rude member of the family had collected *that*? A
piece of the cradle of Christ? There would be no such cradle.
Cradles cost money. There had once been a manger in a cow-
shed in Bethlehem, two thousand years ago. Had it had a
preservation order slapped on it by the Jewish Office of Works,
in AD 1?

He felt sick unto death. He had believed in all these things
for so long. Now they could only be lies, tourist trash, a brisk
line of goods for the hucksters who waylaid the faithful. The
shining look on simple Brother Ninu's face was a measure of
their falsity. They were good enough to fool a friar. They must
be rubbish.

He felt a sweat breaking out on his own brow. My turn,
Veronica... The cell was now stifling, the monastery had
become a harsher prison than Ta' Kordin, the odour of sanctity
worse than a cess-pit's. Brother Ninu, looking up from his
adoration, noticed the change, and was instantly concerned.

'Dun Salv! Are you all right?'

'I feel a little faint, Ninu. I think it's the heat. Will you ask
the *Gwardjan* if I can see him?'

'Immediately!'

But when Father Salvatore saw the head of the monastery, it
was not to seek his help. It was to say that he was going for a
walk.

For the *Gwardjan*, an old monk with the sad brown eyes of a
man who had not found in life the dreamed-of road to glory,
this was his first real dilemma for many years. He was the ruler

of this domain, and it had never proved difficult to control a flock which was not high on the Church's tables of precedence.

If there was ever disobedience, it concerned over-loud talking, or the late burning of candles; if there were quarrels, they were petty matters of who-was-putting-on-airs, who-took-my-bread-when-I-wasn't-looking, who-sang-too-loud-and-spoiled-the-music. Father Salvatore, and his strange request to interrupt his retreat, was not of this quality.

Father Salvatore seemed very determined, even desperate, for private reasons which the *Gwardjan* hesitated to probe. Father Salvatore was not only a famous man – the catacombs were always being talked of – but technically his superior, though within the confines of the monastery this was arguable. Conversely, the bishop had hinted – no, it was Monsignor Scholti who had hinted – that his retreat was in some sense a disciplinary matter. Yet it was a great honour to have him here, and he must certainly be humoured. And then there was always his mother.

The Most Noble Baroness, and her illustrious family, had long been generous benefactors of the Church. There was already talk of a souvenir gift, to mark her son's stay with the Capuchins : new altar cloths, or even a *golden* pyx to house the consecrated Host. It was not easy to say 'No' to such a man.

The *Gwardjan* temporized. 'Believe me, I do understand. The cell is small, like all the other cells, and life here must seem very confined. But perhaps a daily walk in the gardens? I know they are not at their best in this heat—'

It was not an acceptable answer. Father Salvatore did not exactly want to go for a walk. That was only the beginning of it. He wanted to walk *out*. He wanted to leave his retreat for some days. How many, he could not say.

'I will have to seek the bishop's permission,' the *Gwardjan* told him. 'Since he made all the arrangements. I'm sure you appreciate that.'

'It would take too long,' Father Salvatore interrupted him, and indeed he felt, and must have looked, like a man for whom even an extra five minutes in the monastery would have been insupportable. He *must* have fresh air, freedom, a space for the soul to breathe. He feared – he truly feared – that unless he left his cell, and wandered at will, he would choke, or be poisoned by his own evil thoughts. He was already in terror of these.

He had not felt so fouled since – since, as a boy, he had vowed himself to God.

Lord, I do believe. Help Thou my unbelief.

'Brother, I *must* go. Today.'

'Very well. I will see if I can telephone the bishop.'

While this was being done, Father Salvatore collected his small store of money, made a parcel of some spare socks, an undershirt, a razor, and his breviary, walked past a dozing gate-keeper, and went on down the hill to Marsalforn – and into blessed liberty.

Gozo was different. He had forgotten how different; he had forgotten its simplicity and peace, not at all impaired by the 'refugees' from Malta who had crowded in, and dispersed, and been eaten by the sister isle. It was said that Gozo, tiny as it was, could swallow a whale and spit out *vopi* – the nearest thing to a small sardine which this stretch of the middle sea produced.

The impolite phrase only meant that Gozo remained an utterly private place, an island *in petto* – within the breast – and lucky was the man who could find the key, turn the lock, and vanish inside.

A policeman, searching for a murderer whose tight-lipped friends outnumbered the fleas on a dog, had once told him : 'I would rather question goats with their mouths sewn up, than Gozitans.'

It was Calypso's island, where Odysseus had spent seven years with the importunate nymph-goddess, and had to lie his way out when their second son was born, and sailed home to Ithaca as the first recorded star-navigator whose rule-of-thumb was set down by Homer as the simplest in the world – 'He never closed his eyes in sleep, but fixed them on the Pleiades and the Great Bear, which for seventeen days he held on his left hand'.

Why Gozo? Even the name kept its own secret. It had been called Gaulos by the Greeks: γαυλος was their word for the round-hulled merchant ships of the Phoenicians, whom they hated. Now it was Ghawdex – and this was only *hawdesh*, the Arabic for the litter which sat on a camel's back, not so different from what the island looked like from the sea. Who could tell where the truth lay?

But whether camel's back or ship's bottom, this was his haven, his new-found paradise. A half-day's walk to Marsalforn became a walk round the whole island, stretching slowly to more than a week. His aching tiredness, his self-disgust, gently vanished. As day succeeded day, he refused to think, only to feel.

Westwards from Marsalforn lay the salt-pans: a half-acre of big and little squares, shallow cisterns cut out of the rock at the very edge of the sea. In the tideless Mediterranean, they were filled only by storm waves; when peace returned, the captured sea-water lay under the burning sun, and evaporated, and left behind cakes of the roughest salt which at the appointed time were hacked out and sold.

It was a way of earning a living so strange, and yet so much at one with nature and the sea, that Father Salvatore, sitting on a rock above this ancient factory, could only be delighted. It was a delight not shared by the very old man who presently came past, and stopped to greet him cheerfully enough – this was a priest, and thus could not be a thief or a business rival – and then relapsed into grumbling and bad temper.

The war was ruining his salt-pans! How could that be? Well, there had been this bomb, and it had knocked off a little corner of rock at the edge, and much of the water had drained away, wasted before it could turn into profitable salt. It had been *deliberate*! No mistake about that.

But surely there were still enough pans left, and the sea-water would flood in again with the next northerly wind?

The old man looked at Father Salvatore with hatred, as if he were a mad enemy. 'I've lost a month's salt,' he snarled. 'It's all very well for—' but he did not finish the sentence. Instead he stumped off down the hill, muttering certain old-fashioned curses, and disappeared behind the wall guarding his property.

It was all very well for priests, no doubt: those feckless parasites... Father Salvatore smiled. It was not a day for taking offence. In fact, on this day it *was* all very well for priests.

He wandered a little way down the coast, away from the old man and his troubles, and found a beach with a tiny patch of sand. On an impulse, he bent down, and took off his boots: poor Michael Ainslie's boots, which had served him so well for almost a year. Then he stepped barefoot into the water, and began to paddle like a boy.

I am discalced! he thought joyously. He had always loved the word, because it had been his very first question in seminary Latin, and he had got it right first time. ('Derivation, Santo-Nobile!' 'Sir, *dis* meaning off, and *calcaneum*, the bone of the heel. *Discalceare*, to take off the shoes. A discalced friar is a barefoot—' 'That's enough! Next boy—') Now he loved the action as much as the word.

The touch of the warm sea-water on his imprisoned feet was delicious. Since there was no one to watch, he hitched up his cassock and waded out till the water reached his knees. What bliss! What heavenly happiness! Within an hour of loosing the monastery's grip, and retreating in disorder from his shameful thoughts, he had become free.

He was free to wander further, and to climb the hill below the lighthouse of Ta'-Gordan, and see the whole map of the island spread out below him. It was a time between seasons, between harvests. The last of the onions had been picked, and stacked in bags, waiting for collection. The purple grapes were just fattening; the tomatoes were small and green, the merest promise of a crop next month.

Pumpkins lay large and yellowing, while the clover ricks were turning black, in a valley burnt dry and bleached as old bones. But already hopeful men were attacking the soil again, forcing it towards its next harvest.

There was a man below him in a little patch of field walled in by prickly pear, breaking the earth with a flailing hoe. Did he love the earth, or hate it? It seemed that he hated it: he brought the hoe down with a vicious curving sweep, with all his strength, with as much tenderness as a murderer making sure that his victim would never speak again.

He held, clenched in his mouth, a corner of a sack, to filter the dust he was raising. Presently he paused, and seemed to spit out the sack, and then, still staring down at the earth, began to shout.

Was he mad? No, he was speaking to another man, five fields away across the valley, a man who soon shouted back from the same crouched position, not looking in his direction at all. They were talking about prices. Prices were good, but not good enough.

Something else moved within Father Salvatore's vision, and he shifted his gaze. It was a huge straggling flock of goats,

ambling down a dusty track to their next feeding ground. They
were led by a girl, a girl who really did look mad : an occasionally screaming girl with filthy matted hair, more like a goat
than a woman. But she knew how to guard her flock. If, after
she screamed at them, they still loitered, she bent down, as if
to pick up a stone. Promptly the goats galloped to catch up.

They seemed to know that, though she had not actually
thrown a stone for many months, one day she might.

He slept that night at the priest's house in Gharb : a priest
surprised to see him, but glad of the news he brought, the
account of the world outside. Then he moved on, walking the
rim of the island with the free feet of a wanderer. The days
passed : sometimes he slept rough, sometimes he found a friend,
once he bedded down in a police cell which had not been used
since a certain political meeting in 1931.

No one followed him; no one seemed to care who he was or
what he was doing. As in the monastery, they might stare;
perhaps they talked afterwards; but here his cassock was
enough. He was a priest. They were always doing something.
Perhaps he was looking for somebody.

He was looking for nothing; for no one, not even himself.
The briny smell of the sea, the scorched smell of the earth, were
all he wanted from Gozo. It was still, blessedly, a time to feel,
and not to think at all.

There came a day when he had to buy bread, and he walked
into San Lawrenz. He knew it as 'the good village'; there had
never – proud boast – been a case of slander there, for as long
as anyone could remember. The main street was quiet, and
shuttered against the sun; but on the shady side a few women
sat on stools at their front doors, facing inwards according to
custom, and hooked lace on the worn wooden bobbins which
might have been old in their grandmothers' day.

Lace-making was a hallowed trade, in Malta and Gozo both.
He remembered once reading that when British rule was established in Malta, it had been domestically confirmed by Queen
Victoria. To encourage the lace industry, she had placed an
order for sixteen dozen pairs of long and short mittens, and a
scarf.

One-hundred-and-ninety-two mittens, and *one* scarf? He
would never understand kings and queens.

The people, good as they were reputed to be, seemed glum. Of course, it was hot, and there was the war and the poor food, and a dusty old priest plodding up the street was not very interesting. Only once did he have a proper smile, from a girl who turned from her front door and her lace-making, and greeted him. She was perhaps thirty, dressed in the drab black which custom and poverty decreed for such communities as this, but still lively and pretty. A young boy sat on the doorstep beside her, a baby lay in a wooden box at her feet. Clearly she was busy, but not too busy for a stranger, even a stranger in a cassock.

He bought a loaf – priests didn't seem to need bread-coupons in San Lawrenz – and a little wicker basket of sheep's cheese, and filled his water-bottle, at a shop in the shadow of the church. Then, walking back up the road, he was attracted by sound and movement in a nearby field.

The sound was the steady chuff-and-chug of an old steam threshing-machine, and the movement the disciplined team-work of a gang of twenty harvesters, old men and young boys, lifting the corn-sheaves upwards, feeding them into the hopper, stacking the straw as it came out, and raking up the ears of corn which a clattering fan blew into a pile at the side.

Dust was everywhere, surrounding the thresher with a choking yellow cloud, floating away across the valley. Every man, every boy scurrying about at this task, though stripped to the waist, was pouring with sweat. But the work went on without a pause. After this field there would be the next one, and threshing time, with work by night impossible, was short.

There was one figure who stood out from the working team. All the corn-sheaves were being carried up a ladder till they could reach the top of the machine. But one man, one huge man, disdained to use it. He, and only he, could hoist a sheaf, and balance it on his shoulder, and then toss it upwards with a single heave. He must be a giant.

He was a giant indeed. Waiting his chance, the man turned away from the haze to spit the dust from his throat, and then stretched his stiff neck upwards. It was Rafel Vella.

Father Salvatore the *kappillan*, and Rafel his former sacristan, caught sight of each other at the same moment. The *kappillan* stood with a smile as the giant let out a great shout, and ran forward like a moving mountain of bare flesh, and dropped on to his knees to kiss his hand, and then rose to embrace him.

'Dun Salv!'

'Bongornu, Rafel.'

'Dun Salv!' Rafel could not believe it. 'Bongu, bongu! Bless me, for the love of God!'

'Tkun imbierek.' Father Salvatore loosed himself from the huge naked embrace, and stood back. 'Rafel... How well you are looking. And strong too. Gozo must be good for you.'

The harvest team was watching them, smiling also. One man called out: 'Ejja, Rafel! Anything to get out of work, eh?' But it could not be true, and the laughter was very friendly.

After the emotion of the first greeting, Rafel was suddenly embarrassed, as if he remembered more of the past than he wanted to. 'Have you come to find me, Dun Salv?'

'No, it was just by chance.'

'Have you come for the festa, then?'

'No. Is it your festa?'

'But of course! It's this evening. Before dark. Not like the old days.' But Rafel was dealing with one thing at a time. 'Then why are you in San Lawrenz, Dun Salv?'

'Just a little holiday.'

'Ah... Good, good. If anybody in the world deserves one... Are you still angry with me?'

'I blessed you, didn't I?... I was never angry, Rafel. I was very sad that you had to leave.'

'And I was so ashamed... But please understand. I had to get away.'

'I know.'

They talked a little more, and then some audible grumbling in the background recalled Rafel to his duty.

'Dun Salv, I must get back to the machine, or they won't pay me. But please come to the festa. Five o'clock. I'll tell my mother, and you can have something to eat with us afterwards.'

'Is she coming to the festa too?'

The giant's face clouded. 'No. She is still very strict. She says, with no murtali there can be no proper festa.' The murtali, the giant petards which banged and roared and exploded into cascading stars, without ceasing, throughout festa time, had been forbidden by authority. There was enough of such nerve-racking uproar already. 'Also she is not satisfied with the kappillan... But I will be there. Will you meet me?'

'Of course.'
'How wonderful!'

It was a poor, sad little *festa*, and no one could pretend otherwise. There were no *murtali*, no bells, no flickering torches: no band playing on the *pjazza*, hardly any drinking – wine was hard to come by – and no *pasti* or big tomato sandwiches to be wolfed at the end of a long happy day. The statue of the saint was lifted from his pedestal, and borne through the village streets, and carried up the steps and into the church. That was all – a bare hour of devotion, and no fun.

Even St Lawrence looked sad about it. Pious hands had painted his face pink, and his robes blue, and his halo golden, and the gridiron in his hand – on which he had been roasted alive in martyrdom – a rusty red. He carried a book in the other hand. Father Salvatore had once been told of a tourist's comment: 'I suppose it's a cookery book.' The heretic joke would have amused the saint, a merry man who, even in his torments over a slow fire, had asked his executioners to turn him over. 'That side is done,' he informed them – a better and braver joke than anyone else's on any other day.

But St Lawrence, on this evening of war and short rations, could not be merry. There was so little to look down on. He must be missing the noise and the music and the children darting in and out of the torchlight, the frequent pauses at the wine-shops. All he had to see was tired plodding people, and, for fireworks, some distant gunfire to the south, no substitute at all for a rip-roaring battery of petards just above his halo.

Once again, the only smiling and generous face seemed to belong to the lace-making girl in black, who had greeted Father Salvatore that same morning. Her bright-eyed son had lent a manful hand when St Lawrence needed a little help going up the steps into the church; and the girl herself, who stood alone as she watched the saint's progress, seemed ready to share her enjoyment with anyone who would catch her eye.

Walking back from a *pjazza* now sinking into gloomy shadow, reassuring Rafel about the *festa* ('But it was *very* good. I would not have missed it for the world!') Father Salvatore asked him who she was.

The giant was not at all complimentary. 'Oh, *that* one. Maddelena something – I can't remember the name. If she *has* a name, which we doubt.' The 'we' was especially telling. Rafel now spoke as a pillar of the San Lawrenz establishment. 'There's bad blood there, Dun Salv. Must be. But she came into a bit of money from an uncle – if he *was* an uncle – so there she lives, within fifty yards of the church, and there's nothing to be done about it. Two children.'

'But where is her husband?'

'What husband?... You should hear mother talking about her!'

Father Salvatore heard plenty from mother during the course of the evening. One had only to listen to Mrs Vella for five minutes to wonder how on earth San Lawrenz maintained its slander-free repute. The old woman, a malevolent figure in black with her Carmelite badge prominent on her breast, greeted him from a corner of the miserable home and gave him a Christian welcome. Almost as soon as he entered, she launched into denunciation, firing away (as Michael Ainslie had once said) with both barrels and the maker's name as well.

She had no good word for anyone or anything. No one in the whole of San Lawrenz knew how to behave. The *festa* had been plain sacrilege, because the rules had been broken. When Rafel unwisely mentioned Maddelena, his mother pounced like a harpy, and the Great Whore of Babylon seemed to enter the room, lie down, and spread her loathsome wares for all to see.

Above all, old Mrs Vella was deeply suspicious as to why Father Salvatore had come to San Lawrenz. If he wanted to take Rafel away again, he could not be so cruel. If that Turkish girl (Rafel's wife for thirty-two years) thought she could entice him back to Malta, then she had better think again. If it was something to do with the church in the catacombs, then Rafel had no business there. By all accounts, it was doing quite all right without him. In its own irregular way.

One thing only was clear: her son's place was *here*. She needed Rafel as never before. Her rheumatism was wicked: her hip a constant torment: both her legs as useless as rotten old bamboo sticks. If Father Salvatore, on any pretext, planned to rob her of her only child, then a curse – she knew this was a very strong thing to say to a priest, but she could not help herself – a curse would rest upon the man who did it.

Father Salvatore, feeling that a substantial curse was resting on him already, did his best. He assured her that he was in San Lawrenz by chance. It had been wonderful to see Rafel again, but he was not needed in the catacombs. Little Nero Cassar was doing an excellent job.

'*Better than Rafel?*' Mrs Vella asked menacingly.

'Now, mother. . .'

'As good as Rafel,' Father Salvatore answered, with all the appeasement at his command. He smiled at the giant. 'And I can't possibly say more than that.'

'Well, I don't know,' said Mrs Vella, subsiding into grumbling instead of spite. 'All I can say is. . .' but she seemed to have said it already, because she fell silent. Then she got up from her chair, pitifully slow, tortured by every creaking joint in her body, and moved towards the kitchen. 'I suppose I'd better get you a bite to eat.'

The bite was a wretched meal, grudgingly served, of bread, slices of raw onion, and a soup made from turnip stalks. When this was finished, Rafel rubbed his hands in anticipation. 'Now for the rabbit!' he said.

His mother stared back at him. 'What rabbit?'

Rafel was abashed. 'I thought you said you would kill a rabbit for Dun Salv.'

'Whoever heard of such a thing! There was an egg in the soup!'

A moment which normally would have been deeply embarrassing was brushed aside by Mrs Vella herself. She returned to the iniquities of the *festa* again, and began yet another denunciation. The war was no excuse at all for not doing things properly. If there was no band, then there was no proper procession, and therefore no *festa*. And was it really true that the statue had been lowered from its pedestal *before* the time of the angelus? What a thing to do! They would all be punished – or rather, *those responsible* would be punished. There was only *one* way to serve God, and that was by strict observance of His sacred laws.

Much as he loved Rafel, Father Salvatore found that he could not stay long. He had hoped to sleep the night there, but the house had become intolerable, and the woman odious. He took his leave, saying that he was going back to the monastery, embraced and blessed his friend on the doorstep, and went off down the street.

As the door closed, and the bolt slammed, he heard old Mrs
Vella begin, once more, a long and bitter monologue, a *post
mortem* on the sins and omissions of every other person in the
world.

He awoke at dawn, stiff and cold, not knowing where he was.
All he could remember was that he had wandered down-hill
from San Lawrenz, in a sour mood of disappointment and
despair, and found a black shadow which was a clover rick on
a little slip of land perched above the sea, and there passed the
night. Bad dreams, wild phantoms, assailed him: the noise of
the sea was restless, unceasing: but his exhausted body prevailed. By the time he was fully awake, it was half-way to
sunrise, and he had slept for seven hours.

With a warm, stiff wind playing on his face, he found himself staring down at a land-locked bay, and a huge black rock
at its farther end. On top of the rock was a reddish-brown
fringe which must be some kind of plant. He had never seen
the rock before, but he recognized it immediately, from postcards, from a dozen pictures on calendars and photographs in
the tourist shops of Merchants Street. He could even give it an
advertising man's label – 'Gozo's Famed Fungus Rock'.

Fungus Rock was the tourist name: and *il-ġebla tal-Ġeneral* –
the rock of the General – its traditional title; and both of them
for excellent reasons. The growth on top was a scrubby plant,
unknown anywhere else in Malta, which was believed to have
styptic qualities – it could staunch bleeding when packed on
top of a wound; and it had gained its *'General'* status because
Grand Master Pinto, hearing of its virtues, had placed a per-
manent armed guard on the rock-island, reserving the mysterious plant for himself.

The penalty for landing and stealing was three years in the
galleys. If anyone was going to bleed to death, it would not be
the Knights of 1750.

The sun came up, putting a sparkle on the sea and deep
shadows on the cliffs all round him; and with the sun came the
wind, which suddenly increased to unbearable force, blowing
full in his face. Soon he was finding it difficult to breathe. This
was a *sirocco* wind from the south, a hot wind howling out of
Africa as if straight out of hell: it brought with it a dust storm;
a myriad tiny particles of sand ripped up from the desert and

blown two hundred miles across the sea to plague and hurt Malta.

It was in his eyes, his nose and mouth, everywhere. He got up, and groped his way towards some sort of cover, anything which would give him relief and a chance to fill his lungs. The wind howled, and tore at his cassock, as he crept among the rocks, blindly seeking shelter in the whirling gloom. Presently he found a cave, a crack in the cliffs near the sea-shore, and clambered inside, nursing a bleeding hand, and there, panting, took refuge.

There had been a hymn which his father, who led the Sunday services when he was on board ship, used sometimes to sing at home. It had a noble tune, with words to match. *'Rock of ages, cleft for me,'* Commander Hugo Westgate-Saul was wont to sing, when he was shaving, or when he stopped reading the newspaper, or when he was happy : *'Let me hide myself in thee.'*

The idea of his father needing to hide himself anywhere was ridiculous. But now his son, not a sailor, only a priest, was hiding in a rock, cleft by God for him.

The choking feeling which had assailed him at the monastery, and again in Rafel's house, returned in full strength. He looked down at his blood-stained hand. Virtue was going out of him : he was *bleeding* virtue. Now at last, at this foul moment of his life, in a hot roaring sand-storm, he was being forced to think instead of to feel.

He clung to the side of the cave in terror. Poor mad Hamlet had called such a moment of chaos 'Crawling between earth and heaven'. All his terrible thoughts, his jeering relic thoughts, flooded in again.

Moment by moment, he seemed to be growing unfit to be a priest.

He doubted all things, silly things, sacred things, wildly flying scraps of the faith by which he had lived for forty years. He suddenly thought, for no reason at all, of the Last Supper. Had it really been such a solemn pompous festival, with wine which turned to blood for the next two thousand years, the eating of bread which became the Saviour's flesh ?

It wasn't like that at all. It was a marvellous Man who knew that he must die, taking leave of his friends – fishermen and

carpenters who liked a party – and raising his goblet at the end
of a cheerful evening, and telling them: 'Don't forget – when
I'm gone, have a drink on me.'

It must have been a lot more fun than at old Mrs Vella's.

The wind continued to howl and tug at the mouth of the
cave, while the murk shut out the bay below, where the sea's
noise was now a furious growl. Drifts of sand and grit began to
pile up at the entrance to his lair. Would he soon be entombed,
and discovered a hundred years later, as the tattered skeleton of
a mad old priest who had disappeared in disgraceful circumstances? Would it matter if this happened?

'*Yes it would!*' he shouted, against the wind and the waves.
Yet he knew that he wanted to live, *now*, because his own
church was in love with death.

In Malta especially, the festival of Christmas, the tender birth,
always seemed of much less account than Easter, the gory
death; and funeral pomp was absurdly prized. Birth, life, and
hope on earth were made to sound unimportant; death and
after-life was the true goal. Why? It was all wrong. *Jesus was
not like that.* He said nothing like that, nor did he live such an
arid myth. The denial of man-on-earth, the idea of keeping
people submissive, humble, and patient, while they fixed their
hopes on heaven and fled there thankfully as soon as they
could – how Christ would have laughed at such miserable,
mousy thinking.

Christ loved life, talking, joking, arguing: he loved children,
rogues, and naughty girls. He loved the whole mixture of man;
if he mocked anything, it was always the pompous and the
proud, the non-givers. He came to teach *living* hope and love
on earth: not the ceremonial worship of death. He was a
carpenter, not a coffin-maker.

Would he have loved a rich church? Gorgeous vestments?
Bishops in solemn sanctimonious procession, looking down on
the lowly, graciously allowing a jewelled ring to be kissed?
Never! He would have been standing on the street corner,
pricking the absurd bubble of pride and consequence in any
way he could. He would have called out: 'Here come the
rascals! Watch your purses!'

He would have given the prelates as rough a time as he gave
the Pharisees.

This was awful, unbelievable, blasphemous, degrading... But

Father Salvatore could not stop the impious tide of thought. As well as a life-time of faith, there must have been a parallel life-time of doubt and question, petty jealousy and sometimes rebellion, simmering away like some forgotten stew-pot in a dark recess of the kitchen. Now it was all coming into his cave, as sewage could seep through the foundations of a shaky house, and he could not stop it.

He did not know how. He had been robbed of his spirit, while Christ within him slept – or, more awful still, simply watched and waited.

Perhaps he was already mad... Now Jesus was at the wedding in Cana of Galilee, enjoying himself. He liked a good party. He certainly did not go to this one in order to sanctify the holy state of matrimony. Who said so? He went because there was a jolly wedding feast for some of the friends and relatives, and he had been invited. When the wine ran out, threatening to spoil the evening, he snapped his sacred fingers for more, and more appeared. What a guest to have!

Weddings meant beddings, splendid nights of love, conceptions, babies at breast... A vision of that relic in which he could not believe, the Milk of the Virgin, rose up to torture him. *Oh God! Oh loving Christ!* he prayed, with all the insane fervour left within his racked brain: *Keep my thoughts away from the Virgin Birth.* If I lose that, then I have lost all.

Blessedly, miraculously, the filthy thoughts ebbed again, and he was left only with a silly joke from long ago in Rome. Two English diplomats watching a cricket match, in a garden near St Peter's. A bowler was taking wicket after wicket. First Englishman: 'Jones is absolutely infallible today.' Second Englishman: 'Ah, but he's bowling from the Vatican end.'

The wind and the sand-storm blew very hard for most of that day, while Father Salvatore crouched in his cave, sometimes close to the mercy of unconsciousness, sometimes waking to the sweat, the abject terror of his degradation. In lucid moments, he knew that he must have wasted his life. Even a good priest was nothing much: a passenger in the turning world, cheating on the fare. Now he had become a blaspheming priest as well, a vile apostate, an insolent rebel. He could never get back. He was lost in limbo for ever.

The worst insult to God was that the temptation *not* to return to the world of faith and reason was just as strong as his conviction of guilt.

Towards evening, as so often happened in this turbulent sea, the wind dropped and fell to nothing, so that a tormented man could look out of a window – or the mouth of a cave – and wonder what had been troubling him. Had the wind really been howling about his ears, buffeting his face? On a tranquil day such as this?... With the passing of the storm, some of Father Salvatore's own peace returned, and his thoughts, like the waves trapped in the bay below, retreated from their curling spite to mere tumbled confusion. He could not tell what had possessed him. It had just happened.

He must have been exhausted – far more than he had realized – and in coming to Gozo he had unwound the skein of tension to its last strand. In the process, a disgusting fluid of evil, an excrement of the faith, had made its escape. In the process, a poor feeble priest, tested by adversity, had proved worthless.

At sunset he rose and went to the cave's entrance, kicking aside the dust and the drifting sand, and stood looking down at the bay. This was peace at last: peace for the world, if not for him. Drained of everything except fear and self-disgust, hungry but not deserving to eat, he waited for the sun to quench itself in the sea, and then went inside the cave again, and dropped on his knees.

But prayer would not come, and he knew why: words without heart could never reach heaven. For the second night, exhausted sleep – the coward's relief – came to his rescue, with a drowsy thought which was at least spoken by holy lips: Sufficient unto the day is the evil thereof.

He was not to know that far worse was to come.

The boy who arrived at sunrise had heralded his approach from a long way away. He was a cheerful whistling boy, and his passage across the rocks to the mouth of the cave was not at all silent. Father Salvatore waited in the half-darkness of his refuge until the hesitant summons came.

'Dun Salv? Are you there?'

He called back, and came out. They met at the mouth of the cave. The boy, who carried a fishing-rod and a little sack on his shoulder, was smiling up at him, with a touch of wonder in his face. A priest hiding in a cave!... Father Salvatore smiled back at the son of Maddelena.

'*Bonġornu*. How do you know my name?'

'I know Rafel,' the boy answered. 'He told me. He's a friend of mine. Well, sometimes... I wish I was as big as him.'

'Perhaps you will be, one day... What's your own name?'

'Ganni.'

'How did you know I was here, Ganni?'

'I was fishing last night, and I saw you. I told Mother when I got home.' He unshouldered his sack, and held it out. 'She sent some food for you.'

The generous thought was enough to make him weep. 'How very kind of her! I *was* getting a bit hungry.'

Ganni grinned. 'She said, "Does he think there are shops down there?"'

Father Salvatore opened the sack, and found riches. There was a bottle of wine, a loaf of bread, a cheese wrapped in vine leaves, and two rock melons, warm from the sun. The sight made him absolutely ravenous. He broke off a piece of the crust, and crammed it into his mouth.

Obviously Ganni had a fellow-feeling about this. 'Start eating if you want to, Dun Salv.' Then he peered past the *kappillan* into the rock entrance. 'What are you doing in the cave?'

Father Salvatore swallowed a big chunk of the cheese before answering : 'Just resting. I'm having a holiday.'

'I wish I could live in a cave... Mother says, if you get hungry again, come and eat with us. Or if you want to stay at the house, that's fine too.' With a generous swig of wine, Father Salvatore had returned to his meal, and the boy, after watching him, said : 'You *are* hungry.' But boys had better things to do than look at old priests eating. He began to fidget. 'Well, the fish won't wait, Dun Salv. I caught a *pixxispad* last night!'

'A *pixxispad*?' The Maltese sword-fish could be eight feet long. 'Are you sure?'

'I think it was a baby. I think it was *lost*... Shall I say you're coming?'

'I don't know. I don't think so. But please thank your mother very much for the food.'

'She's a good cook too. *Sahha*, Dun Salv.' Then he shouldered his rod, and the empty sack, and ran off towards the beckoning water. Though the whistling faded away down the rocks, it lifted the heart on its journey.

So did the food.

The crusty bread and soft wet cheese were delicious: the melon honey-sweet, and the strong Gozo wine, deep yellow and smoky on the tongue, was a blessing. He drank half the bottle, sitting at ease in the mouth of the cave, seeing the sparkling water turn from pale grey to deepest blue, watching a tiny figure at the margin of the bay casting and re-casting his line, seeking fresh triumphs.

Then, feeling stronger and happier than for many a day, Father Salvatore decided that it was time for another walk. He shaved as best he could, with a dry blade and no mirror; then he packed the wine and the rest of the bread and cheese, and set off up the hill. The noise of bombing from the distant south only proved how wise he was to be so far away.

He spent the day in the valley west of San Lawrenz: a fair day, full of sunshine, unclouded, benign. In this paradise, the fall of man – the fall of this man – started when he noticed a farmer coming towards him across the valley, leading a breeding ram to its day's engagements.

It was done with a delicacy which delighted him. The approach of man and beast was at first silent: the farmer slowly plodding along the top of a dividing wall, the ram at the end of a rope, picking its way from stone to stone with all the sure-footed ease of a rustic celebrity.

But halfway across, there was a change of emphasis, a subtle enlargement of policy. The man stopped, and drew from his pocket a bell, and tied it round the ram's neck. When they took up their progress again, it was to the sound of music: a continuous tinkling melody which told the world, and all who might wish to be involved, that help was on the way.

Father Salvatore, with a certain shadow of lewdity in his mind, divined the purpose of this rural minuet. The bell was the traditional call to action, familiar to the customers. When the ram left its home village it was making no promises – indeed, it was breaking faith; therefore the bell must, for mercy's sake, be silent. But as it entered hospitable territory, it was not ashamed to announce the fact.

The man and his diligent friend drew near to where Father Salvatore was sitting. Greetings were exchanged. The farmer stood patting and fondling his prize; the ram, whose endowments were manifest – a ram grown old in sin or in legal intercourse – waited and munched and looked up the road.

Did a ram have an address book in its head? Could it make appointments, solemn undertakings, promises of devotion, in a way independent of its proprietor? Meet me at the barn door... I'll be wearing my bell... I'll get rid of this old fool... The linked pair passed on up the road, to the sound of music, the music of the spheres.

Father Salvatore should have been instantly on his guard, but he was not. The wine which he now drank, and the drowsy peace of the day, and the pastoral sensuality of this encounter, all lulled him into acceptance. Instead of praying, or reading his neglected Office of the Day, he relaxed, and slept in the shadow of the wall. When he awoke, it was to see the ram being led back, its manifold duties done. It walked with lowered head; it was not even very steady on its feet. O happy ram! O contented sheep! O ram of God...

The frightful thoughts which now descended took Father Salvatore with them, straight to hell. They were thoughts not only blasphemous, but grossly sexual. He was tempted of the devil to think of his own organs, and of others, male and female, and of all things vile and defiling. The mounting ram became the prick to manhood, which he had forsworn for ever, nearly a quarter of a century before.

A sensual daydream grew to a nightmare of the obscene and lustful: worse still, to a conscious search for forgotten carrion on which to feed this appetite. He remembered – not with shame, but with a sick sense of recognition, since it must have been lurking and lying in wait for him ever since it was told him, with a snigger, by the seminary lecher – he remembered a certain story.

It was of an old priest warning his flock against excesses, malpractices, which were not permissible even within the marital bond. 'Beware of filthy lusts!' he exhorted them from the pulpit. 'Beware of trying to increase sexual pleasure by disgusting means. In particular, *never* give way to the vile practice of placing a pillow beneath your wife—'

He thundered on. Presently he became aware that he was addressing an empty church. To a man, to a woman, the faithful, who had never before heard a whisper of this agreeable trick, were rushing home to try it.

Father Salvatore found that he could not stop thinking such thoughts. Presently he did not try. The devil was in his loins, after all the years of chastity and continence, and would not be exorcised. He had been sure that the day of the sand-storm, the day of doubt and blasphemy, had been conquered and put away. But it had only been skulking, like the story of the pillow, like a sacrilegious thief spying on the altar of God, and now it was taking a great engulfing leap forward to whirl him, with loathsome power, into the pit.

A fresh surge of this assault came with another forgotten memory, of that angry young man in the waterfront bar who, on the very first day of the war, had made the finger-biting gesture against the Italian bombers. Then, nothing had stirred within Father Salvatore; now he recalled its companion story, a crude Maltese joke, and a revolting, contemptuous insult to the Church and the faith.

Where had he heard it? In unspeakable company? How could that be? But now it emerged into daylight, like some blinking, slavering monster – *not to terrify him but to make him laugh.*

An errant young priest was trying to achieve sexual intercourse, in emergency circumstances. But there were difficulties. When he held up the girl's dress, his cassock fell down. When he held up his cassock, the girl was similarly inaccessible. No good could come of this...

Then, on the road above him, he saw a man, seemingly angry, making the furious finger-biting gesture in his direction, and he gave up, for very shame. Passing the man on the road, he said: 'Please don't be angry. I saw you biting your finger at me. But I did not harm the girl.'

'Angry?' the man answered. 'Why should I be angry? All I meant was, hold your cassock in your teeth.'

The diseased beast of prey which was temptation would not give him rest: not until it was slaked and sated – having made its kill. It was now near sunset. He rose, and with willing feet, to the sound of gunfire and the far-off turmoil of some murderous attack, he went through the village towards Maddelena's house.

In the tiny cottage on the Rabat road, small as a stable but neat and clean within, he found a welcome which was like balm. Maddelena was drying the baby after its bath, and then powdering it with stone-dust; soon she laid it down to sleep, and

came back, with a smile, to her guest. She did not seem surprised by his sudden appearance. Perhaps she was never surprised
by anything.

Close to, she was a handsome woman with a fine generous
figure; whatever the extravagance of her life, she had kept her
looks to a degree unusual in rural Malta, where girls, often
quite ravishing at sixteen, grew harassed after long five-year
engagements, were often plain and lifeless by the time they
became brides, and were then automatically pregnant for the
next twenty years.

The recipe, designed to produce fat slatterns clinging forlornly
to late middle-age when they should have been approaching the
full pride of womanhood, was a *diktat* of so many pressures
that the guilt could be palmed off, as with any other confidence trick. It had not happened here.

Returning from the back room where she had put the baby
down, Maddelena had given him a glass of wine. He found that
he could not quite ignore her circumstances.

'That's a fine-looking child,' he said. 'Tell me about his father.'

'Nothing much to tell.' But she was not sulky, nor mutinous.
'He was killed. We were going to be married.'

'And Ganni?'

'I was seventeen. We didn't know anything.'

That was all. He was meant to understand it, and he did. He
sipped his wine, which was the same wine as had furnished the
tumultuous day. Now the innocent girl of seventeen had become the woman of thirty, who knew everything: a calm and
comely sinner who might be sorry, but would never be sad. He
remembered once overhearing another woman, trying to help
one stranger identify another, ask: 'Is he a man or a priest?'
Maddelena was treating him like a man.

Before long Ganni burst into the house, full of his fishing
though bereft of fish. There had been one as big as this – the
small arms stretched to their very limit – which had *just* got
away!... But he had other news for Dun Salv.

'I saw Rafel on the way home. He just met a man from
Malta. They say there's a huge convoy coming in at last. That's
what all the bombing means. Only nearly all the ships have
been sunk. He said a friend of yours had been hurt as well.'

'What friend was that, Ganni?'

'Some little man.'

'Nero Cassar?'

'That's it!' Ganni was delighted, as if he had made the discovery himself. 'Little Nero, Rafel said. He was hit by a bomb, about a week ago, and his wife was killed.'

Such was the corruption of this day that even now Father Salvatore could not treat the awful news as it deserved. It was as if he were hearing a fable of long-ago, a piece of dead history which could not affect the living. Though he said, 'What a terrible thing to happen,' he might have been speaking, and thinking, of a train-accident in some far-off country, a bridge collapsing in Australia. He did not *want* to think otherwise. He did not want to be interrupted. He wanted everything in his life to be here and now.

Presently Maddelena produced the succulent rabbit pie which Mrs Vella had denied him, and they ate in warm family companionship. Darkness fell; an oil lamp glowed in the shadowy room; more of the Gozo wine filled and refilled his glass; the atmosphere, which had been domestic, grew charged with frank feeling, need, want. Ganni went unwillingly to bed. Across the room the girl's bright eyes met his : the girl fated to be a sensual spur to all she met, the object of desire and its hungry accomplice.

Was he a man or a priest? He was a man! Even now, his manhood was proving it, inescapably.

In the end, it was no more than a moment of terrible confusion. Maddelena stood up, indolent, melting, signalling unmistakably. Her big strong body, so ready, so easy to use, so accustomed to receive and to enjoy, confronted him. Already his desire was beyond control. He stood up also, and she was so close that his body brushed against hers. At the single touch, in a searing flicker of flame, it was all over.

She felt it happen, and said, 'You poor man!' and made as if to clasp him. With a groan, in agony, in a violent tempest of shame, he fled from the house.

On a dark street corner, at the far limits of the village, God appeared in shadowy form and said, with great compassion : 'Thou fool.'

He began to walk, almost to run, towards the monastery, as if to the last blind cave in the world.

The Dawning Day
of Father Salvatore

15 August 1942

A trembling and dejected man was not so unusual in Malta, where life could, on an instant, become harsh, violent, and destructive. In Gozo, such a man was not to be met every day or every night, since the small sister island escaped the worst hammer-blows of war. A trembling and dejected *priest* was a novelty.

Father Salvatore, the novelty, sat in a corner of a small waterfront bar, and waited for word that the *luzzu* was ready to take him across to Malta. At midnight, the bar should not have been open, but it was: many rules, enforceable elsewhere, were seen here as fussy interference with a man's freedom to do what he liked in his own time and on his own ground, and were disregarded.

Thus the bar was open, and would remain so until people chose to stop drinking and talking – or, on this particular night, until certain transactions had taken place. If a policeman chose to poke his nose in, so much the worse for him. He would get a flea in his ear tonight, and another from his auntie tomorrow.

Certainly the shaky old priest stuck out like a sore thumb, and had at first been looked at with suspicion. But presently the word went round that he was clear. He was not a spy, and not on holy duty. He just wanted to cross to Malta, which was forbidden during the hours of darkness. Since he must have his reasons, good luck to him – as long as he paid the fare, and forgot all the faces. Before very long, Father Salvatore was left alone.

If the gentle sound of lapping water had been the loudest noise of the night, he might have found it easier to compose himself. But his still-thudding heart had a brutal echo from outside – a continuous thunder of gunfire and bombs, and huge flashes in the night-sky over Malta which could even penetrate the gloom of the bar. Beset by this, as well as all the rest, he sat alone in a corner, drinking his coffee with trembling lips, and tried desperately to fix his mind on something better than bombs and bar-room customers and the fearful trail of sin he had left behind him.

His self-loathing was absolute. There was a Maltese saying about 'Grey eyes which lure men from the streets'. Maddelena had grey eyes, like many Gozitans, but he could not blame his fall on a Maltese proverb, nor on her either. Though the worst sin of all, the breaking of his sacred vow, could not be charged to him, yet the intention had been there, and thus the hideous guilt.

It was the eve, and now the day, of Santa Marija, the assumption of the Blessed Virgin into heaven. Fearful irony, unspeakable blasphemy!... He had spent forty days in this wilderness: now it was more than time to leave and, whatever fresh horror the enemy might be inflicting on Malta and his people, to go back to the catacombs. He had changed his mind, and come to this resolve, on the road to the monastery. Only by returning home could he begin to make amends.

No matter what the scale of disobedience, or the guilt which he would carry with him, he must go. It was 'Come over into Macedonia and help us' all over again, as it had been on the first day of the war. He must go back to his flock, and to poor wounded and bereaved Nero. Nero must have been part of his punishment, a first instalment on a debt which loomed like a mountain, like a volcano spouting filth and fire.

His earlier reaction to the news had been so contemptible, so obscene, that it was past thinking about. It was worse than— no, it was *not* worse than that. But it was on the same scale of horror. Robbed of honour, a cripple of the faith, he *must* return to his sole service, even if only for a short hour. 'They that wait upon the Lord shall renew their strength.' He prayed with all his might that it would prove so.

The tattered and grimy piece of fish-net which served as a door to the bar was pushed aside, and a man came in. Father Salvatore looked up. It was the man he was waiting for.

The *kappillan* knew him only as Twanny, a Gozo corruption of Antoine: the man who had been fetched when he asked about a boat to Malta. Twanny looked like a pirate, and possibly was – or at least a smuggler of sorts, intent on his Christian duty of fetching things for people who needed them. He was square as Fungus Rock, with a big foxy face and shoulders like certain fanciful statues of Hercules. In fact, a *brikkun*, a real rogue – and the very man Father Salvatore needed tonight.

Twanny looked round the bar, nodded once or twice to friends as if to say, 'It's all taken care of', and then crossed to Father Salvatore's corner, and sat down. The bar owner, unasked, brought a tumbler of wine, the colour of bull's blood, and Twanny swallowed half of it before he spoke. Then he leant across the table.

'Ten minutes more.' He had a voice to match his looks, as rough as barnacles long overdue for a scraping. 'Then we're off. It took a bit longer to load than I thought.'

'What are you taking across?'

'Oh, bits and pieces.' No good to ask why bits and pieces went across by night instead of by day. A sudden surge of gunfire across the straits changed the subject for them. 'They say a big convoy got in today. Five ships... God knows we need them.' Twanny took another swig of wine, and then winked, using at least half of his huge face. 'They say a little convoy got in here, too... Are you feeling all right, Father?'

'Yes, yes.' It was his shaking hands which had made the cup rattle in the saucer, and he dropped them into his lap. 'I'm a little tired, that's all.'

'Not much sleep tonight.' Twanny turned to survey the bar, and to give a few more confederate nods, before he went on : 'We're going to St Paul's Bay, not Marfa. It won't be quick. Can't use the engine except in the middle, off Comino. But it's a nice wind. Ten minutes. All right?'

'Yes.'

'Just walk to the end of the beach. You'll see the *luzzu* there.' He got up. 'There's someone else coming with us. But don't let it bother you. We're all friends.'

Father Salvatore waited an exact ten minutes, and then paid his bill and left the bar. Outside, close to the beach and the ripple of water, he found himself moving very carefully until his eyes grew accustomed to the dark. He was deadly tired already, and there was a long night ahead, and not much promise in the dawn. To the south, the giant flashes of light continued to rend the sky : the thud of bombs reached him like open-handed punches, slapping at his face and chest, samples of the real thing. That shadowy voice which had so gently chided him with 'Thou fool' should have added more: 'Thou fool! This night is thy soul required of thee.'

He was ready. But there would be so much left undone.

A little way from the shore, he saw the outline of the promised *luzzu*, and the immense figure of Twanny standing thigh deep and holding its prow. There was another figure waiting on dry land; a tall man with his back to the shore, staring out at the *luzzu*, ready to move. It must be the other passenger.

When his footsteps drew near, the tall stranger turned. There was just enough moonlight for both of them to see, to recognize, and then to gasp out their greeting.

'Uncle Salvu!'

'Michael!'

It was Michael Ainslie.

Father Salvatore, for all sorts of tender reasons, could have embraced him, weeping, but that was not the British way. However, the British way seemed to have undergone some modifications. Within a moment, he found himself clasped in strong arms, and almost lifted off his feet by the warmth of welcome.

Choking, he said: 'Thank God! Thank God!' and Michael, not less moved, managed to answer with: 'Why doesn't someone tell me these things?' Then they stood back, and looked at each other.

There was enough light to see that Michael Ainslie was tonight not so much a Fleet Air Arm pilot as a walking derelict. He was dressed in filthy rags, which might have started life as some kind of boiler-suit, but were ending it as bird-scaring material: in fact, he looked like a scarecrow himself — gaunt, scruffy, burned dark by the sun, thin as a rail, and with a beard partially hacked off by a blunt instrument. He smelled of all sorts of things: garlic, sea-salt, tar, sweat, diesel oil, cheap wine, and one extra ingredient which Father Salvatore could not place.

He could not have been more welcome, nor more loved, if he had been dressed in robes of purest white, gazing down from the portals of heaven.

Amazingly, the heavenly spirit was still there. Michael was tremendously keyed up, and his exhausted body full of life.

'Have you come to meet me? That's what I call service!'

'Well, no. I'm here by chance. But where have you come from? How did you get across?'

'Sicily,' Michael answered. The words came bubbling out, like the wine of youth. 'Delightful country, and I mean that. And a marvellous place to say goodbye to. Oh, I sailed across. Now we're on the second leg of the cruise... But fancy you going over in Twanny's *luzzu*! Surely you're not in this racket too?' He did not wait for an answer. 'How's Marija, Uncle Salvu? I've been thinking of nothing else but her, and a *really* good sirloin steak with onion rings, since the tenth of May. That's ninety-six days, and this marvellous night makes it ninety-seven. But how is she? When did you last see her?'

'She's very well, Michael. Sad, of course, but she won't be sad in a few hours. I've been in Gozo quite a long time, but when I last saw her she was' – what did lovers want to hear? – 'as beautiful as ever, and longing to see you again.'

Michael gave a great sigh. 'After all this, we've *got* to get married.'

'I think that's a very good idea. But how did you escape?'

There was a warning whistle, on an imperative note, from the darkness, and then Twanny's voice called out: 'Come on! You'll wake the dead!'

'I'll tell you on the way over,' Michael said. 'Let's get started... After three months on the run, you tend to grab all the chances there are... Have you any luggage?'

'No.'

'Just a couple of orphans.'

He led the way out to the *luzzu*, and Father Salvatore followed close behind. As they waded, the water splashed and gurgled round their legs, spreading ripples in the track of the moon. Soon they were gripping the side of the *luzzu*, and the *luzzu* itself was gently sliding away from the shore. The painted eye of Osiris gleamed steadfastly on its bow.

Michael whispered: 'This is a different boat, Twanny.'

'It's my other one... You know each other?'

'Certainly,' Father Salvatore answered. 'He's going to marry my niece.'

'Better feed him up...' But Twanny, guiding his boat into deep water, found time to free one of his hands, and to slap Michael on the back, with evident pride. '*Come sta, ragazzo?* Export from Italy? All aboard!'

First they rowed; or rather, Twanny manned the giant sweeps as if they were matchsticks, and propelled the *luzzu* out of harbour by the weight of his shoulders, while Michael Ainslie leant back against the stern-post and steered. 'Just to the left of the moon' was Twanny's helm-order, and it was enough to take them clear of the bay. Then they hoisted the lateen sail, and silence fell as it filled to the south-west wind, and the little waves ran cheerfully against the bow. After they cleared Comino, it was safe to start the engine, and they were on their way.

Father Salvatore – not a sailor, only a priest – made the best of inactivity by sitting in utter peace and loving his surroundings: the great arc of the night sky, the noise of the water, the creak of the sail on its yard, the presence of strong men who knew what they were doing.

The *luzzu* was loaded deep, with mysterious bales half-hidden under a pile of straw. All he knew was that they seemed to smell like – well, like Michael Ainslie. When Twanny, moving huge and cat-like on bare feet, came aft to take the tiller, the passengers were free to talk.

There was so much to ask, and so much to hear, that it was difficult to know how to begin. But Michael, though still excited beyond measure by the blessed fact of freedom, made it, after all, a simple coherent story.

'It's funny when it actually happens,' he told Father Salvatore, and his voice came out of the calm darkness like a responsible child's – a child giving a good account of the day before the bedtime hour. 'I mean, you always wonder when it's going to be your turn, and what it will feel like, and whether you'll bleed to death, or fry to a crisp, or go out like a light, or float down like an angel. I was lucky... Angel Ainslie... There was a colossal bang, and half the plane fell off, and the rest caught fire, and I was swinging on the end of a parachute, trying to work out how to steer clear of the mess down below – the mess we'd made ourselves.'

He had steered clear, with luck, with the skill to be found set out in the drill-book, if one remembered the drill-book when all hell broke loose: when the neat examination answers came up against the test of fear and shock, and the sick wish to let it all happen – the *real* examination.

He had parachuted down north of Catania, on the first wild

slopes of Mount Etna, and into utter silence. He might, he said, have landed in the middle of the Sahara on a bank holiday... He went through certain prescribed drills: burying his parachute, stripping off most of his uniform but leaving enough for identification, to avoid being shot as a spy: making ready thousands of *lire*, in case money was the answer; and hiding in a ditch, till dawn.

First came some soldiers, but they missed him. Then some children who saw him and ran away. Then lots more soldiers, but by that time he had left the ditch and hidden in a barn. Then a child, but a different kind of child: a little girl with large eyes, who stared and stared, and did not panic or run away, but put her fingers to her lips and disappeared at a pace curiously sedate, as ordinary as doing nothing.

Then came a man on a bicycle, pedalling very slowly – perhaps all the best people in the world moved slowly – who tacked up the road, and stopped by the barn, and carefully turned his back on it, and called out: 'Hallo. Hallo. Englishman!' After that, it was easy.

'*Partigiani*,' Michael explained. 'Some fool called them the spaghetti underground... The most gorgeous bunch of cutthroats I've ever seen. And a couple of professors, and a pianist, and some crazy girls, and a priest, God bless him. Bless 'em all! They all had one thing – they loathed Mussolini. *And* the Germans. They hid me, and fed me, and passed me from hand to hand like a pet mouse, but always southwards, and got me nearer to the coast, and then further away, and then right down to the beach. Then they gave me a pair of water-wings – waterwings! I remember even my mother saying they weren't any good – and pushed me out towards a fishing-boat in the middle of a hurricane. They all kissed me goodbye – you know, I *love* the Italians! That was – let's see – eight days ago. Eight days for sixty miles – plus a little help from our friend.'

Michael nodded towards Twanny, now steering a steady course with the aid of a faithfully chugging engine. They were standing off the northern tip of Malta, and ahead of them violent things were going on which happily drowned a small *luzzu*'s engine: the flicker and then the crack of far-off antiaircraft shells, the triumphant *whoomph!* of the bombs, the bark of naval guns.

'Here we go again,' said Michael. 'I should have stayed in

Sicily... It was so peaceful there, even though it was run-and-hide, hide-and-run, all the time, and the next man you saw coming up the road could be the man who was going to kill you... But I met some marvellous people... There was a man who played the guitar – no, it was the mandolin, and he always said: "Puccini – pfui! Verdi – *bellissimo!* Have some more Chianti. You want a girl?" That's about all he knew... There was a priest – he was rather like you, Uncle Salvu – who said: "We have Michelangelo. You have Isaac Newton. The Americans have Benjamin Franklin. How can we lose?" Honestly, I didn't have a clue... But I've never had such a wild time in my life. And all through it, Marija.'

He fell silent, looking up at the stars. Perhaps he had done so for hours every night, in hope or in fear. Then, absurdly, it had been an enemy sky; now these same bright candles were the stars of freedom. Father Salvatore gently prompted him. 'Marija?'

Michael sighed his gusty sigh again. 'She was the only thing that kept me going. Of course, I wanted to win the war, *in theory*, especially with all those sweet people helping me. Otherwise, what a waste of effort... But half the time I kept thinking: Give yourself up, Ainslie. Don't get shot or lynched. Give up, settle for a year or two years in the cooler, *survive*. By then it *must* be over, and you can come home as a hero, or come back alive anyway, with all that pay as well. *But I just had to get back!* To her. And to finishing the job. And I suppose – though it sounds stupid – to Malta. It was all wrapped up in one piece.' He returned to that fatal lure of surrender. 'I used to wake up sweating in some oven under the roof, wanting to live at any price, wanting to be captured alive, and sleep soft, and eat three square meals a day in prison. And then I used to think, "*No!* Absolutely *no!* More people need me than want to see me dead. And I need more of those people." So' – he spread his hands, like a man loosing a burden, and his voice, which had been strong and determined, dropped to a most moving gentleness – '"Home is the sailor, home from sea, and the hunter home from the hill"... I never thought that bit would come in useful.'

Father Salvatore was glad that his face could not be seen, for he was crying. The recital of simple faith, strong resolve – the things which he himself had lost or soiled, and Michael had gained and glorified – had been too much for him. Choking sobs overwhelmed him; if the noise had not been masked by the sounds of war, and the sea slapping against their hull, he would have been utterly betrayed. As it was, he had to drop his head in his hands, and draw in deep gulps of air, and swallow for his very life, before he could regain control. Michael, seeing that something was amiss, leant over him.

'Uncle Salvu? Are you all right?'

He managed to answer slowly: 'Yes, yes... I felt a little faint, that's all... I'm afraid I haven't been very well, Michael. That's why I was in Gozo, on a sort of holiday.' White lies, at least, were better than black treachery. He tried a smile. 'I'm not a very good sailor, either.'

Michael was still concerned. 'And there was I, burbling on. I'm so sorry. Let's give it a rest. This can't take much longer.' He turned his head. 'How much longer, Twanny?'

'Half an hour.'

'There you are. Sit back and have a nap.'

But Father Salvatore was now himself again. 'You weren't *burbling* at all! It was marvellous to hear! Please finish your story.'

'Are you sure?'

'Of course. What happened after you got on board?'

'Well, it was slow. We pretended to fish for a couple of days, fairly close to land but edging south all the time, and then we hauled in our gear and ran towards Malta. Then we had to stop, because after all there's a war on, and we waited for Twanny in his big *luzzu* to find us; and *he* had to be careful not to go too far north, or the Italian navy would have picked him up. Talk about cloak-and-dagger stuff! I really felt quite important, till I realized what it was all about. It wasn't me at all. You know what? These chaps were smuggling cheese! I was just shovelled in with the Gorgonzola.'

'That's it!' Father Salvatore exclaimed.

'What?'

'I smelt it. Gorgonzola. But I couldn't quite place it.'

'You can place it firmly over the side, as far as I'm concerned. I've been sleeping on Gorgonzola for a week. I swear I felt it moving, once or twice... Well, that's about all, Uncle Salvu. Twanny found us – spot-on navigation, worthy of the highest traditions of the service – and collected his cargo, and me, and swanned down to Gozo again, fishing all the way. Gozo is where he keeps the main cache. Then he takes it across to Malta in small doses, like tonight. The price is better that way. He's a real character, that one: all bad... But he got me home, bless his little crooked heart... I should have rung up my masters from Gozo, but I promised not to. Officially, I somehow got direct to Malta. Will you remember that?'

'Yes. And Michael—'

'What?'

'I couldn't be more happy to see you, and listen to you, if I was Marija herself.'

'Well, what a sweet thing to say... Do you think there'll be any trouble about marrying her?'

'There'll be trouble if you don't.'

When, in a deserted corner of St Paul's Bay, the time came to say goodbye, Father Salvatore began counting out the agreed price for his passage. But he was forestalled by Michael.

'Have this one on me. I've got an expense account.' He drew out a thick wad of banknotes. 'Twanny, you've been marvellous. Take all this. I wish it was a thousand pounds instead of about two hundred... I'm afraid it's only Italian money.'

Twanny, steadying the boat against the quay, laughed deep down in his throat, as if he was afraid to let it have full freedom.

'No problem... *Grazzi*. Mikiel. Come back any time.'

'Never! But I can't thank you enough, Twanny.'

'Nor I,' said Father Salvatore.

'Then we're all happy.' Twanny's voice became conspiratorial again. 'If you want to buy any of this cheese, try a lad called Wenzu Tonna on St Nicholas Street. Tell him I sent you.'

'But I know Wenzu!'

'*Do* you? I'm surprised at you, Father. *Sahha*.'

Then they walked along the edge of the beach, keeping in the moon-shadows, and began to climb the Steps of St Paul.

'Better to marry than to burn. Who said that, Uncle Salvu?'

'Are you joking? Don't you really know?'

They were lying in the darkness by the roadside after the long weary climb up to the Victoria Lines. Half-way to the top of the hill, Father Salvatore had said: 'I'm sorry, Michael – I *must* rest,' and Michael had answered: 'You just beat me to it. My

feet are killing me. My everything is killing me.' Then he
flopped down on the grass verge, and Father Salvatore followed
him. He felt as if every bone in his body had its separate ache,
and his own feet were not killing him – they were keeping
him alive, with refined skill and careful malice, to extract the
last ounce and inch of torture.

'You won't get many jokes out of me,' Michael answered,
though gently. 'I lost the knack, some time last week... No, I
don't know who said it.'

'St Paul. The man who climbed the steps with us.'

'With us?'

'He is always there.'

Michael sighed. 'It must be wonderful, to believe like that.
But did he mean – well, that you go to hell if you don't marry
the girl? It seems a bit harsh.'

'I don't think he meant that at all. He was the most compassionate of men, and it wasn't his job to consign people to
hell... I *think* he meant: Don't destroy yourself with longing.
It's better to marry than to burn with unfulfilled desire.'

'That's *much* better!' Michael stretched out his arms and legs
to the sky. 'Oh, I can't wait to get back!... I must say, this
already feels like the longest night of my life.'

'It won't go on for ever,' Father Salvatore said, though he did
not feel convinced of this. 'Don't forget that Chinese proverb:
"At midnight, noon is born".'

'I wish it would get its skates on...' But Michael sat up, with
the energy which was continuously astonishing. 'Well – shall
we press on regardless?'

'Can you pull me up?'

'Any time!'

'Then off we go.'

It had been after three o'clock when they landed from the
luzzu; now it was after four. The moon was down, and of the
stars, only Orion and the mariners' faithful Dog Star, low in
the sky, were trustworthy. Already there were signs of the
dawn, though no bird had yet been hopeful enough to hail it.
The faint light from the east had to contend with the massive
fireworks of man. Since they started their walk, the noise and
the glare of battle, below the southern horizon, had never
ceased.

In an hour, they had walked and stumbled two bone-weary

miles: past closed shutters, and barking dogs which snarled their way back to sleep, and ghostly fields which smelled of burnt crops and tired soil. Though they had expected to be stopped on the road, no soldier had challenged them. Nor had anyone else. The world was sunk in sleep, or was holding its breath in fear of what might happen next, or else it did not want to know.

Breasting the last slope to the summit of the Victoria Lines, Michael said:

'What's happened to security tonight? These brown jobs are jolly slack. By rights we should have been shot long ago. But I suppose they're busy with all that rubbish.' All that rubbish was a sudden crescendo of explosions ahead of them. 'I wonder what on earth's happening. Well, press on, press on.'

Presently he said: 'There must be some way of getting arrested,' and began to sing. He sang 'Ainslie from the Isle of Man' in a cracked voice and with a new variation:

> 'She left me on my own-i-o,
> Now I'm all alone-i-o,
> Has anybody here seen Ainslie?
> Ainslie from Cat-an-i-a.'

Then he shouted: 'Come on! Didn't you hear? Hasn't anybody seen me? I'm from Catania! I've just parachuted down. You could all be murdered in your beds!'

It recalled to Father Salvatore, struggling between laughter and the tears of exhaustion to put one aching foot in front of another, that Michael as yet knew nothing of Lewis Debrincat, and his aid and comfort to the enemy, and his disgrace. But when he told the story, with painful slowness, Michael only said:

'Poor Mrs Debrincat. It's so unfair to her. Poor kids too. I hope Pietru didn't take it too hard... But isn't it silly? Isn't it awful? Some darling Italians helped me to escape, at the risk of their lives, and I love them for it. My prospective father-in-law, God bless him, does *exactly* the same thing, in reverse, and now he's some kind of a pole-cat... That's why war is such a joke. The only thing to remember is, you've got to win it. Otherwise the winner will make a joke out of you.'

They were coming up to the crest of the hill where, as far

as Father Salvatore was concerned, they *must* rest again. By now, the dawn had gained on the night, and was proving it by the broadest brush-strokes in the universe; by now, they could see each other's faces, they could see their own weary feet, they could see the road ahead, still stretching over the hills and far away, an endless marathon still to be run.

At the top of the Victoria Lines, they paused – and they would have used any excuse in the book of behaviour – to read a marble plaque set into the stone-work:

'The Victoria Lines constructed during the administration of His Excellency General Sir Arthur Lyon Fremantle were so named to commemorate the Diamond Jubilee of Her Majesty, 1897.'

'*I'm so glad,*' said Michael, on a savage note. 'I'd hate to think this was any common old rubbish.'

'I wonder why they were built. In 1897? Facing Gozo? Who were they afraid of?'

'Twanny, I should think.' They found themselves staring at each other, perhaps each wondering how long the other could go on, and Michael said: 'You know, we do look a couple of wrecks.'

A pebble, dislodged from the small bastion above them, rattled downwards and fell into the roadway. Then a head popped up against the pale skyline, and a soldier with a gun said:

'Halt! Who goes there?'

It was a shock, but Michael had become used to shocks and ambuscades. He had also become slightly light-headed.

'About time too! Come, come, my man! Asleep on sentry-duty? Penalty, *death!* – or such other punishment—'

The soldier now revealed himself as a stocky red-faced corporal who did indeed look as if he had just woken up. He slithered down the hill, and confronted them with a rifle at the ready and a broad North-Country accent.

'Who goes there, was what I said. Identify yourselves.'

'Lancashire Fusiliers.'

'Eh? What the hell! *We're* the Lancashire Fusiliers.'

'Now, now – careless talk. Take me to your leader.'

'Don't get cheeky with me, or I'll clump you.' The corporal seemed to notice Father Salvatore for the first time. 'Are you an actual father?'

'What a thing to say to a priest!'

It was time for a priest to intervene. 'It's all right. I'm a Maltese parish priest, and this is a Fleet Air Arm lieutenant. We've just landed from Gozo. The lieutenant has come from Sicily.'

'My friend is lying,' said Michael, who really seemed to have taken leave of his senses, and to be enjoying it. 'I—'

Another more authoritative voice from above them called out: 'What's going on down there?'

'Gawd knows, sir,' the corporal shouted back. 'A couple of loonies from Sicily.'

'Where?'

'Sicily!'

An extraordinary roar of military alarm took precedence over all other sounds. 'Turn out the guard! Watch them, Corporal! Where's my helmet?'

Their troubles were over.

A blood-red rising sun was staring them straight in the eye as they were driven, like gentlemen of leisure, towards Valletta. It was a new day and, astonishingly, they need no longer use their feet. On the outskirts of Floriana, they said goodbye, and Michael Ainslie, the important one, prepared to continue on to his appointment with the people waiting for him at Hal-Far airfield. But there were one or two things remaining, out of their strange night.

'Would you like me to ring up Marija?' Father Salvatore asked.

'No, thank you. I think I'll do that myself. As soon as I can.' Then, as he stood by the army truck with its engine still roaring, Michael changed his mind. 'Come to think of it, you *would* do it much better than I can. I don't want the dear girl to die of shock. Not now. In an ideal world' – he still retained traces of overnight eccentricity – 'we would have driven straight to Sliema, and stormed the portals. But I don't want to meet her looking like this. And I *must* report to the winko, and put him out of his misery, or they'll do something awful to me. Can you fix it for me, Uncle Salvu? Prepare the ground for the horrid shock?'

'Yes, of course. What shall I say?'

'Just that I'm alive, and I love her, and I'll get away as soon as—' he changed his mind again. 'No, no! This is so stupid! They can't keep me locked up *today*. Honestly, I've become such a mouse lately ... Tell her I'll meet her at *exactly* ten o'clock. On the bastions – all the best things have happened on the bastions, and they're going to happen again.' Michael, whose clothes in full daylight were seen to be falling off him in filthy strips, and whose young-old face was like a mask to frighten children at Hallowe'en, held out his hand. '*Arrividerci, padre mio*... I must go and comb my hair... If you'd like to come along with Marija, we won't mind at all.'

2

He had a much better idea than ringing up Marija, which was to go direct to the Sliema house and break the joyful news in person. But he could hardly walk another step, his legs having stiffened agonizingly on the drive from the Victoria Lines, and he had difficulty in finding a *karrozzin*. The extraordinary activity in the harbour, and the sounds of battle – or sounds of something – in the sea approaches to Malta, seemed to have emptied Floriana of everyone except people queueing at the paraffin shops and children playing hide-and-seek among the ruins of what had once been a decent and orderly town.

He waited on the street corner, sitting on an upturned biscuit box which had somehow escaped the scavengers. Finally he attracted the attention of a *karrozzin* driver. But it was a merciless bargain.

'Two pounds to Sliema.'

'*Two pounds!* It's never been more than five shillings!'

'This is a special day,' said the man, who seemed unduly elated, or acquisitive, or both. He jerked his head backwards towards Grand Harbour. 'Do you think I want to leave, with all that going on? Ships are coming in! It's a convoy! Four big ones already, and another on the way. I want to watch it.'

Father Salvatore could not forget that he had survived worse things than this, during the past few days. 'All right. Watch it.'

'Now, Father, that's not very reasonable. I'm making a special offer, in special circumstances. I *want* to stay and watch, but I *have* to earn a living.'

'Ten shillings.' But the man was already turning his head

aside, in the classic denial of an insulting offer. It was a desperate moment. 'All right. One pound. It's all I have.'

'All I have is a horse, and a wife, and six children. Do you want us all to starve?'

The un-Christian answer was Yes, if that's what it costs to keep you all alive. But it would not do, on such a happy day as this. It would not do, in any single day in the future. And he had crossed from Gozo to Malta for nothing... He suddenly said: 'Very well. Two pounds.'

It worked. The driver, who must have been startled, pretended not to hear. 'I'll tell you what. Let's say, one pound and ten shillings, and a blessing.'

They clip-clopped down the hill to the music of compromise, and the diminishing drum-beat of war.

When they reached the Casa Debrincat he got out and paid the driver, who said with rare enthusiasm: 'Now I'm going back to the bastions!' He could well afford to... As the noise of hoof-beats died away, Father Salvatore stood on the pavement, alone in a deserted street. It was barely six o'clock: much too early to wake the household, even on such an errand. But as he hesitated, a low gruff voice somewhere above gave him an eerie greeting:

'Halt! Who goes there?'

He looked up, disconcerted, and then saw the head of Pietru Pawl Debrincat, three storeys up, peeping over the edge of the roof-parapet. He waved, and got an instant response.

'Uncle Salvu! You've come back!'

He put his finger to his lips. 'Sh'h. Not too loud. It's so early. How are you, Peter Paul?'

'As well as can be expected.' But Pietru's delighted grin was at variance with this formality. 'Have you seen the ship coming in?'

'Not yet.'

'It's marvellous! There were bombs all round it... I'll come down and let you in.'

The light patter of feet on the tiled floor within was the prelude to slamming bolts and a door flung wide open. Pietru, in pyjamas which advertised Mickey Mouse, stood ready to welcome him.

'Is anything the matter? Why are you limping, Uncle Salvu? Have you been wounded?'

'No.' They were still whispering to each other. 'I've been walking a long way, that's all.' He paused. 'With Michael.'

'*What?*' This was no whisper, but a squeal of delight. 'Has he come back?'

Father Salvatore nodded, full of emotion now shared with another happy person. Pietru was hopping up and down, unable to control his excitement. 'Yes,' his uncle said after a moment. 'He escaped from Sicily, and came over in a fishing boat. He's alive!'

'But where is he? Why didn't he come with you?'

'He had to report first.'

Pietru, steeped in the traditions of the Fleet Air Arm, accepted this immediately. 'Oh yes. Of course. Shall I tell Marija?'

'Not yet. I want to speak to your mother first.'

'She's at Mass.' Then Pietru looked beyond Father Salvatore, and down the front steps. 'No, she isn't... Mother! Michael's come back!'

Giovanna Debrincat, formally dressed in grey, with the white head-scarf which proclaimed her holy errand, stopped dead on the second step, as if a magic word had been spoken. Perhaps this was not far from the truth. It was a moment of pure joy to see her face, which had been blank and preoccupied, change on the instant to a rapturous happiness. She said: 'No! It's not possible!' and almost ran up the steps into the house. 'Oh, Salvu! If you only knew how I've *prayed*!'

'Well, your prayers have been answered.' He embraced her, and felt her body trembling. His weariness was forgotten. What pride and pleasure and deep emotion there was, in being the bearer of such happy news. If only he had been worthy, if he had deserved to speak the words... He said: 'Come in. Sit down,' and closed the door behind her.

'Have you really seen him?' Giovanna asked, struggling to calm herself. 'Or has there been a message?'

'I've seen him, touched him, spoken to him, walked all the way from St Paul's Bay with him!' The words had a biblical ring; it was the ecstatic account of the Risen Lord, told by disciples first bemused and then beside themselves with wonder. *It was not blasphemous...*

'But is he all right?' Pietru asked. 'Was he tortured?'

'He is—' Father Salvatore began, and then stopped. At the head of the stairs, Marija appeared in a silk dressing-gown.

Fresh from sleep, she looked beautiful, and young, and not yet with the waking world. When she saw him she called out: 'Uncle Salvu!' and her hand went to her mouth. She could not see in him a messenger of good tidings. 'Is it some news?' Her voice showed that she hardly dared put the question. After ninety-seven days of hopeless nothing, what else could be expected?

He held out his arms. 'Come down, Marija. I have something wonderful to tell you.'

It was hardly possible to see anything from the bastions. Soon after dawn, tremendous crowds had begun to stream out from Valletta, from the Floriana Ditch, from every hiding hole in old Mount Sceberras, to welcome the four ships of the Santa Marija convoy, now lying under the shore guns, and the rumoured arrival of a fifth. A convoy at last!... Big ships, deep laden, after all the miserable months of starvation! It was no wonder that the crowd, now grown till the bastions were black with people, was singing and cheering, praying and weeping, as they gazed at the evidence of a siege raised, a blessing bestowed on this holiest and happiest of days.

Great clouds of smoke drifted across the harbour, loaded with the acrid smell of war. Father Salvatore, leading a bewildered, wildly elated Marija by the hand round and round the outskirts of the crowd, wondered if their search was going to fail. What a place to meet one man, even a man in uniform.

Against the background of the years, past and to come, it would not greatly matter, compared with the fact that Michael was safe and sound; but on this single day of joy, to miss him would be disaster, ruin... He turned to Marija.

'I didn't know there would be so many people, or I would have arranged to meet somewhere else. If we don't find him—'

'We will. He will.' Marija's beautiful eyes, searching hither and thither among the crowd, were unclouded, confident and expectant as a child's whose perfect birthday treat had been promised long ago, and could not possibly be denied.

'Well, I hope so.' His legs were flagging already, but he would not have confessed it for the world. 'I must warn you again, Marija, he's had a very bad time, these last few weeks. He's very thin, and exhausted—'

'He's not!' she said suddenly. 'He's absolutely perfect!'

'How—'

'Because *there* he is!'

She released his guiding hand, and darted forward. Michael had appeared on the high ground at the back of the bastions, and was walking swiftly towards them. It could not be denied that, with all the miraculous vitality of youth, he looked nothing at all like the ragged wreck with whom Father Salvatore had passed the night. The *kappillan* could have laughed aloud at the transformation. Michael was now simply a tall slim naval officer, deeply tanned, immaculately dressed, on whose intent face was all the pride and urgency of love.

Father Salvatore took plenty of time before he joined them. But it would have been difficult to interrupt before interrupting-time was due. He had never seen two people more closely wrapped in each other's arms. The few watchers nearby at the back of the bastions were all smiling. Ah, the brave sailor and his beautiful Maltese girl... No one, not even a priest, could be ashamed to witness such a loving encounter.

It was Michael, being taller, who first took note of his approach. He raised one hand in salute, keeping the other one where it belonged, and beckoned him. Marija, lost to the world, was a good deal slower to realize that her uncle had joined the party.

'Uncle Salvu!' Michael said joyously. *'Padre mio*... How are the feet?'

'Terrible,' Father Salvatore answered. 'But the heart makes up for them.'

'Spoken for both of us...' He kissed Marija again, and then made an attempt at concentration. 'I'm twenty minutes late, and I'm desperately sorry. But did I have trouble getting away! The quack wanted to send me to hospital! A very ugly scene indeed...'

'Michael, you *are* a bit thin,' Marija reminded him.

'Just what the man said. Such impudence. After all that spaghetti. Can you cook spaghetti?' he asked her fondly.

'Of course.'

'Well, don't. Roast beef and Yorkshire pudding is our motto, from now on. Steak-and-kidney pie to follow.' He kissed her once more, and by chance a sudden burst of cheering erupted, the length and breadth of the bastions, at the same moment. 'Well, isn't that nice?... Are they cheering us?'

'No,' said Father Salvatore, who had turned away to look towards the harbour. 'They could be, but believe it or not, there's something else happening. Look there.'

He pointed downwards, to the smoky focus of Grand Harbour. Above the heads of the crowd, they all saw what the crowd had been cheering : a ghastly ruin of a ship, nursed like a dying man, which was turning the last corner of her voyage, about to come alongside.

After the cheering there came a hush, as the people on watch gradually took in the details of what they had been staring at. It was the wreck of a very large tanker, which must once have been tough and good-looking, but now seemed to be sinking foot by foot as she approached the quay. She had been wire-strapped between two destroyers as the only possible support for her mangled hull, and was being pushed and pulled by tugs using the gentleness of surgeons – surgeons without anaesthetics – who knew that one false probe could bring agonizing death.

The watchers on the bastions had seen the four others in the convoy come in, and they were used to the sight of ships almost falling apart by the time they reached harbour. They had seen, in the last twenty-four hours, a ship with a bomb-buckled side like a sheet of crinkled paper, and another with a gaping torpedo wound, and a third with its bows blown off, struggling into port with a few feet of freeboard. But this last survivor had taken more terrible punishment than all the others put together.

She had her own cavernous torpedo-hole, under a mass of twisted plating at the bows, and another further aft. Her decks were ploughed up from end to end, as if the world's biggest can-opener had been at work, and some of her derricks were canted like saplings after a storm. On the fire-charred upper deck, amid a tangle of piping, two separate scrapheaps of metal which were crashed aircraft, still smouldering, added a freak element to disaster.

The tanker was so low in the water, so mortally wounded, that a man could be seen sitting on deck and trailing his fingers in Grand Harbour.

Michael Ainslie, the returning lover with many other things on his mind, was moved to sum it up :

'Even poor old *Illustrious* wasn't as bad as that.'

But on the other side of the account, on the day of the Mother of God, the four ships, and now this last fugitive from the Santa Marija convoy, had brought their cargoes safely in. The tremendous cheering which now broke out again as the ship was nudged towards her berth, the waving of flags and handkerchiefs, hailed the miracle. No convoy in the history of island siege has ever been more desperately needed, nor more loved when at last it arrived.

In spite of the *Welshman* and other lone blockade-runners, in spite of the submarines bringing in their modest parcels of supplies, Malta's target date – the date on which the island must give up – had approached relentlessly. There had been one massive try at a breakthrough since *Welshman*'s run in May : a two-pronged convoy of eleven ships from Alexandria, and six from Gibraltar, which had set out in June, hoping to converge on the island and bring it relief. It was a brave idea at a moment of high endeavour, but it failed.

The eleven-ship convoy from the east was brought to a bloody halt, and routed : the six-ship contingent from the west fought to the bitter end, and finally delivered two full cargoes. Thus two successful ships out of seventeen triers was the best that could be claimed, at a cost in naval escorts which could not possibly be accepted. The miserable score was only a reflection of what had happened to convoys since the turn of the year, in the effort to sustain Malta.

In cold print, they had to be set down as : thirty-one ships trying to get through : ten sunk : eleven damaged or forced to turn back : and ten docked at Malta – out of which three were wrecked in harbour. The final tally was thus seven safe arrivals out of thirty-one, at a price in escort strength, sailors' lives, which tore out an entire page of naval history.

Even so, it was still unthinkable that the island should be allowed to die. It had deserved rescue a hundred times over, and now it was needed as never before. The strategic position in North Africa was the worst it had ever been, in the whole history of this war; by the end of June, Tobruk had once again been overrun by Rommel, and the Allies had withdrawn to a last ditch called Alamein, sixty miles from Alexandria.

If this fell, for lack of supply, for lack of spirit, the Middle Sea would be lost, and half a continent with it.

Malta was once more the essential supply link, the spring-board, the safe harbour. But Malta itself could not live on nothing, and by August nothing was what it was living on. Preparations were made for one more immense armada, of fourteen big ships with a total escort of fifty-four, to have one more try, and thus to extend the guarantee on the island. The effort was to take priority over all the other demands which the Royal Navy had to meet, from the Arctic to the Far East.

It might have been thought that a convoy of fourteen ships escorted by two battleships, four carriers, seven cruisers, twenty-four destroyers, eight submarines, four corvettes, four minesweepers, and a tug – that such a convoy with four escorts for each merchant ship, would have a very fair chance of scoring 100 per cent. But perhaps its enormous size was a fatal flaw; it was far too big for secrecy, and having been spied on by commercial aircraft and venal fishermen it was waylaid, well in advance, by E-boats, bombers, and torpedo-bombers from Sicily, and a whole line of U-boats patrolling between Algiers and Majorca.

'Pedestal', the code-name for this monster effort, the biggest fleet at large in the Mediterranean since the rout of the Turks at the Battle of Lepanto in 1571, came nothing near to 100 per cent success. In the space of three days it ran into every conceivable kind of trouble, and at the end of the voyage only five out of its fourteen ships reached Grand Harbour.

To begin with, the escorts took the punishment, and then the easier targets, stripped of their cover, were knocked off like ducks on a pond. First to go was the veteran aircraft carrier *Eagle*, hit by a salvo of four torpedoes and sunk in eight minutes. The planes cascading off her deck as she began to roll over might have served as a preview of 'Pedestal's' epitaph.

Shortly afterwards the cruiser *Manchester* ran into a minefield, and had to be sunk. Then another carrier, *Victorious*, fell, for an unusual, most imaginative stratagem which only the Italians would have thought of, and brilliantly brought off : two Reggione bombers, disguised as Hurricanes, mixed in with the aircraft coming in to land on her flight deck, then peeled off and plastered her with bombs. A destroyer was sunk, and then a third carrier, *Indomitable*, hit and put out of action.

With such a prelude, 'Pedestal' entered the worst part of the journey, the narrows and shoals of Cape Bon, and was promptly shattered by the U-boats, E-boats, and aircraft forming up to take their turn. Cruiser *Cairo* was torpedoed, cruiser *Nigeria* was torpedoed; two minesweepers were torpedoed. While the escort was in total disarray (*Nigeria* was the flagship, and her admiral had to transfer elsewhere), the real killing started, signalled by an ammunition ship called the *Clan Ferguson* which, between one minute and the next, disappeared from the face of the waters after a torpedo-bomber hit.

By dawn next morning, only six ships were left afloat, and one more was sent to the bottom by midday. Then there were five – and five, every one of which had been hit by something, was the number that completed the journey : four big freighters averaging 10,000 tons each, and a tanker of 14,000 tons, the *Ohio*.

Though the wounded survivors of 'Pedestal' brought in 55,000 tons of priceless supplies, which pushed the target date back by many precious weeks, it cost the navy certain irreplaceable ships, twenty-nine aircraft, and 350 sailors. It was especially sad about the first casualty, the *Eagle*, an old faithful making her tenth delivery of aircraft to Malta in that year alone. At twenty-five years old, she deserved something better than her contemptuous death.

But apart from food and arms for Malta, the prime offering of this convoy was the thousands of tons of aviation spirit carried in the *Ohio*. Her load was nearly lost altogether; the big tanker had the worst passage of all.

It was really inconceivable that this ship ever got through. In the 'Pedestal' action, she received more flailing blows, and suffered more damage, than any ship could be built to endure. If she had not been tough as a rock, with a very brave captain to match, she would have been abandoned two days short of Malta, and left to burn and then to sink.

Ohio, launched in America only two years earlier, belonged to Texaco and had been lent to Britain for wartime purposes. She looked what she was – a big new modern tanker – and she was thus, in this convoy, a ship marked out for special attention : the largest of the fleet, and the greatest prize. She carried, on this voyage, tons of highly inflammable aviation spirit, ready to be poured into any Spitfire's tanks; barring a few anti-aircraft guns, she was not a fighting ship at all, but a big oil drum ready to explode if a single match were put in the right place.

She was the first ship to be hit as the convoy, suddenly short of escorts, entered the Cape Bon narrows at dusk. The fact that,

lagging behind after desperate days and nights, she spent a day
longer at sea than anyone else, and was the only remaining
target, and *still* made Grand Harbour, was a triumph for her
builders, her crew, the three other ships which took turns at
towing her for forty-eight hours, and for her master, Captain
D. W. Mason, who made a private resolve against all the odds
that it could be done, and never changed his mind.

That first hit by torpedo came from an Italian E-boat, and it
was almost enough to take *Ohio* out of the fight at one stroke.
It knocked out her steering gear, buckled the lids of some
kerosene tanks which started to leak, and thus set her on fire.
But the torpedo-hole was a monstrous twenty-five foot square
cavern, and this helped to douse the flames. Then, without
compasses, and hand-steering from aft, she worked up to seven
knots again and began a hazardous night journey through the
shoals and mine-fields of the narrows.

At dawn she was already a lone straggler, and the first flight
of bombers found her easily enough. She was shaken and holed
by six near-misses; she passed right through some blazing oil
from a ship which had blown up ahead of her; and then a
plane, shot down by an escort, landed on a big wave, bounced
fifty feet in the air, and crashed on to her foredeck.

Captain Mason had barely started to clean up this mess and
plug a few of the wounds when a second plane did exactly the
same thing, this time landing on the stern and restarting the
fires. Shocked and tired men, even with such a resolute captain
to lead them, were slow to bring the blaze under control, and
meanwhile, worse things were happening.

Down below, the shaken engines and boilers were beginning
to surrender. Towards dusk, after a few labouring miles amid
near-misses which lifted her bodily out of the water, she took a
direct hit. The fuel pumps died; one boiler blew up, and then a
second. She came to a dead stop, 150 miles from home. There
would be no more steaming on that day, nor on any other. *Ohio*
had now become two halves of a ship, held together by a strip
of keel and some tangled scrap-metal above. Both halves were
lifeless.

Now she was taken in tow, but with the great gulf in her
side, her rudder jammed, and her splintered keel drawing thirty-
eight feet, she was almost impossible to manage. The tow-lines
kept breaking, sometimes by sudden strain, sometimes by near-

misses. She went in circles, or she sagged sideways, dragging
the towing destroyer with her until they were facing different
ways, neither of them towards Malta. She would move forward
a hundred yards, and then the tow would part, and she would
drift to a groaning standstill again.

Once, on the second afternoon of this, they abandoned her
altogether, because one towing ship could not keep this enormous deadweight of oil and water and crumbling steel moving,
and they must wait for help. Powerless until someone else
turned up, captain and crew had a meal and a few hours'
doze on board the destroyer *Penn*. Then, with fresh help at
hand, Captain Mason, who had been three whole days and
nights without a break of any kind, led his exhausted men back
on board, and they took up their voyage again.

Ohio was lower in the water now, and she was to be lower
still. At dawn on the third day, as she was making her agonized
way towards safety through air attacks which never slackened,
a near-miss from a huge bomb blew a hole in her stern. Tons
more sea-water poured into the dead hull. The tow-lines snubbed
and parted. *Ohio* stopped and settled once more.

But Malta, after this grinding progress of yards at a time, was
now only seventy miles away, with air-cover at last available;
and to Malta she presently came, strapped between two
destroyers which also served as splints, with a third ship astern
acting as a rudder. She was more of a spineless fish than a ship :
sagging like a corpse, but still bearing her cargo.

As every last gallon of this was pumped out, she settled on
the bottom and there broke her back.

The watchers on the bastions could not know the dark side of
the story; they could only see the good news, which was the
four solid ships already unloading, and the fifth, battered but
alive, now secured alongside an oiler and preparing to deliver
her cargo. It was enough – more than enough – to keep the
spirits of all Malta at a tempestuous level of delight, after a
famine so long continued that even hope had gone off the ration.

They might not have eaten today, but by God's help they
would eat tomorrow!

The cheering rose and fell, and never stopped. The waving
flags made a forest of welcome all along the bastions, from St
Elmo Fort to Floriana, and across the harbour in the Three

Cities. The Royal Marine band, which had played *Ohio* in with a version, always so appropriate, of 'A Life on the Ocean Wave', now struck up 'Rule, Britannia!', and the tune, with any words that would fit, was taken up by the crowd.

Michael Ainslie, holding Marija close, said: 'I know the chap who's conducting. You ought to hear him singing "Colonel Bogie".' Receiving no answer, he looked down at his beautiful girl, and exclaimed: 'Marija! You're crying! Just like me.'

'It's so *marvellous*!' She clung to him, as if for her life. 'I didn't know I had any tears left. I'm sorry, Michael.'

'Don't you worry. Use them all up now. We won't be needing any more.'

'Oh, *darling*!'

It was time for Father Salvatore to take his leave.

When he said so, they pressed him to stay, to come back with them for lunch. But the answer could only be No. Today, these two did not really need anyone else in the world, and the moment had come for him to take a different path. He must go to the catacombs, as he had resolved in the black depths of yesterday.

It seemed like the division of his life. The morning of Santa Marija... No day in the future would be the same. Not for him, not for Michael and Marija, perhaps not for Malta. He said, 'I wish I could, but I have so much work to do.' Then he blessed them and said goodbye, and watched them go, hand in hand, smiling at all the world as if it had been invented for their delight. Let it last, he prayed. Let it last for ever.

He sat down on a fallen stone of the bastion wall, alone, shrinking towards the smaller stature which he must now accept as true. The sound of cheering receded as he dropped his head in his hands. The bright children had taken happiness with them. He felt drained of everything, yet he must somehow summon strength for the next step.

From this high point of the bastions, his way – his 'different path' – could only lie down-hill. He must go to the catacombs, find Nero and comfort him, greet his people and perhaps speak to them. It might be the last time for all these things.

Tomorrow, at the latest, he would have to see the bishop, and confess his disobedience, and accept any verdict in consequence. He would not resist. There was nothing that the old man might say to him which he had not said to himself already, in anguish and loathing. Expelled from the Order as a putrid and stinking member – *self*-expelled from the Order... He would submit. If it was his priesthood, he would submit that also.

The thud of an explosion, not too far off, made him raise his head and look about him, as did almost everyone else on the bastions. The cheering and singing died away as they searched anxiously for the cause. There had been no warning. It could not be an air-raid – the sky was clear and innocent. A delayed action bomb? Something gone wrong on board the big tanker?... Then a man, shouting 'Look there!', pointed, and heads turned, and Father Salvatore's head turned also, with a foreboding which gripped his heart.

A cloud of smoke and dust was billowing up, half a mile away near the crown of Valletta. It must be the Auberge de Castile... No, it was nearer, much nearer, to the Palazzo Santo-Nobile... He rose, forgetting his aching legs, and began to walk towards the city: and then, as his course grew more exact and more terrible in its implication, to run.

3

As prelude to a sad and savage nightmare, the postern door was hanging drunkenly from a single hinge. It invited the curious, repelled with threatening horror anyone whose heart might lie within the *palazzo*. Father Salvatore, panting after his swift journey, stepped past it and inside, and was confronted by everything he had trembled to think of since that first moment of panic on the bastions – a scene from a sun-lit hell.

Something – some awful force – must have ripped through the *palazzo*, with a searing breath which not even this ancient fortress could withstand. At the head of the courtyard, the main doors, thick as a strong man's thigh, lay splintered and flat on the ground. The balustrade which Manwel Azzopardi had repaired with such loving pride was sagging like some tawdry fire-escape, and the bougainvillea, growing valiantly until it was a tree, had been torn from it, as if the secret malice of a hundred years had finally struck, and taken its multitudes of blood-red flowers as tribute.

The great well-head with the Santo-Nobile arms lay shattered. It had once proclaimed '*Stabilitas Contra Mundum*', and now was mocked insultingly. Windows were broken everywhere, leaking their tapestried curtains down like flags of surrender. Part of the portico, where the old coaches and *calèches* had delighted a small boy, had now collapsed, and buried all their musty magnificence under tons of rubble.

Father Salvatore, a terrified mourner, had hardly taken in half of this horror when he was interrupted. It was a police inspector whom he knew, from many another cruel disaster like this one, many a bloody 'incident' of the past. Who would have thought that they were destined to meet on home ground? He became aware that there were lots of other people in the courtyard. This one was only the nearest and the first.

'What happened, Leli? There was no air-raid, was there?'

The policeman, who was dusty and haggard, like so many to be met at such times, shook his head. 'Delayed-action job, they say. It was from outside. Some men were digging just up the street, and they must have touched off a bomb. I'm afraid a lot of people were killed. But here' – he gestured round the ruins of the great house – 'it must have caught the main blast. It *tore* through it like a storm – you can see... I'm sorry, Dun Salv. It was so beautiful.'

But where, amid this wrecked splendour, was the human being most precious of all to him? Trembling, he asked.

'Over there.' The policeman pointed across the courtyard towards the armoury, and then looked inside. 'The doctor is with her.'

There were ambulance men whom he recognized, and who also avoided his eye. Stepping over a pile of stones, and a twisted wrought-iron grille which had once kept the world at bay, he heard a soldier, a corporal in a demolition squad – yet another known face, a friend in the society of friends which suffering Malta had banded together – saying: 'All this lot will have to come down. It could go any minute.'

Outside the armoury door, two frightened girls turned as he approached. They were weeping. 'Thank God you've come, Dun Salv,' one of them said. It was the girl who had dropped the sauce-boat at the terrible Christmas lunch, and had exclaimed *'Gesu Marija!'* to the consternation of the faithful. Let her say it again now, in true pleading humility... He remembered her name.

'How is the Baroness, Anna?'

'Oh, Dun Salv!'

As he made to step past them, and enter, one more friendly face – did he know every single actor in Malta's tragedy? – swam into his blurred view. This time it was a hospital doctor, Anton Farrugia; they had been partners many times, often at that desolate moment when a doctor shook his head and yielded to a priest. Beyond Farrugia he caught a glimpse of a shattered room, with a ceiling from which torn plaster hung like bleached seaweed, and of a nun bending over a bed.

The armoury, which he had always told his mother to trust, must have turned traitor. It had not proved strong enough.

Anton Farrugia's face was as grave as he had often seen it, but from the moment he caught sight of Father Salvatore something was added to it: a special intimacy and compassion, as when a man comes upon a child crying in the dark, and finds that it is his own. He put out his arm, and touched the *kappillan* on the shoulder.

'Salvu! What a day to meet! It's God's will that you are here.'

'What's happened, Anton?' The touch of the hand on his shoulder was deeply ominous: he had made the gesture himself a thousand times before, and always as a prelude to grief. Only now did he discover what a mortal blow this lightest of contacts could be. 'How is my mother?'

Doctor and priest met each other's eyes. After an appalling moment, Anton Farrugia answered:

'At her age... The explosion was a terrible shock. A lot of the plaster from the ceiling fell on her too. There has been some internal bleeding. I've decided not to move her.' Again the touch on the shoulder, the message of No. 'I don't think I can do anything, Salvu.'

'And I can?'

'My dear friend – yes.'

It was the tide of punishment again. First Nero, then his own mother. Why did it have to be other people? 'So God dresses us for heaven,' he thought. But in the torn flesh of others?...

He trod his way forward, through crumbling stone-dust and strips of wood from the ceiling, towards the bed. The nun, who was old and calm, whispered a greeting, and backed away.

He saw what he must see: what he had always been destined to see, in one shape or another. Under a shroud of white plaster, the Most Noble Celeste Emilia Santo-Nobile lay like a grey corpse. The beautiful face, thank God, was unmarked, but it was wafer-thin, as if the fullness of life had already ebbed away. In this bed where she had been born, where she had lain as a bride, as a mother, as a widow, his beloved mother now lay in death.

Near death. There was still to be seen the rise and fall of shallow breathing, but the pallor which was earthly dust was also the hue of mortality. There could not be much more time.

He took out the little golden phial containing the holy oil, exquisitely shaped under the hand of a Roman master two centuries ago, which his mother had given him when he first became a priest. So it returned to her... He began to pray, and then to anoint, with the gentlest hands of a life-time of ministry.

His voice was as strong as he could make it, at such a moment. 'Through this holy anointing and His tender mercy, may the Lord forgive whatever sins you may have committed through the eyes—' his hands were shaking, but he forced himself to touch her, to brush with oil the dying features, 'through the ears – through the nostrils – through the mouth – through the hands – through the feet... Amen. Amen.'

When he turned back towards her pillow, uncertain whether life still lingered, or whether he was alone, he found that her eyes were open. They were full of shadows, like a window into the unknown, but they were fixed on him.

Her lips opened also. He moved swiftly, and bent to catch her words.

'Salvatore...' It was the merest rustle of dry breath. 'You did that very well – for a young fellow...'

He had forgotten that he had ever told her that long-ago story. While he was still remembering, she smiled, as if pleased with this last surprise for a dear son, and closed her eyes, and was gone from the room, and from life.

After a long moment he bent to kiss her, and thanked God for a soul at peace. Then he was on his knees, and weeping bitterly, as a son was entitled to do; and then slowly resolving his soul, as a priest once more.

He would remember this till the day of his own death... But he *must* believe what he had told countless others, at the same moment of anguish... Since underneath were the everlasting arms, no grief need be insupportable... If one believed, if one believed.

4

Everything seemed to be happening for the last time. Even
crossing Grand Harbour had something of a farewell feeling
about it; whatever happened on the morrow, it was unlikely
that he would pass this way again, on this particular journey,
for months or years which could not even be guessed at.

The harbour itself, despite the activity on board the big
tanker, had its usual air of mourning; there were some new
headstones in the old graveyard – the mast-tops and funnels of
a recent wreck, the gantry of a floating crane which seemed to
be growing out of the sea-bed like a giant fungus, the rusting
hulk of a barge sunk between ship and shore – but it was the
same graveyard, overgrown with all the weeds of war, never to
be reclaimed by the hopeful hand of man.

When he came to the Three Cities, and began his accustomed
journey through the outskirts of Cospicua, the picture of ruin
was complete. He had often spoken of hope. Where, in this
desert of destruction, was hope to be found?

But then – then it all changed. The nearer he got to the catacombs, the more his spirit revived. He felt that he was at last
moving towards something real: something which lived, and
had always refused to die. He had taken a hand in this: not a
humble hand, though his thanks for the gift of service must be
humble. In the Cottonera Lines, which he had grown to love,
there was still a living faith to be found. If it was only one of
many places in Malta with such a claim on greatness, he need
not be humble about that, either.

The welcome he received on his return was enough to warm
the heart of any man, no matter what his mood was. There was
only one message for the *kappillan*. How he had been missed!

He had forgotten the enormous vitality of this tomb. In the
abundant fellowship of their refuge, people crowded round
him, wanting nothing more than to shake his hand and take
him back to their hearts. He had been away too long. He must
never leave them again. And the convoy – had he heard about
the convoy? Thousands of tons of everything! They could live
for ever on what the ships had brought in. And the big tanker!
What a sight – and what a stroke of luck. On the very day of

Santa Marija. It would keep the Spitfires in the air till the end of the war. Malta would never be bombed again!

He went from group to group among the smoky caverns of his domain, shaking hands, embracing, blessing. There was only one thing they were ready to be sad about, but as soon as he reassured them, cheerfulness overflowed again. It was the matter of the Palazzo Santo-Nobile.

They had heard that it had been bombed. Was it true? Well, there had been a little damage. And his blessed mother, who had been so generous? Had anything—

'She is resting peacefully,' he told them.

'Thanks be to God and Santa Marija!'

Now he had his own questions. How was Nero? Where was Nero?

'He's here in your very own cell, Dun Salv,' an old street-hawker answered. 'You'd think he was the pope himself... Excuse me, but you know what I mean. It was the best place to put him.'

'But how is he?'

'Oh, full of life. Try to keep that one down! You know he lost his leg?'

Even in the summer heat of the catacombs, Father Salvatore felt a cold chill at the appalling news. 'No, I didn't know. I was told he had been hurt, that's all.'

But here at home, there had been more time to get used to it.

'These things happen. Sliced off, clean as a chicken's head. And the girl was killed, too. But you know about that, surely?'

'Yes. I *must* go and see him.'

'Soon, soon. But first – come and look at the new cooking-stoves. You know who gave them to us? The bishop himself! Ah, what it is to have influence! Who needs a saint in heaven?'

It was not quite within the pure doctrine of the church's teaching, but Father Salvatore let it go. He was moved at the bishop's generosity, yet not at all surprised. The marvellous old man had a heart as big as the faith itself. He also had an exact sense of who should be punished, and who should not.

Even the reunion with Nero, which a moment before he had been dreading, turned out to be a joyful one. Once again, he had forgotten the spirit of the catacombs.

The dwarf lay in his stone cot, a rug over the lower part of his body, although the night was warm. There was pain in his face, as there must have been pain in all the rest of his tiny frame. His eyes especially gave tell-tale signals of distress, beyond any disguising. But as soon as he caught sight of the *kappillan*, he was transformed.

'Dun Salv! You've come back!' He made as if to rise, and then remembered, as they both remembered. 'Ah, this stupid leg... I've so many things to ask you, and to tell you, I don't know where to begin. Give me a blessing, first.'

'God bless you, Nero.'

'Now I'm better... But I must get out of here. It's your room, after all. Why didn't you send a message that you were coming back?'

'I didn't know, Nero. It all happened so quickly. But you mustn't think of moving. There's plenty of time.'

'But where will you live?'

'We'll see... Please tell me what happened. You know how sorry I am.'

'You can't be more sorry than me...' Yet it was a joke, not a complaint. The dwarf was not in mourning for himself, whatever else he might find pitiful or wretched. He was a man of the catacombs. 'It was so stupid, the whole thing. I took Teresa out for the evening. I liked to – well, I liked to show her off. You know how it is... We were so happy, Dun Salv, you wouldn't believe. We went to that bar on St Ursula Street. It might have been any other bar in the whole of Valletta, but it had to be that one. And then' – he made a great sweep with a little arm – 'down came the bomb. We actually heard it coming. It makes a noise like – like a mad woman screaming at you before she cracks you on the head. When I woke up, I was in hospital, with a funny feeling in my leg – only there was no leg there – and they told me she was dead.'

Living it all again, his face was so stark in suffering that it could be felt in every corner of the cell. But what struck Father Salvatore was the greatness of spirit here. Though the worst wounds of a young life had been inflicted, Nero seemed already capable of absorbing them. It could be heard in the way he told his story : the straight account of a hideous upheaval.

There had been promise running all the way through it. In the fullness and weariness of time, a different day would dawn : a day when Nero would again be talking as he had talked, long ago, at their first meeting on the *dghajsa* crossing Grand Harbour: with the same cheerful, bouncing vitality, the credo of 'We're not dead yet!' – 'Let's *do* something about the war!' which had been so enormously attractive, so heartening. Nero himself, lying in his cot, looking down at the half-filled rug, summed it up bravely:

'Well, never mind – it was a very small leg.'

Almost choking, Father Salvatore said: 'You're teaching me a wonderful lesson, Nero.'

Nero opened his eyes wide. 'Me teach *you*? – pigs will be flying next! What I say is, it's lucky it wasn't *both* legs. Then I really *would* be walking close to the ground...' Swiftly his tone changed. 'But Teresa – that's quite different, isn't it? What a wicked waste!' He turned his head aside on the pillow, and whispered: 'Everything was just starting... I must tell you something. We were hoping – we were almost certain she was going to have a baby.'

Father Salvatore did his best, in the desperate urge to comfort. 'Nero, there's hardly anything I can say. It's the most awful thing in the world. I needn't tell you to be brave. You *are* brave. Try to remember, she has gone to God.'

'I need her more than God!' It was a sudden ferocious snarl, the bitter protest from the depths of a resentful heart. 'What's the matter with Him? Was He jealous of me?'

'Nero, Nero.'

'I'm sorry, Dun Salv. Give me a little time.'

Then it was quiet in the tiny stone cell, while outside the voices of the catacombs rose and fell as people started gathering for the night. The cooking smells wafted upwards; the children called, the lights would be flickering in their niches, and the little dead brothers peeping down on a strange new world. God also looked down... Father Salvatore thanked God that Nero had found his answer, though it was the one which no one could ever believe, at that first cruel stabbing which was the loss of love.

Yet time did dull everything – pain, memory, rage, despair, the iniquitous robbery of bereavement. To say so was often heartless. To *believe* so, within a suffering soul, was divine mercy.

Presently a subdued Nero asked: 'When did you hear about it?'

'Only yesterday. I was still in Gozo. When did it happen, Nero?'

'Eight days ago... Who told you?'

'Well – it was Rafel. Someone brought a message from him. I'd met him earlier.'

'Rafel! You really saw that old mountain man?'

'Oh yes. He sent all sorts of remembrances. I think he misses the catacombs.'

Nero looked wary. 'Well, he had his chance, didn't he? I hope you won't think – we don't need him back, Dun Salv.'

'There's no question of that. He couldn't come, and why should he, anyway?'

'Right! In a couple of weeks, I'll be hopping about like a flea. A flea on crutches – think of that! People will come from miles around...' Suddenly Nero clapped his hands together. 'I was forgetting! All my own troubles! We heard the *palazzo* had a bomb. Is it true? Is your mother all right?'

'She is resting peacefully,' he answered, as before.

'That's good. And isn't it wonderful about the convoy? At this rate we can hold out for ever. I *knew* it would turn out like this. So did you. You always told us to trust God, and to hope.'

'It has *never* failed.' Looking at the dwarf, Father Salvatore knew that he was growing exhausted; the small lined face was grey with fatigue. He got up from the bed. 'It's time I left you, Nero. Why don't you have a little nap?'

'I'll have a think, anyway...' Nero lay back on the pillow, and closed his eyes. His voice came sleepily. 'I've had a lot of thoughts, lying here. Dun Salv. Not bad thoughts. How could they be bad, in your cell?... I *still* don't see why we had to have a war. Why God allows it. Malta never did any harm to anyone. Yet it always seems to happen, like you've been telling us. And so many people get killed and hurt, or their lives are spoiled... But if it's a plan, then it's a plan.'

'It is one of the greatest mysteries, Nero.'

'Then you won't expect the answer from me.' Nero's eyes were still closed, but now he was smiling. 'Oh, we've missed you so much, Dun Salv! It's been months... How long?'

'Forty days.'

'You mustn't go away again.'

'You hardly need me now.'

'You'd be surprised! They caught a man helping himself to the spare altar-candles, last week!... Will you talk to us tonight?'

'I think so. But not for long. I'm rather tired myself.'

'Ten words would do! And I'll be listening, if they have to hoist me up like a saint!'

'Now, Nero.'

A man came hesitantly to the cell door, to ask about Mass, and Father Salvatore touched the dwarf gently on the forehead, and left him. He did not really feel equal to speaking tonight, but it would come, it would come. At a moment of private grief and public joy, he had been privileged to be joined with his people. What else could he do but tell them once more of peace and strength, life and hope?

HEXAMERON!

AD 1917.
Pax Britannica et Melitensis

The *kappillan* could always surprise them.

'When I was a young man of twenty-two,' he began, 'I sailed into Grand Harbour on the bridge of a destroyer, just like the one that came in today, holding up the big tanker. No, I was not in the navy, though I certainly wanted to be. I wanted to be the captain! But I was dedicated to God already – a young seminarian who would be a priest in two years' time. Perhaps it was the only moment, in nearly twenty-five years, when I wanted to be anything but a priest. I tell you this tonight, because tonight I feel very close to you again, and we are all happy, and people who are close and happy should have no secrets.'

He waited for them to quieten down. The idea of Dun Salv wanting to be a naval officer must have seemed very odd to them. He hoped, somehow, to show them why it had been so.

'That was in the first world war, in 1917,' he went on, 'and I was coming back from Rome to Malta. You must remember that Italy was an ally in that war. I was only a passenger in the destroyer, and I was on a sad errand: returning from the seminary for the Requiem Mass for my father, who had been killed at a big naval battle called Jutland, just a year before. But the sad journey of 1917 turned into a glorious one. In fact it was a great day when we came into Grand Harbour, a day just like today, when all the news is good, when we can at last see an end to war and a chance of peace. In 1917, the war had not yet been won, but it had been won *here* – because of what I saw when we arrived.'

He looked down on the close-packed people, his people, and then to an upper gallery, where Nero could be seen, listening intently, chin on hand, hand on the stone parapet. It was very important that he told them everything.

'On the voyage from Naples, where we started, I had made friends with two men – well, a boy and a man. One was a midshipman, coming out to Malta to join his new ship. The other was a Maltese messman, a steward. They were two very different people: one was eighteen, the other about fifty. But they had one thing in common: they were both troubled. They were not happy, because they did not like the present and they feared the future. Yet when we sailed into harbour, they were both transformed by what they saw there, just as I was. What they saw was strength and security and hopes of peace, all in a single picture.

'I want to tell you tonight about that young English boy and that middle-aged Maltese – and the destroyer, and her captain, and what we all found when we got here. First, the midshipman—'

The midshipman, who was lively and goodlooking, with all his lifetime of service before him, was the most harassed human being young Salvatore had ever met. It was hardly possible to believe it! He had a most beautiful uniform, with gleaming brass buttons and white shoulder patches: he even carried a dirk! Salvatore had been deeply envious, as soon as he saw him. But after a day in his company, even a seminarian, beset by so many rules, watched by so many eyes, subject to such steely discipline, could not possibly feel jealous. By contrast with a Royal Navy midshipman, a Roman Catholic priest-to-be might think himself in heaven already.

'But aren't you looking forward to it?' Salvatore asked the worried young man who seemed to have so many wonderful things ahead of him. They were sitting on the after-deck in the warm evening sun, feeling the thrust of the propeller shafts beneath them, watching the creamy green water racing past the rail.

There was not another ship to be seen, all round the horizon, and not a cloud in the sky. Mount Etna was looming up from the south, topped by a drift of purple smoke for identification. It was a day for doing nothing in absolute peace, but destroyers, Salvatore knew, were always in a hurry. 'I mean,' he went on, 'going to a new ship... This one is so exciting.'

'Oh, *Scorpion*'s all right,' the midshipman answered. '*Beagle* class – you can't beat them... Destroyers must be marvellous to serve in... *Scorpion* was cock of the whole fleet at coaling ship last year. A hundred and twenty tons in an hour, all shovelled by hand into those awful sacks and hoisted on board from the collier. They weigh two hundred-weight each!... She must be really well-run... Have you met the owner?'

'Who?'

'The captain – Commander Cunningham.'

'Oh... Only to say good-morning, when I came on board.'

'A. B. Cunningham,' the midshipman said. 'I'd like to serve with him. I can tell you, he's got a hot reputation... Destroyers are marvellous,' he repeated. 'Give me a small ship, every time. Much more chummy. Only six or seven officers. I mean, you actually *know* the captain. In a battleship, he's like a big black cloud a thousand miles away. All you ever meet is the blasted lieutenant who terrorizes the gun-room, and he's more than enough... *That's* what I'm going to. I was in a cruiser first, and she was all right. Then in a battlewagon, and it was awful. Now another battlewagon, and I suppose she'll be worse.'

'But why is it so awful?'

The midshipman, who should have been so happy, was looking sad and nervous even at the thought of it. 'Just the way we live, and the things they do to us. If you're a wart in a big ship—'

'A what?'

'We're called warts,' said the midshipman. 'Nice, isn't it? The lowest form of animal life... We sleep in hammocks in the steerage flat' – it sounded terrible already – 'and we live and eat in the gun-room, which is a sort of steel sweat-box with too many people in it. That's our little cage in the zoo, and the head zoo-keeper is the gun-room lieutenant. He can be all right, or he can be an absolute brute. All I've met so far is brutes... If he wants to, he can make life hell. My last one had brought it down to a fine art.'

Salvatore waited. The midshipman's language would not have been acceptable in the seminary, where the word 'hell' was not one to be lightly used. In the silence, there was some activity near them: one gun's crew was changing over with another, and the gun was being tested with much slamming and banging and barked-out orders. The midshipman watched it with a professional eye.

'They didn't muster the ready-use ammunition,' he said. 'Otherwise all right...' He picked up his story. 'To begin with, you get beaten for everything you do or don't do... Up to six strokes with a scabbard, and that's no joke. You get beaten for forgetting things, or for being late, or for looking insubordinate, or for wearing your cap at the wrong angle, or for not saluting when the man is twenty yards away and dodging behind a funnel. You get beaten because you haven't been beaten lately... How do they punish you at that jolly old seminary? Do they beat you?'

'No,' Salvatore answered. 'It's more – moral.' He tried to make it clearer. 'I mean, the rules are there, and if you break them, it's such a disgrace that the Vice-Rector only has to look at you... I suppose you could say that it's taken for granted that you would never disobey the rules. Not on purpose, anyway.'

'Ah,' said the midshipman, 'I can see the Pope has his head screwed on the right way.' This was freedom of speech even more unusual, but it was such a free and easy evening that it did not matter. 'Just like the First Sea Lord. *He* knows you're doing your best, and if you do something wrong, it's probably just a mistake. So does the captain, if he's ever aware of your existence. So does the commander, who can dock your pay or cancel your leave if you've been really stupid. But they do take it for granted that at least you're trying. It's only the man actually sitting on your neck, the gun-room lieutenant, who doesn't care whether you're trying or not. He's just out for blood. And if he can't catch you breaking the rules, he gets the blood some other way.'

'What way?'

'Oh, it's all so childish,' said the eighteen-year-old midshipman, sad and exasperated at the same time. 'A lot of it's traditional. They say it turns out good naval officers, but I think they'd turn out all right anyway, without all the nonsense... You've got to remember that the gun-room lieutenant has *absolute power*.' He made it sound a very real element of misery, which perhaps it was. 'He can start any stupid game he likes, and you've got to join in, and if you're the loser, guess what happens... Out comes that jolly old scabbard... There's a game called torpedoes. The junior wart is picked up by about six other lads, and swung to and fro to work up speed, and then sent sliding down the dining table. If he lands flat on his chest with his arms tight behind him, he's a good boy. If he tries to break his fall, he's a coward... There used to be a game of making us climb out of one porthole and into the next one, but they lost a midshipman overboard – he was too small to bridge the gap – so they've kindly put a stop to that one.'

'Good heavens!' said Salvatore.

'Oh, it's a merry life on the ocean wave... The lieutenant in my last ship used to suddenly stick a dirk in the deck-head, any time during dinner, and if you spoke after that – even if it was just "Pass the salt", because you hadn't noticed him doing it – you were for the high jump... Or he'd shout "All warts out!" and the last one out of the gun-room had to climb up to the spotting-top and back again, in the pitch dark, however filthy the weather was. Once he said: "All warts double round the forward turret, carrying their plates!" In the middle of the meal! When we came back, we found the gun-room door was shut, and this damned lunatic was shouting: "You're all late for dinner! Four strokes!" Honestly, what can you do with a man like that?... I suppose he was bullied when he was a wart himself, and now he was paying it off... The silly thing is, it *has* produced a marvellous navy... Best in the world... Like Nelson did, in spite of all that flogging round the fleet.'

The sun was going down, an enormous copper disc sliding gently into a placid sea. Already the mountains of Calabria on their left hand were filling up with shadows. *Scorpion* romped onwards, making for the straits between Italy and Sicily. The midshipman, darkly brooding – but perhaps he was not unhappy all the time, just when he felt like it – looked at his watch.

'Seven o'clock... Half an hour to watch-keepers' eats... I get so hungry at sea... Thank goodness there's none of that "All warts out" nonsense in destroyers... There's nothing wrong with the Grey Funnel Line except some of the people... A good owner makes a difference. Like this one. Like old Westgate-Saul.'

'*Who?*'

The midshipman was surprised at his vehemence. 'Captain Westgate-Saul. My first skipper, in *Black Prince*. Did you know him?'

Salvatore was almost trembling. 'He was my father.'

'*What?*'

All he heard, for the rest of that evening, was what a marvellous, wonderful man his father had been: how he ran the tautest ship in the navy, *and* kept a kindly eye on the midshipmen so that they didn't get murdered in the gun-room: how all the best fellows had been killed at Jutland... This was the dear father for whose soul he, and his mother, and brother Benedict, and little sister Giovanna, would be praying with all the devotion in their barren hearts, the day after tomorrow.

Some of them were crying: tiny Nero, who had always been closest to him, and was also the newest acquaintance of death, had dropped his head in his hands, and was sobbing. He had not meant to make anyone cry, just to hold up a picture, and turn it this way and that, so that they would remember it, and him, when he was no longer there to show it. Yet man could often see, through tears, what sunshine blotted out. He would hold it up a little longer, and not yet make it a brighter picture, nor the exact one which would lift their hearts to view, in astonished rapture, the dawn.

Scorpion ran steadily on, making a smooth passage through a velvet night. But Salvatore continued to lie awake. It was his first real holiday for years: even to think of it as 'liberation' was a sin of some kind, and to have said so out loud would have caused such hissing reproach, such a rumble of denunciation, that even a midshipman would have been glad to be elsewhere.

But the thought was with him, none the less, as real as the fact of careless freedom. He would have plenty of time to repent when freedom was over.

After such a day, he sought sleep in vain. He had heard too much that was new, the noises of the throbbing ship were too close, the slit of cabin next to the wardroom too hot. About an hour before midnight, he got up, and dressed again, and went out on deck.

Above him there was a noble arch of stars, as far as the eye could reach, and dark masses of land on either side. The pulse of the engines had slowed, the thresh of water at their bows had subsided to a gentle sighing. As he looked about him, glad of the cooler air, he became aware of a figure near by, leaning over the after-rail, also enjoying the night. Soon a Maltese voice said : 'Good evening, sir.'

He knew who it was immediately : Joe the chief steward, who was looking after him, and the midshipman, and all the wardroom officers, with the same zealous skill. No one else in the world would have called him 'Sir', anyway... But to make sure he asked :

'Who's that?'

'Joe Zejt, sir.'

Joe Zejt... The figure beside him was only the stocky black bulk of a man, but Salvatore could fill in the details, from a day's observation. Joe Zejt was old, by seminarian standards, but brisk and competent : a fair-haired Maltese, which was unusual, and a tough and swarthy one, which was normal. The only other thing about him, and the most noticeable, was his morose air, which never seemed to change. It was not sulkiness; it was a deep and private resignation. Someone in the wardroom had said : 'Old Joe doesn't smile. Sometimes his face creaks a bit.'

Why was that?

Joe Zejt said : 'Come up for a bit of air?'

'Yes. I couldn't sleep.' Salvatore's eyes had become used to the black of night, and he pointed towards the looming bulk of land on either side. 'Where are we?'

'Straits of Messina,' Joe answered. 'They get wider soon. This is the tricky bit. After that it's a straight run home.'

'Where's home, Joe?'

'*Il-Belt*.'

Salvatore smiled in the darkness. *'Il-Belt'* was 'the town', and to a Maltese the only town in the world worthy of the name was Valletta. It made him feel homesick already... Wanting to know more, eager for human contact after so disturbing a day, he asked : 'How long have you been in the navy?'

'Too long.'

The harsh words came as a surprise, and then one remembered what Joe's daylight face looked like, and they were not a surprise any longer. They sounded like his life story.

Salvatore, who was beginning to learn the duty of compassion, who might even have been practising for that far-off day when he would be listening within the confessional, asked : 'Why do you say that? Would you like to tell me?'

Joe Zejt said unexpectedly : 'You're a good kid, if you don't mind me saying so.' It was a very long way from the first 'Sir', but the 'good kid' enjoyed it limitlessly. 'Well, I'm Maltese, like you. So I'm a steward. A chief steward. It's a good job, but I won't go any higher. I started as a boy, and that means thirty-six years in the navy. Year before last, I was at Gallipoli, escorting the Australian corps. But only as a steward. Suppose I ought to be satisfied. My trouble was, I always wanted to be a sailor.'

'But you *are* a sailor.'

'Tell that to the navy.' The bitter tone, coming out of the embracing darkness, had the same shock as the earlier 'Too long'. It was the sound of a man eaten by frustration, by disappointment. 'We're stewards. Officers' servants.'

'But don't you like this ship?'

'I like this ship very much.' The answer was forthright. 'They treat me like a human being. Maybe because they don't owe me any money. But I'm only on temporary draft, for a big diplomatic do in Naples. I've got to go back to my own ship. Battle-cruiser. I'm the chief steward there too. *And* the messman.'

Salvatore was becoming confused. What was the meaning of those words about 'owing me money'? How could that happen? He temporized. 'What's a "messman" mean?'

'Best job in the fleet, if you know how to work it. For a start, it means you have a bit of money saved. It's not monkey business. It's part of the perks, and you have to scrub hard for it. So you make a little extra money out of this and that. If I buy fish for the wardroom, I want to be sure it's always fresh.

The man has to back up his reputation. If Ganni Mizzi from Hamrun wants a contract to supply the fruit and vegetables, he has to see me first. And why not? His stuff is as good as the rest... So you have a little money put by, and everyone knows it. Who knows it best of all? The young officers! They never have a penny in their pockets after the fifteenth of the month. So they borrow from the messman. So I'm a money-lender.'

Salvatore waited in silence. It was an unknown world. He could not tell whether it was 'monkey business' or not. All he knew was that at some unknown point of time it had poisoned the spirit of a man. Though guilt could never become innocence, it could be seen as pitiful human frailty, on which the Saviour had never passed a harsh judgement.

'You know what people think of money-lenders,' Joe Zejt went on. 'They treat them like dirt... What's the name of that Jew in the book?'

'Shylock,' Salvatore ventured.

'That's the laddie! One minute they're cursing you for taking your pound of flesh, and the next they slip into the pantry, and it's "Joe – let me have another fiver till the end of the month. Please, Joe. Usual interest". Of course I charge interest! One shilling in the pound a month. Just like the Bank of England! Think of the risk I'm taking. An officer gets posted somewhere else, and the next thing you hear, he's an admiral. You don't go asking an admiral for a bit on account. He's probably in China anyway. But even when they pay up, they despise us just the same.'

'I'm sure they don't mean it.'

'I'm sure they do... I'm sure some of them do. There's one proper bastard on board my ship.' Salvatore was hearing more terrible language from sailors on this voyage than during all the last six years in Rome. It could hardly be otherwise. 'He's the torpedo officer. Torps, they call him. Very popular in the wardroom. Oh yes...' Joe's voice changed to scornful mimicry. '*Drinks all round. Now then, no heel-taps. It's my shout, old chap...* So Torps owes me over seventy pounds.'

Salvatore, whose financial life was constricted to the point of penury, was surprised. 'That's a lot of money.'

'Oh, I'll get it back. Bit by bit. Torps has got a rich daddy, only he's afraid of him... But is he grateful for a bit of help? *No he is not!* He treats me like muck, all the time. He found out that Zejt means oil in his language, so he makes fun of it. "Zejt! Bring me a pink gin! Without oil!" You know something? I could make a joke too. His wife is called Sybil. We all know what that means, don't we?'

Salvatore almost blushed. Sybil was near enough to *zibel*, a very rude word indeed which was never heard within seminary walls, and rarely outside. But Joe Zejt had more in his resentful soul, seemingly stored up against the night when only the black hills of Sicily, and a little novice-priest of no account, could overhear.

'Then he was going on about my fair hair. No, he's not one of them. Just nosey, and wanting to show which is the upper class, and looking for something to spit back. So I told him, my granny said we had a bit of Greek in the family. "Greeks?" he said. "They're worse than the Maltese!" And *that's* the man I've baled out of trouble a hundred times, and I still have to salute when I slip him the money.'

Salvatore, at a loss in this desert of the spirit, remembered something. 'It isn't just you. It isn't just stewards and officers. They treat their own midshipmen worse, don't they?'

'You've heard that, have you? Well, you could certainly win a bet on it. Poor little rabbits... Whenever I get depressed I think, well I'm not as bad off as a midshipman.'

Scorpion, by her engine beat, was picking up speed again. They seemed to be in open water now, with the Sicilian shoreline dropping away on the right hand, and nothing on the left but a restless sea, silver-gilt in the moonlight. There was a very faint smell in the air ahead, the burnt smell of Africa. Joe Zejt, turning from the rail, stretched and yawned. Then he said:

'Clear run now... It's time I turned in... Do you want any duty-free stuff?'

'I don't think so.'

'Go on. Take your ma a bottle of brandy. Only six bob.'

'Well, if it's all right—'

'Of course it is! You're down on my books, aren't you? Wardroom mess, additional for passage. That means you're entitled. And if you haven't got enough cash to pay—'

There was laughter, self-mocking, in the chief steward's voice. Salvatore found that he liked Joe Zejt very much. But he *was* sad, and it seemed that he was sad for ever... When they parted, Joe said: 'You're a priest. Well, going to be. Who knows

— maybe you'll be a bishop one day. *But I'll never be an officer!* Nor my son. He's a cook-boy at St Angelo. Chief steward, if he's lucky, in 1950. That's what's wrong with Malta!'

They made their landfall, in misty morning sunshine, at Ta'-Gordan lighthouse on the northern point of Gozo, and then ran on down the coast, past Marsalforn, and red Ramla Bay, and little Comino island, towards Malta. The ship seemed cheerful everywhere, from the sailors hosing down the decks to the grimy stoker who came up for a breath of air and stayed to puff a cigarette in the shadow of the whaler.

Scorpion had been away, on detached duty, for more than a month : she was due for a boiler-clean — whatever a boiler-clean might be; but it involved a rest and a spell of leave, which was all that mattered.

Then came a surprise. Salvatore, engrossed in the peerless view of home, and the very island in the arm of St Paul's Bay where the saint had been cast ashore, felt a touch of his elbow. It was Joe Zejt again, but a much more formal Joe. The chief steward actually saluted.

'Captain's compliments, sir, and would you like to come up on the bridge?'

Salvatore knew enough about the navy to realize that this was indeed a compliment. He dusted himself carefully, brushed his hair, and polished his boots before ascending.

As he came to the top of the bridge ladder, Commander Andrew Browne Cunningham — Salvatore had been perusing the Navy List in the wardroom library, which contained four other books: *King's Regulations & Admiralty Instructions, Part One*, the *Manual of Seamanship*, the Bible, and an exciting-looking novel called *The Riddle of the Sands* — Commander Cunningham turned from the wing of the bridge to greet him.

'Up you come, young fellow! I thought you'd like to watch us entering Grand Harbour.'

The captain was a tall, fair-haired man with a merry face and a very sharp eye. He was dressed in gleaming whites, and had a telescope tucked under his arm. Salvatore thanked him gratefully for his invitation.

'That's all right,' the captain said. 'It's a bit dull at the blunt end... I hear you're Westgate-Saul's son.'

'Yes, sir.'

'Great chap! We were shipmates in the old *Suffolk*, and he was very kind to me. Sorry he's gone... Now – do you know where you are?'

Salvatore did know, exactly. They were gliding past the handsome watch-tower on Sliema front; just ahead lay Dragut Point, and beyond it the magnificent bastion of St Elmo. He was nearly home, and it was a breathless delight.

'Right,' Commander Cunningham said to him, five minutes later. He had been the calm centre of great activity: signals were being flashed to shore, flags hoisted, a rebuke sent to the engine-room for making a single puff of smoke, a chart brought to him for a quick glance, and orders relayed down to the fo'c'sle, where a line of immaculate soldiers had fallen in. 'I think you'd better keep out of sight while we actually go in. Rig-of-the-day isn't cassocks, even though this *is* Sunday.' But he said it with much friendliness. 'Duck in there' – he pointed – 'at the back of the signal bridge. You won't miss anything, but the Commander-in-Chief will miss you.'

They made a slow turn round St Elmo, and then the whole length of Grand Harbour opened up, and with it the most incredible sight Salvatore had ever seen. It was the Mediterranean Fleet.

There were so many ships that, from where they were entering harbour, one could almost have walked ashore. Line upon line of them came into view: five big ones which must be battleships, attendant cruisers, at least twenty destroyers: all trim and grey, all at rest, and secure in their strength. Gazing at them, Salvatore could have sung with pride and happiness, or wept that he was not a sailor.

There was an instant message here, clear and strong, and he was part of it because of the voyage he had shared with *Scorpion*: a declaration that peace-keeping had virtue, and virtue did not die in war: that out of bad things like cruelty and degradation, out of death and suffering, endurance and courage, there could come a mighty tranquillity.

His father should have been here, to enjoy this moment... But perhaps his father *was* here, standing back with his hands on his hips and his head up, able to declare: 'I have fought a good fight, I have finished my course, I have kept the faith,' and able also to know that there could be no mourning, when his place was so well taken.

Commander Cunningham's voice interrupted. 'Stop engines!' he called out suddenly; and then, to his first lieutenant: 'We'll wait two minutes, Number One. They're just finishing church.' He caught sight of Salvatore, peeping out from behind a curtain of signal flags, and smiled. 'Good timing! You brought us luck!'

Across the waters of Grand Harbour, from the nearest big ship, there came the sound of a brass band striking up, and then of men singing in full-throated chorus. The last hymn, in any congregation, was always the most popular... Salvatore recognized the tune immediately: it was the Protestant hymn which started 'Eternal Father, strong to save, Whose arm hath bound the restless wave', and it might have been the beginning of his father's own Requiem.

He had so often sung it, not in worship but as something to accompany shaving, bathing, strolling in the garden, relieving his feelings after a dull party. When it came to the part which said: 'Oh hear us when we cry to Thee, for those in peril on the sea', he used to give it all the vigour of an unmusical man who could hold a tune with the best of them...

Once, on some forgotten afternoon, he had added, for anyone who cared to hear: 'Those in peril on the sea should also make damn sure their gun-turrets are on the top line.' Mother had answered him with a long grave look, and after a moment he had raised his hands in mock surrender. But she did not tell him that what he had said was untrue. All she murmured was: 'It's not very nice for the children.'

The closing hymn died away. Bugle-calls sounded all over the harbour. Commander Cunningham, who had sharp ears as well as eyes, said: 'Slow ahead both!' and *Scorpion* began to weave through the fleet towards her mooring-buoy.

As they passed ship after ship, pipes shrilled, and were answered: men came to attention: salutes were returned, ensigns were lowered and then raised, obeying some intricate pattern of courtesy which Salvatore could not follow. But once again the message was clear. *Scorpion* was rejoining a company of mariners, manning ships which, as a fleet-in-being, need not fight again. Now, under this shield impregnable, not a mouse stirred in the Mediterranean.

It was a fleet which had slowly cleansed the Middle Sea of all save a few free-booting U-boats, and had made of Malta a staging-post for the great seaway to India and the Far East, a fortress not even to be approached on any pretext, and a refuge for the weak, as the old Knights Hospitallers had decreed.

In the past three years Malta, 'the nurse of the Mediterranean', had established twenty-seven hospitals and 25,000 beds, where all the wounded and battle-weary men from Gallipoli, Salonika, Italy, and France could come and be cared for. Here they were safe, and here everything else was safe, within a framework of the twin elements of life on earth: the valour of man and the glory of the Lord.

The duty picket-boat which came alongside to collect *Scorpion's* passengers was a gorgeous plaything which was more than enough reason for joining the navy, even as a midshipman: a paragon of small-ship design, with a bell-mouthed funnel of burnished brass, and bright vermilion paint within her ven-tilator-cowls.

As she approached, sailors fore and aft did a positive ballet dance with their boathooks – shouldering them, raising them, swinging them round, then using them, while the midshipman in charge actually had the privilege of steering this, his first command... She edged alongside *Scorpion's* ladder as if drawn by a magnet, as gentle as Sunday morning itself.

'Not bad,' said the midshipman from the *Scorpion*. 'I would have gone astern a little later myself.'

But as they sped ashore, past the ships lying closer to land, past a line of destroyers ranged in exact order, like toy boats in a benevolent pond, he became entranced with all that he saw. He reeled off the names of ships as if they were favourite cousins, favourite *children*.

He said, again and again, 'It's so marvellous to be here, after that awful Scapa Flow!' He said: 'Did you see my ship? *Inflexible*. She's the flagship! She was at the Battle of the Falkland Islands!' He said: 'I wonder how soon I can get on board.'

Though Chief Steward Joe Zejt, the third passenger, was still morose and self-contained, even he was observed to smile as he looked back at the might of the Mediterranean Fleet, and said: 'It makes up for a lot of things, doesn't it?'

They landed at Customs House steps. It was the good firm rock of Malta again. Salvatore could only think of his father,

who should have been here today. But he would be here tomorrow. Tomorrow they would pray, and remember, and thank
God for his life. What better could one wish for than that, and
a poet's loving farewell to go with it; a blessing for everyone,
past, present, and to come:

> 'Sleep after toil, port after stormy seas,
> Ease after war, death after life doth greatly please.'

*Father Salvatore, now pale with fatigue and care, fell silent,
and the silence was not interrupted for a long time. He had
held up his picture, and it had filled their hearts to overflowing. Peace! Peace at last! Peace would come, just as it
had done before; now it had been promised! There would be
heaven on earth, after all their hellish ordeals; and after that
there was still heaven in heaven. What more could a man
ask? Miracles?*

They were not to know, on that night, that it would be left to
Nero to announce what was indeed a sort of little confused
miracle, at a moment of wild rejoicing: Nero who, only a year
and a month later, madly excited like everyone else, forgetting
his lost leg and all his other miseries, told his hearers:

'Do you remember the last story Dun Salv showed us? About
the destroyer, long ago in the first war, and the captain called
Cunningham? It's all come true! He saw it, more than a year
ago! It's in the paper today!'

He jabbed triumphantly at the newspaper of September 1943,
and showed them the story: where it said that this was the end
of the war for Malta, and how the signal which proved it had
just been sent off – in a funny sort of language, but still good
enough to understand.

He pointed to the name of the man who had sent it, Admiral
of the Fleet Sir Andrew Browne Cunningham, Commander-in-
Chief, Mediterranean, and then to what he had said:

'Be pleased to inform their Lordships that the Italian battle
fleet now lies at anchor under the guns of the fortress of Malta.'

Memoirs of a
Day~Tripper 2

The hearse had long disappeared from sight. The procession of the mourners – every kind of man and woman, under the Maltese sun – had plodded away down the dusty road; as they passed by, the standing crowds of Marsalforn had joined in, a broad ebbing stream of humanity which presently emptied the town of all who could move and follow.

Now the bell tolled, not only for the dead priest but for us left solitary on the street-corner: the dwarf, and the giant, and the privileged intruder.

They had shed tears. *We* had shed tears – no one who had seen a black-plumed, black-caparisoned horse go by, hauling the mortal remnants of someone on whom so much love and longing centred, could be aloof from feeling. Perhaps we had shed other things as well: myself, a cool detachment, and the dwarf, the cutting edge of sorrow.

For the last time he wiped his eyes, without pretence, as did the guardian giant behind him.

'That was a very good funeral,' he said.

At a first hearing, the comment seemed to have lost something in translation. Then I realized that he had spoken the exact truth.

Since he was now so composed, I made the most of it. 'Can I ask some more questions?'

'Why not?'

'Did Father Salvatore ever build his church? The one that was bombed at the beginning?'

The dwarf shook his head. 'No. He left Malta before it was possible. He went here in the middle of the war – only it was nearly won – and he stayed in Gozo for ever. We never saw him again.'

'But didn't he keep in touch with you?'

There was another shake of the head. 'We tried many times,

but the answer was always the same. He was in a closed part of the monastery, and could not see anyone. It was said that when the gardener died, Dun Salv took over all the growing. He was always very strong, like a farmer. It was said that he grew more beans and onions and melons than they could ever eat! But that was just a rumour.'

I remembered. 'Someone I met this morning said that he lived in a cave.'

The dwarf looked surprised. 'We all lived in a cave.'

'No – here in Gozo.'

'I don't think that's true.' He half-turned his head, and said something to the giant at his back. They spoke together for quite a long time. Then the dwarf turned back.

'This old man met him, for one evening when he was here. He says there was a lot of talk about what Dun Salv did here. Even bad talk. He might have sheltered in a cave for a night. There *was* a big storm. But no one knows for certain, and now it's all forgotten.'

There was no more to be found out, on that point. I still had others.

'Do you remember, you said that Father Salvatore might come again, if he was needed?'

The dwarf gave me a very close glance, under bushy black eyebrows. He countered with his own questions. 'Do you believe that he *could* come again?'

'Well – no.'

'Ah – a true answer! That's the best kind.'

'But why would you need him again?'

He took longer to reply to this. I had the feeling that, though I had not yet become a nuisance, Maltese courtesy would not last indefinitely. The other feeling – that I owed this man, and this moment, quite enough already – was about to take over, and to silence an inquisitive mouth, for certain old-fashioned reasons, for ever.

Finally the dwarf answered: 'Troubles never end, do they? Malta has always had troubles. Why should they stop for us? Dun Salv taught us that it has always been the same. Malta is in the way of people, so they want to take it. We've tried to say No, time after time. Now we want to say No for always.'

'On your own?'

'If we can.'

'So you don't want any outsiders?'

'We want tourists.' He grinned: he was in full command of
this exchange, and we both knew it, and I did not mind. 'Just
like rich America, or London. But we don't want soldiers or
sailors.' He must have caught a wary look in my eye, for he
continued swiftly: 'I'm sorry. It's not my idea. I like sailors.
Dun Salv liked sailors. Once he said he really wanted to be a
sailor, like his dad. But Malta has been the country of everyone
else, for hundreds, thousands of years. Now it is ours, and we
must prove it. We must be strong ourselves.' He sighed. 'Oh, I
know it sounds mad. It might make us poor. We *are* poor. But
not for ever.'

Under the bright sunshine there was a gang of children
coming back up the road, truants from the solemn procession.
Not for them the dull part... When they saw the dwarf they
gathered round him, as if the little man was the one person they
really wanted to see, in all the world. A small barefoot girl gave
him a bunch of ragged wild flowers, pink and yellow, picked
for private reasons and now awarded with all the generous
impulse of the heart.

While the gentle giant beamed, the dwarf thanked her very
formally, adding something which made her squeal with delight. But his last word was for me:

'You see – it has started already. No one is poor today.'

An acknowledgement

While saluting many other Maltese and Gozitan friends, among them Austin Camilleri, Peter Paul Grech, George Xerri, Father Gregory Vella and Dun Guzepp, Gozo Commissioner J. Micallef, Lorry Piscopo, Dr Eddie Rapa, Anton Vassallo, John and Roger Portelli, Dr Anton Calleja, Frank Grima, and Gozo librarian Paul Cassar, I must record a special debt of gratitude to one man.

This is Monsignor Anthony Gauci, DD, Canon of Gozo Cathedral and Acting Headmaster of the Gozo Lyceum, who read my manuscript as it came off the typewriter, corrected its errors of fact and fancy, and instructed me in certain intricacies of his faith, which is not my own.

He is not to be burdened with anything which is wrong with this book, only with what is right. Above all, he should *not* be identified with any of its characters, whether sacred or profane.

San Lawrenz, Gozo, 1970–1973   NICHOLAS MONSARRAT

Nicholas Monsarrat
The Pillow Fight 80p

Passion, conflict and infidelity are vividly depicted in a gripping story of
two people and their marriage. Set against the glittering background of
glamorous high life in South Africa, New York and Barbados, an
idealistic young writer tastes the corrupting values of success and a
beautiful career girl starts to question her former values . . .

The Nylon Pirates 80p

Carl, the poker-playing mastermind . . . Diane and Kathy, two
fast-working sirens . . . Louis, the vicious young gigolo . . . The
Professor, their 'respectable' treasurer . . . these are the pirates of the
twentieth-century sea lanes – ruthless, cunning, lying in wait for their
pleasure-seeking victims . . .

'All good unclean fun' TIMES LITERARY SUPPLEMENT

The Ship That Died of Shame
and other stories 90p

The story of a gunboat, dishonoured by smugglers, which took its
revenge in a raging sea . . . the tale of a honeymoon-turned-manhunt
when an ex-commando employs the tricks of his trade, in 'Licensed to
Kill' . . . and in 'The Thousand Islands Snatch' we read of days of terror
for a beautiful girl – hostage for a fortune . . .

Richer than all His Tribe 80p

This scorching sequel to *The Tribe That Lost Its Head* reveals how the
African island of Pharamaul betrays her independence. In Pharamaul
lechery and treachery soon replace principles and idealism.
Corruption and extravagance reap civil war and cannibalism. And
Dinamaula, now dictator, dreams of fresh empires . . .

John le Carré
The Naive and Sentimental Lover £1.75

In describing the agony of a man caught between the two sides of his
paradoxical nature, John le Carré has lost nothing of his skill in
narrative and suspense. But in the humour, the pain and the love with
which he relates the rise and fall of Aldo Cassidy, we witness the full
flowering of his talents.

'Sad, funny, captivating, and stunningly fertile' SUNDAY EXPRESS

Tinker Tailor Soldier Spy £1.25

'A great thriller, the best le Carré has written . . . marks the return of
his finest creation, George Smiley, brilliant spy and totally inadequate
man' SPECTATOR

'His best book since *The Spy Who Came in from the Cold* . . . plenty of
flashback travel . . . interdepartmental skulduggery . . . rapid action at
intervals and a red peppering of violence' OBSERVER

The Spy Who Came in from the Cold £1.25

A topical and terrible story of an English agent . . . the monstrous
realities behind the news paragraphs which record the shifts and
tensions of the Cold War . . .

'Superbly constructed, with an atmosphere of chilly hell'
J. B. PRIESTLEY

A Small Town in Germany £1.20

A race against time – to find Leo Harting, who has vanished from the
British Embassy with secret files – before Germany's past, present and
future collide in a nightmare of violence and death.

'Brilliant, unforgettable . . . a masterpiece' NEW STATESMAN

Alexander Fullerton
Sixty Minutes for St George 75p

The Royal Navy's desperate raid on the German base at Zeebrugge . . .
eleven VCs and hundreds killed or wounded in one of the finest feats of
arms of the Great War. Now a lieutenant in the legendary Dover
patrol. Nick Everard, who won his spurs at Jutland, is second in
command of the destroyer *Mackerel* when the Navy goes in on the most
daring assault of its history . . .

'Fullerton's speciality is the meticulous re-creation of hazardous
seamanship, the noise of battle and the minutiae of bloodshed'
SUNDAY TIMES

Zeno
The Four Sergeants 75p

Sicily 1943: A sabotage operation behind enemy lines, to blow a bridge
behind a Panzer Division and smash Axis withdrawal strategy. The men
– a hand-picked Airborne platoon – include a section of German Jews
. . . soldiers who can never allow themselves to be taken alive . . .

'In the war yarn class, this book rates high . . . tense, authentic'
SUNDAY TELEGRAPH